VOLUME 1

VOLUME 1

JOHNATHAN MCCLAIN
AND
SETH MCDUFFEE

Podium

Cover design by GrafitArt and Ryan Willwerscheid

ISBN: 978-1-0394-5540-5

Published in 2024 by Podium Publishing
www.podiumaudio.com

Podium

For anyone reading this . . . thank you for sharing in the journey.

VOLUME 1

ACT ONE

IN THE (NEW) BEGINNING

PROLOGUE

Kinship of Spirits, Riftbreaker Book Ten, Chapter Fifty

*C*arpathian! Stand! Stand! Carpathian! You cannot give up!"

There was a time when the desperate imploring of Teleri Nightwind, who had for so long remained by Carpathian Einzgear's side as his confederate, his ally . . . his friend, would have compelled Carpathian to find the strength to do as she was asking. To stand. To fight. To continue the quest. There was a time when her urging would have been sufficient.

But that time had passed.

Indeed, he could hardly even recall when that time might have been.

Now, here, on the threshold of his own mortality, her exigency held less sway than it once had, the sound of her pained pleas seeming hollow and distant as the lights continued to dim around him.

Through the narrowing pinprick that stood as the last remnants of his vision, Carpathian Einzgear saw the walls of the Tower of Zuria, home to the Ninth Guardian and their precious Nexus Core, yet unbreached. The seemingly impenetrable parapets streaked with the blood of the thousands who had died in their futile assault on it.

Humans, Elves, Dwarves, Ridisha, Ishilden . . .

Even mighty beasts—Tentasaurians, Drakonars, Zephyrixia . . .

All dead.

Dead because of a foolhardy call to arms issued by Carpathian himself. "The World Saviour," a sobriquet he never requested, left him ever uneasy, and, at this moment . . . felt like the cruelest kind of joke. He had failed to reach the core and reopen the flow of Mezmer, the world's essential life force, back to its people. He had failed to unmask the Ninth Guardian. He was a Saviour who had, in the end, failed to save . . . anything.

"Carpa—!"

The sound of Teleri's voice shouting his name was cut short, replaced by a horrible gurgling. One known well by any who had ever trod this land and seen their comrades, their loved ones, fall. A truth about this world—and perhaps all worlds—that was inescapable: Death arrives for everyone in its own, individual manner but leaves in precisely the same way.

"Teleri!" Carpathian managed. Or, at least, thought he managed. It is possible that the intended bellowing of her name was happening only inside his mind. At this point, it made no difference. Reality and fiction had become commingled into a morass of indecipherable consequences. And, as Almeister had once reminded him, quoting an old bit of wisdom shared often throughout the land, "At the setting of the suns, intentions are irrelevant. All that matters . . . is consequence."

Almeister.

Xanaraxa.

Zerastian.

Mael.

He had failed them as well.

Almeister, held captive in the Tower, awaiting a trial that was to be no trial at all. A sideshow for the entertainment of the High Council. Its own unique form of torture.

Xanaraxa, enslaved by zealots. Captured by members of the Disciples of the Ninth Guardian and forced to do their bidding, subjected to the kinds of horrors that Carpathian could only have nightmares about. On the rare occasions when he slept.

Zerastian, lost to the sands of the Great Desert. Carpathian could still see her delicate hand waving goodbye as the dust storm engulfed her.

Mael . . . Poor Mael. His most fervent apostle. The one who willingly forfeit his own preeminence so that he might serve what he saw as a greater good. The strongest of them all, save for Carpathian himself, brought hard to his knees by . . .

No.

It hurt too much to even think of Mael's fate. So, Carpathian tried not to.

And now, it would seem . . . Teleri.

As Carpathian attempted to turn his head in the direction from whence he heard her calling, he felt a pressure on his spine. A nudge.

It was Pergamon. Grown now to his combat size, using his shell to deflect the barrage of Mezmerically infused projectiles intended to finish Carpathian once and for all. With all the strength he had remaining in his snail's exoskeletal frame, he pushed and prodded the famously recalcitrant World Saviour with his antennae.

"Carpathian! You must summon your will!" shouted the Saviour's steadfast companion, the rich, rugged tone of his Mezmerically granted voice which had once so amused Carpathian now seeming stretched and thin. Anxious. Bordering on hysteria.

It made Carpathian sad in a way he could not quite express.

"Carpathian Einzgear!" Carpathian's loyal, unfaltering familiar continued urging. If anyone or anything might impel the Saviour to find one last drop of resilience within his depleted reservoir of hope, it would be Pergamon. True to his form, Pergamon's steady, measured reason had saved Carpathian more times than could be counted. The Saviour might find cause to continue the fight in honor of his most constant companion if but for nothing else. "You must—" the snail cried.

But, not unlike Teleri's aborted exhortation moments earlier, Pergamon's voice was clipped short by a blade that Carpathian could not see . . . but could feel.

The enchanted steel penetrated the snail's shell with its Mezmeric energy and, in so doing, pierced both the soft, fragile body beneath it, as well as the soft, fragile body of Carpathian himself.

"Nooooo!" Carpathian cried out, this time with certainty. It was unquestionable. Because the next sound he heard was laughing. Laughter that morphed into mockery.

"Nooooo," the voice mimicked. Carpathian could see the Super Vizier striding over to him casually, the smoldering husks of disabled conveyance vehicles, hastily appropriated for war, creating a macabre yet eerily beautiful tableau of destruction around her. She arrived at Carpathian's prostrate body, half buried under the weight of his now dead companion, and stood above him.

"Nooooo," she said again, this time quieter and somehow with even more contempt as she came to stand beside Moridius, who was holding the weapon that had just ended Pergamon's life and come within centimeters of puncturing Carpathian's mechanical Heart and ending his as well.

Moridius—the Templar who had for so long dreamed of the day when he might be the one to snuff the Saviour's candle—offered a satisfied smile to the Super Vizier and stepped away, withdrawing his blade, dragging with it the limp carcass of the now dead Pergamon.

Carpathian began to weep.

The Super Vizier leaned over him, her smile as bright as the second sun.

"Oh, Einzgear," she said in the condescending, pitying tone Carpathian knew so well. "You reckless fool. You stupid. Unconscionable. Blithering. Reckless fool. You have been a prickly nuisance of a thorn for so long, and now . . ." She surveyed the field of battle, blighted with the freshly slain corpses of true believers. "All these beings. All these poor, misguided souls who were naive enough to follow you blindly. There is something comforting about the fact that you will die knowing you are responsible for their deaths as well."

Carpathian coughed and felt pain. Pain he had not experienced in a very, very long time. There was something oddly soothing about it, as it reminded him of eras long gone. Ages before. Before his legend had grown so great that he felt he could no longer shoulder its weight. It reminded him . . . that he was human. Of Meridia born.

He wept harder.

The Super Vizier's grin widened to the point that it threatened to split her cheeks. She drew herself closer still to Carpathian's ear and whispered, "And now that you are gone . . . so, too, will be all you tried so hard to protect. All that which was sanctified by your having been its . . . shall we say . . . custodian, we will destroy. For that is all you were, Einzgear. Behind the bluster and pomp and pretense, you were nothing more than a glorified janitor, frantically attempting to clean messes for which, let us be honest, you were responsible from the start. So, I hope your last thoughts are to imagine what will happen next. The absolute ruin that shall be made of what you once held dear will be unlike anything ever witnessed on this plane."

She ran her hand condescendingly across his long, sweat-soaked hair, brushing it from his tear-stained cheeks. She was so close to him. Closer than she had ever been. Close enough for him to reach up and end her, had he the strength—or the will—remaining. She was close enough that he could smell her skin. An unmistakable scent of lilac. An offensively lovely smell that completely embodied the besotting evil of the Super Vizier and all those who followed the path of the Ninth Guardian.

It was, as it had always been, the most sinister of all the Ninth Guardian's contemptible deceits: The fact that they could turn that which was once good into an object of despair.

The smell entering his nostrils caused his Heart to beat faster.

"His" Heart. This thing in his chest that had landed there what now seemed like five lifetimes ago. This mechanical surrogate for the real thing. It granted him strength and powers beyond his one-time imagining, but it was also the source of so much of his burden and regret.

Every pulse of the clockwork life force was a bridge to ages forgotten and futures not yet written. And today . . . that had been his undoing.

These glimpses into the river of time that had always offered Carpathian the upper hand, allowing him to dance steps ahead of his adversaries, were now showing him a glance beyond the horizon of futures where he saw a discordant event, a shadow of something unexpected.

An aberration.

Darkness.

And it caused him to laugh.

"What is it?" the Super Vizier asked, the faintest hint of worry sprinkled upon the question. "What are you laughing at?"

He did not answer. He could not. The laughter was set to overtake him. It caused him pain—deep, immutable, agonizing pain. And the more he felt it, the harder he laughed.

"Stop it," the Super Vizier said, working to maintain her composure. Then, "STOP IT!" she cried, deciding that maintaining her composure was no longer a priority.

He would have explained it if he could. Would have explicated the ways in which her greed would be her own undoing. How her vituperation would lead to her downfall. How she would not be spared, and the darkness would engulf her as well.

But there was no time to elucidate such things. Because with neither he nor the Super Vizier noticing, Teleri, clinging to the bleeding edge of her own life force, had dragged her small, eviscerated frame to where Carpathian lay and placed her hand on his chest.

And with the last remaining breath she had to beckon, she uttered a phrase . . .

"Yn Vastr."

. . . and the air around Carpathian began to shudder.

The power within him, his Mezmer, swelled, rushing through his veins like an undammed river.

His spear—the Arm of Hearts—began pulsing darkly in his weakened grip, the life force from his slain foes fueling its function. And as his Mezmer surged, he felt the connection to his armor, his weapons, all the artifacts he'd collected in his journey—the Blade of the Starfallen, the Gauntlet of Sorenthali, the Obsidian Shield of Baelus, the Cerulean Tunic of the Seafarer—begin to fade, each item shimmering like a thousand gems in a diadem.

"What is happening?" the Super Vizier squawked.

"There will be another," Teleri whispered, barely audible over the swirling cyclone of Mezmer forming around Carpathian and the still raging battle being fought valiantly but futilely by a remaining few on the desiccated Fields of Rendalia.

"WHAT HAVE YOU DONE?!" the Super Vizier shrieked.

Teleri did not answer. She could not. She had used the last bit of voice she possessed to offer this world the assurance that although she and Carpathian would not live to see it . . . another might rise. A Saviour furnished in a way that Carpathian was not. A true hero.

And having fulfilled the promise she made to Carpathian lo' those many seasons ago—a promise to never leave his side—she died, a small smile enshrined on her lips forever.

And as flights of angels carried her to her rest, so did they ferry away the burdens of Carpathian's station. The long-shouldered weight of his responsibility to this world dissolved from view, leaving Carpathian stripped free of its bitter history.

He felt lighter as he let his head fall gently to the ground.

"No!" the Super Vizier shouted to the deaf heavens. "There will be no others! Bring him home!"

"Mistress?" Moridius questioned.

"Bring him back to Bell's View. That is where his journey began."

"Mistress, I—"

"Bring him back, so that all those who might be tempted to follow in his path may see the folly in their choice! Bring him back, sever him into fourths, and display the disunited parts of his desecrated carcass throughout the land as a warning to any who might fancy themselves audacious enough to trod in his footsteps!"

Moridius hesitated. Not because he was resistant to fulfill the order but because of the hysteria present in the commandment. He had never seen the Super Vizier oriented thus. And it gave him pause.

"Mistress," he repeated once more, "are you—?"

"Do it!" she demanded.

"Yes, ma'am," Moridius replied with genuflection, stifling the urge to reach out and stroke her cheek. Others were present, and there were appearances to maintain. No one could know that beneath her venom and cruelty, the Super Vizier was capable of loving and of being loved. It was now, as it had ever been, paramount to all else that she be feared.

And though Carpathian could hear the conversation, it sounded as though it was happening somewhere deep in the recesses of his mind. And he felt no fear. A twinge of regret, perhaps, but not fear.

Everyone he'd ever cared about was dead or gone. Some long forgotten, some soon to be. Everything he had tried to achieve, he had failed at. All he'd once thought good was a lie. And thanks to the heroics of Teleri, there was a chance—however faint—that all might not be lost for those still alive who wanted to fight.

But that fight was no longer his.

He remembered something Xanaraxa had once said to him. Xanaraxa, the philosopher-poet, always quick with a verse that cut through the din of the world's noise *with precision and the clear-eyed wisdom of a soul who could see beyond the horizon, who intoned:*

The greatest gift for which we can hope,
Is that hope be not here.
For when hope, the deceiver, is struck away,
Then so too is fear.
Knowing that the end is nigh,
The mind can clear and find the time
To see that fear with all its wiles
May be left behind like a faded smile.
Thus . . .
If the wish is for pain be gone
To embrace the coming of the dawn
Free from struggle and hurt and sorrow
Then hold not hope
That there may be 'morrow.

Simply put, Carpathian thought, accepting that the end is the end liberates one from fear because one no longer clings to the desperate hope that there will be anything more.

Thinking on it made him sigh, long and low, as if attempting to hasten the expulsion of air from his lungs so that hope, fear, and all the rest of it might rapidly disperse into the ether like so much collected baggage from off his corpse.

A cold, icy chill, indicating the full separation of his corporeal being from the world that he inhabited, swept across his body. And as the suns dipped below Meridia's distant horizon, surrendering the planet to the gentle caress of night, Carpathian looked on, his silhouette etched against the twilight.

The avowed Saviour at the end of his journey, not with a triumphant roar but with a peaceful sigh. The most unexpected hero one could ever have imagined, with all of his irrelevant intentions and inevitable consequences disappearing quietly into the comforting embrace of the setting suns . . .

CHAPTER ONE

"Are you fucking kidding me?"

"What?"

"He dies?"

"Uh . . ."

"Carpathian *DIES*?"

"Um . . . I mean . . . yeah?"

"ARE. YOU. FUCKING. KIDDING ME?"

As I place the manuscript down on my desk, having just read the final few chapters aloud to Brittany, and pick up a slice of room-temperature pizza, the prevailing thought I have at this moment is . . . *Yeah. This is pretty much what I was expecting.*

I'm actually amazed she waited until the end. I tried not to look at her as I was reading, knowing that if I did, I'd see her increasingly slack-jawed reaction and start to feel a twinge of regret. Because I'm not delusional. I get what a big deal this is. But I need to maintain my composure, so, taking a bite of the slice, I try to chill everybody out.

(And by *everybody*, I mean Brittany.)

"Brit, listen, just calm—"

"Don't tell me to calm down. Bruce, I swear to Christ, do not—"

"I wasn't going to!" It comes out muffled by the cheese and sauce, so I swallow and emphasize, "I promise."

It's an obvious lie. I already got out the "calm" part. But honestly, while I prepped myself for *a* strong response, I was not entirely prepared for *this* level of anger. I knew she might have some robust pushback, but nothing quite like this.

No, that's also a lie.

I feared it would be exactly like this. I was just hoping for something different.

Hope and fear. Kissing cousins.

But I know Brittany too well. She's always been my toughest critic. Or . . . That's not fair. *Tough*'s the wrong word. *Candid evaluator of my prose.* Maybe that's more accurate. Or at least more polite. Regardless, being frank about my writing is part of what I pay her for, and she's good at it. Just . . . there's an unusually hot heat coming at me in this moment. Even for her.

Ooooh. Know what? I bet I know what it is.

"Are you . . . ?" I start, but stop myself before I can finish the thought, remembering that the last time I asked her what I was about to ask, she very nearly punched a hole in the sky. "Never mind."

She stares at me. "Am I what?"

"Nothing."

"No. No. Am I what? What were you going to ask?"

"I wasn't going to ask anything."

There's a long beat before she says, "You were going to ask me if I'm on my period, weren't you?" Another beat. "*Weren't you?*"

I need to answer this very, very carefully.

". . . Are you?"

"What the hell is wrong with you?!"

Shit.

Okay, look, maybe I should have seen this coming. No, of course I should have. I knew it would be a shock. I didn't tell her what I was planning. How I was intending to end the series. Or, for that matter, *that* I was intending to end it. To be very honest, I didn't really know myself that I was going to until it happened.

And I already had her doing research for book eleven. We had even started discussing a rough outline for books twelve through fifteen. In her mind, everything was full steam ahead for the next . . . god . . . however many years of our, I guess, partnership. (Which isn't actually a *partnership*, per se. I mean, she's my assistant, but still . . .)

So, I understand her surprise. But now that she's gotten it out of her system, I can try and explain why I—

"And *I* die too?!"

Oh, she wasn't done. My bad.

"What do you mean, *you* die?"

"Me, Teleri, whatever. *We* die? Why do *we* die?"

I take a moment to consider what she's asking, then offer, cautiously, "You know that you're not *actually* Teleri, right?"

She looks at me with an *are you stupid?* face. "Yes, of course I know I'm not *actually* Teleri. But there's a lot of me in there."

I take an odd kind of offense to that for some reason. "Okay, hang on. Now, not *a lot*—"

"*Not a lot?* Teleri is a five-foot three-inch lesbian who speaks six languages and who, before 'the Great Expunging,' was pursuing a postgraduate degree in 'sorcerology.'" She pauses to let the point land and then sniffs derisively. "*Not a lot.*"

I start to protest again, but then stop myself and acquiesce. "Alright, fine. But still, Teleri's primarily an invention of my imagination. Just like everything."

She chews at her lip. Squints at me. "When did you introduce Teleri? As a character?"

"I-I don't— Around book three? I guess?"

"And when did I start working for you?" She sticks her neck forward, jutting out her chin and raising her eyebrows in a *Hmm?* implying manner.

I sigh out through my nose, start to say something, stop, make my way over to the aquarium so I can sprinkle in some ground eggshells for Gonzo to nibble on (because even though I've had him for a long time, I only recently learned that ground eggshells are apparently the preferred snack of the Mexican Turbo Snail, and Gonzo really seems to enjoy them), and turn to face her.

"Any similarity to situations, persons, or animals, living or dead, is purely coincidental."

She stares at me, laughs sort of bitterly to herself, then says, "You're missing the point. I'm not mad that you wrote me into the books. Honestly, I've always thought it was kind of flattering. But . . ."

"But what?"

"I dunno! It's pissing me off that you killed me without checking with me first! I know it doesn't make sense, but whatever! I only just found out about it! I haven't had time to explore the psychological implications! I'm just annoyed!" She has her hands on her hips. For someone so much physically smaller than I am, I find her oddly intimidating at this moment. "What happened to the plan?"

"Which plan?"

"The plan for the next however the hell many books you were going to write?"

I shrug. "Dunno. Story took me this way instead."

"Took you that way," she scoffs. "Okay."

"What? What are you snorting at? What does that mean, *okay*?"

She levels a gaze that is half glare, half eye roll. "It means I'm not your shrink, Bruce, but killing yourself off all dramatically—"

"Whoa, whoa, whoa, whoa, whoa, whoa, whoa. Killing *myself*? What do you mean, killing *myself*? You think—? Brit, I'm not Carpathian."

She tilts her head at me. There's yet another long beat (I hope these don't become a habit. I hate awkward silences.) before she says, "Bruce. Please. Please, don't pretend that—"

"I'm not!" I take a breath to gather my thoughts before continuing, "I mean, look, of course, yes, obviously, there are maybe parts of me written into him, but—"

"*Parts*? Dude, the city Carpathian is from is called *Santus Luminous*."

"Yeah?"

"We're in ST. LOUIS right *now*!"

"I don't—"

"Before 'the Great Expunging,' Carpathian was a 'Public Conveyance Conductor.'"

"So?"

"So? You used to be a goddamn *BUS DRIVER*, Bruce!" She blinks several times and says, mostly to herself, "*Puta merda. Kuso chikushou. Putain. Tu te moques de moi?*" Which is what happens when she's really, really angry. She almost reflexively begins swearing in as many different languages as possible. I think it has something to do with not wanting to be confined to one manner of rageful expression. Then she switches back to English and asks, "Is this a joke? Is this some new, weird-ass hidden camera show? Am I gonna wind up on TikTok or some bullshit?"

"Brit—"

"Bruce . . ." She takes a breath. It's a familiar pattern. She gets upset about something, comes charging out of the blocks like Usain Bolt, then—once the initial burst has subsided—lets her shoulders drop. It's a pattern I've watched her replay dozens of times over the past few years.

Beneath the bluster, she's a really, really nice person and a solid friend, and I don't think I could've enjoyed all the success I have without her. I sincerely don't. But you just kinda gotta weather the storm before you get to her bright sky. And I'm the type of person who can do that. Things like people yelling don't get to me, usually. I tend to be a real go-with-the-flow, live-and-let-scream sort of a cat. Externally, anyway. Most of my frustration and anxiety stays tucked away inside in a nice, tight little ball that I think doctors might technically call an "ulcer."

But, again, that's me. Most people don't make it past Brit's first wave of fury. Which is why she got kicked out of her sociology PhD program in the first place (the lawsuit involving the professor whose hand she stabbed with a pencil remains ongoing) and I helped her out by offering her a gig working as my Girl Friday. (Though she's much less Hildy Johnson than she is Wednesday Addams, so maybe it's more appropriate to call her my Girl Wednes—)

"Bruce . . ." She says my name a second time, which usually indicates she's gathering her thoughts. When you work as closely with someone as we have for the last seven books, you get to know their idiosyncrasies better than your own. "Why?"

She plops herself in the wingback chair in my home office and folds her hands in her lap, waiting for me to answer. Even though she's ten years younger than I am and her feet barely touch the ground when she sits, she still manages to project an overwhelming "disappointed parent" energy.

I finish tapping the eggshells into the snail habitat, pop the remaining pizza crust into my mouth, step over to the wingback's companion chaise-longue, and lay myself upon it, therapy patient style.

"Because," I start, still chewing, "I'm . . . Tired." She doesn't respond, presumably waiting to see if I plan to expound on the point. So, I honor the unspoken request. "I just . . . I dunno. I'm not . . . happy anymore. Doing this."

"Which part?"

"I mean, all of it. The coming up with new ideas. The hours of research. The—"

"*AHHHHHHHNNNNNN.*" She makes a sound like a wrong-answer game show buzzer. "Bullshit. You don't 'come up' with new ideas."

"Of course I do."

"Come on, man. It's not like you sit around for hours ruminating over details and plotting shit out. You just . . . whatever the hell you call it."

"Get into a flow state?"

"Yeah," she says, with what might be a touch of sarcasm. "Get into a *flow state*. You're a regular James Joyce." Which she says with what is most decidedly sarcasm. "And I do all of the research. No excuse there. Not buying it. What else?"

I take a deep breath through my nose. Let it out the same way. "Honestly?"

"No, lie to me. Yes, honestly! Jesus."

I'm struggling to keep my emotions from surfacing. But despite the attempt, thoughts of unanswered calls from friends, missed birthday parties, failed relationships, and countless nights spent hammering out chapters flood my mind. And all of it in service to . . . what? A bunch of made-up stories that . . . that . . . That accomplish what? I don't know. That's the problem. The weight of it all threatens to suffocate me.

I rub my hands down my cheeks, feeling the three-day stubble. "I feel . . . trapped."

"Trapped. You're probably one of the most successful authors in, maybe, the world today—"

"Okay, hold on. Not in the *world*."

"Your last three books all topped the *New York Times,* and you've been nominated for *four* Hugo Awards."

"Exactly. I've never won."

She pounds her fists against the side of her head. "Whatever! You're living a dream that, if you'd told yourself ten years ago you'd be living, you wouldn't have believed was even possible. And you feel . . . *trapped*."

I nod slightly, my head making a soft rubbing sound against the upholstery of the chaise's Roman arm, and say simply, "Yes. I do." I keep going before she can tell me how broken that is. "And hey, I get it, okay? I know that sounds . . . Goddammit. I'm not ungrateful; I'm really not. This has been an incredible ride. I mean, Christ, all I wanted to do initially was just distract myself from how much I hated my stupid job by writing fan fiction on my lunch breaks. That's it. That was enough for me."

She eyeballs me with skepticism.

"No bullshit. I mean it. I had given up on dreams of being a successful author well before then, and, y'know, at *that* time, I was just writing for me. To . . . Whatever. Remind myself that I could? I suppose? I dunno. Look, I just wanted to be able to escape into a fantasy world of my own creation. That's all. I genuinely never thought it would result in all *this*." I gesture out at nothing in particular, intending to indicate the house, the pool, the guest house, the Porsche Panamera Platinum Edition in my driveway. (I need to say that a second time: The. Porsche. Panamera. Plat. In. Um. Edishy-ition. Deep Black with black interior. Twenty-one-inch sport wheels in satin platinum. I named her Sheila. So, I mean, I know I'm a lucky bastard. However . . .) "And I feel so, so, *so* fortunate, but . . ." I trail off, realizing how much I must sound like an unappreciative prick despite my claim to the contrary.

"Buuuuut?" Brittany draws out. "But what?"

"None of it feels the way I thought it was supposed to."

"How'd you think it was supposed to feel?"

"Not sure. But not like it does." I swing my legs to the floor and sit up, facing her in an attempt to articulate it more clearly. "It doesn't feel like it's mine anymore. Y'know?"

"No. I don't. What does that mean?"

"It means that the story, Carpathian's story . . . I feel like I have all these . . . responsibilities, or obligations, now to . . . I don't know. To *deliver* something? I guess? Or . . . satisfy some kind of set of expectations, or— I dunno! I dunno. I just . . . It just doesn't feel like it's *mine* anymore," I repeat for emphasis. I take a pause to try and work out if there's a better way to explain it. When I can't find one, I ask, "Does that make any sense?"

She studies me as I try as hard as I can to project anything at all that might resemble contriteness. Then she sighs.

"Of course it does."

"Yeah?"

"Yeah. Because it isn't." She says it with an impressive mixture of pity and disappointment. She is a complicated young woman.

"I don't— What are you saying?" I ask.

"God, dude. For someone so smart and talented, you can be a real dink sometimes, you know that?"

". . . Thanks?"

She stands, moves over to the bookshelf, takes down the first book—*Seasons of Rebellion,* novel one of the Riftbreaker series by Bruce Silver—and holds it consideringly.

"When you make something, and then you put it out into the universe and ask people to engage with it—book, movie, TV show, music, art, whatever— you're making an agreement with them. A compact. You're saying that you are surrendering the thing you've created to them, and that by them picking it up, it is no longer exclusively yours. It is a shared experience. And that by consuming it, they become part of the life cycle of the thing. Honestly, it's debatable whether or not ideas are proprietary in the first place. If Elizabeth Gilbert is to be believed, an idea starts somewhere out in the cosmos, looks for a willing vessel to funnel it into existence, and then passes through that vessel to wind up in the hands of the audience who is destined to find it, appreciate it, and become affected by it. So no, bro, of course it's not 'yours.' It was never *yours* to begin with. It's bigger than you."

She finishes her soliloquy by coming close to me, putting her hands on mine, kneeling down, and looking up to peer into my eyes with something like sincere belief.

"Who's Elizabeth Gilbert again?"

That is, apparently, not the response she was hoping for.

"What is *wrong* with you?!" she, like, bellows.

"I'm sorry! I just . . . I know the name. I just can't remember—"

"She wrote fuckin' *Eat, Pray, Love.* And yeah, I know, whatever, not my shit either, but she gave a TED Talk one time about . . . Doesn't matter! It's on YouTube! Look it up! The point is that you don't get to just *quit* a thing because you're *tired.* Jesus!" She slaps the book back into place on the shelf and stares at me. "So what do you want?"

"What do you mean?"

"You don't wanna do *this* anymore. What *do* you want to do? You wanna write something else?"

"Maybe? I'm not sure. I mean, I left the door open a crack. Teleri cast that spell on him at the end. Maybe, someday, I'll do a sequel or something where someone else comes to pick up the story." I pause again because I don't want to lie to her. "Or not. But I don't want to think about it now. Now, I just want to sit on a beach somewhere for a while and, like, chill."

"Chill?"

"Or . . . get inspired again. Rediscover myself. I feel like, somehow, I've lost my . . . I'm not sure. But I wanna find it again. Whatever it is. And I know it sounds . . . I know how it sounds, but . . ." I sigh, searching for the right way to convey what I'm feeling and not finding it, so I land on, "I just want to try and shut off my brain for a while. Clear it out. Start fresh. That's all."

She stares at me more, her head listing side to side like she's considering her next sentence. Finally . . . "Your readers are going to pretty much *hate* you for this. You know that, right?" she demands more than asks. "They're going to feel betrayed."

I try to shrug it away. "I can't allow myself to worry about that. Worrying about what could happen in the future is nothing but wasted energy. If you have the time to worry about a thing happening, it means that everything is fine *right now*. Because if whatever you're worrying about were actually *happening*, you'd be too busy dealing with it to worry over it. So . . ."

She stares at me for an astonished beat. Then she shakes her head and her eyes narrow.

"Yeah, okay, Tony Robbins."

"Please don't—"

"I'm sorry, but . . ." She takes a deep breath. "Dude, I think it's super that you wanna go on this 'spiritual journey' or 'vision quest' or whatever the hell it is, but just . . . don't talk to me like I'm other people. Okay? I know you. You once chased a food delivery guy ten blocks to give him a dollar because you accidentally shortchanged his tip and didn't want him to think you were cheap. You can't *not* worry about it." She blows out her lips with a motorboat-sputtering sound, then says simply, "There are people who have fallen in *love* with Carpathian."

"Maybe some people have. There are lots of people who think he's—"

"Okay, but I'm not talking about them. I'm talking about the ones . . . the ones who've gotten tattoos, who've named their kids after him. *Kids*. Named *Car. Pay Thee-an*. The ones who go to the conventions—actual conventions; do you get what a big deal that is?—dedicated to this world you've built. The ones who stand in line to get your autograph. The ones who tell you how much what you've written means to them. Like that one lady who named all of her cats after characters from the books? Her *cats*, bro. Do you know how invested people get in their goddamn cats? *That's* who I'm talking about. Cat lady and the rest of them. Those are the ones who are devoted to what you've made. And those are the ones you'll be pulling the rug out from under. I mean, you don't feel any responsibility to them to, y'know, not blow it the hell up?"

I try to think of the right thing to say, but realizing there probably is no "right" thing, I just say the first thing that comes to mind.

"I never asked anyone to do all that stuff."

I expect another Krakatoa eruption or at least a Chernobyl meltdown, but what I get is neither. What I get looks more like, honestly, sorrow. And maybe a little fear.

". . . I suppose I shouldn't be upset, right?" she half whispers. "Because it is me who's constantly encouraging you to worry less about what everyone thinks."

"This isn't your—"

"Doesn't matter. Doesn't matter if it is or isn't. Beside the point. The point is that, sure, okay, fine. You 'never asked anyone to do all that stuff.' Fair enough. But . . . you did ask me for something." I feel like someone just sucked all the air out of the room. "You asked me to help you. To come along on this journey with you. And I did. Because I believed in you and what you were making and . . . All of it. And then you decide to end it like this? Without even . . . telling me? Forget 'asking' or 'consulting.' You just decided to do this on your own and . . . ?"

She trails off. And it's way, way worse than her yelling at me. The hurt. The vulnerability. It brings what she apparently sees as my . . . *betrayal* . . . into way starker focus than any amount of verbal battery might. Then she lands a quiet, finishing blow . . .

"It just feels pretty goddamn selfish."

Somewhere in the recesses of my mind, I hear a voice call out, *Fatality!*

"Hey. Hey, look—" I reach out to put a hand on her shoulder, but she pushes it away.

"No. No, you don't get to do that. You don't get to do your whole 'It's all good, fam. I'm just super chill Bruce Silvert from St. Louis who don't cause no trouble and is everybody's charming, occasionally-stoned-but-in-a-fun-way best bud.' Not tonight, man. I'm sorry."

Ouch. That . . . Yeah, that stings. Not so much the mocking my personality part. Because, to be fair, she's not wrong. (And, because I *do*, in fact, work hard to be kinda chill about things, it would be horribly ironic to get bent out of shape about her noting it.)

No, the part that stings is that she uses my name. My real name. My full name. I hate that. My dad used to call me by my full name when he was particularly annoyed with me—which was often—and I definitely harbor some PTSD around hearing it. Fortunately, I don't very often because Brittany is the only person I know who still refers to me by my actual last name. (Bruce Silver just seemed kinda sexier on the cover than Silvert. The only other Silvert I've ever known is a company that makes adaptive clothing for seniors. No shade. It's super-comfy-looking casual wear. It's just not the vibe I was going for.)

But my point is that her use of it highlights how well she and I know each other and how close we've gotten over time, and sort of further underlines how selfish this decision of mine *may* have been. She's right. She's not other people. But . . .

Shit. No. *No.* I can't let remorse or any other random emotion steer me from what I *know* is the correct decision. Perhaps I've not gone about executing it in the most elegant possible way, but I believe, in my heart of hearts, that it is the best decision for me to make.

I think.

Maybe.

She turns and starts to head out of the room.

"Where are you going?"

"To the pool house."

"Why?"

"Because I live there and because I don't have anything else to say at the moment."

"What? Wait, wait, wait, no— Come on, Brit, it's not— Hey, have a slice with me and let's—"

"No."

"But can't we just—?"

"No. We can't. Not now."

Roughly fifty different ideas run through my head about how to try and persuade her to stick around and keep hashing this out. I hate conflict. That's probably why I'm in this situation. I don't need to start tracking how every decision I've ever made has been by virtue of conflict avoidance. The origins of why that is trace back a long way, but I feel that it really cemented itself as, like, my whole personality when I became a bus driver instead of a novelist when I was eighteen—even though it had been my dream to be a novelist since I was, like, five—because driving buses is what my dad did, and I didn't want to piss him off when he got me the job.

Sort of funny in an absolutely not-at-all-funny-and-really-shitty-way that *stopping* writing is what's triggered this new calamity.

"Hey," I call after her. She stops moving but doesn't turn to face me. I say to her back, "Y'know, if you're worried about money or anything, don't be. I'll still—"

The pained look on her face as she spins around sharply causes me to stop talking.

There is a beat before she offers, quietly, "Wow," and shakes her head, slowly. "It's not about money, Bruce. It's never been about money. I'm a smart gal. There are plenty of other things I could have chosen to do. I wanted to work for you because I liked the job and believed in what you . . . *we* . . . were making." (I take note that she speaks about it in the past tense.) "And the idea that you would reduce it to something as trivial as . . ." She squeezes her eyes shut tight, the way a person does when they want to avoid crying, and takes a deep breath.

"Can we . . ." I begin, trying to calculate anything else I can say that won't sound overly placating at best or condescending at worst. I come up with, "Can we just talk about it in the morning? Please?"

She studies me almost sympathetically and then says, "Sure." I sigh out in relief. At least until she adds, "If I'm still here."

She spins away from me once more, and as she swings open the door that leads to the backyard, a cold, icy chill comes swooping into the room.

Which I probably wouldn't necessarily notice that much? Except . . .

. . . it's August.

CHAPTER TWO

I think he's breathing! The covers is movin' up and down!"

The voice sounds vaguely . . . British? Maybe? Kind of "Renaissance Faire" British.

"No, they're not. It's just a trick of the light. Stop being fokken weird, mate. He's dead. Proper dead. Look at him. How friable and brittle he be."

The second voice sounds similar. It feels like I . . . recognize them? Somehow? Though I'm not quite sure from where. I think I'm dreaming? But it must be a lucid dream because I am acutely aware that I'm dreaming. Although I'm also not sure what I'm dreaming about.

"Don't *friable* and *brittle* mean the same thing?" the first voice asks.

"Who fokken cares? I know dead! And *that's* fokken dead."

"Maybe he was always friable and/or brittle and we couldn't tell. We don't know. First time I've laid eyes on him without his armor and all."

There's a vague pressure in my chest, a pulsing rhythm that feels odd. And the voices keep nattering as I attempt to rouse myself from this half-sleep-state thing I'm in.

"Are we sure it's even really him?" a female voice asks. "What's happened to his hair?"

"His fokken hair?"

"Yeah. Them long, lustrous tresses. Where'd they go?"

"Maybe you ain't never heard of . . . a hair. Cut?"

"But his beard . . ." the female voice continues. "Never seen him all scruffy, baby-face like. So much more rugged he always was. Just, how can we know for *certain* that this ain't a decoy figure or the like? Could be some type of Spell that—"

"Oi! The herald said this is where we'd find him, and this is where he be. In front of us. Right now. It's him, yer all making excuses, and I've had enough of it. So, get to it."

The first voice starts begging. "Please, no. *Please*? Please, don't make *me* touch him?"

"For fok's— Why the FOK NOT? He's. Fokken. Dead!"

"He disappeared three Lunar Rotations ago. We don't know what he's been up to between then and now. Got his hairs cut, trimmed that beard up all tidy. We don't know his game. Mayhaps he's just playin' at dead. I were there at the Battle of Floraisient. I seen what he done. Played dead right up to the moment when someone laid a hand on him, and then he took that hand clean off, along with the arm, the neck, and the head attached to it." I feel a tentative poking at my ribs through the duvet. "Hey! Saviour! You dead in there?"

Savior?

"Oi! It don't matter! If he ain't dead now, he will be once he's carved up into cutlets. So. Get. To. Carvin'. This is a fokken honor, mate. I'm giving you the chance to be the one to make the first cut. And if you want that promotion you've been whining about . . ."

"I do, I do," the first voice, in fact, whines. "I just—"

"It's alright," the female voice says. "Don't be afeared, Draven. I'm here to back you up, ya need."

"Then you do it, Yolanda."

"I . . . I would, but, erm . . . Moridius gave you the order. Chain o' command and that."

Moridius? Draven? Yolanda? Battle of Floraisient? Wait. These are . . .

They're characters. My *characters. For crying out— Please don't tell me I'm going to now be* dreaming *about them. I put them all out of my misery for a reason. Jesu—*

"For the love of Kentavion, will someone just fokken—"

"ACH! HE STIRS!"

I squint my eyes open to see . . .

. . . three figures looming over me. Two men and a woman. Two men and a woman I know even though I've never met them before. They're dressed in all-black, semitranslucent armor. They appear wide-eyed with something akin to fear, and have their hands at the ready on the swords they have slid into scabbards attached to their belts.

Exactly as I described them when I wrote them.

"Oi! Make no sudden moves, Einzgear! This can be easy or fokken brutal, mate!" The speaker is a big, hulking brute with a shaved head and more scars than smooth flesh.

Supreme Templar Commander Moridius Wreathnestle, of the Springswallow Wreathnestles, introduced in *Cataclysm's Spawn*, book seven of the Riftbreaker series. Originally conceived as a love interest to the Super Vizier—just to offer her character some additional dimension and complexity—he went on over the last three books to become something of a chief rival to Carpathian. Especially after Carpathian took his brother Charlemond's life.

(To be fair to Carpathian, he was actually trying to save Charlemond when it happened. Charlemond was dangling from a cliff's edge, and Carpathian was swooping in to keep him from falling when he was pummeled from behind by a Cidaswan. It was complicated.)

Regardless, Moridius didn't want to hear it, and it's what's fueled his personal animus toward Carpathian. So, given his prominence in my consciousness over the last few volumes, I probably shouldn't be so shocked that he's showing up in a semi-waking dream.

Draven Pistolstarter and Yolanda HoneyBunny on the other hand . . . I am surprised to be dreaming about them. Side-characters who've never been much more than comic relief. Puck and Bottom. The Rude Mechanicals of my universe.

Then again, I am having a late summer night's dream, so . . .

God. I can't stuff my face with pizza so close to bedtime anymore. It wreaks absolute mayhem on my circadian rhythms.

I blink my eyes a couple of times to try and rid my mind of the dream-images standing in front of me. *What time is it, anyway?*

I turn my head to look at the clock and, when I do, a blade slashes down in front of my face, missing chopping my nose off by millimeters. And not just any old blade. A fireblade. A Mezmerically enchanted blade.

Mezmerically enchanted?

"*Yeah, you heard me,*" a voice inside my head answers.

"*Who's that? Who's there?*" I ask, internally.

"*You, I think,*" the voice responds. "*Bruce,*" it adds for clarity.

"*Me?*" I emphasize. "*You're me?*"

"*I think?*"

"*You're me.*"

"*Best I can tell.*"

"*So, I'm talking to myself?*"

"*I guess?*"

What in the Moon Knight-*Issue-Number-14 is happening???*

"AHHHHH!" is the sound I make as I roll away from the pulsing blue flame emanating from the enchanted metal of the blade.

This isn't real. Relax. Just pull your shit together, wake up, and—

SCHOMP! Another blade slices down, blocking me from rolling to the other side of the bed, and that's when I realize that the blades haven't just pinned me in—they've turned the edges of my California King into a smoking pile of pulsating electric dust. Exactly like the Mezmerically enchanted swords do in Riftbreaker.

"Oi! Don't make this no harder than it has to be, Einzgear! You're lucky I have instructions to make it timely, else I'd take my dear time watching you suffer!" Moridius bellows.

Moridius bellows? C'mon. No. Stop. This isn't really—

"Yolanda! Grab his feet!"

"Moridius! Don't reveal our names to Carpathian! That's suicide!" Yolanda HoneyBunny, whose name I already knew (because I made it up as an homage to *Pulp Fiction*) cries out.

Alright, Bruce. Pull it together. Shake this off. Wake up. Wake up. Wake up, wake up, wake up, wake—

"Reveal our . . . ? We been after him for a dozen moon cycles! You think he don't know?! Draven, Yolanda, you're both getting written up! And know that your bonuses this year will reflect your pathetic display of fearificatiousness! You're a hard one to kill, Einzgear. I'll give you that! But anything worth doin' comes with its labors, don't it?" Moridius says, wrapping his husky meat hooks around my naked ankles.

Okay, this no longer feels like a dream. I mean, it didn't really feel like a "dream" before. But that's the thing about dreams. When you're in the middle of one, they're as real as anything that happens in waking life, which is both why Wes Craven's classic *Nightmare on Elm Street* franchise is so successful and why it's not improbable to think that the world is nothing but a simulation. But that latter point is a bit of navel gazing that can get tabled for another time because, at present, the shit that's happening in my bedroom feels VERY real to me.

Which is when I have a terrifying realization: This isn't a dream. This is . . . Oh god.

This is a B&E! These three cosplaying superfans have gotten my address and broken into my home, and are here to terrorize me because they somehow heard about how I have chosen to end the series! Oh shit!

How did they find out? The only person on the planet besides me who knows is Brittany, and she . . .

No. There's no way Brittany would've done something like post a spoiler on social media or some fan page or something. Would she? I can't imagine. And even if she had, there's no way these three would have already gotten their shit together to come storming in here all willy-nilly, carving up my bed and bodying me around.

Carving up my bed?

Whatever. Not the time to get mired in the details. I've got some wackadoos up in this funky joint, and I need to get out of here. Because there's also no way the cops'll get here in time to do anything now. This is all on me. I really, *really* wish I wasn't in my pajamas. I feel so Holden Caulfield-ish.

"Okay, alright!" I shout, kicking at cosplay Moridius. "Just . . . Just . . . take it easy! Alright?! Whatever this is, we can work it out. Just—"

But that's all I get out before he yanks me, feet first, off the bed, smacking the back of my skull on the footboard as he does, and I crash hard to the bedroom floor.

"Ow!" That's me. But the jolt I feel is less from the impact of hitting the floor and more from the . . . I dunno . . . whirring? I feel in my chest.

What in the cardiac arrest is that?

"Look out!" "Draven" shouts, pointing. "His chest! The Heart!"

"The heart?" What is he—?

Oh shit. My chest. It appears to be . . . *Glowing?* No. Glowing. Period. Not a question. That's what it's doing. It's most definitely glowing.

"Are you sure this isn't a dream, Bruce?"

"Who gives a good goddamn, Bruce? Run, you Simple Simon–looking son of a bitch!"

I do as I instruct myself. Without thinking about it any further, I leap to my feet and dash out of the room, leaving the motley crew behind. The sudden burst of adrenaline makes me feel like I've been mainlining espresso.

As I dart away, they scramble after me, tripping over each other in their haste.

"Get him!" "Yolanda" shouts, but "Moridius," in his attempt to grab me, ends up tackling her instead. They both crash into a bookshelf, sending my collection of first editions tumbling to the ground.

I race down the stairs, taking them three at a time. *Good Christ, why do I have so many stairs?* As I reach the bottom, I discover that there are *more* dress-up Templars waiting in my living room! What the flimflam?

One of the goons, spotting me, shouts, "Block the door!"

My bare feet skid to a halt as I look for another way out. The kitchen? My eyes land on the doggy door. I always meant to get a new kitchen door after Baxter ran off, but I continued to hold out faint hope that maybe he would—

"NOT THE TIME, BRUCE!"

Yeah, alright, fair enough, me.

I squeak down the hallway, slipping a little and cursing the fact that I just *had* to have the hardwood buffed and polished a week ago. I dive for the doggy door, squeezing through with surprising ease. *And Brittany says hot yoga has no real-world applications. Ha! Take that, Brit, ya cynic!*

Once outside, I take a moment to catch my breath, ready to make a beeline for the guest house to warn my cynical assistant about . . . whatever the hell is going down, but I stop dead in my tracks. Because while *my property* seems untouched, everything beyond the edge of the driveway is, well, wrong.

The St. Louis skyline is . . . not. It's . . . changed. Or something.

The skyscrapers in the distance are twisted and bent at odd angles. Black smoke curls off from somewhere far away. Even the sky is . . . incorrect. Those aren't stars. Or, they kind of are, but they're not the ones I normally see floating around out there in the night.

The fu—?

And then . . .

I see the Arch, the most famous identifying characteristic about this town. The "Gateway to the West." Except it isn't. I mean . . . No. It is. But it—

It looks as though someone's beefed it up in Photoshop. It's *huge*. Enormous. And crazy-looking. Red light shining out of the top like a beacon of ill-intent.

What in the Country Grammar *is going on? This doesn't look like my home anymore. It looks exactly like what I . . .*

And then, through the big bay windows that allow me to see from the back of the house to where delivery drivers slam-dunk packages on the front stoop . . . I spot the vehicles parked on the lawn.

At first glance, they look like motorcycles, but on closer inspection, they're . . . *magecycles?* Just like the Super Vizier's lackeys ride, with intricate symbols—runes—etched into their frames. The engines hum. Idling.

Ach! Why does my chest still feel so weird?

What the hell was in that pizza? Oh! Mushrooms! I ordered mushrooms! Goddammit! I'm tripping balls! Son of a bitch! The little hoodlums who work at the pizza place are up to tomfoolery! Tomfoolery, I say! No! Brucefoolery! Oh, someone at corporate is getting a sternly worded letter from this disgruntled and extremely high customer, I'll tell you that! Dominoes will fall, I say! Domino's! Will! Fall! Oh! I made a word joke! I get it! Ha-ha!

"Search the whole place!" a muffled voice calls from inside, then I hear crashing as my would-be abductors begin turning shit over, and I realize . . .

Gonzo!

My sweet, dear, harmless pet snail who has never once in all the years I've had him tried to escape on me like Baxter the Labradoodle is all alone in there with them! Shit. I need to go back and, at the least, rescue Gonz. He's a snail! There's no way he can outrun them on his own!

This is so much to process!

Too much, it seems. Because instead of making moves, I find myself enervated by the overwhelming stimuli. So, I just stand here, dumbfounded, trying to comprehend what's happening. The world I knew is gone, replaced by what looks like Meridia, my fictional world. People dressed like Templars are looking for "Carpathian" . . .

And as this is all settling on me, I hear footsteps approaching.

I wheel in place with an approximation of a karate stance. I think. I've only taken a couple of classes in my life, but I have watched *Kung Fu Hustle* about a hundred times, and I've always fancied myself a decent mimic.

But instead of one of the home invaders, I see Brittany. She's disheveled, clearly having just woken up, buttoning up a pair of cutoff jean shorts and wearing a white tank top emblazoned with "Feminist Is My Second Favorite F-Word." Her hair is in a bun, and she sports a look of astonishment. Wide-eyed, slack-jawed astonishment. Which is very unlike her.

Brittany is a lot of things, but easily flabbergasted is not one.

"What. The . . ." she starts, but doesn't even get the rest out. The staccato "What. The. F?" that I've heard her utter probably a thousand times appears to be stuck in her throat as she stares ahead at the bizarre landscape. Does she see what I—?

"What?" I gasp. "What's wrong?"

"Santus Luminous," she whispers.

"What? What are you saying?" I feel like the patron deity of confusion.

"It's Santus Luminous," she repeats. "How did—?"

"He's outside!" I hear "Draven" shout from inside the house.

"It's not really Draven, Bruce!"

"I know, Bruce! But I didn't stop to get the asshole's real name! Cut me a break! I'm working with limited intel here!"

"And he's got the sorceress with him!" "Draven" continues. "She's alive as well!"

Sorceress? Wha—?

"Sorcer*er*!" I hear "Yolanda" respond.

"What?" yells "Draven."

"Sorcer*er*. We've talked about it twenty times, Dray. It's not gender specific. You wouldn't call me a Templaress, would you?"

"I didn't mean it in an offensive way, Yolanda! My intention wasn't to—"

"At the setting of the suns, intentions are irrelevant. All that matters is consequence."

Oh, Christ. They're quoting my own books as they rampage through my house.

"You're right, you're right!" "Draven" calls. "That's on me! I'm still evolving; I'll have a look at it! But the fact remains that the *sorcerer* is also still alive, and they are outside!"

I grab Brit by the shoulders. "Brittany! Do you have your phone? We have to call the cops. Shit's gone sideways. There's a bunch of lunatics in the house—superfans. They—"

"What did we do?" she murmurs, almost catatonically, still staring at the sky.

"What? What did who do?"

"You. What did you do?"

"Who do?"

After a long pause, she mumbles out, "Voodoo," and shudders.

It's the shudder that takes it from being a poor excuse for an Abbott and Costello routine and turns it into something authentically spine-tingling.

Then she turns to me, her face trapped somewhere between terror and realization, and adds, "We're here."

"What do you mean? Here? Here where? What are you saying?"

"Quickly! Don't let them get away!" comes from inside as I hear booted feet start charging toward the door.

"Santus Luminous," Brittany says, stone-faced. Serious as cancer.

"What?" I reply. For, like, the hundredth time in the last five minutes. "Oh, no. Brit . . . Did you come back in after I went upstairs and have some of the pizza too? Oh shit, I—"

FWOOM!

"THE HELL?!" I scream as a bullet from inside the house pierces the air, cracking past my head. No. Not a bullet. I've heard bullets before, and they don't sound like that. At least not bullets from any guns on Earth. However, as I wrote about it in the books, what I heard *might* sound an awful lot like a shot from a . . . *switchsaw?*

A *real* switchsaw?

The hell? Why aren't my neighbors doing anything?! This is supposed to be a safe neighborhood! Where are all my HOA fees going?!

And then, in this desperate moment, light erupts from my chest.

"AHH!" I shout. Yet again.

So many questions and so much shouting. This is the opposite of how I generally like shit to be. Since I finished reading the end of book ten to Brittany, things have been extremely uncomfortable in a way that I absolutely do not enjoy.

And something in the back of my brain tells me that it's not going to cool out anytime soon.

Or maybe it's not in the back of my brain.

It's more accurate to say that it's right in front of my eyes. Because . . .

"Oh shit . . ." Brittany mutters half-in-awe, half-in-barely-contained panic.

"What? What is it?" I grind out as the light from my sternum expands, carrying a not insignificant amount of discomfort with it.

She doesn't respond with words, just points with repeated urgency at the air before me. I have to squint to see what she's trying to indicate. Something inside me feels pulled taut, making it hard for me to focus.

Straining, I can begin to make out . . . I can begin to make out . . .

Oh my god. I can begin to make out a display of gears attending the projection-like beam of light pouring from my chest. Cogs shift seemingly without end until I can finally identify words.

>**Mezmer Type:** [Review Required]
>**Foundation:** [Review Required}
>**Resonance Tier:** [Review Required]
>**Affinity:** [Review Required]
>**Statistics:** [Review Required]

>**Armament(s):**
Mechanical Heart

>**Inventory:** [None]
>**Abilities:** [None]

>**Spell(s):**
Control

. . . What? Oh, god. No. No. It can't be . . . The Heart? The Mechanical Heart.

The Heart that Carpathian's guide and mentor, Almeister, replaced his actual heart with early on in *Seasons of Rebellion* to give Carpathian an advantage as he began his journey toward becoming the World Saviour. It was the linchpin of his entire rise to power.

This is the way the Mechanical Heart works in Riftbreaker. Exactly as I wrote it. None of this makes sense.

I stare numbly at the words for what feels like a long moment. I feel a hand land on my arm. I turn to look. Brittany. She's glaring ahead at the air in front of me as well. I see her chest rising and falling with her breathing, saucer-like eyes glistening with tears of what appears to be wonder and maybe terror. Her muscles tighten, causing her to quake. Her lips press together and part again as she struggles to stave off hyperventilation, and between short, sharp stabs of breath, she manages to utter out . . .

". . . Select Spells."

CHAPTER THREE

What are you talking about? You can see that?" I ask, even though I obviously know the answer.

FWOOM!

Another blindly fired switchsaw blast. This one even closer.

"Select Spells, Bruce!" she shouts as she reaches out and does it for me.

In a burst, I feel a rush of energy course through me and I start sweating.

Not sweating because of the blast of energy itself but because I am experiencing—in real time, in real life—things that I *wrote about* in my books. The literary depictions of what happened to Carpathian when he first interacted with his own powers and Abilities in a world of my invention are occurring within *me*. At this very moment.

And, to be overly simplistic about it, it's a real head trip.

New words now appear just above the (*gulp*) open inventory slots.

Dear [New User],
You are currently under assault by [Templars]. These [Templars]
cannot be defeated given your current Level(s). In order to both
fully verify and enjoy the possibility of upgrading your Level(s), you
must visit a Pulse Well. Thus, given the circumstances, it would be
prudent to move with greater haste. Or, perhaps, simply flee!
{COURTESY MESSAGE #1}

Okay. So, here's the thing that's insane. (*The* thing. As if there's only one.) I know exactly what that all means. Because I came up with it. I crafted the world, the rules, and functionality—all of it—that I'm apparently in the middle of right now. But I'm finding myself having a hard time engaging with it. And not just because I'm still not totally sure I'm not hanging on to the fringes of a flying carpet taking me on a magic shroom ride.

It's because . . . It's tough to explain. It's kind of like, I suppose, the difference between theoretical physics and applied physics. One is academic. On paper. Y'know—theoretical. The other is . . . well . . . applied. And right now, I'm having to *apply* ideas that previously only existed *theoretically* in my imagination and on my computer screen.

Christ. All this confusificatiousness is not doing much to speed up any decision-making process I might be needing to engage with. Fortunately, Brittany appears much less gobsmacked than I am by all this, and is seemingly down to clown.

"Press Control!" she yells, pointing at the lone available Spell.

"What?"

"Oi!" I hear, then look to see "Moridius" charging through the back door, switchsaw (twenty blasts in the clip, one in the chamber) drawn and pointed right at me.

"Fuckin' press it, dude!" Brit shouts again, simultaneously reaching past me and pressing a word floating in the air in front of us for the second time.

Jiminy Kris Kross, there's an awful lot going on right now.

As she activates it, I hear a *ZZZWWWAAAHHHMMM* sound, and the world seems to slow. Time compresses dramatically. I can feel something happening inside me. An actual, physical feeling washing through my body. My twitch response and muscle awareness is suddenly heightened. Not a lot, maybe ten percent or something, if I had to guess, but my . . . well, *control* over my physical instrument, my body, feels elevated in a small but perceptible way.

"Diiid iiit wooork?" Brittany ask-yells. But her voice sounds muddy, distant, slowed down.

"I dooon't knooow. Maaaaaybe?" I answer, my voice sounding the same. Kind of how people in movies sound when they're on an acid trip. "Whaaat waaas suppooosed to haaappen?"

"Whyyy aaare yooou aaaskiiiing meee? Yooou creaaaaated the Syyyyystem!"

Oh, god. "The System." Aka "the universe." Aka the thing that governs how all of life on Meridia operates. (To paraphrase Douglas Adams: In the beginning, Bruce created the System, and that is now proving to have made some people very angry and is appearing to have been a very bad move.)

Hearing her say it—*You created the System*—causes a scrum of thoughts to collide in my brain.

They say "write what you know," and although Riftbreaker is primarily a product of my overactive imagination, that overactive imagination is influenced by a fairly eclectic set of interests. Consequently, a lot of the ideas in Riftbreaker are inspired by a motley mélange of some of my favorite diversions in life: fantasy novels, classic literature, poetry, music, movies . . . Shakespeare . . . um, professional wrestling . . . video games . . .

(I like to think of myself as Whitman wrote: "Do I contradict myself? Very well, then, I contradict myself . . . *I contain multitudes.*" Others might refer to me less poetically and suggest that I am simply "easily distracted." Who's to say who's right?)

Regardless, pulling from the bric-a-brac shop inside my brain, Meridia and its mechanics are based, like, forty percent on standard, medieval fantasy tropes, forty percent on a dystopian, *Mad Max* meets *The Terminator* type vibe, and maybe twenty percent on survival horror games like *Resident Evil* and big, open world shoot-em-ups like *Red Dead Redemption*.

(Less charitable critics of my work have referred to this manner of inspiration, pejoratively, as "derivative" and "pandering." I have always fancied it as something more of an *homage*.)

So think, Bruce, think. Control was Carpathian's first real Spell. It was the cornerstone of all of his eventual strengths and Abilities. How did it work in the early days . . . ?

Ah! Right! I remember . . . !

At its most rudimentary, most uncomplicated level, Control is a Spell designed to give the user basic mastery over their environment. The intention being that if things ever got too out of hand or started moving at too chaotic a pace for Carpathian to manage, he could . . .

Slow.

It.

All.

Down.

Thus allowing him to see the entire field of action unfolding in front of him and, well, *control* how those circumstances played out.

But. Because I didn't want to turn him into some kind of superhero right from jump, back in the beginning, this meant that Carpathian lived *inside* the effect along with everybody else. Later on, when he *increased* his Abilities and Spells and everything, he became more like the Flash, where he'd be able to speed up or stay at a constant pace while the world around him ground to a crawl, but as an Initiate, it meant that *everything* that was happening came to almost a halt, including Carpathian.

The one key difference for him was that because he knew it was happening, he could maneuver himself to alter the action taking place, while everyone else had to follow through with what they had committed to before time got warped.

I guess it's kind of like entering Bullet Time in *The Matrix*. Neo also moves slowly, along with the bullets coming at him, but he's able to dodge them and whatnot, whereas the bullets themselves—and Agent Smith—have to continue the course they're already on.

(Huh. In fact, now that I think about it, that's *exactly* what Control is like . . . Eh, I'm sure it's fine. Nobody's ever sued me or anything.)

"Eiiiiinnnnnnzgeeeeeaaaaarrrrr!" "Moridius"'s' voice is louder and perhaps *slightly* less echoey than mine and Brittany's were just a second ago. He's still moving in slowish motion, but the slo-mo effect of Control is starting to wear off, the light emanating from my chest is starting to dim, and this aberration in space-time is returning to a standard twenty-four frames per second (or fps, as they say in the movie game). Which lets me know that the time dilation is already almost at its end.

Shit. I forgot just how crappy *it was back in the beginning before Carpathian got all OP. Back when he was just a regular, easygoing guy, plucked up by the forces of the universe and told he was destined to become the World Saviour.*

. . . Oh god.

. . . Oh no.

. . . Oh god.

. . . Oh, no, no, no.

Oh me-oh my-oh, oh Toledo, Ohio!

SHIT.

I think I get what's happening. But how . . . ?

FWOOOOOM!

I see another blast of Mezmerically enhanced plasma heading for Brittany at half-speed. And, without thinking, I grab her arm, spinning her to the side and out of the way of the blast radius, circling elegantly, if slowly, away from the shot like some kind of bizarre, post-apocalyptic Fred Astaire and Ginger Rogers. We complete several balletic maneuvers as we continue rotating apart from the baddies who are firing at us.

And then . . . a sound. A sort of a *SHWOOOOOOOOOOMMMMMPPP*, like when your ears have been filled with water and it's finally draining out. I take a huge inhalation of breath, like I just erupted from being submerged in that same water as the effect of Control wears off, and we fall desperately into a wall of privacy shrubbery that encircles the backyard, which I meant to have trimmed up months ago but am now glad I never did because it gives us much needed cover for a moment, I hope.

And, once more, life comes at us fast, as the saying goes.

"Yeah, I think it worked," I gasp out.

She looks at me, globe-eyed. "Is that it?"

"Is what it?"

"Control! The Control effect. Is that all you get? How long before it fills up again?"

"I-I don't know."

"Why not? Isn't there . . . Isn't there, like, a timer or a gauge or something? That's what Carpathian has in the books."

Brittany has a hard-won trait about her that she calls "accept and adapt." She bounced around a lot of places when she was a kid, and says that one thing it taught her is how to take in the given circumstances of a new environment without resistance, thus allowing her to move right away to figuring out how to function within it. It's a pretty useful attribute, and I feel like it's why she's currently able to embrace the idea that we're not both just experiencing some type of shared hysteria event much more readily than I am.

"I mean, yeah. But I don't . . ."

"Don't what?"

"I don't really remember."

"What do you mean you 'don't remember'?!"

"I just . . . Flow state!! I just write things down as they come to me! You're the one who's supposed to keep track of that stuff! Why don't *you* know how long it takes?"

"Are you serious??"

And just then, almost as if the Heart could hear us bickering over it, an icon— a pulsing representation of the Heart's beating energy—appears, cast in the air in the same way the gears appeared moments before.

Thump-thump. Thump-thump.

It's even. Methodical. In stark contrast to the chaotic mess of the world around us. And the icon possesses an almost black color—drained of life. A blackness that is refilling with something more like a rich redness with each *thump* it thumps. But it is doing so *slooooowwwly*.

FWOOM!

Yet another blast, carving up the vegetation just a few feet away.

"Not as soon as I would like!" I confess hoarsely, and see the muscles in Brit's jaw tighten near her mandible. It looks like a fish's gills when it's been pulled out of water and is trying to survive.

"Einzgear! Sorceress!" "Moridius" calls out.

"It's just *sorcerer*, Moridius." I hear "Draven" correct.

"Thank you, Draven," "Yolanda" appreciates.

"Fokken hell! Fine! *Sorcerer!* Einzgear! Come out! You're only prolonging the inevitable! We *will* find you!"

"I don't understand what's happening!" I whisper-shout.

"What's happening is that we're both somehow now in Santus Luminous, you and me, the two of us," she says redundantly. "And there are Templars trying to ether our shit!"

"But . . . how?"

"Not the priority, Bruce! We can figure out WTFuck when we get the hell outta here, but first, we gotta *get the hell outta here!*"

"Come out, Einzgear! I want to be able to look ye in the eye when I take yer life! Civilized-like!"

"Shit. Just . . . lemme think for a second," I manage to squeak out.

Okay. Okay. If this is real—and I feel like it's still a big if—*I need to maybe put myself in the mind of Carpathian Einzgear, since that's who they think I am.*

I've heard actors call it "The Magic If." When approaching a character they'll be like, "If *I* were this person in such-and-such situation, what would *I* do?" Theoretically, it should be easy. I did, in fact, invent Carpathian, and I put him in all kinds of scrapes and difficult-to-escape situations over the years. And he always got out of them.

The problem is that I'm not kidding; I can barely remember back to the beginning of Riftbreaker, before Carpathian had all his powers and stuff. Back then, I was still just sort of making it up as I went along. It wasn't until Brittany came on around the third book that anything like an order or catalogue got put into place. Hell, she even made maps of Santus Luminous and all the other major locations in Meridia so we'd have a common frame of reference for where events were occurring.

Maps.

"Maps!" I shout. Hushed-ly.

"Maps?"

"You made all those maps of Meridia, remember?"

"Of course I do. I took an online cartography class."

If I'm a go-with-the-flow kinda dude, Brittany is . . . whatever the exact opposite of that is. Her attention to detail is both impressive and exhausting.

"They're in my office. Along with my car keys and Gonz."

She looks at me for a second, then prompts, ". . . Okay?"

"We need to sneak past these whoever-they-ares, grab Gonz, my keys, *and* the maps, and then try to get to a Pulse Well—you know, the ones where people go to verify their upgrades and take possession of new Abilities and recharge Mezmer and formulate game plans and such which is a sentence I just said that I feel reasonably confident has never been spoken by anyone else in the history of time or at least not in that order I dunno I can't be sure but whatever that's what I think we gotta do," I . . . vomit out in an unpunctuated, borderline coherent tumbling jumble.

I'm expecting Brit to say something like, "That's *your best idea?? Are you f'ing kidding me?*"

(Obviously, she wouldn't say "f'ing." She'd use the actual word. But I stay away from saying it for the most part. Not because I have anything against it or because I'm prudish or something. It's just because she uses it so much that it's almost like . . . her signature? It's *her* thing. And I don't wanna bite her thing. Everybody needs a thing they can call their own.)

In any case, it's not what she says. Instead, she just goes . . .

"Okay."

She gets really dialed in when life around her turns chaotic. It's like this super-power she has that was borne of a particular brand of childhood trauma. Goes hand in hand with the hyper-organized thing. And makes her a very good person to have next to you in a crisis. Like this one time? I was baking a cake? And the milk I had was expired, and . . .

Know what? Doesn't matter! Another time!

(Tangential streams of consciousness are one of *my* childhood trauma-borne superpowers. Arguably less useful at the moment.)

"You move toward the house; I'll distract them," she whispers.

"How?"

"I dunno. I'll think of something."

"What?"

"I dunno, Bruce! I haven't thought of it yet! Just start creeping that way . . ."

"Shit," I say, clipped, and start trying to sneak through the foliage toward the door.

"There! The shrubberies is a-movin'!" I hear Draven call, and I brace for what I feel certain is going to be a very painful dollop of magically endowed energy ripping through me. But then, I hear . . .

"Hey! *Haan gesigte!*"

Is that . . . Afrikaans? Holy shit. I didn't even know she had that one in the chamber.

I peek through the leafy greenery and spy Brittany stepping out from the berm to confront the assembly of my imagination.

What is she doing? They're going to blow her to tiny Brittereens!

"Yeah, you! Dicks!" she barks out, hands on hips, chin lifted in challenge.

"Nightwind . . ." Moridius growls. "Holy *Keletas*. How did you get here as well? I saw you die on the Fields of Rendalia with mine own eyes."

"Yeah, well . . . eyewitness accounts are statistically responsible for seventy-five percent of wrongful convictions."

Moridius and the other Templars gathered next to my pool (again, probably never been said before in history) stare at her, confused.

". . . What? What does that mean?"

"It means you can't always believe your lying eyes, ya taint-twizzling bitch whistle."

Moridius looks around at the others, who just kind of shrug.

Is this her plan? To verbally berate them into confused submission? Whatever. It's giving me enough of a window that I think I can make it inside. Maybe.

I look in front of me and see that the Heart icon is, like, maybe a twelfth refilled. Barely any amount at all, but it's better than nothing, I suppose. I try to think.

How did Carpathian summon his Stats and Spells and stuff in the books back in the beginning?

"He didn't, Bruce. They just sort of appeared when he needed them. The Heart determined when it snapped into action and when it didn't."

"What? Why did I do that?"

"Something about teaching him the power of self-reliance or something? I dunno. It was all kind of hazy there for a while. What do you want from me, man? I am you."

Well, that's just—

ZZZWWWAAAHHHMMM.

Okay. It seems that, fortunately, the Heart has decided, in this moment, that I *do*, in fact, need its aid.

Alright. Well. Yay.

Thump-thump, thump-thump . . .

I can feel the Control effect pulsing inside me once more. But the *thump-thump* is decidedly weaker than it was, and getting weaker with each thump.

Great. May as well not even have it at all.

"Hey! Remember what Almeister told Carpathian. Don't look a gift Mechanical Heart Control Spell in the aorta, Bruce."

". . . Annnd wheeere diiid sheee geeet thiiis straaange attiiire?" I hear Draven ask in thick, molasses-like speech as I spin my way smoothly free from my tiny jungle and directly through the still-ajar back door just as . . .

Thump . . .

Thump . . .

SHWOOOOOOOOOOOMMMMMPPP.

And I take another huge inhalation of gasping breath as the effect of Control wears off once more, having given all it has to give at the moment.

I look left, right, and seeing no one there, hustle it down the hall toward my office, the soles of my bare feet slapping on the hardwood floor in the model of many a great and under-habilimented hero, dating back to Achilles.

Although, Achilles . . . um . . . Not a great prototype. Things went badly for my man A-Kill. Dating back to . . . Uh, John McClane? Heck yeah! Greatest action hero of all time! Yippee ki-yay, mother—Oh no . . .

"He's here!" shouts a beefy Templar blocking the doorway into my office. "At the entrance to the library!"

(He makes it sound much fancier than it is. It's really just a spare bedroom that I threw some bookcases and a desk into. I mean, I'd love to have built a proper library, but when I got into the permitting process with the city it started to seem just like a whole big thing. Because, see, the Ward Ten Alderman and I went to high school together and we never really saw eye-to—)

"Not the time, Bruce!"

I turn and race up the stairs. Which is, quite clearly, a *terrible* idea, but it's where the signal from my overwhelmed brain sends my adrenalized legs running off to.

"Moridius! I've got him!" Beefy shouts, following behind me just as the . . . um . . . power (?) of Control really starts to fade. It's like I had had a tiny shot of Dexedrine helping me become all "Bradley Cooper in *Limitless,*" and now it's worn off.

Upon reaching the second-floor landing, I realize that all I've managed to do is a) bring myself back to the exact place I was running away *from*, and b) kind of trap myself here.

I spin to see the Templar land a heavy, booted foot just behind me, and I start backing up as he continues his deliberate approach.

"Okay, listen," I start.

"I know I should wait for Moridius so he can see it happen himself, but my uncle was one of the ones you led to his death, fighting *your* battle for you on the Fields of Rendalia. One of the ones you got to believe in you and then betrayed, false prophet. So, I don't think anyone'll mind if I make the first cut. I owe you at least that much."

His uncle? False prophet? What the hell is he . . . ?

I start tapping my chest, frantically, trying to get the Heart to wake up or whatever it does. In *Seasons of Rebellion*, the Heart was acquired by Almeister from Richemerion, the Warden of Protection, one of the Elder Mystics of the world.

I had initially thought of the Heart almost as a joke. Because the Heart *landed* in Carpathian. So . . . Heart? Landed? *Heart. LANDED . . . ? Heartland?* Because I'm from Missouri, and—?

Whatever! Not the point!

The point is it's a Mechanical Heart bequeathed by an Elder Warden, inherited-and-used-reluctantly by Carpathian as both his inner guide and his inner armor.

A literal deus ex machina.

(Technically, it's a deus ex machina that's also a machina ex deus—god from a machine by way of a machine from the gods—and I initially worried that the whole gimmick was too on-the-nose. But, at the end of the day, most people didn't seem to pay too much attention to the metaphor or care about its provenance, and just thought the idea of a mechanical heart was fire, so I stuck with it.)

Regardless, I could sure as hell use it right now.

"Hey," I say, tapping harder. "Hey, hello?" I whistle. "You still in there? Little help?"

"What's that?" Beefy asks, nervous. "Whatchu doin' there?" The Templar takes on a look of real anxiety as he draws his sword with one hand and his switch-saw with the other, and I tap my chest harder, like I'm practicing some aggressive form of EFT. "Stop that! Hey! Whatever you're doing, d-don't!"

I see that he's got an itchy trigger finger and is just about to use it when . . .

. . . I hear a scream from outside.

Oh god, no.

One of my worst fears— No, my *worst* fear: harm coming to people I care about, especially because of something *I* have done, sounds like it's getting real-ized fifty feet away from me in my backyard.

Something awful is happening to Brittany. And it's my fault.

I have the impulse to just run at the beefy Templar, damn the consequences, and try to bowl him over so I can make it to Brittany's side and aid her in what-ever small way I can.

But I don't.

I don't run.

I freeze in place instead.

Because after the initial shock of hearing the bloodcurdling wail passes, I become aware . . .

. . . It's not Brittany who's doing the screaming.

CHAPTER FOUR

What's all that?" the Templar asks. I have to presume, rhetorically.

A second shriek pierces the air. Neither triumphant nor joyous. This is what someone sounds like when they've been introduced to a fresh kind of hell.

A lot like the persistent scream that I realize has been echoing in the back of my brain since I was so rudely ripped from the womb of my slumber and ass-spanked into this new reality that I find myself steadily, if reluctantly, accepting is, in fact, reality.

The same way Carpathian once did.

I am sad, scared, and kind of weirdly intrigued at the same time.

Beefy and I lock eyes and, as if by unspoken agreement, we both charge to a hallway bathroom where there's a window that looks out onto the backyard. Standing side by side, peering out, we're presented with a simultaneously fascinating and horrifying sight.

A big-ass lizard.

And not just any big-ass lizard. THE big-ass lizard. A colossal, colorful creature. The very embodiment of a chaotic mind run amok.

The Tentasaurian.

It's the size of a house and looks like a cross between a Gila monster and a calamari who grew up on steroids and hate.

With wings.

And it breathes fire.

Basically, it's the bastard cousin of a vine dragon, but more importantly, it's the primary and *only* summon that Teleri Nightwind was able to conjure when she first came on the scene.

Did Brittany . . . ? Could she even . . . ? How . . . ?

Doesn't make a difference. Regardless of how or why it has shown up, there is, right now, a goddamn Tentasaurian in my backyard. And somewhat fortunately, I suppose, it's doing the job we need it to do, which is to scare the ever-loving hoopty out of the Templars on the ground.

(I also note, albeit briefly, that I just thought of them, without qualification, *as* Templars. Definitively. No hesitation. Because . . . that is what they are. Not cosplayers or figments of my imagination. They are Templars. Minions of the Super Vizier. Just like the one gawking out the window with me.)

And on cue: "That's a Tentasaaaaaaaaaahhhhh!" Beefy screams as the Tentasaurian lets loose with a blast of irradiating flame from deep inside its Tentasaurical belly—or wherever the fire comes from. I actually have no knowledge of the thing's biology. I just wrote a bunch of stuff down this one time when I was on peyote, and when I read it back the next day, the Tentasaurian stuff was all that was sort of legible.

Irrespective of the fire's provenance, it's intense and close and real, and it LIGHTS UP the yard, raining down a white-hot monsoon of flame that incinerates all my well-curated lawn furniture, and also somehow simultaneously causes the water in my pool to erupt into a boiling cauldron of chaos.

Which I guess makes sense? I mean, it's not *just* fire. It's magical fire. Mezmerically enhanced fire. Fire that causes the seas to boil and melts the most enchanted steel.

Christ. Why did I have to make up so much shit that can kill a person? Why couldn't I have written a nice, cozy series about . . . magical trout fishing or something?

The now boiling pool water typhoons up and over the coping in a small tidal wave of *oh holy shit here it comes!* causing Moridius, Yolanda, Draven, and the others to run from its drenching fury as the Tentasaurian continues shrieking and immolating everything in its path.

Everything, that is . . . except Brittany.

Brittany just stands there, the explosion spilling out from behind her and blowing her hair loose from its bun like she's Charlie McGee in *Firestarter*. (The Drew Barrymore one, not the Zac Efron remake. No hate to Zac Efron. He's a great talent and a stone-cold hunk, but I'm a purist.) But just like in both versions, hellfire is quite literally erupting all around her while Brit remains stock-still, allowing it to happen, appearing somehow unworried and remaining untouched by the destructive force of the Tentasaurian's rage.

Or, as the great punk band, the Dead Milkmen, might say: There's a *Big Lizard in My Backyard*, apparently called into being by the "Punk Rock Girl" who lives in my pool house, and so right now, we need to get into my bitchin' Porsche and get the hell out of here!

(I know the third song title is actually "Bitchin' Camaro," but it's the middle of the night and the Chevrolet dealership isn't open, and even if it were, we're too busy fighting for our lives for me to take the time to go buy a Camaro and bring it back to the house just to make all the retro-punk song references work.)

In any case, at seeing all of this unfolding before my eyes—and because my brain clearly tends to do what it wants, when it wants, irrespective of circumstance or appropriateness—my mind shifts yet again, even farther into the deep cuts of 1980s pop culture, and "Shadrach" by Beastie Boys starts playing inside my head . . .

For about half a second, even I am baffled as to why *this* would be the case at a time like this, until it comes to me . . .

"Shadrach" is so named because it features a sample of "Loose Booty" by Sly and the Family Stone. And, in the middle of "Loose Booty," Sylvester Stewart, aka Sly, begins chanting, in funkified syncopation, "Shadrach, Meshach, Abednego. Shadrach, Meshach, Abednego," completely randomly, since the story of Shadrach, Meshach, and Abednego comes from the Torah (aka the Old Testament, for those Christianically inclined) and is about three young men who refused to bow down before a golden statue of Nebuchadnezzar, choosing instead to allow themselves to be thrown into a fiery furnace as punishment. But, instead of letting them get burned alive, Hashem rewarded their faith in Him by protecting them, and they were seen walking around inside the flames, unharmed.

What that story has to do with someone having a loose booty is anyone's guess. Pretty sure Sly's imagination was just about as recklessly out of control as mine. Also, I have to assume he was pretty high when he recorded it.

Regardless, that is the sample the Beasties used for the song "Shadrach" and—as at the moment, Brit appears to be saturated by light and flame that should otherwise be turning her into a charcoal briquette, but isn't—it has leaped into my auditory canal as something of a soundtrack, I suppose.

Shadrach, Meshach, Abednego, Shadrach, Meshach, Abednego, Sly's funkdafied voice echoes over and over as the Tentasaurian's Belly Blasts continue, causing Beefy to jerk himself back from the window and retreat to the far corner of the bathroom.

"Don't move, so-called Saviour!" he shouts. "You're coming with me!"

How he thinks I will be able to not move and simultaneously come with him is a riddle for another day because, at the moment, I have to figure out how to *both move* and *not* come with him, in direct contradiction to what he would prefer.

I turn to face him fully, hoping to eye some manner of escape that doesn't require me leaping out of a window into a torrent of flame and Templars, when I catch a glimpse of myself in the bathroom mirror. There is still a faint glow emanating from my chest, appearing to intermingle and dance with the light from the flames outside the window. It creates an image that is . . . angelic?

Is that too grand a description? Or too obvious? If I were writing this, how would I depict it?

I might suggest that it has . . . "crafted an illusion that I, myself, have in some way become part of the fire, at synergistic oneness with the same life-force from which the universe was created. Not simply of its sweltering womb borne, but *part* of the very genesis itself."

I dunno. Something like that. Brittany'd make sure it got tightened up in editing.

Point is, it's a pretty hard-ass visual, I gotta say.

And I'm not the only one who thinks it's impressive. The fear in Beefy's eyes confirms that I am looking to him like the cover of an old Iron Maiden album or something, because he bangs his shoulders against the wall as he backs up and levels his fireblade and switchsaw at me.

Holy Jabroni, these are even more intimidating in life than when I imagined them.

The fireblade is, well, pretty much what it sounds like. Kind of a cross between a classic knight's broadsword and a lightsaber. Pretty standard fantasy fare. The switchsaw . . .

The switchsaw is something I introduced in book two after I had finished binging a reality series about lumberjacks.

At their essence, they're guns, albeit really, really honking big ones with a barrel that would make Dirty Harry uneasy. But they aren't *just* guns. They are something of a sleek marriage between a revolver and a chainsaw. Each equipped with a Bowie knife–length bayonet of spinning chain extending menacingly from the barrel. Basically, it's samurai-wielding tradition and modern-day technology all bound up in one deadly package. Y'know, in case you shoot at an enemy who can't be harmed with traditional firepower, you'll still have the chance to disembowel them in a grotesquerie of hand-to-hand combat once they are finally upon you.

(Inventing an obscene number of ways for things to kill and be killed is one of my literary strengths, I like to believe.)

Point is, one would think, that with both of these instruments of carnage pointed directly at me, I would be the one quaking in my . . . bare feet.

But I'm not. At least not comparatively. It's actually Beefy who still seems terrified.

"Stay back!" he shouts. "I'm warning you!"

"Okay, look," I start, raising my hands in the universal gesture of *I'm unarmed, don't do anything we'll both regret, and by "both" I mean* me.

But my hands in the air seem to do little to calm his nerves. In fact, they do just the opposite. Because the second I have my palms up . . . he fires on me.

BOOM. BOOM.

Shit! I have no time to . . . Anything! I can't even—

ZZZWWWAAAHHHMMM.

Thump-thump. Thump-thump.

Ow! The Heart. The Control effect. It's back. But it . . . it hurts, kind of.

I narrow my eyes in pain, and when I open them, I can see why it stings. The meter is almost pure black now. And it's quivering. Vibrating. Like the Heart is squeezing every last bit of Mezmer it might possess out of itself to try and keep me alive.

With the air around us slowed to a crawl, I can eyeball the blasts, and am able to pivot myself *just* enough to avoid them striking me. They crash into the wall behind me in slow motion, ripping holes in the plaster.

BOOOOOM. BOOOOOM.

Two more shots. I dodge those as well and, without many other places to go, find myself pirouetting right in the direction of Beefy's outstretched switchsaw hand.

My eyes meet his, and his go f'ing wide. Wide? No. F'ING WIDE. Like, cartoonishly so. Like, Wile E. Coyote wide. And the last thing I hear is . . .

Thump . . .

Thump . . .

Thump.

Right before a . . .

SHWOOOOOOOOOOOMMMMMPPP.

As the Control effect wears off yet again, everything goes back to a highly adrenalized pace, and . . .

Rrrrrrrrriiiinnnnn. Rrrrrrrrriiiinnnnn. Rrrrrrrrriiiinnnnn.

The "saw" part of Beefy's switchsaw fires up.

CHAPTER FIVE

R*rrrriiin, rrrrriiin! Rrrrriiin, rrrrriiin!* is the horrifying sound that provokes a horrified, "ACH!" sound from me.

I jump back as the Templar waves his fireblade around with one hand and
jabs the switchsaw toward me with the other, all the while saying, "Don't come
closer!"

Which, I mean . . . It's just a weird thing to say. Like, bro, you're holding quite
literally ALL the weapons and I'm in pajamas with no shoes. The hell you think
I'm gonna do?

Just then, he seems to find his courage. Or at least recognize that he is absolutely in the high-status position when it comes to our little face-off, because he
summons up an "AHHHHH!" as he lunges forward with the switchsaw, aiming
right for my gut. Or my neck. Or my everything.

Honestly, it's hard to tell because of what happens next.

ZZZZZWWWWWAAAAAHHHHHMMMMMMMMMM.

Thuuummmp.

Thuuuuummmmmp.

Just as Beefy lunges, inside my chest, the Heart seems to dig deep for whatever
last, tiny bit of Bruce-Assist it might have left at its disposal and grinds out as
much Control as it can possibly muster.

As he's inches—or probably less; call it micro-meters—from driving the
slowly spinning, *rrrrriiin, rrrrriiin, rrrrriiin, rrrrriiining* set of tiny blades into
my extremely rrrrriiin-rrrrriiin-averse body, the Control effect gives itself and me
one. Last. Gasp. The icon looking like it's about to tear apart and is holding on for
(my) dear life. Just enough for me to spin to the side one final time and do some
kind of, like, Aikido move on Beefy.

I would use the exact word for what it is, but unfortunately, I dropped out of
my Aikido classes after the third lesson.

It occurs to me, quite abruptly, that I have started and stopped, suddenly, a
variety of combat hobbies in my life. Karate, Aikido, Wing Chun, boxing . . .
pottery. (Not technically a combat hobby, I suppose, but you do "throw" clay, so
I feel like it counts.)

I'm not a quitter. I'm really not. I just . . . happen to . . . *quit* . . . things . . .
a lot.

But! In my defense, the Aikido quitting was because I found the sensei to be
kind of a Chad.

Coincidentally, his name happened to *be* Chad, so I dunno if it was his fault
or if he was just set up for failure in that regard from the start—nature/nurture
and all—but whatever the reason, it felt to me like he took a certain amount of
pleasure in knowing more than everyone else, and I found it to be off-putting.

I wound up basing a minor character in Riftbreaker on him.

Guy called Timbolloree.

He fell into a well and no one bothered to rescue him.

Anyway. The point is that while I don't know the name of the move, I pull it off with a degree of skill, grace, and acumen that I feel I absolutely should *not* have, given the fact that I only ever had three lessons.

As Beefy thrusts the switchsaw at me, I rotate-slash-pivot to the side, manipulating this momofuku's elbow and shoulder in such a way as to propel him forward, the weight of the heavy weapons he's carrying assisting him in careening in the direction of the sink.

I'm not gonna lie; it feels kinda cool to do a slick Aikido move on someone in a real life-and-death situation.

The arm I push on, the one carrying the switchsaw, goes across the front of his body, causing . . . Well, causing the rotating, *rrrrriiin, rrrrriiining* switchsaw blade to, uh, saw? Right through his opposite thigh? By which I mean . . . exactly that. That's what it does.

It doesn't "cut" into his leg or "embed itself into the soft, sinewy flesh" or anything even remotely as gory or descriptive as that. It, quite literally, just saws his lower limb off right above the knee in a clean, fast *chomp*.

I'm obviously horrified by this. Truly. This is not how I intended the pushy-offy to work out. I just wanted him not to drive the thing into *me*, not necessarily to sever part of his body from the rest of his body. But, as much as I feel a sense of startle-eyed regret for about a nanosecond, I quickly remember that he was trying to do the same, if not worse, to me.

And so, as his now off-balance, one-legged frame tumbles forward, collapsing like a six-foot five-inch or so sized tree that's been felled in the woods, his head happens to smash hard onto the edge of the sink.

Like, really hard. Like really, really hard. Like cracking-off-part-of-the-basin-and-absolutely-giving-himself-a-concussion hard, like we're in a goddamn Charlie Chaplin movie.

Or, y'know, maybe it *kills* him? Less funny, but to be candid, I'm not a hundred percent certain I can bring myself to get absorbed in it just at the moment, partially because . . .

Thummmmmmmmmmp.

SHWOOOOOOOOOOMMMMMPPP.

I suck a huge intake of air, and something inside me tells me that may be the last boon I get to my ability to dodge things and slow down time for a little while.

Literally. Something inside me tells me that.

You have reached a threshold of your Mezmeric Resonance that is deemed [DANGEROUS!] You will need to rest before it is advised that you use more Mezmer.

Is what I see projected into the air in front of me.

Super. That's just perfect.

But I can mourn my deficits later. Seeing this as my chance to grab up the things I came back into the house for, I start to make for the door. But then I pause. Sort of. *Pause* is more of a euphemism. Actually, what happens is I stop dead in my tracks because I now see another message populate the open space in front of me that I call "the air."

You might consider attempting to retrieve the gentleman's footwear and weapons before you abscond any farther. It will, one must assume, prevent another obstacle such as the one you are currently confronting, allowing you to focus a greater amount of your much needed attention on far more pressing concerns.
It's not as though he shall be requiring them further.
{COURTESY MESSAGE #2}

What's curious is that in my imagining of the Heart, I always kind of *anthropomorphized* its general affect as being one of a John Cleese/Basil Fawlty–like character? Replete with all the attendant cheekiness that implies? But I didn't *write* it that way. In the books, it's very serious and businesslike. The Notifications I'm getting seem to be appreciably more . . . jaunty.

But, regardless of the messenger, I have to shake my head because, while the Heart is right, it is very disconcerting having these Notifications coming from out of nowhere periodically to offer their input at random. I wonder if it felt as confusing to Carpathian when he first got the Heart installed in him.

What the hell am I talking about? I created Carpathian. He isn't real. He never experienced anything I didn't tell him to.

"Didn't he, Bruce? Didn't he?"

Stop. I don't have time to indulge my potentially multiversal existential rumination right now, but if—*once*—I get out of here, and am not facing imminent destruction, I'm really going to need to figure some shit out.

Besides, the Heart is right. When John McClane was trapped in the Nakatomi building, his lack of shoes caused him no end of pain and suffering. The one time he did try and scoop up some kind of foot covering, he was met with the misfortune of having expelled a bad guy whose feet were smaller than his sister's. Which is funny and kind of clever when you see it in a movie. In real life, being in a situation of mortal peril—shoeless—is appreciably less charming.

Luckily, Beefy's feet don't look like they'll present a sister-size-foot problem. If anything, his Templar boots might be a size or two too large for my totally normal-size, regular-guy feet.

So, I do as the Heart suggests, prying Beefy's one big black magecycle boot off his still connected leg, and then . . .

Ugh. Nooooo, really?

"Yes, Bruce, really. Sack up and yank the bootie off the recently detached leg that still seems to be spurting arterial blood."

"But I don't—"

"GRAB THE BOOT FROM THE SEVERED LIMB, BOY!"

(I hear that last directive in my dad's voice. Don't suppose I need to call Dr. Finkelstein to figure out why that is.)

Obeying the command, I . . . pick up . . . *gulp* . . . the leg . . . *blurp* . . . trying not to . . . *oh god* . . . throw up all over the interior of Beefy's now-no-longer-attached limb . . . *waaahhh* . . . yank it off . . . *pizza, no, no, no* . . . and somehow manage to work it and the other one onto my feet . . . *hang in there* . . . without hurling everywhere.

"Good job, Bruce! I knew you could do it!"

"Thanks, Bruce. That means a lot."

They are, in fact, too big, but what's that old saying? Any boot in a storm of flame and mayhem provoked by the sudden and violent transportation of someone into an alternate reality? Pretty sure that's how that aphorism goes.

I go to grab the fireblade, as the Notification also encouraged me to do, only to discover that it turns out I don't really know how it works? Because the second I touch the hilt, a geyser of flame tears out from the thing and lights up one of my new hand towels. Which, in and of itself, would not be that big of a deal. Yeah, they're nice towels, and I only just got them, but, y'know. Seems, comparatively, like a small worry.

However, a far more significant worry is that it appears that magically enhanced fire spreads a might quicker than the conventional type I'm familiar with. Because, in an instant, the hand towel touches the wall, and that entire side of the bathroom is consumed by an urgent, shrieking red and a frantic, piercing blue.

The intensity of the heat it generates causes me to jump back a few feet. I start to run, but then, glancing at the switchsaw, I consider that I really *should* have something to protect myself with, so I reach for the handle. But, again, it seems as though I could benefit from some kind of user manual, because the instant I touch the thing, it *rrrrriiin, rrrrriiins* into action and spins its way out of my grasp, smashing through the glass shower and imbedding itself into the wall.

Hm. Upon further consideration, perhaps it is advisable that you forgo your attempts at looting for now, and simply place your focus into surviving the utter cataclysm that has been unleashed. Yes. That seems the more prudent course of action at present. Let's go with that, shall we?
{COURTESY MESSAGE #3}

Heeding the Notification's sound advice, I tuck my pajama pants into the tops of the boots and clomp, clomp, clompity clomp clomp my way down to the office. Lurching for the desk, I grab my car keys and begin opening desk drawers, looking for the maps. Finding them buried under a pile of random papers and receipts I thoughtlessly tossed on top of them, I am reminded of how I sort of . . . well, not exactly *mocked* Brit when she first showed them to me, but definitely failed to show the appropriate amount of gratitude and awe at what she had done.

Now? Now, they might be the one thing that saves us both from an untimely and utterly unexpectedly brutal end.

If we survive, I really gotta—

FWOOOOOMMMMM!

A raging fireball comes crashing through the window, immediately incinerating half of the office. Fortunately, it's the half I'm not currently standing in, but here's the thing about giant balls of magical fire: They don't have to hit you square in the face to make it *feel* like you've been hit square in the face.

"AHHHHH!" is the sound of me screaming. Again.

My house is so, so on fire.

I pull the maps close to my chest and start to galumph clumsily away when I remember . . .

Gonzo. Shit. I can't leave him here. Sure, yes, he's just a snail and, sure, yes, it's weird for someone to have developed as deeply an emotional attachment to a snail as I have to Gonz, but . . . he's Gonz! I got him back before I even started writing Riftbreaker. And even though Mexican Turbo Snails aren't supposed to be able to live that long in a reef tank, Gonz and I are going on damn near twelve years together. Twelve! That's gotta be some kind of record!

And, of course, despite my somewhat nakedly bullshit declarations to the contrary just a few hours ago, Gonz was obviously my inspiration for Pergamon.

Just like Brit was my inspiration for Teleri.

Just like, I suppose, on some latent level, I was the prototype for Carpathian. Or, at least, the idealized version of myself was the prototype.

A reluctant hero who never asked for all the responsibility he was handed.

Whatever. Point is, Gonzo is my guy, and I'm not gonna let my guy perish here.

"Like Carpathian did Pergamon?"

"Oh, shut the hell up, me. Just let me grab the damn crustacean."

As I reach in to scoop Gonzo out of his spacious aquarium and drop him into his more portable travel aquarium—or as I like to call it, the "snail-mobile"—I can almost swear that he cocks his head. Like he's looking at me with a "what in the world have you done, chum?" expression.

If he starts talking to me in a rich, rugged, Pergamon voice, I swear I'll . . .

. . . Nothing. I'll do nothing. Just add it to the list of things that are happening that I would have found laughably impossible, like, twenty minutes ago.

Gonzo, maps, and keys firmly in hand, I once again commence clip-clopping toward . . . I'm not sure, but it has to be better than here.

Approaching the kitchen, another fireball zips past, feet from my face, obliterating another section of my now uninhabitable house.

With the back door a no-go, I stumble, bumble, and fumble out the front instead. Stepping outside, I see the Templars all racing for their magecycles, the Tentasaurian chasing after, leaving strips of scorched earth at their sixes as they rev away. Then, I hear Brittany's voice.

"Bruce?!" she yells, rounding the house, which I notice is starting to . . . waver? Wobble? Kind of . . . *dematerialize?* As the fire is expanding and fully engulfing it.

"Brit?!" I shout back. "Was that . . . *you?!* Did you summon . . . ?"

"I dunno," she says, breathlessly, as she grabs my arm, causing me to drop the maps on the ground and nearly drop Gonzo.

"The maps?" she asks, and I nod. She squats down, picking them up. "Keys?" I reach into my jammies pocket, holding them up and jingling them at her. "Gimme Gonz. You drive. I'll navigate."

My inquisitive and sometimes procrastinating nature compels me to want to ask, "*Navigate to where?*" but I stifle the impulse, hand her the snail-mobile, and with a *beep-boop*, unlock the car.

Sliding behind the wheel, I glance through the windshield and see the house now actually and unequivocally disintegrating and . . . I don't know . . . floating in tiny snowflake-like fragments, away into the darkness of the night sky. Like embers from a bonfire swimming against gravity and up into infinity.

Except it's not the fire that's causing it. The fire itself feels like it's a part of the dissolution. The expulsion of all that was mine being absorbed into this new world.

This new world I created. And of which I am now, it would seem, a living, breathing part.

The passenger door slams shut as Brittany plops down next to me, Gonz and a passel of painstakingly hand-drawn maps in her lap.

"Okay," I breathe out. "So . . . where do we go?"

"I need a second," she says, opening up the maps and looking through them.

I look again through the car's front window and see that my house, the back-yard, the pool, all of it, is now gone. Almost like . . . a black hole closing in on itself. Or some kind of *portal* or something? I dunno. I'm no astronomer or astrophysicist by any stretch, which is why I chose to write fantasy and not sci-fi. (Which, at the moment especially, seems fortuitous. At least I don't also have to figure out how to get oxygen in the middle of all this massive suckery.)

But whatever you call it, it's . . . *eating* . . . all that once was.

Which is concerning for a couple of reasons:

1. It's EATING ALL THAT ONCE WAS.

And . . .

2. It's not stopping at the house.

It's expanding. The consumption is creeping along the driveway toward the car.

"Um, Brit?"

"I said I need a second, Bruce!" she snaps, head down, still studying the maps.

"Okay." Then I add, "Cool, it's been a second. We gotta go."

"What? No. I—"

"We gotta go, Brit!" I thunder, and she looks up to see what I see: A stifling blackness, a literal rending apart of our prior lives, undulating toward us with haste.

I slam the car into reverse and punch the accelerator, firing us backward with a screech of tires, just escaping having the car and its cargo devoured by the unforgiving nothingness.

And then, with a *SHHHHHWWWWWAAAAAWWWWWP!* it's all gone.

The house, the place where I sat and crafted the stories that have now become my violent reality, disappeared.

And having fully engulfed the last vestiges of the driveway, leaving no trace of the before and us abandoned in the here and now, the unseen force that claimed it appears momentarily satisfied, and all is quiet.

Almost quiet. In the distance, I can still hear the revving engines of the magecycles and the braying call of the Tentasaurian chasing them away. I turn around in the driver's seat to see barren terrain stretched out around us, twisted buildings and the overamplified "Arch of Raylion" beyond.

"Alright," Brit says, swallowing and looking again at a map. "I think . . . Yeah, go that way." She points to the right.

"What's that way?"

"If we're approximately where I think we are, then that's where Bell's View is."

"Bell's View? Are you sure?"

She looks at me in that way she does.

"*Sure?* Am I sure, based on the fact that we've been inexplicably thrown into a world your fucked-up imagination invented, that the made-up-ass maps I created to try and give it all some sense of order and verisimilitude are pointing us in the right direction so we don't get our nuts handed to us by any of the inhabitants of said world?" She lets it hang for a moment before answering herself, "Yeah, Bruce. I'm *sure*."

I'm worried the ensuing eye roll is going to cause her to detach a retina.

I sigh, exhausted. I'm drained. I feel like I haven't slept in a month. It feels like my *soul* is sleepy.

"Okay," I say after a moment. "If you're sure."

I don't need to look over to know her jaw is constricting and her fist is balled up.

My knuckles tighten around the steering wheel. I look ahead at the road in front of us; it is neither straight nor safe looking, nor, explicitly, a road. But forward is really our only option unless we want to just sit here and wait for fate to come to us.

If we want to survive, we're going to have to be decisive and, as the one ability I would appear to have at my disposal right now might suggest, in control.

I steal a look at Brittany, legs crossed under her lap in the passenger seat, Gonz sitting with her, as she studies the maps.

"Hey, Brit?" I start, before shutting myself off.

"Yeah?" she says after a bit of a freighted moment.

". . . Nothing. This way?"

She nods, and I turn the wheel, press down on the accelerator, and Sheila begins ferrying us toward what I suppose can only be called . . .

. . . a purgatory of my own making.

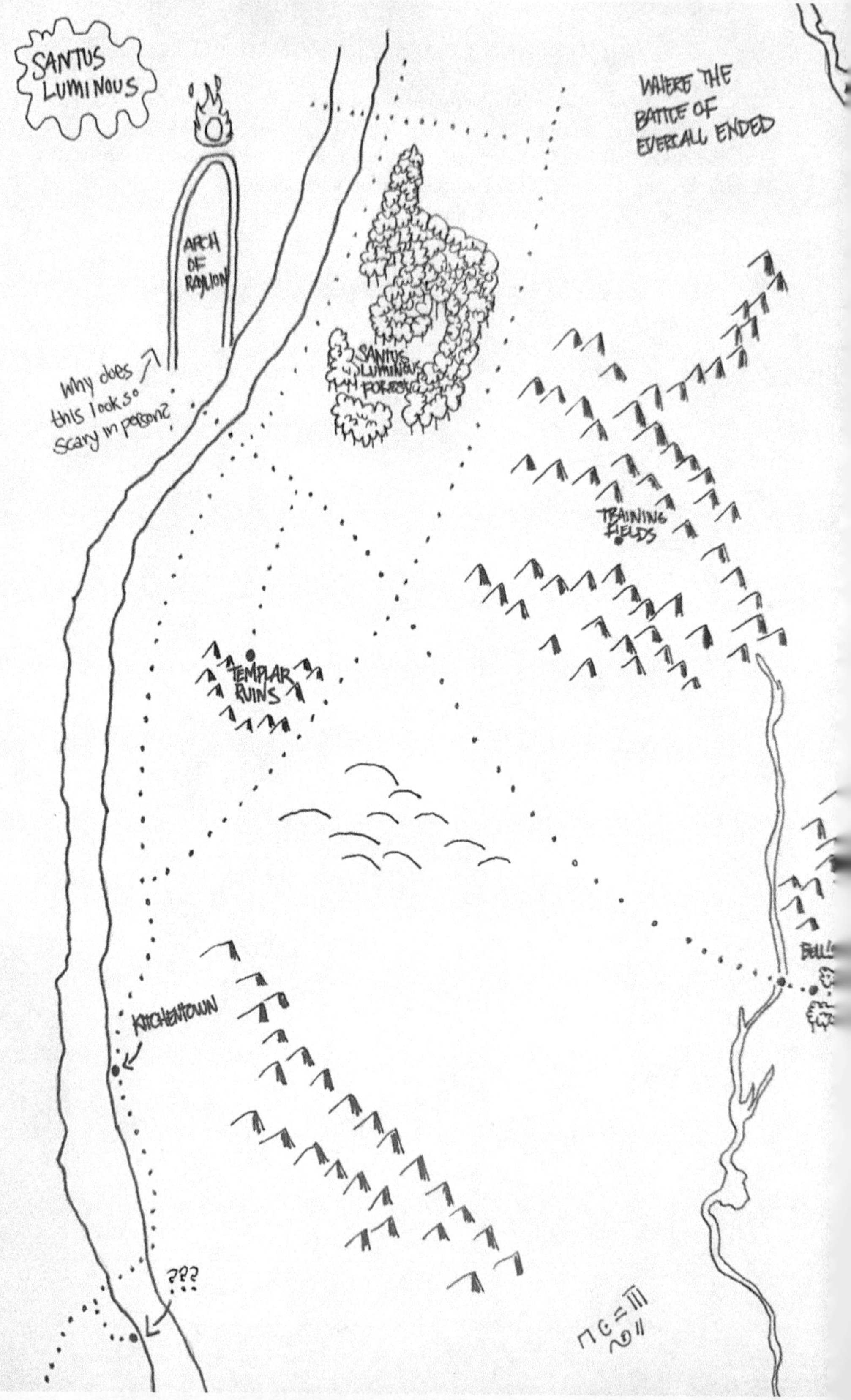
SANTUS LUMINOUS
ARCH OF RAYLION
WHERE THE BATTLE OF EVERFALL ENDED
SANTUS LUMINOUS FOREST
Why does this look so scary in person?
TRAINING FIELDS
TEMPLAR RUINS
KITCHENTOWN
???

ACT TWO

PARADISE (PRETTY MUCH) LOST

CHAPTER SIX

Seasons of Rebellion, Riftbreaker Book One, Chapter Eight

I can't do it!" Carpathian moaned from his splayed prostration on the ground. If his recent training had taught him anything, it was what the view of the heavens looked like when observed from a prone position on the cobblestone streets of Bell's View.

"You can," Almeister said to him in his fatherly way. "And you will."

Almeister reached his hand toward the fallen Carpathian, who stared upon his new mentor for a long moment before finally grasping the old man's palm and allowing himself to be pulled back to his feet. Once standing him up to his full height, the ancient wizard dusted off Carpathian's ragged conveyance conductor's uniform, took him by the shoulders, and looked him in the eye.

"You were chosen for a reason, Carpathian. Even if you cannot yet understand it."

In the short time since Almeister had first stepped foot on Carpathian's conveyance shuttle and informed the disbelieving conductor that the Grand Convocation of Elder Wardens had identified him as the one prophesied to counter the cultish evil of the Ninth Guardian, he had heard the old man say it again and again: "You were chosen for a reason. Even if you cannot yet see it."

Carpathian wondered when he would see it. When it would start to become clear to him why he was the one the Wardens had supposedly identified as the "World Saviour." Because, at that moment, he felt that he was anything but.

"Perhaps the Wardens are mistaken," Carpathian said, dejection ringing through his tone.

"The Wardens are merely following the path upon which the prophecy has led them. They did not choose. The System chose. The System itself is abused by the Ninth Guardian's apostasy as much as the citizens of this world. Thus, as the citizens will come to believe in and trust in you, the Saviour, you must also learn to Trust the System."

Carpathian considered the statement. It struck him not so much as a word of advice but as more of a pattern of existence by which he was being asked to live.

"What if the System is mistaken?" he asked.

"The System is never mistaken," Almeister countered. "The System merely is."

"I don't understand."

"You will."

Carpathian's patience wore thin. "I cannot control the Mezmer!" he shouted.

"That is why we train," Almeister replied, unperturbed.

"But . . . the Mezmeration feels as though it will never take hold."

"Again, my boy. Why we train," Almeister said with the patience of a man possessing infinite reservoirs of the quality.

"But . . ." Carpathian started again, pausing before summoning the courage to finish his thought. "I don't feel like a Saviour," he insisted.

Almeister scoffed at his recalcitrance. "And how is it that you believe a Saviour must feel?"

"I don't know. Not like me," Carpathian admitted, dejectedly.

Almeister twisted his head from side to side, studying the young man, a small smile teasing his lips.

"What?" Carpathian asked, now even more self-conscious. "What is it?"

"I have something for you."

Carpathian allowed his eye to follow Almeister's hand as he reached into the folds of his garments and withdrew a box. A small box, not considerably bigger than the width of the wizard's hand.

"What's that?"

"A gift."

"A gift?" Almeister nodded. "For me?" Almeister nodded again. "From who?"

"Whom," Almeister corrected. Carpathian continued to think it annoying that in addition to all the physical matriculations he was being asked to endure, he also found his grammar being habitually held under scrutiny.

"From whom," Carpathian adjusted.

"Richemerion."

"Lord Richemerion?" Almeister nodded. "You've held audience with the Warden of Protection themself?"

"Many times," the wizard responded, amused by the asking.

Carpathian wasn't sure if he could believe that the old man was telling him the truth or not. Almeister had told him many things since the two of them first met, and Carpathian remained uncertain of whether the wizard was truly all he purported to be or just a daft old fool who had managed to prey on the young Einzgear's naiveté. But, at this point, in for a farthing, in for a pound, Carpathian had decided.

"And Lord Richemerion gave you a gift . . . for me?"

Almeister nodded once, slowly, and with his knotted, weathered fingers, grasped the lid of the box and drew it back on its hinges, allowing Carpathian full view of what was inside. Upon seeing it, his eyes grew wide, and his jaw fell open. Somewhere in the great, far beyond, Carpathian could swear he heard a remote crash of thunder. And, much closer, he heard a deep, resonant thump-thump. Thump-thump. Thump-thump.

Carpathian swallowed hard and reached his hand out to touch the object, but pulled back at the last moment, suddenly afraid in a way he had never before felt fear.

"What . . . ?" he started. "What is that?"

The smile fell from Almeister's lips but remained flickering in his eyes as he answered. "An upgrade. Of sorts."

"It looks like a heart."

"As well it should."

"What is it intended to do?" Carpathian asked.

Looking at it, thumping before him in the box, his own heart began to beat faster. Which, in turn, caused the thing in the box to pound in syncopated rhythm, as if mimicking the tangled muscle living inside Carpathian's body.

Almeister did not answer directly, instead saying, "All your questions will be answered in time."

He positioned his free hand on Carpathian's chest, in the place where the former conveyance conductor's very spirit was now thundering as if it wished to escape. Carpathian's eyes went wide and his breathing became shallow, while the pounding of the Heart in the box accelerated and the beating of his own seemed to simultaneously slow.

"What . . . What's happening?" he asked, gasping for breath.

Almeister looked at him with a kindness that belied his normally stern countenance. "Don't worry," he said, his smile returning fully. "It is all part of the prophecy. Do not doubt. Trust. Trust that everything is happening exactly as it should. Trust . . . the System."

Carpathian began to shudder, every fiber, every sinew inside of him pulled taut. He did not trust. He did not trust at all. But he also could not move, as much as he might have wished to run. To flee. To escape his fate.

He was fixed in place. Nearly a statue, unable to tear itself from its plinth.

The pulsing in his chest slowed to a stop as the thudding mechanism being held by Almeister became more and more vigorous in its vibration.

Carpathian looked down at the wizard's other hand still pressed against his body, seeming to be the only thing holding him to his feet, and then back up into Almeister's twinkling eyes before . . .

. . . the entirety of the world around him . . .

. . . went black.

CHAPTER SEVEN

Ahhhhh!" That's me. Shouting. Again.

The jolt causes me to realize I've been checked out, mentally, for the last little bit here, and I'm suddenly aware that we've been driving for a good while. Probably not the safest thing for me to have been conveying us to wherever we're supposed to be going while in a total lack of consciousness, but based on what's happened so far this evening, *safety* is feeling like a relative concept.

"You okay?" Brit asks, reaching over to touch my arm and sloshing Gonzo around a little in the process.

"My chest," I groan, squinting my eyes and clenching my teeth. "It's doing it again. God, *The Grinch* is such a bullshit story. If his heart really grew three sizes that day, he'd be MORE pissed, not all happy and handing out presents and shit. Seuss, you're a goddamn charlatan."

And then, through my tapered vision, I see . . .

Partial Standings are available for perusal. Would you like to review them now?
[Yes] [No]

"Yes, we would," Brittany says, reaching to press [Yes].

"You really can see that too?" I ask.

"So it seems."

"How?"

"Is this genuinely what we're worried about at the moment?"

"I'm just asking questions. Seems like we're likely to have a few."

She *errrrrrgs*, then says, "You wrote it so that Teleri could 'peer into the unknown voids of Carpathian's truth,' or whatever-the-shit, didn't you?"

"Yeah? I guess."

"Well, so, there ya go." She reaches forward, presses [Yes], and my body tenses as I grip the steering wheel tighter and the menu flashes out of my chest, projecting onto the windshield.

>Mezmer Type:
Unknown
[Review Required (Please Visit Pulse Well)]

>Foundation:
None
[Review Required (Please Visit Pulse Well)]
>Mental: *Etherflint Level 1*

>**Physical:** *Etherflint Level 1*
>**Aura:** *Etherflint Level 1*
>**Animus:** *Etherflint Level 1*

>**Resonance Tier:**
Etherflint

>**Affinity:**
Unknown

>**Armament(s):**
Mechanical Heart

>**Spell(s):**
Control

"Okay," I breathe, taking in the anemic state of, I guess, *my* trivial status. "That's a drag."

"Yeah," Brittany sighs. There's a still moment before she adds, "But it's your fault."

"Excuse me? What's my fault? What the hell is that supposed to mean?"

"*You're* the one who had Carpathian just toss off everything he acquired on his journey through ten friggin' books. The Blade of the Starfallen, the Arm of Hearts, the Gauntlet of Sorenthali, the Obsidian Shield, the Cerulean Tunic . . . You had him send all his shit off into the wherever *when you killed him.*" She really leans into that last bit. "That's what *you* wrote. So, if *you're* now him, *you're* gonna have to start over basically from the beginning. You're . . . whattaya call it? Remorted. That's it. You're remorted. You're a remort, bro. A remort. Ya fuckin' remort."

I don't know how she's able to make it sound like a word that would get you canceled for saying it in public, but she does.

I nibble at my lip as I consider what she's suggesting. Then, hesitantly, because I know it's not going to be received well, I offer, ". . . Teleri."

"What?"

"You're misremembering. Carpathian didn't send it away. Teleri did. When she laid her hand over his—er, my? Whoever. Carpathian's Heart. So technically, it's . . . *your*? Fault?"

I flash a toothy smile. Not because I'm *trying* to be cute; it's just my default position to want to attempt to be charming at all times.

I can feel her staring bolts of murderous intent at me before she says, "I will rip off your arms and beat you to death with them."

We drive on in silence for another minute or two, both of us taking in the world outside.

Then, "Why is this happening?" I ask.

"I dunno," she says, continuing to stare out the window.

Another beat as I look through the moonroof.

I suppose I imagined it more or less like this when I created it, but there are a variety of things that don't exactly comport. Like, for example, in my mind, the sea of stars above us was vast and complex in a somewhat geometric style. (I think I called it "an intricately woven manifold of near-computative majesty," which I wrote because I had been watching this docuseries on famous mathematicians, and because I think the word "manifold" is embarrassingly underused.) But now, here, I can see it's *far* more ornate and complex than anything I ever envisioned.

It's like how I suspect George Lucas might have felt his first time arriving at a Star Wars–inspired theme park. Sorta like déjà vu from a dream I barely remember.

I blow out some air and mutter to myself, "There are more things in Heaven and Earth, Horatio, than are dreamt of in your philosophy."

". . . What?" Brittany asks.

"What what?"

"Why are you quoting Shakespeare?"

"I . . . dunno. Just 'cause?"

"Don't."

"Why not?"

"It makes me nervous."

"How come?"

"Because that's what you do in the books when you can't think up anything of your own that you like. You sneak in Shakespeare."

"Well—"

"And you usually do it when it precedes something awful happening."

I consider this. "Okay, but this isn't a boo—"

"Just don't. Alright? Please? Can you not? For me? Please?"

". . . Okay." There's a beat before I note, "Shakespeare was just a really good writer."

There's another brief silence. I hear the water splashing gently in Gonzo's snail-mobile.

Then, "I'm not Carpathian."

Brittany sniffs. "Okay."

"'Okay'? Okay what?"

"Just like I'm not Teleri?" I start to argue, but she doesn't give me the chance. "Whatever. Who the hell cares? Does it really matter? Those Templars back at the house thought you were Carpathian. In the same way they think I'm Teleri. So, regardless of what you *claim* you intended or didn't intend, it seems like this is who we are *now*."

"But—" I begin before she cuts me short again.

"I don't wanna get into an ontological debate, Bruce. It doesn't make a difference. Perception is truth, at least to the people perceiving it. So, if this is how this world sees us, this is who we are. And we're just gonna have to get our heads around it until we figure out . . ." She trails off.

"Figure out what?"

". . . How we got here? Why we're here? How we get back? All that shit."

Another pregnant pause.

"Did you summon the Tentasaurian?" I ask, breaking the moment. "To attack the Templars?"

"I'm not sure. I just had this . . . feeling that if I confronted them, something would happen."

Slosh, slosh.

Oh no. Does all this mean that whoever we encounter will also see Gonzo as *Pergamon*? That's going to be a problem. In Riftbreaker, Pergamon is endowed with the power of speech and all kinds of Mezmeric enchantments. He can cause himself to grow in size for combat and shrink down for reconnaissance. He can move as fast as a cheetah when circumstances call for it. He's one bad motorfinger. But Gonz is just . . .

He's just a harmless Mexican Turbo Snail whom I may have based Pergamon on, but who IS NOT actually Pergamon!

Man, this blows.

"SCREEEEEEEEEECH!"

The sound is off somewhere in the distance. Far, but not so far it isn't terrifyingly audible.

"Goddammit," Brittany moans. "What is *that* now?"

"I'm not sure. Did it sound like a Drakonar to you?"

"How am I supposed to know what the hell a Drakonar sounds like?"

"I don't know. How did the guy who did the audiobooks make them sound?"

"Are you kidding?"

"Where are we right now?" I ask.

She opens up one of the maps and studies it. "We're . . ." She looks out the window and back at the map. "I think we're just south of the Sea of Swans."

The Sea of Swans. Its vast expanse is akin to a bottomless chasm spreading out like petty gossip. It is a Grand Canyon–size pit that furrows deep into the earth, filled with birds and Mezmeric beasts that are . . . also similar to birds.

(Sometimes it's hard to come up with new shit.)

In any case, even shrouded in the blanket of the night, we can hear the haunting cries of soaring monsters echoing from the depths beyond. The calls of these creatures send an involuntary shiver down my spine, reminding me of some of the darker chapters I penned. The land surrounding it is rent and distorted, a tortured terrain which seems to constantly pull my eyes toward it.

"Just south. So we're about to be . . ."

"In Bell's View," she finishes.

Bell's View. The town where Almeister trained Carpathian.

And remembering that causes me to have yet *another* unpleasant realization.

"Almeister . . ." I mumble aloud.

"What about him?" Brit says.

"He's being held in the Tower of Zuria."

"Yeah? So?"

"So, if all this"—I indicate the environment outside the vehicle—"is real. Like, really real. Then . . ."

I don't look, but I can feel the awareness washing over her as well.

"Then . . . there's probably, definitely, really an Almeister, and he's probably, definitely, really being held captive."

"Yeah." I swallow hard.

Brittany continues. "And so . . . Xanaraxa. Zerastian . . . Mael."

"Yeah," I say, quieter this time. I know what her next words are going to be. And it's going to suck.

"They're very likely real people who are also very likely really . . . Oh, shit."

We did some horrible things to them. Or, I suppose, I did. Brit just did the research for me on awful ways to torture someone and that kind of thing. (Her browser history would look incredibly alarming to anyone who stumbled upon it.) At the time I was writing it all, I couldn't have known that I might be imperiling and abusing actual living beings. But it seems as though it's possible that—

"Turn here," Brittany says suddenly.

I jerk the wheel and drive us past a sign that reads "Now Entering Bell's View."

Bell's View was conceived as a real classic type of fantasy hamlet. Taverns and inns and all that stuff, but accented with an array of postapocalyptic-style weapons merchants and vehicle repair shoppes. (Spelled "shoppe" for no other purpose than it is the cool, fantasy way to spell *shop*. Same reason I chose to spell "Saviour" with a superfluous *u* after the *o* even though I'm neither British nor Canadian. Some people have called my various affectations "pretentious," or, more colloquially, "douchey." They're not necessarily wrong, but I'm committed to it now. In for a farthing, in for a pound, I reckon.)

What's noticeably disturbing, driving along the streets of Bell's View, is that the town is in shambles. No one to be seen. The carcasses of abandoned buildings the only evidence that this was once a thriving community.

"What happened?" I wonder aloud.

"I . . . don't know. I thought Bell's View—"

"It was," I interrupt, knowing what she was going to say.

"So how . . . ?"

"I have no idea. I didn't do this. I mean, I wouldn't have . . . I didn't do . . . whatever all this is."

There's more silence as we creep by the skeletal remains of what was once a fundamental anchor of Meridia.

I can almost hear Brittany thinking. Her brain is loud.

"This is where Carpathian first acquired *that*"—she points at my chest to indicate the Mechanical Heart—"isn't it?"

"Yeah?"

"And, as a consequence, Bell's View was always granted some type of special Mezmeric dispensation, right? Even as the rest of Meridia was being ravaged at the direction of the Ninth Guardian, Bell's View remained protected?"

"Well, sure. I mean, it had to, *narratively*, because . . ." I let the thought drift off.

"Because why?" she asks.

I wrestle with the answer because there is no actual narrative reason for it to have remained under enchantment and protection. Not really. It was just . . .

"Because," I finally admit, "because it was one of the very first locations I came up with when I started world-building, and because it was the place where Carpathian found his strength and his purpose and did get"—I tap at my chest, still marveling over the fact that it's real—"this. So, I think I . . . I just . . ." I take in a breath and make myself say it. "I developed an irrationally sentimental attachment to the place and could never bring myself to have the Disciples of the Ninth Guardian destroy it. That's why," I say, half expecting her to give me shit over getting all emotional about a formerly imaginary place from a book I wrote.

But she doesn't.

". . . I get it," she says.

"You do?

"Of course I do."

I look at her, and she gives me a small smile. I nod in return. "Yeah."

"So, okay," she goes on. "But so my point is . . . what did you write? When you friggin' killed Carpathian?"

"Hey! I didn't *kill* anyone. He chose to die."

"Bruce . . . he 'chose' to die because you wrote it that way, and now we've been transported here—I have to assume—as some sort of cosmic consequence for the choices you've made, so don't goddamn tomato/tomahto me on this one. You know what I mean."

". . . Fine," I acquiesce after a moment. "What are you thinking?"

"What you read to me. The thing you read. What the Super Vizier said?"

"That the . . . ?" It takes me a second to realize what she's saying. But then, it lands so hard in my brain that I almost get a nonimpact concussion. "You mean: 'All that which was sanctified by your having been its custodian, we will destroy'?"

"Uh, yeah," she replies. "That."

I look out of the window and think about the rest of the line: *The absolute ruin that shall be made of what you once held dear will be unlike anything ever witnessed on this plane.*

And now, I'm shuddering like I just took a cold plunge in Saskatchewan in January.

"So you're saying . . . ?" I begin.

She finishes the thought. "I'm saying that when Carpathian . . . *departed this mortal coil*"—She gives me a kind of snotty, "since you love Shakespeare so much" grin—"he took his Mezmeric protections with him. Like you wrote."

"I—You—I—" I stutter ineloquently. "You really think that's possible?"

"I dunno. I'm just spitballing, but . . . Is it possible that the enchantment Almeister cast on Bell's View to protect it while he was training Carpathian and that it subsequently retained was somehow stripped from it? Yeah. I suppose it might be possible, bro."

The look I give her must project my feeling that what she's saying sounds insane because she responds quickly with, "I don't fuckin' know! I'm not the maker-upper of shit! That's you! I'm just trying to apply something resembling logic to this monumentally illogical snatchtastrophy of a crotch grab we find ourselves in!"

Jesus Christ. Did I . . . ?

"No," I declare with a conviction that is definitely not warranted. "There's no way that—"

But then I stop myself because while her theory is weird and crazy in its way, it is—I have to admit—*not* without logic. But no. No.

"No," I continue. "No, that's . . . Sure, I wrote that that's what was *going* to happen. But I didn't actually write it *happening*. So there's no way that . . . No. No, I reject the theory. That can't be how all this works."

"Why not?"

"Why not?"

"Why not? I mean, Bruce. It's looking to me like everything here kind of does its own thing autonomously, whether you dictated it or not. Maybe Elizabeth Gilbert was right."

"Elizabeth—*Eat, Pray, Whatchacallit?*"

She nods.

"In what way?"

"Just . . . I don't know. Maybe . . . Maybe Meridia exists independent of your imagining, and you're just the vessel through which its stories funnel."

There is a weird, uncomfortable, dawning revelation climbing up the back of my neck.

"What are you saying?"

"I'm saying, if that's the case . . ." She pauses.

In my chest, I can feel the Heart beating. *Thump-thump, thump-thump, thump-thump.*

"*If* that's the case," she repeats, "then . . . you didn't choose to write Riftbreaker . . ."

Thump.

"Riftbreaker . . ."

Thump.

". . . chose you."

CHAPTER EIGHT

There's a thing in movies where the camera lens zooms in while the camera itself dollies backward, creating the effect that the subject on the screen is falling away and coming forward at the same time. It was originally conceived by Alfred Hitchcock and is called a "dolly zoom." In filmmaking, it's become a quintessential way of communicating visually when a character has just had everything they thought they understood or believed to be true about their world turned upside down.

If there were a camera on my face right now, I suspect it's what would be happening to me.

"Riftbreaker . . . chose *me*?" I manage to squeak out.

"Maybe?" She shrugs. "Again, just spitballing." She raises her eyebrows, her face illuminated by the faint glow of the four moons.

Chunk, chunk, chunk.

"What, what, what is *that*?" Brittany nearly whines.

"I don't know. It sounds like," I start, getting out an almost comical "the car," before, with one last tragic *chunk*, the Panamera stops dead in its tracks, drained of gasoline.

"Are you kidding me?" Brit says to no one in particular. "Little heads-up woulda been nice!"

"Sorry. I wasn't paying attention to the notifications. The car ones, I mean. Not . . ." I drift off.

She takes a breath and says, "Okay. Okay. So, how do we refuel? Do we think there are any hidden gas stations somewhere that we don't know about?"

"What?" I'm still a little distracted and a bit stuck on the whole "Riftbreaker chose you" business. "Oh, uh, I'm not sure. I mean, I don't know if the car is, um, transformed too?"

"Transformed? You mean like . . . ?"

I lift my shoulders. "Yeah, I don't know. Maybe?"

In Riftbreaker, vehicles, like pretty much everything else, are powered by some version of the world's Mezmer. Mezmer isn't interchangeable, per se; there are rules about what can operate with what types of magic—courtesy of a spreadsheet Brit made—but no matter what the power source, none of them are fossil fuels.

"We should look," she says.

"Sorry?"

"Under the hood. I guess let's pop this bitch's top and see what she's working with."

I glance out the driver's side window and see a burned-out building that looks like it used to be a doctor's office, perhaps. We both just sit there for a moment, looking out of all the windows and trying to do, I guess, a potential threat assessment of the town. The distant cawing of . . . whatever is doing the cawing the only faint noise I can perceive.

After a moment, I glance in Brittany's direction to see her watching me, expectantly.

"What?" I ask, slightly defensive.

"Are you getting out?"

"Um . . . I—Maybe it would be safer to wait."

"Wait for what?"

"I don't know. Morning?"

"You think waiting for morning's going to make this situation somehow better?"

"Maybe? 'Joy cometh with the morning,' and all that."

". . . Are you really now quoting *the Bible* to me?"

"Technically, I suppose? I actually remember it from an old episode of *The West Wing.*"

The dead-eyed, heavy-lidded look of "please kill me" that comes over her would be almost funny in a wide variety of other situations.

She throws the door open and hops out, leaving Gonzo and the maps on the seat. He's munching on a residual eggshell and, I think, watching me.

"She really does seem to be adjusting to this new life more quickly than I am," I tell him as he keeps chewing.

Is *this a new life? This isn't going to become our brand standard, is it? Surely there's a way out of this messed-up* Pagemaster *situation we've found ourselves in.*

. . . Right?

I step out and look all around. No one. Nothing. Completely and totally abandoned. All of Bell's View.

The safe haven, the sanctuary, destroyed. Paradise lost.

Brit snaps open the latch on the hood of the car and lifts it up. "Um . . . well. Huh," she says.

"What? What is it?" I ask, coming around to see what she sees.

Staring down into the well where the engine should be, I see that it's no longer there. Instead, it's been replaced by a complicated-looking contraption that resembles nothing so much as a . . . well . . . as a heart. Kind of like the one currently beating in my chest.

"Ay ca-yi-yi-ramba," Brit whispers. "What is . . . *that?*"

"Oh, wow."

"What?"

"This is my car."

"Yeah, no shit. What're you—?"

"No," I interrupt. "I mean this is *my* car." I incline my head toward her so that she gets it.

"*Oooooh,*" she realizes. "Oh, wow."

"Yeah."

The whole deal with vehicles in Riftbreaker is that they are either free-range and can be commandeered by whoever has the appropriate Mezmer to fuel them, *or* they're owner specific and operate almost as an extension of the handler themselves, meaning that the latter are *bonded* to the driver. Other people *can* drive them, but typically only with the owner's permission, and even then, they will only be able to operate at, like, eighty percent capacity relative to what they're capable of doing in the owner's hands.

It's a really, really big deal to get your own *dedicated* vehicle. Hell, some members of the High Council don't even have one. You typically have to be either really, *really* wealthy and powerful or really, *really* special in some other way.

And, up until now, I never actually gave Carpathian an exclusive one of his own. As a one-time public conveyance conductor, he had the ability to drive just about anything on wheels, and with Control, he was straight-up Lando Norris when he was in the driver's seat, but like everything else about him, his skill and expertise built up over time. I was kicking around the idea of rewarding him with a seriously fire-ass whip once we got to book eleven; felt like he had gained enough power and influence that it was maybe finally time.

(Obviously, I didn't. I, uh, killed him instead. Different direction.)

However, I suppose if there were to have been a book eleven, Brit, Gonz, and I are now living in it, so when seen through that prism, I *did* wind up giving him his own chariot, after all.

Good god. I may be on the verge of having to question my lifelong rejection of the idea that there is such a thing as "fate."

"So," Brit starts, "how do we top it off?"

"Top it—? Um, I, uh . . . I dunno."

". . . Excuse me?"

"I dunno. I never wrote a scene where someone had to re-Mezmerate one. Never came up."

She stares at me, exhausted. "You're killing me, man."

"I'm sorry!" I exclaim, more out of frustration than anything else. "How the hell was I supposed to know that . . ." I trail off, acknowledging the . . . everything.

She rubs her palms together hard, like she's scrubbing them with soap. "Okay." She runs a hand through her hair. "So, okay, well, thinking about this from the perspective of how Mezmer works, generally, and judging by the car's similarities to your . . . internal situation, feel like we're probably going to need to find a Pulse Well and get you loaded with the complementary Mezmer required to fill it up."

"Complementary?"

"Yeah. I mean, if this is "Carpathian"s' car," Brit continues, "it would stand to reason that it operates using the same brand of core Mezmer as Carpathian himself."

"Does it?"

"What? Stand to reason?"

I nod.

"I have no idea, bro. I'm doing the best I can given the outlandishness of the situation. We're in a world born of that unending maze of a thing that lives in your skull. If you don't have the answers, I'm not sure I can be expected to know much more." She sighs long and hard, making a kind of a "*blehhh*" sound at the end. "Is *your* Heart still charged up? Maybe it knows something." She taps at my chest.

"Stop it," I say, slapping her hand away.

We both wait for a moment, and I brace myself to see if the Heart responds with a Notification or something of some kind.

It does not. Only the eerie quiet of an abandoned Bell's View and the still distant cawing fills the air.

"Isn't it supposed to help when help is needed?" she asks, knowing just as much—or as little—as I do, but asking anyway. "It's Carpathian's personal concierge, is it not?"

"I mean, yes and no." I rub my eyes, trying to think. "The concierge thing is just . . . more like an *attribution* I gave because I thought it was funny."

"Oh, yeah, well . . . well done. It's a hoot."

"I'm just saying it's more than simply an asset or, like, an assist tool. The Heart is *actually* supposed to be a personalized embodiment of the System itself. I mean . . . it exists inside Carpathian to do a lot of things: It allows him to 'see' the world, provides extradimensional storage, serves as the unifying force that holds all his armaments together—"

"His armaments? The armaments you had him send off to we're-fucked-with-out-them-ville? Those armaments?"

I ignore the rhetoric and continue. "Allows him to make object modifications, provides him the unique ability to see certain System Notifications and statistics and so forth—which, of course, no one else really gets to have, which is part of what makes him unique and grants him a certain kind of advantage. Um, allows Teleri and other Party members to engage with it as part of his Heart Guard, which is *how* she can 'peer into the unknown voids of Carpathian's truth . . .'"

"Jesus Christ, I don't know that I realized before just how much you burdened that one lonely plot device with." I offer my palms up in a *whattaya want from me* gesture. "Yeah, I know," she says. "Flow state." She growls in her throat then slaps her hands on her thighs. "Well then, let's find a damn Pulse Well, plug in, and see if there's any intel on upgrades or enhancements or whatever-the-shit that might help us."

She looks at the map.

In the books, whenever someone surpasses a Resonance Tier (aka "levels up") they need to visit a Pulse Well to verify their new Spells, Attributes, and the like so they can fully access it all.

I say "verify" because, very technically, the Pulse Wells don't actually *give* you new tools. They just kind of confirm that you've earned them. It's predicated on the idea that like ninety percent of success is just having confidence in yourself.

I had this friend who was a runner, and she always used to say, "I know I can go faster; I can feel it. I just don't know how to access that gear."

Well, a Pulse Well would show you that you *already* have access to it. And then, you'd be off to the races, so to speak.

So, you *earn* experience and enhancements and all the rest of it via training and your actual experiences in the world, but a Pulse Well identifies what those things are; specifically, lets you make certain decisions, and then validates (both literally and figuratively) everything you are now in possession of. Like, you may possess a natural talent as a Wind Walker, but you would likely still be stuck to the ground until you saw and had it confirmed. It's the difference between, "I think I can fly," and "Oh shit! I can fly!"

And while Carpathian can view certain stats and receive Notifications at more or less any time because of his Heart, Pulse Wells are also the only place *other* people can go to find out that information about themselves. I guess the best metaphor is that it's kind of like everyone else needs to step on a scale to see how much they weigh, while Carpathian has a scale sort of built into himself so he can get those details whenever he needs.

But that's it. The Heart just gives him the approximate 411 on what's available; it can't *apply* it. It's not full service. It's like when your car gives you a Check Engine notification. You know you need to poke around and see what's going on, but until you get it on a lift and have a look, you won't know for sure what the deal is.

Carpathian has to have everything verified and validated just like everyone else. It's one of a handful of ways that I used to make sure he didn't get too powerful too quickly. I have a thing about parity in Riftbreaker; it's more interesting to me when characters are rewarded for being smart and clever and working hard than just having access to the best Abilities or the coolest toys.

The more obstacles a character has to overcome, the more rewarding the payoff when they finally get where they're going.

In any case, the *downside* of stopping at a Pulse Well is that it leaves one completely *exposed* while one is checking in and revving up, but once you come away from it, you're typically endowed with new, important, shiny Abilities. And, more significantly, usually also with a *plan* for where to go next and how to best put to use your upgraded status.

(Side note: There was always a small but heated online debate raging between readers who thought Pulse Wells were genius because stopping at them allowed me to dole out exposition as necessary without it feeling especially clunky or obvious, and other readers who argued that it was just lazy writing. Anyway . . .)

"I don't think there's gonna be a Pulse Well here," I tell Brittany.

"Why not?"

"Because there's no temple, is there?"

That's another rule about Pulse Wells. They're required to be located in a "Temple of the Body," aka shrines found in various locations where you can train, modify, meditate, and essentially upgrade yourself in whatever capacity makes sense, etc. A Mezmeric gym, basically.

"No," she says with some frustration. "No. There's no temple. Goddammit, Bruce."

"Why 'goddammit, Bruce'? What'd I do?"

"Nothing. Never mind."

She doesn't have to say it. I know. She's annoyed at the fact that even though I created the world of Riftbreaker, I am woefully inarticulate when it comes to discussing a lot about the more pedestrian aspects of its details and mechanics.

And I recognize that, looking at it from the outside, one might think I'm a big *fan* of hypertangled messes because of how often they show up in my work, but I'm really not. I mean, I like Christopher Nolan as much as the next cinephile, but I ain't out here trying to make *Tenet*, if you know what I mean. It's not a *choice*. It's always been more just, I dunno, me being held hostage by the whims of my own creative juices. Ideas come as they come and then I let them go where they want to go. Just how it works.

Which is something we in the writing game call "being a pantser." As in, "writing by the seat of your pants," aka, "stream of consciousness."

Many great writers have been pantsers. James Joyce, of course. Faulkner, Beckett, Kerouac, Proust, Virginia Woolf. Gaiman, I hear. I mean . . . *Gaiman*. If it's good enough for Gaiman, it's certainly good enough for old Bruce Silver.

But it's why I have trouble remembering a lot of the stuff I've written. It's also the thing that drives Brittany crazy—or one of the things—as she's tasked with having to come behind and help make it all coherent. However, the probable upside is that this particular way of working has resulted in me selling seven million books worldwide, and—at the time of this . . . unfortunate turn of events— I've just entered into negotiations for the film and TV rights, so . . .

Oh shit. The film and TV thing. I was supposed to have a call with my attorney about that in the morning. The studio executives have apparently asked if it's okay to make Pergamon a giraffe instead of a snail. Dammit, I really gotta figure out how to get outta here and back home.

Wait, what was I thinking about?

Giraffe, Gaiman, Nolan, Temple of the Body . . . Oh. Pulse Wells. That's right.

"I'm sorry," I say. And I mean it. It's one thing to not have a clear plan or grasp of direction when what's at stake is a work of fiction. It's another thing entirely to be lost at sea, as it were, when what's at stake is . . . well, considerably higher. "Okay? I'm sorry. I know. I know; I made all this up. You'd think I'd have a better understanding of it all. I get it."

She blows out her lips and says, "Don't be sorry. Just because you make something doesn't mean you're ultimately responsible for it."

"Doesn't it?"

"I have no idea, but what is it your dad always says? 'You may have come from me, Bruce, but I'll be damned if I understand you'?"

There's a quiet beat or two. There are a lot of things I think to say in response, but what comes out of my mouth is, "We could try the Candy Shoppe."

"The candy shop?" she repeats, then, "Oh . . . right," she mumbles with a certain degree of judgment. "*The Candy Shoppe*."

The Candy Shoppe. So named because, in the lore of Riftbreaker, it had once been an actual candy factory. A bit of a nod to Willy Wonka. But it's also a double entendre because it's the first place I created to patch up wounds and give out potions and upgrades and whatnot.

Initially, it was going to be what I called all the spots Carpathian would stop and do his whole "leveling up" thing. Candy Shoppes, a place where one goes to get treats. Seemed fun and kind of clever, I thought. But when the first book came out, I discovered that people were making lots of jokes and memes about it like, *"What? Carpathian gonna have to fight 50 Cent?"* and shit like that, and I got self-conscious, so I wound up ditching it as a thing and changed the name of the upgrade areas to Pulse Wells. But the original Candy Shoppe might still be here.

"I mean, it's worth seeing if we can at least try to find it. Unless you've got another idea."

Brittany stares at the map. "It's not even on here . . . but, yeah, screw it. Let's see if—"

Before she can finish, we hear something. A kind of a growl or . . . something.

"What is that?" she asks.

"I have no idea." I spin my head around to see if I can find where the sound came from. "I don't think I ever described anything with a . . . yawp like that."

"With a *what* like that?"

"A yawp."

"A yawp?"

"A yawp. From 'Song of Myself'? The Walt Whitman poem? 'I sound my barbaric yawp over the roofs of the world'? A yawp."

We hear it again. Louder this time.

"Yeah, to me it just sounds like a cat trying to sing a Whitney Houston song."

Not exactly as poetic as Whitman, but she's not wrong.

"Let's just get the hell away from whatever it is, see if we can find the god-damn Candy Shoppe, and then figure out how to Mezmerize the car and keep moving. To where, I don't know, but we can't just dick around here and wait to be fingerbanged by whatever's making that noise."

I pull my head back, a little surprised. "Did you just make that up?"

"Make what up? Fingerbang? No. It means when someone—"

"No, *Mezmerize*," I clarify. "Mezmer. Ize. Mezmerize."

"Oh. I guess? I dunno. Why? Why does it matter?"

"Because it's such an obviously cool play on words. How come I never thought to call it that in the books? When something got influenced by Mezmer, that it would be Mezmerized? As opposed to Mezmerated. Which is what I wrote.

"Mezmerize. That's awesome. How did I write ten books and never think of it myself?"

She looks at me like I'm mentally unfit for service and shakes her head. "Yeah, I have no idea, and frankly, Bruce, could give a fat baby's ass right at this moment."

I nod, acknowledging that I'm just making nervous small talk the way I am wont to do when I get anxious, and then start looking around again to see where the yawp-slash-massacred Whitney joint might be coming from.

"So," Brittany starts, examining the map again, "Candy Shoppe's not that way, it can't be that way, and I hope to Christ it's not that way." She points in various directions. "If it's anywhere, it must be this way." She starts off. I don't immediately follow. "You coming?"

I nod once more, trying my best to adorn my face with something like resolve.

"Lemme just grab Gonz." I open the passenger door and pick the little guy up. "C'mon, buddy. The adventure continues." I look at him, and it appears as though he's not looking back at me, but almost like he's . . . looking *around* me. Like he's peering at something behind my back.

I turn.

"What is it? You see something?" Brit asks.

"I'm . . . not sure. But let me just . . ."

Beep-boop.

Upon hearing the sound, Brittany's eyelids get heavy. "Did you just lock your car?"

"Yeah?"

"Why?"

"I don't want anyone to steal anything."

She starts to say something, stops herself, starts again, stops a second time, then points at me, starts to say something else, stops yet again, shakes her head, waves her hand in the air, rubs the bridge of her nose between her eyes, and heads off once more. This time I do follow.

But just as I take a step, I hear the noise again. This time, it sounds less like an abstract something and more like a specific something. In fact, I would swear it sounds like *EIIIIINNNZZZGGGEEEAAARRR.*

I still can't spy anything myself, but when I look down at Gonzo, I note that he continues to appear distracted by whatever it is that has caught his eye.

And an odd but, I think, completely reasonable thought pops into my head.

I wonder if he'd be able to see it better if he were a giraffe.

CHAPTER NINE

I think it might be up ahead?" I say, glaring at two identical ends of a T-intersection.

"Up ahead which way?" Brit asks, staring at the map.

Both of our heads track from left to right as we examine the path. Then we look at one another, then forward again. We sigh simultaneously.

"This is so friggin' bizarre," she says.

"I know."

"If you had told me six years ago, when I got on your bus for the first time and you happened to randomly notice that I was reading *The Way of Kings*, that having a conversation with you would eventually wind me up here?" She gestures all around us, then stops talking.

Wind blows. I hear something creaking somewhere. The water in Gonzo's snail-mobile slops gently.

"You would've walked instead?" I ask, by way of completing the thought.

She looks at me and chews at her lip. "Shit. I dunno. I probably still woulda done everything the same. I make bad choices." She points at a building sitting directly at our twelve o'clock that looks like it was a tavern before whatever happened here . . . happened. "Is that maybe Jeomandi's?" she asks.

Jeomandi's Pub and Pints was the only tavern I'd ever written about that had enough of a role in the story to earn a proper name. It was sort of a rogue's gallery where outcasts, troublemakers, and ne'er-do-wells of all kinds would meet up and exchange information, formulate schemes, that kind of thing. A real Creature Cantina type of joint. It was actually the site of the first major throw down Carpathian got into in *Seasons of Rebellion*.

Almeister had intentionally spread a rumor that Carpathian was trying to steal the wife of one of the Reapers of Agony—who, as their name might imply, were not inclined to shy away from a fight—and then snuck out the back of the pub, locking Carpathian in when shit started popping off. It was a real come-to-Carpathian moment that forced him to take a true accounting of himself, and also showed him he had more skill and ability than he knew.

Especially with an enchanted Mechanical Heart that allowed him to *take a punch*. Which, following the old adage of "that which does not kill us makes us stronger," is one of the primary ways someone gains proficiency and power in Meridia. If you can endure getting knocked down and keep pulling yourself back to your feet, you'll get rewarded for it. Leveling Up happens, in part, via the building of metaphysical (and sometimes actual) scar tissue.

So while Carpathian wasn't yet the greatest fighter in the world when he encountered the Reapers, he was already tougher than buffalo hide and really, *really* hard to bring down. Which, as the series went along and he added more tools to his toolkit, translated to him becoming damn near impossible to kill.

Which, consequently, required me doing some extremely intricate maneuvering in this last book to get him into a state where it could be plausibly believed that he might succumb to his injuries.

(Ultimately, I had to just have him throw in the towel of his own accord. I know it's a little bit of a cop out, but giving up is an even more assured way to die than a blast to the chest from a rune cannon.)

Also, early on, I used his durability as something surprising and off-putting that could get him out of a difficult situation. Enemies would eventually just get worn down by smashing their fists into the equivalent of a slab of calcified rock and either give up out of exhaustion or break their knuckles or whatever. Or sometimes, he'd bleed all over them like Tyler Durden in *Fight Club* and they'd freak.

Never underestimate the power of being able to ick someone out.

In any case, this can't be Jeomandi's. And I tell her so.

"This can't be Jeomandi's."

"Why not?"

"Jeomandi's wasn't technically in Bell's View. It was just a ways away, close to Revelation's Pass? Near that creek? The one where Carpathian found Pergamon." I hold up Gonzo kind of without thinking, indicating him in a way that suggests he is, in fact, Pergamon.

I get self-conscious, lower the tank, and stare awkwardly at the ground.

Brittany sucks at her teeth, says, "Oh. Right," and looks at the map again.

I'm starting to worry that her maps are, possibly, not going to be of as much utility as I had initially hoped. I just keep being aware that there's all this stuff I suppose I kind of intrinsically knew was here but never thought to include or write about. When I would close my eyes and picture Bell's View, this is what it looked like, but it's all rendered in appreciably more graphic detail than I wrote about.

Because, I mean, let's be honest . . . generally speaking, people ain't wanna be reading all that. No disrespect to Melville, but I always felt like I would've enjoyed *Moby Dick* just as much had I not been granted such languorous insight into whaling vessel carpentry or, y'know, had to read an entire chapter about how one cuts up a whale's cock to fashion it into a robe. It's like, Herman, c'mon! Let's just get to the friggin' harpooning already!

But back to the matter at hand, I don't know if we're ultimately going to be aided by Brittany's maps as much as I would have wanted, owing to the fact that Jeomandi's—with all its weatherworn oak garnered from the forests of Ristania and its finely polished brass, rubbed religiously to a gleaming, glistening, almost mirrorlike shine by the arthritic hands of the pub's longtime barkeeper, Clavion (herself a third-generation bartender, having been taught the profession by her mother, Jerustus, who had, in turn, learned the craft from her father, Symphonium)—doesn't appear to be the desiccated remains of the pub that's before us.

"Goddammit," Brittany says to herself, slapping the map against her leg before asking, "should we just pick a direction and go?"

"Lemme see if I can . . ." I close my eyes and attempt to concentrate.

"What are you doing?" she asks.

"Shhh," I shhh. "Lemme just . . ."

I scrunch my eyelids together tightly, trying to summon some kind of aware-ness into being. I invented all this (or, potentially, had it all funneled through my brain and onto the page by mystic forces I don't yet understand. Thanks for that, Elizabeth Gilbert); I *should* be able to conjure *some* kind of clarity about where we need to go next. Maybe?

I open my eyes.

"Left," I say, pointing.

She lowers her head and draws her chin in, looking at me almost through her eyelids. A semiglobal expression of "you certain about that?"

"You're sure?" she asks, not at all buying my extremely confident suggestion.

Abruptly, we once again hear the sound we heard back by the car. Only, this time, it sounds clearer. Closer. And even more precise. Like it's definitely uttering the word:

*EIIIIIIIIIIIIIIIIIIIIINNNNNNNNNNNNNNNZZZZZZZ
ZZGGGEEEEEAAAAARRR.*

"No," I admit, "I'm not sure. But standing here just hoping we figure it out doesn't seem like the move." She rubs at her forehead in, I presume, frustration. And probably a little fear. Or maybe I'm just projecting. "So, when Almeister brought Carpathian to the Candy Shoppe, I wrote that there were crows circling the area."

"Okay."

"Because it seemed super creepy and ominous."

"Alright."

"And Almeister didn't tell him where they were going."

"Uh-huh."

"Because I thought it would be a cool misdirect, right? Like, 'Ooooh, some-thing bad is going to happen,' but then it just turned out to be this training zone for Carpathian where—"

"Bruce, will you get to the fucking point, please?" She looks over her shoulder. Somewhere in the great distance, we can hear the faint roar of engines.

"Look." I point at three crows circling near the entrance to an alley. She tilts her head up to see them, then back to me. I lift my shoulders and raise my hands. "I remember some things."

*EIIIIIIIIIIIIIIIIIIIIINNNNNNNNNNNNNNNZZZZZZZ
ZZGGGEEEEEAAAAARRR.*

"Shit," I gasp. "Do you hear that?"

"Of course I do. I can't tell if it's 'I Will Always Love You' or 'Greatest Love of All.'"

"I don't think it's either. I think . . . I think it's saying *Einzgear*."

"Einzgear? You think it's addressing Carpathian directly?"

"What it sounds like to me. Not to you?"

Her brow furrows. "I dunno. Hard to know if you're right or it's just your particular brand of narcissism manifesting itself."

Before I have the chance to get automatically defensive, I see something. In slow motion. Exiting the swinging bar doors that adorn the front of the burned-out pub across the street.

Two glimmering, black bullets heading slowly toward us. The kind of thing that you'd expect to make a person jump out of the way or dive for cover. A real Wyatt Earp, O.K. Corral kind of a situation.

But I don't dive out of the way, and neither does Brittany.

Because they're not bullets.

They're *eyes*.

Radiating pure enmity, moons light glinting off them.

Arresting.

Attention-grabbing.

And finally, once my own eyes adjust and I can better understand what I'm looking at, I have a stark and heart-palpitating realization that I'd feel a whole lot better if there were actual bullets heading our way instead of . . .

"Shit. There," I whisper hoarsely, pointing.

Brittany looks.

"What the . . ." she starts, seeing what I see. "Holy Mickey Mouse."

There's a reason she chooses that particular coinage to express her shock and awe.

Imagine a rat. A grimy, filthy, New York City subway rat with big sharp teeth and a clear case of bubonic plague. Now imagine that even uglier and more hellish and approximately the size of a Great Dane.

And then cut out the middle portion of the rat's body and replace it with the body of a lion. A strong, alpha feline with a thick, tufted mane running down its spine until it reaches the hind quarters, and then it becomes a rat body and legs again.

That's this thing. And it looks pissed. And deliberate. And, somehow, like it's been actively waiting for us.

It starts moving in our direction, and it once again calls out . . .

"*EIIIIIIIIIIIIIIIIIIINNNNNNNNNNNNNNNNNZZZZZZZZ ZZGGGEEEEEAAAAARRR.*"

"What in the why-is-this-happening-to-us is that?!" Brittany says, trying to catch her breath.

"I don't know! It doesn't look like anything I ever wrote about!"

And I never would have. I hate rats. I hate them so much that I would never even have entertained the *notion* of writing about one.

When I was five-years-old, probably a year or so before my mom died, I was exploring this old, abandoned house that my dad had forbidden me going into. So *obviously*, I was gonna go poking around. Partially because Dad had forbidden it, but partially because Mom had been reading *The Lion, the Witch, and the Wardrobe* to me, and I was super bummed that the closet in my room didn't have a portal to another dimension where I could hang out with and talk to lions. Felt like a real architectural oversight.

But this creepy old place down the street just *had* to have one, I decided.

So, even though Dad had made it *abundantly* clear that I wasn't to ever go in because it had been condemned by the city, I concluded that the real reason he was so against it was because it just *had* to have a doorway to another universe.

Spoiler: It didn't.

What it *did* have was an extremely rotten set of floorboards that, when five-year-old Bruce stepped through a bedroom closet door onto them, transported him not to a magical universe with creepy witches handing out Turkish delight with abandon but directly down into the basement.

The basement that was *crawling* with rats. I mean an *Indiana Jones and the Last Crusade* amount of rats.

And just as young Bruce Wayne was scarred for life by falling into a cave and encountering the rat's flying cousin, so too have I been terrified of the squeaky little vermin ever since.

(However, unlike Bruce Wayne, I did not choose to "turn my fear into a strength" by adopting a weird rat kink and making rats my whole identity. I mean, no judgment, but just . . . no.)

I'm saying I'm so antirat that even as much of a movie junkie as I have ever been, I had to look away the first time I saw the "Rodents of Unusual Size" scene in *The Princess Bride*, and I wouldn't deign to go see *Ratatouille* precisely because I think it's irresponsible to try and normalize rat culture, even in an animated format. *That's* how much disdain I have for rats.

And so, it's no small irony that here I find myself being advanced upon by some kind of mutated rat-lion mash-up who has an ability to pronounce Carpathian's last name, and . . .

Wait. Wait. Rat . . . Lion? Mash-up? What? Why would . . . ?

"Bruce . . ." Brittany says, interrupting my thoughts and starting to back away.

"Yeah?" I say in return.

"Bruce . . . ?" she repeats.

"Yeah . . . ?" I say again, more strongly.

"BRUCE?!" she says louder. "Fuckin' run!"

We do. We take off as fast as we can, given that she's in flip-flops and I'm wearing boots that are at least a size too big and carrying a travel aquarium that houses an ironically so-named Mexican Turbo Snail.

The thing, whatever it is, comes darting out of the pub at us, moving faster than we can run to escape it.

I'm *ca-lomp, ca-lomping* along, and Brittany's cheap, nail salon–issued flip-flops *slap, slap, slap* on the ground. But the sound that dominates the air is the land-pounding, earthquaking *CLUMP, CLUMP, CLUMP* of the beast's paws behind us and its horrifying battle cry.

" *EIIIIIIIIIIIIIIIIIIIIINNNNNNNNNNNNNNNNZZZZZZZZ ZZGGGGEEEEEAAAAARRR!*"

CHAPTER TEN

Why is it shouting your name?!" Brittany yells out.

"It's not!" I return in kind.

"It sounds like it's saying 'Einzgear'!"

"Yeah, but I'm. Not. Carpathian!" I repeat emphatically.

"Oh, good! Tell it that! I'm sure it'll be all, 'Sorry, bro! Thought you were someone else!'"

We're zigzagging through the narrow streets of this ghost town, Brittany right ahead of me. Poor Gonzo is left to the whims of our flight, sloshing around inside the snail-mobile as I clutch it to my chest. Looking toward her, I notice that Brit is gasping for breath, but I also notice that, to my surprise, I am not. I'm staying behind her only so I can make sure I don't lose proximity and keep myself between her and the thing chasing us, because I feel as though I could go some unknown percentage faster and blow right past her if I wanted to.

It has to be the Mechanical Heart. Just as it made Carpathian resilient and strong, it seems to be granting those same privileges to me. I mean, I'm not exactly out of shape, but I don't typically spend my evening hours at a full-on dead sprint. So, I'm amazed by how little this likely death race feels like it's affecting me at all.

Physically, anyway.

Mentally, I'm huffing straight chaos. But I can still move, so I do, my eyes darting along the road to try to find any avenue of emergency egress.

Aha!

Spotting a low-resting drainage awning up ahead, I make a split-second decision, darting past Brittany and pulling her with me. But then, I hear the approach of the beast.

"*EEEIIIIIIIIIIINZZZZZGGGGGEEEAAAAAR!*" it continues to bellow as I think very seriously about pooping my PJs.

And then . . . it pounces.

My mind goes into overdrive like any time in my life where I've felt near death. Like that time I was driving the bus and discovered someone had put a *BOMB* on it, and if the *SPEED* of the bus fell below—

"Not the time for jokes, Bruce!"

"I know, but this is what I mean by my mind going into overdrive!"

For whatever reason, the Notification that popped up earlier when shit went FUBAR is not offering its services this time, so I take matters into my own hands and try to, I suppose, *focus* on the Control spell that I *know* is stored somewhere within—I suppose—my Mezmeric channels.

Since everyone in Meridia has Mezmeric channels, I'm aware that, because I cast it once, I should now have a rudimentary understanding for whereabouts it lives in my body. That's how Carpathian began to commandeer his power, and I've described the action a hundred or more times in the books through the medium of Carpathian and his journey. It's just that now, as noted, we've gone from charming distant theory to hulking, hyperpresent practice.

I dial in on my intention, direct my mind to seek out the place within me where I believe Control *must* be, and even though I can't name it, I can *sense* it somehow. And then . . .

ZZZZZWWWWWAAAAAHHHHHMMMMM.

Thump-thump. Thump-thump.

SHUUUUU-DUD-DUD-DUUUUUD-DUUUUUD. SHOOM.

Everything begins screeching to a crawl. The monster, Brit's barely contained throat noises of panic because she hadn't opened her mouth fully before she started screaming, hell, even the air feels a bit more . . . *tangible* in this decelerated atmosphere.

I turn to look and see the disgusting rat-lion suspended in midair, its filthy rodent mouth open, its dumb, twitchy, maybe-they're-cute-in-cartoons-but-in-real-life-they're-oogie-as-balls whiskers looking like the bristles of a dirty old push broom.

But it worked!

It worked! I controlled Control myself! Look at that! I've been in this world for all of maybe a couple of hours and already—

SHWOOOOOOOOOOOMMMMMPPP.

I gasp as the effect disappears from within me. Suddenly.

Shit. Guess I need to stay focused to keep it going. Okay. Good note. Lesson learned.

I yank Brit out of the way and drag her time-shaken ass toward the little crescent-shaped awning at the base of the wall just as things start spinning back into their usual velocity and . . .

SLAM!

The airborne beast behind us crashes hard into the side of a building, unable to stop itself.

I don't wait. Ignoring Brit's now full-blown screams, I shove her under the awning and dive right behind her. As we slither underneath, my pajama top catches and scrapes against the cold metal, ripping a hole in the side.

"Goddammit!" I shout.

"What?!" Brit yells anxiously. "What is it?!"

"These are Italian silk! They cost like five hundred bucks!"

I can tell Brittany is well and truly afraid because she doesn't even threaten to donkey punch me in the kidneys or anything. If there was any doubt before about how serious things are, it may be now abandoned.

We burst through a barely visible opening, a passage that leads us into a closed-off, dimly lit back alley filled with forgotten doodads and overgrown weeds. Without missing a beat, we take another sharp turn, darting behind a stack of decaying wooden crates, momentarily pausing to catch our breath. Just as we're about to make our next move, the guttural bark of the beast echoes through the narrow passageways. It's still pursuing us relentlessly, its paw beats growing louder and closer with each passing second.

"What the hell is it?" Brit demands in a frantic whisper. "I don't remember that thing coming up at *all* in the story! Something from a rough draft?"

"No way!" I say, peeking over the crates, trying and failing to calm myself down. "You know how much I hate rats! I don't even like *imagining* them, let alone filling a story with any. It's the reason I put monster crabs in the sewers of Priello instead. Can you do something?"

"Me? The hell do you expect me to do?"

"Summon another Tentasaurian, maybe?"

"Dude, I dunno how I did it the first time. Or if I even did. Might have just been a coincidence."

"You believe that?"

"No! Of course I did it! But like I told you, I just had an instinct. Shit, man, Teleri studied beast mastery in school; I studied social change with an emphasis on population and demographics. If you want me to ask it a bunch of census questions, I got you. Other than that, it's gonna take me some time to get up to speed."

I dare to peer up over the crates once more and see the thing, whatever it is, prowling. It's still purring out Carpathian's surname, only quieter. Which is somehow even more frightening.

I'm trying to steady my shaking hands so that the rolling water in Gonzo's tank doesn't give us away when Brit pops her head up next to mine from behind the crates.

"Door!" she says, spotting an open doorway in a house directly across the road from us.

The beast turns in our direction.

Oh, it has superhearing too. That's nice for it.

In an instant, it's charging.

"Shit! Shit!" I yell. And then I'm darting toward that slightly ajar door across the way like my life depends on it. Because, y'know, I'm pretty sure *my life depends on it.*

Brittany's right behind me, her breaths synchronized with my own rapid inhales and exhales. We plunge into the darkness of the forgotten dwelling as our feet trip over memories: fractured furniture, abandoned photographs, relics of lives once lived. Not imagined or dreamt of, but truly lived. The air is heavy with both dust and some ineffable essence of the past.

Behind us, the creature bursts in, an avalanche of muscle and instinct. The doorframe barely survives its entry, and the thing slams headfirst into a China cabinet that once held someone's treasured heirlooms. A cacophony of shattering porcelain and splintering wood reverberates like a violent symphony.

As the beast finds itself momentarily entangled within the wooden shrapnel and shattered breakfront, a burst of adrenaline sharpens my senses. This is my window—a fragile moment of opportunity that's closing fast. I've *got* to slow this thing down, or we're going to be rat-cat food.

My eyes dart around, spotting several wooden splinters and shards scattered across the floor, remnants of the now destroyed cupboard. Hands trembling, I tuck the snail-mobile under my arm and grab a handful of the detritus.

With a gulp, I take aim and throw the first shard. It sails through the air, propelled more by desperation than any skill, and—as is to be expected—misses its target entirely. A spike of panic shoots through me. I grab another piece quickly and throw it. (Because it worked so well the first time.) This one at least makes contact, but it's a glancing blow, hitting the beast on its thick-skinned flank. It snarls, apparently unfazed, and continues to disentangle itself.

My Heart pounds in my chest; every miss narrows our window for escape.

Third attempt. This shard is jagged, longer, more substantial. With a deep breath to steady my trembling hands, I throw it as ferociously as I can. The shard spirals through the air, and then . . . contact, striking the beast square on its snout.

The creature lets out an earsplitting shriek, and its eyes blaze with what can only be described as furious disorientation. It staggers back a step, shaking its massive head as if trying to rid itself of the pain, the indignity, or both.

"Upstairs!" Brittany's voice slices through the frenzy. We make a mad dash for the staircase, our footfalls muffled by years of dust that's settled into the carpet. Reaching the landing, our eyes lock onto a likely sanctuary—a bedroom. We don't hesitate, slamming the door shut with a sense of finality and barricading ourselves in by shoving an old dresser against it.

A shadow creeps in past the threshold, and we hear the creature's haunting breaths.

"What do we—?" Brit starts to ask, but before she can finish, the door disintegrates, bursting into virtual nothingness.

And now . . . the beast is here, filling the entryway with its malevolent presence, its eyes fixed on us, predatory and unyielding. Brittany acts on pure survival instinct, I imagine, her hand gripping my arm as she catapults both of us toward the window. Glass shatters, and we tumble through, landing on the hard cobblestones below. Or, more accurately, I land on the cobblestones, holding Gonzo in the air to keep his case from shattering, and Brittany lands squarely on my stomach, knocking the wind out of me.

"Oh, shit!" she shouts. Which I find funny, considering I'm the one who just got Jimmy "Superfly" Snuka'd. "Come on!" she yells, jumping up. "Let's go!"

I have no idea whatsoever if it's the adrenaline or the ability to *take a beating* that Carpathian enjoyed, but somehow, I manage to struggle to my feet just in time to see . . .

CRASSSSSSHHHHHHHHHHH!

The nasty bastard of an unholy union betwixt cat and mouse *bounds* through the window from which we just made our clumsy descent, and before I can take another breath or think another thought . . . It. Is. In. My. Face.

"Come on, Bruce!" Brittany shouts from just up beyond me.

I can feel, actually *feel*, the rat face's breath. More than that, I can smell it. It is . . . whatever. I'm out of descriptors. It's really bad.

I can't move. I feel like Carpathian did when confronted by the Mechanical Heart still in the box. Afraid in ways that are altogether new, and yet unable to run. Ways that I don't even know if I fully understand. A new fear coupled with an ancient one and . . . a kind of sorrow that I kind of recognize but haven't felt in a very long time.

I feel like I'm going to throw up. And, yet again, I wish I had not eaten late-night pizza. An odd thought, perhaps, but I hear that right at the moment a person realizes they're going to die, any number of random ideas might dart through their brain. Unfortunately, my brain is primarily occupied dually by not *wanting* to die—and the goddamn pizza.

The last thing I hear is a roared, "*EIIIIIIIIIIIIIIIIIINNNNNNNNNNNNNN NNZZZ*" all up in my grill, just before . . .

A noise like a thunderclap erupts in the fractional space between me and my doom, and some manner of energy blasts me and Gonzo backward about fifteen feet, sending the monster from my nightmares tumbling off to the side in a violent, wrenchlike manipulation, finding itself abruptly and unceremoniously impaled through its leonine torso by a random shaft of barbed metal protruding from some kind of abandoned, deathmobile-looking vehicle.

"ACH!" is the thing I say as I tumble back, struggling to maintain a hold on the snail-mobile.

The hell? What's going on? I was all super-chill-in-the-face-of-imminent-destruction, too-fast-to-live-too-young-to-die Bruce Silver, my final moments seeming Gucci as all giddyup; ready to be sent to my maker at peace and one with the universe. And now I'm freaked out again! What just happened?!

"Bruce!" Brittany comes running over to me, grabbing my arm and attempting to pull me back to my feet. "What was that?!"

"I dunno," I say, struggling to stand, feeling the grinding gears of the Heart in my chest working overtime. "I thought it was about to—"

The air in front of us starts to shimmer and vibrate. Like the ripples on a lake after a stone has been thrown in and settled at the bottom, and the water is stilling itself back to its state of natural placidity. I blink a couple of times and squint, even though it does nothing to actually help clarify Jack Sprat. What *does* clarify matters is the now obvious materialization of a form. A human form. Not humanish or humanlike—actually human.

The person—for they are undoubtedly that—is imposing, shrouded in a dark, billowing cloak that seems to further absorb what little amount of dim moons light there is. The edges of the cloak flutter slightly, as if there's a sudden breeze. Beneath the hood, two piercing eyes gleam with an unsettling intensity, the rest of the face obscured in shadow.

Brittany tugs at my arm, trying to draw me away. "Who is that?" she asks.

I stare at the eyes looking at us and they peer intensely back. I twist my head to the left. The partially hidden newcomer twists their head to the right. I twist my head to the right, still studying, and they continue to mirror, twisting their head to the left.

"Bruce? Who is that?!" Brittany repeats more emphatically.

The new arrival has now settled into a fully molecular being. A solid composition, completely formed, and I can feel their energy, their life force, decanting in our direction.

The sense, or perhaps *quality* I receive from it is . . .

. . . kindness.

I know them. They are someone I have not thought about in a long while but once upon a time thought they were going to be very, very important to the story I was telling.

"Oh shit," Brittany says, realizing as well. "Is that—?"

The person lifts their free hand and pulls the hood of the cloak back to reveal . . .

. . . a woman.

Red hair. Sharp, clear, almost impossibly green eyes. Alabaster skin. Pretty in the kind of way that makes you feel safe and wanting at the same time. The absolute apotheosis of what perfection in human beauty as filtered through the lens of great literature must be, in the mold of classic heroines from fantasy novels throughout time immemorial.

"Persephone?" I ask, shaking my head slightly to try and grasp what, or who, I'm seeing.

"Hello, Carpathian," she says, tears starting to form in her impossibly emerald eyes. Then she smiles, cocks her head like a puppy hearing something it can't process, looks me up and down, standing here in PJs and Templar boots, and asks, "What in the name of Richemerion are you wearing?"

CHAPTER ELEVEN

Seasons of Rebellion, Riftbreaker Book One, Chapter Twenty

I am disappointed in you, Carpathian."

Hearing the old man say the words cut Carpathian deep in his recently instated Heart. It was a phrase he had heard uttered numerous times over the years by his own father, and to now hear it spoken by the wizard who had taken him under his tutelage and had, thus far, been nothing but a compassionate and beneficent surrogate, caused him to feel a shame he could not turn away from.

"What? Why?" Carpathian fumfered as the two men watched Arec, the leader of the Reapers, retreat from the bludgeoning he had just been dealt.

Finding the Reaper once again—following the beating Carpathian had previously suffered—and offering unto the man the brutal repayment he had just administered, left his Heart glowing, grinding, and whirring at roughly five thousand RPMs. At least twice as powerfully as the most highly charged engine Carpathian had ever seen or serviced, even back in Conveyance Mechanic's School, when he had worked on the mighty MPVs, the Mezmer Propulsion Vehicles, that were said to possess the greatest internal Mezmer-generating energy ever harnessed. "I thought you'd be happy," Carpathian continued.

"Happy that you used the most formidable gift that can be bestowed upon a human for such an insignificant purpose as petty revenge?"

"Happy that I'm learning how to harness it," he said, tapping at his chest. "Happy that—"

"You were chosen so that you might stand in defense of those who cannot defend themselves. Not so that you can punch down merely to appease your own ego."

"But—"

"They did not threaten you this time, Carpathian Einzgear." Hearing Almeister call him by his full name caused an odd tremble to reverberate throughout his body. "You sought them out. You became the aggressor. You chose to challenge them because you knew you could win."

"Almeister, please," Carpathian began. "I didn't—"

"Perhaps I have been naive," the wizard considered.

"About what?" Carpathian asked, nervously.

"It may be possible that the System can be wrong, after all."

Almeister turned and moved swiftly away, leaving a stunned and speechless Carpathian standing there, trapped between his desire to chase after his sworn mentor and his embarrassment over what he had done to disillusion the man so. After a long moment in suspended animation, Carpathian felt a chill before hearing a voice from behind call his name.

"Carpathian . . . ?"

He spun around to see a crystal chalice filled with some type of nectar floating in midair.

"Persephone?" he inquired.

The young sorcerer began to materialize, her bright, green eyes coming into focus and showing Carpathian something resembling a mixture of compassion and sorrow.

"Hi," she said, sheepishly.

"Why are you Shadow Casting?"

"When I approached and saw that you and father were having a disagreement, I summoned Pellucidity. I didn't want to interfere. Here." She reached forward with the chalice she was holding and offered it to Carpathian.

"You don't think he might have noticed a goblet mysteriously levitating itself?" he asked, attempting to cover his shame with a joke and a smile as he took the nectar from her.

"It was reflexive," she replied coyly. The subtle retraction of her chin and the bowing of her head caused Carpathian's Heart to whir ever that much faster.

"What is this?" Carpathian asked, referring to the vessel he now held in his hand.

"It is a mixture I have been toying with."

"What is it intended to do?"

"Insight."

"Insight?"

"Yes," she said. "It is intended to offer insight."

"Insight into what?" he asked.

She didn't answer the question, instead saying, "He's frightened."

"What?" Carpathian asked. "What do you mean? Who is?"

"Father," she replied, quietly. "He's scared of what will happen to this world if . . ." She trailed off, reticent to conclude the thought.

He did not to need to ask "If what?" for he already knew the answer. If you fail, she would say.

"I did not imagine him to be the type to feel fear," Carpathian told her.

"Of course he does. He has much to lose. We all do," she responded thoughtfully. "Everyone feels fear, Carpathian. It is why the Ninth Guardian is conspiring to do the things they are conspiring to do. They too are afraid. They are afraid that if the Mezmeric Concordance that has been prophesied comes to pass, they will no longer be able to force their will on the people of this world. They are afraid that there will be harmony. Harmony is their greatest horror, for it is only within the disharmony they have fabricated that they can preserve their power."

Carpathian considered this, and realized in that moment why Almeister had become so upset with him. It was one thing to be afraid and strong enough to fight in defense. To fight for survival. It was another thing entirely to turn that fear into aggression—which was exactly what the Ninth Guardian had done. It caused a small part of Carpathian to feel sympathy for the faceless Guardian.

But only a small part.

Persephone grinned.

"What are you smiling about?" Carpathian asked, trying as much as he was able not to be distracted by the sun that seemed to live in her eyes, the sparkle that seemed to shine off her lips, or the abrupt realization that the daughter of his mentor and guide tended to wear the tunic under her bodice so loosely tied that it fell open quite a bit more than it probably should, exposing more of the creamy white skin of her chest than he imagined he should be seeing. "Seriously," he said, forcing his eyes back onto her face, "what has you so pleased?"

"I'm just happy that it's so effective."

"That what is?"

"The nectar. You didn't even have a sip of it yet, and it has already granted you Insight."

"Insight into what? I didn't say anything."

"You don't have to."

Carpathian's eyes widened a bit, realizing that Persephone must be able to see inside his thoughts. He wasn't sure if this pleased or terrified him, but he did notice, as she walked away, that she seemed to casually toss her hair over her shoulder a bit more—he would call it—coquettishly than usual . . .

CHAPTER TWELVE

It's called a Ronine," Persephone says, placing two mugs of steaming-hot something in front of me and Brittany, and a thimbleful in front of Gonzo. She brought us to her workshop (which I'm envisaging for the first time because I never wrote about it explicitly and only sort of peripherally knew it even existed) and has been explaining about how the town was ransacked just recently. "It has been crafted by the High Council expressly for the purpose of anticipating your rearrival."

A Ronine. A play on "Ronin," I imagine. It also could just be a shortened version of "leonine rodent." Maybe it's both, a bit of a low-key double entendre. As much as I remain repulsed by the idea of it, I have to give it up for the High Council's cleverness when it comes to naming conventions.

"What do you mean, my rearrival?" I ask.

"It was their suspicion—as has been all of ours who are privy to the details of the day—that you might reemerge here. In Bell's View. Where your journey once began. And you did." Persephone says the last with an unmistakable breath of relief. "Though you have modified your style of presentation with your attire, your nascent-hirsute countenance, and your tonsorial adaptation, you remain unambiguously . . . you." She takes on an impish grin. "I will admit I have thought of you often, Carpathian. I asked father about you frequently . . ."

There is a trailing sadness in her voice.

Of course there is. Her father, Almeister, is trapped in a damn tower because of me. Shame and regret continue to rapidly outpace confusion and anxiety as my dominant emotions.

It's surreal to be with her. Persephone. If I'm being honest (and at this point, honesty feels like the securest thing to hang on to), Persephone is based on a woman I was dating at the time I started writing Riftbreaker. Mollie was her name. Mollie Kincaid. I liked her. A lot. I think I may have loved her, but I can't know for sure because I also think I'm nearly pathologically reluctant to allow myself to fall in love. Which has to do with me being reluctant to allow myself to feel much of anything too deeply. Which has to do with . . .

Whatever. Doesn't matter now. I'm saying I have issues with commitment.

Point is that Mollie was really cool and smart and pretty and nice, and I thought . . . I dunno, that there might be something there. We had, I guess, what people like to call "chemistry." (Which I've always thought is a misnomer when it comes to talking about relationships. I contend that if you're able to find someone you wanna be with, it should be called having "alchemy" with them. Because chemistry is science, but finding someone you like being around . . . ? Like, *really* like being around . . . ? That's damn near magic.)

Anyway, whatever you wanna call it, Mollie and I seemed to have it, so I wrote her as a character into my first book, which is, I reckon, less of a risky thing to do than getting her name tattooed on my eyelids or whatever. Because, y'know, if it wound up not working out, I could always just write her out of the story and move on. And, obviously, that's what happened. It didn't. Work out. With Mollie and me.

So once Carpathian left Bell's View, he left Persephone behind, and that was, for the most part, that. I mean, Persephone is Almeister's daughter, and up until Almeister got imprisoned in the Tower of Zuria, he might have mentioned her from time to time, but after Teleri showed up to become Carpathian's lady-sorcerer ride-or-die, Carpathian never really thought about Persephone that much again.

But based on all the things she's been saying, it would appear that Persephone never really *stopped* thinking about Carpathian.

"So the Ronine's sole purpose was to hunt Carpathian?" I seek clarification. She tilts her head, and I realize . . . "I mean, me? To hunt me?"

"Yes," she breathes out. "And I wouldn't say *was*."

"Why?"

"I can guarantee with certainty that when we return to where we confronted it, it will be gone."

"But . . . you blasted it away, and it impaled itself on—"

"It does not matter. That will only slow it temporarily. The Ronine has no feelings, no wit, no sapience, no purpose other than to hunt and kill, and it will neither cease nor wane until it has fulfilled its purpose."

"Yikes. Well, that sounds—"

"Defeating it absolutely is only possible at the hands of the Saviour himself."

"Say again?"

"Not in your current state, obviously. But once you have regained your strength and your tools. Owing to the Ninth Guardian's failures to subdue you in the past with more conventional, corporeal foes—Azteral the Punisher; Vylleritus the Dark Scion; Strafe Mortallus the Merchant of Condemnation . . ."

She's naming all the Big Bads, the world bosses that Carpathian had to defeat in each book in order to continue his march toward his final confrontation with the Super Vizier and the Ninth Guardian. This is so trippy.

". . . Posthumarcron the—"

"Right, yeah, no, I know who he—I. Who *I* had to, y'know, 'best' in order to . . . whatever. But I did have aid in those, um, endeavors. Teleri, for example, dealt the finishing blow to Oppenkinder the Wanderer."

Brittany—who is only half-paying attention, marking the maps with this new location and scribbling notes in the margins—raises her hand in the air before dropping it back down to trace something with her finger.

I continue. "So why is defeating the Ronine only possible by *my* hands?"

"Because, unlike those of Meridia-borne with inherent imperfections that could be exploited, the Ronine was crafted with the express intent of counter-manding your powers. The Ninth Guardian and High Council took all they have learned of your potential weaknesses—of which there are precious few!—and manufactured a creature designed specifically to penetrate your vulnerabilities. So it is only by clotting those vulnerabilities that it can be beaten."

My vulnerabilities? She means Carpathian, I know, but . . . *Bruce* is the guy who hates rats. *Bruce* is the guy who associates lions (and, to a lesser degree, witches and wardrobes) with the death of his mom . . . She's not just talking about *my* vulnerabilities. She's talking about MY vulnerabilities.

Christ. I feel like I'm in friggin' *Wheel of Time* all of a sudden.

"Okay, so let me understand this," Brittany says, going through her notes. "Ever since Carpathian left"—she pauses, remembers she's technically now talking about me, and points at me with her pen—"him, I mean. Him. Carpathian here. Ever since he left on his first assigned Quest back in the day to seek the Blade of the Starfallen, everything's been cool with Bell's View? Like, no one's come sniffing around trying to fuck with anything? Up until just the last week or whenever?"

Persephone regards her with curiosity. "You are vastly unlike the ways in which I have heard my father speak of you, Teleri Nightwind."

"Oh . . ." Brittany says, her attention pulled from her focused scribbling. "Oh, uh, yeah, well . . . Resurrection changes a person, I suppose."

Resurrection, or remorting, or reconstitution (or even Mezmerated recarbonification, as I have called it before in a reckless desire to not just keep typing the same phrases over and over) is not completely uncommon in Meridia. It doesn't happen every day, but characters who have been dead will occasionally pop back up from time to time.

I always considered it both a way of giving myself ample opportunity to surprise the story and, in the event people got really, *really* mad that I killed off one of their favorites, an open door to suggest, "*Hey, don't give up hope; they might still make it.*"

I mean, that's exactly what I did with Carpathian at the end of this last book. And yes, I'm aware it's a very noncommittal, kind of messed-up, *Walking Dead* thing to do, but up until season seven (when it is universally agreed upon that the train went off the tracks for the TV version), they managed to make it work, so, y'know . . . *homage.*

The point is that this is why even though the news of Carpathian's demise spread throughout the land, it doesn't appear to have come as a shock to Persephone that "Carpathian" and "Teleri" are here with her now. To the contrary, she seems downright tickled to see them. Or . . . us. Or at least, me, or . . . Carpathian, or whatever. The hug he . . . I . . . *we* got was . . . *familiar.* I'm not complaining about it. After all the shit I've already been through here, getting a friendly . . . cuddly hello was . . . not unwelcome.

But no, the part that she seems to be bumping on is the amount of swearing that "Teleri" is doing. Brit swears a lot for anybody, but Teleri was always identified as "an academic" and "to the manner of sorcery borne" and stuff like that, so one wouldn't really anticipate quite so many f-bombs.

(Persephone also seemed as confused over Brittany's tank top and jean shorts as she was me in my pajamas. She tried sounding out the words on the T-shirt phonetically, so to Persephone, Brit's shirt reads: /Fem-eyen-eye-sam is me second favor-eyet fword/.)

"I suppose it does," Persephone replies to Brittany's suggestion about reincarnation changing a person. In our case, literally. I also get the impression that she's regarding Brit with a fair amount of skepticism. And maybe, possibly, just a hint of jealousy.

"In any matter," Persephone goes on, "yes, until the Saviour's *presumed* exhaustion in Rendalia"—she kind of smirks on *presumed*—"no one dared to approach Bell's View. Not even DONG."

There is a beat before I feel compelled to ask the, I feel like, extremely obvious question. "Um . . . *dong?*"

She regards me like I'm not all there, then says, "Yes. DONG. The Disciples of the Ninth Guardian. DONG."

Brittany looks at me. I look at her. She silently projects her patented *Are. You. F'ing. Kidding me?* and I try not to bury my dumb face in my stupid, stupid hands that apparently typed out the name of a mythic, terrifying, all-powerful cabal, dozens upon dozens of times over the course of ten books, the acronym of which happens to be friggin' *DONG, and I never noticed.*

I deserve whatever awful shit is going to happen to me here. I really do.

"Oh, of course," I attempt to cover. "DONG. Yeah. Right. DONG. I know DONG."

"Yes," Persephone says, curiously. Then asks, "When one reconstitutes, does the System perform some manner of memory wipe as well?"

"Oh, uh—Maybe? It's pretty jarring." (An understatement, to say the least.)

She looks at me with pity. "I'm sure. And I suppose that also explains why Pergamon has remained silent." She looks at Gonzo, sipping from his thimble. "He has not yet uttered a word, and as I remember him, he was always so loquacious."

"Oh, right," I continue stammering. "Well, yes, I think that . . . You have to remember," I say, trying to remember myself, "that when Carpa—*I*. When *I* found Pergamon at the edge of the creek near Jeomandi's, he was just, well, as he is now. It wasn't until your father served him the elixir that imbued within him Philological Consciousness that he started to . . . uh . . . talk. And all that."

Speaking of talking, I'm trying hard to remember to talk *like* Carpathian, just so I don't have to have a bunch of additional conversations about why my own shit is so off-kilter. Yet another thing that seems like it should be no big deal. I wrote ten books in Carpathian's voice. But, as I'm sure Brittany would attest, it's kind of like learning a foreign language: Easier when you have the time to think about it and write it all down than it is to have an actual conversation. To which end—

"So, wait, wait, wait, wait," Brit says, jumping back in. "So lemme get this timeline right. When did, uh, *DONG*"—she raises an eyebrow at me. (Oh, please. She never caught it either.)—"come through and tear this place apart?"

"The very night that . . ." She trails off, looking at me with simultaneously sad yet somewhat flirtatious eyes. "Three Lunar Rotations ago."

I didn't really change the way time works on Meridia. It's exactly like Earth time, just with different verbiage and operating on a lunar calendar. So "three Lunar Rotations" simply indicates three days.

Brittany looks at me and whispers, "When did you finish?"

"Finish what?" I ask.

"The . . ." She makes a gesture like she's writing with a quill. (How I know it's a quill that she's miming, I'm not sure. I'm just really good at identifying space objects from an improv class I took once.)

"Oh, I guess . . ." Realization dawns on me like the sun rising on a nuclear winter. ". . . about three . . . uh . . . Lunar Rotations ago."

It feels like the temperature in here dropped about ten degrees. Brit and I stare at each other in stupefied silence.

"Finished what?" Persephone asks.

"Oh, uh, nothing. Hey, why are you still here?" I ask, changing the subject.

"What do you mean?" she returns without guile.

"I mean, why are you still here? In Bell's View? Why didn't you escape when DONG"—I'm never going to feel good about saying that—"came to destroy the town? Or before that, even?"

Once again, she looks at me with confusion. "I . . . can't," she says. "It is my sworn task to remain here."

"Why?"

"Because . . ." She takes a moment to think. "Because of the Mezmeric enchant-ment. Bell's View is the genesis of your path. The commencement of your journey toward becoming the World Saviour. It is the wellspring of all that is right and pure and good. It was always assumed that its desecration would result in irreparable consequence. And it has been my honour to serve as its protector. Until now . . ."

Her face drops, her effort to sustain a sunny countenance setting quickly. It's comingled with a hint of bafflement as well, like she's never really had to answer the question before. And now, upon reflecting on it, she can't quite make sense of the reasoning.

Because of course she can't. Because the real answer to the question is much simpler:

She never left because I never allowed her to. I kept writing ahead and left her behind.

That's the real reason she's still here.

She furrows her brow, still holding on to a faraway look. Then she compels herself to brighten. "But it's alright. None of that is of concern now." She raises her chin with pride and renewed vigor. "Because you're here. I knew the absurd rumours were false."

"Rumors?" I note. "What rumors?"

"Rumors?" she echoes me, then corrects, "No. I said *rumours*."

"Yes. No, I understand. Rumors. That's what I said. What rumors?"

Her lips tighten, and her jaw fixes in a kind of tiny frustration. "I don't . . . You're pronouncing it oddly. *Rumooouuuuurs*," she says again, drawing out the second syllable so that I can clearly hear the superfluous *U* after the *O* that would appear on the page were it being written down.

I press my lips together and nod. Because I did this to myself. "Right. Rum*OURS*," I emphasize. "What kind of rum*OURS*?"

"Oh, just . . . silly things. That . . . That your *presumed* fatality on the battle-field was somehow a *choice*. That you had voluntarily forfeit yourself and forsaken the Rebellion! Preposterous! As if that would ever happen!"

I try not to meet her eye. Because . . . Because . . .

Because.

"I didn't believe it, obviously," she goes on. "Of course, I did grow worried when I heard that you were to be quartered so that you might not recarbonify, and that your component parts were to be displayed prominently throughout Meridia to strike fear in the hearts of all those who might dare to take up the cause that you had, *supposedly*, abandoned." Her back stiffens with pride. "But that was all just *a fiction*. I knew you'd return. And now, the work may begin again."

She smiles, exuberantly.

"What work . . . ?" I ask, cautiously, already anticipating the answer.

"The work of unseating the Ninth Guardian. Of unlocking the Nexus Core and allowing Mezmer to once more stream freely to all those on Meridia who are denied it. Of thwarting the destructive, malignant, all-consuming intentions of the High Council and the Super Vizier, and unmasking the insidious visage of the Ninth Guardian themself."

Brittany looks at me, raising yet another eyebrow. I snap my fingers nervously.

"Yes, yes . . . yes," I say. "Of course. Doing all that. Um . . . But, so, here's the thing—"

"The first step, obviously, will be freeing father from the Tower of Zuria," she interrupts.

I now raise both of my eyebrows to no one in particular.

"Right. Your father. Almeister. Yeah . . . So . . ." I debate with myself about how to handle this. I feel like, maybe, the best thing to do would be to try and explain to her that I'm not actually Carpathian. That I'm . . . Bruce. The guy who created Carpathian. That I made him up. Unless, as has been proposed, I didn't, and somehow, I actually *am* him? Or . . . ?

Suddenly, I hear the AC/DC song "Who Made Who" from the soundtrack to the Stephen King movie *Maximum Overdrive* blaring in my brain, Brian Johnson's raspy voice asking the lyrical question, "Who made who? Who made you?"

(Jesus Christ, I've seen a lot of movies.)

But before I have the chance to weigh any further how to address the "I'm not actually Carpathian" issue, I seize up in mild alarm and great discomfort once more as a beam of light bursts yet again from my chest, and a Notification is projected forth into the air.

My eyes start to water. The pain in my chest increases, amplifying to a degree that it hasn't in the previous instances of this kind of thing happening.

Reading the words that now loom in the air before me, I have a suspicion that it's not the physical sensation that's causing my augmented unease.

It's the Notification itself.

You have been offered a Quest!
"Rescue Almeister from Imprisonment in the Tower of Zuria."
Do you wish to accept this Quest?
[Yes] [No]

CHAPTER THIRTEEN

You have to do it."

Brittany is whispering.

We're huddled together just outside the door to the workshop. I started hyperventilating when I saw the Quest Notification and then stepped away. Persephone began to follow, but I convinced her that I just needed a second because I'm still adjusting to having been remortified (which is a term with multiple meanings if I've ever heard one) and asked her to watch after Gonz. Or *Pergamon*, as it were.

I could see her bristle when Brittany followed me, but I honestly can't bring myself to worry too much about the jealousy of a person I only just found out was real toward a person who isn't real but who Persephone thinks is real but also isn't the person she thinks she is.

So, Brit and I are standing in an alley that I've kind of been presuming is protected in some way by Persephone's Mezmer, because the workshop is the only place I've seen in Bell's View that isn't totally wrecked, but I'm suddenly concerned that only the workshop itself is shielded and that we might be exposing ourselves by coming out here to confab. I can hear unfamiliar sounds of living things and recently familiar sounds of mechanized things like magecycles in the distance.

Brittany repeats herself. "Bruce. You have to."

"I have to? Yeah, I really don't! I can't! I don't . . ."

"You don't what?"

"I don't even know how to start going about doing something like rescuing someone from a tower. How am I supposed to—?"

"We'll figure it out. Carpathian didn't know how to do any of the things he did either until he learned how and acquired the necessary Abilities and tools and all that shit to make it possible."

"You're serious."

"Damn right, I'm serious."

"But—"

"Look," she says, grabbing me by the arms and staring me in the face, "as far as I can see, it's our best shot at maybe getting back."

"Back where?"

"Home. Back to where we came here from."

"I don't see how—"

"Think, man. We're here for some reason. We have to be. And, based on the limited information I have at the moment, it appears probable that *that* reason is to set shit right. Whether you created all this yourself or whether you were just the unwitting scribe writing it all down, the choice you made to kill off the last hope for salvation that the assholes who live here had has placed this whole goddamn world in jeopardy.

"You said it earlier . . . Almeister, Xanaraxa, Zerastian, Mael . . . We now know that these are all real people with real lives that you just fucked with for the sake of 'telling a cool story,' and now, you have the chance to unfuck them. You can write them a new story. Only . . . figuratively this time. Ironically."

I squeeze my eyes closed.

My worst fear. Harm coming to people I care about. Especially because of something I have done.

When I open my eyes again, I see Persephone through the workshop window gently stroking Gonzo's head as he appears to sip from the thimble.

Shit.

"But okay, great. Let's say we go around and manage to make right all the damage we didn't know we were doing—"

"*We?*"

"Fine! Me! Whatever! The damage *I* didn't know *I* was doing! And somehow succeed in *not* getting cut into multiple pieces and scattered hither and yon as some kind of 'hero deterrent.' How do you think that helps us get back home, Dorothy?"

She gives me a sharp look.

"Don't you start with me, bro. If I'm Dorothy, then you're the chickenshit Cowardly Lion, the dumbass Scarecrow, and the cocksucking Tin Man"—she taps my chest for emphasis—"all rolled into one."

She sighs. "I'm just saying that since Almeister is Carpathian's mentor, his guide, the one dude who seems to have a deep and abiding understanding of how Meridia works—like, actually works, like for real—then it's possible that he might be able to . . . Hell, I dunno. I'm just guessing, given my narrow comprehension and best instincts, but . . . maybe wave some Mezmeric wand or something and get us the Judy Garland outta here."

Hearing her idea, I'm wrestling with myself not to say what I'm thinking.

"What?" she asks, clearly observing my internal struggle. "What is it?"

"Nothing," I let out. "Just . . . I mean, he *is* a wizard. And if our goal is to go off to *see* the wizard and find out if he can—OW!"

I know she pulls her punches with me because we're friends. I shudder to think what her striking me with her full force would feel like.

"We have to do this, Bruce. We don't really have a choice."

I try to think through all the other remotely plausible options I can come up with.

"Why don't we just let ourselves get caught?" I offer.

"Caught?"

"Caught, captured, killed, whatever. Maybe this is really all some kind of wretched dream or shared fugue state thing, and we'll wake up back home again."

She blinks and shakes her head at me in the way people do when they're trying to wrap their heads around what you're saying.

"Or, y'know," I go on, "worst-case scenario, we'll end up resurrected and can figure it out from there. You saw *Edge of Tomorrow*. You know how this kind of thing works."

She opens her mouth, but only pops of air from the back of her throat emerge as she attempts to decide what, exactly, she wants to say. Finally, she settles on, "Are you stupid?"

"Depends on who you ask. Why?"

She makes a grinding sound deep in her larynx then yells, "Because!" She looks around, self-conscious, and continues more quietly. "Because, dude. Have you forgotten how it works? You don't just get to keep coming back. In Riftbreaker, *if* you're one of the lucky ones who gets to remort, you only get to do it *once*. One time. That's it. The original gets one shot at a resurrection. One more try to get shit right. But if the copy fails, that's it. It's done. Game over."

"No, of course I didn't forget." I really didn't. I may get hazy on lots of things, but not something as integral to the mythology as that. (C'mon, Brit. Give a guy *some* credit.) "Of course I didn't," I repeat. "But . . . we're not copies. We're us. You aren't Teleri; I ain't Carpathian. So, let's say this is really real. Okay, well, fine. So we get to use our rebirth credit confirming it. And, if it's not real, then we're out of here. No harm, no foul." I let that linger in the air before following up with, "It's worth a try, don't you think?"

She mulls it over for a moment before saying, "Almeister already remorted in book six."

"Yeah, I know. It was tragic as hell, but then turned into the happiest day of Carpathian's life. Why are you . . . ?" I trail off. Because I realize, of course, why she's bringing it up. The sham trial Almeister is being subjected to already has a predetermined outcome. It's going to be a clown show resulting in him being found guilty of "Treasonous acts in defiance of the Ninth Guardian" and put to death. Probably extremely painfully. I hadn't yet worked out exactly what that was going to look like, but it was gonna be gruesome.

Of course, Carpathian would have swooped in and saved him. I kind of had this loose idea worked out about Carpathian and Teleri crashing the trial in a super dramatic fashion, battling a bunch of Disciples, and rescuing Almeister from the prisoner's box in the courtroom. But then, Carpathian died.

So.

Y'know.

That didn't happen.

Anyway.

"Okay, but still—" I begin before Brit cuts me off.

"And as far as we go . . ." She pauses before finishing, "You sure you wanna gamble that we *aren't* already on our second go 'round? Technically? Maybe the System can't distinguish us from the actual Teleri and Carpathian. You've seen that not everything here operates exactly like it was conceived of in the books. So . . . do you really want to take the chance?"

I think about my answer. Sincerely. She's not wrong. While I suppose there's a nonzero possibility that we *might* wind up back in Kansas again, metaphorically, there's an equally decent chance that that'd be it. End of book. Cover closed. The last chapter in the story of Bruce Silver.

Which is an awfully big risk to take on something so fraught with unknowns.

And even though the plot of this incipient tale is also unknown and feeling like it's extremely out of my control just now, the feeling of a narrative doing its own thing and being extremely out of my control is something I at least have experience with.

I blow out a heavy breath. "Yeah, okay," I concede, adding, "I will take the Ring, though I do not know the way."

Brit's heavy-lidded look makes no attempt to disguise what is already her clear exhaustion. "Are you gonna do that a lot?"

"What? Quote Tolkien?"

"Tolkien, Pratchett, Martin, Jordan, Lewis . . . the Wachowskis . . . whoever. Biting other people's shit gonna be your thing on this dumb hero's journey?"

"First of all, it's not biting—it's *homage*. Second, there are no new ideas under the sun. As I always say, you should never feel bad about borrowing great ideas, because whoever you're borrowing them from probably borrowed them from someone else."

Her eyes narrow at me. "That's what *you* always say?"

"I mean . . . maybe not *always*, but—"

"Sure you didn't steal it? *From Michael Caine?* Who said, 'If you see an actor do something stunningly effective, steal it. Because you can be sure they stole it in the first place'?"

I pause, recognizing that she's right. That is where I heard that before. But I query, "Is it technically stealing if you don't remember where you got it from?"

She grinds out, "Mm-hmm, mm-hmm, mm-hmm," and takes a deep breath before we head back inside.

"Are you alright?" Persephone asks as we enter the room. "You didn't soil yourself as you did upon your first encounter with the Raiflorax, did you?"

Oh, Christ. Once upon a time, I thought it would be a charming moment of levity to have Carpathian tinkle his pants when he came face-to-face with his first great, nonhuman foe. Now, I'm finding myself both regretful and inexplicably embarrassed at having written it.

"No. No, no. All is . . . well."

"So, you are committed, then?" she questions, uncertainly but hopeful. "You will be accepting the Quest to retrieve Father?"

At the asking, once again, my whole torso seizes up as the Quest is broadcast into the air in front of my face.

"Yep, absolutely," I moan, reaching out and pressing [Yes].

Another Notification appears in the prior's place.

Quest: "Rescue Almeister from Imprisonment in the Tower of Zuria."
[ACCEPTED]

Quest Requirements:

Requires Artifact: [Blade of the Starfallen]
Requires Spell(s): [Stealth]

Quest Restrictions:
[None]
(You're going to need all the help you can get!)

Time Allowed for Completion:
[Seven Lunar Rotations]

(Upgrades may be available. Please visit the nearest Pulse Well to
access options.)

Oooookay. Welp. We're in it now.

So, not only do I have to figure out how the hell to pull off this rescue, I have to first be in possession of the Blade of the Starfallen and some kind of Stealth Spell. And, I only have seven Lunar Rotations in which to make it all happen. Dynamite. That's just great.

A bundle of thoughts gets kicked over and tumbles rapidly across the landscape of my brain.

No restrictions. Alright, well, that's . . . compelling. I'd always write Quests so that there would be some limitation on the questor's abilities. Felt like by creating an extra obstacle for them to overcome, it raised the stakes and made things more interesting. Like for example, if it was a battle against a winged opponent, I'd make it so that Carpathian had boundaries on how much he could use his Flight Ability or something. Or this one time Teleri was forced to forego use of any of her most powerful Spells and had to rely exclusively on her One-Inch Punch Ability. (RIP, Bruce Lee.)

But this . . . this Quest . . . has *no* restrictions? None at all? I can't imagine that bodes favorably.

I do suppose the timeline makes sense. It corresponds to how I left things for Almeister in the last book. His trial was scheduled to happen at dawn, a fortnight from his capture. (Supposedly to give his High Council–appointed barrister time to prepare, but it was really just so I could create a bunch of horrible scenarios in Carpathian's mind about what awful things were being done to his mentor.)

The capture happened four Lunar Rotations before Carpathian launched his failed assault on the Tower. And it's been three Lunar Rotations since then. So yeah, seven nights left until he's given his sham hearing bright and early the following morning. Or at least, what I assume will be a sham hearing. That was how it was advertised.

I wonder if tonight counts as the first night? In which case, I'll actually only have six Lunar Rotations to get this thing done. Not that it matters, given how little I know about what I'm wading into, but I'd still prefer more time than less to figure it out . . .

On a positive note, at least upgrades appear to be available. Unfortunately, as previously established, there are no Pulse Wells nearby to see precisely what they are and implement them. At least no Pulse Wells that either Brittany or I can remember.

So I suppose we still need to find the Candy Shoppe and see what's what.

Okay.

Okay.

Okay.

Let's do this thing.

"Alright . . ." I sigh out on a deep, centering breath. "Done. So, um, is, uh, is the Candy Shoppe still . . . functional? I need to do a proper inventory of . . . things. And get Mezmer for . . . my car."

Persephone takes on a sad look. "Yes. It's here. Unfortunately, it was not spared as DONG rampaged through Bell's View. I had only enough agency to protect but one besieged area, and . . . I chose to protect this place, my workshop, instead. I'm . . . sorry. I . . ." She trails off, turning her head away like she's ashamed.

"Hey, hey," I say, approaching her. "Don't apologize. There's nothing to be sorry for. You couldn't have known for sure that Carp— I was going to be back. You had to guard what you thought was most worthy of guarding. You did what you had to."

"But it's so selfish," she protests. "You would never do something so self-serving. You would have put the greater good ahead of your own impulses."

I try not to make eye contact with Brittany, who I can feel is boring holes in the side of my head with her glare.

"No," I reply. "No, I . . . That's . . . Whatever. Doesn't matter. Nobody's perfect. Just . . . Is there anything operational left in the Candy Shoppe? Does the Interlocutrix still work?"

The Interlocutrix. The very first device I conceived of for Carpathian to access his upgrades and Abilities and so forth. It was built exclusively for him, to get his Heart up and running. A way of reinforcing that even though he wasn't OP at the time, he was still special. I suppose I could have skipped the whole Candy Shoppe, Pulse Wells, machine-necessary upgrade component of the world writ large, but I didn't for two reasons:

1. After Carpathian got his Heart, he was tempted to use the strength it granted him recklessly, like how it played out when he confronted the Reapers. So Almeister had the Heart's System rules altered in such a way as to force Carpathian to take a moment if he wanted to "power up," as it were. Because it compelled him to take a beat and think things through.

(Ironic, I know, that I, of all people, would make my characters take the very kind of methodical approach I tend to eschew, but . . . despite mounting suggestions to the contrary . . . *I am not Carpathian.* I'm really not.)

And,

2. It always seemed like it added an extra level of tension and stakes to me. (I'm all about tension and stakes. To my now great misfortune.) Plus, it extends

the whole car/automotive motif I have running throughout. When a car runs low on fuel, you don't just snap your fingers and suddenly have it again. You have to find a place to stop and top off. That's how it works for Carpathian too.

Ultimately, I just felt like if Carpathian could do whatever he wanted whenever he felt like it, it would make him less . . . I dunno. Human. Somehow.

While Carpathian was special insofar as he was "Chosen," his ascent wasn't marked by some kind of unique, superior set of talents or Abilities that only he possessed. He was just this regular guy who, by virtue of his commitment, dedication, tenacity, and (eventual) belief in himself, wound up becoming who he ultimately became.

Basically, I wanted anyone who found the books to feel like they could be Carpathian too. To be able to see themselves in him. And having him need to make a pit stop every now and again to buff up seemed like a cool way to do that.

Although, now, I'm really wishing he could just take a shot of some kind of magical super elixir and turn into an indestructible He-Man on the spot.

Speaking of elixir . . .

Ting, ting, ting.

That's the sound of the thimble Gonzo has been drinking out of tumbling off the table and onto the floor. Looks like he's sucked down the entire thing, and he appears to be . . . wobbling? Kind of like he's drunk?

"What was in there?" Brittany asks Persephone.

"While you were outside, I refilled Pergamon's chalice with the same formulation Father once gave him."

"You . . . what now?" I ask.

"The elixir of Philological Consciousness. I thought it would be useful in helping expedite his recarbonification process."

I turn, wide-eyed, to Brittany, who's wearing a not dissimilarly saucer-eyed look of her own. Simultaneously, both of our heads turn to see . . .

. . . Gonzo. Still appearing to stagger around on the tabletop, his tiny snail body wavering and quavering, his small features beginning to take on a more . . . *humanized* . . . affect.

And then . . . a sound. A sound emerging from his up-until-this-very-moment-non-sound-making mouth.

"Mmmmm . . ."

Oh, dear heavenly baby Yeshua in the manger. What is happening?

"Mmmmm . . ." Gonzo grunts again.

Oh god. I think my brain is going to explode. Or implode. Maybe both. My sweet, pet Mexican Turbo Snail has been granted the enchantment of speech. Is he going to sound like Pergamon? Rich, rough, and wise, kind of like Richard Harris as Dumbledore? Or rich, rough, and wise kind of like Michael Gambon as Dumbledore? Or rich, rough, and wise, kind of like—

"MmmmmAN! Dios. ¿Todo esto que está pasando? This some trippy shit, huh, homes?"

Like Danny Trejo?

CHAPTER FOURTEEN

Seasons of Rebellion, Riftbreaker Book One, Chapter Fifteen

This is the Candy Shoppe?" Carpathian asked, looking around with an almost childlike wonder at the space.

It resembled nothing at all like the type of thing he had imagined.

Rather than a dark, secretive burrow that might be typical of a wizard's lair, the Candy Shoppe resembled more a small factory. Which was, of course, what it had once been. Brightly lit and immaculately kept, dazzlingly colored potions adorned the shelves, and sophisticated, intricately constructed devices were curated and arranged thoughtfully throughout the large space, all of which tugged at Carpathian's imagination, causing him to wonder over what they might be. Or do.

"It is," Almeister responded.

"What does—?" Carpathian started to ask about a device that drew his eye particularly. But, before he could finish the thought, Almeister directed his attention to a contraption that banished all other distractions from Carpathian's mind.

"Over here," Almeister said, pointing.

In the corner of the room stood an apparatus that, even with as many types of machinery as Carpathian had encountered in his lifetime, looked like nothing he had ever seen. It seemed to him to be some mixture of organic matter and high technology. Not unlike Carpathian himself in his current incarnation.

A pulsing green light radiated from the center of the thing. It teemed with some manner of electricity but appeared simultaneously as if it had been built within a hollowed-out tree.

"What is it?" Carpathian asked, wonder in his tone, eyes wide, almost hypnotized.

"It is an Interlocutrix," Almeister answered. "It is a device I have created with which you may interact to take the fullest advantage of your endowments."

Carpathian wandered in the direction of the machine as if being pulled by an invisible string, almost as though the Interlocutrix was beckoning him. He approached it the way one approaches a wild animal, fearful but wanting—needing—to make contact for reasons not altogether clear.

"How does it work?" Carpathian asked, his voice barely more than a whisper.

"Step forward and you shall see," the old wizard responded.

Carpathian looked at his mentor then back at the Interlocutrix, and did as Almeister commanded.

Immediately upon stepping onto a small platform, light erupted from the machine and wrapped Carpathian in its warm embrace. It caused him to feel protected in a way he had never before known protection. Swaddled in a kind of loving embrace that had been lost as a child and ever yearned to find again. And lo, after the *passage of many years, Carpathian felt, for the first time in quite a long time indeed, that he was safe.*

And then, showing in the air before him, a Notification. One that, even though no actual voice accompanied it, he could somehow hear inside himself . . .

Welcome, [CARPATHIAN EINZGEAR]
You have successfully coupled with the [INTERLOCUTRIX]. Your current standings are as follows:

>Mezmer Type:
Three-Type

>Foundation:
Vanguard

>Resonance Tier:
Etherflint

>Affinity:
Dreamweave [Perfect]
Nexabind [High]
Chronoshift [High]

>Statistics:
Mental: Etherflint Level 3
Physical: Etherflint Level 5
Aura: Etherflint Level 4
Animus: Etherflint Level 2

>Armament(s):
Mechanical Heart

Carpathian stared at the words, an admixture of joy, fright, and awe coursing through him.

"What does it all mean?" he managed, his voice breaking with emotion.

Almeister approached from behind and rested a hand on the young man's shoulder. "All in good time, my boy. All in good time."

"Excuse me," a rugged, newly acquired but already familiar voice echoed through the room from the entrance to the Candy Shoppe. The light from the Interlocutrix faded as both Carpathian and Almeister turned to see the currently diminutive form of Pergamon approaching.

"Pergamon," Almeister said. "What is the matter? You appear concerned."

Carpathian had to smile to himself. He had not yet learned how to interpret the recently consciously awakened animal's mood and expressions as Almeister had.

"Templars," Pergamon said with a deep register of worry, "have been seen advancing upon Bell's View."

Almeister smiled gently. "Well, then," he said, "as they are not able to enter, perhaps we had best go to meet them."

He inclined his head toward Carpathian, who took a deep breath, nodded at Almeister, and grabbed up Pergamon in his hands as he moved to continue his engagement with his destiny.

CHAPTER FIFTEEN

E*ntonces, ¿has podido entendernos a Bruce y a mí todo este tiempo?*" I hear Brittany say.

"*Obviamente, chica. Soy un caracol, no un idiota,*" Gonzo . . . um . . . responds.

"What is this strange tongue they are speaking?" Persephone asks as we walk behind the two.

"Oh . . . It's, uh . . . It's a remort thing. Don't worry about it."

There's a brief flash of something that crosses Persephone's face. If I didn't know better, I'd say it was frustration. But I do know better. And it's not.

It's disappointment.

"I am glad you were able to find a suitable companion on your journey, Carpathian," she says.

"A suitable . . . ?" I start, then realize what she's implying. "Oh. Oh. Oh, no. No, no, no. No. No. Like, really, really no," I offer. Ardently. "No, Brittany's, uh, uh, Teleri's not my . . . She's not my *companion.*"

"She's not?" Persephone asks with maybe a hint of hopefulness.

"No. I mean, she *is*, obviously, in the most basic definition of the word. But she's not . . . No. Not in the way that . . . I mean, among other things, she's not interested in me. Like that."

She appears dubious. "Really? Not interested in the World Saviour? I have never met one such as she who would not be."

I don't think I realized how desirable I made Carpathian out to be to Persephone. I'm like sweet ambrosia up in this piece. "Right. Right," I ruminate. "Well, that's . . . sweet, but Br—Um, Teleri is a lesbian. Which you probably didn't know. But she is. So . . ."

Persephone cocks her head. "A what?"

Oh shit. Yeah. Teleri never explicitly identified herself as a lesbian in the books. Or, I suppose, technically *I* didn't identify her as such. Not for any other reason, really, than "lesbian" is derived etymologically from ancient Greek, which, of course, is both a language and a concept that doesn't exist here. I just kind of *implied* she was one. And then only because I didn't want people to think that there would ever be anything romantic between Carpathian and Teleri.

Riftbreaker may be a fantasy, but it's not that kind of fantasy.

"Um," I continue trying to course correct inelegantly. "Just . . . no. Teleri's not . . . She's just a friend. That's all. Honestly, she's . . . like a sister to me."

Persephone nods, seeming to be mollified by the explanation, and smiles. She places her hand gently on my back, and I feel her touch on my naked skin where the fabric of my pajama top is torn. Apart from being yanked out of bed by Moridius, it's the first *actual* physical contact I've had with someone in this world.

My Heart whirs faster.

"Such odd garments in which to be reconstituted."

"Yeah. Yes. Well, you know, 'fashion wears out more apparel than the man.'"

Her eyes light up. "That's beautiful. Did you just coin that, Carpathian?"

"Uhhh . . ."

"By the spirits of Extrania, even with all the other eventual endowments you are likely to regain, you now find yourself *a bard* as well?"

"A bard? Hehe. Well . . . um . . . Well, yeah! I guess! Sure does seem like it, huh?!"

Apparently, being transported here has left me with a fair amount of ambivalence about plagiarizing better writers than myself.

She continues smiling and shakes her head.

Man, I really did Persephone dirty. I mean, I had no idea I was doing it, but she's been stuck here in this town, pining for Carpathian, for who knows how long, and . . .

I truly did a number on all of these people. Jesus.

"It's right here," she says, moving ahead of Brit and Gonzo—who have continued nattering to each other in Spanish—and approaching a door. It looms before us. Ajar.

The stench of this place is awful, overpowering; a vile confluence of urine and decay. It causes me to retch a tiny bit. *Good gravy, how long is it going to take for this pizza to digest?*

"Is *this* the Candy Shoppe?" Brit asks.

"Yeah, fool, this is it? This shit looks jacked up," Gonzo echoes, to my still fresh bafflement.

Persephone titters. "Pergamon, your recarbonified form is so peculiar."

"It's not the only thing around here that's peculiar, *chica*. You should get homeboy here to tell you what's really going—"

"Yep!" I intercede. "This is the Candy Shoppe!" I can't be any more certain than Brit and Gonz are, but I have to trust that Persephone isn't leading us on some kind of spurned-lover goose chase just to get revenge for having been abandoned here . . .

. . . Which is an *incredibly* specific thought I just had that has me feeling all kinds of uncomfortable.

Wait. *Is it* possible *that . . . ?*

"After you." Persephone gestures to the absolutely repellent-looking door.

"Oh, uh . . ." I mumble, unexpectedly quite out of sorts.

This is the kind of thing I did all the time in Riftbreaker. I'd woo a character into a false sense of comfort with an apparent ally, and then have the ally turn on them owing to some long-harbored resentment or other behind-the-scenes scheme the first character didn't know about.

"Yeah, *Carpathian*," Brittany croons, "after you."

"Yeah, *Carp*," Gonzo mocks, "open the door, big homie."

Both of them seem to be dumping an awful lot of salt on me for no reason. We all share looks. My eyes narrow at Brit and then at Gonzo in her hand. Her eyes narrow at me. I can't really tell what Gonzo's eyes are doing because he's a flippin' snail, but I can feel his disdain.

Persephone just stares at the three of us placidly, hands folded in front of her.

Finally, after a moment, Brit shakes her head, chomps her teeth together like a snapping turtle, thrusts Gonzo at me with a "here," and places her own hand on the door.

I hold my breath, abruptly and possibly irrationally but also deeply worried that we are most definitely walking into some kind of vengeance-oriented trap.

"Oh, god," Brit says, jerking her hand back.

"What is it? What's wrong?" I ask urgently, looking to see if Persephone's face has gone from smiling politely to grinning maliciously.

"It's slimy," Brit says, making an *Ugh* face.

"Slimy?"

"I stutter? It's fine. It's just . . . gross."

Brittany is one of the cleanest people I've ever known. I wouldn't necessarily call her a germaphobe or anything, but she's definitely tidy. I would maybe go so far as to say she's fastidious. It's in line with her sense of order and organization.

I'm not a slob, per se, but I'm not above leaving a pair of jeans on the bedroom floor or letting a dish or two sit in the sink overnight. Brit's the kind of person who checks into a hotel room and has to have everything unpacked and put away properly in the drawers before she can go out again, so I know that, for her, having her hand covered in the putrid filth of a transversal door to the unknown is likely to be not her favorite.

"But that's it?" I question. "Just slimy? No other strange, Mezmeric shock to the system or anything?" I look once more at Persephone, who maintains her pretty, guileless deportment.

"If it summons a hard manner of nostalgia for you to enter, Carpathian, I understand. Allow me. Follow whenever you feel ready. I will warn you, however, it is . . . in a truly frightful state."

What does she mean by that? *Does she mean it's going to be frightening to see? Or that* I'm *going to get a fright? Or both? Or . . . What is the game here?*

Whooooosh. With a wave of her hand, the door opens, and she disappears into the darkness beyond, leaving us here and me still pondering awful thoughts about her motives. Which feels simultaneously terrible but also like the right thing to be doing.

"She coulda just fuckin' done that all along?" Brittany bites out, noting the open door, and wiping her hand on her shorts. Then she reaches into her pockets, pulling out the map and a pen, and starts drawing.

"What are you doing?" I ask.

"Updating the maps."

"Why?"

"Why? Because now that we're here, like HERE, we may actually need them for something real, other than just approximating shit and making sure you don't forget where the Battle of Crystal Falls was supposed to have taken place."

"Do you always keep a pen in your pocket?"

"Of course."

I consider this, then start to guess, "Because you never know when I'm gonna—?"

"Because I never know when you're gonna throw out some rando-ass idea that I'll need to make sure you don't forget, yes," she finishes as she clicks the pen into its cylinder and tucks it away.

There's a beat before Gonzo says, "Okay. So let's do this thing, yo."

Now that we're alone, I feel like I finally have the opportunity to ask, "Gonzo . . . what—?"

"Call me Pergamon."

"Sorry?"

"You heard me, *ese*. Now that I get a vote in shit and you can hear what I say, you think I'm going to let you keep up with your racist bullshit?"

I snap my head toward Brittany, who shrugs.

"Racist . . . ? I—"

"I said what I said, homeboy. *Gonzo? Gonzo?* You named me *Gonzo?*"

"Yeeeahhh," I begin slowly. "It's short for—"

"For Speedy Gonzales. I know, bitch. I know what it's short for, *puto culero.*"

"He called you a fucking bitch ass," Brittany adds helpfully.

"I—Wha—Bu—No!" I get out. "That's not . . . No! That's not racist. *I'm* not racist! I just thought it was . . . You're a Mexican Turbo Snail! So, y'know, you're slow, and you're Mexican, so I thought it would be, like, funny and ironic to name you—"

"Speedy Gonzales! One of the most racist-ass cartoon characters ever? Just out there inculcating children with subtle, psychologically imperialist dogma about American superiority for like seventy years? *That* Speedy Gonzales?"

"Uh—"

"Oh," he says, going really nasal and doing a not-terrible Speedy impression. "'Oh, ¡Arriba, arriba! ¡Ándale, ándale! Look at me, kids! I'm Speedy Gonzales! Your friendly little neighborhood mouse who runs around entertaining you with his oversize sombrero and animated hijinks! Aren't I funny? Aren't I a good time? Aren't I subtly and insidiously embedding into your developing consciousness the idea that Mexicans are nothing more than hilarious *RODENTS?!* Just amusing little vermin who eat cheese and make you laugh?!' Damn, fool. I'm shocked you could even get past your pussy-ass phobia of mice to make the 'joke,' as you call it."

Suggesting that I'm stunned should, at this point, be passé. But I'm *stunned*. And not because I'm in an alternate reality with a Mechanical Heart and a talking snail, but because . . . I love Gonzo. I'd do anything for him. My brain moves so fast and in so many directions all the time that having him in my life, looking at him all methodical and calm in his tank in my office, would always help chill me out. I never meant to stress *him* like this.

Oh, and also . . .

"I'm *so* not racist! I'm like the least racist person I know!"

"That's what racists always say, *ese*."

I look to Brittany for help. She shrugs.

"Well . . ." I mumble. "I'm . . . sorry. It was never my intention to—"

"'At the setting of the suns, intentions are irrelevant. All that matters is consequence.' Think I heard someone say that one time," Gonzo chides. Snarkily.

"Okay," I accede. "You're right. You're right. I'll . . . take a look at that."

There's a brief moment before Gonzo shakes his tiny snail head and says, "Nah, it's cool. I think it's just been building for a long time. And I only just got the ability to express that shit when your hot sorcerer lady friend gave me that spooky juice. Now, if you had named me after Speedy's cousin, Slowpoke Rodriguez, we'd be done, homes." He proceeds to do, once again, a pretty decent Slowpoke Rodriguez impression. "'*Hola*, my name is Slowpoke Rodriguez. I am not as fast as my cousin, Speedy Gonz—' Bro, Looney Tunes can shove it up their *culo*!"

So, SO much to unpack here, but the thing foremost in my mind is, "How do you know all this stuff?"

"You spend a lot of hours jerking around on YouTube when you should be writing, big homie."

I take a deep inhalation of breath. "Well. Again. I'm sorry."

"*No hay problema*. Glad we chopped it up. We gonna see what's behind this creepy murder door, or what?"

Then he . . . *jumps* . . . like, literally *jumps* out of my hand and onto the ground, where he proceeds to shuffle himself along through the entrance with, I'd say, ten percent more pace than I've seen him move in the past.

Brit looks at me, starts to say something, stops, shakes her head, and follows.

"I have written some outlandish shit in my time, but . . ." I say aloud to myself, trailing off before heading through the door after them.

Inside is a barely visible space, dimly lit by a number of exposed light bulbs hanging here and there. And, despite all the reasons I shouldn't be amused right now, I have to stifle a chuckle. Because I remember when Brittany started working for me and read the first couple of books to catch herself up.

"*How is there electricity?*" she had asked.

I told her I didn't understand the question, which prompted a lengthy monologue about medieval lighting implements, which then somehow digressed into a story about Thomas Edison, George Westinghouse, Nikola Tesla, and the legal battle to patent the light bulb. When she was finally finished, I just looked at her and said, "*Yeah, I dunno. I just thought it would be cool. Maybe they're Mezmer powered or something?*"

That was probably the first indication she got that this job was going to be a lot more challenging than simply picking up my dry cleaning.

Regardless of how the bulbs in this room are being powered, what they show causes my heart to break a little bit. (Which, now that it's a Mechanical Heart, could happen quite literally.)

It's the Candy Shoppe alright, right here in front of my eyes. Except . . . it's in ruins. Crates are stacked haphazardly, their contents destroyed. The dim bulbs cast eerie shadows, making it all feel even more foreboding. This place that I wrote about as a marvel of clockwork and alchemy now lies in ruins. Brightly colored potions—shattered and spilled—stain the floor. All the different machinery I'd written about being intricate and beautiful is now just broken debris.

Looking up, I see the skylight is shattered. Some pieces of smashed glass hang valiantly to the framing of the broken roof, but most are now just shards on the ground that crunch under our feet as we continue treading cautiously through the remnants of what once was.

"Fuck. Me," Brit mutters.

"This some messed-up shit, yo," Gonzo—er, I guess, now officially Pergamon?—contributes.

"Yeah," I concur.

"Where's Persephone?" Brittany asks.

"I'm over here," Persephone calls, waving us to her.

I hate this feeling of foreboding I have with her. I can't tell if I'm just being paranoid or—

I stop myself thinking more about it because I see something.

My eyes lock on a platform near a far corner of the room, tarnished and covered in grime.

The Interlocutrix.

Now that I'm really looking at it, I'm reminded of my initial stimulus for the thing, *Star Trek: Voyager.* I'd envisioned it pretty similarly to the Borg alcove that Seven of Nine uses to recharge herself.

And by "pretty similarly" I mean . . . that's it. That's basically what it is.

I remember crafting it that way because, well, it just seemed to work. The Borg alcove had this weird mix of organic and mechanical that felt both alien and familiar. I'd come up with something even better later on when I invented the Pulse Wells and Temples of the Body, but here is the mother of that invention; the patient zero of my madness.

In an absolutely wretched state.

"Come," Persephone says, still waving us come-hither.

Brit and Gonz—Shit, *Pergamon* (going to take some getting used to) move her way.

Seeing me hanging back, Brit asks, "Hey. What's going on? You're being weird."

I'm *being weird. Yeah, okay.*

"I'm coming," I say, forcing myself to edge closer to the Interlocutrix.

"As I said," Persephone nearly whispers, eyes looking toward the ground, "I wasn't able to save it from DONG's fearful terrorization, but I believe it still works. Would you care to step onto the platform and see what use it might still offer, Carpathian?"

Looking into her eyes, there is an earnestness that I can't believe is fabricated. And I mentally admonish myself for being so mistrusting.

Brittany's right. I am being weird.

"Yeah, for sure," I say, moving closer to examine it.

Suddenly, there's a hum. It's subtle, almost imperceptible, but it's there. The closer I get, the more pronounced it becomes. And then . . .

The Mechanical Heart suddenly starts to react as well. And by *react*, I mean freak the ever-loving flickety-flack the funk out.

"Ahhhhhhhhh!" I holler out in the way that is apparently my SOP whenever the Heart does its heart thing.

Oh, shit! I've been had! Took! Hoodwinked! Bamboozled! Carpathian felt powerful and cool when the Heart did its Heart stuff in the Interlocutrix! My awesome fantasy world is supposed to be crazy-sexy cool and far less screamy!

Light spills out of my chest from behind my pajama top, flashing like a Russian police light, syncing up with the hum. Brittany comes running to my side, her eyes wide.

"What's happening?" she shouts as she approaches.

"I'm not . . . sure!" I call back.

"What's going on?" she asks Persephone. "It's not supposed to be like this!"

"I . . . don't know . . ." Persephone responds, appearing equally confused. Which is comforting in its way? I suppose?

"Make it stop!" Brit hollers.

"I don't know that I can," Persephone responds. "Only Carpathian and my father have full access to its functions. I don't—"

"It looks like his face is going to melt off," the snail formerly known as Gonzo offers.

All at once, the Interlocutrix spurts itself clunkily into action, firing up fully and spitting out a bizarre light show that resembles nothing so much as the footage from the end of The Who's iconic 1978 performance of "Won't Get Fooled Again" at Shepperton Studios. Which is honestly not uncool.

Hell with it. You know what? I've had a good run. I've done more with my life than I ever imagined I would. So, I suppose if I wind up dying in the next few seconds, at least I'll go out rocking with the sound of Roger Daltrey screaming in my ears.

"*Although, it'll be kind of ironic. Because you* will *have been fooled, Bruce.*"

"Oh, shut up, Bruce. You're a real wet blanket on this whole hero's journey thing, you know that?"

But then . . . I don't.

Die, I mean. Instead, the discomfort abates, and Notifications start broadcasting themselves into the air.

Welcome back, [Carpathian Einzgear]!
It appears there have been some changes to your Mechanical Heart
functions since you last used this terminal. Would you like to delve?
[Yes] [No]

"Delve?" I hear Brittany say. "Delve into what? Bruce, what's happening?!"

"I have no idea," I grit out.

Note: Please be aware, this terminal will be down for scheduled upgrades on [Date Missing].

Okay, so, that seems bad. I shudder once more as a new bolt of energy is hammered through me, and I watch another Notification being broadcast that, well, that is probably the last thing you want to see in a situation like this . . .

[Error Retrieving Data]
[Foundation Altered]
[Terminal 13.2 Reaching Dangerous Threshold of Mezmer]
[Please Stand By . . .]

CHAPTER SIXTEEN

E*rror retrieving data?" "Foundation altered?" What does all* that *mean?*

"What does all that *mean*?!" Brittany shouts, giving open voice to the very good question.

"What does what mean?" I hear Persephone reply, confusion rimming her tone.

"All that shit in the air!" she bellows, gesticulating at the space around me. "That! All that! 'Dangerous threshold,' etcetera! You can't see that?"

"No, I can't."

"Why not?"

"Because I'm not a part of his Heart Guard. Only those with access to his Heart can engage with its functions fully," she says sadly.

Well . . . there's a metaphor if I've ever heard one.

"Gon—" Brittany starts before being cut off by the snail.

"Pergamon, girlie."

"*Pergamon*, do you see all that?"

"Yeah. I can see it."

"Do *YOU* know what it means?"

Obviously, Pergamon doesn't. Even in the books, Pergamon didn't know—

"Of course I do," he says. *Oh. That's surprising.* "It's like if he adjusted his car seat for his body and then went away for the summer and had a growth spurt or something. When he came back, he'd have to reconfigure the settings for his new dimensions. Only, in this case, it's like homes went away for the summer and shrank down to, like, a baby. Get used to it. He's going to be Benjamin Buttoning his way through shit for a minute, I'm guessing."

"How do you know all that?" Brittany asks.

Persephone responds, "I mixed a dram of Insight into the Philological Consciousness elixir. I thought, as Carpathian is still reassuming his footing here, it might be helpful to have a guide well versed on the current state of affairs as you make your journey to attend to Father's captivity. A surrogate for Father; someone to fill his role until you all are able to retrieve him directly. He does not possess the full complement of Father's wisdom, of course, but his heightened awareness and comprehension should prove to be a useful tool in certain circumstances."

"Yeah, seems like I got the 411 on some shit, fool," Gon— *Dammit.* Pergamon affirms.

I see Brittany shake her head and start purposefully toward the machine with an energy that suggests she's going to rip everything apart with her bare hands.

"Teleri Nightwind, what are you doing?" Persephone asks as I feel my Heart and the machine continue to cement their apparent love connection.

Pulse, pulse, pulse. Hum, hum, hum.
"Shutting it down. I don't like this."
"I don't feel that is safe," Persephone conjectures.
"For real; I wouldn't do that, little homie," Pergamon concurs.
Pulse. Hum.
"And what's happening now looks *safe*?" she says over the sound of whatever this is that's going on as she attempts to look for, I guess, some kind of power source or off button or something. When she can't find anything that clearly indicates how to shut it down, she grabs up a discarded piece of pipe from nearby and goes to whack it.
"Don't!" I shout.
"What? Why not?" she shouts back.
"Because they're right! We don't know—" But before I can finish the thought, a new message appears.

[Data Error Corrected]
[Update Finished]
[Data Cache Recovered]
Welcome back, [Carpathian Einzgear]!
Unfortunately, the totality of your historical function could not be retrieved, as it appears there have been some changes to your Mechanical Heart functions since the last time you attempted to use this terminal. The most recent information, however, was successfully recalled. Additional settings have been revised. Would you care to delve?
[Yes] [No]

There is a sigh of momentary relief, and before I can think too much more about it or let anyone tell me not to, I reach my arm up and press [Yes].

Good choice. Assessing Mechanical Heart now. Please stand by.

There's a fresh moment of nothing, almost as if my brain has left my body, before a heavy *clunk* in my chest, and a new message appears.

It looks as though you have survived a dangerous encounter with a group of [Templars] dispatched by the [Disciples of the Ninth Guardian] under orders from the [High Council]. Congratulations! You proved yourself to be ORSS! One Real Slick Sally! {COURTESY MESSAGE #4}

"Why is it messaging like that?" Brittany asks.
"I don't know."
"Messaging like what?" Persephone asks.

"All cheeky and sassy."

"It's been doing that," I acknowledge.

"Why?" Brit persists.

"I continue to not know."

"That's closer to how you talk than the way shit sounds in the books."

"I am aware and, for a third time, do not have an answer as to why."

"What books?" Persephone says.

Below you will find an overview of the Updated Model of your Attributes. Delve at your leisure! (But also, be quick about it.)

>Mezmer Type: [*Assessing—One Moment Please*]
>Foundation: [*Assessing—One Moment Please*]

>Resonance Tier:
Etherflint

>Affinity: [*Assessing—One Moment Please*]

>Statistics:
Mental: *Etherflint Level 1*
Physical: *Etherflint Level 1*
Aura: *Etherflint Level 1*
Animus: *Etherflint Level 1*

>Armament(s):
Mechanical Heart

>Inventory: [None]

>Abilities: [None]

>Spell(s):

Control
[1 New Available!]

I stare at the words, taking in the information. Truthfully, it's been a hot second since I've actually had to look at any of this stuff in depth. In part because . . .

Okay, so, full disclosure, while Brittany didn't actually *write* any of the books (and she would never suggest she did; she's way too honest to do something like that. Frankly, sometimes I would prefer if she were *less* honest.), she *did* take over a lot of the . . . *crunchier* stuff so that I could focus on just making shit up. So, as we went along, more and more of the statistical items and cataloguing and so forth fell to her to generate. So she's not so much a "ghost writer" as a "ghost contributor," I suppose.

(I do thank her in the credits of every book and did give her a free place to live, plus a pretty decent salary with bennies, so I don't feel too bad about it.)

"Who you trying to convince there, Bruce?"

"Oh, stick a sock in it, me. I'm still processing a lot."

The other part of why I haven't had to dig into all this mechanical stuff in a while is because the further I got into Riftbreaker, the less I relied on the Attributes and Notifications and so forth that had made it so popular to begin with. There was a certain amount of blowback I had to weather from the readers who are really into all the mechanics and details of how things work here, but I expected as much and had to make an executive decision.

I decided I could justify it because, in my defense, when your main character has leveled up to essentially somewhere in the realm of a minor god, you have to start getting creative. Which, I mean, I've always prided myself on being something of a . . . Well, not a *visionary*; I'm not arrogant enough to suggest that. But, you know, I'm a creative *type*.

Whatever. Semantics.

Speaking of types, currently, the Mezmer Type isn't showing. It just reads "Assessing," so . . . maybe it's part of the previous data error?

"Careful, Bruce. You start trying to use too much reason on things now, and you might just create a disharmonic convergence."

"I'm gonna slap you twist legged, Bruce."

It is unclear if it's just stress causing me to have conversations with the bifurcated other half of my psyche or if I'm going through an actual psychotic break. Neither one seems ideal, but at least the prior of the two won't result in me winding up in some kind of M. Night Shyamalan reckoning later on, where I realize that I was actually Carpathian all along and Bruce Silver was the figment of *his* imagination. So, I mean . . . let's everyone just keep fingers crossed.

Ignoring my split personality's caution against rationalizing my way through things—and in a cataloguing of specifics that would surely delight any hardcore details enthusiast were this to be the kind of stuff I was writing down in a book rather than just ruminating over—I try to let myself remember the nuanced particulars of how this was all originally set up back in the day.

So . . .

The "Types" are the foundation for Mezmeric abilities here. It's kinda like . . . mystical DNA—the core essence, if you will—that dictates what kind of Spells you can use and what powers you have. "Foundation" *also* needs review. It's what fresh-faced, baby Bruce, a handful of years ago, decided was a wonderful alternative term to the idea of classes; just like "Mezmer" is a jaunty and more specific way of saying *magic*, and "Super Vizier" is a jaunty but still hopefully obvious way of saying *Supervisor*.

(That was done in an attempt to see to it that if my old supervisor at the Metro St. Louis Transit Agency—who always seemed to hate me—ever happened to read the books, she would be able to know how I felt about her in print while avoiding getting sued. As previously noted: I am creative.)

Statistics is easy. "Mental" I crafted after binge-watching a bunch of psychology documentaries. I thought it'd be cool to have characters with high adaptability, like changing strategies on the fly and such. (Of course, then I got distracted by a video on how to make the perfect grilled cheese and never really fleshed it out much beyond that.)

It's the same with Physical, Aura, and Animus. They're aggregate statistics that cover a lot of what you might call "strength" and "dexterity" and "charisma" and all that jazz. Physical is anything having to do with the body. Animus relates to Mezmer and its associated companions. And Aura is . . . general likeability, presence, and willpower.

I'll admit that the System is a little flawed, but what system isn't? Does anyone really think that whoever created the system for Earth didn't get distracted by grilled cheese videos? Take a look at a platypus sometime and tell me that shit wasn't the byproduct of a drug-induced stream of consciousness.

Anyway.

Resonance Tiers. *These* are the real meat and potatoes of the whole Mezmeric organization. The lowest—which of course is where I'm at in my "journey"—is Etherflint. The scale goes up from there, but ultimately, there are Tiers after it called Ironspark, Steelshard, and Manasteel. These were designed to give a sense of progression in the world. Conveniently, they're also parceled out in levels (because why not?) in ranks of Level One through Level Ten in each Resonance Tier.

"Hey," I can hear Brittany say tentatively. "What's going on?"

I guess I didn't realize that I sort of checked out while I've been taking everything in. I have no idea how long I've been standing here, ensorcelled by the manifestly bewildering nature of the uptown-funkified Heart-to-Interlocutrix conversation taking place before my eyes.

"I'm just sorting things through," I answer. "I don't want to be reckless with anything the way . . ." I start to say, *the way Carpathian was*, but then look over to remember that Persephone is still with us. I'm going to have to get into the habit of not talking about Carpathian in the third person, since I'm *technically* him. For now. In the same way that Gonzo is now Pergamon.

So I need to get used to being Carpathian Einzgear himself.

Brittany's right. The Templars and the Ronine clearly don't give a good goddamn that I'm not, and getting mired in trying to explain otherwise is time that could be better spent not getting shot, gutted, or eaten.

". . . the way *I* was," I continue, "that one time I was in a hurry to escape from the Charging Arm of Particulareon and misallocated my physical boosts into my Aura, making me more personally appealing but still unable to lift the Trident of Retribution, so I had to charm my way out of it instead?"

"Fuckin' mess that was," Brittany mutters.

Persephone giggles. "I heard tell of that misadventure. It is one of the many tales of Carpathian that have become legend."

"Oh. Yeah. That's funny," I breathe.

Back to the business at hand . . .

Type, Foundation, and Affinity assessment nearing completion. Just another moment, please.

I'm intensely curious to find out what the assessment reveals, because the lore that, to a greater or lesser degree, drives every choice and action in the world of Riftbreaker is that once upon a time, Meridia was a Utopia. Nearly Eden. It was verdant and full and at peace, in part because all of the inhabitants of Meridia possessed Mezmer. Some had more, some had less, but for millennia, everyone had a shot at . . . whatever. Leveling Up, and growing in the world.

And then, one day, along comes this shadowy, mythic figure calling themself the "Ninth Guardian," who manages to convince certain swaths of society that Mezmer shouldn't just be allocated to everybody by default but that it should happen on an ad hoc basis. The question being: Who determines "ad hoc"? Who decides who deserves it and who doesn't?

Complicating things . . . the Ninth Guardian's true identity is a mystery, but their own Mezmer is so powerful that they inspire a vast cult of followers to do their bidding.

(To be fair, no one knows who the Ninth Guardian is because I don't really know who the Ninth Guardian is. It's just a cool name I invented in *Seasons of Rebellion* and ran with. It's been the subject of more than one disagreement between me and Brit, with her saying, *"You can't just write about this mega-boss baddie and have no idea who they are!"* And me saying, *"It's fine. They'll reveal themselves to me when they're ready."* And then she'd say something like, *"Darth Vader literally means Dark Father! You think Lucas didn't have that shit planned out?!"* At which point I'd usually pretend to get distracted by something else. Or actually get distracted by something else. Sometimes, the prior would lead to the latter.)

Anyway, it's this mysterious Ninth Guardian who, owing to the force of their Mezmer and charisma, was able to rise to power and put together a High Council—of which the Super Vizier is the chief custodian—in order to limit who can have Mezmer and who can't by restricting the world's access to the Nexus Core. Which is, like, the wellspring from which all Mezmer originally flows.

Because Mezmer isn't just some abstract concept or idea; it's a living thing. As tangible as any basic necessity—food, shelter, whatever. I mean, in order to survive and thrive in a magical world, a being obviously needs to have access to magic. But since the Ninth Guardian controls the primary Mezmeric faucet, as it were, and the manner of distribution, they get to determine who wins and who loses. Swear fealty to them and you get the juice. Don't, and you don't.

So, DONG— (erg, so annoying) DONG, the High Council, the Super Vizier, and all of their evangelists are the villains seeking to maintain power by keeping Mezmer in the hands of the few, and Carpathian, Teleri, Pergamon, Almeister, et al. are the heroes trying to ensure there will remain an equitable distribution of mystical energy so that everyone has an equal shot at life.

It gets more complex than that, of course, with the Rebellion attempting to build their own countervailing Nexus Core, and some characters occupying a gray area alongside some characters who don't really care at all and have been beaten into submission and accepted that they're probably never going to get Mezmer, etcetera, but at its most bare-bones subbasement, that's what Riftbreaker is all about.

It's a simple morality tale driven by a fantasy engine that I thought was pretty neat.

Now, as it got more and more popular, did a bunch of people online accuse me of pursuing some kind of "woke" agenda and start calling me a "dickless, socialist, cuck snowflake"? Yes. But did I let that cause me to question my decision to write it the way I wanted and consider changing things? Maybe, a little, absolutely. As Brittany is quick to point out, I am famously confrontation averse.

I just didn't want people walking around thinking I had any kind of agenda at all. Because I really didn't. I simply told the story I wanted to tell and figured if people liked it, great, and if they didn't . . . Well, I guess I assumed they'd just not read it, ignore it, and go on about their day. Which I know probably sounds naive, but, y'know, I'm about fantasy in all ways, I suppose.

(The socialist thing, in particular, is one assignation lobbed my way that I could never make sense of. I drive a Panamera, for crying out loud.)

Anyway, ultimately, I decided to hell with it. Who cares? People can say what they want. What I wrote made for great storytelling. Everybody can understand why there'll always be friction between the haves and the have-nots, even if they don't always agree on which is which.

And, to keep it all shaken up, I'd periodically misdirect the characters (and the readers), by making them think someone was weak when they were really strong and vice versa. That's part of why nobody can see anyone else's Attributes, and why only Carpathian gets updates and Notifications in real time while most everyone else has to go to a Pulse Well to discover what kind of bumps up they're earning and what lofty—or not-so-lofty—plateaus they're on.

There's something inherently suspenseful and dangerous about engaging an enemy when you don't know what kind of powers or Abilities they may have. Even more so when *they* may not even know themselves. It creates tension when there's a real possibility that the clear-cut path you *think* you know the story is going to follow suddenly doesn't. And, of course, it's that very unknowability that allowed for me to craft a scenario in which the seemingly undefeatable World Saviour met his end.

Obviously, knowing what I know now about what the consequences of that action would lead to, I might have been more thoughtful about throwing around Mezmeric allocations all willy-nilly. Unfortunately, unlike the soothsayer, Caramodial the Prescient, from book five, *Merchant of Condemnation*, I couldn't warn myself about the Drakonar lurking in the darkness.

At least I did sort of put rules in place for how *many* Types of Mezmer a person could use at once. I'm pretty sure Brit created a chart for who can do what and when, because there are a *ton* of Types. The most basic version is One-Type, which is when someone can use only one kind of Mezmer from the substantial (and honestly, continually ever-growing) list.

Carpathian was established as a Three-Type from jump (using Dreamweave, Nexabind, and Chronoshift), which was rare according to my lore, but necessary to give him a shot at success. Especially considering the Super Vizier and some of the other High Council members could use at least four Types. His Foundation wasn't anything particularly impressive at the start, save that it worked well in tandem with his Types.

Where "Types" are *what* kind of Mezmer someone can use, "Foundations" are *how* someone activates or channels their powers. Carpathian was a Vanguard. As a Vanguard, he could integrate his Mezmer into his martial skill, the focal point of his power being his weapon. (Though, while the weapon didn't matter necessarily, the more powerful it was, the better it was.)

And *that's* all a somewhat detailed and certainly *very* crunchy way of saying that . . .

. . . I have a knot in the pit of my stomach as I not-so-patiently wait to find out what the hell's taking so long.

Assessment Complete!
Please take a moment to acquaint yourself fully with *all* revisions
made to device [Mechanical Heart] since your last interaction with
this terminal. And remember to . . . Always Trust the System.
{COURTESY MESSAGE #5}

Okay, so, that seems . . . ominous. And mildly threatening. But let's see what—

>[NEW] Foundation:
Synchron

>[NEW] Mezmer Type:
All-Type

Wait. What? Seriously?
Brit must feel the same way upon reading it because she echoes my thoughts. "Wait. What? Seriously?"

"For real," Pergamon says.

"Seriously what?" Persephone asks. "About what are we being serious?"

I'm too distracted to answer. I read through the description, trying to wrap my mind around this curiosity.

>Foundation:
SYNCHRON

Synchron Mezmer users possess the unique ability to synchronize and harmonize with fellow wielders. Their primary function is to amplify group spells and facilitate coordinated, large-scale operations. Within a group setting, they serve as the cohesive element, ensuring stability and unity in collective Mezmeric endeavors. This is performed primarily through ensuring a strong and reliable Mezmeric waveform.
Mama say whaaaaaaaat?

>Mezmer Type:
ALL-TYPE

All-Type users possess a natural affinity for every known Mezmer Type. Their innate adaptability allows them to fluidly transition between different energies, making them versatile and unpredictable in Mezmeric operations. All-Type users can tap in to the full spectrum of Mezmeric abilities, though their Resonance may suit certain types better than others.
Mama Say Mama Sa Mama Coosa!

"Bruce . . . ?" Brittany begins.

"I know, I know," I tell her. Which could be in response to multiple things she might have been about to say, but it doesn't matter. It's true for all of them.

And now, the Affinity allocation finishes assessing itself as well.

>Highest Affinities:
Function [Average]
Mirrorweave [Average]
Gravitate [Average]

Oh! Okay. That's actually really neat. Despite the fact that I apparently have access to all Mezmer Types, it's showing the ones that best make me me? Rhetorical. That is what it's doing.

Basically, if my Type is DNA, then *this* is my ancestral breakdown. My magical 23andMe results, as it were. (My actual 23andMe results showed that I'm a direct descendant of Genghis Khan. Which I thought might explain why I always charge into pizza places like I'm about to set fire to their horses. But then I found out that something like one out of every two hundred people on Earth are also related to Genghis Khan, so the pizza thing might just be that I also have a little Caesar in me.)

Regardless, a new message appears.

Would you like to select your [1] New Available Spell?
[Yes] [No]

Here we go.

I press [Yes]. I know exactly what I'm looking for. I need to find a Spell that grants me a decent Stealth Ability of some kind so that I can at least knock out that Quest prerequisite. And, since I'm only at Level One and my Affinities are Average, it shouldn't take—

. . . Whoa.

There is a shift, and the menu fills with options. And I mean FILLS with options. Spells upon Spells populate and force a scroll bar to be created off to the side because there're so many that it doesn't all fit in the dimensions of the space in front of me.

Holy cats, there's a bunch of these. Looking from the top, I can see it's in alphabetical order by the origin Mezmer Type, and a couple of spells from each of the branches.

>Phase Touch [Aetherpulse] [Etherflint]
>Wisp Sight [Aetherpulse] [Etherflint]
>Calm Creature I [Beastcore] [Etherflint]
>Feral Gaze I [Beastcore] [Etherflint]
>Temporal Glimpse I [Chronoshift] [Etherflint]
>Sensorial Actuation I [Chrono—

The list goes on and on, each entry showing a different Etherflint (what Brittany came to classify as a "basic bitch") Spell in the arsenal to choose from. I don't know how to process it all, considering this is a development I don't have copious amounts of time to shoegaze on and ruminate over.

"Good god, there are some here that I never even—"

"May I ask a question?" Persephone asks. Which, of course, means she already *did* ask a question, and normally I'd say that, turning the whole thing into a little joke, but it doesn't feel like the time. *I hate letting a moment of levity escape, but one has to read the room.*

"Of course," I say, still only half-paying attention as I try and absorb the sheer scope and breadth of the options in front of me. Even though the decision should be somewhat clear based on my current needs, I still find myself feeling like Jeremy Renner in *The Hurt Locker* when he came back from Baghdad having managed to avoid getting blown up during his whole tour of duty, and then found himself stymied by having to pick out a box of cereal at the supermarket. The one seemingly simple task—allocating myself a Spell—is now so overwhelmed by options that I feel completely paralyzed by the choices before me.

But then, Persephone asks (what is *technically*) her second question, and the decision of which Spell to pick feels appreciably less important than it just did.

"Why does she keep calling you Bruce?"

CHAPTER SEVENTEEN

Ahhh!" is the sound of me ripping myself unceremoniously away from the Inter-locutrix, as well as a sound I'm getting pretty damn tired of hearing myself make.

"Oh, my. Are you alright?" Persephone asks.

"Uh, yeah, yeah, no, I'm okay."

The thing I'm realizing is that all this stuff with the Mechanical Heart doesn't actually *hurt* so much as it is just really, *really* shocking. I think the physical response I've been having is more psychosomatic than it is painful. Maybe I'll get used to it.

"If you live long enough."

"Oh, pipe down, Bruce. You're being a ninny."

And speaking of ninnies called Bruce . . .

"So, uh, what was that?" I ask Persephone, rubbing at my chest and feigning like I didn't hear the exact question she just asked.

"Teleri. She has now called you twice by another name. 'Bruce.' Why so?"

I look at Brit; her eyes go wide at me. She tilts her head to the side in a "Sorry?" gesture. I clear my throat.

"Why does she, uh . . . ? *Bruce*, you say? Huh."

Persephone maintains her placid gaze upon me, hands still folded politely, chest still heaving with each breath she takes. (Which isn't explicitly necessary to notice relative to the situation at hand but is one I notice anyway. It would seem.)

"Yes," she offers after another moment of me not saying anything. "Is she making a joke?"

"A joke?"

"Yes. Concerning the prophecy."

"The prophecy?"

I hope I'm not turning into one of those people who answers questions by just repeating the last two words of the previously asked question, turning it into a new question. *Man, I'm also just now realizing there are so many pitfalls and contemplations within the world of question asking. I wonder why that is? Doesn't matter. Rhetorical.*

Anyway . . .

"Yes," Persephone goes on. "The prophecy about the one called Brucillian."

I glance at Brit, who raises her eyebrows and shakes her head a tiny bit. I can feel my lips tighten and pull against my teeth, and my brow furrow and neck twist when I look back to Persephone and say, "Bruce who-what-now?"

Persephone opens her mouth to respond, but before she gets a chance, a small snail with a loud voice chimes in.

"Brucillian. The one who, in some circles of the lesser informed, has long been rumoured and prophesied to be the *true* World Saviour. And, while once easily dismissed, since the felling of Carpathian on the field of battle, these rumours have seemed to exponentially increase their hold over the imaginations of the citizens of Meridia. Because while in the past, only the dunderheaded and naive might have bought into what is ultimately a silly children's story, talk of Brucillian's portended coming has, of recent, spread throughout the land like dragon's fire as a popular subject for debate, assuming a place of prominence around all manner of supper tables in Meridia."

I feel like Brittany did back in my house. Like I'm being punk'd or something.

"Anyway, homeboy," Pergamon says, affecting a less soliloquy-like tone, "that's prolly why old girl thinks T. Night over here was making with the name-joke hilariousnesses."

Persephone regards the snail for a moment, then smiles, looks at me, and says, "That's right."

I look to Brittany yet again and mouth out *Brucillian?* but only get another pair of raised eyebrows and a concomitant shoulder shrug.

"Okay, um, yeah, listen . . ." I start. "Out of curiosity, I have to ask, why didn't you just give me the Insigh—?"

"I know," Persephone interrupts sheepishly. "I probably should have offered the tincture to you directly, but . . ." She trails off, a wistful look on her face. "But the last time I proffered Insight to you, it . . . led you to . . ." She doesn't finish, but I know what the rest of the sentence is: *It led you to leave here and forget about me.* "I'm sorry," she goes on. "If you'd like, I'll still be happy to . . ." She stares at the floor, letting the thought go unfinished once more.

I should take her up on it. The smart thing to do would be to gain as much knowledge and Insight about the world of Meridia as I can. The *real* world of Meridia. Because, obviously, I'm not my character, and also because correlation is not causation. Never once did it cross *my* mind that Carpathian left Persephone because . . . because of some acute perception of the depth of her feelings for him. That he maybe got scared off by her emotions and that's why he left and never came back.

But that's very evidently what *she* thinks. And if given a second chance, past experiences might cause one to want to make different choices the next go 'round. Just in case . . .

"No," I tell her, putting on what I think is an understanding smile. "No. That's okay. Pergamon should have Insight. He should be our guide. That makes—" I cut myself off because something strikes me. "Wait. Are you not planning on coming with us?" That creeping feeling that something is not quite right is crawling up my spine again.

Her expression turns quizzical.

"I . . . I . . ." she stammers. "I did not think I would be welcome."

And like a flippin' stone landing in the pit of my stomach, I instantly gain something like *non*-Mezmerically induced insight. Or what one might call *awareness*.

Oh. OH. That feeling I've been having that she's looking to get some kind of revenge. It's not prescience or suspicion at all . . . it's guilt.

She's not out to seek retribution for me having abandoned her. Not even a little bit. I think . . . I think I just kind of want her to. Because then I won't have to feel so shitty about it.

My skepticism isn't about *her* feelings toward me. It's about *mine.* Toward myself.

I can be slower than a Mexican Turbo Snail sometimes.

"Of course you're welcome! We obviously want you to come!" I exclaim, probably overenthusiastically, but whatever.

"Really?" she asks, hope in her voice.

I look at Brittany, who shrugs again with a "Yeah, sure, more the merrier" implication.

"Yeah. Really. Absolutely," I respond, meaning it more than I think I expected.

"Well . . ." Persephone says, sounding like a person who's been holding their breath for a very long time and can finally let it out, "then let us step you back into the Interlocutrix so you might become emboldened by your options and have at your disposal the requisite endowments necessary to sally forth!"

"Yeah," I agree, less enthusiastic about getting back into the Interlocutrix than I'd like. "Let's do that."

Maybe it'll be better now that I understand it's not really painful and it's just me not being used to it. Maybe— "Ahhhhhhh!" Nope. Still not great.

/ / /

"Careful," Persephone cautions as we approach the area where we last saw the Ronine. She and Brittany are leading the way as we peep and creep back toward where we abandoned Sheila.

"It's over there. About a tenth of a klick that way," Brit says, looking at the map and pointing.

"A klick?" Persephone asks.

"Oh. Yeah. It's a military term."

"I did not know you served in the military. What is your rank? I apologize if I have not been addressing you by your appropriate title."

"Oh, no, not me. My mom. I was a military brat."

"A what?"

I see Brittany gather herself, figuring out how to spin it.

"My mother was a . . . commander . . . in the . . . Rendalian army."

"Was she?" Persephone asks, surprised. "I did not know that." *Of course she didn't. Because I never wrote anything about Teleri's backstory. She just showed up one day and never left.*

"There is much I do not know about you, Teleri Nightwind," Persephone ponders.

"Well. Yeah," Brit says. "Yeah, she was. My mom. So, we moved around a lot. Which is why . . . Anyway. *Klick*. It's a military term."

"Klick," Persephone says, letting the word settle. "I like that. Klick. Klick. Like Elves' shoes on cobblestones, yes? Klick, klick, klick. Is that where the word comes from?"

"Sure? Probably?" Brittany says.

She looks back over her shoulder at me and I nod, giving her a covert thumbs-up.

Persephone regards Brittany with much less uncertainty and more warmth than before, which comforts me. One less thing to worry about. Which is good, because . . .

"It ain't there no more, *ese*." That's Gon— Shit. Pergamon. That's Pergamon. I'm back to carrying him in his snail-mobile for ease of transport.

"What's not there any—? Oh."

The Ronine. It's gone. Just like Persephone said it would be.

Well, that's just aces. Makes me feel like I picked the right Spell from the impossibly robust set of options available from the Interlocutrix.

After standing there for what felt like until forever o'clock, I finally just selected CloakRender I, which allows *me* to disappear. Literally. Turn myself invisible. I know it's really just a basic Aetherpulse type, but it was the only thing suggesting a Stealth or Sneaking Spell that I could find on the list available to me right now. I know there are others, but most of them must be buried somewhere deeper in the fantasy forest, and there isn't time to go on a casual ramble looking for them. Urgency is pretty well kicking the door in and threatening to ransack the place.

And, at any rate, it accomplishes the bare minimum of what I need: It sets me up to go on this Quest with at least that aspect of things in hand. Stealth ability required. Stealth ability attained. Yay, me.

I don't yet know exactly what its application will be. When I wrote about the Blade of the Starfallen the first time, Carpathian just had to dislodge it from where it was embedded in stone, King Arthur style. But things here ain't like they used to was, as my great-grandmammy would always say. (Truth be told, I didn't actually know my great-grandmammy, nor do I have any idea if she ever said something like that, but it's not impossible to think that she did. I come from a long line of real daughter-of-the-soil types on my dad's side.)

The biggest downside I can observe is that, at its current Level, there are limitations on how long I can remain unseen when using CloakRender. And it doesn't allow me to do any of the cool stuff that the higher level Aetherpulse Spells accommodate—like passing through walls or, at their ultimate capacities, interacting with the Spirit Realm—but for now, it will have to suffice. I'm not a hundred percent sure, but I think I have a decent handle on how it works.

Not a hundred percent sure. Yeah. Honestly, I have *no* idea. This is all new stuff that I never wrote into anything, so I'm just free soloing this mountain and gambling on my knowledge of all things fantastical and gamer-y to back up that I'm making good choices.

If nothing else, having an ability that lets me sneak around undetected seems like it'll be cool. Some of my favorite books I've ever read feature characters who are super sneaky.

In any case . . .

Owing to the fact that the Quest notification said there are no restrictions and I'm going to need all the help I can get, I had hoped there would be more boost-'em-ups available to me, but no such luck. My best interpretation of the situation is that this particular Quest is well beyond my current Level of Abilities as a theoretically recarbonified soul, and I'll want to get myself OP much quicker than Carpathian did in the books. But for the moment, I've had to content myself with just nabbing the one Spell and loading my Mezmer up enough to refill Sheila so we can get moving again.

I will say that suddenly being in possession of All-Type is not too shabby, and while I have no idea how something like this could happen, I'm not gonna look a gift Mezmer in the mouth, but I still have a long way to go before—

EIIIIIIIIIINNNNNZZZZZGGGEEEAAARRR.

I stop dead. Spin myself around three-hundred and sixty degrees, looking everywhere.

"Did you all hear that?" I say, voice shaking.

"Hear what, fool?" Pergamon asks.

"I didn't hear anything," Brittany volunteers.

"What did you hear, Carpathian?" Persephone asks.

EIIIIIIIIIINNNNNZZZZZGGGEEEAAARRR.

It sounds like it's at a distance, but I definitely hear it.

"The Ronine. You can't hear it?"

"The Saviour would be able to sense its presence first. You can hear it calling?" I nod, still glancing around. "Then we must hurry. Quickly, to the transport. We must imbue it with its necessary Mezmer. Hurry."

Seeing the car up ahead, we pick up our pace to run and trot over to the abandoned Porsche.

Arriving by Sheila's side, Persephone stops abruptly and mumbles, "This is . . . yours?"

"Um . . . yeah," I say. "Yep. That's . . . That's, um, Sheila."

"Sheeeeeeila," she purrs, letting the word sort of waterfall from her mouth in a very ASMR kind of a way as she wanders over to the car and slowly strokes her finger down the side like she's in a cheesy *Car and Driver* online marketing video. "Where did you acquire it?"

"Oh, uh—" I start, but she interrupts.

"It is unlike anything I have seen," she says dreamily. "It's beautiful."

She's clearly entranced by the sleek lines and overall sexiness of the ride. (Which, I mean, she's not *wrong*, but it's really not the time.)

But all of the sudden, I find myself irrationally filled with pride. I say *irrationally* because as much of a gearhead as I kind of am, I've never been one of those people who sees their car as an extension of themselves. You know, one of those whose vehicle somehow becomes a substitute for their personality. It's just never been the way I interact with inanimate objects.

But here, now, in this world, it very much *is* an extension of me. Literally. It's bonded to me. It requires my Mezmeric enchantments to operate to its full potential, and while I haven't had the opportunity to really test it out yet, when I'm behind the wheel, it should be able to behave in ways that no one else could cause it to perform.

EIIIIIIIIINNNNNZZZZZGGGEEEAAARRR.

We'll find out soon enough.

"Okay, so, let's get it filled up and get going, yeah?"

Persephone doesn't respond. She just continues gawking, mesmerized by Sheila. But I need her to pull it together so we can . . . um . . . Mezmerize . . . Sheila.

Oh, riiight. That's why I went with Mezmerated, because mesmerize and Mezmerize could get confusing if you're, I dunno . . . whatever, reading it aloud or something. And Brittany says I never bother to think anything through. Ha.

EIIIIIIIIIIIIIIIIIIINNNNNNNNNNNZZZZZZZZZZGGGEEEAAARRR.

"Shit," Brit says.

"What is it?"

"I hear it now."

"You do?"

"I do too, homes." Pergamon says.

That seems to pull Persephone's attention back to the matter at hand.

"Yes, we must with haste away. Once the members of your Heart Guard can also sense it . . ." She doesn't finish the thought. Instead, she zips to the front of the car, pops the hood like she's been doing it for years (everyone in Meridia has a least a base-level skill at Grease Monkey), and waves me over. "Quickly," she says.

I hand Pergamon off to Brit *("Yo! Easy with the sloshy-sloshy, homeboy.")* and stand next to Persephone, staring at the massive dark heart under the hood of my car.

"Alright," Persephone says.

"Alright what?"

"Commence. Re-Mezmerate your vehicle so that it might—"

"Yeah, no, I know. Just . . . *how* do I do that?"

"Oh," Persephone says, realizing . . . something. "The recarbonification has stripped you of your knowledge of Vehicular Re-Mezmeration, hasn't it?"

"I . . . guess so?"

"Well, since it is . . . *yours,*" she says decisively and *kind* of inappropriately(?), "it should simply sense your presence and draw from you whatever amount it needs, provided you are in a non-fatigued enough state to share."

"Riiight. Right. Okay, yeah, I remember that. Right," I say, convincing probably no one.

EIIIIIIIIIIIIIIIIIIIINNNNNNNNNNNNZZZZZZZZZZGGGEEEAAARRR.

"Bru—Uh, Carp?" Brittany calls. "Maybe let's . . . ?"

"Yeah, yeah," I affirm, standing in front of Sheila, waiting for her to . . . draw from me. But . . .

Nothing happens.

I change my positioning to see if maybe I'm in the wrong place.

Nope. Still nothing.

I assume something kind of like a Spider-Man pose.

"What are you doing?" Persephone asks.

"Um. Not . . . ? I don't . . . ? It doesn't seem to be working."

"This is *yours*? Yes?" Again, she really hits the "*yours*."

"I mean, yeah, yeah, she's mine. Fully paid for. I own the title and everything."

She puts her hand to her chin, thinking. "Then, I do not . . ." She stops, awareness dawning. "Did you not complete the binding ceremony before setting off with it?"

"Complete the which now?"

She looks distraught. "The reentry into this world has cost you so much." *She has no idea.* "Before you can fully engage with a vehicle unto which you only it has been bestowed," she explains, "you must first bind with it as its proprietor." *Oh. I get what she's saying. Like how I had to register my profile with Sheila on the app. I get it.* "Quickly, take off your garments."

Okay, maybe I don't get it.

"Excuse me?"

"Disrobe so that you may begin the Mezmeration of the vehicle."

"Dis-who-so-what now?"

I look at Brit because, as previously noted, it was she who made all the charts about how this kind of thing works, but she just shakes her head and shrugs her shoulders.

Persephone huffs out the kind of sigh that attends someone in a state of great urgency who has to stop and explain something that every five-year-old should know.

"As is child of parent borne and sustains itself by mother's milk, so too shall the vehicle of driver be bound by the natural connection you share."

"You're saying he has to breastfeed the thing?!" Brit exclaims.

"No," Persephone counters. "It is not literal. It simply means that the driver must be unencumbered during the initial binding process. Most people perform this thaumaturgy in the privacy of their vehicular stables before they commence their first journey. Did yours not indicate to you that it yet required your consummation?"

"*Consummation*? No!" I declare. "Or, maybe? I didn't notice! There's been a lot happening!"

I have two thoughts:

1. This has always been my hesitation about buying an electric car. I think they're cool and they're fast—all torque all the time—and they're good for the planet and all that stuff, but I worry about range anxiety!

And,

2. Good god. I've got a fertile kind of creativity, but this whole feed-the-car-your-nudity is both weird and semi-erotic in a way I don't think even I could have come up with.

"*EIIIIIIIIIIIIIIIIIIIINNNNNNNNNNNZZZZZZZZZZGGGEEEAAARRR!*"

Shit.

"I hear it now, too!" Persephone cries. "Swiftly! We haven't—"

But that's all she gets out before the Ronine materializes in front of us. From thin air, right in the middle of the street. It looks even bigger than it did before. Maybe I just misperceived its size as I was running from it, but it seems even rattier and more lion-y at once.

"So *what* do I do?!"

"Bare yourself, and it will draw from you what it needs! I shall keep the Ronine at a distance!"

"But—"

"Now, Carpathian! Please!"

It's the "please" that gets me. It's so primal and desperate that I stop thinking about everything and just do as she says.

Stripping the torn pajama top over my head, I glance down to see . . . abs. Really, really good abs. An eight pack, at least.

Again, I've always been in okayish shape, but this . . . this is some Michael Phelps sinewy, ripped, shredded, broad-chested, and ready-for-the-gold kind of a thing I'm looking at.

I touch my torso to make sure it's really me.

"Yo, Narcissus!" Brittany shouts. "Indulge your self-adulation later! Let's get to naked-ing!"

Acknowledging with a quick nod, I stumble to kick the too-big boots off my feet using the heel-toe method. And then . . . I hesitate. Unexpectedly.

I'm not a prude by any means. I even wrote a diatribe in book five about how all bodies are beautiful and that we should celebrate them all equally and stuff like that. (I had just watched a News Channel KSDK special report on what they called a "body-shaming epidemic" and felt like I needed to contribute to the conversation.) But, I dunno, I'm not historically given to waving my tallywhacker around in public.

"Just do it, man!" Brittany implores. "I don't give a shit!"

"Yeah, bro, it's nothing I haven't seen before!" Pergamon lends.

Oh, right. I do like to write in the buff sometimes. Makes me feel less constrained somehow. Like the ideas flow more naturally when I'm not encumbered by—

Oh. Ohhhhh. *Ooooooooooooooooh.* I get it. I think? This is *that.*

This car thing is somehow derivative of that part of *my* process. Holy mascarpone. Things are making more sense. (Sort of.) Even the stuff here that I didn't create, per se, is still a byproduct of me and the choices I have made. Wow. That's some heavy woo-woo.

As is child of parent borne . . .

"Homie!" Pergamon yells way louder than I think he should be able to relative to his size, pulling me out of my head. "Stop, drop, and open up your drawers so you can get to making with the boom-boom on the vroom-vroom!"

"Goddammit," I whisper as I rip my pajama pants down my legs and step out of them.

BOOM!

I jerk my head to see the Ronine being blasted back by Persephone, just as she did earlier. She's generating and handling glimmering balls of Mezmer like she's A.I. (By which I mean the great Allen Iverson, who, as a writer, is the only A.I. I will ever have respect for.) She's aiming the balls of fiery magic straight at the beast and hitting it dead-on, but it just keeps coming.

I'm not sure how much Mezmer Persephone has in her at the moment. If, like Almeister, she can generate reservoirs of her own, or she has to re-up like everyone else when they use up what they're working with. But I don't want to have to find out, so as she cradles the balls of Mezmer in her hands, I grab hold of *my own*—

"*NOPE! Nope. Not gonna let you do it, Bruce. It is a lazy, adolescent joke that is beneath you, and we'll have none of it today.*"

"*You're right, Bruce. I'm sorry. My head's not clear right now.*"

"*Don't worry about it, Bruce. Now go screw your car back to life again.*"

I take two steps toward the car when suddenly . . .

ZYYYYYOOOOOOOOOOP!

It's just like the times previous when the Heart has sprung to life, except that's a lie, and when I frame it more accurately, it's not *just* like it at all. It doesn't startle or shock me or anything of the like. It feels . . . strengthening, in its way. Like I am no longer just me, but in some way, greater than myself. If I had to describe it beyond that, I'm not sure I'd be able to find the words, but in the least amount of words possible, I feel . . . unafraid.

Which is a relief, I must say.

My arms are out at my sides, and my legs are apart. I didn't move myself this way; something has pulled me into this stance. A golden, gauzy hue has bubbled up, surrounding both me and the car, as in front of me I see . . .

Vehicle: [Sheila]
Titleholder: [Carpathian Einzgear]
Vehicle Rarity: [Unquantified]
Vehicle Class: [Lightning Rider]

And then, like a big, chunky power switch being flipped on . . .

VROOOOOM!

Sheila roars to life.

CHAPTER EIGHTEEN

Vroom, vroom, vroom, vroom vroom!" Sheila . . . *says*? Sorta?

Which is not to suggest that the car itself is talking and going "vroom, vroom, vroom." Because that would be silly. And *kind* of funny? But mostly silly. People can judge me all they want, but I've always thought the premise for *Knight Rider* was lame. A talking car? Like, what, Michael, you can't make any real friends? Seriously. The hero of your show's sidekick/bestie is a talking car? Makes him seem sad to me. And in no world I had a hand in crafting would something like a car become sentient.

Again, hate if one must, but it's just so . . . I dunno . . . unserious seeming somehow. And for all its high-concept world-building and occasional flights of fancy into the potentially absurd, one thing I never wanted Riftbreaker to become was some kind of a joke.

"Big homie! We gonna bounce, or you just gonna penis gaze all day?!"

Emphasizing the point, the formerly named Gonzo, newly christened Pergamon, yells at me urgently in his Danny Trejo–sounding voice to draw my focus away from my naked form and back into action, reminding me, quickly, of the gravity and seriousness of our circumstances.

"Almost there!" I shout back. Because now I see it. Instantly viewable to me now that I've bonded with the car is its Energy Meter. It's gone from zero percent to ninety in less than the snap of a finger. The vroom, vroom, vroom blaring from the engine—while not literally speaking to me as such—is still, somehow, the car communicating *with* me. It's beckoning to me, letting me know that it's ready and rearing to go.

I suppose it's probably similar to the way people who ride horses describe their connection to a beast of burden they love. There's a private language they share. Animal and human.

Mollie, the woman I based Persephone on, rode horses. She used to say—

"GO!" The actual Persephone—the one who is currently battling off a newly to me discovered beast called a Ronine—shouts as she sends another blast of Mezmer in the monstrosity's direction.

But I notice it's weaker. The blast, not the Ronine. The blast's impact is less effective than the ones she was hitting it with even just moments before. Which, I suppose, answers my question of whether or not she can maintain her power without having to endure some type of cooldown period. I'm not sure how deep her Mezmer channels go, but they're clearly not boundless. The Ronine is now able to push into the energy, forcing itself closer to her. And me.

"We gotta get to steppin'!" Brittany shouts.

Everyone's right. Of course we do. But, despite the need to flee, I find myself quite completely enthralled by what I see Persephone doing.

I never assigned her a specific Mezmer Type as far as I remember, so I didn't know what kinds of things she might be capable of, but watching her now and considering the way she appeared out of thin air and all the other qualities I've observed within her, it's clear that she is *a Dreamweaver.*

Her hands move in a swift, intricate dance, and suddenly, the air shimmers around her.

In a dazzling display reminiscent of the grand finale of a Broadway show, at least a dozen copies of her materialize. These illusory doubles, like backup dancers hitting their marks, twirl and weave around the Ronine. Each one moves in perfect harmony with the others, a dazzling spectacle that leaves the beast snapping at phantoms.

The real Persephone, amid this sea of duplicates, becomes impossible to pinpoint. The juxtaposition of the Ronine's grotesque form with Persephone's graceful illusions is . . . well, it's something. The light from her spells casts eerie shadows, making the scene look like something out of a simultaneously terrifying and beautiful nightmare.

"Yo!" Pergamon shouts. "You crying, *ese*?! Yo, girlie, our boy's glue is melting off! Homeboy's waterworks are flowing!"

What? What's Pergamon saying?

And, in the midst of the far-too-much-to-keep-track-of, I can feel what he's talking about.

My eyes are wet. There are tears running down my cheeks. Not "flowing" or "gushing" or anything as dramatic as that, but just . . . gently tumbling out of the corners of my vision and glissading down the contours of my face.

This is awful. This is terrifying. This is ridiculous. This is impossible. And yet, it is all so profoundly . . .

"*Another time, Bruce! You can indulge it all another time. For now, you need to get your friends, your car, and your privates together, and get on the road, Jackson!*"

Annnnnd we're back.

Hell of a thing that my mind can wander even in a time like this, but hey . . . part of the gig of being Bruce Silver!

"You okay?!" Brittany yells toward me.

"Yep! Yep, good, fine!" I reply, wiping my tears away and looking at Sheila, who is revving her engine in a way that I interpret clearly as *hurry the hell up.*

But before I can take a step forward, the Ronine begins making a sound. An awful, obscene sound. Worse than a roar or anything of the kind; it sounds like . . . like . . . like it's trying to cough up a furball?

The hell?

And then, from its mouth (*from its MOUTH*) comes pouring a freaky, horrifying conglomeration of creatures.

They are smallish, but not so small as to be insignificant. Most are about the stature of a really healthy Parisian gutter rat. They are likewise a Frankenstein's mix of rat and cat, miniature versions of the Ronine itself. Except . . .

. . . instead of legs, they have wheels.

Wheels?

WHEELS!

What in the H.P. Lovecraft is going on?!

"What are those?!" I shriek.

"They are Rapprentices," one of the Persephones, whom I take to be the original, calls between her ever-weakening blasts.

Before I can make some kind of smartass comment about how no matter how clever the name "Ronine" might be, "Rapprentice" is absolutely pathetic (is it short for, like, Ronine Apprentice? I guess?), I see one of the other Persephones get absolutely *mopped* by a powerful swipe from the Ronine. She screams in pain as she is ripped in half and dematerializes.

"Ahhh!" cries the Persephone who was speaking to me, confirming my suspicion that she's the true one.

"Seph!" I bellow to her, assuming a level of casual comfort in shortening her name that I don't think I've earned but am running with anyway.

I bend down, grab my pants, and go to slide them on my legs, but then realize they're not my pants, are actually my top, and now I've got my foot caught in one of the armholes and wind up falling face-first onto the hard cobblestone.

"Ow! Shit!" I shout. Obviously.

And, looking up, I see coming toward us from an intersection maybe half a mile away human riders. On magecycles. With black, retro-futuristic armor adorned with symbols and runes.

Templars.

"Saviouuuuuuuuuuuuuuuuurrrrr!" the one riding in front shouts, somehow audible over the tsunami/earthquake/big bang happening all around.

Moridius. I recognize his thunderous braying from before.

Brittany is at the door handle of the Panamera, tugging, with Gonz—Shit. *Pergamon* now on her shoulder, shouting, "Unlock it! Bruce, keys!"

And, quite literally everywhere else . . .

Two of the Persephones break free from the Ronine to fire upon the approaching Templars.

Two more dispatch themselves to rumble with the dumbly named Rapprentices.

And one is still engaged in Mezmer-to-fang combat with the primary rat-lion.

She's fighting everything everywhere all at once like she's Michelle Yeoh, doing all in her not-unimpressive power to allow us to escape.

Meanwhile, I'm flat on the ground, pajama top around my ankles, bare ass to the heavens, and feeling awfully, awfully . . . vulnerable . . . and useless, I gotta tell you.

"*Bruce . . .*" the voice inside my head calls out quietly. Softly. It sounds different somehow. Gentler. But I'm still able to recognize myself.

"*Bruce? Is that you?*"

"*Listen to me . . .*"

". . . *Okay.*"

"*Look into your Heart.*"

"*What?*"

"*You have to remember to look into your Heart.*"

"*Look into my—*"

"*I know it must feel like you are starting all over again, but you have abilities and knowledge you did not have before. You survived once. You thrived once. You will again. Just look into your Heart. Salvation is within.*"

What? Why is the voice in my head getting all Deepak Chopra all of a sudden?

"*What do you mean, salva—?*" I start before a blast from a Templar's boom stick shatters the air next to my prone, buck naked prostration.

"Bruce!" Brittany calls out.

Look into my Heart. I get it. The voice means it literally. Although there's probably some broader metaphor at work that—

BOOM!

Nope. Not the time for self-reflection.

Okay, so look into my Heart. Look into my Heart . . .

Oh!

I can choose how and when to engage with it. My Heart. That's what the voice means. I don't have to wait for it to show up. I don't have to WAIT for Control. I can SEIZE Control. I touched the top layer of it earlier when we hid from the Ronine, but I can really, really learn to manage it. I just have to decide that I want to. Carpathian was reticent too because of the responsibility, but he got over his fear. I can too. I can too. I can too.

I close my eyes, focus, and . . .

Snap.

Not a big snap. A tiny, little snap. The sound of the Heart clicking into action and engaging.

Control: [Activated]

You have activated the Control Spell. Well done, you.
(There was some concern you had forgotten it was available.)
{COURTESY MESSAGE #6}

Were I not otherwise monumentally predisposed, I would take another second to reflect on the odd combo-parlance the System is using. Which is definitely half the way I wrote it and half like the way I would joke to Brittany about having it communicate. But I am. Otherwise monumentally predisposed, I mean, so . . .

ZZZZZZZZZZWWWWWWAAAAAHHHHHMMMMM.

And. Everything. Slows. Down.

Thump-thump.

I can see the meter. It's showing marginally more rich redness than before. Not let's-smoke-these-fools-and-set-the-world-ablaze amounts more, but more than before the Interlocutrix.

Which should be enough.

I roll my foolish nakedness over the cobblestones (which has its own array of discomforts but, on balance, is not a big enough deal to make a thing out of) and scoop up my PJ pants, sliding *them* onto my legs and feeling in the pocket for Sheila's fob.

Beep-boop.

"Geeeeet iiiiinnnnn!" I shout, hearing my own voice as drawn out and echoey.

Brittany, carrying Pergamon, grabs shotgun. Again, slowly, but just fast enough to take a seat and slam the door closed before any of these douchey things that are out to kill us (Me? Us, probably) can do her damage.

That's possible, of course, because Persephone is still holding everything off single-handedly. Well . . . not technically single-handedly, because there are still multiples of her, but the sentiment remains generally true.

Ignoring my top and the oversize boots (which look like they've given me a blister anyway, so to hell with 'em), I dart over to Persephone (again, *dart* is relative, but I'm not sure phonology is a priority just at this instant) and, without warning, grab her around the waist.

Thump-thump. Thump-thump.

"Caaarpaaaaathiiiaaaaan? Whaaaaat aaare yooou doooooiiing?" she asks, the words coming out slow and syrupy.

I choose not to answer because it doesn't matter. Either my Synchron Foundation operates in concert with my All-Type Mezmer the way I interpret, or it doesn't.

We'll know in a hurry.

Thump-thump. Thump . . . Thump.

Shit, Control is almost expired. Dear Richemerion, I hope this works.

Thump . . . Thump.

Thump . . .

Thump . . .

. . .

BOOM!

It's like that old footage of the first explosion that happened outside Los Alamos. Like, *exactly* like that. A huge sphere of energy ballooning out and blowing back everything within its radius. Which, it would seem, is substantial.

Thump.

Thump.

SHWOOOOOOOOOOOMMMMMPPP.

Annnnnd, again, we're back.

I note that my intake of breath isn't quite as desperate this time around. It's more like I'd only been holding it for a little while and less like I'd just survived a wipeout at Pipeline.

I also take note of the fact that the other iterations of Persephone were not spared the effects of the fissionlike kaboom we caused. Just as the big blam blew back the baddies, it also banished the other battling babes.

(Ugh. I did not mean to do that. I swear. It just happened. My brain . . .)

And now, Persephone, still clutching at my spine as I clutch at hers, pulls her head back and, with a look of astonishment in her eyes, asks, "What was *that*?"

"It seems I now have the ability to sync with fellow blah, blah, and can transition between meow-meow, in the event that yadda, yadda."

"What?"

"Doesn't matter. Let's pound bricks." I pull away and tug at her wrist to come with, but she holds herself in place. "What's going on? We gotta take it on the heel and toe, Seph!"

". . . You go."

"*What?!*" I ask with a completely reasonable amount of WTF.

"You have created a chance for escape. You must take it."

"But—"

"Look," she says, pointing.

The Ronine has been blasted almost comically into the side of a building, ripping bricks and infrastructure free all around it, but it is not dead. Not that, apparently, it actually *can* die—at least not now—but it's not even dead-appearing, as it was before. It just looks annoyed as it steps away from being embedded in the rubble and begins prowling toward us again.

"Right!" I exclaim. "So—!"

Rrr-rrr-rrr-rrr-rrr-rr. Rrr-rrr-rrr-rrr-rrr-rr. In the distance.

Gods. Damn. It. The Templars and the Rapprentices are revving back up again. Shit. This has to be a result of the fact that while I *have* All-Type Synchron, it's still baby-size in terms of its efficacy. Son of a—

"Carpathian," she says again, looking me in the eye and placing her hand on my bare, muscly chest, which is . . . feelings. "Go. And do all you can to avoid detection as you Quest for Father."

"But—"

"I will find you," she says with a cinematically Mechanical Heart–wrenching blend of resoluteness, assurance, and affection.

"*EIIIIIIIIIINNNNZZZGGGEEEAAARRR!*"

"Go," she says a third time, quietly. And with finality.

And, damn, shit, shittety damn, son of a fickety shuck, I release my grip on her wrist and sprint toward the Panamera, Brittany waving me to hurry. *Like I'm not, Brit! Jiminy!*

Sliding behind the wheel and slamming the door shut, a voice greets me. Feminine and vaguely German.

"Hello, Carpathian. To where are we headed?"

"What? Are you—? Sheila?"

"Yes, Carpathian. It is I, Sheila. Where shall we venture to?"

Aww, for the love of . . . Are you kidding?!

"Uh, to where . . . ?" I just about stutter, both put off by the fact that I now have A TALKING CAR and the fact that I have no idea where to head next.

Brittany is fiddling with the maps, also trying to figure it out. "Shit. I . . . I don't—"

"Would you like autopropulsion to determine the best course to charter?"

"Auto—?"

"*EIIIIIIIIIINNNZZZGGGEEEAAARRR!*"

"Yes, sure, yes! Auto-whatever us the hell out of here!"

"Excellent. Please ensure your seatbelts are buckled securely."

And then we're in one of those Tesla videos of people experiencing Insane Mode for the first time. Which is to say: We scream like we just hit our first big roller-coaster drop and got pushed off a bungee-jumping bridge at the same time.

Kind of an AHHHHHMYYYYYHOLYYYWHAAAWWWWWAAAAAHHH that *starts* as a scream and ends as a whiny-ish cry as we are whipped off into the night.

But we're not home free yet because, looking in the rearview, I see a passel of Rapprentices kick into high gear as they come chasing after us.

"Dammit," I mutter.

"What is it?" Brittany asks, turning in her seat to look behind. "Oh shit," she says, seeing the ridiculously monikered mini monsters bearing down from behind, their tiny rat-lion bodies churning up dust and debris from their wheel treads as they rocket ahead, right on our six.

"What do you think they do?" Pergamon asks. "Like, shoot lasers from their eyes or—?"

"I don't know! I don't wanna find out!" I say, pressing down on the accelerator to try and put more distance between us. But, even with as much haste as we are making, the stupid little microbeasties are somehow sticking with us.

"Incoming threat detected on rear of the vehicle. Would you like to deploy a countermeasure?" Sheila asks.

"Huh?" I respond ineloquently.

And then, on the PCM—the Porsche Communication Management screen— I see a list of options appear:

*Chaos Chain
*Fog of Decimation
*Sonic Torment
*Oscillating Vortex
*Lightning Rider Strike

"What the hell is an 'Oscillating Vortex'?" Brit asks.

"I have no idea," I admit. But as I can see a wide-jawed, sharp-fanged, rat-suffused killbot, its mouth open and light glowing from within its jaws as it prepares to unleash whatever Mezmeric volley it has in store upon my car, I just push the button on the screen that's closest to my finger: Lightning Rider Strike.

And with the force of the unbridled heavens loosing fire from the sky, a bolt of shock lightning blasts from the tailpipe, and I watch in the mirror as it immediately absorbs the Rapprentice in a smothering blanket of fury, torching it completely and causing it to disappear.

Upon seeing this, the remaining Rapprentices chasing us stop dead in their tracks and turn to head back the direction from whence they came.

"Well," I say, finding it curious how swiftly they seem to have given up, "that was relatively easy."

Brittany, more robust in her response, declares a mighty, "Hell yeah!" as she looks behind us through the rear window at the now escaping menaces. "Eat a dick, ya freaks!"

And as Sheila continues rocketing us away from danger, I manage to force a small smile.

Which evaporates quickly when I glance in the rearview one last time to see—in the rapidly shrinking far distance—a now tiny vision of Persephone . . .

. . . being hit square in the chest by a blast from a switchsaw.

At the very same moment she is beset upon by Templars . . .

. . . and the Ronine . . .

. . . and the returning Rapprentices . . .

. . . the name for which suddenly seems much less silly as the last thing I see before the scene behind us dissolves entirely from my view is Persephone's mouth opening wide in a silent—but agonizing-looking—scream.

CHAPTER NINETEEN

Seasons of Rebellion, Riftbreaker Book One,
Chapter Twenty-Five

I understand," Persephone said, her face betraying no hint of emotion, though the Insight with which she had not so long ago abled Carpathian led him to know better.

"I wish you could come with us," he told her so sympathetically that he almost believed it himself, "but it's not me. It's your father. He's worried about what might happen to you if you join us on this next Quest."

The lie was easily disproven. All Persephone might have to do would be to ask her father directly. But Carpathian knew she wouldn't, for that was not the nature of things between Almeister and his only child. And beyond that, Carpathian knew well enough that Almeister, entrenched as he was in the ancient ways, already bristled at the notion that his daughter chose to follow in his footsteps. Owing to her unique Abilities and deep wellspring of empathy, she likely never had a choice, but Almeister held hope out just the same that she might instead have dedicated herself to a path that would have put her less in the sights of the Ninth Guardian.

So, Carpathian gambled—as was his wont—on the probability that she would take him at his word. Such as his word was.

"As I say," she nodded stoically, "I understand."

He gave her an affirming grin and, with a nod of his head, slapped her on the shoulder. "I knew you would," he replied.

He did not see it as coldness or cruelty, just as what it was: The conclusion of a chapter that he had thought might have finished differently but, in the end, was probably for the best.

Carpathian knew well and good that with the burdens being foist upon him, he would have no place for weakness. For vulnerability. And given how much grace she had shown him and how ardently she believed in him, he knew that a time might come when he would disappoint her. Or worse. And that was an additional burden that even his Heart's capacity for storing assets large and small could not bear.

Or, at the very least, it was the yarn he had woven to ensure he would not labor under any misgivings about the decision he was making in requesting that she remain in Bell's View.

"So," he began speaking again, awkward as a schoolboy, "thank you for everything. Truly. For the support, the encouragement, the . . . Insight . . . all of it. You've been a tremendous friend, Persephone Vizardsdottir."

She regarded his extended hand with a mixture of amusement and pity, choosing not to shake but to instead force her smile to curl her lips fractionally more than they might otherwise as she turned her back on him and walked away, leaving him feeling not quite foolish, but certainly close.

As she departed, almost seeming to float away down the dark streets of Bell's View, Almeister approached Carpathian, noticing his extended hand.

"Where is my daughter going? Is she choosing not to attend us on our journey?"

"No," Carpathian replied, slightly startled as he ever was by the silent appearance of the old man. "No, she said she thinks it would be better for her to stay and look after the town."

"Did she?" Almeister asked, clear wonderment peppering the question. "Really? That does not sound like her. She's forever asking to be more involved with my endeavours. Particularly when they also happen to involve you . . ." He arched an eyebrow at the young man who had now told enough lies that to retreat from any one of them might mean compromising a dozen others.

"She's . . . mercurial," Carpathian worked out.

His mentor regarded him for a long, long moment. Even longer than usual.

Finally, he said, "Yes. Well. Very good. Shall we fetch the snail, then, and be on our way? We haven't the time to wait any longer, and though you are not fully ready . . . you are ready enough."

"Yes," Carpathian answered, an unearned confidence swelling inside him.

"Alright, then," the old wizard said, his cloak circling as he spun to leave.

Before he followed, Carpathian turned his head to see Persephone one final time. But it was too late. She had disappeared into the night, leaving only the warm lights emanating from the inns and pubs and spilling onto the streets to greet his glare.

Something about it gave him comfort. For he knew, if nothing else, Bell's View—this place that, in its way, had birthed him anew, granting him power and purpose he never imagined himself having . . .

. . . would always be safe.

NORTHERN SWAMP

SOUTHERN SWAMP

SEA OF SWANS

Fuck this place →

REVELATION'S PASS

JEOMANDI'S PUB & PINTS

WHERE CARPATHIAN X FOUND PERGAMON

???

BELL'S VIEW HILLS

BELL'S VIEW

I fell asleep here

Where are we going, Bruce?
↖ UP

Sometown we never named

ACT THREE

PARADISE (SORT OF) FOUND

CHAPTER TWENTY

"Maybe she's okay."

It's the third or fourth time she's said it, and while I appreciate Brit trying to be optimistic and bolster my spirits . . . I don't, actually.

In fact, it's annoying the shit out of me.

"Yeah, homeboy. Girlie's right. Sexy redheaded other girlie seems like she bad as hell, *ese*."

And the chatty snail isn't helping.

I don't respond. Again. Just white knuckle the steering wheel as Sheila guides us to . . . wherever it is she's taking us. I have no clue where we are other than there's some river or creek or something running alongside. I've tapped on the GPS screen multiple times, but all it shows is a dot with a message that reads "You are here."

"And, I mean, as far as we know, she's never remorted," Brit tosses in. "So—"

"You still updating those maps?" I ask brusquely.

A chilled silence comes over the car so that the endless blackness and faint calls of mythic beasts outside seem all the more endless and mythic.

"Yeah," she says after a lengthy moment. "Yeah, sure." She unfolds a map, looks around, says, "Think we're probably in the vicinity of Revelation's Pass," pulls the pen from her pocket, and starts scribbling. She may be updating them or just writing "all work and no play makes Bruce a grouchy boy" over and over. Right now, I don't really care.

Godsdammit. I . . .

Actually? No. Know what? Doesn't matter. I don't need to rehash the whole thing. I *want* to. I really *want* to replay all my actions and emotions in my brain because it creates the illusion that I might be able to do something about it now, but . . . but that's just me closing the barn door after the horses have—*Mollie rode horses, and Persephone is crafted in Mollie's likeness, and . . .* Jesus! I can't even NOT think my way out of a mind spiral!

Okay. Okay. Okay, okay, okay. Pull it together, Bruce. Just . . . Just . . . focus on the Quest at hand. Things don't have to be more complicated than that.

"*Really, Bruce?*"

"*Sure, Bruce. One of your, it would seem, myriad problems is concentrating on only one thing at a time.*"

"*I know. I'm sorry.*"

"*Hey. Don't beat yourself up, tiger. You have many other good qualities.*"

"*I do?*"

"*Sure you do. You . . . have a great head of hair.*"

. . . Great head of hair? The best pep talk my split personality can offer me is that I have good tonsorial endowments? Super.

Other me *is* right, though. I need to just keep moving forward; hope, if not presume, that Persephone is alright, and figure out how to get her father out of the Tower of Zuria.

Which means I first need to get my hands on the Blade of the Starfallen.

"Do you remember exactly where he first acquired it?" I ask.

"Acquired what?" Brittany rightly responds, owing to the fact that I was having that whole conversation with myself and provided her no context.

"The Blade of the Starfallen. The Quest requires that we be in possession of it in order to rescue Almeister. Carpathian pulled it out of that rock, but I don't remember where I said it was specifically. So, y'know, do *you*?" I ask, with probably more annoyance in my voice than I intend. But frankly, I *am* annoyed, so I can't be bothered to care that I sound like I am.

Given the edge in my voice, I'm half expecting another pointed comment about my inability to remember things I should be able to, but I don't get it. Maybe *because* of the edge in my voice.

Without fanfare, Brit just answers, "The base of Mount Saatus."

"That's right."

"Saatus means *fate* in Estonian."

"Yeah, no, I remember. Okay. So is that where we're headed? Are we being navigated that direction? Best you can tell?"

She ruffles through the paper in her lap. It looks like Perg is helping her seek. (I just this moment decided I'm going to start calling him Perg. Unless that's offensive too. To . . . I don't know, whoever. Friggin' people who don't like having their names shortened.)

I know I'm not making any sense. I'm frustrated. And agitated, which are not things I allow myself to feel-slash-become very often, so I don't know quite how to distribute them properly.

"I see it," Perg says.

"Yeah, yeah, I see it too," Brittany echoes. Then a weight enters her voice. "Shit. I forgot . . ."

"Forgot what? What is it? Is it far?"

"I mean, yeah, it is. But it's not so much just that it's far as it is . . ." She drifts off.

"What?" I prod.

"It's in a pretty shitty neighborhood, fool," Perg says.

"Huh?"

Brittany sighs. "It's right beside the Cavern of Sorrows. Like, *right* beside."

"It is?"

"Yeah."

"*It is?*"

"Yeah, Bruce. It is."

"But. No. That's not right. That can't be right. When I wrote about the Cavern of Sorrows—"

"When you wrote about the Cavern of Sorrows, you wrote it with the express intention of leaving *Mael* there as the big book eight cliffhanger."

"Right, so—"

"And then, when Carpathian and Almeister went to try and save Mael, and Almeister got tricked by fuckin' *DONG*"—*I know she's gonna make a point of highlighting it every chance she gets*—"he wound up imprisoned in the Tower of Zuria as the big book *nine* cliffy. Which, I know it's maybe not the time to point this out, but who gives a shit? I had thought that the whole *point* of book ten was supposed to be that Carpathian realized, even as he approached god-tier status, that not having those around him who helped him arrive there still weakened him."

"I mean . . . it was. It did! The whole reason he was *able* to be killed is because he lacked the *true* source of his power, which was never the armaments or his Leveling up but the *people* who helped him acquire it all. It's an allegory about—"

"Oh, fuck an allegory, bro. The allegory would've worked the exact same if the next part of the series had been about saving the people who saved him and helped him become who he was. Instead of killing him off. Only, y'know, it would've been happy and nice and . . . not all self-sabotage-y. But okay!" She snorts, then adds, "Goddammit, dude. This is what happens when you go off and do shit without including me. We get sucked into a universe you created and have to do in real life the shit you coulda just done on paper."

(I would hasten to point out that that's only happened once and thus doesn't feel like a fair consequence to hang her argument on, but not the time.)

A new, fresh, chilled silence overtakes the car. Only this time, the chill is coming from the passenger seat.

"But," I start, breaking up the absence of people talking and trying to stay on mission, "why would I have built the Cavern of Sorrows next to Mount Saatus? Was I trying to say something about the intertwining of sorrow and fate, or—?"

"Who knows, Bruce?" she asks, rhetorically, her own aggravation now on full display. "If you don't know, then how the hell am I supposed to? When I proofed book eight, it read clearly to me that the whole thing was going down for Mael next to the same place where Carpathian originally received the Blade, so that's why it's there. Because you never gave an indication that it wasn't, and so I just went ahead and assumed it was what you intended it to be."

There's another beat before Perg chimes in at Brittany with the same thing I'm thinking but am too apprehensive to say. "Well, then technically, isn't it *your* fault that the shit is in the same place?"

The roads in Meridia are pretty jacked up, so this isn't the smoothest ride already, but the vibrating I now feel inside the car isn't coming from rough terrain; it's coming from the bubbling Vesuvius that is Brittany Patricia McAfee.

". . . Excuse me?" she finally grinds out.

"I'm just saying," Perg goes on, "that if you're the one who's supposed to be checking homeboy's shit, and *you're* the one who made the maps and kept track of—"

"Kept track of what?!" she . . . yowls. "Kept track of every convoluted, contradictory idea that runs through Retcon Johnson's goddamn maze of a brain?!"

(I know I should be offended by that, but "Retcon Johnson" would actually be a pretty cool name for a character who shows up in a story and changes the past in some way. I'm gonna keep that one tucked away for something in the future. Ironically.)

"Let's call it the Candy Shoppe!"

. . . Oh, right. Brittany's still pissed.

"Oh, no, wait," she keeps going, "let's call it *Pulse Wells* instead. In one book, we'll say that the Amulet of Soren can only be activated by the tears of a newborn celestial entity, and in the next book, we'll just say it's activated at random by dropping it accidentally into the Lake of Alumos!"

I wince. Because she brings that up, like, once a month. I mean, she's not *wrong.* My initial draft of book four, *Ages of Alumos,* was, to be generous, a catastrophe. It was a maze of convoluted timelines, conflicting Mezmeric laws, and plot holes you could drive a semi through.

Brittany had come aboard Team Riftbreaker on the book previous, and I think I was just so excited to have someone to bounce ideas off of and spitball with that I let myself get carried away with the lore and the worldbuilding and the rules and all. But in my defense, that's the joy of writing fantasy. You get to explore the what-ifs without the limitations of the real world.

Brittany hadn't shared my reasoning. "*You're a really talented guy,*" she had said, "*but it's like you've got Rembrandt-level skill and you're using it to make some Jackson Pollock shit.*"

That was a real splash of water to the face because we had recently had a talk about how if I ever got enough money, I thought it would be cool to go to an art auction and do the whole "lift a paddle casually and place a bid" thing. She'd asked what kind of art I was into, and I'd told her that while I was no, like, collector, I'd always thought the Baroque style was the prettiest. She had been surprised, saying that she took me for more of an abstract impressionism type of guy, and I told her that I thought most abstract impressionism looked sloppy. Like, I can't ever figure out where my eye is supposed to go.

So, to have her contextualize my work that way was a wake-up call of sorts. Although . . .

It may also have been the moment I actually started to see writing Riftbreaker as more *work* than *fun.*

I dunno. Doesn't matter much now, I suppose.

She goes on listing things that she's had to come behind me and try to clean up:

"Let's introduce a character called Rufrict in book six and build up this whole goddamn plotline around her and her obsession with Teleri, only to basically forget about her and just have her disappear by book seven! And when good ole Brittany points that out, let's say, AND I QUOTE, 'Don't worry about it. The fans *didn't like her.*'"

Okay, this one I have to push back on a little because, I mean . . . they didn't.

I tried to give Teleri a love interest, but Riftbreakerers (which is an absolutely terrible name for a fan base, but no one ever seemed to best it, so it stuck) just simply DID. NOT. LIKE. Rufrict. I could never understand why. I thought she was funny. And quirky. Kinda sorta an Alyson Hannigan-as-Willow type from *Buffy*.

But man, people thought she was annoying.

Honestly? And I hate to shift blame on anyone else or point fingers, but . . . honestly? I *kinda* think at least part of the fault falls on the shoulders of the guy who did the audiobooks.

I feel bad even thinking it because he's an absolute world-class actor and one of the nicest people I've ever met, AND I think he's a huge part of the reason why the books did so well in the beginning. Because he's got a decent-size fan base, and I'm sure a lot of the folks who discovered the books early on did so because they were followers of his. (Turns out, a lot more people listen to audiobooks than I knew before I started this whole thing.) But . . .

Erg. He just . . . He picked this *voice* for Rufrict that . . . it made her sound . . . well . . .

It's not the choice *I* would've made. That's all I'm saying.

Anyway. That's why I didn't write about her again.

But no. No, I'm *not* gonna push back on it right now, if for no other reason than Brit's on one, and when she's on one, it's best to let it work itself out. But also because, like I said, I hate blame shifting. So, whatever.

Largely speaking, her point is valid. She's done the best job of herding the passel of cats that is my imagination that she can. And we're all under a lot of stress, so best just to let her—

"Not to mention the fact that while I'm doing all THAT SHIT," she continues yelling at Perg, "I'm also trying to coordinate meetings and conventions and make sure bitch remembers to go to his dentist appointments, so maybe you're gonna wanna back off with the . . . What do you have? Not fingers. Antennae? The antenna pointing? Yeah. That. Maybe back that shit up a step, *coño*."

Out of the corner of my eye, I see Perg's head retract on its long, snaily neck. First time he's gotten a fistful of Brittany, I guess. I remember what it was like the first time. Catches you off guard.

"Okay, well, so . . . Okay," I jump in to try and save the snail from further abuse. "So the Blade is *near* the Cavern of Sorrows. That doesn't mean we have to *enter* the Cavern of Sorrows, does it?"

"No," Brit replies. "No, we don't *have* to."

"Right. So why—?"

"*Because* it's where Mael is," she says decisively.

I turn my head to see the expression of *"I mean, don't you think we should?"* in her eyes.

"Oh. Well, okay, look . . . No. Not . . . No. We can't just—"

"Bruce—"

"I know, I know. But . . . Jesus Christ. We've got a metric ton of shit to deal with already. Let's just . . . Let's just focus on the task that we've actually agreed to. The Quest we have accepted. We'll get to everything else we need to do, but . . . for now . . ."

I drift off uncomfortably. Because Mael is one of her favorite characters. Hell, Mael is just about everyone's favorite character. Over time, he came to be Carpathian's biggest cheerleader and staunchest ally. Even when others doubted Carpathian, Mael would encourage them to continue believing.

Which is made all the more impressive when one considers that Mael *himself* was chosen to be a Saviour. (A Tribal Saviour, not the *World* Saviour, but still.) Mael is possibly the least selfish, most righteous figure in all of Riftbreaker, so knowing that we'll be that close to where he's languishing and not attempt to try and help him is pretty shitty, but—

"We are arriving at our destination."

I stop ruminating over Mael's plight and strain my eyes to see what's up ahead. At first it looks like more nothing. Just blackness. And then, like the lights of Las Vegas manifesting from out of nowhere after you've been driving for miles at night in the middle of the dark desert, it appears.

A sign.

Gaudy and glitzy and neonlike (if neon actually blazed with living flame), broadcasting loudly that we are about to come upon . . .

Jeomandi's Pub and Pints
"A Place Where Friends Meet."

CHAPTER TWENTY-ONE

Holy shit," Brittany says upon seeing the place coming into view through the windshield, looming larger and larger as we approach like some kind of netherworld carnival tent.

"Yeah," I agree. When I first introduced it, I described it as being the kind of a place where "*one might find a werewolf arm wrestling with a banshee,*" and that's absolutely what it appears to be in real life. Once again, my imagining of it is *mostly* what I see, but it's even more intensely chaotic than I perceived it.

The parking lot—which isn't a lot of any kind, just a big pile of dirt in front of the place—is filled with every manner of mechanized, motorized transport conceivable, all parked wantonly with no seeming order or reason to the orchestration. People—and other beings of various species that one finds in Meridia—mill about, drinking, talking, burning donuts in the sand, all the stuff one does at a scary dive bar where bad shit goes down.

I see a really jacked Elf punch something that looks like a . . . I have no idea.

"What is *that*?" I ask aloud, seeing something that I can't quite wrap my mind around.

"Dunno," Brittany says, peering ahead. "Looks like the spawn of a fish that learned to walk and then had sex with a grizzly bear."

"You never made a character sheet for something like that, did you?"

She shakes her head, then says with a start, "No! Wait. It's maybe kind of like a doodle I drew once when you asked me to come up with something 'mega freaky' to have Carpathian battle with. I thought it was dumb, so I never showed it to you, but . . ."

She goes silent, realizing now, I imagine, the same thing I am: that it's not just MY creativity finding itself represented here. The implications of which are . . . I'm not sure. But it suggests that, somehow, anything *either* of us may have ever dreamed up or dreamt of or entered our consciousnesses, even casually, could exist here.

Which is even more(?) . . . unnerving? If that's possible?

I put my foot on the brake, manually overriding the autopropulsion that Sheila's been using and—despite how dumb I know I'm going to feel talking to a car—ask her the obvious question.

"Sheila? Why are we at Jeomandi's?"

"Arriving at: Jeomandi's Pub and Pints. Would you like to see what people are ordering?"

"What? No. I asked WHY we are at Jeomandi's."

"Okay. I won't tell you, then."

"The fuck?" inquires Brittany in her Brittany-anic way.

"I dunno."

"Sounds like she's not sentient, yo," Perg offers up. "Seems like she's just more of a regular virtual assistant, machine-learning type of *chica*."

"But . . . why?" I ask.

"Dunno, fool. Because you have a natural inclination toward inconsistency, and rules only apply for you insofar as they do or don't propel your particular narratives, and that has extended over into the broader reality of the circumstances into which you find yourself now injected? Best guess."

I rub at my forehead. I'm conflicted. While I'm, I suppose, happy to know that I don't *actually* now have a fully sentient car, owing to my natural repulsion to such a concept, it would be nice to have an awareness of what Sheila's onboard guidance knows about why we're here that I don't. "Okay. Well. Super," I breathe out. "Do *you* have any idea why we're at Jeomandi's?"

"Me?" Perg asks. "Why would I know anything about it? I didn't read your shit. I only just learned I can read when I saw the sign above the bar. Unexpected. I would've thought Jeomandi's was spelled *J.I.O.*, not *J.E.O.* This world is a truly remarkable one of never-ending wonder."

"Yeah, but . . . Persephone gave you Insight, right? So, quite technically, you might currently be the most knowledgeable of the three of us about what's going on in Meridia."

I hear him huff out a small, derisive laugh. "Well, that's *loco*. That a snail you happened to buy at the aquarium store would know more about the place that you spent ten books writing about than you do?"

"Yes. I know. But—"

"That's the very definition of irony, fool."

"I—" I pause. Because I really shouldn't get distracted by this detail, but . . . "I actually don't think that's *the* definition," I counter.

"Oh, no? What is the definition then, Miriam Webster?"

"It's Merriam-Webster. Merriam with an *e*," I correct.

"Who gives a shit, homes? You know what I mean. Explain irony to me, Mr. Oxford English."

"Irony? Irony is . . ." Huh. *I'm just realizing that I'm not sure I actually can. I use the word all the time, but maybe I don't know the exact definition?* "Uh . . . I mean. It's a concept that . . ."

"Irony is when something happens in the opposite way to what is expected, typically causing wry amusement," Brittany chimes in. "That's the actual, literal definition."

Since I can't really see Perg's expression I don't know how I know it's one of smugness. I just know that it is when he says, "Sounds like the *exact* thing that we got going on here, fool."

I pat my palms together in the approximation of a golf clap for some reason. "Okay, fine, great. So then, can you please use your *ironic* wellspring of possible Insight into this situation to determine the purpose in us having been brought here?"

There's a beat while he . . . eyes(?) me? And then he says, "Sure, why not? Lemme try. Put me up where I can see things, girlie?"

Brittany lifts him and sets him on the dashboard so he can get a full view of the place. I can hear him taking deep breaths in and out. It seems to syncopate with the hum of the idling car engine. Then, Perg starts to hum as well, sort of a modified "Om," like he's performing a Zen ritual of some kind. His little snail antennae begin wobbling around.

"Oooooooooooooooom. Oooooooooooooooom. Oooooooooooooooom," he goes.

Then, all of a sudden . . .

POP.

He EXPANDS in size, filling up pretty much the entire dashboard, his shell pressing against the roof of the car and damn near clocking me and Brittany in the jaw.

"The hell, dude?!" Brittany shouts, spinning her head and neck out of the way to avoid being socked in the chops.

"That's weird, huh?" Perg says casually.

"What did you just do?" I ask, finding the seat controls with my left hand and edging myself backward to create some distance from the newly miniature-pony-size snail on my dash.

"I'm not sure. Just happened. But this is dope," he replies, wriggling around.

"Careful!" I warn. "Your shell is pressing against the glass. You'll crack the window."

"I ain't gonna crack nothing, Nancy Worries-Too-Much. Relax."

"Can you go back to the size you were?" Brit wonders aloud, pressing her hand against Perg's . . . I guess . . . butt? To keep it out of her face.

"Not sure, but why would I want to? This is fire. I like having some heft."

"I appreciate that," I start, attempting to use reason in a remarkably unreasonable situation. "But will you see if you can? It would be nice to know if you can choose your sizing at your discretion. Seems like it'll be a helpful tool to have at our disposal."

"You sure you just don't want me small to maintain your sense of dominion over me?"

"What?"

"Your primacy. Your need to believe that, as a human, you maintain supremacy in the natural order of things. You're not just racist; you're speciesist, fool."

"Speciesist? I—"

"I'm just clowning on you, homeboy." He laughs. "Lemme see."

He begins his deep breathing again, coupled with a low, steady hum, and after a moment, there's a *CLUCK* sound—like someone snapping their tongue against the roof of their mouth—and he's back to his traditional size, the remnants of his enlargement visible as a shiny residue on the area just above the console.

The three of us sit in silence for a moment.

"So, yeah," he says after a couple of beats. "Seems like I can control the little-big thing. But I still don't know why we're here."

I let my head fall back onto the seat rest and run my hands through my hair. "Okay. Okay. Okay, okay, okay. Let's . . . Let's go see . . . what we can find out, I guess."

I put Sheila in drive, and we edge slowly up toward the morass of other cars parked willy-nilly all over the place. A handful of extremely menacing-looking toughs mill about, drinking from tankards or straight from the bottles, all of them giving off intense "something very bad is going to happen at the roadhouse tonight" vibes. The Elf and the fish-bear seem to have made up and now appear to be making out.

And that's when I realize that it actually must almost be dawn, because I can see what appears to be dawn light starting to show off in the distance to the north. Which presumably means that the first Lunar Rotation of the Quest is nearly at its end, and we've barely even started on the path to rescue Almeister. *So what in Meridia are we doing at Jeomandi's?*

I can't tell if it's the late-night/early-morning blue or the screaming neon that's casting the hue on our faces through the windshield, but it's extremely *Twin Peaks* chic.

The people outside of the tavern are starting to notice us. Their heads turn in our direction, and all of them have the same look: On-guard curiosity blended with a kind of anxiety at not being able to figure out who the hell this is rolling up all stealthlike. And that's when I see them.

Three figures, standing like sentinels outside the entrance to the pub.

Reapers.

It's hard to mistake the air of danger that emanates from their outlandish outfits. Their clothes are a mishmash of leather and armor adorned with metal spikes, glowing trinkets, and an array of exotic weapons. A cyberpunk, anachronistic fantasy biker gang, the patch on the back of their cuts the gruesome image of the Grim Reaper holding up an impaled baby, and the letters R.O.A. stitched underneath. Reapers of Agony.

(One would not need to search one's brain too hard to determine which TV show I might have been binging at the time I came up with the idea for the Reapers.)

Upon seeing them, a brief rush of adrenaline courses through me. They look cool as shit, exactly as I wrote them, appearing in front of me in vivid clarity, just as I described them. There's a sense of satisfaction I feel in having rendered them in such precise terms as I now see them to be. Maybe it's weird, but rather than anything like fear or trepidation, I feel—not for the first time in all this—pride. The writer's ego, I suppose, but I'd rather feel proud of their creation than any of the seventy other things I could feel at the sight of them.

I don't know if I can pick them out as individuals—we're not close enough for me to see the names on their cuts—but there are three of them. One man, one woman, and one of indeterminate gender with long, thick dreadlocks and wearing an intricate and masterfully crafted silver cat mask.

The woman is clad in leather that looks like it's seen a lot of action, scarred and scraped from years of what I can only assume is brawling. Her eyes scan the car skeptically, calculating.

But it's the guy with the hatchet scar on his face that grabs my attention the most. His nose is missing, just a flat area of scar tissue, and his left eye is not an eye at all but an Ocularum Bond, a meld of cybernetics and Mezmer. It glows a cold blue, almost metallic. That's when I realize that I do know who this one is. The leader of the group of Reapers that Carpathian tussled with in *Seasons of Rebellion.* A bad, bad dude, to put it mildly.

"Arec . . ." I whisper, more to myself than anyone else.

"What?" Brit asks. "What'd you say?"

"Arec," I say a little louder, lifting my chin in his direction.

Brittany fixes her eyes on where I'm signaling. "Oh, shit," she says.

"Who's Eric?" Perg asks.

"Not Eric. A-rec. *A.R.E.C.* Arec. As in 'A. Wreck-ing ball of a human being.' He's the president of the Revelation's Pass chapter of the R.O.A."

Perg wiggles his head around to see. "Oh. Oh shit. That's a bad-looking *güey.*"

"Yeah. That's how I wrote him."

"Well . . ." Brit starts. "What do you want to do? Go in? Keep driving? What?"

"I dunno. I need to think for a second."

I sit for a tick, trying to dial in on myself. Or, more specifically, my Heart. Thus far, it's done a reasonably okay job of pulling my coattails when it has information I can use, and even though it's only been a few hours (*A few* hours? *Jesus.*) I can already feel myself starting to get a better handle on its function. Maybe it'll provide some kind of guidance.

I place my hand on my chest the way Carpathian would sometimes do to get in touch with his Heart. Literally.

Nothing happens.

I massage my shirtless sternum and breathe in and out slowly to try and, I dunno, activate it.

I hear, "Yo, fool. What are you doing? This ain't no time for an autoerotic tantra session."

"Shh," I hiss. "Shh."

I try to get some kind of something to happen, but since I'm not even really sure what it is I'm looking for, I'm not completely shocked when nothing does. But it is frustrating.

"Goddammit," I huff.

"What is it?" Brit.

"Why are we here? The Quest is to rescue Almeister. Why aren't we just heading straight to the things we need to fulfill the objective?"

"Because, Bruce," she says, "that's not how this shit works. C'mon, bro. You know the deal. You get a Quest, and then you have to do a bunch of stuff to give you the requisite Abilities and boosts and all that crap to complete the Quest.

Y'know, Side Quests and all that. Look at us. I'm pretty sure none of us are *Leveled Up* enough to do shit right now. And until we can get near a Temple of the goddamn Body and find a Pulse Well, neither I nor Gonzo—"

"Pergamon. Don't make me call HR on you," Perg says.

"Jesus. *Pergamon* here can even see what *our* Stats are. I mean, I can *maybe* summon a Tentasaurian, but I don't really know how"—she points at Perg— "and this one seems to know just enough to probably get us into trouble but not enough to get us out, and only just found out he can enlarge himself—"

"I wanna use embiggen. Sounds classier," Perg interrupts. Brittany ignores.

"And you . . . Well, I mean, let's face it. You're a far cry from being the Carpathian we need right now."

"First of all: Not Carpathian! So . . . y'know. And second of all, what do you mean I'm a far cry from being what we need?!" I don't know why I find myself simultaneously rejecting my Carpathianic role and yet offended that I'm not Carpathianic *enough.*

Oh, no, wait, yes I do. It's because I don't want to shoulder the load but still want to be celebrated for hauling it up the mountain.

You're a real conundrum, Bruce Silver.

"*No, you're not, Bruce. You're just kind of a humble narcissist.*"

"*Shut up, Bruce. Don't be a vibe killer.*"

"Dude," Brittany says, bringing me out of my mental shamble, "you're not at World Saviour Level yet. Not even close. I think you're forgetting just how vulnerable Carpathian was at the beginning."

"Yeah, trust me, I really don't think I am."

"Okay, well." She considers. "Then I guess what I'm suggesting is that you're maybe gonna have to go through some shit, just like Carpathian did, to build experience and skill and all that hoo-ha until you've got enough oomph to do what needs to be done."

"You think that's why we're here? For me to get my head bashed in?!"

"Maybe. Jeomandi's was where Carpathian took his first, hardcore, real-world beatdown. But it's also where he gained an ass-ton of experience and knowledge and wisdom. So . . . I dunno. Maybe the System—of which *that* thing"—she taps my chest—"is an extension—is directing you exactly where you're supposed to be. And, until you gain total . . . whatever, *harmony* with it, I suppose you just have to have faith that it knows what it's doing. Y'know, 'Trust the System' or whatever?"

"Damn, yo. Girlie didn't even drink no Insight brew and she's coming in hot with the mad intellectuals, fool. Good job, *chica.*"

"Thanks."

I sigh. Because . . . she's probably right. Shit. I'm not looking forward to what is surely going to occur when we get out of this car. But, I suppose, it's unavoidable.

I nod in the direction of the Reapers. "You think *they'll* see me as Carpathian?"

"Everybody else has," Brit acknowledges.

I sigh once more. "Okay," I finally accede. "Let's . . . go . . . see if we can . . . *glean* why we're supposed to be here."

I open the door and step out. Brit opens hers, takes up Perg in her hand, and steps out as well. Then the three of us begin striding toward the motley assemblage before us. I try to imagine how we look, Brit in her flip-flops and cutoffs, carrying a snail; me, wearing only Italian silk pajama bottoms and nothing else.

We probably look pretty badass.

(I mean, obviously, we *do not*. But that kind of thinking isn't going to help anyone, so better to just live in the delusion.)

As we get closer, I can feel all eyes on us, hard, and I gulp. Because even if this is what I'm *supposed* to be doing to fulfill my . . . whatever . . . *obligation* . . . these are not the kinds of people I'm eager to have conflict with. They're just not. They're hardened, miserable, and always looking for a fight.

Yes, Carpathian had to get the hell kicked out of him upon his first encounter with the Reapers in order for him to ultimately grow, but those are growing pains (quite literally) that I'd just as soon avoid.

But then I think . . . *Okay. Relax. Maybe—just maybe—we'll get lucky, and they won't see me the same way everyone else has. It's possible(?) they might not recognize me as—*

"Carpathian," Arec hisses the name like a curse. "Carpathian Einzgear."

Or they absolutely, one hundred percent will.

CHAPTER TWENTY-TWO

Einzgear?" declares the woman in leather. "HERE?"

I don't move except to swallow and clench my fist. Tension crackles in the air like a live wire, threatening to shatter the fragile peace of the early morn. ("Peace" being a relative term.)

The atmosphere is charged, heavy with the unspoken understanding that this moment, this intersection of lives, could erupt into chaos at any second. The burbling of the creek that runs just off to the side of the tavern is amplified in my ears, sounding more like a gushing waterfall. The three Reapers shift uncomfortably on their feet. Arec's Ocularum Bond cycles through a range of colors, settling on a menacing red that sets my skin crawling.

I feel Brit tense beside me, her body coiled like a spring. I don't know what she thinks she'll do when shit starts popping off, but I appreciate her fighting spirit. Perg looks like he's trying to retreat into his shell, like a turtle, but as he is not a turtle, he succeeds only in scrunching up his neck so that he looks like a wrinkly old sock that won't stay stretched out anymore and pleats itself about a hundred times as it falls down your ankle. (Maybe he's actually readying himself like a cobra, getting ready to str—Oh. Nope. No, now he's turning around and trying to run away up Brittany's arm. Okay, good to know where he stands when it comes to squabbles.)

I swallow, readying myself for the beats to my noggin' I'm going to have to withstand. If this plays out like it did for Carpathian, I hope I can take the same pounding he did.

"*See if you can talk your way out of it, Bruce,*" my head voice advises.

"*What?*"

"*Why not? Can't hurt. Maybe you can do things differently than Carpathian did.*"

"*Yeahhh. Yeah. You're right. If the idea is that I can clean up some of the things that happened here, maybe I CAN take a different path with them this time. That's a good thought, Bruce!*"

"*Thanks, Bruce. I try.*"

"Okay, listen . . ." I start, putting my hands up in a nonconfrontational manner. But before I can get out another word, Arec steps back and says, with a degree of nervousness, "What are you doing here, Einzgear? We had heard you was extinguished."

"He's been recarbonified?" the leather-clad woman offers by way of both question and explanation.

"Obviously that," Arec replies, his eye socket throbbing with its red glow. "But why's he here? Why you here, *Saviour*?" He puts a whole lot of cynical-sounding torque on the last word. "Been a long time. Why would a remorted World Saviour be back at this shithole?"

It's a reasonable question; it has been a long time. Nine whole books, to be precise. For them, it's got to have been at least . . . uh . . . I really have no idea. Keeping track of the exact timeline is Brittany's job. To which point . . .

"I, uh . . ." I start to answer the Reaper, looking over at Brittany for some kind of reassurance, I suppose. She nods at me with a "don't worry, I've got your back" seriousness. "I, uh . . . I'm not sure. What I'm doing here," I say haltingly, deciding that telling the truth might just be easier than making up a whole big whatever.

The answer causes Arec's brow to furrow, and he now looks me up and down, like he's only just seeing me for the first time.

"Looks like reconstituting's been a bit unkind, eh?" His initial hesitation at seeing me seems to have dissipated, and he steps appreciably closer to my face than is comfortable. His Ocularum Bond appears to be judging me somehow. "Is this what happens when you've betrayed your oath? You come back around like . . . this?"

He scoffs a little as he nods up at down at my pajama-bottomed body. Which, candidly, hurts my feelings a little bit. I'm just here for a physical beating, not an emotional one.

Also . . . what does he mean by *betrayed my oath*?

I brush aside the judgment (mostly) and start to ask.

"My oa—?"

"My nephew believed in you," the woman in leather says, stepping up to stand beside Arec.

"Your neph—?"

"My little nephew!" she shouts, continuing to not let me get words out. "He was a nice kid, never getting involved with *politics* and all that. Always focused, as a lad should be, on the three Rs." *The three Rs?* "Ridin', robbin', and rapin'. Like a good boy." *Okay. Not the three Rs I was thinking of, but—* "And then he fell under the sway of 'the Saviour' and all his grand ideas. And you led him to follow you to his death on the Fields of Rendalia!"

She spits in my face. Which is not only insulting, but really, really gross. I guess I had kind of a vague understanding of how unhygienic a dystopian fantasy world could be, but it feels like all of Meridia could really use a heavy loofah-ing.

But, more importantly, none of what she's on about is actually my fault. I mean, sure. I wrote all that stuff, and so . . . uh . . . in that regard, I suppose . . . But . . .

Oh, whatever! I didn't know it was actually happening to actual living beings! I'm not accountable for some rando I didn't even know existed following Carpathian to their inevitable death! Everybody get off my currently shirtless back!

"Listen," I say, trying again to talk my way out of this even though I am realizing the chances of that are in the negative integer range, "I'm sorry about your nephew, but I—"

Arec takes another step toward me, close enough that I can hear the whirling of the synthetic eye in his skull. He pokes me in my naked chest with a hairy index finger. "You got a lotta sack, Einzgear. I'll give you that."

Brittany stiffens even more rigidly beside me, and Perg appears to disappear into her hair. I find myself debating whether I should use Control and just scoot us away from here. This doesn't feel like a replication of Carpathian's initial journey. This feels like something else. Something more sinister. And punitive.

But . . . no. If Brittany's right—and she's usually right about things that go on in Riftbreaker—then I need to just go through some trials so that I can, whatever. Level Up, I guess.

Man. I never thought I'd miss the days of two weeks of vacation a year plus bennies I had when I worked for the city, but in this exact moment . . .

"I know we didn't have a lot of success teaching you a lesson about not touching Reaper property back in the day, but maybe we can still learn you something. Besides, we owe you for what you done to Arec when you met the second time . . ." Leather Lady reaches into her cut and pulls out a mace. The iron rings clink as it unfurls, and she swings the spiky metal ball around in a tiny circle.

"Well," I volunteer, feeling my brain start spinning, "I mean, first of all, I'm sorry about that last bit. If it matters, I got quite a tongue-lashing when it happened. So . . . Second! I never did sleep with anyone's wife, okay? That was . . . That was just a rumor—or, I guess, rumOUR—that . . . Doesn't matter. But, for the record, it's not really cool to call someone's wife 'property.' I mean, I know that, culturally, certain customs don't translate, but I feel like—"

That's all I get out before I see the woman draw the mace back and make to bring it smashing spiked-ball-first into my face. At which point, it will become painfully clear (again . . . literally) just how much I do or do not share the inherent toughness of Carpathian Einzgear. So if this is why we're here, to let me walk a mile in Carpathian's boots, then let's get to stepping.

But before the mace makes contact with my jaw, I hear a sound. A . . . *POP.*

And then a cry of, "*Puta mierda!*" as Perg takes the full hit of the mace to the back of his embiggened shell.

CHAPTER TWENTY-THREE

Seasons of Rebellion, Riftbreaker Book One, Chapter Eleven

Come back, you cowards! Come back and fight!" Carpathian Einzgear called out semi-coherently through his bruised and bloodied lips as Arec and the other Reapers of Agony mounted their Thundercycles and roared away from Jeomandi's Pub and Pints, the sound of their engines screaming into the night.

"Why won't he DIE?!" Arec had shouted as he leveled punishing blow after punishing blow from the mace he carried at his hip onto Carpathian's seemingly unbreakable skull.

Carpathian had wondered the same thing.

What form of Mezmer Arec and the others possessed, Carpathian did not know. But one thing that had become quite literally painfully apparent was that whatever strength and Spells the Reapers had at their disposal, they were insufficient to rob Carpathian of his life. That his own Mezmeric capacity, powered by the Heart, could stand as a fortress against a far greater assault than he had imagined.

Thump-thump. Thump-thump.

The Heart continued beating strong inside of him. Even if, at this exact moment, he might have wished it would not.

Carpathian braced himself against the doorframe, trying not to fall onto the hard, dusty ground beneath his feet. He could see—although barely, through his swollen eyelids—the gaggle of Jeomandi's frequenters staring at him. The looks on the faces he could observe were, uniformly, of stunned horror. He saw a Minotaur—a creature known for its unusually high threshold for tolerating the vile and disgusting—vomit onto a small Dwarf by its side. The Dwarf vomited in turn, causing an assembly-linelike torrent of regurgitation to take place all throughout the vehicle dismounting area.

"Son," a voice spoke from behind him. It was the voice of Clavion, the gentle barkeeper whose family Jeomandi's had been maintained by for generations, and would surely remain for generations more.

Carpathian turned to see the kindly woman, her eyes filled with sympathy, staring at him. "Yes?" he uttered. Though, given the state of his lips, tongue, and teeth, it came out sounding like "Esh?"

Clavion put her hand, softly, in the place where his shoulder once was and which was now just an empty socket, the arm having come fully disengaged from the muscles and ligaments to which it had previously been attached. Carpathian winced as he looked into her gauzy, blurry visage and forced a grotesque smile, as if to assure her he would be alright.

She nodded her head at him, slowly, and then, with a tender lilt to her voice, said, "Please, please don't ever come back to my pub again."

She then stepped back inside and closed the door in Carpathian's face, forcing him to remove his hand from the frame that had been his support, causing him thus to fall to the ground.

He lay there for a moment, wondering over the point of this . . . exercise. Wondering over why Almeister would have put him in such an awful position. The most charitable interpretation he could assign was that, perhaps, it was an attempt to show him that he was stronger than he had imagined himself. That he possessed resilience and fortitude.

That was the charitable interpretation.

The less charitable, and, at the moment, less hopeful but more probable analysis that his traumatized, concussed brain could conceive of was that, perhaps, it was to illustrate to Carpathian that he was alone. That there would be no one there for him on this journey for which he had been supposedly chosen.

Perhaps, he thought, this was merely an initial offering—an appetizer—to set the stage for the buffet of suffering and anguish that was yet to come.

It was possible, he thought, that this was an opportunity of sorts. A chance being presented to Carpathian for him to step away. Now. To reject this burden before it was too late. To separate himself from the responsibility before others might be drawn in to face consequences similar to his. Or worse.

In other words: He thought this might be his chance to give up.

And that was the moment, as he lay there in the dirt, blood and dust and spittle and tears all comingling together, that Carpathian Einzgear made a decision.

He would not give up.

He would see it through. He would prove to both himself and all those who had ever doubted him that he was capable and strong and worthy and . . . enough.

That he, Carpathian Einzgear, public conveyance conductor number seventy-six thousand, eight hundred and forty-three, was enough.

Enough to take on whatever task was foist upon him.

Enough to shoulder the burdens of this struggle and become a leader of others.

To stand for both himself and for those who could not stand for themselves.

And to exact justice upon those who might wish to do harm.

Now that the ringing in his ears was beginning to abate, and the sound of conveyor-beltlike vomiting was starting to quell, Carpathian could hear the gurgle of running water.

He lifted his head from the dirt and looked ahead to see the creek that cut through Revelation's Pass burbling along, unaware that anything at all might be the matter. Carpathian began dragging his splayed form toward the water, fingernails digging into the terrain, pulling himself fractured bit by fractured bit toward its welcoming, cooling, restorative invitation.

Upon arriving at the bank, he reached into the wash with his tired, ruptured hands and scooped up puddles of cleansing water to splash onto his face. The sensation of it hitting his wounds caused him to flinch, but at the same time, it felt to him like a rebirth. A baptism. He would now be remade in the image of the Saviour that Almeister had told him he was destined to be.

Some of the water sloshed into his open mouth, and he drank it down, relishing in the feel of the purity draining down his throat. Greedy for more, he plunged his hands in again, ready to take another gulp, when he noticed . . .

A small, delicate-looking snail sitting in his cupped palms, appearing to stare at him curiously.

Carpathian had never before been so close to a snail's countenance, so he did not know if they always looked as though they were issuing a quizzical stare or not, and thus, he was unable to determine if this was its natural mien or if there was something unique about this one.

"Hello," Carpathian mumbled aloud, fully aware that the snail could not possibly respond in kind but nonetheless feeling compelled to communicate with the tiny thing. "It looks worse than it is," he went on, in an attempt at a joke that caused him to laugh. Which, in turn, caused him to groan in pain at the feeling in his ribs.

Rather than retreating, the snail, in the most unexpected of unexpected responses, began edging its way along Carpathian's forearm. It took several long moments, but it finally reached the upper part of his bicep where his dislocated shoulder rested against his cheek. And then . . .

The snail nuzzled itself there.

Carpathian was struck dumb at the act. He blinked several times, ignoring the discomfort in his eyelids—and the rest of him, for that matter—as he contorted his neck to look at the miniature beast.

The two stared at each other for what seemed to Carpathian like a very long time, their faces illuminated by the flickering light of the sign above the tavern. The sign reading . . .

Jeomandi's Pub and Pints
"A Place Where Friends Meet."

CHAPTER TWENTY-FOUR

Holy shit, that hurt!" Perg wails as the mace-wielding Reaper falls back, the pinging of the metal spikes off Perg's shell sending her stumbling.

He's even bigger than he was in the car when he made himself large. And now, in this moment, I can see clearly—after having known him for all these years—that he has a moustache. A properly groomed, long, lush, and altogether triumphant moustache that would make Salvador Dali proud. It looks great on him, which is a feat. Not everyone can pull that off.

Still, this is not what I was expecting to happen.

"Perg!" I shout. "What are you doing?"

"Helping my boy, fool!" he says, then adds for confirmation, "That's you; you're my boy. But I'll be honest, yo! If I had to do it all over again . . . ?" He makes a groaning sound before he shakes his head from side to side in a signal of, *"I'm not so sure I'd make the same choice."*

"What's the matter, Einzgear? Can't even fight your own fight?!" Arec yells in return as he reaches for the arcanum blaster on his hip. (At least, it looks like what I described as an arcanum blaster. Could be an eldritch flintlock. Hard to tell with so much going on.)

I feel every muscle in my body tense. The Mechanical Heart starts pounding faster, which I guess I'm hoping is a good sign? Like it knows I'm about to suffer some abuse, and it's revving up for it? Hell, I dunno. I'm just making up rationales for things as they come at me.

"Time to say goodnight, false prophet," Arec says as he points the weapon at my face and . . .

And suddenly cries out, "OW! WHAT IN THE SEVEN HELLS?!" as his wrist is bent backward, and he is disarmed in one swift motion by the *other*, previously unmoving Reaper. The one wearing the cat mask.

That's strange. Why would they stop a fellow Reaper?

"I don't think they are a Reaper, Bruce," other Bruce in my head says.

"Really, Bruce?"

"Yeah, Bruce, look. They're not wearing a Reaper cut. I think they just happened to be standing here."

Huh. Brain Bruce is right. They appear to be not-a-Reaper. But that still doesn't explain why they're intervening.

Regardless, the leather-bound, mace-twirling Reaper regains her footing and lunges at Cat Mask, but Cat Mask takes the weapon by the chain, yanks it free, and then spins it around in their own hand before wrapping it fluidly around Arec's neck. His Ocularum Bond starts spinning wildly, presenting a frenzied panoply of colors as he gasps for breath.

The female Reaper makes another attempt to subdue Cat Mask, but Cat Mask points what was, until recently, Arec's sidearm at her, and she stops.

The image before me of this dreadlocked, masked figure with both arms outstretched, holding two Reapers at bay, is quite the sight. Like some sort of perverse and violent representation of the cross of salvation. (When you get right down to it, the cross *itself* is kind of a violent and perverse symbol, but that's a whole hornet's nest I don't have time to get into.)

Cat Mask yanks Arec forward, staring at him in his one good eye and whispering so quietly that I almost don't hear it, "Go," before lowering the pistol and letting the mace loose, allowing Arec to pull it free as he coughs and sputters.

"Who the hells . . . ?!" he hacks.

Then he and the leather-bound woman stare at Cat Mask, debating whether or not they should continue this fight. It takes all of about two seconds for Arec to look at me, over to Cat Mask, then back at me, and declare, "Why won't you just die FOR ONCE?!"

Then he and the woman in leather jump onto their nearby Thundercycles and, true to the name, thunder off into the still-emerging early-morning light.

There is a long, long beat as a guy in pajama pants, a woman in cutoffs and a tank top, and a three-foot-tall snail stretching its neck out from having been hit in the shell by a mace stare at a being who looks kind of like the titular character from the Predator movies. But, y'know, wearing a cat mask.

There is an odd kind of tickling in the back of my brain. Cat Mask doesn't take their eyes off me. And I don't take my eyes off them.

Then . . . they start to . . .

. . . slowly back away, disappearing around the rear side of Jeomandi's . . .

. . . and are gone.

"What? Was that?" Brittany asks. Or . . . says. It's obviously not a question as much as a declaration of confusion. Which I share.

"Yeah. I'm not sure," I reply. "Perg, are you okay?"

He continues stretching his neck as he speaks. "I feel like I need a massage. You think they got one of those inside?"

"I doubt it."

"Well, then . . ."

POP.

Suddenly, he's back to his regular snail size.

"Pick me up, girlie," he directs up to Brittany, who obliges by bending down and scooping him.

"You didn't have to do that," I tell him. "In fact, the next time someone wants to hit me with something, I need you to let them. It's the only way I'll know if I'm as, um, durable as Carpathian was."

"If that's what you want, fool," he says, slightly indignant. Then he mutters, "Try and have a homie's back and . . ." before he starts mussitating in Spanish.

"Who was that person? In the cat mask?" Brittany asks.

"I dunno," I respond. *Although that may not be completely true. But I can't be sure.*

"Do you think it was—?" she starts, clearly thinking the same thing I am.

"I don't know."

"But do you think—?"

"This game of you asking questions I don't have answers to feels like it has no winner," I tell her, feeling exhausted and battered. Even though I'm not *as* battered as I could be.

"Okay," she replies, arch. "Then I won't ask. Dick."

"Alright, fool, everybody settle down," Perg attempts to placate. "I think we're all just a little tired. And hungry. Y'know, maybe that's why we're here. To get something to eat," Perg says.

"You think we're here for food?" Brittany asks.

"I dunno. Maybe. Why not? Like, maybe the car or the Mechanical Heart or whatever knows I've only had *estúpidos* eggshells for the last three months."

So, the very—and I mean *very*—least important thing for me to focus on in this instant is Perg voicing displeasure at what I've been feeding him lately. In fact, there is an argument that nothing could be less important. But . . . I'm me. And my brain has locked onto the words, so . . .

"You don't like them? I thought eggshells were supposed to be your preferred snack."

"They're goddamn *eggshells*, fool. YOU like eating that shit?"

"But I read that—"

"You believe everything you read?"

I consider the answer, then suggest, "Before all this? Probably not. Now? Who know what's true and what isn't?"

"Fair point," he agrees. "But no, homie, they taste like . . . eggshells, I guess. I don't really know what to compare them to. I haven't had a chance to cultivate the most expansive palate."

"It actually wouldn't kill us to eat something," Brit offers. "I mean, one thing all machines have in common: they need fuel to keep themselves running."

Unbelievably, in spite of everything, and still not completely sure I'm not going to throw up as-yet-undigested pizza at some point, I do find myself kind of peckish. All this imminent danger works up an appetite.

"Yeah . . ." I finally say. "Okay. Let's go . . . see what's going on inside, I guess."

The moment we cross the threshold into Jeomandi's, I have to take a breath. It's overwhelming; all these creatures and people. A menagerie of various beings that I dreamed up in assorted instances of inspiration or madness.

There's a table where a Ridisha—which has a man's upper half but a bestial body and six legs covered in gilded fur—is locked in a debate with an exceptionally hairy Dwarf. They're both sipping on what has to be Vylian mead, a drink that glows like a fallen star.

Farther on, I see a Satyr sitting between two Gnomes, eating a meat pie. He's really tearing into that thing while his companions speak to one another from over the stretch of his back.

There are also plenty of humans. In fact, the vast majority of oxygen-based life-forms filling up the joint look to be Homo sapiens, many of them showing clear symptoms of having been cradled preciously within the womb of a land nourished by highly caffeinated, progression-fantasy-infused LitRPG java with just the tiniest soupçon of dystopian sci-fi sprinkled over the top for zest.

Elves, Dwarves, River People, bikers, Gearheads, Squee Ballers, RyderDies, warlocks, witches, concubines . . . flying monkeys . . .

"*Wow. Where's the Wicked Witch, Bruce?*"

"*Goddammit! It's not stealing! It's—*"

"*I know. It's* homage."

"*Shut up, Bruce! People like it! You don't mess with success!*"

Allll these creatures and people just . . . here. Living their lives. Totally unaware that I exist.

SCREEEEEEEEEEECH.

That's the sound that happens.

Sort of. Not literally. There's not an actual screech. It's just that, in my head, that's the kind of needle-scratching-the-record sound that occurs as everyone STOPS what they're doing and looks DIRECTLY AT US. Standing here. Like we're the guys from Delta in *Animal House* and just showed up at the club where Otis Day and the Knights are playing. Like we do *not* belong here.

And, to complicate matters further, they look angry. Not just angry like drunk, angry barflies can look by default, but like they're very specifically angry . . . at us. Or at least, at me.

We stare at them. They stare back.

"Bruce . . ." Brittany whispers.

"I know," I mutter, teeth gritted.

"Big homie . . ." Perg says.

"*I said I know!*" I grit out, louder.

It's dead quiet. A chair squeaks on the floor. Someone suppresses a cough. And then . . .

They all go back to what they were doing, arguing and drinking and being generally bawdy. Which is, more or less, exactly what happened the first time Carpathian entered Jeomandi's. I look over at Brittany and see her staring up in wonder at various neon signs flickering above the bar, ablaze with Mezmeric fire.

All of them written in languages *she* invented.

"Quorxic . . ." she marvels in a hushed whisper. And then, "*Eldrali!*" she coughs out with a gasp. "Oh my god . . ."

"Wow," I agree sincerely. Because I know how hard she worked to come up with all of the languages she did, but Eldrali in particular.

Eldrali is the "language of the abyss," spoken by the hill folk of the Unending Valley. I wanted something really complex but that would also be pronounceable by anyone reading it (and the audiobook narrator, of course) for book . . . *Wow.* I forget which one I had her create it for now, but it was . . . one of the middle ones.

Anyway.

She used a combination of her own multilingual gifts obtained from years of traveling the world as a kid wherever her mom was stationed, and some dead languages that she researched, like Coptic and Akkadian. I mean, she went all in. She even had Zooms with David J. Peterson, the conlanger who created Dothraki for the *Game of Thrones* TV series. (He offered to help craft the Eldrali language himself, but when Brittany found out what he charges, she got indignant and intensely protective, and they kind of had it out in Old Ravkan from *Shadow and Bone*. I couldn't understand what they were saying, but it sounded like it got pretty surly.)

I lean in, trying to be respectful of the moment she's having, and ask, "What do they say?"

"Huh?" She shakes herself from her word trance. "Oh. That one"—she points—"says, 'Vanar Dreambrau, sixty-five silver.' And that one says, 'You worked hard today. Reward yourself with a flagon of Rilkawing's Toxic Ale. It'll make ye' forget everything.'"

"They're . . . ads for booze?"

"Yeah," she sighs dreamily, as if she just heard the greatest love poem ever written.

Eh, I get it. It's cool to see the evidence of your hard work in action.

"How much silver we got, *ese*? A Vanar Dreambrau could really hit the spot."

I ignore Perg and continue making my way into the space. If I felt reasonably vulnerable when the Templars attacked me in my full pajama set back at my house that no longer exists—which I did—then I'm feeling pretty much a showing-up-at-school-naked level of insecurity now. Only way, way more self-conscious. Because I *am* practically naked, and this is far worse than Trig class.

(Okay, maybe not *far* worse. Trig was awful, but this is still rougher by a decent margin. I don't know by how much of a margin, specifically, because division isn't really my jam either. Honestly, I'm terrible at all math, but this is still appreciably more anxiety inducing than being naked in math class. No one had broadswords in math class. That I could see, anyway.)

Moving through the space, eyes meet mine. And it's like we have something in common. Their looks suggest that they feel like they maybe know who I am but aren't a thousand percent sure? And I feel the exact same way.

Brittany's once-more pragmatic voice breaks through my cogitating. "We need clothes."

"We?" I echo with the clear implication that it is *Bruce* who needs clothes.

"You gonna start doing that a lot, Bruce?"

"Doing what, Bruce?"

"Referring to yourself in the third person?"

"I dunno, Bruce. Maybe I was talking about you."

"Don't get cute, Bruce."

"Yes, *we*," she affirms. "We're bringing too much attention to ourselves. I think it's part of the reason people are staring at us. That and, y'know, the fact that some of them clearly recognize the remorted presence of Carpathian Einzgear in their midst."

"I'm not—"

She shoves the palm not carrying Perg in my face. "I can't even right now, bro. Not even."

I let it go.

"Maybe the Grubble can help," I say, gesturing to the bartender. "They tend to know everyone and everything. He'll probably have a bead on where we can cop some gear."

Grubbles. A species whose entire conceptualization was fueled by nothing but Red Bull and a looming deadline. Short, pebbly skinned, big, floppy ears . . . I mean, if I'm being completely honest with myself—which, generally speaking, I'm not, but in this instance, I will be—they're basically goblins.

But I've always found the caricature of how goblins are intimated in fantasy to be a bit . . . obvious. I mean, the way they look, how they come across; it's easy to suggest that they're kinda . . . Renfield-like. Desperate, over-the-top kook-a-loos. Which is such a "book by its cover" way to think of them. I wanted to subvert the trope, so instead, I made them intelligent—cunning, even—and charismatic.

They're pretty neutral parties where any political or socioeconomic or civil issues are concerned, unless there's something in it for them, explicitly. So, y'know, sociopaths. But charming ones. Real Machiavelli types, you could say. (Not to be confused with a *Makavelli* type, aka Tupac, upon whom I crafted the character of Xanaraxa, the philosopher poet. *Who I'm surely also gonna have to rescue from DONG at some point if I wanna go home. Awww, maaaaannnnn . . .)*

"Where's Clavion?" Brittany asks.

"Clavion? I dunno."

"I thought she was the only barkeeper. Having been taught the profession by her mother, Jerustus, who, herself, had learned the profession from—"

"Yeah, no, I know who Clavion is. I don't . . . Let's just . . . Come talk to the friggin' Grubble with me, okay?"

"You think that's a good idea?"

"Why?"

"I dunno. Because what's in Riftbreaker is that Jeomandi's has been in Clavion's family for generations."

"Okay."

"And now Clavion's not here."

"Okay."

"Which means that it's another perturbation."

"A perturbation?"

"Yeah."

"To what?"

"What she's saying, fool," Perg pipes up, "is that this appears to be yet another affirmation that life here in Meridia does whatever it wants, irrespective of you having influence over it or knowledge of it. And thus, it might be prudent for you to more carefully gauge the actions you choose to entertain. For, while in a book, individuals will frequently take reckless steps forward for the purposes of plot progression, in this, the real world, it is much more advisable that you employ discretion when you interact with the inhabitants of this place, i.e. formulate a clearer picture of who they are and what they're all about before you go dashing into engagement with them, especially given that you are, for all intents and purposes, no longer you, but in fact, the manifest embodiment of your creation. And one who is very much at odds with the hegemonic forces in this universe. Basically . . . look before you leap, homeboy."

"Yeah. Something like that," Brittany confirms.

"Insight?" I say to Perg.

He shrugs, insomuch as he can shrug, and replies, "I know what I know, bro."

I take a peek at the Grubble, who appears to be giving us a long, assessing stare. When he sees me see him looking, he slaps on a radiant smile.

I hesitate, thinking over Perg's insightful counsel toward caution. He's right. In the books, I'd have characters initiate actions that one probably wouldn't in life because I *needed* them to. In order to keep the story moving and keep readers invested, I had to have them look before they leapt and occasionally exhibit activities that, while not explicitly stretching the bounds of credulity, are the kinds of things that anyone with a brain and a tendency toward self-preservation would think twice about.

I give this notion its due reflection before saying, "Fair enough, but we can't just stand here forever, waiting on something to happen, so . . ." and begin walking toward the bar.

The Grubble never takes his eyes off of us as we cross the room, his forced but broad smile unwavering.

"Travelers," he says in a very "hail fellow, well met" type of a way. "Welcome to Jeomandi's. What can I get you?"

"Um, we're actually just wondering if you know where we can, uh, fetch some, um, manner of, uh, new raiment," I say, smooth as a gristmill.

His smile tightens, never quite reaching his eyes, and he says, "New vines, eh?" Then he laughs. "This here's Jeomandi's Pub and Pints, me old son, not Hardonion's House of Haberdashery."

"No, I know, I just thought you might be able to—"

"Where's Clavion?" Brit interjects. "Is she not here tonight?"

The Grubble looks at her curiously. "Clavion? Well, there's a name I haven't heard in a while. You knew Clavion?"

"Uh, yeah," Brittany says. "I used to come here. Before."

His eyes narrow, and his smile widens. "Before? Musta been long before."

"What do you mean?"

"I bought this place from Clavion probably nine, maybe ten rotation cycles ago. Just after Carpathian Einzgear had his famed row with the Reapers. Said she didn't need the headache of owning a pub anymore, how often she'd have to repair it when it would get busted up and all." He stops talking as his gaze traces me up and down, then he smiles again and adds, "But Einzgear is dead now, so at least he won't be a problem anymore, eh?!" He laughs way, *way* too obviously and slaps the bar top in the most inelegant attempt at a lie I've ever seen.

Clearly, he recognizes me. Or, not *me*, but who he thinks I must be. Or . . . whatever. Doesn't matter. The point is that it's clear he believes me to be Carpathian, just like everyone else, but for some reason is trying to act like he doesn't. *I wonder why he—*

"In any case, what can I get ye? Drink? Food?" he interrupts the thought.

Perg jumps onto the bar. "Yeah, bro, we could eat. What kind of food you got, fool?"

Taking in the small snail, the barkeeper laughs and says, "I believe we might have some Frangilonian eggshells back here somewhere."

I can see Perg's antennae droop. "Eggshells?"

"I thought your kind liked that sort of thing."

Perg turns his tiny head toward me as if he expects me to gloat or something. I put my hands up, indicating that I remain on his side and take no pleasure in someone else being casually speciesist.

"Or," the Grubble continues, obsequiously, "if that's not to your liking, we also have Rendalian buffalo wings." He points to a giant of a man—an oversized Viking-looking fellow—who is munching down on literal wings from a Rendalian Flying Buffalo. The wings don't appear to be cooked, just marinated in what looks like probably the buffalo's own blood and slapped onto a plate. "The buffalo was killed just this morning," the Grubble bartender goes on, "so its wings are still fresh."

Perg watches the Viking pick a feather out of his teeth and says, "Nah, I'm good." Then I hear him murmur to himself, "*Estúpido bar.*"

The bartender cocks his head before smiling again. "Alright. What about the two of you?"

"Um," Brittany starts, "maybe just some, uh . . ." Then, quite abruptly, she stops. Like she forgot what she was saying. "Uh . . . actually, we *should* probably get going. It's almost morning, and I'll bet Hardonion's is going to be open soon, so . . ."

"No!" the Grubble exclaims, a little overemphatically if you ask me. Then, he course corrects and smiles once again. "No," he repeats, syrupy. "No, they won't be open for hours. Let me get you all plates of nourishment and some goblets of thirst quenching. On the house."

On the house? Why? That is, in my rendering of Grubbles, very un-Grubble-like.

"No, that's okay," Brit insists. "We really need to—"

"HEY!" the massive Viking yells out. "*Goomrish nor t'shan devolkerer!*"

The barkeeper puts his finger up in the direction of the big man as he looks at us and says, "Don't go anywhere. Be right back." He smiles wider still and goes to tend to the mountain masquerading as a person.

I turn to Brit.

"Do you know what he said?"

"Yeah, he asked for more blood sauce in Staratzanish. We gotta get out of here."

"Why?"

"Because," she says, pointing behind the bar, "of that."

I look. And there, sitting next to a line of half-drained bottles of various colors and compositions, I see it. A flyer. A sheet of paper with two things printed on it:

1. Me. A picture of me, I mean. But an image of MY face. ME. Bruce Silvert. Plain as day. And not just any picture. The picture that was on my ID badge back when I still drove a bus. Dopey smile, stupid blue polyester shirt, and clip-on tie, the whole nine.

And . . .

2. Words. Right above my dumb haircut from back in the day. Words that read: "WANTED. CARPATHIAN EINZGEAR. DEAD." (No, "OR ALIVE," just, "DEAD.") And beneath the photo: "IF SEEN, DO NOT ATTEMPT TO ENGAGE! CONTACT YOUR LOCAL TEMPLAR OFFICE IMMEDIATELY."

I stare for probably a lot longer than I should, especially given the implications of what it is I'm seeing, but I'm having a hard time wrapping my mind around it.

"What the . . ." I start to question, but before I can get out whatever curse was about to pass my lips, Brittany grabs my arm, scoops Perg off the bar, and shuttles us toward the rear door, the one Almeister snuck out of when he locked Carpathian in here to battle the Reapers the first time. And, also just like Carpathian then, upon arriving at the door, we find it barred and locked.

"Shit!" Brittany says as quietly as she can.

"Maybe . . ." I start, trying to think it through. "Maybe we can make it out the front."

"Seriously?"

"I dunno! I don't have a better idea. Perg, you got anything?"

"Insight only extends to amplified impressions about certain mechanics or possible intentions within the construct of the broader realities here, not how to do an impromptu jailbreak from a roadhouse bar. Sorry, homie."

Before I can say anything else, I wince as I get a cold chill up and down my bare torso. Not for any emotional or psychological reason, but for a completely terrestrially physical one.

The front door of Jeomandi's has just opened, letting in a shaft of burgeoning dawn's light and a gust of unusually brisk morning air. It makes my skin pebble.

And looking in that direction, I *do* then get a belatedly emotional shiver running up and down my naked back. Because in the doorway, silhouetted by the early-morning sunshine, I see that . . .

. . . a Templar has just entered Jeomandi's Pub and Pints.

CHAPTER TWENTY-FIVE

What the hell do we do?" Brittany asks.

Looking around, I notice another door. One that I had no idea existed nor have any idea where it leads, but it's the only thing I can see right now that might lead anywhere, so . . .

"Here," I say quickly, "over here."

I jerk them both with me and grab at the handle. It opens! We sneak breezily and quietly through to find ourselves in . . .

. . . a tight, cramped, windowless storage room that smells like rotting meat and pickle juice.

"Oh, fuck," Brittany says, gagging.

I gag too. Because it is unbelievably awful. (But on a tiny, bright note, when I gag, it just tastes like regular old bile with no pizza afterburn. So, y'know, small victories.)

There's a crack in the doorway by the hinges. We press our faces against it in an attempt to take in more regular, foul-smelling Jeomandi's funk than the supercharged, foul-smelling, makes-you-want-to-kill-yourself funk of the storage room. It doesn't really work, but it does give us the marginal advantage of *kind* of being able to see what's going on outside? But it's only a sliver of a view. I can't see all the way to the front door, so I don't know precisely where the Templar is.

"Perg," I start. "Can you get a better view?"

"Bet," he replies. "Post me up, girlie?" Brit lifts him to a place where he can fit pretty much his entire head through. "Damn, fool," he says.

"What? What is it?"

"I think that Templar Elf saw us."

"Elf?" I ask. "She's not an Elf."

"Really? You sure?"

"Yes, I'm sure. I saw her. She's not an Elf."

"What is she?"

"An Ishilden."

"An Ishilden?"

"An Ishilden."

Ishilden. One of my most prized creations. Tall, slender creatures with pointed ears, eerily beautiful no matter their gender.

Stunning. Original. Unmistakable.

"Okay, well, I mistook her for an Elf," he says.

"How could . . . ? She's *blue*. Elves aren't blue."

"I dunno. I just figured she's a blue Elf. Because, you know, she looks like an Elf. But blue."

"This conversation feels unimportant and stupid!" Brittany admonishes. "The important thing is that she's a fucking *Templar*."

"And that she saw us," Perg adds.

"How do you know she saw us?" I ask.

"Because she's heading this way."

Shit.

My mind is racing for a million reasons; mostly, though, about how is my old work ID photo on a WANTED poster sitting behind the bar at Jeomandi's Pub and Pints in Meridia? Like, HOW does that happen?

Also, *why*? Is *this* why we've been brought here? Brittany's theory about the System guiding us where we need to go in order to gain the necessary Abilities to make things right . . . Is *this* actually what that entails? Not just fighting some Reapers or whatever, but . . . this?

Maybe . . .

Maybe it's more high stakes than when Carpathian went through it the first time because the *world* is more high stakes. Maybe that's it? The first time through, DONG and the Super Vizier were just beginning their ascent to power, just like Carpathian. So, they all grew in concert with one another, matching each other, Carpathian countering their ever-darkening evil with his ever-purifying light.

But now, they still have their power, and I . . . or . . . no. *No. Just because people think I'm him and . . . my . . . face is on a WANTED poster doesn't mean it's true. So . . .*

They still have their power, and *Carpathian* has been stripped back down to almost zero. So maybe, in order to get to where he . . . I . . . we . . . need to get to, maybe we're going to have to face stiffer odds and overcome greater obstacles. So . . . So the System is creating scenarios with higher risk. Because it's setting us up for success more rapidly.

Makes sense.

Kind of.

In any case, I need to think about how to play this, because I feel like confronting a fully armed Templar with an order to capture Carpathian, "dead only," is still maybe a bit of a high-risk challenge for the state I find myself in. So, I should at least try and figure out how to use what we have available to us now to get us out of here, master-strategist style. That's a way to gain experience as well.

For sure I can use Control to try and slow things down for a moment or two. And now that we know Perg can grow in size . . . Well, I'm actually not sure how that helps us in this situation exactly, but it's something. And Brit . . . well . . . If we can puzzle out precisely *how* she can summon up a Tentasaurian, then it's possible that—

"I think maybe I was wrong," Brittany says, putting a stop to my escape-plan spitballing.

"Wrong about what?" I ask.

"I dunno. All of it?"

"All of—?" I don't even get out the word "what" before Perg says, "Oooooh shit, girlie. I feel you. I mean, like, literally. I can feel what you're thinking."

"You can?" I ask. "What's she thinking?"

"You can?" she also asks.

"Yeah," he replies. "I think so."

"Well, I can't," I volunteer. "So does somebody wanna—?"

"Can *you* tell if I'm right or not?" She ignores me.

"Nah," Perg says. "Not really. I think I probably need more exposure or evidence or . . . I'm not sure. It's a new trip; I'm still figuring it all out. I mean, shit, I only just learned I can get big a little while ago."

"Yeah, can somebody tell me what you're talking—?"

"I think the System might have different intentions in bringing us here than I originally thought," Brit says.

"Really? That's crazy, because that's sort of what I was just thinking."

"You were?"

"Yeah. I was thinking that it—"

"Might actually be trying to fuck us up."

I kind of gnaw at my bottom lip for a second before saying, "No. No. In fact, that's . . . almost exactly the *opposite* of what I . . . Wait, what are you saying?"

"I'm saying that I'm wondering if its intent is *not* to help you—us—climb the ladder back up to OP or whatever so that you can clean up the messes that got made, but is really to . . . I dunno . . . punish you for making them."

I shake my head a little bit involuntarily because I'm not sure I completely understand what she's suggesting. "*Punish? Me?* I don't . . . What are you—?"

"She's saying that you jacked shit up, fool," Perg weighs in. "You set up a world where your guy, Carpathian, was supposed to save people and bring about justice and all that shit. But instead, what happened was that he led thousands of people to their deaths, betraying a bunch of his most ardent believers, and then he just dipped. She's saying maybe the System is pissed. Maybe it's out to take the person responsible, the real one—you—and make them pay for what they did to this place. That is what you're saying, right, girlie?"

Brittany nods. "Yeah. Yeah, that's what I'm saying."

I feel myself starting to hyperventilate, the beating of the Mechanical Heart getting louder.

"Shh, fool," Perg says. "You need to quiet that shit down. We're supposed to be hiding."

"But . . . But, no," I manage out. "No, that's not . . . No, no way. I mean, the Heart is itself a personalized embodiment of the System *inside* Carpathian—me. So that would mean that, if what you're saying is true, then . . ."

"Then the call is coming from inside the house!" Brittany gasps. (Which, while kind of a stretched metaphorical reference to the 1979 horror classic *When a Stranger Calls*, still carries enough impact to freak me out as well.)

I gasp too, which results in me breathing in some of the putrid air, and I gag. Pulling myself together and putting my face close to Brittany's and Perg's near the crack in the door, I whisper, "You really think that the point in us having been brought here could be for me to pay some kind of price for the things Carpathian did?!"

"Goddammit, Bruce!" Brittany barks stiffly, balling her fists. "For all intents and purposes, for better or worse, you ARE Carpathian. That picture on the WANTED poster under the name Carpathian Einzgear is not of some random guy we've never seen before. It's a picture of YOU. Carpathian did the things he did—or didn't do things he should have—because it's what *you* made him do or not do. You're one and the same, bro! Stop dodging responsibility!"

Before I can respond or dig too much deeper into the theorizing part of this little distraction to our existing circumstance, Perg draws our focus back to the matter at hand.

"Oh shit!" he exclaims. "The not-Elf Templar *chica* is at the bar! She's talking to the Grubble barkeeper homie!"

"What are they saying?" I ask, momentarily less interested in the mind-bending, existential accountability debate I'm having with Brittany.

"I can't hear them," Perg replies, "but it's pretty animated. The Grubble has his hand out. Which, y'know, not even using Insight—just guessing—is probably something like, 'Where my reward money at, homegirl?'"

"What's she doing?" Brittany asks. "The Templar?"

"She's just chilling, letting him rant. Like, just lying back in the cut and—OH SHIT!"

"What?! What's happened?!" That's me.

"She just sawed fool in half with a sword! Like, SHRVOOM at a diagonal, and my man is now in two separate Pythagorean-ass slices of Grubble on the deck, fool!"

"What?!"

"What's happening now?" Brittany asks.

"Now she's kind of looking around at everyone else in the place."

"What are they doing?" Me asking.

"Nothing. Just . . . Oh, okay, now they're pointing."

"At what?" Brittany says.

"Us. They all just pointed in our direction at the same time like they choreographed the shit." Perg jerks his head back inside the room. "And now she's marching toward the door. So. It hasn't technically been *nice* knowing you, but it's been real."

"Shit!" Brittany shouts, retching a bit at having opened her mouth so wide. "Quick! Barricade the door!"

"You want to make us be *more* stuck in here?" Perg asks. "I mean, if we get sliced in half, at least we'll die quick, as opposed to suffocating in this room with the smell of a pig's butthole stuck in our nostrils forever." (I want to ask how he knows what a pig's butthole smells like, but, again . . . priorities.)

I try to think, but my brain seems to be malfunctioning because the only thing that comes out of my mouth is, "What kind of sword?"

"What?" Perg asks.

"What kind of sword is she carrying? Did you get a look?"

"Damn, fool. I dunno! How'm I supposed to know what fantastical weapon-of-slicing the person who is not an Elf, *but most definitely is*, is packing? I ain't got no Blade Master Ability."

"You know that there's such a thing as a Blade Master Ability?" Brittany asks.

"Apparently!" Perg shouts.

"Why, Bruce? Why does it matter?" Brittany continues.

There is a jiggling at the door handle, and we all jump backward, propelling ourselves even deeper into the chamber of noxious odor.

"Saviour?" the Ishilden Templar says in a high, clipped tone. "Saviour? I'm going to need you to open the door so that I might . . . um . . . well . . . I was going to say, 'have a word,' but everyone knows that's just a euphemism for, 'run you through and then fractionalize your lifeless body,' so . . . can you open up? Please?"

"She's courteous," Perg says. "That's something."

"Why, Bruce? Why does the type of blade matter?" Brittany asks again.

"If we know what kind of weapon she's carrying, it might give us a hint as to what type of Mezmer she possesses. And, given what we have at our disposal, if we knew that . . ." I trail off.

"What?!" Brittany urges.

"Given what we have at our disposal, if we knew that . . . we'd . . . probably still die. But we'd die informed. I dunno! I'm just saying shit!"

POUND, POUND, POUND.

A heavy, Templar-gloved banging at the door is followed by, "Saviour! Open up! It's been a long week; we've been on high alert since you went missing. I just want to have a shower, a goblet of Vanar Dreambrau, and put my feet up. *Both* of 'em. We heard what happened with Kickelmustron earlier."

Kickelmustron? Beefy! That's his name.

"*Oh, that's ironic, huh, Bruce? 'Cause he won't be kicking anything again! Elmustron or otherwise! Huh? Huh? Amirite?*"

"*This is not the time for wordplay, Bruce!*"

"*Any time is a time for wordplay, Bruce. Don't be such a killjoymustron*".

"I have an idea!" I exclaim.

"What?!" Brit asks, frantic anxiety almost choking off the word.

"CloakRender."

"You wanna go on a coke bender?" Perg asks. "Not the time, fool."

"No." I can't believe I have to clarify. "CloakRender. I can go invisible and sneak by her."

"Great for you," Brit replies. "What about us?"

"No, listen, if she comes in and doesn't see me, it should confuse her for at least long enough to allow me to get behind her and take her out," I proclaim with an amount of excited certainty that is massively unearned.

Brittany does not appear to share my enthusiasm, but with no better options on the table, says, "Yeah, okay. Let's try it."

I take a breath and try to touch in with the Heart. I don't actually know if "touch in" is the right way to describe it, but it's the best way I've got at the moment. I can feel it beating, and it seems like I'm connected with it.

I close my eyes and try to attach, specifically, to the Aetherpulse channel I now possess. (If we survive, Brittany's gonna have a field day cataloguing my All-Type abilities.)

POUND, POUND, POUND.

"Last chance, Saviour! I don't condone destruction of property, but I will break down this door if I have to!"

She'll slice the owner of the place in half but draws a line at property destruction? Seems like someone's priorities need realignment.

"Bruce . . ." Brittany urges.

"I'm on it. I'm on it. Hold on. Just . . ." I breathe out, breathe in, take one last, meditative inhale, and hear Brittany gasp.

"Bruce, it worked."

"Really?"

I ask because I don't feel any different. But then, I hold my hand up in front of my face and see that . . . it's not there.

Instead, floating in the air where the flesh of my palm should be, I see the words:

CloakRender: [Activated]

CHAPTER TWENTY-SIX

Oh shit, homie! Where'd you go?!" Perg exclaims.

"Ohmigod," I bark back. "You can't see me?"

"No," Brit says. "You literally just vanished before our eyes."

"Okay, okay, wow, okay, then let's let her in and—"

Before I can utter another syllable, *BOOM!* The door fairly well explodes. Just disintegrates from the violent blow dealt by . . .

Oh shit.

It's a spellsword. Son of a . . . The Ishilden is holding a damn spellsword.

As if my expectation of how absolutely boned we are couldn't get any more . . . uh . . . expectant . . . the sight of the spellsword disabuses me of whatever illusions I might have harbored.

The spellsword is another extremely obvious nod to the lightsaber, just like the fireblade, I suppose. (And, I know, I know. Now I'm stealing from—um, *paying homage to*—myself. But lightsabers are really cool weapons! Everybody leave me alone!)

One of the differences between a fireblade and a spellsword, however, is that whereas the fireblade channels one very specific type of Mezmeric force—Flame Energy—the spellsword uses the Mezmer Type of the *user* to draw its power. Which means, of course, owing to the rules that govern this place, there's no way to tell what type of Mezmer is inside the blade unless you know what the wielder's Mezmeric core is all about or until you get hit by it. At which point, it really doesn't matter anymore.

The spellsword pulses with energy, casting an eerie green glow around the room.

Green. Green. A green glow. Green might indicate . . . Shit. I can't remember. I wonder if Brittany—

"In the name of Kentavion, it smells like a pig's anus in here!" the Templar proclaims, covering her nose with her bracer.

How do so many people know what a pig's—? Whatever. Doesn't matter. Another time.

The Templar lowers her arm from in front of her nose and cocks her head to one side then the other. And that's when I remember . . . she can't see me.

I splay my fingers in front of my face and wave my palm up and down.

Nothing. No reaction from her at all. *Ha! She can't SEE ME!*

I begin moving carefully to try and get around her back without giving myself away.

"Where is he?" the Templar asks.

"Uh . . . who?" Brittany responds innocently.

"Don't toy with me, Nightwind! You're next, as soon as I dispatch Einzgear, which I reckon will tender me some much-needed time off. Thinking of going to the Shore of Edenswell, in fact. Maybe rent an overwater bungalow. So where is he?"

I continue creeping carefully in her direction and, just like when Control is active, I can hear the *thump-thump* of the Heart letting me know that the CloakRender Spell is working.

"I, uh . . . don't know," Brittany replies, vamping and looking around. She's not lying; she literally doesn't know where I am at this exact instant.

Unfortunately, it is in this same exact instant that I hear, *Schwink!*

And . . .

CloakRender: [Time Expired]

. . . pops up in front of my face.

Are you kidding? It lasted barely ten seconds!"

"Yeah, well, sorry, Bruce. But you knew there were time limitations when you picked it."

"But not ten seconds!"

"What do you want from me? I know as little as you do about—Oh shit! She sees you!

I've barely taken two steps forward when I spy my own raised hand reappearing before my eyes, coming back into full, corporeal opacity. Which is, to say the least, disappointing.

The Templar blinks and then looks at me, confused. "What are you doing? What's that you're doing with your hand there?"

I continue to give it a half-hearted wave and say, with a deflation I cannot hide, "You can't see me?"

The Ishilden considers then replies, "In fact, I can."

"Yeah, no, I know. I just . . . It's a catchphrase this wrestler used to—"

She points the spellsword directly at me, and I stop talking.

"Well . . ." She smirks, a bitter smile on her lips. "I have to say, this is not how I imagined you would present yourself." She looks me up and down, disappointment on her face. She looks at Brittany and Perg in a similar manner. Like she was kind of excited to confront the World Saviour and his cohorts, and now she almost feels sorry for us. "Looks like someone's not as mighty as they used to was, is they?"

Putting aside my desire to correct the horrible grammar, I try to think what I can possibly do. Maybe . . . Maybe if I lean into the whole WWE bravado thing, I can bluff our way out of here. It's a terrible idea, but at least it's an idea, as opposed to just standing here getting spellsworded into oblivion.

"Alright," I growl, affecting a very SummerSlam Promo kind of voice. "Listen, it doesn't have to go this way, Ishilden. You can walk out of here today, or they can carry you out." The expression on Brittany's face is one of, let's call it, horrified worry. "Just . . . Just let us leave, Templar. You do that, and . . . and . . . and we'll let you live." I add an, "Oooh, yeah," for no particular reason.

She stares at me quizzically for a long moment before finally saying, "Yeah, alright."

"*Holy cats, Bruce, it worked!*"

Then she begins striding into the room, lifting the spellsword up to attack as she sighs, "Let's just be done with this foolishness."

"*Oh no, it didn't work! Uh-oh! Quick, suplex her off the top turnbuckle!*"

It takes her all of three paces to land in front of me with her arm raised above her head. This is about to be over in less than a second, but before she's able to strike . . .

ZZZZZWWWWWAAAAAHHHHHMMMMM.

Control: [Activated]

Thump-thump. Thump-thump.

I'm not sure if I did that this time or if the Heart did it on its own, since there's no additional Notification beneath it, but right now, I don't care.

The spellsword is coming down slow. Slower than slow. I would say *glacially*, but given how climate change has—

"*Not the time for pontificating, Bruce!*"

"*My bad, Bruce.*"

It's *veeerrry, verrrrry* slow, is my point.

"Briiiiit," I say, "greeeeeeeeeeen."

"Greeeeeeeeeeen? Whaaat dooo yooou meeeaaan?"

Thump-thump. Thump-thump.

"The tyyyyype of Meeeeezzzmer sheeeee's uuuuusing. Dooooo yooooou knooooow whaaat iiiiit iiiiis?"

The blade, while slow, is still moving in my direction, and Control, while a welcome addition, is still not stable enough to last for any amount of time that would allow us to have a lengthy ponder over what type of Mezmer might be what. So, if Brit doesn't know right off the top of her head . . .

"IIIII dooooon't knooooow riiiiight ooooooff theeeee toooooop ooooof myyy heeeeeaaad," she replies. Painfully slowly.

Shit. If she knew for sure what it was, I might be able to determine if I thought I could survive taking a hit from it. Because either Brittany's right and the System is out to absolutely rail us, or I'm right and this is all just a more high-octane version of what happened to Carpathian at Jeomandi's the first go 'round.

Thump-thump.

If it's the former, then nothing matters, and we're cooked anyway, but if it's the latter . . .

Thump.

If it's the latter, then . . . I dunno. Then I might just be able to take the bludgeoning from the spellsword and survive. If the Heart makes it possible for me to endure a pummeling from the right kind of Mezmer, I could absorb the blow and then use Control once more to, I dunno, drop-kick the Templar in the face.

Thump.

And then, Bob's your uncle, we could get out of here before she'd be able to ready the spellsword for another go.

Thump.

I can't keep running forever. At some point, I'm going to have to stand and fight. That was what Almeister was trying to teach Carpathian back when he locked him in Jeomandi's the first time.

Thump.

But if I'm gonna do this, I gotta decide now. The Heart continues to drain, and the more time I use up, the longer it'll take to refill so that I can use Control again. Shit.

Shit, shit, shit, shit, shit shit shit.

To hell with it. Nothing ventured, nothing . . . something.

"Bruuuuuce?" Brittany asks, still slow and languid. "Whyyy dooo yooou waaaaant tooooo knooooow?"

SHWOOOOOOOOOOOMMMMMPPP.

GAAAAAAAAAAAAAAAAAAAASPPPPPPPPPP.

I take in a deep breath, less this time because I need to and more because I'm preparing myself for what's about to happen.

And that's when—just as my lungs fill with oxygen and the world resumes its relentless tempo—I hear Brittany screaming, "BRUCE!"

. . . And feel the blade of the spellsword smash hard into my skull.

CHAPTER TWENTY-SEVEN

*B*ruce*?*"

"*Who's that? Who's there? Bruce? That you?*"

"*You're okay. You're okay. It's all going to be fine. You're okay.*"

Just like back in Bell's View, before we escaped, the voice sounds kind. Gentle. Or rather, *I* sound kind and gentle. To myself. I guess.

"*Everything's going to be alright, Bruce. I promise.*"

"*Why are you being so nice right now?*" I ask myself.

"*Because you need it.*"

"*I* need *it? What does that—?*" I start, but as also happened the last time I attempted to get into it with my self-affirming other half, I am interrupted by a different voice calling my name. One that's very much not inside my head.

"BRUCE!" Brittany yells a second time.

"OW!" I now hear myself shouting as my awareness returns and (what I can only assume is) blood pours from the top of my shattered cranium down into my eyes, blotting out my vision. But, at least I can hear myself calling out in pain, which I guess is a good sign?

"What are you doing?!" Brit bellows.

"I'm . . . testing to see if I can withstand a hit from . . ." I put my hand to my face to touch the blood. It's not as sticky and hot as I was anticipating. And, for that matter, it's not really . . . red. Huh.

And that's when I realize, it's not blood in my eyes.

It's . . .

Oh, gross!

It's pickle juice!

Rancid, putrid, fetid pickle juice!

Oh, god! And it's in my mouth!

"Ach! Ach! Ach! Pttt! Pttt! Pttt!" But of course, all spitting like that does is cause me to take in even more pickle juice than if I had just kept my mouth closed. "What happened?! What's happening?!"

It's hard to see because the DISGUSTING PICKLE JUICE(!) IS IN MY EYES, but I hear a CRASH! and then the Templar yelling, "Oh my gods!" in kind of a disgusted way.

Barely lifting open my eyelids, I can sort of make out . . .

The Templar has somehow been knocked over and smashed into the shelving that houses the unholy brine and, it would seem, racks and racks of who-knows-how-long-it's-been-sitting-out-and-decaying meat, with flies the size of hummingbirds circling all around it. She continues screaming and wailing, slashing at the air with her spellsword, which continues pulsing with green Mezmer.

As I have said before, never underestimate the power of being able to ick someone out.

Blasts of Mezmeric energy slash forth with her wanton hacking, and I have to duck to avoid one of the jolts hitting me in the side of the head. And it's when I duck that I come face-to-face with . . . Perg.

Big Perg. Even bigger than he was outside when he embiggened. Like, almost-eye-level-with-me big. Just over six feet tall.

"What did you do?!" I shriek.

"I saved your bacon bits, fool! I pumped myself up at exactly the right time and *blocked* old girl's chop-chop with my shell shield, homie. Again."

"What?"

"Hells yeah. *And*," he goes on, "an additional unintended but most decidedly *asombrosa* consequence is that the power generated by my sudden embiggening busted shit up in here, yo!"

"But I need to— I'm trying to— If you—!"

I'm attempting to explain that if I'm ever going to get anywhere in this world, I have to start taking some hits! Or at the least, I need to fight my own battles and not have Perg or whomever jump in every time. I mean, Perg has clearly been rewarded for having taken the mace blow outside; he's already twice as big as he was before. I'll bet when he gets to a Pulse Well, it'll verify that he jumped up, I dunno, maybe even a whole Level just from that one act alone. At this rate, everybody around me is gonna wind up all fancy and OP in no time, and I'm still gonna be . . . RP, I guess. Regular P. And nobody wants to go through life RP. Might as well stand for "real pathetic."

I grimace through the gush of foulness spilling down my face and abruptly realize that the sensation I *thought* was the spellsword crashing into my dome was actually one of the pickle jars that must have fallen when Perg *popped* into his supersize self and disrupted the fragile order in this chamber of hellscape foodstuffs.

"It *tastes* like a pig's anus as well!" the Templar shouts, likewise attempting to spit out onto the floor whatever evil has made its way into her mouth.

Okay, I'm sorry. I just have to know. HOW does she know what a pig's anus TAS—?

"C'mon!" Brit shouts, grabbing at my arm.

Yanking me up, she tugs me away, and we dart out of the room of digestive horrors and out into the (comparatively) welcome air of Jeomandi's main drinkin' and fightin' area, where pretty much everybody has stopped the drinkin' they were doing to watch all the fightin' going on.

It's worth noting that when I say "we dart" out of the storage room and into the primary part of the pub, I do literally mean *we* dart. *We*. Dart. All three of us.

What I'm saying is that Perg is moving just as fast as me and Brittany. Maybe faster. In this, his enlarged state, my man has some friggin' *wheels*.

We get about halfway across the room when the front door crashes open once more and in storms another figure. Another Templar, to be precise.

"Cosma! What's happening in here? Did you get Einz—?" That's as much as he gets out before seeing me, Brit, and Perg hustling his direction and immediately pulls big, chunky gloves from his belt and yanks them on. They ignite with an *orange* glow, and I realize, of course, that they are Mezmerated chunky gloves.

Ah, shit. Orange, orange, what does orange . . . ? I think as he thrusts his gloved hands toward us and calls, "Don't move another step, false prophet!"

Before I can think another thought, there is an *eruption* compelled into existence by the Templar's protracted fist. Not an eruption of flame, but of earth. A spear of stone explodes from the floor directly in front of us, showering the room with chunks of rock and debris.

Oooh. Orange is Stoneheart Elemist. That tracks.

That's the term I coined for those like him who can control geological elements. Stonehearts deal with earth, shaping it to their will, a facet of lore I'd been pretty proud of if only for what I thought of as a boss naming convention. Now, however, I wish I had named them Softhearts and had them control only plush toys. Next time . . .

"Oh, shit!" Brit shouts, stopping in her tracks before she collides with the stalagmite, causing me to smash into her back. Perg, however, doesn't slow himself in time and winds up skidding directly into the giant Viking fellow, who appears to be the only person in here who is nonplussed by the mayhem and is content to continue chowing down on his buffalo wings.

That is, until Perg bangs into the table, spilling the wings and the blood sauce all over the floor. It's at that point that the giant notices the disruption, stands to his full, giant-y height (which has to be at least nine feet), nearly battering his horned helmet against a chandelier, and bellows out, "*Razjnazzee, faltroom eikdeveyeli!*"

"What did he say?!" I ask Brit again.

"He says he just got back from a month-long journey to the Ardendale Lands and that it was a challenging and brutal time, and he's been longing for Rendalian buffalo wings for weeks, and now that he has them, he just wants everybody to shut up so he can eat in peace!"

"He said all *that*?"

"Staratzanish is a very efficient language!"

The Viking smacks Perg out of the way as he moves toward the recently entered Templar.

"Perg!" I shout as his shell collides with the bar, cracking the wood but looking as though the impact has left his shell intact.

"Damn, bro!" Perg shouts in the direction of the Viking. "Shit was an accident! It wasn't personal, fool!"

But it seems as though the Viking is, in fact, taking the upending of his meal quite personally as he looks around trying to determine who he wants to tear limb from limb first. His head pivots back and forth from me and Brit to the newly entered Templar. I don't know if he eeny meeny miny moes it or if it's just that

Brit and I look like we wouldn't put up enough of a challenge, but for whatever reason, the Viking chooses to take up his grievance with the Stoneheart.

"Stay back, you," the Templar warns, pointing his gloved fist at the mountain. "This ain't got nothing to do with you. Walk away and—"

But that's all he's able to say before the Viking wraps his hand around the man's throat and—

POOOOOOOOOOF!

And nothing. Because before he can do anything else, an irradiating blast of green Mezmer hits the Viking in the back, electrocuting him where he stands, causing his body to jerk and sizzle and boil and then, after an agonizingly long moment, kind of . . . well . . . *erupt* into sections of Viking that splatter all over Jeomandi's. And I do mean *all* over. No one is spared being caked in Viking residue.

Oh. Right. I remember now. Green is indicative of Scorchheart Mezmer. Because in The Green Mile, that's what happened to poor John Coffey when he was put in the electric chair. Bit of a circuitous route to take for that particular homage, but it is, apparently, quite effective.

"Fucking gross!" Brittany yells. I would say I feel for her, but as I am now covered in both the devil's pickle juice and Viking entrails, I'm finding it hard to work up the sympathy for anyone but myself as far as feeling oogy goes.

And, yet once more, I find myself with a decision to make. We have a Templar in front of us, a Templar behind us, and a bar full of other miscreants who, given how pissed it would seem everyone is at Carpathian (not to mention the apparent bounty on his head), are not going to risk their lives, happy instead to watch the show. So the way I see it, I have a couple of options:

1. I can try and use Control once more to facilitate some kind of escape for me, Brit, and Perg. Except we're pretty far from the door, and I don't know if there's enough slowdown in the Control tank for us to make it out.

When I was in the Interlocutrix, I had the option to upgrade Control with a Pace Aberration augmentation Spell, which would have stepped me further in the direction of being able to move at a more normalized speed than everyone else stuck in the time dilation; that's what Carpathian did back when he first started upgrading his Spells. But I needed goddamn CloakRender to go on the Quest, so . . .

2. I can do what I was trying to do a moment ago: take the hit and see if I can withstand the trauma. Then, if I *don't* die, I can probably use the moment it takes for the spellsword to reset to activate Control and extend the amount of time I can *sustain* CloakRender, and then, assuming that works, hope I can a) somehow get close enough to disable the Templars, or b) at least create enough of a distraction to allow Brit and Perg to make it out of here.

I realize that in the second scenario, my chances of taking a dirt nap are exponentially increased, but . . . well . . . unlike in the books, where I could always manufacture a way of getting Carpathian out of sticky situations by, I dunno, having some unexpected back door open up for him in the form of another character arriving (or, in some cases, an actual back door), I've got no moves here. And here's the thing: If it's a choice between shitty odds of saving all three of us versus slightly less shitty odds of saving at least two-thirds of us . . . I gotta go with that one.

I'll either survive and know that I can—presumably being rewarded for my troubles with some kind of enhancements or advancements or enchantments or . . . other kinds of -ments in the process—or . . .

Or I'll not survive, and either get remorted or not. Because I already have been.

But whatever the ultimate outcome, at least Brit and Perg will have a chance to make it out of here and to, I hope, safety.

Honestly, it's not even a debate.

So. Here goes marginally less than nothing, I suppose.

I feel in my pocket for my keys, my old house set that is on the clip with the Panamera fob. My fingers find them and, weaving them through my knuckles, I yank them out of my pajama pants pocket and start waving my fist around in the air, shouting, "Don't come closer!"

To my great wonder, both of the Templars jump back.

"Careful, Cosma! He has a weapon!" the Stoneheart shouts.

The Ishilden—Cosma—squints her eyes and leans in to see. "Boff, you idiot! It's just a vehicular ignition device!"

"What?" Boff shouts back.

Cosma sighs. "Keys! He's holding a set of keys!"

"Am I?!" I proclaim, trying a different version of the only thing I know how to do in situations like this, which is to attempt to put *just* enough doubt in the mind of the person threatening me to make them wonder if I'm more badass than I appear. Or, at least, crazier; gotten me out of more than one bar fight over the years. Might as well dance with the horse that brung ya. "Am I?!" I shout again, louder. "You sure they're not some type of special keys of reckoning gifted to me by the gods? You willing to bet your life on it? Huh? You wanna get nuts?! Do ya?! Well then, let's get nuts!"

Cosma stares at me for a long moment. The whole pub has gone quiet, save for the *drip-drip-drip* of the Viking's viscera hitting the floor from all over. Then, after what feels like five minutes but can't be more than five seconds, she says, in the same tired voice with which she uttered it before, "Yeah. Alright."

. . . And blasts the shit out of me with a thrust of Scorchheart power from the tip of her spellsword.

CHAPTER TWENTY-EIGHT

B*ruce . . . ? C'mon inside, boy. Dinner's ready.*"

"*Five more minutes, Dad? Please? I'm just about to escape from the clutches of the evil prince of—*"

"*Bruce Thomas Silvert, no you're not. You're hiding in the bushes, probably getting deer ticks on you! Stop acting a fool, get your butt in the house, and wash yourself up for dinner. Don't make me come drag you in here and put a tan on that hide of yours. I'll do it, Bruce.*"

"*I know. I know. I just—*"

"*Now, boy.*"

"*Okay, Dad. I'm sorry . . .*"

I don't know what it is about getting hit by the Scorchheart Mezmer that makes my mind go there; it feels incredibly random. But as I look down at the smoking, charred area on my left arm where the skin is bubbling and popping and burning in a way I've never imagined the idea of even considering the possibility of perhaps feeling this kind of pain, it's the memory that pops up.

From my shoulder all the way down to my wrist, my arm looks like it's been ripped off, put on a spit, and slow-roasted all day for tonight's luau. In contrast to the smooth, baby-fresh flesh of the rest of my naked torso, which only recently had the benefit of a grade-A seaweed wrap at New Seasons Spa and Salon (ask for Melissa), the arm is particularly hideous.

Gonna take a lot more than a talented level-three aesthetician to sort this situation out.

"Bruce!" Brittany shouts at the same time Perg yells, "Big homie!"

They both start dashing toward me, which is the exact *opposite* of what I want. I want them running toward the door.

Silver lining? The place I got nailed hurts like hell, but . . . I'm still alive. I took the hit. I took a blast from a spellsword that not a hundred and twenty seconds ago absolutely torched a big, bad, nine-foot Viking, and I'm still standing.

> **Congratulations! You have withstood a blow from a [Templar]'s Spellsword and lived to tell the tale! You, my friend, are made of sterner stuff than the average bear! Which is not that much of a compliment because bears are notoriously susceptible to being set aflame, but nonetheless, you've done alright! Good on you!**
>
> **Please seek a Temple of the Body, that you might Verify new Abilities at a Pulse Well!**
> **{COURTESY MESSAGE #7}**

I was right! Brit was wrong (or at least, conspiracy-minded), and I was right. The System *isn't* out to screw me. Or not as such, anyway. It's *testing* me. I'm being put through the same kinds of challenges Carpathian was, only amplified. And . . . I'm surviving.

Holy shit.

And while that's cool and all, and I'm pleased as Hi-C Fruit Punch, we need to get the flip outta here. At least, some of us do.

"Run!" I shout to Brit and Perg as they approach.

"What?!" Perg hollers back. "Bro, your arm is jacked up! You need—"

"I need you to run! I'll follow! I just . . . Just go!"

I don't have time to explain my (admittedly flawed and kind of dumb) idea for getting them out of here while I try to create a diversion by combining Control and CloakRender. (Like, why didn't I just try that *before* I took the shot?)

Because— Because I needed to know. I needed to understand how sturdy I really am and what I can handle. It feels important for me to make myself aware of how much abuse I can take.

Regardless, now that I know I'm capable of absorbing the blows, I can try to—

POOOOOOOOOOF!

"OOOOOWWWWW!"

The first sound is another flare from Cosma's spellsword making its way in my direction, and the second is the eardrum-shattering caterwaul I make as the shot incinerates my leg.

Well, not *incinerates* exactly. "Incinerates" implies that it's gone. It's not gone. It's just more that it's now seared stalks of tibia and fibula than anything resembling what I have heretofore thought of as "my leg."

My pajama bottoms, on the other hand . . . The leg of those *is* incinerated. Which, while not the worst thing about the circumstance, still totally bums me out. They were the exact shade of blue that I like, and I don't know if I'll be able to find 'em again. Man, this whole thing just gets more and more sucky.

Thump-thump. Thump-thump.

The Heart. I can hear it. I can hear it like I hear it when Control is active. But looking in the air for some kind of Notification, I see nothing. Moreover, something about this beating seems different than when Control is in effect, in the same way that time feels like it's slowing down but also in a way that's distinct from the Control Spell being put to use.

So if this isn't Control taking over, then what is it?

"*I think, Bruce, you might be dying.*"

"*Really, Bruce?*"

"*Maybe. We've never died before, so I can't totally be sure.*"

Oh my. Apologies, I believe I may have been wrong; you do appear to be an average bear. It is profoundly likely that you are now going to die. Shame. But it has been a jolly good pleasure knowing you,

and just remember as you cross over to the great beyond . . . you kind of brought this all on yourself. Morose last thought, I know, but it's honest.
{COURTESY (and possibly final) MESSAGE #8}

Oh shit. Brittany WAS right. The System is out to screw me!

Or at least confuse the shit out of me. Which, if that's its objective, then mission accomplished! Bravo on the stupefaction, I guess?

But . . . hell. It's not wrong. I suppose I kind of did bring this all on myself.

Man, it's strange. I've written about death dozens of times, maybe hundreds. I've killed many, many characters over the years, but I've never been sat in Death's waiting room myself.

I mean, yes, of course, in the broader sense, I know we're all just waiting to die all the time. That when all is said and done, life is nothing more than a brief pit stop between not having been in the first place and being no more, and that existence is less than a blip on the radar of the infinite, and the angle from which you choose to view it and how you use the time spent waiting determines for each individual what it means to be alive . . .

"Wow, Bruce. That was kind of profound."

"Thanks, Bruce. I always felt like if the book thing didn't work out, I could have made a real go of it in the fortune-cookie-writing game."

. . . but being this close to the conclusion of *my* story is different than anything I imagined.

It feels like . . . like coming in from outside when it's freezing and immediately being submerged in a hot, steaming bath. Yeah. Like that.

It's not awful, actually.

And, for deeply personal reasons, that gives me enormous comfort.

My eyelids feel heavy. Sleepy. So, so tired. And through the gauzy amber haze that now clouds my vision, I see Cosma, the Ishilden Templar, a look of venomous contentment on her face as she points her spellsword at me once more. I wonder what part of me she plans to shoot to finish me off. If the Super Vizier's intention is still to sever my body into pieces and display me around the land, she'd better pick wisely. At this rate, there won't be much of me left.

I have to kind of appreciate that she chose to take out my leg. I feel like she probably did that as revenge for what happened to Kickelmustron. At least that's what I'm telling myself. Something about believing she did it out of a dedicated attention to narrative cohesion in the midst of all this chaos is oddly reassuring.

I can hear Brit and Perg still screaming my name, but it sounds like they're calling from a great distance away. And maybe I don't hear them anymore. Maybe what I hear are just the echoes of them shouting for me in my own mind.

That's nice. To hear your friends calling for you at the end. I like that. It certainly sounds nicer than—

RN-N-N-N-N-N-N-N-N-N-N-N-N! RRRN-RN-RN-RRRN!

Which is what I hear now, and which is most definitely not an echo but very much grounded in the present moment.

What in the name of Aunt Fanny's fanny pack is that?

It's a brutal sound. Mechanical. Loud as yellow sin. Coming from just outside. And then . . .

The door bursts open with such force it nearly unhinges, and it's like a splash of cold water to the face. The violent opposite of the warm mortality bath I was enjoying. It wakes me up.

My eyes pop open wide, and I struggle to stay standing, putting most of my weight on my one, still mostly functional leg. I wobble in place and gawk like a drunk guy fighting to maintain balance as he attempts to make sense of something he sees that has startled him.

What in the hell . . . ?

With the seeming preordination of an avenging angel dispatched by some greater force to rain down unbridled retribution upon all, is a figure. A figure silhouetted by the blazing light of a new day who careens into the room, gliding across the wooden floor on their knees, sparks shooting up from their metallic knee plates, suns glinting off the futura-punk armor they wear, thick, ropey dreadlocks coasting in the air behind their head.

Blinking to try and get a handle on what I'm witnessing, I can see that this person, whoever they are, is sporting a silver feline mask.

The not-Reaper. The one wearing the cat mask. Thus, the name I've assigned them—Cat Mask. It may not be clever, but it's accurate.

What are they doing here? Why are they back? Saving my day a second time?

And that's when I notice something else that causes me to snap completely out of whatever distant dream of death I might have been having and back into a state of acute awareness in the present. (As if all the rest of what's going on wasn't enough.) Even with all the pyrotechnics on display that accompany the arrival of this emissary of ruin, what draws my attention most is not the shower of sparks or the grand, savage entrance, or even the mask itself. No, my gaze is drawn principally to their hands.

More precisely, to the dual switchsaws they're wielding.

Cat Mask twirls these lethal instruments around their index fingers, not in a showy way but with precise control, as if they're an extension of their own body. The spinning seems to defy physics, each rotation perfectly balanced. Calculated menace.

RRRN-RN-RN-N-N-N-RN!

With a motion as smooth as silk pajamas, Cat Mask swipes one of the switchsaws horizontally across the back of Boff's knees as they glide past him. The whirling chain bites through cloth and flesh like a hungry lawnmower. Bright red fountains into the air, followed by Boff's scream of anguish. He collapses in a pool of his blood like a marionette with its strings cut, arms flailing.

His outstretched hand clenches into a fist, but whatever Spell he was intending to cast fizzles out. The room quakes, and a column of stone bursts down from the ceiling, raining shards of rock and dust onto the floor.

The entire sequence, from the door flying open to the gravel falling, might have spanned only a couple of seconds, but in my mind, it has unfolded like an epic, each frame filled with intricate details that would look so friggin' cool in 70mm slo-mo that I almost forget where I am for a second, imagining myself instead sitting in a DreamLounger seat at Marcus Ronnie's IMAX, big bucket of popcorn in my lap and giant root beer at my side.

But then I am pulled back into what is currently passing for reality.

Cat Mask doesn't waste a second. They pirouette gracefully to their feet, twirling one switchsaw around their finger before aiming it at Cosma. Two shots ring out almost simultaneously. The first bullet collides with Cosma's spellsword as the Templar attempts to block, disrupting its Mezmeric energy and shattering the sword into fragments. The second finds its mark on the side of her head, and she falls, lifeless before she even hits the ground.

It all happens so quickly. Just like that, Cat Mask is the attendant who has entered the waiting room and, without ceremony, beckoned Cosma back into Death's cold, impersonal exam room.

The tavern goes silent once more, save for the fading echo of the switchsaw blasts, the idling hum of their blades, and the thud of Cosma's body crumpling to the ground. I'm unsure of what to do. I don't know who this is or why they came to save us or . . . what's going to happen to my charbroiled limbs, because they STILL REALLY HURT.

So I just stare, dumbfounded and in pain.

Goodness gracious! What a Tilt-a-Whirl that was, eh? So, I must retract my previous retraction and reaffirm that you ARE, indeed, a lucky bear! You lucky bear!
To which end . . .
Would you care to review your Standings? You've earned the right!
[Yes] [No]

Sure? I guess?
I reach out, weakly press [Yes], and this is what I see:

>**Mezmer Type:**
All-Type

>**Foundation:**
Synchron

>**Resonance Tier:**
Etherflint

Statistics:
>**Mental advanced (Please visit a Pulse Well)**

>Physical advanced (Please visit a Pulse Well)
>Aura advanced (Please visit a Pulse Well)
>Animus advanced (Please visit a Pulse Well)

>Highest Affinities:
Aetherpulse [Average]
Function [Average]
Mirrorweave [Average]

>Armament(s):
Mechanical Heart

> Inventory:
[NEW!] [2 Slots Available!]

>Abilities: [None]
[2 New Available! (Please visit a Pulse Well)]

>Spell(s):
Control
CloakRender 1
[2 New Available! (Please visit a Pulse Well)]]

I can't quite get a handle on what I'm looking at because I remain pretty out of it, but it seems like . . . like there's something odd about this set of advancements. How could I possibly have jumped several levels in each ability? That's just . . . not possible. Is it? Carpathian took FOR. EH. VER. to bump up, and he's the motherflippin' *Saviour.*

I've just read so many stories where the main character flies to the top of their class, and by the end, they're overpowered as all hell. I mean, people complained that Carpathian's ascent was too slow (it literally took two-and-a-quarter books for him to get to Ironspark, which is the next Tier up from Etherflint), but if I had gone any faster with it, I'm sure there'd have been a whole coterie of readers who would've been like, *"Oh, so I'm supposed to believe that one day, dude is a public conveyance conductor, and the next day he's friggin' Thor?"*

And, as hard as it is for me to get peace with the notion of disappointing people, I learned a while back to stop trying to appeal to *everyone*—at least as much as I'm able—because when you do that, you just wind up in some sort of creamy middle zone where you're not really doing *anything.*

And even though I don't love rubbing people the wrong way in life, the last thing I wanna be is the guy who tries to make a piece of art that people finish and then go, *"Eh. It was fine. What's for dinner?"* So I made the choices for my work that *I* would have wanted to read about.

Still and all, I'll cop to the fact that I definitely dragged Carpathian's progress out for a bit longer than I maybe would have if I had to do it over. But this? I've been here for less than one full Lunar Rotation, and I'm skipping up the daisy chain this fast?

I'm not complaining. It's just strange, is all I'm sayin'.

But whatever. I just had my whole body blown to hell and appear to have quite a bit of decent booty headed my way in return. If I can survive and make it to a Pulse Well.

I wonder if Brittany and Perg are equally well rewarded now?

Before I can spare it all another thought, Cat Mask saunters over with an appropriate amount of feline grace to stand directly in front of me. They're tall. I'm still struggling to stay upright, but giving it a fair try. I don't want to fall down in front of someone I don't know; that's a bad way to start a new relationship.

The patrons inside Jeomandi's have remained stock-still as this whole affair has played out, and they show no signs of moving now. The stunned quiet continues to fill the air. The stark, white light from Meridia's recently risen suns penetrates the dark interior of the bar, framing the figure in the cat mask, painting them in shadow. I squint and strain to try and make them out, but the light hurts. I want to know who they are. Why they're here. Why they came back. Why they seem to have crafted a rescue as they appear to have done.

But before I can make my mouth address any of these queries, they obviate the need by stepping to the side, out of the direct suns light, so that I have a better look at them. And as they raise their hand to the chin of the mask to lift it up, I see a tattoo on the back of their fist. I don't know how I missed it before, but it's easy to spy now because of how dark their skin is and how much it contrasts with the bright white of the ink that looks almost as if it's crafted from the suns' light itself.

And seeing it, the suspicion I had about who this might be is triggered anew.

Because the tattoo is a Tri-Venn. A modified triquetra—the three-cornered Celtic knot—combined with a Venn Diagram. I know it straight away. Because I invented it. It's how I described the tattoo that Mael wore on the back of his hand.

Could it be . . . ? Were Brittany and I right in what we were both thinking before? Is it possible that us talking about him somehow . . . ?

Cat Mask continues lifting the face cover to reveal . . .

Not Mael.

A woman. A woman I feel like I should know. A woman whom I'm sure I must.

Ohhh. Cat mask. Cat. Like Catarinci. Like Clan Catarinci, I realize.

So I take an exceptionally well-educated guess at whom she might be and say, "Lonnaigh? Is that you?"

The imposing human with the flawless chocolate complexion and piercing blue eyes gestures at my wounds and answers in the Irish brogue that I am expecting.

"Carpathian. Looks like ye' got yerself quite the feckin' scratch there."

Her eyes narrow, and she smiles a satisfied grin. I smile half-heartedly in return.

Then feel my body crashing to the floor.

CHAPTER TWENTY-NINE

Merchant of Condemnation, Riftbreaker Book Five, Chapter Ten

As Mael Anderbariach steered the megaton delivery vessel away from the Ninth Guardian storage yard from whence he recently borrowed it, he glanced over to see his sister, Lonnaigh, gripping tightly onto the seat between the two of them, her fist shaking.

"Ye alright?" Mael asked. Lonnaigh gave a tight, sharp nod. "Really?" he followed. "Because ye seem quite a bit far from alright, Lon, m'dear."

"I just . . ." she began. "I don't like it, May."

"Don't like what?"

"All of it. This 'plan,' if'n it can e'en be called that. We don't e'en know what we're hauling, for feck's sake." She lifted her shaking fist and jabbed a thumb behind her to indicate the massive storage container they were dragging.

"'S Mezmer," he replied with a small shrug.

"Yeah, brother, I know it's Mezmer, but we dunno what kind, or if it even—"

"It's fine," he said, cutting her off. "Carpathian says—"

"I don't care what feckin' Carpathian says!" she exclaimed. "You are the chosen Saviour of Clan Catarinci. Since when did ye decide it's all fine and good for ye to be Carpathian's errand boy?"

Mael twisted his thick, trunklike neck, feeling his long dreadlocks sweep across his shoulders. He gripped the wheel of the vessel, causing the Tri-Venn tattoo on the back of his hand to stretch and morph. He glanced at it then nodded to his closed fist, saying, "Do ye know what it symbolizes?"

"What?" she asked. "Yer tattoo? 'Course I do. It—"

"It symbolizes infinity, interconnectedness, and unification. A meeting in the middle."

"Yeah, May. I know what it—"

"I may have been chosen to be the Saviour of Clan Catarinci, but I am also a citizen of Meridia. And Carpathian Einzgear was chosen by the System to be the World Saviour. What I do at the behest of him, I do for the benefit of myself and for all those who breathe the same air as I." He paused then smiled. "I do it for ye, Lon," he said, reaching out and rubbing the top of her head, ruffling the nascent dreadlocks budding on her scalp.

"Stop," she said, pushing his hand away. "I'm not a child anymore, brother."

She knew she would always be his younger sister, but after the Battle of Floraisient, she had also started to become known as a warrior in her own right. And that was how she wished to be treated. Even in private. Because, she hoped, if she were treated as such, she might one day come to believe it herself.

"Don't worry," he said, his deep, resonant intoning and seeming lack of concern almost sufficient enough to cause her to heed his direction. "I won't let anything happen to ye."

She rolled her eyes and began to respond, but before she was able, an explosion of such force and magnitude that, even though it did not impact their vehicle directly, it still sent the transport careening off its wheels and onto its side, skidding across the barren, desecrated earth with the intensity of ten Drakonar blasts.

"May!" Lonnaigh screamed as the massive machine continued its violent, unnatural bowling along the Meridian plain.

Mael did not respond. He could not, for the unexpected eruption had occurred on his side of the cabin and immediately knocked the mighty warrior unconscious, the attendant radiation from the event searing all the flesh on the side of his body that was exposed to the conflagration.

After what seemed to Lonnaigh like an interminably long amount of time, the transport finally came to a dusty rest. She could hear a creaking, keening noise coming from the storage container just behind her head.

It was an unnerving sound. The sound of highly concentrated Mezmer having been disrupted and now in danger of spilling forth from its casket, unleashing an unknown brand of power out upon the land.

Carpathian. This was Carpathian's fault. He had assured them that this transportation channel was clear. That Mael would be able to steal the container of alchemical supply and return back to Carvesend unmolested. That they would be in no danger, and that the bounty would be able to be harnessed in the alternative Nexus Core the Rebellion was constructing, and that the wizard, Almeister, would be able to convert it into whatever core Mezmer was needed so that the Rebellion would have access to the necessary tools to defeat the Ninth Guardian and their Disciples, thus allowing Mezmer to once again flow freely to all of the citizens of Meridia.

That . . . was her mistake. Believing that anything the "World Saviour" said was true. She had ever been suspicious of this Einzgear, of this potentially false prophet who had so blinded her brother and earned his loyalty, even though Carpathian did not possess even one-hundredth of Mael's integrity and power.

And then, through the shattered windscreen, she could see him approach. A sweltering illusion of a figure swaggering insouciantly toward her, coming more and more into petrifying focus the closer he strode.

Strafe Mortallus. The Merchant of Condemnation, as he had come to be known.

The worst kind of villain, in Lonnaigh's eyes. Someone who had presented himself as an ally, and then turned on the Rebellion, proving himself willing to be bought by the highest bidder.

And it was Carpathian who had told them to trust. Trust that this Strafe, this childhood friend of Einzgear's, could be counted upon to provide them with the tools they required to best the Disciples of the Ninth Guardian once and for all.

Liars. All of them. All of them. Liars.

If word got back to the High Council about Carvesend and the Rebellion's Core, all would be lost.

Smiling at her, Strafe Mortallus reached into his vest and withdrew a switchsaw. He pointed it at the cracked windshield and the newly bloodied face of Lonnaigh Anderbariach, favorite daughter of Clan Catarinci, and pulled the trigger.

The booming energy of Mezmeric inevitability spat through the air at supersonic speed, so fast that one might not even be able to hear it approach. If there was comfort to be taken in Lonnaigh's demise, it would be in knowing that her end had come so quickly she barely had time to fear it.

Or that would have been the story one would tell oneself if her death had happened in that moment.

But it did not.

Because, even more swiftly than the shot from the merchant's switchsaw, Pergamon—made large to the point that his size rivaled that of a fully grown Tentasaurian—moved his body in between the line of fire and the cracked glass, deflecting the shot with his massive shell and sending it back in the direction from whence it came.

Where had he come from? How was he able to intercept the Merchant's intended death blast so suddenly?

These were the questions Lonnaigh asked herself as the snail bellowed with monumental, bone-quaking thunder, "Are you alright?!" Lonnaigh was able to work out a shocked nod. "Your brother. Mael. Is he alive?!"

Lonnaigh blinked, shaking her head, attempting to gather her focus. She strained to reach for her brother in the driver's seat, swiping his long dreadlocks away and feeling his neck for a pulse.

"Aye," she yelped out, for yelping seemed to be that of which she was most capable at the moment, "'tis."

"We must get him to Almei—" Pergamon was able to offer before another shot, this one even more ferocious than the first, sent him airborne, away from his place as a shield of protection for Lonnaigh and Mael.

Twisting her head painfully to the side, Lonnaigh could see where the blast had come from. A militia of Ninth Guardian extremists were approaching the now disabled vehicle. With a Foundry Canon, a traveling Mezmer-generating workshop that had been promised by Strafe to the Rebellion, but which had instead been sold to the High Council behind the Rebellion's back. The very tool that was to have been a jewel in the Rebellion's arsenal, now being used against them by the Disciples of the Ninth Guardian. The insult hurt almost more than the myriad injuries they had suffered.

Almost.

Lonnaigh reached for her seating restraint, attempting to disengage herself so that she might throw her body on top of Mael's. She did not think she could possibly free him and pull him out of harm's way, but she did think she might at least be able to absorb any further assault on the vehicle and, perhaps, die in his stead. More realistically, however, she simply wanted to be as close by his side as she could in their last moments together.

Her fingers fumbled for the release mechanism, but she could not find it. She tugged at the strap covering her chest, but to no avail. A tear formed in her eye and just as quickly loosed itself to cascade down her cheek. She breathed out in sharp, jagged stabs through her nose, a full complement of companion tears set to join the first when a white, blinding light engulfed the cabin of the toppled transport. It caused Lonnaigh to have to shield her eyes lest she be blinded.

It took less than a second for her pupils to adjust to this new assault, and when she opened them, she saw . . .

Carpathian Einzgear and Teleri Nightwind hovering in the air beyond the windowpane.

Lonnaigh blinked several times in quick succession, trying to comprehend what she was witnessing. She had known the two for only a short time. Weeks. And she had seen them wield impressive Abilities and show an unusual brand of Mezmer on occasion, but she had not before seen them . . . defy gravity itself.

But there they were, quite literally floating in the air in front of her eyes. Teleri, her arms moving in some virtual indication of interlocking, concentric circles, which seemed to be the action that was producing the light that surrounded them. A light that, at present, was protecting them all. Lonnaigh could hear another explosive attempt to penetrate the dome of protection Teleri was casting, but it echoed off and did not puncture the Mezmeric insulation keeping them safe.

And Carpathian . . . Carpathian hovered beside her, his favored weapon—the Blade of the Starfallen—drawn in front of him, a concerned look on his face.

He descended from his perch in the sky to land on the engine housing of the transport. With one hand, he ripped the web-shattered window free from the frame and tossed it to the side, entering the cabin and immediately assessing the injuries done to Mael.

"Well," he said, putting on a brave face in spite of the severity of Mael's wounds, "looks as though he's gotten quite the scratch or two, eh?" He smiled at Lonnaigh, careful not to betray his attempt at ameliorating her evident fear. "He'll be alright. But first, we must get him and you back to a safe haven where he might receive healing."

Carpathian was careful not to say aloud the thing he was thinking: Why, when they last visited a Pulse Well, had Mael not taken an upgrade to his Healing capacity, choosing instead to funnel power into his Fortitude?

It was likely that the latter was what had saved his life in this instance, but the absence of the former was going to make it difficult for him to repair himself.

On some unspoken level, Carpathian knew Mael had chosen as he did because he wished to have the same resilience of which Carpathian was in possession. To be more like Carpathian. But Carpathian had the Heart. Without it, Mael—nor anyone that Carpathian had ever met—would be prepossessed of the same Durability he was, but . . .

But he didn't argue with Mael at the time. He did not want to embarrass him.

Now, he wished he hadn't spared the man's feelings, as it may wind up costing him far more than a momentary shame.

"Carpathian," Teleri called out. "I cannot maintain the Disc of Fortification much longer."

"Here," Carpathian said, nodding to Lonnaigh and reaching into his Tunic to retrieve something no bigger than the size of Pergamon at his smallest. "Take this."

"What is it?" Lonnaigh worked out.

Carpathian closed his eyes briefly, and the small object expanded in his hand to become a shield. The Obsidian Shield of Baelus, which Carpathian had used to protect them once before, on the battlefield in Floraisient.

"Take it," he said, offering it to her. "It is not absolute, but it is better than nothing."

Lonnaigh stared at it for a moment, remembering the story she had heard about the trials Carpathian had to endure in order to be awarded with the rare Artifact.

"But—" she started before he stopped her short.

"Do not argue. Take it. Please."

The look of earnestness in his eyes softened Lonnaigh's calcified opinion of the man. She still was not sure she could trust him—she had trusted Strafe, after all—but, in this moment, she concluded that trust and skepticism were equally useless. And at least trust would come with a shield.

She took the item. Carpathian nodded at her, placed his hand on Mael's cheek, placed his lips on Mael's head, and whispered some type of incantation Lonnaigh could not make out. Mael stirred in place, and something inside of Lonnaigh stirred as well.

Then, faster than thrashed lightning, Carpathian flew from the cabin and set off to rejoin the fight.

CHAPTER THIRTY

As my eyes flutter open, I can't make out where I am right away, but the sounds I hear are instantly familiar. They remind me of the transit authority depot where I used to report to work. Metal grinding on metal, hydraulic lifts going up and down, compressed air being blown out from something and into something else.

The smells comport with the noise. Oil, grease, the scent of skin glistening with sweat.

"There, there, lad," a voice soothes. "Take 'er easy. You suffered quite a wounding." It's a feminine voice that sounds similarly accented to Lonnaigh's, a sort of a lilted, Celtic thing.

When I first crafted the character of Mael and the entirety of what became Clan Catarinci, I described them as massive warriors with physical attributes that suggested they would be likely comparable—on Earth—to someone from Jamaica or the West Indies. (Also possibly ancient Moors, in a nod to *Othello*, my fifth favorite Shakespeare play.) But when I presented the text to my audiobook narrator, he sent me an email saying that he didn't feel comfortable trying to do a Jamaican-type accent and asked if I would be okay with him doing a modified Irish instead.

Brittany did some research and confirmed that there was once a Celtic people called the Celtiberians who lived on the Iberian Peninsula. I decided that that detail would be sufficient to satisfy anyone on Reddit or wherever who griped about the seemingly chaotic heterogeneity of culture on offer with these particular characters. (As if just saying, *"It's a fantasy, bro. It doesn't have to turn into a whole thing,"* wouldn't be enough.)

In any case, it's very strange to now be hearing the actual voices of those who previously just sounded like whatever I heard in my head or like my narrator tweaking his vocal cords to present an array of other folk.

Not strange because they sound vastly different than what I had heard or imagined but because they sound almost *exactly* like what I had heard or imagined. And yet once more I find myself confronting the question of which came first. And for that matter, who exactly is the chicken and who is the egg.

I continue squinting, my eyelids flickering and struggling to stay open, until I can finally sort of see the face leering down at me from above. It belongs to what I would describe as a narrow, gritty cocktail of a woman. She's older, maybe in her seventies in Earth years. In Meridia, she could be anywhere from forty to a hundred and forty, depending on her Class and strength.

She has dark brown leathery skin, but there is still a softness to her. Something timeless and generous. Instead of the dreadlocks that Mael and Lonnaigh sport, she has a mane of ivory-white hair that flows like a river of moonlight. Her eyes are sharp, a color I don't think I've ever seen a person's eyes have before, shimmering with a glowing golden hue that calls to mind an unattended fire.

She wears an outfit made of leather, top to bottom. A leather jerkin with a high, military collar. The shirt underneath has black leather sleeves and the hem of it hangs down low, almost to her knees, blending seamlessly with her black leather pants and calf-high, black leather boots. She resembles what I imagine a septuagenarian Beyoncé would look like walking in a Rick Owens runway show. Strapped across her rugged outfit is a bandolier featuring a mini apothecary of vials filled with unknown concoctions.

"Who is she, Bruce? Who is this person?"

"I don't know, Bruce. Even with my own spotty memory, I feel sure I'd remember if I wrote a character like this."

Obviously, I'm not going to know every single creature I encounter in Meridia, but it's an odd feeling to think that I've been getting tended to by someone I didn't write about. That's weird, I know, but . . . for as much as I always eschewed the idea of *controlling* the story, things still responded to what I chose or didn't choose to have happen. Now? Not so much.

"Where . . . Where am I?"

"You're in Garr Haven," Older Beyoncé says.

Garr Haven. Clan Catarinci's workshop, their garage. A literal garage built into the side of Mt. TaumSauk. (Which, I know, is the actual name of the actual mountain in Taum Sauk Mountain State Park and I just combined the two words into one, but I honestly couldn't think of anything better than "TaumSauk," so I went with it. The State of Missouri Tourism Bureau said they've seen visitation to the park rise by almost five percent since the book with Mt. TaumSauk came out, so I feel good that I'm helping the local economy.)

Unlike the real Taum Sauk Mountain on Earth, however, Mt. TaumSauk on Meridia gets no outside visitors. By design. It's hidden from all except those who know the way, because it is also the de facto headquarters for the Rebellion. And now that my eyes are able to focus, I can see more clearly . . . *Holy macaroni. I really am here. I'm actually in Garr Haven.*

Big, muscled members of Clan Catarinci work on vehicles all around the place. And I think . . . ? Yep. Sure enough, they are attended by Grease Monkeys, actual macaque monkeys who were Mezmerated by the Catarinci Clan for the express purpose of assisting in repairing vehicles damaged in road battles with DONG.

Yes, it's a play on words, but there was actually a specific inspiration for creating them.

Back when I used to drive buses for the city, there was an engine repair guy at the depot who had a capuchin. (Which I always used to pronounce as /ka-POO-chin/, but he pronounced it /CAP-uh-chin/, so I started saying it that way because I assumed he was right. I anticipated it might turn into a whole big pronunciation issue in the Riftbreaker audiobooks, which is why in Meridia, they're macaques. Anyway . . .) Sometimes, he'd bring her to work with him and let me feed her pistachios while she picked nits out of my hair. It was always the bright spot of my week. Her name was Crystal. She wore a little beret.

Here in Garr Haven, the Grease Monkeys chitter and scurry around, handing various tools to the chief mechanics doing work on vehicles scattered about the workshop. Hydraulic lifts stand tall like monoliths. Heavy-duty impact wrenches and welding stations are all being utilized to their full capacity. Nobody currently at labor seems to notice or care that I'm here. Or awake. They continue going about their business, repairing and enhancing the Frankenstein machines they've cobbled together.

I have so many questions, so many things I feel like I want to ask. But, as I try to sit up and get a better look at everything, a pain so severe it feels like it's going to cause my body to split in two courses through me. My Heart starts thumping at an alarming rate, which makes everything hurt more.

Oh! Hello! You are awake! My goodness, you gave everyone quite a scare!
Good news/Bad news.
Good news, you're alive! Huzzah! Bad news, your overcooked limbs are in danger of becoming infected and subsequently atrophying to the point that you are at grave risk of losing them forever! Shame, that. Not the headline you had hoped to awaken to, I'm sure, but it does no favors to beat about the bush with such matters, so . . .
Good morning!
{COURTESY MESSAGE #9}

The notification goes on to once more list my Stats and available upgrade options upon reaching a Pulse Well and yadda, yadda, but the part I'm hyper-fixated on is the business about losing my limbs. Looking at the arm and leg that were blasted to bits by Cosma's spellsword, I see that they remain blasted to bits.

"Bruce!" I suddenly hear Brittany calling.

"Big homie!" Perg shouts out as well.

Oh, thank the gods, they're okay. I wouldn't be able to . . . if . . . Anyway, they're okay.

I roll my head to the side to see that I appear to be resting on a cot in the corner of the large, open garage. Brit is approaching at a gallop, with Perg in his snail-sized size riding on her shoulder.

Her pauldron-covered shoulder.

Gone is her sassy tank top and the cutoff shorts; in their stead, she dons what I can only describe as "warrior sorcerer chic." Metal shoulders and breast plate with a leather assassin bodice that has chains all across the midsection. Metallic gauntlets and vambraces. Dark, blood-red tights with metal greaves covering the calves, and a flowing black cape trailing behind her.

Basically, she looks like what would come out if you typed in "cosplay fantasy porn girl" into an AI art generator.

Perg still just looks like a snail.

They arrive beside the cot upon which I'm convalescing, and for a moment, it looks like Brittany wants to give me a hug. But then she stops herself, either because she realizes that I'm still too wounded for physical contact, or because she realizes that it would be a show of emotion that isn't undergirded with a bad attitude and thinks better of it.

"You're . . . Hi. How are you feeling?" she asks.

"Like I've had an arm and leg deep-fried in molten lava."

"Makes sense."

"We thought we had lost you there for a minute, fool," Perg says. "But then, Lon drove us back here to the workshop and Tavrella, she got to business, and kept you from, y'know . . ." He makes a noise with his mouth kind of like fabric ripping, which is, I assume, to vocalize the sound of me dying.

I turn to the striking older woman with the bandolier of ampoules and ask, "You're Tavrella?"

"Aye."

"Are you a healer?"

"Not exactly, more an alchemist. I've tried to cure ye up the best I can, but that was powerful Mezmer ye had put upon ye. And what Mezmer I have access to is fine for some injuries, but Templar Mezmer . . . that comes straight from the core in the Tower of Zuria. Pure. Undiluted. Only so much what can be done with the resources I have on hand. The goal has been to just keep ye alive until ye wake up. Which now ye have." She smiles.

Right then, one of the monkeys comes sauntering over; he wears little grease-stained coveralls and carries a vial of something that glows with a cool, blue light. I notice the simian happens to be smoking a fat spliff.

"Thank ye, Jameson."

Jameson the Macaque raises the joint he's toking into the air in a gesture of "no problem," then he looks at me as he takes a long, languid toke on the blunt and blows the smoke right in the direction of my face. He points at me with the doob and says something that sounds like, "*Coconopo. Rodiofonisu. Astapapana,*" before he nods his head thoughtfully and strolls away.

I cough, which hurts, and ask, "What was that, then?"

"He said that he's glad you're alive. And that he knew the Gospel was heresy and you'd be back soon to set things right," Brittany informs.

"I didn't know Grease Monkeys even had their own language," I tell her.

"I . . . didn't either," she replies, frowning with realization.

"Then, how do you—?"

"I don't know," she says sharply.

Tavrella appears to be smiling to herself.

I think for a moment and then also realize that I have no idea what "Gospel" she's referring to. I never wrote anything about any kind of Gospel.

"What Gospel does he mean?" I ask.

"I don't know that either," Brit answers, slightly agitated. "He just said 'the Gospel.'"

"He's talkin' 'bout the Gospel according to Brucillian, obviously," Tavrella—I assume she believes—clarifies.

Brittany and I now share a worried look and Perg says, "Yeah, fool. I told you all about Brucillian. Don't you remember?"

"No, of course I . . . But there's a Gospel? What's in it?"

"Nothin'," Tavrella says. "Don't ye worry about it. Just drink this." She reaches toward my mouth with the liquid Jameson brought over. I turn my head away.

"No, seriously. What is this Gospel? Is there something about Carp—me? In it? I've been through a lot with the remorting and getting burned alive and all, and feel like if there's something out there in the form of a Gospel that has a monkey saying it's potentially chock-a-block with heresy about me, I deserve to know."

Tavrella takes a breath. "There's a lot of foolishness in it. This and that about false prophets and the coming of the true Saviour, and a bunch of other faff. Don't spend any time on it; it's just in vogue at the moment because of all that's goin' on. A conspiracy without foundation. Nobody who's known the true wonders of the things ye've done cares a whit about it, and soon as the word becomes wide that ye are back again, it'll be quickly forgotten and cast for good onto the dustheap of history." She waves her hand like she's shooing away a gnat.

I wish I shared her cavalier disposition.

"Really. Save yer strength to focus on getting yerself healed properlike," she says. "Now, here. Have a dram o' this. It'll be good for ye." She places the ampoule against my lips, and I take a sip.

The potion hits my tongue, and I wince. Not because it tastes bad but because it tastes delicious. And familiar.

It's exactly like a blue Freezer Pop, my favorite flavor from when I was a kid, which is both comforting and wildly discomfiting all at the same time.

"There ya go," she says as I swallow the liquid, "that's a good boy. Drink it all down."

She has an almost eerily pacifying quality about her. I do as she encourages and suck at my lips to take in all of the tasty, Freezer Poppy goodness.

Tavrella pats my head.

"Hey!" Brit calls, pulling my focus deliberately to her and gesturing up and down at her regalia. "What do you think? I mean, like . . . sick, yeah?"

"It's . . . something." I grimace as I try to sit up. "Where'd you get all that?"

"Where do ye think she got it?" the strong, authoritative voice I now recognize to be Lonnaigh's calls out.

She comes striding over, looking every bit as fierce and expansive as I last described her in book eight of Riftbreaker. To the best of my knowledge, that was the last time Carpathian saw her.

After he was forced to abandon Mael in the Cavern of Sorrows, Mael's last request was that Carpathian look after her. Carpathian had intended to honor the appeal, but when he told Lonnaigh what had happened, how Mael had offered up himself and Carpathian couldn't save him, she rejected the Saviour, undoing three books' worth of goodwill and trust he had worked so hard to engender

204 JOHNATHAN MCCLAIN AND SETH MCDUFFEE

in the warrior called Lonnaigh Anderbariach. He had watched her grow from a reticent, frightened younger sister into the powerful leader of the Rebellion that I see before me today, and then he just shot himself in the foot by betraying her hard-won faith in him.

"*Bruce. What the hell are you talking about? YOU did that. YOU wrote it that way.*"

"*You say tomato, I say Carpathian-did-it-stop-blaming-me-for-shit-that-I-don't-think-is-my-fault.*"

"I gave it to her," Lonnaigh goes on as she arrives cotside.

"What?" I ask, having gotten distracted by the sight of her.

"The vines. Dug 'em up for her. The System did ye both no favors when they remorted ye. Silly form of covers they draped ye in. Or barely draped ye in, in yer case." She points at what remains of my luxury pajama set. Which, to be clear, is a lone pant leg.

(Pant leg? Or pants leg? Is each leg called a "pants," thus making it a "pair of pants"? Or does each leg stand alone as its own "pant," which is what necessitates the pluralization? Is this the kind of thing that should be taking up my focus right now? A million percent not. Is it, however, helping keep my mind off the pain? It was, but now that I'm thinking about it again, OW.)

Lonnaigh must see the agony register on my face. "Slow yerself there, Saviour. We don't need ye ripping yer limbs apart afore we get ye settled right again."

"You brought us back here?" I ask, still trying to piece things together.

"Aye. We loaded ye into the rear seat of yer vehicle and brought ye in. Weren't no easy ride neither."

"What happened?" I grunt as Tavrella smooths my hair back and shushes me softly.

Lonnaigh looks at Brittany and Perg with a twinkle in her eye then back to me, takes a breath, and says, "Well . . ."

CHAPTER THIRTY-ONE

"Once Upon a Time in Meridia."
Part 1

A moan from the prostrate form of Bruce Silver drew Lonnaigh's attention to the back seat. "How's he doing?" she asked.

"His pulse seems okay," replied Perg the Snail from his place sitting upon Bruce's carotid artery, monitoring him carefully. "Not pumping pumping, like 'Oye Cómo Va' or anything, but it's still there. Like 'Bésame Mucho.'"

"We need to keep him alive. If we can get him back to Garr Haven, Tavrella might be able to save him." Lonnaigh breathed heavily, gripping the steering wheel tighter, focusing her eyes ahead on the fallow terrain. It was barely yet full morn and already the untilled land shimmered under the mirage of the suns' heat.

"Tavrella?" Brittany asked.

"Aye," Lonnaigh affirmed. "The alchemist." She looked over to see the puzzled expression on Brittany's face. "What's the matter?"

"I just . . . don't know them."

"Why would ye?"

"Oh, uh," Brittany stammered, trying to find the best way to mask her confusion. "Just, we've had so many, um, adventures together. Feels like I would have met the alchemist at some point."

"Alright," Lonnaigh said without opinion or addition.

"How did you know we'd be there?" Brittany asked. "At Jeomandi's?"

"I didn't," Lonnaigh responded. "I got a Quest notification."

"What?"

"I'd been doing some training with my old blast rifle. Felt certain I was due to receive a boost in my Marksmanship Level. So, I visited the Pulse Well and, sure enough, I had jumped all the way up to Tier Eight Marksman. Rewarded myself with these new beauties"—she slapped the switchsaws in their holsters on her hips—"and then got offered a Quest where I could put 'em to use."

"And the Quest was to rescue us?"

"No," Lonnaigh replied curiously. "It was more, whatchacallit? 'Ambiguous.' The Quest was just to go to Jeomandi's and wait outside with the Reapers. I thought it was odd, but it said the reward would be some manner of surprise. And then you all showed up. It definitely was a surprise." She paused, glanced one more time at Carpathian resting in the back, and added, "I'm still waitin' on the reward."

Silence followed. After a moment, Brittany pulled out one of the hand-drawn maps she had been so diligently maintaining. "Where are we now?" she asked.

Before Lonnaigh could provide an answer, the haunting cries of soaring Mez-meric beasts and the distant sounds of countless flapping wings answered the question for her.

"The Sea of Swans?" Brittany gasped, looking down at the map and then back out the window.

"Aye," Lonnaigh said. "Fastest way to get back to Garr Haven." She side-eyed the paper Brittany was holding and added, "Why d'ye need that? Ye've been there near on a dozen times."

"Oh." Brittany self-consciously folded the map up and placed it back in her pocket. "The . . . recarbonification. It . . . kind of does a sort of memory wipe. About certain things. I guess."

"Does it? Never heard that before."

They drove on in silence for another moment, the not-distant-enough-for-Brittany's-liking roar of creatures she and Bruce had dreamt up as nightmare fuel now powering her waking day. Since being evidently transported to Meridia, Brittany had not allowed herself to question deeply the particulars of how they had come to be there nor why. Now, in the semiquiet aftermath of the previous hours' torment, she couldn't stop herself from wondering in earnest.

Was she right when she posited to Bruce that their presence there was some sort of penance? A chance to engage with the world Bruce and she had so cavalierly rent asunder? Certainly, it seemed, it was at least that much. But how? How could such a thing have transpired? It may not matter, but not having answers to questions that seemed answerable was its own unique form of torment to Brittany McAfee.

Curiosity came naturally to her. Her mother had been a military intelligence officer. Brittany had grown up being taught that rigid adherence to strategic, operational, and tactical planning was the surest way to a successful path in life. Unfortunately, this knowledge was frequently at odds with her somewhat rash temper. A temper she'd developed as a suit of armor to protect her from the mockery of others, as she was always the "new, weird kid." Always.

One thing she'd learned early on: Cultures may be diverse, customs may be varied, languages may separate us, but one unifying constant remains no matter where in the universe you find yourself: People will be dicks. Especially toward those who aren't like them.

And Brittany wasn't like anyone. She was an amalgam, a composition born largely of her own invention and indomitable will to survive. Which was why, when she met someone with whom she felt any kind of connection, she would hold on to that connection as fiercely as a proton held a neutron in an atomic nucleus.

In terms of loyalty, Brittany was a nuclear force.

"Mmmmmm," Bruce moaned from the back, and Lonnaigh pressed down harder on the accelerator.

Brittany started to ask a question; something benign, something like, "how much further?" if for no other reason than to keep worry from overtaking her. But before she could, her thoughts were interrupted by . . .

"EIIIIINNNZZZGGGEEEAAARRR,"

. . . from somewhere that sounded nearby.

"Did you hear that?" she queried.

"Hear what?" Lonnaigh responded.

"Perg?" Brittany followed.

"Yeah, chica, I hear it."

"What? What do ye both hear?" Lonnaigh repeated herself.

But before any answer could be offered, another sound that all could assuredly discern made itself known. A halting, shrieking, unholy piercing of the aural plane.

"Jesus!" Brittany shouted, covering her ears.

"Is that what ye heard?" Lonnaigh barked over the orchestra of horrors.

"No, but what is that?!" Brittany called out, the sharp pain in her eardrums not ameliorated by her cupped palms.

"That," Lonnaigh said flatly, nodding ahead.

Focusing her gaze, Brittany saw a monstrous shape rising into the air before them from somewhere deep in the canyon known as the Sea of Swans. It was all leathery wings and gnarled limbs, with eyes glowing like coals from the ancient crater of Avernus. Its skin a patchwork of scars and scales glistening sickeningly in the morning sun, it presented as an ascending apocalypse, the roar shaking the very air around them.

Brittany's mind raced, doing a rapid-fire inventory of creatures she could recall from within the pages of Riftbreaker.

An Earth Eidolon, she thought. A creation akin to the classical golems of myth. A virtually unbeatable foe, birthed by the very planet upon which they drove.

This was, Brittany thought further, bad.

The creature let out a guttural screech that rattled the Panamera in which they rode. Lonnaigh clutched the steering wheel tighter still, the dark skin of her knuckles turning as white as the Tri-Venn tattoo she wore.

"Hold on!" she shouted.

"What?!" Brittany called, not because she did not hear but because she could not understand why they were continuing to drive forward and not turn away. Then she looked in the side mirror and—seeing what Lonnaigh must have witnessed in the rearview—understood.

Bearing down upon them from behind was a fearsome sight.

The Ronine, accompanied by a phalanx of Rapprentices, and flanked by Templars on magecycles were thundering in their direction, a billowing cloud of dust surrounding their parade of mayhem.

They were trapped. Trapped between probable death and guaranteed death.

"Shite," Lonnaigh cursed.

At that moment, the soothing, melodious, synthetic, lightly accented voice of Sheila rang out throughout the vehicle. "Incoming threat detected on the rear of the vehicle. Would you like to deploy a countermeasure?"

"Godsdamn right," Lonnaigh declared to no one in particular. She dared to remove a hand from the steering column long enough to reach out and press the car's PCM screen. It lit up with options.

"What in the seven hells is an Oscillating Vortex?" Lonnaigh asked.

"I had the same question!" Brittany crowed in return.

Concluding that no harm could come from trying all available choices, Lonnaigh pressed on each of them in succession.

Chaos Chain
Fog of Decimation
Sonic Torment
Oscillating Vortex
Lightning Rider Strike

And . . .

. . . nothing happened.

She tried again. And again. And again. Finally, Sheila responded, saying, "Only the Titleholder is authorized to use these functions. Please request full access from sanctioned Titleholder to continue."

"Shite!" Lonnaigh declared once more.

"Yo!" Pergamon's voice could be heard calling from the rear. "Yo, big homie! You give old girl permission to use all the toys, right? What's that? Yes? You do? That's what I thought! Hey! Car! Big homie says todo bien!"

Unfortunately, Sheila was unresponsive to the dubious affirmation of the recently philologically endowed Turbo Snail, and the PCM screen went dark.

Looking once more into the side mirror, Brittany could see, emerging from the rapidly closing pack of predators . . .

Moridius Wreathnestle.

Propelled by something more than mere obligation—driven hard by devotion and the need for retribution—Moridius pushed his magecycle forward, well beyond its capacity, until he arrived beside the Panamera.

Brittany found herself looking into the eyes of the man as he withdrew his switch-saw and pointed it directly at the glass separating them.

"Homegirl!" Pergamon shouted from the back seat as he closed his eyes and focused on trying to embiggen himself. Perhaps, if he could expand in size, he could shield her from the blast as he had shielded Bruce earlier. But before he was able to effectuate the change in size, the vehicle hit a not insubstantial bump in the pockmarked terrain, breaking his concentration and causing him to fall from his place on Bruce's neck.

Robbed of the chance to play hero once more, he did instead all that he could do to help in this circumstance and shouted, "Duck!" as he toppled to the floor.

Brittany didn't duck. She couldn't. She found herself paralyzed by a kind of fear she had never before known. Or, no . . . Not fear. Something else. Something she couldn't identify. Something that felt both new and ageless at once. Something . . .

"Oh, shit!" Perg shouted once more. "Look!"

Lonnaigh craned her neck to look through the windscreen, and when she did, she saw, soaring through the sky as if appearing from nowhere . . .

"A Tentasaurian!" Lonnaigh shouted.

Brittany did not look. She did not respond in any way. She was frozen, head tilted back as if in a trance, body glowing with an ethereal light.

And so she remained as the Tentasaurian, called to command by the power of the one known as Teleri Nightwind, joined the battle with the Earth Eidolon and the full complement of powers dispatched by the High Council to provide narrowly sufficient cover such that Sheila and her precious cargo might make their escape . . .

CHAPTER THIRTY-TWO

And then blah, blah, blah, etcetera, in the face of certain whatever, we pulled off a darin' so forth and such on and made it back here. Don't matter. We're all still alive, is the upshot. Yer welcome."

I stare at Lonnaigh as she concludes the story, then I look to Brit. "Tentasaurian?"

She shrugs. "Yeah, I called up a Tentasaurian. So what? Big deal."

I nod to myself for a moment. "On purpose?"

Lonnaigh looks at me curiously, then at Brit, who answers pointedly. "Yeah. Obviously. I'm *Teleri Nightwind*. That's what I do."

I take in a deep breath and look at Perg, who also appears to shrug with his tiny body.

"Yeah, big homie. That's what she do. I get embiggened. She summons beasties. You . . . do what you do. It's who we are, fool."

Lonnaigh cocks her head, furrows her brow, and presses her lips together before noting, "The three of ye are vastly different personalities than before your reconstitution."

"Yeah," I breathe out. "Yeah, it's . . . what's happened." Then I realize . . . "Sheila?"

"She's fine," Lonnaigh assures. "She's over there, being tended to." She nods to where I see Sheila being buffed by two Grease Monkeys and one chief mechanic from Clan Catarinci with something that appears to be an oversize diaper. "She handles damn well, Einzgear. Fine machine she is. Too fine, some might say. Sure you're really the Titleholder?"

I ignore the slight. "Well. Thank you," I say with as much sincerity as I can possibly muster. Being hyperaware of the friction between Carpathian and Lonnaigh, I feel I need to do my utmost to try and repair the rift however I can.

To be the "rift repairer," if you will.

"No, Bruce. No. Things are bad enough. Don't make matters worse with indolent attempts at internalized badinage."

"I don't need yer thanks," Lonnaigh says.

"I was just trying to—"

"I need yer damn help, Saviour."

I look to Brittany, who nods in a way that tells me she is aware of what's next. "Help . . . with what?"

"Getting my feckin' brother out of that damn cavern. What d'ya think?"

". . . Right. Well. Of course. I mean, clearly—"

"Clearly? No, not clearly. Ain't nothin' clear 'bout it. He's been languishin' there for damn near a full Lunar Cycle, waiting on you to retrieve him! I'd have gotten him m'self already, but you're the only one who knows exactly where he is!"

When the group—Carpathian, Teleri, Pergamon, Mael, Zerastian, and Xanaraxa (Almeister was off negotiating with a dockmaster at the Great Gulf of Burléon to try and secure a boat)—ventured into the Cavern of Sorrows, it was to retrieve the Cerulean Tunic of the Seafarer, which had been stolen by Nox, the Cavern Troll, who was working in cahoots with the Super Vizier to capture the Party.

Carpathian needed the Tunic in order for them to cross the gulf safely. Draping his Heart Guard in its protection was the only way they could all find safe passage to reach the shores of New Espoiria. But of course, a bunch of shit went sideways, and Mael—because Mael was always the most heroic of the bunch—sacrificed himself to the cavern so the rest could escape.

I mean, it's clearly ripped off from *Fellowship of the Ring*, but it's not like I had Mael saying "Fly, you fools," or anything. (He said, *"Run, you fools."* Totally different. Plus, if I was *really* ripping it off, it would've been Almeister saying it, not Mael. *And* Nox would've called the Tunic "Sweet darling" or something. Which they didn't. And besides, it's a *tunic,* which is in no way a *ring*. It's not my fault the audiobook narrator chose to give Nox almost *exactly* the same voice that Gollum had in the movies. I mean. It— I just— Whatever! *Homage!*)

Anyway . . .

As Brittany reminded me, I did have Almeister and Carpathian try to go rescue Mael in book nine, but Almeister got captured instead. Just a whole, big, messy avalanche of things going wrong. Great for creating drama, bad for the situation in which I currently find myself . . . embathed.

"I know, I know," I say, trying to pacify.

"Only reason I even know he's still alive is because of this!"

She holds up the back of her fist, showing off her tattoo; it palpitates with its white glow. It's the thing that bonds Mael and Lonnaigh's spirits together. She got it from the same Mezmeric artisan who'd crafted Mael's just before he joined Carpathian's Heart Guard. He told her, *"I may share a piece of Carpathian's Heart, sister. But we . . . we share each other's souls. We are kin, we are blood, we are bonded, and we are unbreakable."*

And then there was some crazy Celtic-slash-made-up-language hybrid chanting that Brittany put together and that I can't remember, and then . . . that was it. Mael could feel Lonnaigh's life force and she his. As long as hers pulsates like that, it means Mael is still alive.

"I get it," I say, still trying (and barely succeeding) to keep Lonnaigh from . . . I dunno. Hurting me? More? I guess? "I understand your frustration."

"Oh, do ye?" she asks with more than a little insincerity. "Well, then. Shouldn't be a problem to go grab him up. Ye already have to venture to Mount Saatus to fetch the Blade of the Starfallen, do ye not? The cavern is right there."

I look to Brit, who raises both her hands in a "Sorry, buuuuuuuut what was I supposed to tell her?" gesture.

"I do," I reply slowly. "Yes, that's true. I do have to do that. And then, as soon as we've succeeded in getting Almeister, we can return and—"

"No. Not as soon as anything, mate. Not later. Not after. Not some other, Einzgear. Before. First. Now."

"Lonnaigh, please. The Quest for Almeister has a time . . . Look, it's going to take who knows how long to get to Mount Saatus, and then we have to get all the way back to Santus Luminous, and—" Before I can continue offering arguments as to why I can't possibly make this happen now, there is a ripple of pain in my chest and my everything else as a notification appears.

You have been offered a Quest!
"Rescue Mael from the Cavern of Sorrows."
Do you wish to accept this Quest?
[Yes] [No]

Are you kidding me?!

We've barely made progress in the Quest that we set out on! Is *this* why the autopropulsion charted us to Jeomandi's? And, for that matter, why the System sent Lonnaigh there?

I can't figure out what the System's game is. Is it out to help or to hurt? Is it on my side or working to wreck everything? Why is it gaslighting me?!

Right now, I don't suppose it matters. What matters is that I've got a Quest in front of me that—if I accept it—really puts me against a wall in terms of fulfilling my *first* Quest. We already lost one Lunar Rotation. We only have six days (or, I guess, nights) to save Almeister. And I have a feeling it's going to take every possible second of them to pull it off.

But, if I *don't* accept it, then I'm really screwed with Lonnaigh. And I don't wanna be screwed with Lonnaigh. Carpathian didn't wanna be screwed with her either. It was a horrible position he was put in when he had to choose between Mael and his mission.

But . . . Dammit. No. I have to be smart. And tactical. And . . . just . . . no.

I take a breath, looking at Lonnaigh with as much empathy as I have in me. "Listen, I *want* to get Mael. Of course I do. But it's going to be incredibly dangerous and—"

She snorts a derisive laugh, which interrupts me before I can protest further. "Dangerous . . ." She clucks her tongue. "Y'know, Carpathian Einzgear, when I first met ye, I was unconvinced. I couldn't figure out if ye were for true or just an impostor Saviour with some kind of agenda. If ye meant all the things ye proclaimed about yer intentions and yer commitment to the world, or if ye were just out for yerself. But ye earned my respect by showing me that ye did really care about Meridia.

"Clan Catarinci traces back to before we started recording time. My family is one of the first peoples. So, lest there be any doubt, my allegiance is to the truest good, by which I mean the survival of the planet itself. Ye think if DONG is able to eventually batter the will of the people into compliance, that that'll be the end of it? Once they've cordoned power from the citizenry, they'll need to find something else to fight against, so they'll have nowhere to turn except the ground upon which we stand.

"It's what the Ninth Guardian is. The kind of force who'll never be satiated. And the Guardian and DONG will keep on stripping this world of what makes it worth fighting for until there's nothing left. Literally. Meridia was once a fertile womb that could foster life, and it's been turned into a decaying rock that takes it instead.

"I thought, before ye gave up on the battlefield of Rendalia, that ye shared the belief that we could turn back the sea. I convinced myself, somehow, that Mael had sacrificed himself for someone who shared the values that he and I have. That danger and death and all those things that others fear didn't apply to those like us. I thought . . . ye might be a true leader. Someone who faces reality and owns their responsibility. Maybe ye were. Maybe at some point ye were committed to what's proper right and good. But now . . . the way yer talkin' . . ." She pauses, looks at the floor, and shakes her head before repeating her previous observation.

"Ye are vastly different than I wanted to believe ye were before."

The statement hangs in the air like a noose, and now I have to decide if I'm going to stick my neck through it. She called Carpathian by his full name, and it caused me to feel as much of a chill down my spine as if she'd called me by mine. But—

"*Bruce . . . please. How long are we going to keep this up?*"

The voice of my possibly fractured psyche chimes in with an entirely different tone than it has used previously. More earnest. Almost tutorial.

"*What are you talking about, Bruce?*" I ask myself.

"*The whole 'I'm not Carpathian' runner you keep using. Don't you think it's getting tired?*"

I bristle internally at the fact that the voice in my head used a writing idiom to dismiss the very real situation I'm in.

"*It's not a runner,*" I tell myself indignantly. "*It's the truth. I'm. Not. HIM.*"

The voice replies, "*Carpathian wasn't 'him' either. Not at first. He grew into himself. But insofar as he struggled to accept the reality of what he was called to do before he finally gave over to it, you are* exactly *alike. Carpathian isn't just a person, Bruce. He's an idea. A representation of the possibility that we can become greater than we are if we take ownership of our power. Like Nelson Mandela once said, 'Your playing small does not serve the world. We are all meant to shine, as children do. It's not just in some of us; it is in everyone.'*"

The weight of the idea lands heavy inside me. My Heart whirs in my chest, almost as if it's happy. Like it's been waiting on me to come to this kind of a discovery and is celebrating the fact that I finally have.

There's just one tiny problem with the soliloquy. And while I know . . . I *know* . . . I should let it go, I just . . . *Argh.*

"*Marianne Williamson,*" I tell myself.

There's a long pause before the voice answers, "*What?*"

"*It wasn't Nelson Mandela who said it. It was Marianne Williamson. In her book* A Return to Love."

"*I— Bu— Wha—? You—?*" the voice stammers. "*Marianne Williamson, the woman who ran for president Marianne Williamson?*" it asks.

"*Yeah,*" I say inside my mind.

"*Well . . . why do people think it was Nelson Mandela who said it?*"

"*Dunno. I think it might be literally, and ironically, an application of the Mandela effect, which is when we collectively misremember historical events or people. The coinage comes from when everyone somehow believed that Mandela had died in prison, but in truth—*"

"*I know what the Mandela effect is!*" the voice shouts. "*How do you know it's Marianne and I don't?! I'm YOU! To hell with it! Whatever! Point remains! Sack up, sister! Or I'll go haunt Patrick Rothfuss's mind! I'll do it, Bruce! Don't think I won't! I don't give a TOOT!*"

Awwwwwwwww, dammit . . .

I reach out, press [Yes], and get another wave of owie, owie, ow, ow, as I see:

Excellent!
Quest: "Rescue Mael from the Cavern of Sorrows."
[ACCEPTED]

Quest Requirements:
Requires Item: [Elemental]

Shit. Of course it does. The cavern can only be fully accessed if one is in possession of an Elemental item that grants entry to the various paths of Elemental ingress. Because god forbid I write that someone could simply walk in.

Quest Restrictions:
[Once Quest is commenced, it *must* be completed in order to exit the Cavern.]
(Or you may choose to die there. That's fine too.)

Time Allowed for Completion:
[Two Lunar Rotations]

Reminder: Upgrades are available. Please visit the nearest Pulse Well. Seriously. Taking on another Quest, especially this one, without steeling your resolve is highly, highly, highlyhighlyhighlyhighlyhighly unadvisable.
{COURTESY MESSAGE #10}

Okay. Okay, alright, this is gonna be okay. I've still got six Lunar Rotations to complete the Almeister Quest, so we can make this happen. We can make all of it happen. In fact, it might be for the better.

I was gonna need to find and grab up Mael at some point anyway, probably. And, y'know, Mael is a BEAST. Just an absolute monster of a human. Kind of like what you'd get if you crossed Gregor Clegane from *Game of Thrones* with L'Jarius Sneed of the Kansas City Chiefs. A mountain of a man who can move lightning quick and knows how to knock people the hell out.

Having Stealth is a requirement for the Almeister Quest, so I presume that means I'm gonna have to get all furtive up in that piece at some point, but I can't imagine there also won't be at least a few punches getting thrown, so there's clear value in having him back in the posse when we storm the Tower.

Alright, so lemme put this together real quick. It just needs to go, in order, like this:

First: I get my crispy corpus to a Pulse Well and have someone prop me up long enough to get all of the bounty that's due me.

I would pull up the list again, but every time the Heart notifies me, it makes everything inside feel like there's a passel of bees trying to escape through my skin, so I'll content myself to just knowing it's gonna be a good haul. Like, a handful of Foundational boosts, I think? A new Spell—which means I can get a much-needed Healing Spell—some open inventory slots . . .

I can't remember what else. I had a hard enough time recalling this kind of stuff when I would assign it to Carpathian in the books, and I was *writing that down*. I just know I've earned goodies, and I need to see what they are so I can rock 'em in full effect like the old-skool and criminally underrated *Mantronix* album.

So, that's number one.

Second: We go grab the Blade of the Starfallen. I'm mildly nervous about this because . . . because it was Carpathian's sword. Only the true Saviour could withdraw it from the stone. As noted, not that original an idea, but effective. It happened in the last half of book one and was the moment when Carpathian could no longer even remotely entertain the idea that being the Saviour was not his gig. Again, believing in yourself is more than half the battle.

But, dare I say it for the umptillionth time, and at the risk of alienating the voice in my head . . . *I am not Carpathian*. However, since everyone in this world thinks I am so much that it has even cute little stoned macaques believing it, maybe a mythic sword of legend won't know the difference either. We'll find out, I guess.

Third: We go get Mael.

Which is not as simple as just saying those four words, but I'll have my upgraded self, Brit and whatever upgrades she's surely entitled to, Perg and whatever he's got coming his way, and a switchsaw-spinning, rarely grinning but always winning Lonnaigh at my six. So, there's that.

And then, finally: We rescue Almeister.

Again, easier said than done, especially if it winds up taking the full two Lunar Rotations to handle the Mael sitch, but . . .

But nothing. It's gonna suck, no matter how it's parsed. I can just feel it. And also, the Heart has warned me, in multiple ways, that it's going to be a shit show, so it's not so much that I have a premonition—I've just been warned by a mercurial force that's either trying to prep me for a soft landing or soften me up for the kill.

Whatever. Makes no difference. Almeister is most definitely the key to, if nothing else, unraveling the mystery of how we might be able to get home.

Eventually.

I hope.

And that's it. The whole plan is that linear and that oblique all at once. Oxymoronic. Emphasis on the second part.

But we gotta get moving, so . . .

"Okay," I grunt, forcing my fragile frame up into more of a sitting position and putting myself into my best Carpathian head. "Let's do this thing. Somebody help me get to a Pulse Well so I can sort all of . . . this"—I refer to my body—"out. Come on. Let's make moves. We only have six more Lunar Rotations."

Instead of hopping to, like I just directed, everyone just stares at me.

Hm. This does not do much to inspire confidence in my leadership skills.

"*Maybe you need to shout a little, Bruce.*"

"*You're still here, Bruce?*"

The voice sighs. "*Yes. Like Led Zeppelin once said, 'I can't quit you, baby.' So c'mon, at least try to put some oomph in your voice.*"

"*I dunno, Bruce. I'm not really much of a shouter. I think it'll be weird.*"

"*Nooooo. It's why it'll more effective. The more sparingly you use a tool, the sharper it remains.*"

Bruce is right. Or . . . I'm right, I mean. Control isn't just a cool, time-slowing Spell; it's something you have to take if you want people to respect you.

So I suck in a breath and ready myself to give the order again. This time, more order-y.

But before I get to practice my R. Lee Ermey in *Full Metal Jacket* voice, Brittany speaks up.

"Two," she says, coincidentally quieter than I'm used to hearing her speak.

"What?" I ask. "What was that? Speak up, soldier. I can't hear you."

I think she'll appreciate this new thing I'm trying, her being a military brat and all.

"Two," she repeats, slightly louder. "Two Lunar Rotations. Not six."

I nod slowly, thoughtfully, then ask, "What in the fresh hell are you talking about?"

A notification appears, causing me to jolt.

Ah. I see where the confusion is. You believe you've only been unconscious for a number of hours. In fact, you have been in something of a coma, I suppose you'd call it, for the last Four Lunar Rotations! You really did take quite the drubbing.

In any case, apologies. This all should have been made clear to you when you awoke. There's just so much else happening that the Notification was deprioritized in the queue! Shan't happen again.

"My bad," as you might say. ☺
Time Remaining for Completion of Quest:
"Rescue Almeister from Imprisonment in the Tower of Zuria."
[Two Lunar Rotations]
{COURTESY MESSAGE #11}

CHAPTER THIRTY-THREE

You don't think you should have told me when I first woke up?!" I say, sotto voce, to Brittany and Perg, who are walking beside the wheelchair in which I am being pushed by Tavrella. And yet again, every strained word sends me into paroxysms of agony.

"Careful, dear boy," Tavrella cautions. "Yer still in no state. Soon."

She strokes my hair again, which should feel overly familiar, but, y'know, if somebody who looked like Beyoncé was stroking your hair, you'd not complain either.

Lonnaigh walks up ahead, leading us down the long corridor that attaches Garr Haven to the nearest Temple of the Body and adjoining Pulse Well. It was incredibly convenient to be able to repair vehicles and boost Abilities and train all in the same place, so I set it up this way.

(Is it *overly* convenient and a little bit of a cheat? Yes. Is it as much of a plot convenience as Gero just wantonly making the Androids in *Dragon Ball Z* as powerful as he wanted them to be? I would argue not.)

"I was going to," Brit starts, "but—"

"But we were just happy to see you're still here, fool. Take it as a compliment," Perg chides.

I hear Tavrella laughing politely behind me.

"I don't understand. When this"—I tap at my chest—"reset itself back in the Candy Shoppe, why didn't it reset the Quest parameters as well?"

"Is that a real question?" Brittany asks with a snort. "You think I have the answers to how this whole renegade System works?"

"You're the one who kept all the lists for the books."

Brit turns her head to me sharply, widens her eyes, and tightens her jaw, stopping herself just short of saying, "Ix-nay on the ooks-bay. Averlla-tay is ight-ray ere-thay."

(Pig Latin is one of the only other languages Brittany speaks that I am semiuent-flay in.)

I tilt my head to try and look up at Tavrella to see if she clocked anything or seems put off by the idiosyncrasies of this new and definitely not improved Heart Guard crew, but she just keeps looking straight ahead, a mysterious little smile on her lips.

"How are we possibly going to get all the way to Mount Saatus and the Cavern of Sorrows, then *back* to Santus Luminous in under *two* Lunar Rotations?"

"Glad you asked," Brit replies, withdrawing a map from her fresh new garb from the Meridia Fall Fantasy Collection. "Lonnaigh has been helping me fill in the spotty parts of my memory that were lost when we, y'know, reconstituted." She unfolds the map and points. "That," she says, "is how we get there and back in under two Lunar Rotations."

I look at what she's referring to, slightly confused.

"The Arch?" I say. (The Arch of Raylion, my clever and not at all obvious homage to the Gateway Arch.) "I don't get it."

"Of course you don't. *Because you forgot too*," she emphasizes for Tavrella's benefit, I guess. But Tavrella continues not to seem like she cares all that much.

"It's a portal, homie," Perg chimes in.

"It's a portal?" I repeat.

"It's a portal," Brit affirms. "It's a, y'know, a whatayoucallit. A Quick Travel portal. All we have to do is plug in the proper coordinates, make sure we hit it at exactly a hundred and forty-one point six two two kilostrydes per hour, and it'll take us exactly to where we need to go."

"A hundred and forty-one point six two two?"

"Yuuuuup," Brittany rolls out. She's wearing a kind of raised-eyebrow, knowing look.

"That's . . . specific."

"Yuuuuuuuuuup," she says again, drawing it out longer.

"Why does it need to—?"

"Doesn't matter," she throws out quickly. She takes a breath, clears her throat, and adds, "The good *NEWS* is that if we use the portal, we stand a decent chance of getting there and *BACK IN TIME* to handle the Almeister business." Her eyes widen to accompany her raised eyebrows.

I'm confused. She's clearly attempting to convey something to me, but I don't . . . ?

News? Back in time? What is she trying to—?

And then it hits me.

Oh, dear lord. Seriously? No. Oh my god. Really? It can't be. For the love of . . .

I set the standard measurement of distance on Meridia at something called a kilostryde because . . . I mean . . . it's just a mashup of "kilometer" and "stride" spelled with a *y* instead of an *i*. It's not that deep.

Now, having been born and raised in the great state of Missouri, I couldn't tell you the metric equivalent of jack sprat as converted from the imperial system. In fact, the first time I went to London a few years ago for a Riftbreaker convention, I tried to exercise in the hotel gym not realizing that the twenty-five-pound weights I was attempting to lift were actually twenty-five *kilograms*, or roughly, *fifty-five* pounds. (The dislocated shoulder I suffered was nothing in comparison to the injuries I'm currently sporting, but it definitely slowed down typing for a few weeks.)

Brittany, however, having lived all over the world, is conversant with converting time, temperature, distance, all that. Just like she can speak in a variety of languages.

And one of those languages is "Bruce Silver."

Thus, using her combined expertise in multiple methods of communication, she has just told me that a hundred and forty-one point six two two is equivalent to precisely . . . eighty-eight.

Eighty-eight. Miles. Per hour.

The speed at which the DeLorean in *Back to the Future* needed to be going in order to travel through time, the theme from the original film being the song "Back in Time" by Huey Lewis and the *News*.

I start to reach for the bridge of my nose to rub away the headache I feel coming on, but then realize I'm doing it with my torched hand, and the pain from my burned fingers causes me to forget about the ache in my skull.

"Are you . . . ?" I begin to groan out because, once more, this is not me. I didn't do this. I didn't write about Quick Travel or the Arch being a portal or anything. Once more, things are functioning as art imitating life imitating art imitating life and on and on and on, like a collection of never-ending fun house mirrors.

Now intensely curious about what other tidbits have been discovered while I've been convalescing, I ask, "So, what else have you two been up to for the last four nights?"

"I mean . . . just, y'know, waiting on you to wake up. Getting caught up with Lon. *It's been so long since we've seen her.*" Brittany leans into that part pretty hard, although I am coming to think that Tavrella is the kind of person to whom we could tell our story of transportation here and would just respond with, "*Well, isn't that something?*"

But better safe than sorry. "Yeah, yeah," I say, going along with the charade. "And what'd you find out? About *what's been going on since we saw her last?*" I put some shoulder into the question myself, just for uniformity.

"Oh, not much, just . . . she and some other members of Clan Catarinci went looking for Mael but couldn't find him, so she dispatched a platoon to seek you, but then they were captured by DONG and tortured for information on where to find Garr Haven and Carvesend and the Rebellion's Nexus Core and all that good stuff, but—as far as she knows—none of them gave up anything, since she figures they would've found it by now . . ."

And although one would think I'd be almost fully inured to wild reveals at this point, my mouth opens wider and wider the more she speaks because, what?! All that happened since the end of book eight?

Book nine was the failed attempt to rescue Mael, which resulted in Almeister's capture. And then, book ten was . . . what it was. But neither of them featured Lonnaigh at all because she wouldn't speak to Carpathian anymore, so he just let her be. I always figured there'd be some grand reunion between the two, but . . .

So, in addition to things like Gospels and portals that I didn't know about *at all*, even stuff I thought I had a clear handle on . . . I don't, really. The whole of Meridia continued to just spin in the background as I was off writing about other adventures.

Oh, Elizabeth Gilbert, you really tapped into something, didn't ya?

". . . which is where all the gear came from," Brittany finishes.

Shit. I zoned out again. She's spinning around, showing off her attire, the cape flowing behind her as she circles.

"Sorry. What?" I say.

"It's where Lon got these clothes for me. The Annex."

"The Annex?" Yet another thing that apparently exists that I know nothing about.

"Aye," Tavrella says from behind me. "'Tis where is stored all the looted paraphernalia that Clan Catarinci has captured."

"They've got all kinds of stuff. Old Templar gear. Weapons. It's where I dropped off the gloves," Brittany says.

"Which gloves?"

"The ones I boosted from that Templar at the tavern. The Stoneheart gloves."

"*Oh, wow, Bruce. Look at that, O me of little faith. An ELEMENTAL ITEM. Which you need for the Mael Quest. It's almost like you should just Trust the System.*"

I grit my teeth and tell the voice in my head, "*Bruce, if we ever meet face-to-face, I'm gonna punch you so hard . . .*"

"Why'd you take those?" I ask Brit, curious if she received some sort of command or . . . ?

"Dunno. Just feel like looting is kinda de rigueur. *Et quand à* Meridia . . ." (Oh. Okay. So no command; she's just a thief. Great.) "Woulda scooped up the spellsword too," she continues, "but it was still too hot to grab."

"Why didn't you just put on the gloves first?"

"Don't start, okay? Things were moving at a pace, and getting your overly tanned hide outta there was the priority."

I shudder at the phrase "overly tanned hide." Tavrella seems to sense it and strokes my head again. I can't figure her out. She's, like, extra nice. I mean, her bedside manner is off the chain.

"Here we are," she says as we arrive at the temple door.

It's a grand, ornately carved oak affair, just like I described it in the books. It stands in intentionally anachronistic contrast to the gritty, mechanical nature of Garr Haven and all its machinery. Temples of the Body, wherever they might be found in Meridia, are sacred spaces; temples in every sense of the word. Of the body, for the body, and in service to the temple that is the body itself.

Half dojo and half prayer hall, each one has soaring ramparts, polished marble, and great murals depicting the Battle of Evercall—canonically, the place from whence the very first Pulse Well sprang forth . . . because after the Battle of Evercall, I had written myself into a real corner. Carpathian had gotten JACKED UP in the showdown with Azteral the Punisher—the half-man, half-machine invention of my own imagination who one hundred percent was NOT Arnold Schwarzenegger in *The Terminator*—and needed to get healed up real quick.

I had already established that the Candy Shoppe was one of a kind and way back in Bell's View, which Carpathian had left a whole book and a half previous, so Carpathian crawled into a random abandoned building and asked for Richemerion, the Warden of Protection, to save him somehow. Suddenly, the whole place transformed into a Temple of the Body, replete with a newly monikered Pulse Well.

Looking back on it, it seems wildly convoluted. Like, why couldn't I just have had Almeister use Mezmer on him or, y'know, gone back and done a revision *to make life easier on myself?* (Because "flow state" is a hell of a drug, that's why.)

Regardless of the reason, we're here now. Outside of an actual Temple of the Body. And it's causing my own body to shiver in anticipation.

"Ye alright?" Tavrella asks, noticing my little shimmy.

"Yeah, yeah," I breathe. "All good."

She moves around me to stand in front of the door. Facing me, she places her hands on her hips, looking for all the world like some kind of alchemist warrior queen. "Ready to go inside?"

I swallow and nod before she opens the door to reveal . . .

. . . what looks an awful lot like a Twenty-Four Hour Fitness.

In fact, it looks almost *exactly* like the Twenty-Four Hour Fitness I go to back home.

Hm. Well. Okay.

Brit is clearly as unprepared for this as I am because her mouth falls open a little, and she points. "That . . ."

"I know."

"That doesn't look like . . ."

"It does not."

"Why does it look like . . . ?"

"I don't know, but I think we're gonna have to stop questioning these things."

She takes a breath, puts on her accept-and-adapt face, and gives me a tight military nod.

Tavrella must notice the befuddled expression I'm wearing because she asks, "Ye sure yer alright, there? Ye seem forlorn somehow."

"Forlorn? No. No, no. Not forlorn, just . . ." I look to Brit for help finding a word.

"He's just . . . overwhelmed by the . . . majesty . . . of the temple."

I mouth *Majesty?* She shrugs. Like we're in a sitcom from the '90s or some damn thing.

Tavrella smiles impishly then moves back behind me to wheel me through the door, past a full weight rack, and over to a Smith Press Machine where Lonnaigh stands, waiting.

Draped over the bar of the Smith Press is an assortment of what appears to be clothing.

"What, uh—" I start to ask, pointing.

"It's proper raiment for when ye get out of the Well," she says. "Can't go off on a Quest to save my brother with ye in a loincloth."

"These came from the whatchacallit?"

"The Annex, aye. Combed through and found ye the best options I could come up with. Apart from these." She holds up the Stoneheart gloves Brittany nicked. "It's been a bit o' time since we collected anything new. But it's a damn sight better'n nothin'."

Tavrella rolls me over to inspect it. The first item is a mesh suit that looks like it's going to be formfitting. I pick it up with my good arm and find that it's surprisingly lightweight. Like SPANX. (I know because I had to go to this holiday gala thing a couple of years back and I had enjoyed a particularly robust Thanksgiving, so shoutout to SPANX for helping me squeeze into my tux.) The suit is clearly designed for mobility. The mesh is interwoven with a fine, almost invisible thread that catches the light in an iridescent shimmer.

And next to it is . . .

"Drakonar-scale bracers," Brittany says, hushed.

Her quiet reverence is justified.

The scales themselves have this deep, rich color that seems to dance in the light. Drakonars, as a species, have resistance to certain Mezmer Types. One can tell which Mezmer will fail to affect them depending on the color of their scales; so, these being red tells me that they will have at least a bit of fire invulnerability. Which, looking at the half of my body that remains griddled, occurs to me would have been nice to have come into possession of sooner. But, y'know, don't look a gift Drakonar bracer in the scales.

And, on the floor . . . boots. Nothing fancy. Just boots. They look nice, at least. The last has a form-fitted shape, and they appear to be a Goodyear welt, as opposed to being Blake Stitched, which, while more expensive, suggests that some thoughtful cobbler was thinking of durability. As the late, great shoemaker Stefano Bemer once said, "Quality is remembered long after price is forgotten."

(Way back before Riftbreaker, I wrote a series of short stories about a shoemaker who was murdered by bandits along with his whole family and became a vengeful wraith intent on exacting retribution using his shoemaking skills. It was called *The Sole Gatherer*. Never really caught on as a series, but I did learn a lot about fine footwear.)

"Where did you acquire all this?" I ask, referring to the clothes, mostly because I don't actually recognize the style as being familiar to anything I wrote about. Particularly the mesh suit. It looks like the type of thing designed for when you have a ballet recital at one o'clock, but you have to go to war at three-thirty.

"It was standard Templar-wear long ago," Lonnaigh says.

"Uh . . . Whence? Ago?" I ask.

"From the era of the *last* Rebellion."

"Mm-hmm. Mm-hmm. Mm-hmm. Sure." I nod. I nod. I nod. Then . . . "*Which* Rebellion?"

She looks at me as a disappointed teacher might.

"I know we ne'er talked much about yer life afore ye were 'anointed' Saviour"—she rolls her eyes—"but did ye not attend school of any kind? Did they not teach ye yer history?"

"I, uh . . ." I fumfer. Because, honestly, I don't really know what kind of schooling Carpathian had. I put some amount of thought into his home life and that kind of thing—which may or may not share some similarities to my own—but I didn't do a deep dive into the guy's matriculation other than he aced his public conveyance

conductor exam with such high marks that it brought him to the attention of the
Elder Wardens as the one who would become the Saviour. Some people seek glory,
some have it thrust upon them because they know how to feather a clutch.

"History?" I continue stammering before Perg jumps into the conversation
from Brit's metal-clad shoulder.

"Yeah, fool. This is not the first time Meridia has been threatened."

". . . Sorry, what?"

"Back in the time before time, before the era of bounty into which most
currently walking the planet were born, there were also threats. However, in the
past, they were successfully quelled by a small but dedicated band of fighters, with
Clan Catarinci as the tip of those particular spears. The *last* was the rebellion they
waged to successfully thwart the efforts of the one they called the *Eighth* Guardian. The eighth in the lineage of Guardians who believe their purpose has ever
been to disrupt the System and topple the natural order. And, so, y'know, that's
where they got all this fly gear you see here from. From whooping that Eighth
Guardian ass and holding on to the spoils as trophies. Or, at least, that's the information I seem to have access to right now."

Lonnaigh nods. "Aye," she says, "the snail speaks true."

There is a long, long pause as I try to parse through what I just heard. Brittany is the one to finally speak up. "The *Eighth* Guardian?" she settles on, clearly
as gobsmacked as I am.

"Of course," Lonnaigh starts. "Why do ye think the Ninth Guardian is called
the *Ninth* Guardian? Did ye not have a proper education either? Good thing ye
travel with the snail."

*No. Nonononononono. No, the Ninth Guardian is just a cool-ass sounding
name that I picked because . . . it sounded cool ass!*

"That's tautological of you, Bruce," the voice in my head weighs in.

*"So are you trying to tell me that there have been eight 'Guardians' prior who all
tried to disrupt the stability of things on Meridia . . . and failed?"* I ask myself.

*"I'm not telling you anything, Bruce. I'm also in the dark. But, if your sapient snail
friend who has insight into certain realities of life here is right, then . . . yeah. Sounds
kinda like how it probably went."*

I can't. I just can't. I'm sorry. This is becoming more complicated than *Per-
mutation City.*

"But, no, wait . . ." I begin. "So what's happening is a cycle that has been—"

Lonnaigh heads me off, her patience clearly wearing thin.

"No!" she shouts. "No more waitin'! I'm not wasting energy going over that
which ye should already know! This ain't the time fer a history lesson! And if yer
just tryin' to stall, I've enough of it. My brother's waited damn long enough. I
don't know why the System herself would lead me to find ye again the way she
has, but if it ain't to rescue Mael, then I got no use fer ye."

Tavrella places her hand on my shoulder. It stills me from any reaction I
might otherwise have and subdues me quickly and generously into a place of
quiet compliance.

Thump-thump. Thump. Thump.

My Heart slows. I didn't even know it had started beating faster.

"You're right," I sigh in the direction of Lonnaigh. "You're right. Let's get about the business of . . . what's next. Just . . . let them go first." I nod at Brit and Perg. "They haven't had a chance to verify anything about their statuses since we . . . reconstituted. We're gonna need to know all that we're working with if we're going to formulate a coherent plan for proceeding."

Although the temple resembles nothing that I ever imagined, it's still a Temple of the Body and, I have to presume, works in at least some kind of comparable way to how I wrote about it. As a place to train, modify, meditate, and upgrade. All these workout machines *must* be more than *just* workout machines. Right? Like, they must be Mezmeric machines that allow you to train up your newly verified Abilities and acquired Spells? *Right?*

Either that or the thing in the corner is just a regular old Glute Grinder. But I'm not about to start asking more questions at the moment.

Lonnaigh breathes in through her nose and draws her spine straight. "Aye. Fine, then. Nightwind, let's go."

She strides over to a door with a sign on it reading "Pulse Well Must Be Cleaned After Every Use" and opens it up. When she does, what looks like a transparent glass tanning machine comes zipping out into the larger gym space with a *ZOIIIIINNNNNG* sound, like it's a prop in some wacky Japanese game show.

Lonnaigh waves Brittany to step inside, but Brit doesn't move.

"Hop to," Lonnaigh says, snapping her fingers. "Let's go."

Once more, Brittany stays still. She grimaces a tiny bit and crosses her arms over her chest.

"Bri—?" I start, then gather. "Teleri? What's wrong?"

I can feel Lonnaigh tense up from halfway across the space. "What's the problem?" she asks.

Brittany doesn't respond. I hear Perg whisper loudly into her ear, "You okay, girlie?"

"Hey," I say, reaching out for her with my good arm. "Hey, what's wrong? You don't wanna know what awesome Abilities you have access to that are just hiding inside you, waiting to be unleashed? Or at least confirm at what Level your whole 'Summoning' thing is living?"

She shakes her head, and I notice that her jaw appears to tense when she says, "Yeah, yeah, I'm fine. I'm just remembering . . ." She trails off, snorting a little *hm* to herself.

"Remembering . . . ?" I prompt.

She sucks her teeth. "What happened the *last* time Teleri—um, I. The last time *I* visited a Pulse Well." She shoots me a look.

"What are you . . . ?" I begin to ask before realizing . . . "Oh. Right," I moan a little as I recall the same thing she does . . .

CHAPTER THIRTY-FOUR

Kinship of Spirits, Riftbreaker Book Ten, Chapter Forty-Five

Run!" Einzgear the Saviour shouted to his companions as the Giant Serpent of the Mokeisan rumbled toward him, Nightwind, and Pergamon who, in his largest form, was still no match for the creature. This was the same serpent who had previously stirred the mighty Mokeisan Desert into such a whirlwind that even Zerastian, with her incomparable intellect and premonitory Skill, could not escape its fury and was absorbed completely by the maelstrom it created.

If only . . . Carpathian thought at the time. *If only Mael had been with us,* perhaps his strength could have disturbed the outcome.

But he wasn't there. And Zerastian was taken.

As were they all.

Mael before her.

Xanaraxa after.

And finally, Almeister.

Almeister. Still trapped inside the Tower of Zuria awaiting trial, and Carpathian as yet unsuccessful in retrieving him. What kind of Saviour must he be, he wondered, if he could not even save the person responsible for his ascent to such a lofty perch? A very poor excuse for one, indeed, he answered his own thoughts.

Oh, that they now had with them but one of their number lost, they might stand something of a chance against the serpent's rough, impermeable hide and thunderous rage. But such as they were currently assembled, they stood little chance.

"Teleri!" Carpathian called to one of his last two remaining allies. "You must flee! Now!"

But Teleri Nightwind would none of it. She still believed in the one called the Saviour. She believed that his purpose was true, and that if she but focused intently on her Identify Limitation Spell, she might be able to find some vulnerability in the beast charging toward them, and Carpathian could take fullest advantage of it.

The serpent itself was far too powerful for her to end on her own; she knew that, of course. It was, indeed, far too powerful for any one soul to best without aid.

Except for Carpathian. The Saviour.

He could bring this monster to its conclusion. Of course he could, she thought. He had bettered many another foe with just as advanced a Level, if not greater. And thus, she could not understand why he was so resistant to take up the fight. But she did not know that Carpathian had been harboring doubts. Doubts he believed he had long since banished. Doubts that he, even with all the powers he had been granted, could save this world.

He had been wrong lo those many moons ago outside the pub called Jeomandi's. It was not incumbent upon him that he shoulder the weight of Meridia's fate on his own. There was no shame in admitting that he needed the others. They might not have been to each other's lineage borne, but they had grown to become something not unlike relation.

It was his relationship to them that granted him his truest power. And without them—without them all—he questioned if he would still be able to complete his odyssey as it had been prophesied.

But he had not shared such thoughts with Teleri. Why would he?

And so, she stood fast, eyeing the colossus with intense Focus, trying to pinpoint the likeliest place for Carpathian to launch a Felling Attack. A killing blow. But . . . she could not. The monstrosity's Mantle of Security was too great and obscured her Ability to highlight its disadvantage.

"Fyunccantre," she cursed to herself quietly in Lumivarian. It had been at least a dozen Lunar Rotations since she'd visited a Pulse Well, so while she could feel inside herself that her Ability to focus her Spell was sufficiently advanced to grant her the vision she required, she had yet to verify it, confirm it, and thus be able to access it in a manner that would allow her to employ it in battle.

And given how ferociously the serpent was pursuing them, she thought that even only having the upgrade validated might not be enough. She might need to practice its utility in a Temple of the Body as well. And all of that would take time—time she did not think they could spare.

A feeling of overwhelming regret took her over. A feeling that . . . she had failed them.

If only she knew that she was not alone in her feelings.

Suddenly, she felt a jolt of energy grasping her from behind. Her body was drawn backward, yanked from her defiant position facing down the beast. She whipped through the air as if being pulled by a giant rope around the waist, keeping her eyes on the serpent, its jaws wide, Mezmer flaring from within as it raced to catch her, determined to lay her to waste.

And then, like a masked tussling partner waiting anxiously behind the ropes of one of the scripted grappling battles that were so popular among the citizens of Santus Luminous, Carpathian slapped his palm into hers and—powered by the Gauntlet of Sorenthali—wrenched her farther away as he burst past her to enter the fray, a living embodiment of hope and raw power. She felt the surge of his strength as he propelled her effortlessly, hurling her up and away from danger, the air around him seeming to warp as he activated ChronoHeart Eclipse, bending the very fabric of time around himself.

To Teleri, it appeared as if Carpathian moved within a separate reality where each second stretched into a vast, vibrant infinity as he became less a man and more a blur of desperate determination and unyielding resolve.

"Pergamon, to her aid!" Carpathian's voice thundered, a commanding echo that pierced through the slowed reality. As she receded from danger, Teleri saw Pergamon, his form shifting in response, soaring forth to catch her in a swift, protective embrace.

With Teleri now safe in Pergamon's care, Carpathian faced the serpent alone. The Obsidian Shield, alive with dark energy, flared into being, creating an impenetrable barrier against the beast's Mezmeric assaults. Moving with grace—as only one whose Manasteel Resonance had been forged and refined time and again could—each blow from Carpathian's Gauntlet carried the force of a thousand tempests.

Yet and still, the serpent retaliated. Its massive body—a mosaic of scales and muscle—was quick, quicker than even the World Saviour had guessed it could be. Carpathian met its fury with an artful dance of blades and light, the Cerulean Tunic flickering as he navigated the boundaries of the physical and ethereal realms, diving in and out of view in a blink.

Then, calling on his underlying Nexabind allocation, Carpathian beckoned forth the Aspect Guardians, the ethereal echoes of ancient heroes. Elders of the Elders themselves. They swarmed the serpent in a flurry of blades, creating a dazzling display of light and shadow.

Likewise, the Aspect Guardians' Spell tempered a connection, the rift from which they appeared weeping with Mezmer beyond the permanent plane. Mezmer that the World Saviour could now harness. Carpathian became a channel of divine power and soared to reach Teleri and Pergamon, bringing them under his Aura Shroud.

The Arm of Hearts, charged with the life force of legions, shone with destructive intent.

And with a scream that reverberated across the vastness of space and time, Carpathian—with one branch of his Mezmer holding his friends safe in his charge and another directed with unforgiving vengeance toward the serpent—dove like a comet toward the abomination. The spear struck the beast's heart with apocalyptic force, a collision that shattered the air and resonated through realms unknown.

In a brilliant explosion, the serpent was driven full through, its colossal form finally, mercifully, disintegrating, defeated by Carpathian's overwhelming might and his dogged unwillingness to allow it to live its venomous existence on this plane for another moment.

It was then that Carpathian and his companions, cocooned in a makeshift cradle formed by the Saviour's Aura Shroud, crashed through the roof of the Temple of the Body like a child's rag dolls, the three of them falling onto the floor of the sacred space and rolling to a graceless stop.

They breathed in the sudden, almost unsettling quiet as the suns shone down through the rafters upon their still living spirits, overcome with the knowledge that life would not be abandoning them. Not this day.

Finally, after several moments' pregnant silence, Carpathian spoke.

"We can no longer take such risks."

"I do not feel we take them," Pergamon, now in his Moderate Form, replied. "It seems to me they are forced upon us."

Teleri chuckled a small laugh despite herself.

"In either case," Carpathian continued, "if we are to continue apace, we must make it our priority to reassemble our coterie."

"I thought," Teleri said, pausing to take in a contemplative breath, "that is what we have been doing lo' on these many Rotations."

"We must redouble our efforts," he replied somberly. "And to do that, I feel we must . . ."

The echo of his trailing voice in the sacred chamber hung in the air like a gathering storm.

"Feel we must what? Carpathian?" she prodded.

"Feel we must disband. The three of us. For now."

Bafflement settled on both Teleri and Pergamon.

"Carpathian?" the snail queried. "I don't understand. I thought you just said our goal was to reconvene our Party, not to dispel it further."

Carpathian swallowed before speaking again. "I realize it may seem counterintuitive, but there is a method behind the recommendation." The Saviour's two allies waited with rapt attention. He continued. "It is time that we assemble an army. A true army. A proper army. I had once believed that we few, we happy few, we band of brethren and sistren, might provide an ample enough ocean to quell the fires of those who oppose us, but I see now that is not so."

"But—" Teleri began to protest, but Carpathian would none of it.

"No, Teleri. No. Even with the fullest complement of our collected strength—which we do not have—we are inadequate. I am unconvinced that even the Aspect Guardians are sufficient to lend aid. Just now, I could feel their capacity waning. I fear that they, like all of us . . . are tired."

Teleri and Pergamon observed the Saviour with concern. He had ever been dour, but this . . . this felt like something else.

"We must, I now believe, conscript a proper army. An army of all those on Meridia who do not wish to allow the Ninth Guardian, the High Council, and the Super Vizier to continue expanding their power. Because while we fight for those who cannot fight for themselves, there will come a time when we are no longer able to carry the struggle."

Teleri, forgetting herself, began to contest the Saviour once more, "But—"

Carpathian raised a hand to silence her. "There will. As certain as there will be a 'morrow, we will, eventually, each succumb to the truth of existence. And that is that it is ephemeral. And when that day comes, if we have not created a mechanism through which all might be able to fight for themselves, we will have failed."

A new kind of silence now shrouded the room. One not borne of relief but of concern.

"But . . ." Teleri began yet again. "But the Mezmer the High Council possesses . . . it is too great. And they can always replenish themselves, whereas the rest of Meridia cannot."

"And that is why we must separate. I will seek and marshal the necessary forces to do what must be done to bring the battle to the Tower. It is there that Almeister is held. It is there that the Core is housed. And it is there where we might find the Ninth Guardian. Some may fall, but victory will be assured if you and Pergamon return to Carvesend and see to it that the Rebellion's Nexus Core might finally be functioning properly."

"But Carpathian," Pergamon spoke up cautiously, "we have had but only scattered success with the Rebellion Core. To assemble an army the scope of which you speak and endow such a force with Mezmer to a degree that it might be able to wage a war against—"

"It is not a request, Pergamon," Carpathian interrupted kindly but firmly.

Pergamon quieted and bowed his head.

Teleri and Pergamon were Carpathian's friends, but more than that, they were his apostles. Not in the manner of servitude, as were the Disciples of the Ninth Guardian, but in the manner of loyalists, as perhaps a soldier of lesser rank to that of a superior. Even when they did not understand the Saviour's commands, they followed them.

Had they known Carpathian's plan was flawed at its base, they might have protested further. But not having the precognitive services of Zerastian present—or the wisdom of Almeister, or the philosophy of Xanaraxa, or the brute force of Mael—they acceded to do as Carpathian commanded.

The irony was that Carpathian could have seen it himself, had he chosen to look. He possessed adequate Mezmer across the necessary fields of practice to make himself aware of what was to come. But his fatal flaw had ever been his unwillingness to express aloud those parts of him that remained from before. The parts of Carpathian left dormant but incessant as he grew over time to embrace his role as the Saviour. The parts that were not bred of his ascent but were of his truest, most essential self.

Not that which set him apart from others, but that which bound him to them.

And so, he chose instead to focus only on his current intentions, and thus, willingly blind himself to the probable consequences.

"So it's settled," he concluded, rising to his feet. "Teleri, you and Pergamon should both attend the Pulse Well before you venture out again. Ensure you have access to the richest complement of your Mezmer." They both nodded, suppressing the words that filled their mouths but that they dare not let escape.

Carpathian strode to the door of the temple, cape trailing behind him, and before exiting, looked back over his shoulder at the two who had become—though he still might not speak it aloud—his family. "I'll see you soon."

And then . . . he was gone.

CHAPTER THIRTY-FIVE

So, what happened?" Lonnaigh asks. "Last time she visited a Pulse Well?"

Brit still has her arms crossed. She's tapping her toe and staring at me.

Man. Carpathian never got this kind of disrespect. Feel like I'm getting all the crappy parts of being him with none of the perks.

"Oh, not much," she says. "Carp here just managed to convince me and ol' Perg to go running off to Carvesend and get the Rebellion Core up and running to fuel an entire army. The same army he then led to doom. Which you may have heard about."

Lonnaigh looks shocked. "I know of the battle, obviously, but I ha'not heard that accessing the Core were part o' the plan. There's no way the Rebellion Core is adequate to provide that much Mezmer. Not in its current state."

"Yeah, no shit," Brit replies. "But y'know this one." She points at me. "Never know what wacky idea is gonna fall outta that big Saviour skull of his."

Even though it hurts like hell, I roll my shoulders back to try and avoid launching into some kind of self-defense. Partially because I don't really have one, and partially because Brittany isn't pissed about Pulse Wells or Nexus Cores or even failed battles. She's pissed because that was the point in book ten when I stopped running the chapters by her.

Our normal way of working had evolved into something like: I write a chapter. Then I show it to her. Then she tells me if there's anything in it that I missed or forgot or "flow stated" my way into a corner with or something. If anything was particularly messy or contradictory, I'd go back and do a rewrite, employing her notes. If, as would occasionally happen, everything checked out, then it was full steam ahead to write the next one.

It bears repeating, even if only to myself . . . I truly don't think I would enjoy all the success I have without her.

But of course, that process wasn't how the final five chapters of book ten went.

Brit even said, "*Wow. He's breaking off from Pergamon and Teleri to whip up an army on his own? That's bold. You have any idea what happens next?*"

"*Kind of,*" I had replied. Which wasn't a lie. When I wrote, "*she did not know that Carpathian had been harboring doubts. He had not shared such a thing with her,*" I didn't tell her how true that was for Bruce as well. If I'm being completely transparent with myself, I had been feeling the weight of being "bestselling author Bruce Silver" for a minute. And even though I hadn't committed to the notion of killing off Carpathian and crew until I actually got into typing it, it had been swirling around.

So, just like Carpathian sent Teleri and Pergamon away while he went off alone to . . . I dunno, meet his maker, I hid from Brittany to pound out the final chapters of the life of Carpathian Einzgear alone in the shadows of my own imagination.

(I didn't hide it from Perg, funnily enough. He sat behind me in his aquarium the whole time. If I had known dude was eyeballing me as hard as he was, I probably would've thrown a blanket over the tank or something.)

By the time Teleri and Pergamon made it to the battlefield that Rendalia had become, it was too late to save him. Just like by the time I read the end aloud to Brittany, it was too late to save . . .

Whatever.

Anyway.

That's why she's pissed.

"Yes. Fine," I find myself saying. "What happened was less than ideal. I know. But there's nothing that can be done about it now except to try and correct the mistakes of the past by not repeating them and repairing whatever damage done I can. And that's it. Okay? That's it. And that's what I'm trying to do. So. Yeah. I don't know what else to say. I mean, I'm sorry, alright? I'm sorry and . . . If we can all just get into the damn Pulse Well now, verify our Statuses, and grab whatever strengths and Spells and Abilities and all that that we can, then I vow that I will do all I can to get Mael, get Almeister, get everybody we need to get and set things right by trying to recenter all possible worlds on their damn axes, because *that* seems like the kind of thing I'm *absolutely* qualified for. So, alright? Okay? Can that be . . . ?"

I let it trail away because I really don't know what else to say. I'm sure I don't sound very Saviour-y right now.

"That's the first damn time I've ever heard ye talk like a true Saviour," Lonnaigh says.

Well, that's unexpected.

"It's no secret that I've had my doubts over the time I've known ye, Carpathian, but . . ." She pauses, then says, "A *true* Saviour isn't all about power and might and indestructibility. A true Saviour is about being accountable to that which they are sworn to uphold and defend. That's what my brother has always had." She places her hands on her hips and looks at me with a twinkle in her eye and, like a coda, adds, "So, alright then."

There is a beat where no one speaks, and then . . .

"Sooooo, we good now?" Perg asks. "We set to get Mezmer-swole and go run the fade on some of these cabrones del DONG?"

Brit nods, tightly at first and then more convincingly with each bob of her chin. "Yeah. Yeah, sure," she replies. "Let's get ready to go fuck shit up."

She takes Perg off her shoulder, places him on the arm of my wheelchair deal-y, and strides over to the Pulse Well, waving her hand in front of the access panel. The door opens up, and she looks back at me like, "Well, that was cool." I realize this is her first time really engaging with the tech here on Meridia, and it reminds me of the nervousness and excitement I felt when I first stepped into the Interlocutrix.

Five days ago!

Feels like five centuries. (Maybe it is. Again, I never set the hardest rules for the timeline.)

In any old case, the glass door closes behind her, and the chamber comes instantly to life.

"Whoa!" she shouts as a kaleidoscope of Mezmeric energy swirls around her, each hue more vibrant than the last. "Ooo-whoa! Whoa, whoa, whoa!"

She's lifted into the air, floating in a sudden sea of chromatic brilliance. It looks disorienting, and she closes her eyes, grasping at the air for some kind of anchor, I suppose.

"Is this how this is supposed to work?" she shouts.

Lonnaigh laughs a confused little laugh. "Ye act like ye've n'er been in a Pulse Well before."

"Remort!" Brittany calls. "Technically, I haven't!"

"Oh, right," Lonnaigh says. "Well, yeah, I mean, this is how they work. Dunno who designed the damn things; that's lost to the ash of history. But whoever it was clearly had a fixation with the color spectrum."

That, or they imagined the Pulse Well specifics while on an ayahuasca retreat.

From the ceiling of the Well, a ribbon of light unfurls, a living stream of luminescence, before, with a crescendo of bright energy, the chamber reaches its peak. The walls of the Pulse Well light up, transforming into a massive display that projects onto the far wall. And we can all now see what Brit is working with.

Welcome, [Teleri Nightwind].
It would appear there have been some changes since your last visit.

Oh, no. Here we go. Brit's going to most *definitely* have a negative reaction to the new, snarky, sassified version of the System's Notifications.

Please be advised that you might experience a mote of discomfort
with the process as we delve into the modifications and adaptations
required. Your patience is appreciated.
{COURTESY MESSAGE #1}

What? Why no cheeky, mischievous, "oopsie daisy, you're making a mistake" style of messaging like I've gotten? Brit's visit with System Integration is much more similar to how I wrote it. I'd go so far as to say it's *polite*.

Maybe it's just as afraid to get on her bad side as everyone else is.

Whatever the reason, she is spared having to be condescended to by what I receive as Oscar Wilde meets Ricky Gervais, and the display now shifts as the wall populates additional text.

[Teleri Nightwind], your current attributes are as follows:

[NEW] Mezmer Type:
Three-Type

[NEW] Foundation:
Vanguard

Vanguards are combat-focused users who have trained to integrate their Mezmer seamlessly with physical combat, ensuring they can switch between Spellcasting and martial skill fluidly. Requires a weapon as a focus.

Wow. *Wow.* Brit's a Vanguard. And a Three-Type. That's wild. Teleri was a One-Type Sorcerer. This is . . . *extremely* different than the way things were in the books.

Carpathian was the Three-Type Vanguard, and the fact that he resonated with three specific Mezmer disciplines was a big deal. Now that's what Brittany's got going on? It's like we've been reshuffled and dealt new hands. We're not just Teleri and Carpathian—we're an altogether different rendering of Teleri and Carpathian.

"*Curiouser and curiouser, eh, Bruce?*"

Curiouser indeed.

Her new details continue broadcasting.

>**Resonance Tier:**
Etherflint

>**Affinity:**
Convocationist: [High]
Function (Warmarked): [Average]
Stellari: [Average]

Statistics:
Mental: *Etherflint Level 3*
Physical: *Etherflint Level 3*
Aura: *Etherflint Level 1*
Animus: *Etherflint Level 2*

>**Armament(s):**
Summoner's Cape

>**Abilities:**
Map Maker [Advanced]
Beast Mastery [Intermediate]
>**Spell(s):**
Summoner of Something [Novice]
Randolf's Radiant Ray [Beginner]

So she *does* have a Beast Mastery Ability. Of course she does; that makes sense. And it's already operating at an Intermediate Level. I'm also intrigued to see her in possession of Summoner of Something. So far, that *something* has just been Tentasaurians, but now that it's been verified that she can summon other things too . . .

Man, if she can figure out how to combine all this with her advanced-level knowledge of Population and Demographics, who knows what would be possible. (Eh. Earth-based skillsets probably aren't transferrable to Meridia.)

And, obviously, she's an Advanced Map Maker. Not sure I understand how that will redound to our overall benefit yet, but why would I? I just *invented* it all.

Maybe.

Regardless, the one unexpected thing that really stands out is Randolf's Radiant Ray. That was a Spell Carpathian acquired back when he was still wet behind the ears and learning how Mezmer worked (i.e., Bruce was still figuring out how he wanted Mezmer to work). It's dangerous and unwieldy, especially at the Beginner Level, but when cultivated . . . ? I'm not really sure who I thought Randolf was supposed to be, or why his ray was so radiant, but Triple R, as I took to calling it, could become one hell of a weapon.

I'm freaked out and excited all at the same time. Which is how Brit looks as well.

The Notifications disappear, the color wheel of illumination fades away, and Brittany is gingerly and smoothly placed back onto the ground.

The door whooshes open and she exits the Pulse Well, appearing to feel kind of like how I felt after I went scuba diving this one time. When I was underwater, things were wondrous and still and eternal, and when I emerged, it was like I was a baby being born, leaving the warm, safe embrace of the womb and finding myself tossed into the harsh reality of the world. But, unlike a baby, there was no one there to swaddle me. I had experienced some kind of spiritual communion, and now I was back to the business of figuring out how to navigate life on my own again.

I mean, that only lasted a minute because then a waiter from the boat approached me with a mimosa, and I was all good again. But for a second there, it was a real vulnerable experience.

Brit has that "just been birthed" look about her, is my point.

"You okay?" I ask when she lands next to me again.

She doesn't answer with words, instead scrunching up her face like she's confused and looking at her hands, opening and closing her fingers. She finally nods, blinking her eyes and taking deep breaths.

"Feels different, huh?" I say.

"Yeah," she replies quietly.

"Alright, snail, let's move," Lonnaigh orders Perg.

"You're a bossy *mujer*, you know that?" Perg says back as he hops off the arm of the chair and starts scooting his way across the room.

We all watch him struggle for a moment, Lonnaigh sighing with impatience, before he notices us looking at him, makes his *om* noise, and . . .

POP.

Midsize, he glances at us all, purses his lips—which causes his long, luxurious moustache to twitch—says, "Happy?" and then makes his way much more quickly inside the device.

Again, the door opens, closes behind him, and in moments, the light show begins again.

"¡Ay, ay, ay!" he shouts as he is lifted into the air and the colors engulf him. "This is what I imagine a sick-ass *quinceañera* would be like," he shouts. "Today, I am a woman!"

Welcome, [Pergamon Slow Bottom].

Pergamon has a last name? And it's *Slow Bottom*? But I never . . . *Oh, whatever. Fine.*

It would appear there have been some changes since your last visit, *ese*.

Ese? The System is calling him *ese*? *Ese*. Well . . . that's illuminating, I guess. Seems to be tailoring itself to each of us? Individually? Customizing its communication style to identify with whoever it's speaking to directly, providing a bespoke user experience, as it were, like it's a Savile Row tailor and is literally and figuratively crafting the experience of our interactions for us as individuals.

I still don't know what to make of it, but at least it seems classy.

Please be advised that you might experience a mote of discomfort with the process as we delve into the modifications and adaptations required. Your patience is appreciated, dear homie.
{COURTESY MESSAGE #1}

"This is dope, fool," he calls out. "I'm about to have it verified that I can tear some shit up. I can feel it!"

[PERGAMON SLOW BOTTOM], YOUR CURRENT ATTRIBUTES ARE AS FOLLOWS:

[NEW] Mezmer Type:
One-Type

[NEW] Foundation:
Hexkeeper

Okay. So at least Perg is kind of the same as he was. Or . . . real Perg is like fictional Perg. Or . . . Whatever! I'm saying that in the books, Pergamon is also a Hexkeeper.

Hexkeepers (sometimes called "Vexkeepers" in the colloquial, lore-building, Bruce-can't-ever-choose-just-one-thing aspects of the world) specialize in Protection-type Mezmer. Pergamon prime was conceived as a simple, rock-steady, end-all-be-all of defensive tour de force. Not much of one for starting a fight, but definitely the ally you want having your six. (The amount of abuse he had to take in that last chapter to get him worn down to the point where Moridius could stab through his shell was savage.)

It would seem that's what he is yet again. Only this time, with the added benefit of having been given Insight, which, I suppose, makes him strong, durable, *and* wise. (Or, at least, wordy and opinionated.)

His verified details keep coming.

>**Resonance Tier:**
Etherflint

>**Affinity:**
Mutamorph

>**Statistics:**
Mental: *Etherflint Level 6*
Physical: *Etherflint Level 1*
Aura: *Etherflint Level 3*
Animus: *Etherflint Level 6*

"Hell yeah!" his muffled shout echoes from inside the Well. "¡Claro que sí, cabrones! Eso es todo! Level six in the house, bitches! Two times! Let's *go*! *Me la chupas*, Meridia!"

I look to Brittany.

"It means suck it. He's telling the planet to suck it."

I nod to myself. I understand the impulse.

"Abilities are next, right?" Perg asks with the giddy eagerness of a child getting ready to open the birthday present that they just *know* is going to be the sick-ass Mongoose Outer Limit, twenty-inch mag wheel BMX street machine in orange and black that they've been *waiting* for . . .

>**Abilities:** *Service Mount*

. . . only to discover that they have received a Fruit of the Loom three-pack instead.

"Service Mount? What is that? Is that like some weird sex thing?" he calls.

Lonnaigh answers. "Nay. Means that ye can be mounted, as would any beast, for purposes of transportation and conveyance."

"Conveyance?!" he hollers. "I get one Ability, and it's a labor-based one? What kind of racist-ass, *pendejo* machine is this? This is some bullshit!"

He receives his final Notification.

>Spell(s):
Philological Consciousness
Insight
Exoskeletal Enlarge

The words then fade, the lights dim, and Perg is dropped back to the floor. Unlike Brittany, however, he does not look as though the answer to all of life's mysteries hath alighted upon his consciousness. He just looks pissed. Like he heard he was getting a raise but found out instead that he has to work extra hours for less pay. Which, I guess, technically . . .

He hustles over to me, still in his larger form, and stares me dead in my eye. "You do this?"

"Do what?"

"*Service Mount?*"

"What about it?"

"You set it up like as another"—he makes air quotes with his antennae—"'hilarious joke'?"

"No! No. No, I . . . I told you; I never—"

"So you're telling me 'the System' just picked this shit on its own? You gonna say it's literally 'Systemic' but deny your role in establishing and perpetuating the System?"

"I don't—"

"Einzgear! Let's go!" Lonnaigh calls over, mercifully. "Ye and yer snail friend can bicker on yer own time after we've got my brother back!"

I raise my hand and shrug at Perg because I really don't have any control over any of this, it doesn't feel like. He huffs, causing his moustache to billow and fall, and then Tavrella rolls me to the door of the Well.

"Ye need help, lad? Gettin' in?"

"No. No, I think I got it. Thanks."

She smiles and strokes my head again before stepping away.

I blow out a breath, brace myself with my hands on the arms of the chair, and stand. And when I do, the remainder of my pajama bottoms virtually disintegrates and falls to the floor.

And here's the thing . . .

That should annoy me. Or make me feel embarrassed. Again. Or any other number of disturbing emotions, as the Dalai Lama might call them.

But it doesn't. Because this moment feels too big to allow it. Like, this feels even bigger than when I entered the Interlocutrix. It feels perhaps as though that was just an amuse-bouche, and now, we're onto the main course. An undercard to the main event. A prologue, if you will.

That *this* is the moment when . . . something changes. What that is, I don't know, but . . . something. It's beyond thought or reason. There is just a feeling in my bones. And not only because almost half of my bones are basically exposed.

It's because there is a kind of awesomeness, in the truest sense of the word, in this moment. A worshipfulness. A manner of fear. Not the type that stifles but the type that causes one to marvel at the potency and power of that which is before them. The kind one feels in the presence of true greatness. Of . . . the divine. A kind of spiritual, everlasting, celestial sort of—

"Ye gonna get in, Saviour? Or ye just gon' stand there with yer bits out?" Lonnaigh barks, and I shuffle my naked and burnt-to-a-crisp ass awkwardly into the thing that looks like a fitness club tanning booth.

CHAPTER THIRTY-SIX

Standing nude in the center of the see-through chamber, I don't really feel self-conscious like I did when I revved up Sheila. I don't know if it's because almost half my body looks like an overcooked hot dog, or if it's simply that my priorities have become radically realigned and I don't care anymore, but being butt-ass naked genuinely no longer gives me pause.

What does give me pause is the actual memory of bonding with Sheila.

Because it triggers the recollection of looking in the rearview and seeing Persephone being ripped apart by forces that were dispatched to hunt *me*.

She waited for me. She stayed there, trapped in Bell's View, just waiting. When DONG came through and destroyed the town, she continued waiting, believing I would return. I caused her to die. I wonder if she'll remort? I wonder . . .

And then I stop wondering. Because all of a sudden, I am aware that I am thinking "I." As in *I* am the one she waited for. *I* am the one responsible. Not Carpathian. Me.

WHOOSH!

"Oh, shit!" is what I exclaim as I find myself in the midst of the abruptly activated, swirling phantasmagoria inside the Pulse Well, being lifted into the air by the power of the colors themselves. Each individual hue seems to carry with it a sense of purpose and identity, and touches a different part of my senses. Like synesthesia but amplified to a degree that's beyond sensory and I can understand the colors' intentions in my core. By which I mean both my Mezmeric core and my actual, human gut.

Unlike what I observed with Brittany and Perg, where the details of their persons were simply magnified onto the glass, because of the Heart, the color and light seem to almost penetrate me, pouring through my body and funneling the nature of me through my battered self, assessing me from within. Like it's inventorying me and attempting to interact with and repair me at the same time.

Thump-thump. Thump-thump.

My limbs begin tingling.

Thump-thump. Thump-thump.

And then . . .

WHAM!

My entire being stiffens. And I mean my *entire* being. Every part of anything that makes me *me*, from my skin and bones to my blood and marrow to the unnamable part of my noncorporeal self that is, I suppose, the truest essence of what makes Bruce Bruce.

I start hyperventilating sharply, attempting to swallow and finding that I can feel every sensation involved with the act. The tensing of my larynx, the taste buds on my tongue, the swish of saliva rolling into my throat and flowing down my esophagus—every last element of the wondrous mystery that is existence and being a part of it, magnified to an impossible degree.

The colors swirl around me, through me, feeling alive themselves, each touching a different part of my scorched skin. Like the colors are becoming a part of me as well, joining to reinforce—or perhaps replace—my DNA, taking over as the foundational building blocks of my physical representation on this plane.

It's super trippy.

And that's when it happens.

Hello, [Carpathian Einzgear]! You old so-and-so!

For the love of . . .

Can I just *please* get a quiet moment of contemplation as I float, naked, in a mythical restoration machine while being stared at by my former assistant, my talking snail friend, a character I may or may not have created, and one whom I most definitely didn't but also might have because who knows what's real anymore, for cripes' sake?

Rhetorical. I know the answer is no. Fine. What's next?

Let's be done with the suspense, shall we? I'm sure you're keen to see what it is that now lives within you for you to take advantage of. So! Without further ado . . . !

The information on what I've gained as a result of being fricasseed is broadcast for all to view on the large glass cylinder.

[Carpathian Einzgear, aka "World Saviour"], your current attributes are as follows:
>Mezmer Type: All-Type

>Foundation: Synchron

>Resonance Tier
Etherflint

>Statistics:
Mental: *Etherflint Level 5*
Physical: *Ironspark Level 1*
Aura: *Etherflint Level 5*
Animus: *Etherflint Level 5*

>Highest Affinities:
Aetherpulse [Average]

Function [Average]
Mirrorweave [Average]

>Armament(s):
Mechanical Heart

> Inventory:
Two Item Slots Available

>Abilities:
Scaredy Cat [New!]
Sharpshooter [New!]

Scaredy Cat? Sharpshooter? I've never heard of these. What the hell are they?

He wishes to know what the new Abilities signify! And so, know he shall!

I didn't even say anything; I just thought it. It's like I have an Alexa living in my brain.

Who is this Alexa? Are they cute? Never mind, a question for another time. But to *your* questions, [Saviour], the answers are as follows:

[Scaredy Cat]
Your Physical-component Tier grows to one rank Level higher when you attempt to hide, sneak, or dodge.

[Sharpshooter]
Your Physical-component Tier grows to two rank Levels higher when you fire any projectile at an adversary whilst remaining in Stealth.

Okay. Alright. These seem . . . useful? I guess? Sneakier and sharpshooterier? Was kind of hoping for something like *Impenetrable Soul* or *Stormsong Torch* or something, but it's a process, I suppose. I'm still moving up faster than Carpathian was in Riftbreaker, so that's not nothing.

On to Spells we go.

>Spell(s):
Control
CloakRender
[2 New Available!]

Once again, an almost endless-looking list of options scrolls in front of me.

Etherflint Tier Spells:

>*Phase Touch* [Aetherpulse]
>*Wisp Sight* [Aetherpulse]
>*Calm Creature I* [Beastcore]
>*Feral Gaze I* [Beastcore]
>*Temporal Glimpse I* [Chronoshift]
>*Sensorial Actuation I* [Chronoshift]
>*Error Spike* [Technomancy]
>*Rust Wave* [Deleater]
>*Rumble Shot* [Echo]

And on, and on, and on . . .

The sound in the temple is muted by the Pulse Well, but I do hear Perg shout, "Why does he get choices?! Because he's 'the Saviour'? This fool gets to pick between Rumble Shot and Feral Gaze, but I just get assigned 'Service Mount'?"

Then a long string of obscenities that I can only partially make out. The list keeps on cycling.

>*Gravi-glue* [Gravitate]
>*Blink Bug* [Beastcore]
>*Shadow Puppet* [Elemist - Shadowheart]
>*Vengeful Vines* [Elemist - Florheart]
>*Rival Hand* [Function - Mightmarked] . . .

I have no idea how long this could go on. Given that I'm All-Type, I don't know if it even has an end.

If I look up at the ceiling, I can see a skylight far above that shows the suns beginning to set. Night is upon us. My window of opportunity to fulfill *two* (what I am assuming are going to be) *incredibly* difficult Quests within two Lunar Rotations is closing swiftly. I need to make choices.

But, as frequently illustrated, I suffer famously from what I call "Netflix Syndrome," also known as choice paralysis. It's probably at the root of why my books have so much stuff crammed into them. I get an idea and then another idea and then another, and with my paralytic inability to just follow a thread, I wind up weaving them all in until things look like a pair of Issey Miyake sweatpants.

Somewhere, maybe in the back of my brain, I hear a whine; it almost sounds like my phone alarm. I assume it's my mind telling me, *"Time's up, tiger! Make a choice!"* So after a few more moments of visual flybys, I eye the two that seem most necessary. I don't even reach out to select anything this time; I just focus my energy on them, and suddenly, they take over the place that was held previously as [2 New Available!].

Etherflint Tier Spell Selections:

> *Toxin Dart* [**Mutamorph**]
> *Marrowmancy* [**Mutamorph**]

Done and done. Chosen and chosen.

Mutamorph, which encompasses Mezmer that transforms or otherwise changes you—or, at more powerful Tiers, *other* people and objects—wasn't ever something Carpathian really had any use for. He was *heroic* after all, and it wouldn't have done to give him what are essentially body-horror abilities. Those who use Mutamorph Mezmer in Riftbreaker are historically . . . well, creepy. But me, here, now, I've chosen the Mutamorph Spells for two reasons.

1. I need to be able to heal myself, so Marrowmancy is a no-brainer. And if, as Tavrella says, Healing Mezmer that's sufficient to sort out Templar attacks and the like is in rare supply, I'm gonna need to make sure I've got something on hand—or literally in my bone marrow—that can do the job. I never tested the absolute bounds of Carpathian's natural resilience in the books as fully as I might have, and I'm not keen to keep experimenting on myself.

And,

2. I used to play a lot of *Assassin's Creed* back in the day, and using poison darts was one of my main ways of taking people out. I'd sneak around, hiding in the bushes, and then just blow darts at bad guys until I cleared a path. And given that I now have this Sharpshooter thing going for me, Toxin Dart seems like a logical pickup as well.

Falling under the category of "better late than never," I decide to go ahead and deploy my new Marrowmancy Spell while I'm still in here. Treating the Pulse Well like an O.R., I focus on my Mutamorph channel, and . . . I feel it take hold.

First in my skin. On the surface. All the pain recedes as if someone's gently smoothing over the burns with a cool, soothing balm. My flesh, which a moment ago resembled Dr. Oscar Mayer's Monster, begins to knit together, the raw, exposed areas sealing up as if they're being stitched by invisible hands. It's like watching a time-lapse video of a wound healing, but in real time . . . and done to *myself.*

Then—and this is weird even in a massive world of weird, and I'm not sure exactly what it's about—a small Mezmeric butterfly materializes out of nowhere. I assume it's Mezmeric and didn't just happen to wander in from some garden somewhere because a) there are no gardens left on Meridia since DONG has ravaged the planet, and b) because it's ethereal with wings that are a medley of the same vibrant colors surrounding me.

It flutters around, performing tentative landings on my flesh, each touch of its wings on my skin imbuing me with energy. Vitality. I feel amazing; more than

I might've ever felt. It's as if each touch is erasing *years* of fatigue and exhaustion, replacing it with a vigor I haven't felt in ages. Like I remember feeling when I was a kid playing make-believe in the backyard.

I'm here, fully aware, but awestruck as the Mezmer works its . . . well . . . its *magic*.

In my mind, I hear "A Whole New World" from *Aladdin* start spontaneously playing.

Man, this right here is the real *Magic Kingdom. If they had Pulse Wells at Disney World, the line to get up in here would be out of the park!*

The butterfly's last touch is a gentle kiss on my forehead; a final seal of restoration. I feel whole again, rejuvenated. Reborn. A transformation not just physical but mental and emotional as well.

The whirlwind of colors slowly dissipates, and the butterfly vanishes as mysteriously as it appeared. I'm left alone in the chamber, no longer feeling like a battered, weary fugitive but . . . something else. Something greater than myself.

Tears well up in my eyes yet again, but before they can fall . . .

You're back together! Good as new! Better, even! Better than new!
Pre-new! Before-new! Prior-to-you-new! Woo-hoo!
{COURTESY MESSAGE #12}

Why, oh why, is it like this with me?

The distracting Notification yanks my attention back to the here and now, and . . . lord. There's that whine again. Why is it still ringing in my head? I made my choices. I don't understand—

That's when I hear a muffled voice from outside the Well. This time, it's not Pergamon's—it's Lonnaigh's. And it sounds disconcertingly panicked.

What is she saying? Charm? Harm? Farm? It sounds almost like . . .

"ALARM! The alarm! Garr Haven's under attack!"

CHAPTER THIRTY-SEVEN

What alarm?!" I call out.

Rather than a reply from Lonnaigh or Tavrella, I hear a piercing *EIIIIINNNZ-GEEEAR* break through the blare.

The Pulse Well's magic fizzles out, and I drop like a sack of cottage cheese, hitting the ground with a fleshy *plop*. And, as if things weren't already dramatic enough, when I land, the glass around me shatters, sending shards flying like a snow globe in a blender.

Good lord! I know that in Riftbreaker, the whole point of being defenseless and exposed while in a Pulse Well is to reinforce a sense of anxiety and elevate the potential stakes, but I never threw somebody into one butt-ass naked at the same time. Whatever or whoever has taken over the telling of this story is really pushing the bounds of decency.

"Gahh!" I roar, putting my arms up to protect myself from the descending shards. Disoriented, I open my eyes, trying to make sense of the sudden and rising chaos, to see Lonnaigh and Tavrella being stopped just shy of reaching the door to the corridor that leads back to the garage by Templars. A small platoon of Templars, maybe six, barreling into the temple with weapons drawn.

Oh shit. Oh, god. Brit said that a group from Clan Catarinci was captured and tortured for intel and didn't give up Garr Haven's location, but I've been here for four nights, and . . .

"Ye right bastards!" Lonnaigh yells as she draws her switchsaws and dives to the side, blasting away and falling to the ground behind an Ab Grinder.

She hits one of the Templars square in the face, and their head, well, explodes. I could make it sound more poetic, I guess, but there's really no point. It's like I'm watching *Scanners*.

Tavrella rolls on the floor next to her, reaching for one of the potions in her bandolier. I'm not sure what she plans to do with it because a) I can't imagine she's that keen to assist a Templar, and b) the Templar in question *no longer has a head*. That's not a take-two-aspirin-and-call-me-in-the-morning kind of a wound.

"Carpathian!" I hear a voice call. It's not a voice I recognize. It sounds, more or less, kinda . . . British? Ish? And then I look to see that it's Brittany calling out as she runs toward me.

Oh, yeah, that's good. We need to get much more in the habit of calling each other by our, I guess, character *names. Especially since my name sounds an awful lot like "Brucillian," and I don't wanna wind up in a situation where I find myself as a dude, playing a dude, disguised as another dude. As it were.*

Before I can think much more about it, the Smith Press comes hurtling through the air, crashing into the remaining glass of the Pulse Well and scattering timeworn Templar gear on the floor.

"Shit!" I hiss, scrambling to my feet, feeling every bit the vulnerable, naked guy I am. Standing fully erect, I see—

Wait. No. That didn't—I didn't mean—Oh, who gives a damn?! We're under attack!

Standing up *STRAIGHT*, I see Brit and Perg weaving and dodging switchsaw, spellsword, and fireblade blasts that are lighting the temple up like we're at a Skrillex concert.

"Big homie!" Perg shouts just as an explosion from one of the various forms of assault detonates against the back of his shell. "*¡Puta madre!*" he screams.

Brit grabs the mesh suit from the ground and throws it at me. "Put it on!" she shouts.

I do as she says, noting as I'm sliding both my legs and arms into it how happy I am to have both my legs and arms back and functioning again. It really is the little things.

EIIINZZZGEEEAR! The call of the Ronine is louder now.

"You can hear that, right?!" I yell to my cohorts as I continue trying to get myself suited and avoid getting cooked again after I just got freshly healed up.

They both nod in response, but before I can say another word or make another move, I hear, "Godsdammit!"

Lonnaigh. Shouting. In pain.

Glancing in her direction, I see that a blow from . . . who the hell knows has made impact with what looks to be her right thigh. There's a big, open gash in her pants, and blood appears to be fairly well spouting out through it.

"Saviour! Others! We need yer help!" Tavrella shouts just as she throws one of the potions from her bandolier—the one I saw her drawing out a moment ago—directly at the bunched group of Templars. The bottle lands at their feet and EXPLODES, blowing the lot of them apart, sending bodies flailing through the air like . . . like . . . like Templars who just got blown the hell up by a Mezmeric Molotov cocktail.

Holy cats. Glad she didn't have me accidentally drink the wrong vial.

Before I can even think to lend a hand of any kind, *another* cadre of Templars comes flooding in, like a swarm of angry bees, if bees wore armor and carried magical weaponry. Which, I mean, who's to say they don't? I didn't see the movie *The Secret Life of Bees* but maybe that's what it's about. I don't know.

"Jesus," Brittany huffs, seeing the incoming reinforcements. "We gotta get outta this gym—"

"It's a temple," I correct.

"Shut your Saviour face!" she shouts as the blast waves of Templar fire kick up again and Perg moves to shield us once more from getting hit.

"*¡Ay caramba!*" he screams.

"Whatever you wanna call it," Brittany continues. "There's no way out and we're pinned in, taking enemy fire, while the rest of their phalanx is likely somewhere out there fortifying their command position."

I've heard her use military speak in the past—stuff she picked up from her mom—but I've never heard her employ it in an actual combat situation. It hits different.

I've managed to get myself into the suit, and the boots slid on. Mercifully, they actually fit this time. Which is not, like, the *most* important thing in the world? But comfort is key to living a fully realized life.

I now grab up the bracers and slide them onto my forearms just as a shot of some damn thing makes contact with them. I suppose the shot was aimed at my face, since that's behind where my forearm is currently located as I tug the bracers into place, which is fortunate for me since my unguarded visage is far less fire-retardant than these bracers *most clearly* are.

BAM!

The screaming-hot Mezmer bounces off the bracer and pinballs back from the direction it came, heading directly for the Templar who fired it. A Dwarf. A Dwarf who looks extremely smug until they realize their kill shot is now targeting them instead. They shriek with such an unusually high-pitched yowl that even over the brutal symphony being played on instruments of destruction all around us, it rings out like Renée Fleming singing "Madam Butterfly."

Only, y'know, less lyrical and more bloodcurdling and terror rimmed.

The boomerang blast actually pushes itself *back* into the chamber from which it was fired and causes the whole barrel of the thing to explode and flower out like Bugs Bunny sticking his finger into Yosemite Sam's six shooter in an old Warner Bros. cartoon.

I have to say, that a world can be this deadly and this hilarious at the same time is really quite an achievement. Bravo, Meridia. Well done, you.

As this feat of cartoonish battery is happening, I see Brittany start moving her arms and palms in some virtual indication of interlocking, concentric circles—*which is precisely the way I would occasionally write about Teleri Nightwind activating her Spells*—and just like that, weight plates start levitating.

Levitating.

Weight plates.

In the air.

Like a magic trick.

Or, more accurately, like a Mezmeric Spell.

"Are you doing that?" I shout at her.

"It would appear so!" she yells back.

"How do you know how to do that?!"

"Shut the fuck up, please?! Concentrating!"

The weights—all of them, from the little guys all the way up to the heavy-duty, car tire–size ones—are now swirling in the air, turning into an impromptu buzz saw, deflecting Mezmer shots all around the room and rumbling hysterically toward the squad of Templars, who scatter, immediately recognizing that being bunched up the way they are is not tactical. The downside to this, of course, is that while a small wall of Templars is bad, a fanned-out, mobile, guerilla-style batch of Templars is maybe worse.

"Nightwind!" I yell unexpectedly, surprising myself with how naturally it just left my lips. Brit, however, doesn't seem to register that I'm talking to her and just continues focusing her energy, sending the heaviest plates careening off from the spontaneous blade that she has formed and causing them to behave more like Ninja throwing stars. They smash into equipment and embed themselves in the walls as they seek to strike their Templar targets.

The issue is that, while it's cool that she can do this, she does not have what I might call *complete* command over the Spell. She is still just resonating at an Etherflint Tier with only average Affinities. And she's a newb with it to boot. So, on balance, she's showing up and showing out, but it's not doing much in the way of dealing damage.

"*EIIINZZZGEEEEEEEEEEAAAAAAAAAARRRRR!*"

"Is that that thing?!" Lonnaigh's ragged, pain-tinged voice calls out.

"Shit. *You* can hear it?" I yell in her direction on the ground, where she's still being shielded by Tavrella.

"Aye!" she shouts before groaning and trying to get to her feet.

Dammit. She's too flippin' heroic for her own good. If I don't do something, and I mean now, she's going to attempt to shake off her wound and wind up getting herself killed. I have to protect her, but . . . Christ. I thought we were going to have time to . . . do all the stuff the temple is designed to allow one to do. Practice, hone, sharpen. Maybe get a few deadlifts in. Whatever. But . . .

No time to mourn the loss of a thing that didn't happen. I need to snap to. And now, I should *finally* have the resources to go on offense instead of just trying to figure out how to avoid getting my ass handed to me.

Thus far, I've just been trying to survive. It's time to *thrive*.

"*That's it, Bruce,*" the gentle, affirming version of the voice in my head that I heard in Bell's View and back at Jeomandi's encourages. "*You're starting to get it.*"

Oh, god. Not now. This is not the time for the bifurcated mental meddler in my brain to chime in with its two cents on things. Even if it is trying to be encouraging.

"*Appreciate the thought, but can you not intrude at the moment, Bruce? I have my hands full,*" I ask myself.

There's a pause, and after what feels like a confused beat, I hear in response, "*I'm not sure you're talking to who you think you are.*"

. . .

DOLLY ZOOM!

Huh? Wha—? That wasn't—? Then who—?

That *wasn't* me? Talking to myself? The voice I heard in Bell's View telling me to look into my heart, and then again in Jeomandi's telling me everything was going to be okay, promising that I was going to be alright . . . *isn't* me?!

Have I not actually been talking to myself *this whole time?*

"*No, you have, Bruce. I'm still here. I can hear the other voice too. Weird, huh? Any idea who it is?*"

Jesus! I have TWO voices in my head now?!

"*I'm . . . not sure,*" I start to answer myself. "*I . . . don't . . . Maybe it's—*"

Once again, in what is becoming an almost *too* convenient case of Introspectus Interruptus:

RRRN-RN-RNNN-RN!

The sound of a switchsaw blade—far too close for comfort—fires up. I look in the direction from which I hear it revving and see . . . !

Nothing. Why do I see . . . ? Oh, I know why.

I look down to find the shrieking Dwarf Templar just a couple of paces away from me, running in my direction, waving their now rose-petal-barreled weapon above their head, Chucky doll style. It would appear that the return fire that ruined the barrel of the gun didn't disrupt the functionality of the blade part. And the Dwarf is *ma-aa-aa-aa-ad.*

God, what do I do? There's too much. I can't think. I need . . .

ZZZZZZZZZZWWWWWAAAAAHHHHHMMMMM.

And with that, the Control Spell hums to life in my chest, syncing with my heartbeat. It's an intuitive action, like bracing for the impact of something being thrown one's way. Fist, glass of wine, blast of enchanted fire from a previously thought-to-be-fantasy dimension, etcetera.

Time stretches, elongating. The chaos around me slows, enemies suddenly moving like molasses flowing uphill.

THUMP-thump. THUMP-thump.

The heartbeat is stronger, the icon letting me know how much time I have to do whatever I'm going to do draining slower. Not monumentally so, but slower is slower, and slower is better.

I also feel that I can move marginally faster than everyone around me now. Again, not markedly faster, but enough to make a difference. Like I'm molasses flowing *downhill.*

Now that I have a moment to reason, I do a quick threat assessment and try to determine what's most crucial. The obvious danger looks like it's the amped-up Dwarf with a chainsaw. Which, I mean, if anyone saw that coming at them, they'd probably feel the same.

But when I turn my head, I see Lonnaigh and Tavrella being beset upon by the other five Templars. Switchsaw blasts are nearly frozen in the air between them, and I'm able to clearly identify a look of both pain and fear on Lonnaigh's face, neither of which are attributes I would normally assign to her.

Tavrella is staring . . . at me. It's weird. It's like she's looking to me for help, but there's also something in her eyes that suggests she's worrying after me. Which makes a degree of sense. She did spend the last four Lunar Rotations making sure I didn't die, and I only quite literally *just* became fully repaired to the non-gristled version of myself, but . . . I dunno. Something.

There's almost an artistic poetry to be found in the grotesque tableau. Almost. But not quite. There is, far more than anything elegant, a rabid, pulsing venom in the faces of the Templars, and a shameful vulnerability to be found in the two noble members of Clan Catarinci.

"My family is one of the first peoples. So, lest there be any doubt, my allegiance is to the truest good," Lonnaigh said.

Thump-thump. Thump-thump.

Yeah. Yeah. Yeah. Okay. I know what my priority needs to be.

My eyes pivot to the floor, where I see the gloves. The Stoneheart gloves. My notifications told me that I have two open inventory slots. May as well start grabbing things to fill 'em with.

I bend down to pick them up just as the Dwarf arrives upon me with the switchsaw, the *rrrrriiiiinnnnn, rrrrriiiiinnnnn* ringing out slow and ominous. Malicious. Like a church bell of condemnation. (Which is a labored and overly dramatic metaphor, but it's the best one I can pull up at the moment.)

Bent over as I am, it puts me at perfect blade-smacking height for the Dwarf to rupture my noggin. But as I am *just* thaaaaat much faster than he is, I am able to execute my previously successful and soon to become patented Aikido move (thanks, Chad) with even more finesse and dexterity than I did back in my house. So, before Shorty can do his best carving-the-holiday-bird-that-is-my-skull routine, I spin gracefully away, snatching up the Stoneheart gloves as I do, and . . . well . . . *launch* the Dwarf through the air. Like . . . *LAUNCH*.

Like a projectile.

Like a javelin.

Like I don't know my own strength. Which I technically don't; I only just discovered that my Physical Aptitude is at Ironspark. But I very evidently pack some extra oomph now.

Way, way, *way* up into the air soars the Dwarf, headed directly for the skylight above us, through which it is now visible that darkness has almost fully blanketed Meridia.

The tiny Templar is flying in slow motion, but then . . .

SHWOOOOOOOOOOMMMMMPPP.

. . . things start cranking at full speed again. Which was my choice this time. The Heart icon isn't completely drained, but I just decided that I should hold some Control out in reserve, since I don't know what's waiting for us when we leave this room. It's not a decision I made hyperconsciously. Just like Control starting up, things are starting to happen more instinctively.

"Damn you, Savioooooooooouuuuur," the little guy's little, high-pitched voice echoes out as he crashes hard through the skylight and meets the night sky beyond, looking like a streaking comet.

"Holy shit," Brit says, looking up to see him sail through the ceiling.

"Yeah," I agree.

If this is what Ironspark looks like, I can't wait to see what happens when I hit Steelshard.

First things first, however. Now that Control is off, the pace of the pew-pew is back up to mayhem level. So, I slip the Stoneheart gloves on, once again acting on pure instinct. It's like I already know how to access this portion of Mezmer.

The power of the gloves surges through me, from my hands through the Mechanical Heart and back to my hands, a torrent of untamed force. In a blink, I'm striking out in the direction of the Templars assaulting Lonnaigh and Tavrella.

A stalagmite of razor-sharp rock erupts from the floor, just like back at Jeomandi's. With a focused glare, I will the earth to rise up in a protective wall around the two women, a bastion of stone to shield them from the chaos. I'm bending the earth to my command. It's half battle, half spectacle, the raw, unbridled force at my fingertips cleaving through these clearly low-Tier baddies like they're nothing. The sensation is, I have to say, a little addicting. Like, I-need-to-be-careful-because-this-feels-maybe-too-good addicting.

"EIIINZZZGEEEEEEEEEEAAAAAAAAAARRRRRRRRRR!"

It's now so loud that I physically grab at my ears. Which, fortunately, doesn't make the gloves do anything like drive spikes of marble into my ear-holes or something, but it does cause them to cease working for me. And wouldn't you just know it, the timing of the glove failure coincides with yet *another* wave of Templars. It's like a damn clown car. (Marginally more terrifying than a never-ending stream of clowns exiting a Mini Cooper, but only marginally.)

I go to raise my hands once more because, as the old saying goes, "If you've got Stoneheart Elemist gear, use it," but then I hear Brittany, her voice cutting through the cacophony with a sharp, fear-laden cry that abruptly shifts the tone of the moment.

I whirl around, and the sight that greets me is . . . Well, it's one to see.

Brittany, her face twisted in determined fear, unleashes Randolf's Radiant Ray. It's bigger than I imagined. *Way* bigger. Far, far more impressive than anything I wrote. The light that bursts forth is not just brilliant; it's awe-inspiring.

A colossal beam cuts through the dim in an unwavering line of destruction, sputtering around the edges like an overloaded transformer, vaporizing the air with the hot scent of ozone and sweeping across the space, leaving nothing but devastation in its wake.

And then, just like that . . .

Poof.

It's over.

Silence.

The only sound Brittany's ragged breathing. She's shaking, her eyes wide with fear and disbelief.

"Saviour?" comes Lonnaigh's voice from behind the safety wall. "Saviour? What's happened?"

I stare at Brit, pulsing with power and wonder. Perg even looks a little freaked out.

"EIIINZZZGEEEEEEEEEEAAAAAAAAAARRRRR!"

I grit my teeth at the sound.

"Where the hells is it?" I ask, rhetorically and with certain anxiety in my voice. Not being able to see the villain of the story is always worse than facing it down.

(Well, maybe not *always*, but it's never great.)

Brittany's nostrils flare like a bull's. She takes a breath, calms herself a bit, and says, "Let's go fuckin' find out."

I nod. Because I feel what she must: a sense of intention; a deliberate want to bring the fight to whatever is waiting for us. Not quite a blood*lust*, but a blood-totally-crushing-on-it-super-hard kind of feeling.

Both of us look to Big Perg at the same time to see if he shares our mutual will to see harm done to those who would threaten us. He stares back. Finally, "Yeah, okay. Why not?"

"We'll be back!" I shout to Lonnaigh and Tavrella, hidden behind the improvised stone wall.

"Back? No! Where ye' goin'? Saviour?!"

None of us answer. We just take off, jogging down the corridor that leads back to Garr Haven. I'm wearing the mesh bodysuit, the boots, the Drakonar bracers, and the Stoneheart gloves. I feel like I probably look like the composite spawn of Spider-Man, Wonder Woman, and Deadshot. (I don't really know how superhero procreation works, but I assume the three of them could have some sort of ménage à trois love child.)

There are no more Templars lying in wait that I can see, but I feel, physically, the presence of the Ronine more and more with every step.

The Heart beats harder and heavier.

"You alright?" Brit asks, apparently seeing, or maybe feeling, it happen to me. As a member of my Heart Guard, it could be either.

"Yep," I reply curtly just as we reach the giant doors of the garage.

We share a glance between us before I push them with all my strength. They burst open aggressively in a near explosion, and a cloud of dust from the just-decimated garage doors swells out as the three of us stand there—this time, I feel *certain*—looking legitimately badass and ready for anything and everything that might be waiting for us when the literal dust settles.

Fully prepared for . . .

For . . .

For . . .

. . .

Oh my god.

Not for this.

CHAPTER THIRTY-EIGHT

W-Wha . . . What?" I mumble numbly, staring into the massive garage as the misty, white-gray haze dissipates. Brit and Perg are likewise calcified beside me. Because what we see coming into focus is . . .

Blood.

Everywhere.

Not just "streaking the walls" or "trailing across the floor," but truly *everywhere*, as though Garr Haven was remodeled and finished off with a coat of fresh, sticky, corpuscular red paint. Not simply the residual effect of an act of butchery, but very deliberately and consciously showcased as a brutal display of power, the bodies that once housed the blood barely recognizable as anything more than fragments.

All the women and men of Clan Catarinci, slain. Every single person I saw in here when I awoke not so very long ago, no longer whole.

Likewise, the Grease Monkeys. All massacred. I notice a tiny wisp of ganja smoke dancing up into the air from a macaque-size puddle on the ground, the dying fire of the joint from which it emanates fading rapidly from orange and becoming a sad, ashen grey.

My muscles coil. My Heart beats harder and faster still. I *feel* hurt and sorrow and anger in a way that is inarticulate, not dissimilar to the pain I felt seeing what happened to Bell's View. Because while I didn't know the beings in this place at all, and I'd never been here before now, in some way, I did. And in so many ways, I had.

Brittany's words from a few days ago enter my thoughts:

"*There are people who have fallen in love with Carpathian. There are conventions dedicated to this world you've built. People are invested in what you've made. You don't feel any responsibility to them to not, y'know, blow it the hell up?*"

I get it now. I suppose I've been getting it; I just didn't want to think about it too deeply. But I get it. There's a kind of tug at my heart, both my literal one and my metaphorical one. I can feel myself developing a kind of attachment that is way out of proportion to just having, quote, "written about this place."

And I blew it the hell up.

Before I can think more about it, I am pulled abruptly out of my self-recriminating rumination by a voice I've never heard before saying, casually:

"Hello, Saviour."

The woman is severe but not unattractive. She's thin, wearing tight, fitted trousers and a metallic-looking jacket cinched at the waist. The jacket has wide epaulets from which hangs fringe that looks like dead weeds, and a high, military collar that frames her sharp jaw.

A thick choker rings the entirety of her neck, leaving no skin exposed beneath her chin. Long auburn hair flows down her back, very nearly reaching her hips.

Her eyes are piercing and of no distinguishable color. Almost translucent, like clear glass marbles embedded in the place where eyes *should* be.

She sports a condescending, almost sympathetic smile, the kind that people whose intent it is to manipulate you for their own ends wear when they're saying, *"I'm just trying to help you."*

The Super Vizier.

She looks more like I described her than the description itself. It's what I imagined she would be, but even more than that. She is, quite fully, the living embodiment of both the character I wrote about and the supervisor at my old job upon whom I based the Super Vizier at the same time. She is somehow both Carpathian's great adversary and my former antagonist at once.

She stands at the head of what must be two dozen or more Templars.

I recognize three of them: The one immediately and logically behind her: Moridius Wreathnestle. And just behind him, in the phalanx, also probably predictably: Draven Pistolstarter and Yolanda HoneyBunny.

And at the Super Vizier's side, the Ronine.

She is stroking its rat head gently.

"*Eiiinnnzzzgeeear,*" rumbles quietly from deep in the Ronine's throat. I shudder involuntarily before blinking to make sure this is real.

It is. As real as anything, I guess.

"What—?" I start to ask before the Super Vizier cuts me off by clapping slowly.

"I must give you the credit you well deserve, Einzgear. Your resilience is not a thing to be easily dismissed. It's why I had Moridius send the cadets in first while these"—she gestures to the group behind her—"dealt with matters here. You killed all of them, I presume? The cadets, I mean?"

I start to respond, but she keeps going, clearly uninterested in hearing me speak.

"Of course you did. But, then again, I mean . . . they're cadets. I imagine the Catarincian could've handled them all on her own. That's fine. They're young; a few may reconstitute at some point. Or not. Doesn't really matter. Better safe than sorry, is the point."

She takes a deep breath and then exhales slowly.

"You know," she sighs, "at first, I was terribly disquieted to hear that after all it took to expel you on the Fields of Rendalia, you managed to somehow return. I suppose much of the credit for that must be granted to you, eh?" She points at Brittany. "You are the one who cast . . . whatever it was you cast that allowed him to recarbonify before we were able to cleave him apart and prevent it from happening. Quick thinking, that. Carpathian, I hope you are diligent about giving this one the praise she deserves. Quite the little value-add, isn't she?"

My head is spinning. She's talking about Teleri, but she's also talking about Brittany.

"And, of course," she continues with her James Bond Villain act, which, I have to admit, is pretty solid, down to the unnecessary speechifying and weird pet stroking, "not only have you returned, but you've managed, over these last few rotations, to avoid our best attempts to subdue you still!" She shrugs a little and makes a sardonic face that comes across like, "How delightful!"

"We had thought perhaps the wounds you suffered in your encounter with my Templars at that hole-in-the-planet pub might have been your undoing, as the Ronine here"—she strokes its disgusting head, and I stick my tongue out reactively with a revulsed gag—"lost its connection with your, uh . . ." She waves her finger in a circle toward the direction of my chest. "But then, it suddenly found you again, and Moridius just couldn't wait to resume the hunt and rip you to pieces like a hungry Templar getting ready to feast at a Drakonar-B-Q!"

Moridius's hands tighten around his weapons.

"But then, I had a thought." She taps a finger on her chin as she gears up to do more bloviating. "Instead of continuing to swim against the current, so to speak, why not try and channel the stream to lead us to where we ultimately need to go?"

By "need to go," she means Garr Haven, the home of Clan Catarinci. The home of the Rebellion.

"And by 'need to go,' I of course mean Carvesend." *Oops. My bad.*

Carvesend, the Rebellion's attempt at building a Nexus Core. Which above all else, above any individual or group, is the true threat to the Ninth Guardian. The idea that there might eventually be a mechanism through which all the citizens of Meridia may once again have access to Mezmer. *That* is her greatest fear.

People are never the real enemy. It's always ideas.

Brittany clutches at her garments, inside which she is carrying the maps that, with Lonnaigh's help, she has updated with key locations. Key locations like Carvesend.

Seeing her do so out of the periphery of my vision, I blurt out, "Then why did you do *this*?" surprising even myself with the force and anger driving the unintended words from my lungs. "If you just want to find the Rebellion Core? Why kill everyone here? Why did you have to—?"

"Because," she interrupts. "Because the Rebellion must also be crushed. *Ooooobviously.*" She drags the word out dramatically, like she's exhausted at having to explain. "Because if it is not, it will just continue on, and the Core will be rebuilt and a new Saviour chosen, as we all now know that the Saviour who *was* chosen was not up to the task. No offense."

Not sure how I'm not supposed to take offense to that, but . . .

"And we just can't let that happen. It would be such a waste of all the lives DONG has lost."

I see Moridius's neck twist. Thinking of his brother, Charlemond, I suspect.

And something in me wants to shout, *"What about the lives the Rebellion has lost?! Or all the innocent citizens of Meridia who have suffered under the thumb of the High Council?!"* But something else inside me competes with the urge. Because it feels . . . silly? Maybe? Or at least like . . . like I don't have the right?

"We all know very well how this is supposed to play out," the Super Vizier prattles on. "Meridia goes along on its stupid, thoughtless, merry way until a visionary appears. A Guardian. Someone with the wisdom to see that there is a better option. An option based on worth and merit and being *deserving* of the things this world has to offer, not just *receiving* Meridia's bounty for no reason other than one happens to be of Meridia-borne. As if that makes *any* sense. And, *of course*, in response, a rebellion inevitably arises, a Saviour is chosen, the Rebellion—with the help of the Saviour—finds some way of defeating the Guardian, and peace and blah, blah, blah reign until a new Guardian emerges, and the whole process starts all over again. It's so predictable as to be insulting. We've all read history. We all know the cycle."

I open my mouth to retort, but before any words can emerge . . .

"These ones don't. Seems they never had proper schoolin'."

I turn just in time to see Lonnaigh limping up from behind, Tavrella at her side. They're both covered in fragments of rubble, Lonnaigh sweeping them off her forearms as she hobbles along.

Dammit. Note to self: Next time, throw up two *barriers to protect someone. Especially someone who's just going to want to reject the help.*

Tavrella's eyes find the bloody scene a half second before Lonnaigh's do. The shock and agony in them at seeing the entirety of their company obliterated, wiped completely from existence, and their remains adorning the place now ironically called Garr *Haven,* causes my own heart to ache.

I don't mean the literal Heart, or even my metaphorical heart, but something deeper than that. The very foundation of all that I am weeps at the sight of Tavrella's wounded spirit.

Lonnaigh's response, meanwhile, is much more . . . proactive.

The shift from an attempt at swaggering pride to gutted realization to sudden suffering to uncaged anger happens in less time than I would have thought possible.

Lonnaigh fetches her dual switchsaws and fires on the Super Vizier, very nearly striking me, Brit, and Perg with the blasts in the process.

"Jesus Christ!" Brittany shouts as we dodge out of the way.

I keep my eyes on the action in front of us even as I fall to the ground, and see the switchsaw shots . . . go *right through* the Super Vizier. Literally. They pass through her like she's not even there. Like she's translucent. A wraith. A phantom.

"Fokken hells!" Moridius bellows as he and the other Templars gathered around him all leap free from the incoming fire as well.

Almost all. Two Templars near the rear of the assembly are blown back and land dead on the floor of the garage, their blood intermingling with that of the already fallen.

I glance over my shoulder from my place on the ground and see the same stunned look on Lonnaigh's face that must be on my own. Looking at the Super Vizier, she tilts her head from side to side, still smiling.

"Why would I be there?" she asks with a smirk.

Then, the . . . I dunno. Projection? Hologram? Whatever it is. The Virtual Vizier turns to Moridius, sprawled on the floor, and like she's making a to-do list, says, "Let's go ahead and kill the Catarincians and, um, yeah, kill the snail too. Ugh. Let the Ronine loose on the Saviour because, well, that's what we made it for; might as well get full value out of the High Council's money. But hang on to the girl. Something tells me she's the one who can actually help us. I'm starting to get the feeling that she's the brains of this particular operation."

She turns back to me once more, grin still tightly affixed.

"You know what? Thank you. If you hadn't waged that assault on the Tower, we might still be going 'round and 'round and 'round for who knows how long. But . . . you did. And now. We won't be. So . . . bye."

And then she winks out of existence.

CHAPTER THIRTY-NINE

I'm taken aback for a lot of reasons, not the least of which being that after the Super Vizier's bombastic, periphrastic, not-at-all-fantastic soliloquy, she'd end on such an anticlimactic note. But, then again, that's when you know someone is serious. Big talkers tend to be slow to act. It's those who say the least that you need to watch out for.

Which is a real look-yourself-in-the-mirror-Bruce kind of assessment. Part of the reason I've always been so loquacious, at least within myself, is that it keeps me from having to make any firm decisions about—

"Templars up!"

Oh shit! Here they come!

Upon hearing Moridius's gruff command, the room of Templars all jump to their feet as one. It's super impressive, like watching a well-choreographed dance troupe. (Would actually be kind of sick if their aim were to do some unified pop-locking instead of murdering us.)

A horizontal hail of Templar weapons' fire unleashes in the direction of Perg, Lonnaigh, and Tavrella. Without any kind of warning or indication at all that it's about to happen, Perg gets big.

And I mean BIG.

This is, by far, the biggest he's gotten, taking up almost the entire opening where the large garage doors were just moments ago, shielding Tavrella and Lonnaigh from the incoming fire the way I attempted to protect them with the Stoneheart gloves. He looks like something out of a 1960s Godzilla movie, moving his shell to face the onslaught so the explosions bounce off his back.

"Perg!" I call. "You're . . . huge!"

"And you are observant, Sir Notices-a-Lot!" he shouts back. "Do something, homie!"

"Do what?!"

"OW!" his booming, resonant voice echoes as he takes an absolute torrent of abuse. "I don't give two chinchillas in an eagle's nest!"

"Is that a saying?!"

"Who gives a shit! Help me, fool! I can't do this all night!"

"Then get out o' the way and let me fight my own battles!" I hear Lonnaigh declare from behind Perg, straddling a dangerous line between heroism and hubris.

My mind rifles through my available options for doing damage. It's all still new, so I'm a little overwhelmed and unsure what the best set of tools is for this particular project. We were denied the opportunity to use the temple to train up any kind of facility with our newly verified Abilities and Spells, so everything is going to have to be field-tested in the real world.

It's kind of like saying, "*We* think *the new braking system we've invented to stop this freight train from barreling out of control into a brick wall will work? But let's just throw it on the tracks and see what happens.*"

I still have the Stoneheart gloves on, and that was successful, but do I really want to be that *Fortnite* player who just Thunder Spears everything? Does it matter as long as its effective? I dunno. But variety is the spice of something, so . . .

CloakRender? They've already seen me.

Toxin Dart? Definitely cool, but I haven't used it yet and should probably practice more before I start rolling the dice on that.

I'm built Ironspark tough, so I could just see if I can walk up, take their weapons, and bust heads, but I don't know if *strength* and *durability* are explicitly companionable, and I might not make it that far before I'm lit up and cut down.

Control? Always a fan favorite, but there are *so* many Templars that I'm afraid it'll be like that cutscene at the end of *Red Dead Redemption* where, regardless of how much Eagle Eye you have working for you, it'll never be enough because the game is engineered to kill John Marston at that point no matter what.

Um . . .

"Carpathian!" I hear Brittany yell again in her faux-British accent. It's actually not bad. Her dialect work is super solid.

"Wha—?" is all I get out before I realize *why* she's shouting. My paralysis via analysis has created a situation where I have somehow failed to notice the Ronine barreling toward me, but now I clock its heavy steps vibrating on the concrete floor, and a more fear-based torpor takes over. My calculations scatter, and I can barely keep my thoughts straight. They turn into a swarm of ants in my head, scurrying and colliding into one another.

"Guh!" I spit out, immediately embarrassed that that's the noise I make.

The Ronine slides to a stop in front of me, its presence a hulking mass of machismo menace and muscle, its purpose so singularly focused on me, it causes my stomach to fall out of my butt. Or that's what it feels like. I'm too scared to look and see.

Why isn't it attacking me, though? It's just . . . sitting there, looking at me looking at it. What is it sensing? What is its game?

It comes closer to my face, like the alien pushing up on Ripley in David Fincher's *Alien Resurrection*. And while I agree with all the others who have long regarded that film as the weakest of the Alien bunch, having a nemesis shoving its sharp-fanged mug all up into yours is terrifying in an indescribable way, and maybe I shouldn't have been such a harsh critic.

This, as well as a morass of other inconvenient thoughts, all jumble in my head as I stand here, the Ronine's creepy, soulless eyes fixed on me as if it can see through the facade to the real me. Not Carpathian but Bruce. Bruce Silvert. From St. Louis, Missouri, 63125.

The Ronine's breath, a mix of decay and burnt flesh, washes over me. The Heart pounds so hard I'm next to positive it's gonna burst out of my chest in a shower of shrapnel.

Hey, maybe that would solve the problem! Act like a frag grenade and wipe this sucker out! The heart IS a lonely hunter, after all!

"*Never actually read Carson McCullers, did ya, Bruce?*"

"*No. Why? Is that not what it's about?*"

"*No, it's about a deaf guy meeting people in 1930s Georgia.*"

"*Oh. Well, that's not helpful here.*"

So, okay, the Heart grenade probably isn't going to happen and bail me out, and in the absence of that going down, I find myself forced to confront something: I'm over my head. Way, way over my head in a world I thought I understood but that lets me know more and more, every second I'm here, that I know nothing about it at all.

I stand my ground, though, by golly.

The Ronine tilts its head, eyes narrowing. It's like it's trying to figure me out, or maybe it's just savoring the moment before it does whatever it plans to do. Then, it startles me by growling out "*Eiiinzgeeeaaar?*" in a low, guttural rumble, much quieter than I've heard it. And, well, I might be losing my motherflippin' marbles, but this time, it . . . it sounded like it was presenting the word as a question?

Without warning, it opens its mouth wide, and Rapprentices come spilling out. They are without the tiny wheels this time around, having just tiny, disgusting, rat-lion hybrid legs that scurry up onto my own legs, racing up my body like a squadron of *goddamn rat-lion hybrid creatures that are going to eat my face off!*

"Ahhhhhhhhhh!" I scream, adding an, "Ahhhhh! Ahhhhh! Ahhhhh!" for good measure.

The Ronine keeps vomiting out the little demons, and within seconds, I am fully covered in the animals—or whatever they are—and can feel myself blacking out.

Bruce?!

Mom?!

BRUCE?!

MOM!

Goddammit! I told that boy not to go into that house!

Smash cuts of memories long buried dig themselves out of their graves and pop into my mind at precisely the worst time. I swallow hard, trying to push through the emotional discomfort. Which is way more unpleasant in its way than any of the physical pain I've endured.

WHAM! PEW-PEW-PEW-PEW, WHAM!

What the flip is that?!

It sounds *kind of* like Templar fire, but not exactly. And I come to quickly realize that's because the *pew-pew* effect is not, as it turns out, from an actual pew-pew, but is the noise made by the Rapprentices being *flung* from off my body en masse.

How . . . ?

I force myself to squeeze one eye open a sliver and can just make out Brittany moving her hands in the Tai Chi–like way she did in the temple. In response, the

Rapprentices are being flung from me like droplets of water getting shaken off a wet dog. They're scattered hither and yon around the garage, colliding with force into the Templars, their little claws and fangs grappling onto the Super Vizier's lackeys, latching onto faces, arms, legs, wherever they can find purchase. Causing, of course, the Templars to shriek in pain and freaked-out disbelief.

Which is the right reaction to have. I'd be much more unnerved if they seemed super chill about it.

Now opening both eyes to witness the absurd scene play out in full, I can't help but let out a ragged laugh of shock and sheer, unadulterated relief that I'm pretty sure is a preface to hysteria.

In Riftbreaker, Carpathian would sometimes have moments of—let's call it—*narrative purgation* to assist him when things were most dire (What some ungenerous faultfinders might decry as "plot armor"), but they were almost always aided by the Heart or his own wits.

Watching Teleri sling rodents around like frisbees was not something I would have ever thought to come up with. It's both hilarious and utterly disturbing.

"*EIIINZZZGEEEAAAR!*"

. . . Guh?

The Ronine itself is still up in my face, still readying itself to do whatever awful thing it plans to do to me next. And still, even with all the opportunity in the world to use my new Spells and Abilities to confront it or to run or to, I dunno, ask it if it wants to have tea and talk things through like civilized people (or like one semicivilized person and one nightmare construct fabricated out of fractured memories and suppressed fears), I do nothing. I continue to find myself incapable of moving.

"*Unlike those of Meridia-borne, the Ronine was crafted with the express intent of countermanding your powers. The Ninth Guardian and the High Council took all they have learned of your potential weaknesses and manufactured a creature designed specifically to penetrate your vulnerabilities. So it is only by clotting those vulnerabilities that it can be beaten.*"

Persephone's words spring up in my mind. And I have the same confusion I did upon hearing them the first time. *Bruce's* vulnerabilities are the ones being exploited, not Carpathian's. How could the Ninth Guardian know about things that happened to me as a child? *How?*

Not really worth mulling over right now. Worrying over things is a luxury for people who aren't currently facing the thing they're worried about. Like a Ronine right in their grill.

I should feel compelled to move, to fight, to do something. But I can't. No matter what I try to do to trigger myself into action, my muscles won't respond. I am glued to where I stand.

And then . . .

The Ronine starts to move on its own. Or, no, not on its own. It's being propelled backward, slid almost, like it's on a pallet being dragged away against its will. So, quite literally, the *opposite* of on its own.

It's Brittany. She's doing it. Her jaw is clenched, and her whole body is shaking.

Beast Mastery. She's combining her Summoner of Something Spell and Beast Mastery Ability to drag the beast away from me.

I have to assume that's what's happening.

You would be correct! Remember, you may always take advantage of your Heart Guard Evaluation option. Random guessing is unbecoming of a World Saviour!
{COURTESY MESSAGE #13}

Shit. Right. I forgot that Carpathian can identify what's going on with his cadre in the same way he can peek at himself. The inverse of "peering into the unknown voids of yadda, yadda," which means I should be able to see how much Mezmer she's burning, just like I can keep an eye on the rate at which I'm using up Control with the Heart icon. So I just need to focus my attention on her, and I'll be able to see—

"Oooooof!" The wind is completely knocked out of me as something barrels into me, hard, and slams me back up against a blood-soaked wall.

Moridius.

"Fokken hells, Saviour. You are just about the right luckiest bastard in the whole of Meridia, ain't ya?"

His fists are around my throat. In contrast to the handful of Mezmer shots blasting off the back of Perg's shell as Templars flail and fight against airborne Rapprentices, and the Mezmeric force Brittany is exerting to keep the Ronine at bay, there's something oddly comforting about simply being choked out. It's primal and familiar, as opposed to extra mortal and mystifying.

"I know Mistress said to let the beast have ya, but as your little consort is interfering, I can pick up where it left off."

Thump-thump. Thump-thump.

His grip gets tighter and tighter still, and he's pressing the full weight of his body into mine so that I can't get my arms up to use the Stoneheart gloves in some way, or even try out my new Toxin Darts. And I now feel unpleasantly human.

"I have vowed to repay you for what you done to my brother, Saviour. How you done Charlemond."

"He, um, I," I squeak out, strangled, "was trying to save your—"

"No words!" he screams. His thumbs are pressing into my Adam's apple, and it's denying oxygen to my brain, which is making it hard to stay focused, which is making it hard for me to do anything, like use Control, for example, to slow this merry-go-round down. He is far, far stronger than I would think he could be. As someone special to the Super Vizier, my suspicion is that his access to Mezmer—the good stuff—is far greater than the average recipient might find. "I am glad, though, that ya came back. Because it did give me the chance to run through that bitch girlfriend of yours."

My eyes go wide, not just because they're bugging out of my head due to lack of blood and airflow to my brain, and not just because he's confirming that he killed Persephone, but because of the venomous glee he has in saying it. Like he's relishing in the cruelty. It's not something I'm unfamiliar with; I wrote unspeakable acts of brutality into every one of the books. But hearing it with my own ears is on a whole other level of savagery.

And it's like someone has been shaking up a soda bottle aggressively and has finally uncorked their thumb from holding back the spray.

To be clear, I'm the soda bottle in this metaphor. And I'm shook. But not in the usual way.

Mezmer pulses through me. It's all there—my anger, my fear, my anxiety—all the uncompromising emotions that have been swirling inside me, stultifying and innervating me, now unleashed in the direction of those who would dare to stand in my path.

"I CREATED YOU!" I hear myself roar as I force my arms up, breaking Moridius's hold on me and, with my Ironspark strength, sending him *exploding* across the room to smash hard into the Ronine who, in turn, hammers into Templars and Rapprentices, causing them to tumble like bowling pins.

In my head, I once again hear Aladdin singing.

"Unbelievable sights. Indescribable feeling."

Yep. It's a whole new world, alright.

CHAPTER FORTY

*T*HUMP-THUMP. THUMP-THUMP. THUMP-THUMP.

I can feel the Heart beating with a rhythm that seems to resonate with the very fabric of the universe. It's grounding me, focusing me, giving me clarity. The fear that had been threatening to overwhelm me transforms into something else. A fierce, burning fire of determination.

"Let's go!" I shout at my confederates, but no one moves. Brittany is staring at me, goggle-eyed, and Perg looks down upon me with his giant mustachioed face, confused.

"Big homie?" he says.

"Now!" I order as I direct the force of the Mezmer in my veins toward Sheila in the corner of the garage.

"*VROOM, VROOM, VROOM!*" she says.

(Again, not literally. That would be stupid.)

But that is the sound she makes. Like a thunderclap happening in concert with the green light going off at the Monaco Grand Prix while a space shuttle launches over the top of it all.

"Perg! Get car sized!"

"But I—"

"It's not a request, *hermano!*"

He looks shocked; he's never heard me talk this way before. No one has, because I have never raised my voice like this in my life, I don't think. It almost freaks *me* out.

ZOOOOOMP.

Perg collapses like a building imploding or all the air spilling out of a balloon, and just like that, he's back to his default aquarium size. Lonnaigh and Tavrella are not huddled on the floor cowering but standing there, Lonnaigh, in particular, looking like she's been denied her birthright by not being able to engage in the melee. She shouldn't worry; I have a feeling it won't be her last chance. But first, we have to get loose and stay alive to keep fighting.

"Grab him!" I command Lonnaigh, pointing at Perg, then shout, "Help me get her to the car!" to Tavrella.

There is no pushback, thankfully, as Lonnaigh grabs Perg and Tavrella and I each take a side and begin lumbering Lonnaigh in Sheila's direction.

"Br— Goddammit. *Teleri!* Let's go!" Brittany blinks, looking for all the world like I must have looked just moments ago. Dumbfounded and frozen. "Now, Nightwind, now!" I holler.

It shakes her from her stupor, and she starts running to join us. Team DONG is quickly pulling themselves together, and Brit has taken no more than three steps when a hand attached to a supine Templar body on the floor reaches out and grabs her around the ankle, causing her to fall forward and smack onto the bloody ground.

"Gotcha!" the voice associated with the grabbing hand exclaims.

I recognize the voice. It's the voice of Draven Pistolstarter.

Brittany kicks as hard as she can, but the floor is slick with blood, and she can't seem to manage enough *oomph* to free herself.

"Moridius! I got her! I got the sorceress!"

"Draven," the shrill voice of Yolanda Honeybunny chastises. "How many times are we gonna have to have this conversation! It's sorcer—"

Before she can finish her chiding, a gnarled spike of rock bursts from the floor with a sound like the planet ripping in half. Like an instantly sprouting tree, it springs up, slicing into Draven with a brutal, unforgiving force. Rock spikes burst out of various parts of his body, turning him into a grotesque sculpture of stone and flesh.

Brittany, quaking, looks in my direction, and what she sees is . . . me. Standing beside Sheila, holding Lonnaigh up with one arm while the other is pointed out like . . . I dunno. Iron Man. Spider-Man. Any of the pantheon of superheroes who make shit happen by shoving their hands out at stuff, I guess. A tried-and-true way to shut down a bad guy.

There is a moment of quiet, bewildered silence. Like the still that happens when the ocean retreats just prior to the tsunami that is set to roll in and destroy everything.

"DRAVEN!" Yolanda's pained cry fills the room. It's riddled with suffering. The kind of suffering that accompanies an inconceivable loss.

And then, she goes banshee wild.

She fires her weapons, the weapons next to her, whatever she can get her hands on. She starts launching Mezmer grenades our way, random tools lying around, quite literally anything she can find to pitch at us. She's a one-woman army. Fantasy Rambo.

And we react as one; a single organism driven by survival.

Brittany makes it to Sheila, sliding through the blood and viscera just as the doors, anticipating us, pop open, and we get Lonnaigh and Tavrella dumped inside. Perg jumps to the middle console next to the driver's seat, and I slide in behind the wheel, with Brittany dodging a very close blast of Ice Mezmer from some weapon or another that hits Sheila's passenger door, causing icicles to break off as it slams shut.

"Hello, Carpathian," Sheila says in her far-too-relaxed tone. "Where shall we—?"

"The Arch!" I scream. "The Arch of Raylion! Let's go!"

"The Arch of Raylion. Very good. Please ensure your seat restraints are fastened."

And, once more, we're off, this time smashing through the main entry door to Garr Haven, blasting out the side of Mt. TaumSauk as white-hot Mezmer (so to speak; it's actually a whole variety of colors—would be pretty to look at if its intent wasn't to annihilate you) rains past us and magecycles fire up with the clear objective of trying to chase us down.

I slam the accelerator and we're off, putting enough space between us and the Templars (for now) that I'm able to take a breath.

I'm trying to focus, but Brit and I are both covered in blood that's getting all over everything, and I still have the damn Stoneheart gloves on, and they're interfering with my ability to feel the steering wheel. I know Sheila's some other-worldly supercar now, but she's still my car, and part of that entails us being connected. I need to have the tactile experience of driving her. So, I pull my hands off the wheel long enough to tug the gloves off and hand them to Brit.

"Put these in the glove box."

"What if you need them again?"

"I'll get 'em out when we get where we're going."

"You might forget."

"I won't forget."

"You always put your umbrella in there and forget to bring it, and then it rains, and you're stuck getting wet. If you forget the gloves, you'll get more than wet."

"Will you just—"

Before I can insist, the gloves just kind of *POP!* down to almost the size of a pea.

"What the hell, homie? Are those for me now?" Perg asks.

"No," I reply, having a sudden awareness of what's happening. "No, I have two storage slots and . . ." I trail off because we're being chased, and I don't feel like getting into it.

Brit takes it upon herself to explain. "Unlike some other Mezmeric entities on Meridia, Carpathian's storage isn't explicitly extradimensional in a traditional way. As in, his collected items just become small enough to carry in his pockets without intrusion, and then expand as necessary upon his calling for them. However, he can only shrink down as many items to keep as he has 'storage space' allotted."

There's a fractional beat before Perg asks, "Why?"

"Because he thought shoving things inside himself was gross," she confesses.

She's not wrong. I hand the microgloves to Brit to hold on to since my new bodysuit is pocketless. Which I would call a design flaw, except that I get how pockets would disrupt the clean lines of the silhouette. Whoever conceived of it was thinking fashion over function, and I have to respect that.

"Everybody alive?" I put to the car.

"Aye, we're whole," Lonnaigh answers from the rear.

Which isn't expressly true; Lonnaigh is far from whole. But alive is adequate for now.

The darkness of the Meridian night is all around, speckled with lights from Santus Luminous in the near distance and the blazing flames ahead shooting up from the Arch and touching the heavens. We just have to make it there.

BAM!

The tail of the car is sent bounding into the air before crashing back down again, real, real, *real* hard.

"The hell was that?!" Brittany yells out.

"Sheila, what was that?" I ask.

"The rear of the vehicle has absorbed an impact from a Templar's Mezmeric blast."

"Shit. Are you okay?"

"I am fine. Are *you* okay?" she asks.

"Am . . . Am *I* okay?" I return.

"Yes. You seem concerned."

"I . . . Yeah, I'm concerned! We're being chased by Templars and shit!"

The sounds of nighttime creatures are currently being drowned out by the high-speed chase we're in the middle of, but I know they're out there. Which is when I think to ask . . .

"Uh, Teleri? Can you Summon up something to, y'know? Again? Like you did before?"

"Uh, um, yeah, sure, yeah, lemme . . . I can try. Lemme just . . ."

She closes her eyes and focuses, but nothing happens.

BAM!

Another shot hits the car.

"I am now less fine," Sheila coos. "It would be preferable that we avoid taking much more damage."

"Yeah, no kidding it would be preferable! How we doing, T. Night?"

I just decided in this moment that T. Night is an excellent nickname.

"I . . ." Brit grinds out. "I don't know what's . . . I can't seem to touch it."

"Lemme look," I say.

"Let you? What do you—?

Before she finishes asking, my body stiffens and a beam of Heart light is cast from my chest, connecting itself to Brittany's. She stiffens as well. A Notification appears on the windshield.

Heart Guard Member [Teleri Nightwind] Evaluation:

Mezmer: [Depleted].
All verified Mezmeric functions will operate in Low Power Mode until sufficient time has passed for recuperation.

"You see that?" I ask her.

"Yeah, I see it. I have a friggin' cooldown period?"

"Apparently."

"So, how much—?" *BAM!* "Shit. How much time is *sufficient*?"

"I have no idea."

BAM!

"As the Titleholder's vehicle, I might wish to remind you that you do have access to a host of countermeasures. In the event you have forgotten, they are . . ."

The PCM lights up with:

*Chaos Chain
*Fog of Decimation
*Sonic Torment
*Oscillating Vortex
*Lightning Rider Strike

BAM!

"Ow!" That blast was both harder and louder than the previous. In the rear-view I see the whole damn slate of Templars gaining on us, the Ronine galloping right beside.

Jesus. It's like attempting to defeat the Nameless King in *Dark Souls III*. I tried for weeks and finally just gave up and played *Gran Turismo* for a while instead. This is like trying to kill the king while playing *Gran Turismo*.

I immediately choose Lightning Rider Strike because it got the job done the last time, but when I press it and the bolt of lightning fires back at the oncoming horde, they split, dodge, and avoid taking any damage at all. As if they were expecting it.

"Shit," I say, almost to myself.

Perg speaks up from next to me. "Yeah, homie. Fools pick up on tricks quick around here. They're quick trick pickers, yo."

I glance at him, simultaneously envying and deploring his Insight. I need to grab some Insight from somewhere when we get a chance. This depending-on-Perg business is for the birds. Or . . . the snails. Whatever. I need to know these things.

The Arch is now *juuuuussssst* ahead of us. Which is relative. It's probably about four or five kilostrydes away, but we are *moving*. I glance at the speedometer and see we're going about a hundred and thirty-eight point six seven five kilostrydes per hour. (Sheila's new digital speed readout is *precise*.)

"How fast do we need to be going again?" I ask. "When we hit the Arch?"

"A hundred and forty-one point six two two," Brittany replies.

Almost there. I press down on the accelerator and . . .

BAM!

"Dammit!" I shout as I'm jostled in my seat.

"Select Oscillatin' Vortex!" Lonnaigh commands from the back seat.

"Why? What does it do?"

"No idea, but it's got to be better'n nothin'! Which is what we're doin' now!"

BAM!

We skid and twist, kicking up gravel and dirt.

I press the Oscillating Vortex icon and . . .

ZWAAAAAAAAAAANNNNNNNNNNNNNNNNG.

. . . things get weird. Er. They get weird*er*.

Reality stretches and warps around us, the world outside the car turning into a blur of light. It's like every sci-fi movie's light-speed sequence rolled together and stuffed inside some shadily obtained blunt.

We're definitely still moving, of that I'm certain, but it doesn't really *feel* like it. We're in all places and no place all at once, the Templars and the road and, indeed, Meridia itself stretching into infinity. Or, at least, really, really far. Since there is no edge to infinity, I can't say for certain, but it looks extremely infinity-esque.

And then, with a *FWAWAWAWAWAWAWAWAWAWAWAWOMP!* it's over. As quickly as it started, it stops.

The Templars are nowhere to be seen, nor is the Ronine. All just . . . disappeared.

Brittany looks behind us, to the side, to the other side, in front. "Where'd they go?" she asks.

"They're gone," Tavrella answers, sounding astonished.

"They're what?" Brittany says, like she can't believe it either.

"They're gone," Lonnaigh repeats. "Gone, girl."

Brit opens her mouth to say something, then looks at me and I just shake my head slightly. Not every accidental, Earthly pop-culture reference deserves commentary.

We're almost at the Arch. It's a massive, fiery thing that's even more intimidating up close than it seemed from afar, pulsing with a ferocious power. I look at the speedometer once more. A hundred and forty-one point six two two exactly. Awesome.

I was sure there was going to be *juuuuussssst* one more wrinkle. One more tension-inducing impediment to making it through the Arch successfully. Something silly, like somehow we wouldn't be able to get up to the proper speed, or the Arch would be closed for repairs, or something dumb like that. But it looks like, now that the Templars are off our tail, it's smooth sailing, and all we have to do is just—

"Once we enter the Arch, do you have a destination in mind? Or would you like the Arch to determine the point of exit at random?" Sheila inquires.

"What?!" I bark.

"Aye, Saviour. Ye have to pick where ye wish to go, else the Arch will decide for ye. Did ye truly forget *everything*?"

No. No. I didn't *forget* everything. This is something I literally never knew was a thing.

We are to be upon the Arch imminently. Seconds from passing through it.

Sheila starts to repeat herself. "Again, do you wish to—?"

"Mount Saatus!" Brittany shouts. "Mount Saatus! The Cavern of Sorrows! That's where we want to go!"

We're . . .

"Confirm, Titleholder? Mount Saatus and the Cavern of Sorrows is your preferred destination?"

Almost . . . !

"Yes! Yes! That's where we wanna go! Please, thank you, *danke!*"

THERE . . . !

And as we tear at breakneck speed through the opening of the flaming Arch . . .

. . . we are swallowed whole with a deafening *WHOOOOOOOOOOOM.*

CHAPTER FORTY-ONE

Seasons of Rebellion, Riftbreaker Book One, Chapter Fifty-Seven

In the shadowed ruins of Eldarax, Carpathian crouched behind the crumbling remnant of a Synest obelisk. The air was thick with the electric tang of Mezmeric activity, now a dwindling resource in Carpathian's arsenal. He breathed slowly, conserving the precious Mezmer within him.

Above him, the sky churned with unnatural colors, a canvas of disturbances born by the relentless barrage of Wervar's Spells.

Wervar. A former coworker. A friendly acquaintance turned deadly foe.

He remembered overhearing the man once discussing—joking, really—about the theoretical application of Mezmer and how it could be used to revive one of the broken trams at the Public Conveyance Works. And now . . . now these were lethal realities, searing through the air with a ferocity that betrayed the man's once unassuming nature.

Carpathian found his mind lingering, marveling at the cruel twist of fate. To think that Wervar, someone with whom he had barely exchanged more than a few cursory nods, was now the agent of his potential demise. It was almost laughable, yet here he was, humorlessly bolstering his own survival.

The irony was not lost on him that their paths had converged in such a violent crescendo all because he, Carpathian, had been anointed as the World Saviour, a title that felt more like a curse at this moment. Almeister had once said that none was ever truly an enemy until they were diametrically opposed to what one stood for. He felt the truth of that now, here, crouching behind the carapace of the skeletal remains of a city long ago destroyed by similar machinations of misunderstanding. He did not hate Wervar. Indeed, he had as little reason to feel any sort of way about the man as he ever had toward anyone. Apart from the fact that at the moment, Wervar was attempting to end Carpathian's life.

He did not believe Wervar despised him either. It was merely the cruel hand of fate that had made them devils to one another. Choices had been made, and Wervar, tempted by the potential reality of having the kind of Mezmer of which he could previously only dream, had chosen to follow the Super Vizier instead of Carpathian and the Rebellion.

What might it benefit a man that he gain Mezmer but lose his own soul, thought Carpathian.

Each Spell Wervar cast was a thunderous declaration of his intent to end the Saviour. They crackled and exploded against Carpathian's impromptu shield, an ancient structure never meant to withstand such an onslaught. Carpathian knew he couldn't stay hidden for long. The obelisk was already showing signs of wear, its runes flickering and fading under the strain.

He glanced around, searching for an escape or an advantage, his mind a whirl-wind of desperation. The World Saviour did not want to kill this misguided spirit. He wished to find another way, but every second that passed made it less likely that one might be found.

There was little time. He could feel his own Mezmer draining from the effects of the ritual circle. It was killing his foe as well, he knew, but Wervar was devout. He would see this through no matter the cost.

That is the tragic nature of the zealot.

Wervar released a cry of anguish, a sound of despair and resignation. "It has to be this way, Carpathian!" he shouted, his voice laced with a strange, twisted sense of duty. "No matter if I wish it to be otherwise. See, now. You must see! Before the Templars, I had nothing, was nothing. I owe them everything!"

Carpathian, weaponless and cornered, felt the weight of his destiny pressing down upon him. The notion of grappling Wervar was impossible; the distance and the relent-less deluge of Spells saw to that. In this dire moment, with his back against the ancient obelisk and his Mezmer nearly spent, a desperate plan formed in his mind.

With a deep, resigned breath, Carpathian tapped into the last of his power. Focused on it. Felt the spluttering mote of remaining energy in his core and grasped it. His hands trembled as he conjured a portal, and a swirling vortex materialized before him. It was a wretched, meager thing, hardly larger than his fist, but it was large enough.

Biting back a wave of revulsion, he opened the other end of the gate directly behind Wervar. Whispering a quiet prayer of regret, Carpathian thrust an arm through the swirling Mezmeric port. Then the other. His hands emerged behind Wervar, and he gripped the man's throat in a viselike embrace. Wervar, bewildered, reacted instinctively, releasing a Scorchheart Spell that traveled through the port and hit the Saviour with a shock like lightning, but he held on, his resolve hardened by necessity. His fingers tightened around Wervar's neck, the pressure unrelenting. Wervar struggled, his Spell dissipating as his strength waned.

And then, with a final, crushing grip, Carpathian felt the man's throat and spine splinter at once. Just like that, Wervar was no more. He fell limp, his life extinguished in a moment of savage necessity. The ritual circle's energy, now unchecked, dissipated into the air, leaving a heavy silence in its wake.

Carpathian retracted his arms, the portal closing behind them. He stood alone in the ruins of Eldarax, panting, his Heart heavy with the burden of his actions, the words Almeister had spoken to him rushing into his thoughts: "When you make a man a ghost, a bit of your own soul vanishes in kind."

Carpathian's gaze stayed moored upon his hands, the instruments of Wervar's demise. The weight of what he had just done settled, leaving him with a heavy, hollow feeling. He'd never taken a life before. The last of his innocence was now solidly dispersed with this one final, brutal action. He had always known that the path of the World Saviour would be strewn with challenges, but never had he imagined it would ask that he pay such a personal toll. A life taken by his own strength. Strength granted him so that he might use it to protect.

It was a burden that felt both alien and yet expected in some inexplicable way.

As he lay there, gasping, his body's energy extinguished, the lingering traces of Mezmer in the air felt like whispers of a forgotten promise. A reminder of a path he had once eagerly sought. He remembered the times when he yearned for something more in his life, a calling that would elevate him beyond the mundane existence of a simple conveyance conductor. But this . . . this cold, grim reality of death and duty was never what he had envisioned.

Tears welled in Carpathian's eyes, unbidden yet unashamed. They were for Wervar, for the misguided conviction that drove the man to his end. They were for the cause he deemed worth dying for, for the tragic fate that bound them in this compact. And they were for everything that this war had thus far claimed and promised to claim in legion: lives, dreams, innocence.

In this moment of solitude, Carpathian allowed himself the vulnerability of grief, his exhausted sobs the only sound amidst the ruins.

His sorrow morphed slowly, kindled by the embers of frustration and anger. Rage seethed within him, a fiery counterpoint to his earlier despair. He cursed the Templars, the High Council, the Ninth Guardian themself, though he knew not who they were. All who played a part in this grand scheme that had thrust him into the role of World Saviour were the objects of his contempt. But more than all of these, his fury was directed at the System itself. This System who had seen fit to saddle him with this cursed mantle, who had set him on this path of endless conflict and sacrifice.

Long ago, he had demanded more from life, true. But this was a cruel answer to his plea. There was no glory, no pride in a death in the dirt, in the extinguishing of a life that had once been as ordinary as his own. He had sought significance, but not at the cost of his humanity, not at the price of becoming an instrument of mortality.

Lost in these turbulent thoughts, Carpathian's attention was abruptly pulled back to the present by a sound. A faint clicking—heel on stone—echoed through the ruins, a reminder that he was not alone in this forsaken place. Instinctively, he tensed.

The clacking grew steadily louder, a deliberate, almost casual rhythm that seemed out of place amidst such desolation. Carpathian, his energy nearly spent, turned to see a figure approaching through the debris. It was the Super Vizier, her presence as jarring as her pristine business attire amidst the ruins. Her long auburn hair swayed as she moved, her face betraying a smug sense of satisfaction.

She clapped slowly, her applause mocking.

"Oh, Carpathian, bravo! Truly an impressive display," she cooed, her voice dripping with condescension.

Carpathian's gaze hardened, his exhaustion eclipsed by a surge of contempt. Yet he remained silent, his snarl the only response he mustered.

The Super Vizier continued, her tone light. "How are you feeling? That was quite the performance. First blood is always . . . special, isn't it?" Her words were swollen with rot, meant to provoke, to demean.

Carpathian's fists clenched, but his strength was sapped, his body unresponsive to his anger. The Super Vizier drew closer, her steps unhurried, her confidence unshakable. She reached out, her fingers brushing his hair with a feigned tenderness that made his skin crawl. He wanted to recoil, to swipe her hand away, but his body betrayed him, too worn to resist.

"I do sympathize with you, Carpathian," she said, her voice softening but her eyes cold and calculating. "The world isn't as simple as they make it out to be, is it? Black and white, good and evil. All those lines blur when those who consider themselves heroes are forced to do unheroic things."

Her words were hollow things, barbs poorly disguised as tender flowers, and Carpathian's rage simmered within him. His hatred was bare for this person and the forces that had conspired to bring him to this moment.

Her presence, her patronizing words, only deepened the chasm between the life he had wanted and the grim reality he now faced. The Super Vizier's faint smile suggested she relished this moment of vulnerability. But her victory was fragile, for though she stood unchallenged before him in this now, she faced not a broken man but a World Saviour.

One whose resolve, even in his weakest moment, remained unyielding.

"You're here to take my life?" he demanded.

The Super Vizier's laughter, a sinister sonata, reverberated off the ancient, weather-beaten stones of Eldarax, mocking the solemnity of the ruins.

"Your life?" Her voice was a serenade of malice. "Oh, as tempting as that is, it's not the time. No, no, I'm here for a spectacle far more satisfying than your death."

Carpathian, his voice a mere ghost of its usual strength, asked, "And what might that be?"

"Oh, just to see the cub who aspires to be a lion wallowing in the mud with the rest of the rats."

Her words were glass shards meant to wound, yet Carpathian, ever the unbroken, met her gaze with a defiance contrasting his physical exhaustion.

"There will be more death, Carpathian. So much more," the Super Vizier continued, her voice darkening. "And every scream, every howl of pain and torment from your loss, will be the sweet lullaby that soothes me to sleep." In her words lay a toxic aura, a desire to see him not just defeated but utterly destroyed. Yet . . .

"You know," she mused, "it gnaws at you, killing. Eats you from the inside. It is a drink from a cup that poisons the soul. Unless . . . you simply embrace it; let it become a part of you. It is the only path to freedom in a fractured world, and you'll be better for it. Otherwise, it will consume you."

Carpathian absorbed her words, a stoic statue amidst the ruinous landscape. Her intent was to torment, yet the underlying truth of what she had to say resonated within him, and he found himself strangely emboldened by her twisted wisdom. It was true: The path he walked, the mantle of the World Saviour, was one of perdition paved with tribulation. To accept the harsh realities of his destiny might be his only salvation.

"Enjoy your wallowing, Saviour," she sneered before departing, her footsteps a staccato rhythm fading into the shadows of Eldarax.

Carpathian remained motionless, her words echoing in the silence she left behind. But within him, a new resolve was kindling. As the Super Vizier's presence receded into the ruins, Carpathian summoned his remaining strength. He was the World Saviour, and though the way forward was shrouded, he would traverse it to its very end, for the future was without lamplight, without torch or guideposts, and it was perhaps this fear that prevailed among the people and kept others from seizing the mantle of responsibility.

But her words . . .

One must not turn back just because of shadows and uncertainty. If there was no beacon to follow, then one needed to become the light.

Inhaling deeply, he prepared to step forth from the remnants of Eldarax.

To be the torch that lit the way.

MT. SAATUS

BLADE OF THE STARFALLEN

CAVERN OF SORROWS

ACT FOUR

LAMENTATIONS (LITERALLY)

CHAPTER FORTY-TWO

"AaaaaaaaaaaaaaahhhhhHHHHHHHHHHHHHHHH!"

The screaming happening inside the car escalates in volume as we're spat forth from the other side of the portal into pitch-black darkness.

There is no illumination from the city of Santus Luminous or the Arch of Raylion to provide a glimpse at where we are or what's around us, and to put it bluntly, I can't see shit.

Based on Brittany's map, if Santus Luminous is in the equivalent of where St. Louis is on Earth, then, proportionally, we've been shot out into an even *more* barren and ominous landscape than we departed from, somewhere around where Arches National Park in Utah would be.

Makes sense, I suppose. If you portal through one arch, you have to have a corresponding arch to come out of. I wonder, if we hadn't selected Mount Saatus, where might we have wound up instead. Would we have been tossed out in Palas (Meridia's rough analog to Paris), through the Arc de Triomphe? (Which might still be called the Arc de Triomphe for all I know, since I never set anything there. The Battle for Palas happened mostly around the Tower of Elegiasas and in the Dungeons of Callderondé. Ambitious, I know, to have a book feature *both* a tower *and* a dungeon, but . . .)

Or maybe we would have landed in Nouveau Yosper (aka New York) through the equivalent of the Washington Square Arch. Or been shot out of Meridia's comp to the Wellington Arch and alighted in London (i.e., Faerborough). Or come through what is known on Earth as the India Arch into . . . uh . . . Indaria. (I've had to come up with a lot of names for imaginary places; they're not all gonna be diamonds.)

No. With my luck, if the Arch had been allowed to select our destination, we probably would have wound up deposited at a McDonald's drive-thru in Cedar Rapids.

Still. It's an incredibly rad bit of world design that would have saved Carpathian and company a ton of time as they trudged around the whole of Meridia getting into adventures. I'm a little annoyed that I didn't think of it myself. Or, at least, didn't know it was possible.

Or would be annoyed if I weren't gripping Sheila's steering wheel, holding on for dear life as we fly through the black Meridian night like a shot put, the Porsche's headlamps providing only fractional visibility. I can't tell where the ground below us is or if—

BOOM! BADOOM BOOM BOOM. BOOM BOOM BOOMBOOM-BOOMBOOMBOOM.

Okay, well, that answers that question.

The nose of the car hits the harsh, rocky terrain *hard*. Brit and Perg are slammed up into the ceiling next to me and, glancing in the rearview, I can just make out the shadowed forms of Tavrella and Lonnaigh being tossed around like clothes in a dryer.

"Godsdammit, Saviour!" Lonnaigh hollers, but I'm too focused on trying not to lose control of the car to pay much attention.

Sheila bucks and swerves like some sort of horse-fish hybrid—which I'm sure is an animal that probably exists here—as I work to keep my hands on the wheel, especially because now that I've stopped jostling in my seat, I can see slightly more clearly what's ahead.

And it's not ideal.

A massive, sheer rock wall. A giant monolith. A face of unmoving stone. Or, more simply, a big damn mountain with a narrow passage carved out in the middle that Sheila is far too wide to cut through and that we're about to crash into at a hundred and forty-one point six two two kilostrydes per hour.

"Shit," I cough out, short and clipped, as I slam on the brakes. Our unstoppable force starts spinning in three-hundred-and-sixty-degree circles toward impact with the immovable object before us, and I struggle to maintain control so that we don't all wind up dead. (I mean, if we were gonna die, I would just as soon have done it back at the garage and saved myself the stress.)

Maintain control, I think. *Oh! CONTROL. I wonder . . . if Control . . . extends to Sheila.*

ZZZZZWWWWWAAAAAHHHHHMMMMM.

The moment I think it, it just happens, no extra steps required, which is aces by me.

But, this time, Control doesn't snap into effect the way it has when I've used it previously. It's not a *slowing* of time, per se, as much as it is Sheila simply slowing *herself.* We stop spinning, and instead, she starts kind of hydroplaning to the side, like how a stunt driver can whip a car into a parallel parking position without scratching the paint.

And that's when I realize that it's not just *like* that. That's *exactly* what's happening. Sheila isn't doing this slick maneuver autonomously—she and I are working in concert. Bonded. Truly. Just as it's supposed to happen when a Titleholder is merged with their vehicle.

Well, that's nice. That something *here works like it's supposed to.*

I lean my body into the skid, feather the brake a tad more delicately, and we manage to slide to a gentle stop just inches from slapping against the massive stone sentry. (Which would also have brought us to a stop, but with far less consideration.)

A message pops up unexpectedly on the windshield.

**Congratulations! You just executed a Merge Maneuver with your
vehicle, [Sheila]!
{COURTESY MESSAGE #14}**

That's cool. I wonder if this grants me any new special rewards or skillsets or anything.

**This grants you no new special rewards or skillsets or anything. But
you should feel good about yourself!
{COURTESY MESSAGE #15}**

SHWOOOOOOOOOOMMMMMPP.

The sound of Control wearing off coincides with the sound of Sheila powering down. And then . . . nothing. Heavy breathing in the car and the residual
ringing in my ears is audible but, comparatively, things are quiet.

Perg is the first to speak up. "Well, that was some crazy shit, huh?"

I swallow. Clear my throat. "Little bit."

Brittany presses the interior light above her seat and pulls out the maps. She
unfolds them, looks, and then pulls her chin back.

"Whoa."

"What? What is it?"

She shows me the map she's holding and, well, it's not one of the ones she had
drawn. It is a map. A proper, geographic relief map map. With color and detail
and . . . It's very fancy.

"How'd that happen?"

She shrugs. "I mean, according to the Pulse Well, I do have an Advanced Map
Maker Ability, so . . ."

"So just by you being in possession of it, it'll update itself when we get somewhere new?"

"Certainly looks that way."

"That's handy."

"I'm not mad at it."

She blows out some air, clicks her tongue, and says, "So this looks to be it,
then. Mount Saatus. According to this new and extremely helpful little guide
here, the Blade of the Starfallen and the entrance to the Cavern of Sorrows are
right down the passage there that cuts through the mountain."

Of course. Because there's no way Sheila can possibly squeeze into the slender
tunnel. Because that would make life even just marginally less difficult.

I kick around our options for about a nanosecond before just giving over
to the reality of the situation. We'll have to figure out another way to continue.
There's no point in fighting city hall.

"Really, Bruce?"

Oh god. Not now. Okay. I know I'm gonna regret engaging with myself,
but . . .

"What do you mean, 'really, Bruce?'"

*"I mean, isn't that what this entire thing is about? Fighting city hall? City hall
being the dominant paradigm that sets the rules and keeps everyone who isn't part of
the machine oppressed?"*

"Well, yeah, but—"

*"Maybe what you meant to say is, 'It isn't worth fighting physics.' Or be even more
specific and say, 'It isn't worth fighting the intractable reality that my automobile is*

incapable of finding its way through this narrow opening in this rock wall.' Or something. Words matter, Bruce."

"Oh, please shut up."

"What? Who shut up?" Brittany asks.

I didn't realize I said that aloud.

"Nobody. Just . . . looks like we're going to have to go on foot from here. Sheila can't make it through the passage. Lonnaigh? Do you think you can—?"

"I'm fine," she grits out from the back seat. "I'll be alright. Let's go."

She opens the door and lifts herself out of the car. She looks neither fine nor alright, and her struggle to get out looks neither easy nor painless.

I turn my attention to Tavrella. "I know you said you don't really have the matériel to counteract Templar Mezmer, but don't you have anything that can heal her leg more quickly?"

The car's interior light is still on, and it allows me to see her kind, knowing smile and the sparkle in her crinkled eyes when she says, "Some wounds just take time to heal."

Her eyelids close, her smile widens farther, and then she steps out of the vehicle to join Lonnaigh, closing the door behind her. Before the tiny overhead bulb fades, I notice the blood covering me, Brittany, and much of Sheila, and realize . . . *really* realize what's happened.

Dozens upon dozens of people and monkeys and Templars . . . are dead.

And . . . I killed one of them.

I killed someone.

My god . . .

I remember when I first started writing about Draven Pistolstarter. I was careful to give him little quirks, idiosyncrasies. An identity beyond the pages. I wanted to make him funny and kind of sweet in his way.

In book six, there was this tiny detail, a throwaway line almost, about Draven buying a gift for his niece in Saltburg. It was just to add a layer and show that even the so-called bad guys had families, loved ones, lives outside their roles in the greater conflict. But now, that tiny detail haunts me. It's not only Draven who's gone; it's his niece in Saltburg who's lost an uncle. A girl who will never receive another gift from him, who will never see his face again. The ripple effect of my actions extends far beyond the immediate horror of the violence I've inflicted.

The heartrending scream that Yolanda let out when she saw him fall, it just . . .

I'm reminded of Wervar. From book one of Riftbreaker. He probably had friends, too. A family. A life filled with so much more than I ever knew. People who, by virtue of my actions, I affected without ever meeting them or even knowing they exist.

Draven is the first person I've ever killed. But, then again . . . he's not.

Perg, Brittany, and I sit in the darkened silence for a moment. It's the first time we've been alone together without an existential threat bearing down upon us since what feels like forever o'clock.

And speaking of time . . .

"Can I get a Quest Check?" I say aloud to the cosmos as an open question. It's Sheila's voice that provides the answer.

"Quest Check: You have *one-and-a-half Lunar Rotations* remaining for Quest: 'Rescue Mael from the Cavern of Sorrows.' You have *one-and-a-half Lunar Rotations* remaining for Quest: 'Rescue Almeister from Imprisonment in the Tower of Zuria.' These are all the Quests currently being endeavoured."

A Quest timer appears on Sheila's PCM and starts counting down.

I feel myself grimace. "Goddammit. We're never going to pull this off."

"Well, not with that attitude," Perg says.

I start to shake involuntarily, breathing in and out through my nose, attempting to maintain my composure but failing more and more with each word that comes out of my mouth.

"We have to—and stay with me here—find and retrieve the Blade of the Starfallen, then proceed to the Cavern of SORROWS—which is called THE CAVERN OF SORROWS FOR A REASON—to rescue Mael, who, I might add, we still have to find once we're in there, make it out—ALIVE—which is no guarantee, obviously, and then get back to Santus Luminous, penetrate the Tower of Zuria, and fetch Almeister from the clutches of THE HIGH COUNCIL. The *HIGH* Council! THAT'S what's in front of us. Oh! AND . . . And we have, basically, what on Earth would be thirty-six hours to do it. To confront and overcome a series of obstacles that took TEN BOOKS to set up. So. Tell me again how my attitude is the problem?!"

There's a beat, a filled, freighted, uncomfortable beat, before Perg says, "Okay. I'll tell you again. Your attitude sucks, bro."

"ARE YOU—?!"

Brittany interrupts my gathering emotional typhoon. "He's right, Bruce. I'm sorry, but he is. You can't think like that, or we really will be fucked."

"*Will be?!*" I note.

"More," she says. "More fucked."

"Lonnaigh can barely walk," I point out, trying to get anyone to acknowledge how boned we are. Then I think . . . "Unless . . ."

"Unless what?"

"Maybe I can heal her."

"You? How can you heal her?"

"I took on Marrowmancy, and I have Synchron Foundation now. Why can't I?"

"That's not how Synchron works."

"It's not?"

Brit sighs a little. "No. In the document I made, it states clearly that the Synchron Foundation only allows the possessor of it to sync with another's existing Mezmeric capacities. It's a one-way street. You can draw from someone else to power up and utilize their Mezmer—like you did back in Bell's View—but they can't draw from you and use yours. Unless . . ."

"Unless what?"

"I suppose, logically, if Lonnaigh were a member of your Heart Guard, you could pass along some Healing her way. But that would require her requesting to join the Heart Guard from a place of pure intent and you saying yes. It can't be transactional. And the likelihood of her asking you to bond her indelibly to your Heart because she's such a fan seems unlikely."

I let this swim around in my head for a minute.

"How do you keep track of all this stuff?"

"I dunno, man. I wish I could forget, like, eighty percent of what I've got trapped up here"—she taps her head—"but my brain is like the Hotel California. Once shit checks in, it never leaves." She lets out a long breath. "Maybe she can just stay here. Guard the car. Be on the lookout."

"You wanna be the one to tell her she can't come with us to rescue her brother?"

There's another brief silence. You can almost hear all of our brains whirring. Then . . .

"Shit," Perg says, with something more like resignation than frustration.

"What is it?" Brit asks.

He mumbles to himself in Spanish, but the only word I can make out is "*estúpido*." Then, finally, he sucks in through his teeth and volunteers, "I think I have a solution."

***

"Sit steady, fool! You're slowing me down!"

Lonnaigh rests astride Perg's back, legs dangling down the sides of his embiggened Mount shell as he carries her along the carved-out path in the mountain through which we trudge. (I didn't realize that Mount would also cause a little saddle to manifest on his back. That's a nice touch.)

"Damned ironic," Lonnaigh responds.

"What?" Perg replies.

"That a snail would be complaining about someone slowing it down."

He sputters then says, "That's not what irony is!"

"Actually, lad, I think that's almost the definition of irony," Tavrella weighs in.

The three of them are walking up ahead, Tavrella using a vial of a particularly vibrant, almost pure-white potion of some kind to light the way ahead. There was a moment of real concern when it became clear that despite all the new juice Brittany and I have acquired, neither one of us thought to take on any kind of Illumination Spell. It's always the thing you need most that you don't have handy. A version of Murphy's Law that prevails no matter what universe you're in.

Brit and I trail behind, periodically glancing over our shoulders to make sure no one is sneaking up from our rear. Not that we'd be able to see them even if they were. (It also didn't occur to me to select anything like Night Vision.)

With the light from Tavrella, I can just make out the silhouette of Brittany looking behind us and then back over at me before she says, quietly, "We're gonna get it done."

I don't feel like arguing the point, so I just respond, "Yeah," without putting too much effort into trying to sound convincing.

After another beat, she throws out a "Thank you."

"Thank *me*? For what?"

"For . . . saving me. At Garr Haven."

"You don't have to thank me."

"Yes, I do . . . You okay?"

"I'll be fine." I say it with as much authenticity as I can muster.

We continue walking in silence for a few more steps, listening to Perg complain, before she offers, "Y'know, I, uh, I never saw anyone die before we came here."

"No?"

She shakes her head. "Nuh-uh."

"Really. Hm. I would've thought you probably had, for some reason."

"Why?"

"Not sure. Army brat. All the places you've been, maybe. Things you've seen."

"Oh. Yeah, well, no. I never did." She thinks for a moment before asking, "You?"

I don't answer right away, even though I know the answer right away. After a second of chewing it over, I acknowledge . . .

"Just my mom."

There's a bit of a pause before Brittany says, ". . . Right."

"I mean . . . I was on the other side of the room, coloring in a coloring book with some nurse when the ECG stopped beeping and . . . and then, everybody kinda rushed me out. So I guess, very technically, I didn't actually, y'know . . . But. Anyway. Yeah. Just that."

Things get quiet again, but in a different way than they were before. Some kind of . . . who-the-hell-knows-what caws or shrieks or mews somewhere out in the dark. I note to myself that I don't even flinch.

"You were five?" Brittany asks.

"Six. Five when she got sick. Six when she died."

". . . Do you remember her at all?"

"Uh," I say, sucking in night air, debating with myself how much I feel like getting into it.

"You don't have to . . . We've just never really talked about it, I don't feel like. But don't—"

"No, no, it's . . . fine. Um, I mean, yeah. Yeah. I do. I remember a lot about her."

"Like what?"

"Oh god, um . . . She was really nice. Like, *really* nice. Or maybe she just seemed that nice in comparison to the way my dad is. But . . ." I trail off, considering.

"But what?"

"I dunno. I mean, it's not like Dad was ever all *that* fun to be around, as far as I can recall, but he definitely got more . . . like himself after Mom died."

Brit sighs. "That happens."

"Apparently."

I stop myself before noting that he's a big part of the reason I am the way I am. At least that's what my shrink and I got to, that part of the reason I'm so conflict-averse is because he was always so eager to pick a fight. With me. With everybody. So, it's compensation on my part. To make up for his seeming lack of empathy.

Which is not true. He has plenty of empathy; I know he does. He's just scared of his feelings, which I get. Feelings are scary. He's not that hard to figure out, but it sure did suck growing up.

Whatever. Brit didn't ask about him. Which is fine.

"And, um, what else?" I go back to thinking about Mom instead. "I dunno. Just lots of little things. Like how, when I would go to play at a friend's house or wherever, she'd always say, 'Stay out of trouble. Unless it's trouble worth getting into.'"

"She'd say that?" I can feel the smile creep into Brittany's question.

"Yeah." I laugh. "Yeah. I always thought that was pretty cool."

"Sounds like she was awesome."

"I think she was. I mean, she's the one who turned me on to . . . all this." I gesture around us.

"This? What this? You mean, like, fantasy-and-shit this?"

I nod in the dark. "Yeah. Yeah, she read me a bunch of the stuff when I was little. She'd get my dad situated in front of the TV or whatever and then she'd come into my room to tuck me in and sit on the bed and read me Lewis Carroll or Madeleine L'Engle or . . . C.S. Lewis. Y'know." I pause, remembering. "It's funny. Because that probably only lasted for a couple of years or so? Most? Couldn't have been much more than that since I was so young when she got sick and it all stopped, but . . . it definitely feels like the most important part of my life. Or, at least, the most character defining."

"Sure. That's childhood, right?" Brit says. "I mean . . . Y'know. It's not like I'm the way I am because I have the cuddliest memories of what it was like being a kid."

"What are you talking about, 'the way you are'?"

"Bruce," she whispers, "c'mon, dude. I know who I am. Let's not pretend. I'm aware that I'm a lot to deal with."

"Whaaaaaaaaaat? Stooooop. First I'm hearing of it."

I don't need to be able to see her face in the overwhelming darkness to know that she's giving me an "I will strike you" look.

"It's fine; I'm not trying to deny it. And you've never seemed to have a huge problem with it, so I haven't worried about it with you too much. But, y'know, the rigid adherence to structure, the 'edge,' the keeping people at a distance, all of it . . . Shit's not a mystery. I felt extremely out of control of my life when I was young, so I try to exert control where I can, when I can, because the world is such an out-of-control place."

"Which world?"

"All of 'em, it would appear." She clicks her tongue. "Y'know, sometimes, I wish I could be more like you."

"You really don't." I chuckle.

"No, you're right; I really don't. It seems insane in there." I chuckle a little harder. "But the not being so tightly wound part. That feels like it'd be alright. I mean, look, if I'm being honest . . . Okay, like, the way you write, for example."

"What about it?"

"It's messy and chaotic and . . . Chaotic. And messy. But, I mean, that's how shit is. Life *is* messy and chaotic and doesn't always follow the rules. People aren't logic robots who do things exactly as we want, to adhere to some grand narrative. People go left when you want them to go right. They act in ways that seems counterintuitive. They . . ."

"They die unexpectedly," I suggest. Unexpectedly.

". . . Yeah," she agrees after a moment. "So, anyway, all I'm saying is . . ."

"Yes?"

"All I'm saying is . . . that you've learned to embrace that. And . . . kind of turn it into a superpower. You accept that it's not possible to keep track of *everything* in life. That sometimes life is gonna do what it wants. Sure as hell seems to have done that to us."

"Can't argue that."

"So, what I'm trying to say is . . ." She pauses. "I mean, what I want to get across is that . . ." She pauses again.

"You don't have to—" I try to give her a pass, but she keeps going anyway.

"*What I'm trying to tell you*—and clearly having a hard time doing—is . . . I'm sorry. I'm sorry for all the times I was an asshole or maybe took the fun out of things for you or made it harder than it needed to be when all you wanted to do was just . . . was just . . . was just write the kind of stories that make you happy and remind you of nice times with your mom and that you enjoy. And if me putting pressure on you to 'get it right' or 'keep everything in line' or whatever is in *any* way part of what caused you to decide you needed to—"

"Hey, hey, hey." I have to head her off because it's starting to sound an awful lot like the kind of apology a person makes when they think it might be their last chance to say what they want to say. "No. Stop it. No apologizing. Not necessary for, like, fifty reasons. But mostly because I would not even be where I am today without you."

"Oh, good. Because where we are is so great."

"You know what I mean. I know the Super Vizier wasn't talking about me and you, so to speak, when she called you the brains of the operation, but . . . she's not entirely wrong. You always kept the buses running on time, and I'll never be able to thank you enough for that. So."

I decide—against my habitual nature—to stop talking and just let the moment sit. Because sometimes not saying something communicates what you want better than the jibber jabber.

"You're welcome," I hear her say on a smile, "but it's not me. It's you. Whether it turns out you're the creator of this world or you are just the vessel through which this world chose to have its stories told, it's still *your* brain that it fell out of. I mean, let's be honest. The books are a hit because of their inventiveness and the creativity in them and all that. Not because I made a *bible* that kept track of every little, minute detail and minor throwaway character that gotten written about. I mean, it's not like anyone's staying up at night worrying about whether or not—"

"Help! Help!"

The voice shouting out in the pitch blackness is jarring.

"What's that?" Brit asks, anxiety in the question.

"What is that?" Perg calls out from up ahead.

"Help!" the voice yells out again. "Is someone there?! Oh my gods! It's been . . . I don't even know how . . . Hello?! Can you hear me?"

Tavrella waves her vial of light around, and it expands for a moment, allowing us to better see what's around us.

"Looks like it's coming from over there," Lonnaigh says, pointing.

"Over where?" I ask.

"There." She gestures in the direction of what looks like . . . "There, in that well."

. . .

No. No. No no no. No frick-fracking way. There is no way that . . . You. Have. Got. To. Be . . .

"You can hear me?! Oh, thank you, Richemerion! I've been stuck here for so long! Please, please, please, will you help me get out?!"

You have been offered a Side Quest!

"Get Timbolloree Out of the Well!"

Do you wish to accept this Side Quest?
[Yes] [No]

CHAPTER FORTY-THREE

Hello?! Hello! Oh my gods, I can't believe someone is here!"

The light from Tavrella's vial shining down the well illuminates Timbolloree's desperate, dirty, hopeful face looking up at us like the kid in the human waste pit in *Schindler's List*. (Which I know is a bleak and potentially offensive comparison, but it's not my fault that Steven Spielberg creates such striking and easily referenced visuals.)

Jesus. Timbolloree . . . Something. I have no idea if the guy even has a last name. I never really intended him to be more than anything beyond a joke, which is, of course, the whole problem I'm having to confront here, the old "consequences matter above intentions" of it all really working extra hours to make its point.

God. I can't understand how he's still alive, given that he fell down here in book one. Just like us endeavoring to gather up the Blade now, Carpathian was led to the Blade of the Starfallen by Almeister. It was the true inflection point for him when he finally believed all that was being told to him; all the stuff about him being the World Saviour. Because even with the Mechanical Heart and the confrontation with the Reapers and all the rest of it, he was still holding on to skepticism about his purpose. Until, finally, he wound up here, at the base of Mount Saatus, where it was rumored (or, I guess, rumOURed) that only the one chosen as the Saviour would be able to withdraw the Blade from its place embedded in rock.

Carpathian had a whole hemming and hawing with himself about what the difference between a "prophecy" and a "rumour" is, and ultimately decided that it all came down to belief. After all, a prophecy is just a rumor that someone chooses to believe in. To, I suppose, take on faith (aka trust).

Regardless, the Blade of the Starfallen sequence was the moment when Carpathian finally stopped questioning things quite so much and made the choice to just buy into the myth.

And, because I needed to make an irrefutable show of the fact that Carpathian was the true Saviour, I had a handful of other would-be Saviours present to try their luck at withdrawing the Blade. (Again, big shoutout to Excalibur.) Most of those who failed to extract it just let it go and headed off, dejected, but Timbolloree . . .

Well, as noted, Timbolloree was based on my Aikido instructor, Chad, who was just kind of a dick and who, instead of encouraging me, always made me feel like a chump for not being able to get things right the first time. He also seemed like a bit of a chauvinist and most definitely a skeeve, given how he would put his hands all over women in the class to show them the "right" way to do things while just throwing the guys to the ground to illustrate how to do a move.

Now, obviously, the mature, adult thing to do would have been to take up my concerns with Chad directly. Or, y'know, get over it. But, as a notoriously conflict-averse human who also suppresses his emotions for a variety of reasons, I picked a creative third option and wrote the guy as a character into my book.

So when Timbolloree arrived to attend the Trial of the Blade, he rolled up in what I wrote as basically a fluorescent orange McLaren, top down, with a full harem in tow, and . . .

If I'm being honest, I probably went a little over the top, but when Carpathian finally yanked the Blade out of the stone and Timbolloree didn't, Timbolloree got super embarrassed and decided to get all up in Carpathian's face. So Carpathian casually side-stepped him (Aikido style), letting him fall into the well that I conveniently placed nearby for that exact purpose, and then Carpathian and Almeister had a good laugh and went on their merry way. Which is not *not* a dick move, but in my defense, Timbolloree was a real, *real* big douche bro.

However . . .

Now that I'm facing the repercussive reality of the situation standing here, staring down into the man's panicked, urgent expression, I can't help feeling sorry for him.

Which is something that Brittany has, in the past, called my tragic flaw: My seemingly naive desire to try and find the humanity in people even when they kind of suck.

Achilles had a vulnerable heel; I've got vulnerable feels.

I'm not saying I'm a Pollyanna—I've seen too much crap in my life; I know how the world works. And in the moment someone is being particularly sucky, I may wanna do things like throw them down wells, but when I can finally step back from my own emotions long enough to see that they're probably just scared or sad or whatever it is they're experiencing that's causing them to be the way they are, I'm able to forget the shitty stuff and simply see them as fellow living beings who might be hurting in some way and don't know how to ask for help.

A person can be the biggest, most awful asshole in the world, but if I see them in pain or in trouble, I'll still reach out a hand to help them if I can. Brit thinks that's just me looking at life through rose-colored glasses, and that some people are simply bad apples and no amount of help I offer will change that.

(Case in point: Coincidentally, when she first came to work with me and read book one to get up to speed, she made a particular note of telling me what a dick-bag she thought Timbolloree was, and how she appreciated how I had handled him. I'm saying she had a really, *really* negative reaction to the guy. She said he was *rapey* and nicknamed him "Timbo the Himbo.")

I didn't pry into the whys and wherefores of her feelings about it because a) it's none of my business and b) truthfully? Initially, it made me feel oddly satisfied, because it meant that I'd done a good job of communicating the character and provoking a visceral response. But when I thought about it more, I became worried that I had failed to do the very thing I prize most in my storytelling, which is to make the characters complex and even a little sympathetic. Because I want to believe that, at our *cores*, we're all basically decent, and it's all the shit we encounter outside of ourselves as we go through life that turns us into whatever it is we become. Villain, hero, devil, angel, whatever. You never know what someone's been through.

Frankly, I think that's the thing that causes the folks who enjoy Riftbreaker to feel as strongly about it as they do. Because, for the most part, the inhabitants of Meridia aren't typically two-dimensional cyphers who can be easily classified as good or bad, this or that. They're complicated, which allows them to be identifiable to readers in some meaningful way that transcends tropes and expectations . . . I hope.

I'm sure that sounds grand and even a little pretentious, but it's what I've always gone for because it's also what I find most interesting about the stuff *I'm* into. Action scenes are cool, good world-building is amazing, and I geek out over detailed lore as much as the next Tolkienite, but what keeps me hooked are the characters, their relationships, what they want and need from each other, and what they find in themselves as they travel on their journeys.

Anyway.

The point I'm trying to make is that right now, I'm looking at a random dude I threw in a well ten books ago who is still stuck down there, and I'm suddenly acutely aware of how dirty I did the guy and am feeling really bad about it.

"Please! Please get me out! Please!"

"How'd ye get down there?" Lonnaigh calls out to him.

"Who knows why people do the things they do?" I attempt to deflect.

"Please, just help me! I've lost count of how many Lunar Cycles have passed since I've been here! I've survived by sucking what moisture I can from rocks and eating grubs and dirt! I just want to go home! Please!"

Grubs and dirt? Good Christ.

"Alright! Alright! We'll get you out! Just . . . gimme a second!" I call down. Turning to look at my bloodied and battered crew, I ask, "Thoughts?"

Perg, who is still in Mount form, peers over the edge of the well. "I mean, I can climb walls and shit, but at the size I need to be to drag him along . . ." Perg doesn't have shoulders, but if he did, he'd be shrugging them.

He's right. Both of them can't fit inside the diameter of the pit.

Lonnaigh's no help; she can barely move herself. Tavrella . . . Well, honestly, Tavrella seems to just be a really nice lady who can provide things that taste like Freezer Pops and lob the occasional Molotov cocktail, but apart from having a vial of white stuff that lights up the well enough to see Timbolloree, I'm not sure what she can do in this situation.

So it's down to me and Brit. I could use the gloves to maybe throw down a rock bridge or . . . ? Nah. Probably impale the poor guy or something.

Control? CloakRender? Toxin Darts? Just kill him with a dart to the neck and put him out of his misery?

No, no, and no. Man. Carpathian could fly and stuff, but to be fair, not until much later in the series. So I guess that leaves . . . "Can you Summon him up?"

"I'm not sure."

She shoots me a look, silently reminding me of how she felt about Timbolloree.

"Talk to you for a second?"

I pull her to the side to confab.

"What are you doing up there?! Help me!"

"Hold on!" (God, the guy's been down there forever and a day; you'd think he could wait another minute or two.)

"Brit, come on," I whisper. "The guy—"

"The guy's a scumbag rapist who got what he deserved."

"I . . . I never said he's a rapist. I just said he's a little grabby."

"Bruce—"

"Brit, I . . . Look. We have no idea what his story is, right? We have no clue beyond what I wrote down, and now that we're here . . . What'd you say? These are real people with real lives? The guy's real life has been him *stuck in a well* for who knows how long."

"Okay." She crosses her arms.

I try to think of something that might possibly persuade her, given how entrenched her opinion on the matter seems to be. I know from my experiences in the book community that when someone makes up their mind about a character, it can be extremely hard to convince them to see that character a different way. But . . .

"Look, if I'm to 'Trust the System' and assume everything is happening for a reason, then perhaps this moment is to illustrate the point that no life is inconsequential and that we *all* contain multitudes. That even though Timbolloree was nothing more than a throwaway dig at a type of person who rubbed me the wrong way when I wrote him, in this world, he is a whole entire being who deserves—if not warm fuzzies—at least consideration."

As it pours out of my mouth, the image of Draven, dead on the floor at Garr Haven, pops into my head. The idea of him buying a gift for his niece in Saltburg. Wervar, a guy who wanted a better life for himself and got pulled off the path of righteousness . . .

We *have* to help Timbolloree.

She seems to be considering it but is still resisting. "The Heart said I'm depleted."

"For Summoning up Tentasaurians and whatnot, but surely not so much that you couldn't drag up a skinny guy who's been subsisting on larvae and rock water." I place my hands on her pauldrons. "Please? Can we at least give it a shot?"

She shakes her head a little then lets it turn into a neck stretch. "Move out of the way."

I do, and she begins focusing her energy, rolling her palms around in the air in the Tai Chi manner that directs her Mezmer to Summon. A ball of light forms, glowing faintly but definitely visible, and then starts to expand as we hear, "Oh, my . . . I'm . . . lifting! I'm rising! I'm coming up!"

I peek over the edge to see. Yep, sure enough, Timbolloree the Boy Who Fell Down a Well is levitating, being brought up through the earthen silo inside a shaft of light that Brittany's generating. And now that I can make him out better, I see what truly wretched shape he's in.

He's ghostly white. Beyond ghostly white. Nuclear-winter white. Pallid and papery skin, cuts and bruises all over. His beard is down to below his knees, as is his hair. His clothes are barely more than dusty rags clinging to his emaciated frame.

I feel awful. Truly, truly awful. I can't believe I did this. That this is my fault.

"Just a little more!" he shouts. "I'm almost there!"

Brittany takes a deep breath, squints her eyes tighter, and uses whatever she has left in her Low Power Mode toolkit to help this poor, unfortunate, victimized—

"I'm coming up! I'm coming! I'm coming! I'm almost there!"

Uh . . . Okay. Don't love the way that sounds, but . . .

"Yes, yes, yes, yes!" he shouts as the top of his body elevates above the brick top of the well and Brittany places him delicately on the ground, letting go of the Spell and also allowing herself to flop to the earth, spent.

Timbolloree takes huge gulps of air, trying to catch his breath. He looks so fragile, so very much unlike the Timbolloree I wrote about or imagined. There are tears in his eyes. Then, he looks over, sees Brittany lying near him—huffing and puffing from the exertion—and in an instant, the crying turns to a kind of laugh. Not a pleasant one. It's . . . feral. Lascivious. But . . .

No. No. No, no, no. I'm probably just projecting. He's a person who's had a tough, tough go, and it's likely that's just some part of my brain refusing to let go of an old tape that—

"So," he says, still looking at Brittany, voice hoarse and kind of . . . predatory, "was it as good for you as it was for me?"

The laugh gets louder. And creepier. And altogether gross.

He starts to struggle up to his feet and, when he does, we can all see how . . . *excited* he is . . . to be out of the well.

"Oh, my," Tavrella says as Lonnaigh barks, "For the love o' Kentavion!" and Perg exclaims, "Goddamn, homie! Hide your shame!"

Brittany, still catching her breath, turns to see what we're all looking at and says, "No."

Timbolloree is now on his feet, staggering around and licking his lips.

"Oh yeah. OH, yeah! I been down in that hole a LONG time! A long, *loooooooooong* time. Timbo's got him some catching up to—OH NO!" That's when he sees me. "You!" He staggers back, pointing. "You did this! You're the one who put me down there, you psychopath!"

Lonnaigh looks my way. "Ye did this?"

I try to laugh it off. "Hehe. Times were different."

"Gods, Saviour, I canna believe—"

But that's all she gets out before Timbolloree goes on. "But you can make it up to me!"

"I can make it . . . ? How?" I ask.

He licks his chops and rubs at his . . . thighs. "Weird little harem you got, but beggars can't be whatever they say."

There is an unsettled quiet before Lonnaigh asks, "What?"

"I mean, the old lady, the strong-looking one, and Miss Already-Sucked-Me-Up-a-Tunnel over here are probably enough to get me started. I could do without the snail; snails aren't really my thing, historically, but whatever. Your boy's been down there a looooooooong time, and the saddle looks interesting, so—"

"Bro!" Perg yells. "There's a little thing called consent, fool!"

"Eh," Timbolloree scoffs. "People only whine about that shit when it wasn't any good."

"Dear god, stop!" I shout.

"Nah, nah, nah," he goes on, still . . . experiencing himself. "Ole' Timmy B's been denied that sweet, sweet strusenberry pie for way too long, so I think I'm just gonn—Ahhhh! The hells?!" He is suddenly bathed in light and being lifted into the air again. "What are you doing?!"

The look on Brittany's face would be best described as one of disgusted spite.

"Uh . . . Teleri?" I say. Carefully.

She doesn't respond, just hovers Timbolloree back over the opening to the well as he shouts, "No! No, no, no! No! Please! Don't—AAAAAAAAAAHHHHHHHHHHHHHHHHH!"

The light fades and he goes plummeting to the bottom once more, screaming the whole way down. A Notification appears.

Side Quest: "Get Timbolloree Out of the Well!"
[FAILED]

I watch as Brit wipes her palms together like she's sweeping away dirt, then looks at the rest of us, says, "Blade?" and heads off in the direction the map directs.

We all glance around at one another, then, "I get why ye pitched him down there now." Lonnaigh saddles up onto Perg, and he shuffles her off, complaining the whole time.

Tavrella gives me an amused look, tells me—apropos of nothing as far as I can gather—"Yer a good lad," and then follows the pack into the night.

I take a moment standing here, considering all that's just happened, and upon hearing Timbolloree shouting from deep in the ground below, "Come back! Skanks! Timmy's still got a bone to pick! Hehehehehehehehehehe . . ." I take off my rose-colored glasses and leave them sitting on the edge of the well as I follow the rest of my Party.

"There it is," Brittany says, pointing to the pile of rocks on the ground with the hilt of a blade protruding out of it.

The Blade of the Starfallen. Here. Right in front of me. (Or, the hilt is. The Blade itself is still buried, and only the true Saviour can withdraw it, so . . . this will be informative.)

I wonder if I'm eventually going to have to get back all of the items Carpathian had in his possession that got sent to their places of origin when he died. Man, I hope not. The Cerulean Tunic of the Seafarer is all the way at the bottom of the Zephyrian Sea. I'll have to take on Swimming Abilities and Reoxygenating Spells, and . . . Ugh. It'll just be a whole thing.

"Ow!" Perg barks out as Lonnaigh dismounts. "Do you have spikes on your boots?"

"Why would I not?" Lonnaigh grunts, dropping herself to the ground. "Alright, Saviour. Let's get yer damn sword and get to steppin'."

I take a deep breath, nod to myself, take another deep breath, forgetting that I took the first one, and now I have too much air in my lungs and start having a coughing fit. Tavrella comes over, puts her hand on my back, unscrews the top on a small flask, and makes me drink something that tastes like a Capri Sun.

"Thanks," I say, straightening up and pulling my shoulders back. Like a Saviour does.

Brit gives me a thumbs-up, nods, winks. It could be sarcastic or not; can't really tell.

"Saviour!" Lonnaigh claps her hands. "Yer the one who's so all-fired worried about time. What are ye waiting fer?"

"Nothing. Nothing, I'm . . . just . . . Here I go."

I approach the handle warily.

"It's gonna be fine, Bruce. Just grab the handle, yank out the sword, point it at the sky, yell 'By the power of Grayskull!' or whatever, and Bob's your uncle, we're on our way."

I appreciate the confidence my head voice has. I wish I shared it.

Reaching out, touching the jeweled handle, I carefully wrap my fingers around it. I can feel something. Some kind of . . . I'm not sure how to describe it. Electricity, maybe, pulsing inside the handle and causing my Heart to beat harder.

THUMP-Thump. THUMP-Thump. THUMP-Thump.

My forearm tenses and starts to shake. The current of electricity is now running all the way through my body, head to toes. I can feel my hair wanting to stand on end like when you touch one of those static electricity balls at the St. Louis Science Center.

I swallow, pull on the handle with one, sharp jerk, and . . .

Nothing. The sword doesn't budge. Not a centimeter.

I look at Lonnaigh, who tilts her head at me. "There a problem?"

"No. No, all good. Think maybe my hand's just a little . . ."

I rub my palm against my mesh suit. Dried blood flakes off, so I bend down, grab a handful of dirt, and rub both my hands together quickly. Then I clap, making the dust poof away, and go to try again.

And, just like the first time . . . Nope. Not moving.

Shit, shit, shit, shit, shit.

"*Calm down, Bruce. Take a breath. You're doing great.*"

"*How am I doing great?! You said all I was gonna have to do was yank it out and shout* Grayskull!"

"*I was just trying to buck you up. Don't get mad at* me *just because the sword's obstinate.*"

I wrap my other fist around the handle, now trying to tug it free with both hands. Still no good. I plant my foot on the rock to see if I can get some extra leverage. Nada. Lonnaigh is looking at me with an expression that seems both worried and a little annoyed.

"What in the seven hells is the issue? *Saviour?*" She calls me *Saviour* with some extra spice on the word. As Lonnaigh has never fully trusted Carpathian, this pathetic display isn't helping anything.

"I, uh . . . I'm not . . . I'm not . . ."

I'm not Carpathian! That's the issue! I don't care what anyone says or thinks! I'm not the World Saviour! I'm just Bruce Silvert from St. Louis who, once upon a time, wrote a book for fun, and then got really, really lucky when people read it and liked it. And then got really, really unlucky when the world from the books he wrote decided to teach him a lesson or some shit and dragged him into the middle of the story and tasked him with doing stuff of which he is totally incapable.

Obviously, I'm not gonna say all that. That's just part of the running monologue that I keep going in my brain. The one that, if other people knew about, would cause them to slap me in the face and tell me to snap out of it just like Cher did to Nicholas Cage in *Moonstruck.*

"Um, Carpathian?" Brittany calls, raising her hand and waving me over to her as I did to her back at the well. "Can *I* get a second?"

"The two o' ye sure do seem to share a lot o' secrets."

I attempt to ignore Lonnaigh, cease my futile attempt at sword extraction, and walk over to meet Brittany. Lonnaigh keeps her eyes on me the whole time.

"The hell, bro?" Brit whispers.

"I don't know," I whisper back.

"We need it. And not just because it's a bad look for you not to be able to get it out of the stone but because it's a Quest requirement for rescuing Almeister."

"I am aware. But I can't get it to come out. What do you want me to do?"

She looks down, thinks for a second, then looks back to me.

"It's because you don't believe it."

"What do you mean 'it's because I don't believe it.' Don't believe what?"

"That you're the one. That you're the Saviour."

"Because I'm—"

"I don't wanna hear that shit," she whisper-shouts. Lonnaigh raises her head, trying to listen. "Whether you are or not, you fuckin' need to be right now."

"What are you talking about?"

"I'm talking about fake it 'til you make it, dude. What does the Bible say? Act as if ye have faith, and faith will be given to you?"

I should just roll with it. I *know* I should. I want to, I really do, but . . . dammit . . .

"The Bible doesn't actually say that."

". . . What?"

"That's not from the Bible. It's from the Paul Newman movie *The Verdict*. David Mamet wrote it. I think people think it's from the Bible because it kinda sounds—"

"Who gives a shit?! My point is that, in the same way I hear you giving yourself little affirmations all the time, like 'I'm a good writer,' or 'these jeans make me look cool'—"

"Wait, you hear me saying that stuff? When do you hear me saying that stuff?"

"Sometimes I hear you mumbling when I come up to your room to go over the schedule or whatever, and I just wait outside your door until you're finished. Doesn't matter—you can complain about me invading your privacy another time. I'm trying to say . . ." She pauses and gathers herself. "I'm trying to say that when you wrote that Almeister brought Carpathian here to get the Blade, it wasn't *just* for him to get the Blade, right? It was so he would finally be able to truly, deeply believe in himself, correct? *Believe* that he's the Saviour?"

". . . Yeah?"

"Great. Then I'm just saying . . . reverse the order."

"Reverse . . . ?"

"Dummy, I'm telling you to *believe* that you're the Saviour *first*, and see if that gets it done. Because Carpathian Einzgear isn't just a person—he's an idea, a *symbol*, for what's possible if we all just believe in ourselves."

"*That's what I said, Bruce! Remember? Back in Garr Haven? You were still laid up in bed and I said—*"

"Yes, Nelsonanne Mandelason. I remember. Just, please be quiet for a minute?"

"*Fine. But I want credit for this idea. If it works, I want to be the one you thank when you receive your Saviour of the Year Award.*"

I banish the voice from my thoughts while I consider the implications of what Brit is saying.

Confidence. That's really all she's talking about. Have confidence. At the end of the day, that's what happens when someone steps inside a Pulse Well. They gain confidence. Their powers and Abilities are all already there; they just need to have them validated so they can believe it and know how to use them. Brit's suggesting that I just flip the order. Believe it first, and the rest will fall into place.

Can't hurt to try, I suppose.

Shit. Okay. Here goes.

"What were ye talking about?" Lonnaigh asks as I move to give the handle another try.

"She was just coaching me on my form," I reply, quickly grabbing the hilt to avoid having to discuss it any further.

I take a breath and think to myself: *I am the Saviour. I am the Saviour. I can shoulder the weight of whatever burdens the Saviour must carry. I can. I know I can. Because without me, there is no him. We are the same. We are one.*

I am *the Saviour.*

And, with as much faith in the idea that I can muster, and belief in myself that I can foster . . .

. . . I once again tug on the Blade.

CHAPTER FORTY-FOUR

I'm just saying, it was very anticlimactic," Perg declares as we make our way toward the entrance to the Cavern of Sorrows.

"What were you expecting would happen?"

"I dunno. An explosion, some angelic harp music, big, fancy light show. Something. Not just, 'Oh, cool, the sword was in a rock; now it's not, the end.'"

I get where he's coming from. I thought it was a little bit of a letdown too. But sometimes, pulling a magical blade of legend from its place frozen in the earth is its own reward.

I did get a Notification that read:

You have captured [The Blade of the Starfallen].
Good on you! Use it violently—that's what it's for.
{COURTESY MESSAGE #16}

And then there were a couple of party confetti emojis.

"Not everything is gonna turn into some big, dramatic set piece. Sometimes, things just . . . happen," I advise Perg, spinning the Blade of the Starfallen around at my side.

"Please be careful," Brittany cautions. "Just because you now have it doesn't make you What's-his-name."

"Who's What's-his-name?"

"What's-his-name. The sword guy. The Japanese—?"

"Miyamoto Musashi, Japan's Sword Saint?"

"Yeah. Him. You're not."

She's right. I'm not. But it's hard not to feel like it while I'm holding this thing. Because it's pretty hard ass.

According to, well, me, the Blade of the Starfallen came into being when one of the myriad stars in the skies above Meridia met its life's end and, instead of burning out, exploded, raining a torrent of celestial showers onto the planet for . . . I can't really remember. I wanna say, a full Lunar Cycle or something? Anyway. From the gathered detritus of this fallen star, an ancient artisan forged a blade of unparalleled craftsmanship and imbued it with the essence of the celestial body from whence it was derived.

The blade glimmers with a radiant aura reminiscent of the star's light, while its edge holds the potency of the cosmos itself, yadda, yadda. Legend speaks of its power to rend through darkness and serve as a beacon of hope in the meow, meow, meow and so forth and such on.

And while all that's cool in print, the living version of it puts the description to shame.

The blade of the, uh, Blade glimmers with a metallic sheen that does actually remind me of a starlit night sky. (Or maybe the light show at a Chainsmokers concert.) The sharpness of the Blade's edge looks like it would absolutely lop off a digit or fifty. The craftsmanship is exceptional, with engravings of celestial bodies—comets, stars, nebulas—that spiral elegantly along its length. These intricate designs owe to the fact that the Blade is, indeed, an ode to the talents of the Stellari-using silversmith that forged the thing.

(I think I named her Bonnifer. Or . . . Bathsheba? Belinda? Bonnie Bedelia? Who played Bruce Willis's wife, Holly McClane née Gennaro in *Die Hard*, the greatest action-slash-Christmas movie of all time? Sounds like the kind of thing I'd do.)

Regardless, the hilt is equally impressive, designed so that the cross guard curves protectively around the grip, which is wrapped in *larimhide,* a material I conceived of as one traditionally used for binding powerful scrolls. It's cool to feel how well it works. It's both cushy and kinda sticky, similar to how those epoxy resin countertops make you think your hands are covered in honey residue. It's got a good hold, is what I'm saying.

But the real standout feature is the pommel.

Set within it is a jewel that seems to hold the essence of the Pillars of Creation. It pulsates with a whole gorgeous array of colors: oyster blue, deep purple, king crimson . . . all the classics. In REU, the Riftbreaker Expanded Universe (An exhaustive wiki made for the series. Big ups to ScytheAxeBladeHammer365; terrible screen name but great wiki page editor), this jewel was thought to be the fragment of a star from the heart of a supernova called Epyrean.

Or, I should say, it has come to be thought of that way. That's actually nothing I ever wrote, suggested, or even dreamed about. It's a classic example of enthusiastic speculation by fans of a story linking unrelated elements. Many Riftbreakerers have let their imaginations take over some of the details and built out new angles I never intended. Kind of a Han-shot-first type of a thing.

I guess what happened in this case is that someone must have thought a typo that got skipped by my editor—the word *epyrean*—was intentional, and then let their own imagination run amok. I was trying to describe the way the Blade felt in Carpathian's hand, and had intended to type *em*pyrean, which is another way of saying sublime, but I made a mistake, it got overlooked, and the Epyrean supernova was born. So, I've got no one to blame but myself.

(For the record, I'm not a language elitist. I'm really not. The only reason I use so many magniloquent words when I write is so my language choices don't become supernumerary. But because of that, I can't be too perturbated when some things wind up getting mist.)

In any case, there's now this whole extensive backstory about the Blade that is debated over, when the truth is that I just thought it would be neat if the sword was both deadly *and* pretty. But it doesn't really matter what I intended because, as Brittany was quick to point out, Riftbreaker is no longer exclusively *mine.*

Ha. Ain't that the truth.

However, I *am* the one currently in possession of the real, actual, I'm-touching-it-right-now Blade of the Starfallen. The Blade that can only be wielded by the true World Saviour.

I'm still not sure I feel that much different, to be honest? Like, it's cool that I was able to convince the sword that it should come with me, but part of me thinks I was just able to psych it out.

I dunno. I'm trying not to think about it too, too much. If I were writing all this down in a book, I'd probably be worried that I'm spending too much time in my own head, ruminating over details that are slowing down the pace of the action. I know how much some readers hate it when Carpathian gets too self-reflective, so maybe I should try taking a page out of my own book by . . . uh . . . taking a page . . . out of . . . my own book.

Not mentally writing a whole page of rumination when there're Quests to be completed, is what I'm saying. A couple of mental paragraphs is sufficient for now; I can return to the psychodrama stuff later. We've got shit to do, and—Oh, look, we're here.

"Holy shit, that's a big-ass dungeon," Perg says, his eyes round as he takes in the open mouth of the Cavern of Sorrows.

He's not exaggerating. We're staring at a cave entrance that looks like it's auditioning for the lead role in *Spooky Cavities of the Ancient World*. It looms before us as a colossal and foreboding presence carved into the very heart of the rock face. It's like if Petra in Jordan went goth. It's not just big—it's properly monumental.

If I'm remembering correctly (which I'm sure I'm not, but whatever), the Cavern of Sorrows is so named because back when Meridia was a green Eden, it was actually the palace of a great Meridian leader (Don't ask me their name; I never gave them one) who lived there with their large and cherished family. And then, the Ninth Guardian and DONG came along and jacked it all up because the unnamed Meridian leader tried to resist the Ninth Guardian's pleas to join forces, and yadda, yadda, yadda. Everybody was killed and entombed inside, etcetera.

So, the Disciples having robbed from it all its purity, leaving it to deteriorate and crumble until the underlying earth rose up to consume it, created the worst purgatory imaginable; a place tormented by all manner of wretched beasts and spirits trapped in eternal sorrow, their anguish a palpable presence that weighs heavily upon any who dare to tread within, the very air seeming to thrum with an aura of desolation, leaving all who are bold enough to venture beyond its entrance to ponder the depths of their own sorrow as they navigate its treacherous paths.

Blah, blah, blah. I'm certain I got a bunch of that wrong, but it was something like that.

Regardless of how this place came to be, the descriptions of it were accurate as hell. This joint is scary and intimidating and altogether *gulp*-inducing.

And it's night, so the Scooby Doo yoinks-o-meter that normally tops out at ten is up to about a thirty-five. The four moons bathe the landscape in a surreal, multihued light, refracting and twisting the shadows that dance across the rocky ground, converging on the cave and highlighting its portentous contours and edges. And it's quiet. The kind of quiet that's nearly oppressive because the usual night sounds are conspicuously absent, as if even the fearsome beasts of Meridia know to steer clear of this place.

"Okay," I say, feeling not at all confident about what I'm going to offer next, but throwing it out there anyway because we don't really have much of a choice. "Let's . . . go get Mael."

We take a collective breath and resume making our approach to the mouth. The glow from inside casts shadows that make it look like the walls are moving. Or it's possible that the walls *are* moving. It is filled up to the brim with eternal sorrow; that's gonna leave a mark on a place.

We step into the outer ring that's accessible to anyone, presuming you're the kind of anyone who wants to go sightseeing in a fount of merciless tragedy. Leaving the soupy glow of the moons behind us, my eyes adjust to the dim light, and I can tell we're in a sort of corridor. It stretches out before us, the walls, floor, and ceiling lined with rivulets of multicolored veins that pulse softly. The actual veins of inhumed spirits yearning to be free? Maybe? Who can say? The Mezmeric energy is tangible, though. A subtle vibration that tickles the back of my mind.

"Stop fidgetin', snail. Yer gonna buck me off," Lonnaigh declares.

"Lady, the walls in here are literally pulsing. You want me not to fidget, I'm gonna need about ten shots of Cuervo and maybe some of that sticky icky the monkey back at the garage was smoking."

Speaking of sorrow . . . At the mention of Garr Haven, a weight descends upon us all, and as if the walls can feel our pain, they start pulsing harder.

"Let's, um, try and think happy thoughts," I suggest.

"Are ye jokin', Saviour?" Lonnaigh marvels.

"If you think it's a funny joke and it makes you giggle, then yes. If that question is, as I suspect, not sincere and instead fills you with anger—which is, of course, the surrogate emotion that rises to armor one against feeling a more authentic set of feelings, like fear or sorrow—then forget I asked."

We continue down the hallway, the light from the veins shadowing us in bizarre, elongated forms against the walls. The only sound is our soft, careful footfalls. The corridor then widens, and we step into a vast room.

Before us, guarding the way ahead, stand ten gateways, each a marvel of Mezmeric craftsmanship. They're arrayed in a semicircle, like the court of some ethereal king, each vying for attention yet perfectly in harmony with its neighbors. They are tall, imposing, and framed with ornate designs that suggest a fusion of natural forms and geometric precision. Rather than possessing doors, per se, each one of them is guarded by a pulsing sheet of energy with its own unique, gemlike color. All the recurrent hues that pop up on Meridia to break apart the monotony of the landscape and suggest that *some* kind of hope remains are represented here. Azure, emerald, crimson, violet . . . y'know, the popular kids.

Like the walls, the gates seem alive, as though the very essence of the stones has been distilled and intensified in some way. The air around the gateways shimmers with Mezmeric power. Raw. Dangerous. Essential.

A Notification appears in front of me.

Welcome, welcome, welcome to the Cavern of Sorrows! The Cavern is glad you're here!

(Well, not *glad*, exactly. It is a cavern of SORROWS, but you get the meaning.)

You have arrived at the Gates of Condemnation! Scary! This is where the Trial officially begins.

As a reminder: Once you pass through a gate, you are fully committed. You may not exit the Cavern until your Quest is completed or you are.

(Note: *Completed*, in this context, is a euphemism for dead. Presume you got that, but just making sure.)

You must select the Gateway that aligns with your chosen Elemental Item, so hope you brought one. Good luck, and Richemerion-speed, you gallivanting vagabond!

{COURTESY MESSAGE #17}

"Okay," I breathe.

"Do all the doors lead to the same places?" Lonnaigh asks.

"Uhhh, what's that?"

"The doors. The gates there. They all lead to the same places? We have the correct Elemental item to get to the place where my brother is?"

I *pop* my lips together four times before answering, "*Yeeeeesss?*"

Lonnaigh assesses me before asking, "Ye sure?"

I look to Brittany, who surreptitiously raises her eyebrows and lifts and drops her shoulders.

"Yeeeeesss." It's only marginally more certain, but it's the best I've got. Because I'm not totally sure, and I didn't ever really think about it before this very second, but I assume I'm right.

"Then why are there so many of 'em?"

"Say again, now?"

"If they all go to the same place, then why are there so many options for ingress?"

I suck at my teeth because that is also a good question. And there is no good answer. I just thought it would be cool to have a bunch of fancy gates with sexy-looking Mezmer in multiple colors. And from a visual perspective, that's true. It was one of the things the TV people gravitated toward particularly. Quite frankly, they seemed way less interested in the story and more interested in, as one of the development executives said, "*The cool-ass Riftbreaker theme park ride we're gonna be able to build.*"

But as Lonnaigh *is* interested in tiny little things like . . . any kind of verisimilitude whatsoever, I need to come up with an answer.

"*Becauuuuussse*, um, of theeeee . . . Elemental balance?" I look at both Brittany and Perg with wide eyes, and then just . . . commit to the bit. "The, uh, Elemental *colors* are tied to the Elemental *balance* of the cavern. *Annnnd thuuuuus* . . . each entrance corresponds to a different aspect of Elemental necessity that needs to be kept in harmony for the stability of the cavern itself. Sooooo . . ."

I nod affirmatively like I sure did just say something.

Lonnaigh considers, then asks, "Which one do we have the key fer, then?"

Brittany gestures enthusiastically in the direction of the gates because this *is* something she knows the answer to, as she's the one who came up with the coding system. "Each color represents a school of Elemist Mezmer. Ruby is Pyreheart. Silver is Frostheart. Emerald is—"

"Which. One. Do. *We*. Have?" Lonnaigh demands.

Brittany deflates, which I understand. Being cut off when you're trying to crow about your achievements is a real mood killer.

"That one," she says, pointing petulantly at a glowing citrine gateway, a vibrant orange that signifies, unmistakably, Stoneheart. "That's us."

I approach the glowing gateway, examining it closely. It pulses gently, tongues of Mezmeric energy licking at the confines of the arches.

I stick my free hand out to Brittany like a surgeon asking for a scalpel, and she reaches into her garb, pulling out the microsize Stoneheart Gloves. She nearly drops them in the handoff, and for the first time ever, I realize what a dumb way of handling inventory items this is. Still, though, kilostrydes better than literally shoving crap into my chest or something. Blech.

I grasp the gloves tightly in my fist, call up the menu from my Heart, and select Inventory.

[Accessing Inventory]
1 of 2 Item Slots Available
1 Item Available for Use: Stoneheart Gloves

Would you like to utilize Stoneheart Gloves?
[Yes] [No]

I would. So, I select [Yes], and *pop* go the gloves, inflating to wearable size and springing my hand open. I hand Brit the Blade of the Starfallen while I pull the gloves on, and even cynical Brittany feels compelled to utter, "Wow," when she handles the legendary item.

"Right?" I say back. Gloves now in place, I take a deep breath and channel a surge of Mezmer energy through them, doing my best to form the image in my mind of a small spike of earth that will emerge to convene with the gate like a key entering a lock.

I succeed.

. . . Kind of.

A spike does burst forth from the ground, but in my eagerness, I guess I over-filled the cup, so to speak, because rather than a small, keylike spike of earth, I have called up a six-foot-tall battering ram of stone that smashes hard right into the shimmering wall of color that guards the gateway entrance.

"Shit," I whisper sharply.

"What happened?" Lonnaigh asks. "Did ye break it? Ye broke it, didn't ye?"

"No, I didn't—" There's a rush of Mezmer, a torrent of power that makes the air crackle. The gateway lights up, vibrating violently as if it's going to tear itself apart. "I think I broke it!"

"Hit the dirt, fool! It's gonna blow!" Perg shouts. He throws himself to his side, tossing Lonnaigh to the ground in the process.

"Ow!" she bellows.

Brittany, Tavrella, and I attempt to take cover as well, scrambling away from the gateway as it shudders and shakes. The ground trembles beneath us, and I cover my head with my Drakonar-bracered arms, preparing myself for an explosion.

But, instead of a full-on cataclysm, the violent trembling subsides, the gate-way stabilizes, and as I peek to see what's happened, I discover that the shimmer-ing orange light is gone, and an invitation to venture forward into the Cavern of Sorrows is now extended to us.

A Notification.

Final reminder! Once you step foot through the gate into the Cavern, you are expected to be "'bout that business," as one might say. So . . . last chance to turn back, Action Jackson.
{COURTESY MESSAGE #18}

Thump-thump. Thump-thump.

I blow out a breath, pull myself to my feet, look to my cohorts, and say, "Here we go."

In for a farthing, in for a pound.

CHAPTER FORTY-FIVE

I'm the first to cross through. I'm kind of prepared to, I dunno, *feel* something when I do? Like some sort of weight or pressure or latent memory of a long-forgotten misery of some kind? But I don't. I just feel like me, only now on the other side of the gateway.

Brit steps through next. We do a bit of "making the gloves small, giving them over for safekeeping, handing the sword back to the Saviour" lazzi as Perg shuffles through, and Lonnaigh, no longer trusting of the large snail since he threw her to the ground, limps in behind.

The four of us now await Tavrella, but she doesn't move for a moment. She simply stands there, staring at me directly with her mystically beautiful and kind eyes, looking as though she's not planning on joining.

"Everything okay?" I ask.

"Aye," she says, a grin forming.

"You coming?" I follow up.

"'Course I am," she replies, her smile now in full bloom.

She adjusts her bandolier of alchemical treats and steps through as well. And, as soon as she's crossed over, *BOOMP,* the gate slams shut. Not with the citrine Mezmer but with a solid, hard block of companion stone that shutters down ferociously, declaring in no uncertain terms that we are *here.*

Turning to see what awaits us, I'm . . . Well, you'd think that after all I've now experienced, the ability to be surprised would have been dampened, but expecting a dark, sullen, physical manifestation of the very concept of suffocating loss, and instead finding a beautiful waterfall glittering with an inexplicable light, creating a scene that's almost serene—which is what I see instead—will make you do a double take.

Good to know that I'm not easily jaded, I guess.

"What the hells?" Brittany whispers just loud enough to hear. "This isn't how . . . I remember it." She looks to Lonnaigh and then me.

"Me neither," I acknowledge.

I semi-unconsciously grip the Blade more tightly as I step forward. Getting close enough to the waterfall that I can start to make out what's behind it, I see that it's open on the other side. It's another subcavern inside this larger system that makes up the Cavern of Sorrows. Which, at the moment, appears inaccurately named. Should be the Cavern of Not Too Bads or something.

The energy feels like a static charge as I close in, making the hairs on the nape of my neck stand up. I take a deep breath and step through, expecting . . . I'm not sure what. But the sensation is nothing like I anticipated. It's akin to walking through wet spiderwebs; that clingy, ticklish feeling that is mildly disquieting but ultimately harmless.

Then, I'm through to the other side and standing in another vast cavern. It's kind of like stepping into a dream or a meticulously crafted movie set designed to hit you with a sense of stupefaction. It resembles a Mexican cenote—one of those natural sinkholes that open up to the sky, with water pouring in from the sides. The ceiling is open, and I can see the geometric stars shining down, twinkling all around me like lights reflecting off a mirror ball, giving the place very much a Harlem Renaissance Jazz Club energy.

"What's it like over there?" Brittany calls through the sheet of water between us.

"Like . . . nice?" I reply, pushing my wet hair back on my head. "Come on through."

I shake the water off my hands, and it's that action—seeing the tiny droplets flinging off my skin, smacking against the cavern walls, and rolling down the face of the stone—that triggers a memory. A memory of what water represents in the Cavern of Sorrows.

And it's that memory that causes me to realize . . .

I just made a big, *big* mistake.

"No! Don't!" I yell out, throwing my hand up to stop Brittany and the others from passing through. But it's too late. They've already stepped into the cataract and are coming to meet me.

And that's when I feel it.

An *eruption* of grief.

It starts in the pit of my stomach and causes my breath to catch in my throat. I begin gulping and hyperventilating at the same time, and in an imitation of the waterfall itself, tears start cascading down my face.

Rapid-fire images riddle my thoughts like bullets from a machine gun.

Mom, lying in the hospital bed, the ECG flatlining.

Me in my little boy's suit, standing graveside at her funeral.

Dad, some other time, yelling at me to get my shit together.

Showing up at the bus depot in the pouring rain for my first day of work.

Mollie, the woman I maybe could have loved, walking out of my house for the final time, looking back over her shoulder at me with a tear in her own eye.

Persephone being torn apart by Moridius and the Ronine in Bell's View.

Zerastian being swallowed by the Mokeisan Desert.

Xanaraxa being wrestled to the ground by the Disciples of the Ninth Guardian.

Mael—

Wait. No. What?

Those last ones aren't *my* memories. Those are just things I wrote.

History and fiction are getting commingled somehow, the actual past and the narrative past becoming one.

"Hey! Hey! What's wrong? What happened?! You okay?" Brittany shouts as she exits the passageway of grief and runs over to tend to me, pushing wet hair behind her ears.

I try to answer, but the words are caught in my throat, sobs overtaking me and leaving me helpless. I feel exposed and vulnerable in a way that has no comparison.

I'm appreciably more defenseless in this moment than I have ever been, literally ever. No amount of being naked or having my limbs blasted off or my heart broken by any single event in my life comes even close to compare.

Because I'm not experiencing a single event. I'm experiencing all of them. At the same time. And not in my distant recollection but in the unrelenting present. In the here and the now.

And I am utterly, completely, absolutely, indefensibly, hopelessly . . . laid to waste.

"Look at me!" Brittany shouts in my face, grabbing hold of my arms, attempting to get me to focus. But I can't. I fear I'm beyond retrieval.

For a moment, I consider taking the Blade and running myself through with it just so I won't have to experience this feeling anymore. The impression I'm getting in this instant is that there is no prospect of me ever not experiencing these emotions again, and the only possible way to escape the personal cavern of sorrow into which I have fallen is to end everything.

"What's going on with him?" I hear Lonnaigh shout over the sound of my own agony.

"I don't—" Brit starts, but that's all she gets out before she pulls away and I see her shoulders begin shaking. The same burgeoning hyperventilation I experienced starts to seize hold of her as well. She looks into my eyes, and her own go wide. "Oh, shit," she says. And then . . .

Waterworks. Like a burst pipe, a rushing river, and a monsoon have all collided as one.

"Yo! What's happening, fools?" Perg calls out. But that's the last thing he manages before his oversize snail body is also clutched by a paroxysm of wailing.

And then Tavrella.

And, finally, Lonnaigh.

I think I'm the first to fall to the cavern floor. I can't be sure, but I believe I am the domino that triggers all the others to collapse in succession. Irrespective of who was first, when I wrench open my soaking wet eyes, I am able to see my four compatriots rolling on the ground just as I am, all of us clutching ourselves to keep from tearing apart, rocking from side to side on the cold, hard ground, screeching and howling like a group of colicky babies in an overpacked maternity ward.

Our keening reverberates off the cavern walls, and they pulse and thrum in approval as the deep, hollow emptiness of our sorrow goes on echoing into the uncaring void for what seems like a very, very long time.

"Well, that sucked," Perg says in the understatement of the millennium.

We're traipsing deeper into the cavern, following a path that seems to be taking us . . . somewhere. I have no idea how long we lay there on the ground, caterwauling, but it truly felt as though it was never going to end. It did, mercifully, but . . .

"Yeah," I agree.

"Fool, why did you just let us walk through the boo-hoo fountain if you knew what was gonna happen?"

"I . . . I forgot," I admit.

"You forgot?! How do you forget something like that, homie?"

"I dunno. I was . . . distracted, I think. Because it didn't look like . . . It was pretty. And I just, kind of, got entranced by it. Or something. I mean, ask her; she knows."

I gesture to Brit, who gives a tight nod but doesn't say anything. Her eyebrows are knitted together, looking like she's still trapped inside her thoughts. I know I'm still inside mine.

Now that I've pulled my shit together, a thought that *isn't* a hideous recollection of things I'd just as soon not remember has popped into my head. Something I wrote in this last book.

"It was, as it had always been, the most sinister of all the Ninth Guardian's contemptible deceits: The fact that they could turn that which was once good into an object of despair."

That's what I scribed, but I don't know that I even understood what I meant when I typed it. I just thought it was kind of a cool turn of phrase, but . . .

When I crafted all of the Cavern of Sorrows stuff in book eight, I leaned into the obvious: the creepy, sad, scary dungeon aspects. Which is why, when we got here, I was so amazed to see that it doesn't look like that.

But, the thing is . . . it does. When you look beyond the surface beauty to what lies beneath.

The Cavern of Sorrows isn't an awful place because it *looks* like an awful place. It's an awful place because of the way it lulls you into a false sense of comfort and then pulls the rug from under your feet. Beautiful to look at, harmful to touch. Like a flame, or a poisonous flower, or Victoria Derwin from sixth-grade homeroom. Beauty and agony are more closely related than we like to think.

Just like hope and fear.

I was writing about things I didn't even understand. The ideas just flowed. Like water.

Flow state.

I let out a long, deep breath.

"Hey," I say to Brit, who is shuffling beside me, still looking a little shaken. "What did . . . ?" I wave my finger by the side of my head to indicate that I'm asking what kind of latent tragedies were brought up for her by the Waters of Waah, as I have just decided to start calling it.

She looks at me like "Boy, you know you must be crazy" and says, "No goddamn way."

Fair enough. I let it drop.

"Lonnaigh? How are you holding up?" I ask her.

"I'm fine," she says. Which is a patent lie. She's not fine, neither physically nor emotionally. I don't need to ask what buried sorrows were brought up for her. I can guess. But she seems as annoyed about the fact that her anger, which she uses to obfuscate her pain, was ripped away—revealing the truer emotions beneath—as she is about having felt the honest emotions themselves.

I get it. I don't use anger to mask my true feelings, opting instead for more of a "charming Labrador Retriever" motif that belies any actual agita, but we've all got our armor.

Speaking of those of us with armor . . .

"Big Perg?" I move on to asking. "You?"

"I'm straight, homie," he replies, but I can hear him still gulping down residual tears.

"Anything you wanna—?"

"I said I'm straight, homie!"

I put my hand up, deciding not to push. But I've asked everyone else, so I may as well hit for the cycle.

"Tavrella?"

She takes a deep breath, then lets it out. "I'm alright, lad. I actually needed a good cry. Felt somewhat liberatin', if'm honest."

My brow furrows. I am intensely curious. Tavrella's the only one here that I know literally nothing about, and that answer only serves to ramp up my desire to find out her story, because it's not part of the story *I* wrote. If and when we have some time (big *if* and maybe overly optimistic *when*), I really want to ask her things. Things about herself, about her life, about her experiences on Meridia. She feels familiar and foreign all at once. I may never have written about her, but she is undeniably of this world, and I want to be able to understand how. And why.

Riftbreaker is a fantasy/sci-fi/LitRPG mashup with subtle pop-culture references buried inside, which feels like more than enough genre cross-pollination, but my time here seems to have also added a smidgeon of mystery thriller to the tale. (Which is, frankly, too much. Were I writing the story of what's happening to me here, I might opt to leave out all the cryptic whodunnit bits. Seems like gilding the lily.)

"Where we headed now? This the direction Mael is?" Lonnaigh asks, breaking the reverie.

"Um . . . What does that map say?" I ask Brit.

She pulls it out and looks. Makes a face. "Not much."

"What do you—?"

She shows it to me. There is no map on this section of the map; it appears to have stopped charting the topography back at the entrance to the gateways. Everything after is just a big, empty nothing of blank parchment.

"What's that about?" I ask. "You're designated as an Advanced Mapmaker."

"I have no idea," she says. "Maybe it doesn't apply in dungeons."

"Why?"

The question makes her immediately annoyed. "Because it can't get a Wi-Fi signal? How the hell am I supposed to know?" she whispers loudly.

I get why she's aggravated. We've just endured profound emotional trauma, and beyond that, she can't be expected to know any more than I do.

Lonnaigh stares at us both, waiting on an answer to her question.

"Well . . ." I start, trying to think of anything I can recall about the description of what happened when Mael got trapped in here. "I think if we keep following the path we're on, we'll get there soon. I feel like it's just a bit farther," I lie. Because what else am I going to say?

Trust the System, I think to myself.

The System gave me the Almeister Quest, which necessitated getting the Blade, and then it led us to Jeomandi's, which is where it also led Lonnaigh, and then I got the Mael Quest, presumably because the Blade is right here anyway? So . . . if the System is driving this double-decker of mayhem, it's surely leading us the right way. It has to be.

Except that . . .

It also allowed a Ronine to find me in Bell's View, presumably killed Persephone, brought a bunch of Templars and the Super Vizier to Garr Haven, and slaughtered everyone inside. So . . .

Shit. I dunno. I can't figure it out. The System works in mysterious ways.

"Wait." Brittany stops dead in her tracks, causing the rest of us to pull up short as well. "What is that?"

"What is what? You hear something?" I ask, listening carefully for what I presume is going to be the now all-too-familiar sound of *EIIIIINNNZZZGGGEEE-AAARRR.*

But that's not what I hear. What I hear instead is *CRAAAAAAAAAAAAAAA-AAAAAACK.*

"What *is* that? It's like a . . ."

"It's like a crack," Perg volunteers.

He's not wrong. That is, in fact, *exactly* what it's like.

Another *CRAAAAAAAAAAAAAAAAAAAAACK,* followed by a *CHKA-CHKA-CHKA-CHKA-CHKA-CHKA-CHKA.* A kind of a . . . a . . . scurrying.

Oh, shit.

"Oh, shit," Brittany says aloud at the very moment I think it.

I glance over my shoulder behind us and regret it almost instantly. Shapes, too many to count, are spilling out of the shadows, moving with an unsettling speed. *Oh, crap,* I think to myself, realizing what's happening.

I try to remain calm. "So, we should—"

"Fuckin' run!" Brittany declares, totally scuttling my attempt at keeping things chill.

"Why?!" Lonnaigh asks urgently. "What is it?"

"Shadowscorpions," I answer, probably way too deadpan given the circumstances, but as ever, I can't help feeling like this is my fault. Well, mine and Nat Geo's, as a segment called "Meet the Arizona Bark Scorpion" was what I was watching when I came up with the critters.

And here they come.

They are larger than any scorpion should ever be so bold to attempt being, with glossy carapaces that gleam menacingly in the cavern's ambient light. Their pincers snap aggressively as they scurry, their multitude of legs carrying them with unsettling speed.

It's not enough that the Cavern of Sorrows traps pain inside and then poops it back out all over your head, but there are also monsters? *Why?! Why did I do this?!*

"Because never use one idea when a thousand is more complicated, Bruce."

We all start to run. Or, we almost all start to run. Lonnaigh can't run, so I stop running *away* and instead run toward her, scooping her up in my arms.

"What are ye doin'?" she shouts in protest.

"Not now!" I yell back. "Shadowscorpions!"

With my Ironspark strength, picking her up is nothing, even with the Blade still in my hand. It's not just that she feels light—though she does—it's that what should seem unwieldy isn't at all. I feel like I could carry her, the Blade, and a whole summer vacation's worth of luggage at the same time and have no problem.

And now we're booking it. And I mean *booking* it, the whole pack of us trying to put distance between us and the bad bugs. We're not making the kind of progress I would like, as we're tripping over the uneven, sorrowful terrain, making a real mess of this whole "escape our pursuers" routine we're performing. But, despite all that, we don't slow down, the sounds of the Shadowscorpions just behind us the whole time.

And now, right before us . . .

A dead end. We have been following the path straight into what may as well be a tomb. Because that's what it's about to become.

"Shit!" Brit shouts. "Do you see that?!"

"Yeah!" I call back. "I see it!"

Well, this is what trusting the System gets me.

"I thought you said Mael was this way!" Lonnaigh screams in my face. And, I gotta tell ya, while I understand her impulse, it's super not helpful.

So I place her onto the ground, and her eyes widen.

"What're ye doin'?!"

"Just . . . gimme a second!" I cough out.

Concentrating on my palms, I tap into the Mezmeric energy I'm getting more and more comfortable acknowledging in my own body, feeling the now familiar surge of power. My hands morph, flesh forming into chutes, and . . .

I launch Toxin Darts toward the advancing horde. Given the formfitting mesh suit I'm sporting, I have never felt more like the world's greatest superhero in my life.

"Bruce? I thought you thought Batman was—"

"Not now, Bruce! In this moment, given the situation I'm in and the tools at my disposal, Spidey takes the crown!"

PEW! PEW-PEW, PEW, PEW-PEW-PEW!

I throw all I've got at 'em, but to my grave dismay, the darts prove utterly useless, pinging harmlessly off the Shadowscorpions armored bodies.

"Peter Parker still claim the top spot, Bruce?"

"You shut up, Bruce! Just shut your schizoaffective mouth!"

I start to launch Control, figuring it's my next best bet for trying to orchestrate some kind of way out of this thing. Only Brit and Perg will be direct beneficiaries, as they're the only ones in my Heart Guard. Lonnaigh and Tavrella will just be slowed as well, but maybe—

However, before I can think it through any further, a massive beam of searing light erupts forward, scorching the whole first row of scorpions, transforming them into the consequences of stepping to somebody who has access to Randolf's Radiant Ray. I look to the side and see Brittany, eyes wild and jaw tight with something I would describe as "the unforgiving determination of the vanquisher."

The smell of charred exoskeleton fills the air, and for a moment, the remaining creatures hesitate, their advance slowed by the unexpected onslaught. But, because they seem to possess both a lust for violence and no regard for their own well-being, they begin their charge again.

And then, a strange thing happens.

Brittany, still looking at me, nods.

And I—a slow dawning coming over me—nod back.

Without saying another word, we go marching directly toward the approaching throng.

CHAPTER FORTY-SIX

What do ye think ye are doin'?" Lonnaigh shouts.

Neither one of us responds. We just continue walking to meet head-on the creepy bastards that are kind of, but not exactly, like the scorpions in the Brendan Fraser and Rachel Weisz Mummy movies. Only bigger. And meaner looking. And holding within them not only a vicious sting, but a sting that—upon feeling it—will cause a panoply of painful recollections of losses past to rush into the living present and torment you with an unceasing ruefulness that will carry you across rivers of despair to a restless and never-ending torment, plagued by the conscious reality of all you have forfeit and are never to regain.

Which is how I described it in book eight. And while it's a good description which I'm proud of, it's one I don't want to experience myself.

I spin the Blade of the Starfallen in my hand like I'm one of the Baseball Furies gang in Walter Hill's 1979 cult classic *The Warriors*. And, as the first of the Shadowscorpions approaches, its pincers ready to grab hold of whatever it can find to grab, I draw *back* with the Blade, and *BOOM! Smash* the flibbertigibbet out of it.

It *EXPLODES* the moment the sword makes impact, turning whatever foulness might have made up its essence into a shower of light that comes raining down like the falling tracers of an exploded Roman candle, taking what was, less than a second ago, a terrifying vision of unbridled anguish and rage and converting it into particles of light that shower the cavern in a tawny warmth.

The other Shadowscorpions shriek, and the walls around us pulse once more. There's an almost infinitesimal breath, and then . . . the Shadowscorpions come at us *hard* and *fast*, *28 Days Later*–style, only in the form of carapaced bugs instead of rabid zombies.

I'm swinging away like I'm Stan Musial, absolutely lacerating the ones directly in front of us while Brittany's managing the rear of the pack, lighting them up as if she's got a flamethrower.

We are putting in *work* on these mama jamas.

The whole of the cavern is ignited like a bonfire, Brittany sparking the torch and me turning the orgy of predatory arachnids into nothing more than golden showers.

"*Bruce . . . really?*"

"*I didn't mean it like that and you know it! Stop! I'm fighting for my life!*"

Just then, one of the little buggers manages to somehow slip past me, and is just about to jump onto Brit with its far-too-big-to-be-called-pincers-so-let's-just-call-them-grappling-hooks when . . .

RN-N-N-N-N-N-N-N-N-N! RRRN-RN-RN-RRRN!

BOOM! BOOM!

The shots Lonnaigh unleashes, coupled with the rumble of the chains from her switchsaws, mixes with the sounds of the desperate defense Brittany and I are putting up and the pained screeches from the creatures, creating an almost unbearable cacophony that roars through the cavern. It seems for a moment like we're gaining the upper hand, our combined attacks creating a barrier of pain and destruction that the Shadowscorpions seem hesitant to cross. But there are too many of them, and for every one that falls, two more seem to take its place.

FWOOM!

What the hell was that?!

I hazard a glance and see it's Tavrella. She's launching some of the Mezmeric Molotov cocktails she has in her bandolier, marching forward to stand beside me and Brit, Lonnaigh limping up to join our flank as well. The four of us now represent a wall of ferocious rebuttal to the Shadowscorpions' wave of assault.

"Yo! I can do shit too!" Perg shouts out, coming up to join.

But as he's snailing his way over, the walls, which are already throbbing with a desperate and expanding energy, begin weeping. Weeping? Weeping.

Water pours from the rock and pools at our feet.

"Shit!" I yell out. "Don't touch it! Perg, stay back! We gotta get out of here! Let's go!"

"Go where?" Perg yells back. "It's a dead end, homie!"

"Teleri!" I yell, not even thinking about it. It's starting to just come out more naturally now. "The wall!"

"*The wall?*" Brit returns. "What do you mean, 'the wall'?"

"Triple R! Direct it at the wall! The dead end!"

She turns, blasts the enclosed area with Randolf's Radiant Ray, and it boomerangs back, almost taking Perg's head off in the process.

"Baby *Jesús* in the manger, what are you doing?!"

Brit looks at me, shaking her head. "I'm just at Etherflint. I don't think—"

I spin her, hugging her from behind, wrapping my arms around her chest like a protective big brother might. "Try it again!"

The water is now up to midcalf. The sound of switchsaw blasts and explosive alchemy continues behind my now turned back. I hug Brit as hard as I can, willing every bit of my Synchron Foundation and newly enhanced Tiers to bond with hers.

She spins her hands around in a circular motion once more, and like the old spiritual song "Joshua Fit the Battle of Jericho," the wall comes a'tumblin' down.

"Move! Now!" I command, letting Brittany go and grabbing up Lonnaigh once more. She continues firing on the Shadowscorpion horde as I run with her. Tavrella throws the last remaining vials of blow-'em-up she has in her bandolier, and then she, Perg, and Brit run to catch up to where I am now waiting by the newly blown hole in the wall, Lonnaigh firing away at the reinvigorated and deeply pissed passel of Shadowscorps.

"Through, through, through," I urge, pushing the three past the recently created doorway. Once they're on the other side, I duck in with Lonnaigh as well. "Perg! Block the opening!"

"What?!"

"Spin your shell; block the opening!"

"You just gonna leave me here to get stung all up my backside while you go . . . do whatever it is you're gonna do?!"

"No! Of course not!" I place Lonnaigh down and stick out my hand to Brit. "Gloves!" She reaches into her cloak and grabs the miniaturized Stoneheart gloves. "I'm gonna handle it, but it's gonna take a second."

"*Puta madre. Estúpido planeta con sus estúpidas reglas y pinche Mezmer y esa mierda,*" he mumbles as he blocks the hole with his shell and we hear the sounds of Shadowscorpions crashing into his back, chittering and stinging. "OW! Hurry up, fool! These bitches got bite!"

Taking hold of the tiny hand covers, I once more call up the Heart menu, selecting Inventory.

[Accessing Inventory]

Would you like to utilize Stoneheart Gloves?
[Yes] [No]

"Select [Yes], fool! Select [Yes]!"

I do. The gloves grow to the requisite size, I slip them on, shout out to Perg, "One, two, move!" and when he does, I blast a stone barrier in place to cover up the hole. One of the Shadowscorpions gets caught trying to squeeze through and screams with rage at being pinned in place. It rages and rails at us even from its disadvantageous position until Lonnaigh, switchsaws still spinning, limps over, forces a chain blade into its skull—silencing it forever—and then reholsters the weapons.

For a moment, things are mostly quiet, some faint Shadowscorpion hubbub from the other side of the rock, but comparatively . . . peace.

Congratulations! You and your entire Party have survived an assault
from a [Flock of Shadowscorpions]!

(Bet you didn't know that a group of Shadowscorpions are called
a "flock" did you? Well, they are! Look at that! You survived
and learned something new to share at cocktail parties! What a
wonderful adventure!)

You and your Party have amassed a whole bevy of fun new tricks
and traits. Please visit a Pulse Well to find out what they are that you
might put them to their best uses.
{COURTESY MESSAGE #19}

I bend over, leaning on the Blade of the Starfallen to catch my breath. Although, honestly, I don't explicitly need to catch my breath. I feel fine, which is wild, given what I just went through. But I lean nevertheless because it just seems like the right thing to do.

After a moment, I slide the gloves off, make them small, and hand them back to Brit.

"At some point, you need to get pockets. I'm a sorcerer, not your valet," she notes.

"Saviour?" Lonnaigh's voice chimes. "The feck's m'brother?"

I rub at my forehead because I'm running out of ways to front like I know what the hell I'm doing. I'm seriously debating telling her the truth right now. That I'm not who she thinks I am, and neither is Brit; Perg is maybe half and half, and we're sorry we led her on this wild Mael chase. And then just hope she doesn't immediately whip out her switchsaws again and mow us down.

But the thought only has a brief moment to fleet through my consciousness before a dazzling flash of Mezmer materializes in front of me, and a glittering, rainbow-colored orb appears out of nowhere.

We all jump back out of instinct.

"What is that thing?" Brit asks.

"I don't know," I admit.

"Where did it come from?"

"As I will continue to answer, regardless of what questions you ask, I do not know."

There's a beat as the orb begins expanding and changing shape, turning into something shaped more like a rectangle. A large rectangle, roughly the size of a doorway.

I step forward to study it, now feeling more curious than concerned.

"It looks like a pride flag," Brittany says from behind me.

"Maybe it's telling us to take pride in how far we've come?" Perg offers up.

"Maybe," I mutter to myself, drawn to the colors in it by something I can't identify. Something about . . . the rainbow.

My Heart starts sort of whirring in my chest, which is a new sensation I haven't experienced before. Like it's winding itself up. And I suddenly find myself declaring aloud, "Mael. Mael's through here."

"Really?" Brit asks.

"Yeah," I say, still in kind of a trance. "Really."

"How do you—?"

"Because while Elemental pathways are distinct, they are interconnected, as are all things, and ultimately lead to the same destination. When disparate Elements engage as a unified whole, the harmonious convergence will illuminate a conduit to the shared objective." It all comes out without me thinking, as though I'm only acting as the mouthpiece for some other force.

There's a beat before Perg asks, "You mean actually? Or is that like a metaphor about—?"

"Probably both," I reply, still transfixed on the Mezmeric energy in front of me.

"So you're sure?" Brit again. "You're sure this is how we get to Mael?"

"It is," I hear Lonnaigh say from behind.

I turn around to look and see she's holding up the back of her hand.

Her tattoo. The Tri-Venn. It's glowing. Bright.

I nod to her. She nods back. The whole vibe in here has turned very "SEAL team communicating silently before launching a rescue mission."

I step aside as Lonnaigh limps over to the newly formed portal. She stares at me. I stare back. She stares at me some more. I stare back some more. She— Oh, nope. That's it. No more staring. She just steps forward now and disappears through the portal, which vibrates and shimmers as she passes on to the other side.

Tavrella's next. She pauses, stroking my arm. My Heart whirs louder still. She steps through.

"You're *sure* you're sure about this?" Brit insists.

"I mean . . . yeah? Surer than I have been about anything else."

"This isn't gonna wind up with us howling on the ground and rending our garments again?"

"I don't think so. It doesn't feel that way. And, y'know, I'm trusting the System."

She mulls it over, takes in the rainbow-colored doorway, and smirks a little. "What do you think the chances are we wind up at the Palm Springs' White Party?"

"Hey! Don't—You can't make jokes like that," I admonish.

"Uh, no, dude. *You* can't make jokes like that." She takes a deep breath. There's a hesitancy about her that's usually more my thing. I think she might be suffering from a case of confronting-the-unknown fatigue.

I start saying, "You know, if you wanna just hang here until—" but she interrupts me before I can finish.

"I'm fine." She blows out the breath she's holding, says, "Fuck it," and steps through.

"I think she saw some shit when we went through the waterfall, yo," Perg suggests.

"Yeah," I breathe out, looking after where she just left, then back at Perg. It hasn't been just the two of us alone since we got here. "How *you* holding up?"

"Me? I'm chillero, homes." His eyes narrow, and his snail mouth screws up.

"What's wrong?" I ask.

"How about you, homie? How *you* doing?"

"I'm . . . alright. I'm . . . getting more comfortable, I suppose."

"Word, word . . . You really jacked up those pincher monsters."

"Shadowscorpions."

"That's what you call 'em? Because they're scorpions and they live in the shadows?"

". . . Yeah?"

He looks disappointed. I think. "Eh. I get it. Naming shit is hard. I mean, you named me Gonzo, for the love of Mike."

"Hey, again, I—"

"I know, I know." He laughs. "I'm just playing with you, fool." He sighs out a last laugh then says, "Hey . . . Thank you, *ese*."

I shake my head and shrug, asking, "For what?"

Instead of answering directly, he offers, "My life was supposed to be just creeping along some riverbed at a snail's pace—pun intended—trying not to get eaten by beetles or whatever. I hate goddamn beetles. *Love, love them don't.* Anyway . . . That's not what my life's turned out to be. It's turned out . . ." He nods his head a tiny bit, his moustache bobbing up and down. "It's turned out . . . to be pretty cool, homie." He reaches out with one of his antennae, taps me on the shoulder, and then he's through the doorway as well. And then . . . the strangest thing.

I find myself all alone.

And it's relatively quiet.

And there's nothing attacking me, and no one in my ear, and not a single impediment to me rolling over a whole barrel of thoughts, theories, notions, narratives, and ideas in my head.

But I don't.

My mind stays completely blank so that the quiet is actually just that. Quiet.

I can't remember the last time I just sat and bathed in the quiet stillness of . . . being alive.

But I do now.

Then I blow out a short breath, stretch my shoulders back, spin the Blade of the Starfallen in my hand, and step through the portal.

The passage is immediate. No big, grand light show. No teleportation kind of a deal. Nothing. It's just like walking through any open door I've ever passed through in my life. And on the other side . . .

More cavern.

Bigger and wider than the other parts of the Cavern of Sorrows with which we've engaged, it has a monumental oval obelisk in the center of the space.

Oh, shit. I know where we are.

My four Party members stand before the obelisk, not moving forward. They can't. Because all around the obelisk is a great, almost taunting, wading pool acting as a type of moat, blocking our ability to go any farther without stepping into the grief-inducing water. But that's not the only reason they're frozen in place.

I move forward tentatively to join them at the edge of the forbidding lagoon and look out to see what they do. They're not staring *at* the water, trying to estimate how to get around it. They're staring at what's *in* it:

A seven-foot-tall behemoth of a man with muscles that look like they could bend steel and long, ropey dreadlocks cascading down his back. His dark skin serves as a rich canvas for the intricate network of tattoos swirling across his shirtless body. Notable most of all amidst the artwork that tells a long, complicated story of histories forgotten—the Tri-Venn on the back of his hand, glowing with a light concordant to the one on Lonnaigh's own.

He's on his knees, the water around him rising to the middle of his thighs. His head is bowed. At first, I think there are chains—thick, black chains—draping from the obelisk to hold him in place, but then I realize they're not exactly chains— they're smoke. Tendrils of black smoke, writhing and twisting as they decant *into* him, moving forward in an infinity of slowly traversing waves pouring into his mouth, his eyes, through his flesh.

It has an almost religious aura. Like the glossy print of a painting you'd see on the front of an old Bible, the portrait titled *The Penitent Observer*, or something equally dramatic.

Mael Anderbariach.

Or, at least, what has become of him.

In the books, Mael was a towering monster, an imposing figure that initially acted as a potential obstacle to Carpathian's overarching narrative, but as the story unfolded, he revealed himself to be a tremendous ally, a character who defied expectations, his journey from feared adversary to respected comrade one of the more satisfying arcs I have written. Now, seeing him here, in the flesh, it's heart-wrenching. The Mael I had imagined, full of dignified fury, kneels subdued and silent. A broken husk of a man.

Immediately called to mind is one of my favorite short stories of all time— "Harrison Bergeron," by Kurt Vonnegut—about a boy called Harrison Bergeron who, in the year 2081, when it has been determined that no one is allowed to be smarter, better looking, or more physically able than anyone else, is taken away by the government because he is more physically and mentally capable than his peers, and they see him as a threat.

The plot gets complicated in a very Vonnegut-y way, offering lots of opportunity for debate over the primary themes, but all that stuff isn't the salient part of the story that's causing me to think of it right now. The thing I'm thinking about now is the way the restraints that have been placed on the physically stronger and more powerful Harrison are described, quote, "*Harrison's appearance was Halloween and hardware. Nobody had ever born heavier handicaps.*"

The five of us got splashed for no more than a couple of seconds by the waterfall, and it sent us into spirals of despair that had us regressing to our most primal selves. Our limbic systems were overstimulated to the point that they became the sum total of what we are as living things. The water that touched our skin was the greatest torment I think any of us have ever known.

And Mael is *immersed* in it.

When I wrote it, I just thought of it as a lampshade of some themes I was exploring. How even the strongest can be brought low. How even heroes can find themselves ensnared by forces beyond their control. But there's nothing thematic about seeing him like this. Mael Anderbariach, who I thought was a figment of my imagination, is all too real, and is suffering in a reality that is all too tangible.

I glance to Lonnaigh. Her eyes are starting to glisten with tears prompted by the water, but this time, not because of what it's doing to her. Not directly, at least.

Her lips quiver, and she attempts to speak. Initially, she cannot make the word form, but then she manages to find her voice and out comes a single syllable:

"May?"

The goliath known as Mael Anderbariach doesn't move at first. But then, some kind of current must reach his brain because he twitches almost imperceptibly. His head raises fractionally, just enough that we can see his eyes. They're closed, but he opens them, and . . .

There is nothing behind them. By which I mean, if eyes truly are windows to the soul, then that's what looking through the windows of Mael's eyes reveals. Nothing. Nothing to see. Nothing left. All that was once visible through the windows has been stolen from within, and no trace of it remains.

But then . . .

His Tri-Venn starts glowing brighter, as does Lonnaigh's. Mael begins shivering in place as if a freezing cold has taken hold of him. I see Lonnaigh choke down a lump in her throat, and finally, after several long, torturous seconds of grunting, ragged noises catching in Mael's throat, he manages to force out a single syllable of his own:

"Lon?"

And that's it.

Lonnaigh, unable to contain herself any longer, lunges forward into the pool of water toward her brother.

I scream out an urgent "NO!"

And all seven hells break loose at once.

CHAPTER FORTY-SEVEN

A Falling Reign, Riftbreaker Book Eight, Chapter Forty-Five

The blade of the Arm of Hearts sang through the air—a bright arc amidst the gloom of the Cavern of Sorrows—as Templars swarmed around Carpathian. The air itself, thick with the scent of moss and ancient stone, vibrated with the energy of Mezmer and metal, the clash of power against power. The Saviour wheeled in his levitation, forcing back the teeming Templar throng, and saw his cohorts . . . his companions . . . his Heart Guard . . . enacting their gifts and, as one, attempting to bring an end to this clash and escape from such ancient Mezmer unscathed and with the Cerulean Tunic of the Seafarer still intact.

Teleri, her robes flickering with ethereal light, chanted in a tongue forgotten by time. With a flourish of her hands, the ground beneath a group of advancing Templars shattered, sending them tumbling into the abyss below. Her eyes, aglow with the fierceness of battle, scanned the cavern for their next threat. They were forced to route them, to deceive them. It was the only way forward.

Xanaraxa moved through the chaos with a grace that belied her formidable frame, her six arms a blur, each one holding a different weapon save for one hand which she kept open, manipulating the gravity around her enemies. Templars found themselves either rooted to the spot upon which they were standing by an unseen force or floating helplessly, easy targets for her swift strikes.

Mael, with untamed ferocity, charged through the adversaries, his locks trailing behind him like the mane of a lion. Each blow from his massive fists sent Templars sprawling, the roar of his voice booming over the din of battle, a sound as inspiring as it was intimidating.

Zerastian danced between aura drones and vibration screens that she conjured with a flick of her wrist. Her devices whirred and zipped, disorienting the enemies with sudden flashes of light and deafening blasts. Her laughter, sharp and wild, mingled with the sounds of explosions and collapsing stone.

Pergamon, his body a shield, flashed about the narrow corridors, blocking attacks and baffling the foe. His rich, storied voice offering encouragement or warning, even reprisal—though that was reserved for the horde that assaulted them.

This fraternity, not of blood yet still of Heart, fought on, their synchronicity a notch of pride for Carpathian as Templars faltered in their advance. My Heart Guard, he thought, and though the situation demanded a stoic commander, pride welled within him. He had put them together—whether through circumstance or fate itself, it did not matter. He had done it, and they were what stood against the tide, the highest order of combatants for facing calamity that had ever been assembled.

However, for every enemy that fell, another seemed to take its place, and this reinforcement kept pressing them deeper into the cavern. In order to escape, they would need to find egress through the core of the cavern and to the other side, where the last remaining opportunity for flight waited in the form of the Door of the Divine—the final pathway to salvation from the cavern. The only option left to them.

And, despite all the other obstacles in their way, the greatest still awaited them. The Purgatory Plinth.

In order to reach the path to salvation, they must first navigate their way past the Plinth, an accomplishment never before successfully achieved, for to best the cavern, one of the number must be made sacrifice. And that was a tariff that none who had ever come before could imagine having the resolve to pay. The spirits of all those who had dared to attempt escape had been entombed for all time within, surrendering their suffering to the cavern and becoming a part of the unrelenting, melancholic ardor that fueled its power.

Nox, the Cavern Troll, was still heading the Templar charge. Having made his bargain with the Super Vizier and the High Council to trap Carpathian and his Party inside in exchange for gifts of Mezmer untold, he could not afford to fail. Worse for him still, Carpathian had wrested free the Cerulean Tunic from Nox's knotty grasp. There was no world in which he could allow the Party to escape.

His eyes burning with zeal, he shouted orders, his ragged, strident voice tinged by madness echoing off the ancient walls. "Surround them! The Plinth must not be disturbed! The Council wishes them trapped!"

Carpathian, assessing the situation with a quick glance, knew the odds were swiftly turning against them. "Follow!" he roared through the connection he ever maintained with his Heart Guard.

As they moved to race ahead with the Saviour, Teleri unleashed a Summoning so powerful it drained the color from her face: Hagog, a creature of legendary horror that tore through the Templars with vengeance. Xanaraxa's blades whirled, Mael's fists thundered, and Zerastian's Technomancy wreaked havoc, but the Templars, driven by Nox's fervent command, pressed on, more afraid of what punishment they might suffer at the hands of the Super Vizier than any fate that might befall them inside the cavern's walls.

The chamber shook, dust and small stones raining from the ceiling as the battle reached a fever pitch. Carpathian's gaze locked with Nox's, a silent acknowledgment of the inevitable clash between them.

The Purgatory Plinth's dark promise loomed large, both balefire and curse, the path to salvation it guarded as daunting as the multitude they still faced. With a nod to his companions, a silent command passed between them, and Carpathian steeled himself for the sacrifice that might yet be demanded of him. The door to the chamber was open, and within, he could now see it.

The Purgatory Plinth.

They entered swiftly, trailed by their pursuers. Xanaraxa, fleetest among them, was nearly to the other side when both sets of doors were suddenly wrested shut, snapping themselves closed. She skidded to a stop, wheeling to look back at Carpathian and the others, gaze wild.

"A trap!" she shouted, though it was needless, as they all understood the meaning of the cavern's response. Carpathian cursed as he heard the quiet weeping begin broadcasting its woe from the walls of the core. His Heart thudded to keep pace with the adrenaline in his blood as the walls of this chamber, wealthy with pain and punishment, began to weep.

"A trap!" came the near-simultaneous roar from the Templars, fractionally slower to react to the doom they'd also now stumbled into. But the timing of the realization was irrelevant; there could be no escape for any of them. All were now confined within the walls of a chamber that was impermeable enough to contain the power of the Elder Wardens themselves; a handful of lesser beings would have no hope of escape. There was nothing any of them might be able to do to fight their way free.

Not even a World Saviour.

One of them would need be offered as sacrifice, or all would perish.

And so it was, in that moment, that Carpathian Einzgear realized what he must do.

The chamber's sobs grew louder as Tears of Judgment poured freely, and a current of desperation and defiance swept across Carpathian and his Heart Guard. The gloom between them and the trapped Templars was thick with the agony of epochs past and the impending reality that in moments, they were all to be drowned in an ocean of bereavement.

Nox, eyes alight with a cold fury, commanded the forces with a zealot's fervor. "Do not let them past the Plinth! Their doom shall be the cavern's embrace!" His voice, a sinister echo against the leaking stone, spurred the Templars into a frenzied assault, their determination fueled by the promise of trapping Carpathian and his allies for eternity within the cavern's merciless ache.

Carpathian, amidst the chaos, locked sight with Nox, a silent vow of defiance shining in his gaze. "I will be the sacrifice!" he bellowed over the din of battle, his declaration a beacon of resolve for his beleaguered Party. He fought his way toward the Purgatory Plinth, each step a battle against the relentless tide pooling about his ankles and the inexorable advance of the undaunted Templar battalion.

Mael, witnessing Carpathian's perilous advance, felt a surge of resolve. The thought of his leader, his friend, sacrificing himself while any breath remained in Mael's body was unacceptable. He would not allow it. He could not.

As Carpathian cut down a Templar with a swift strike of his blade, preparing to make his final dash for the Plinth, Mael acted. With a burst of unmatched strength, he barreled through the fray, intercepting Carpathian. Before the Saviour could reach the Plinth, Mael's strength, undeniable and unyielding, manifested not in a blow but in a forceful shove that sent Carpathian sprawling away from his grim objective. The suddenness of the act, the raw power behind it, left no room for recovery or rebuttal.

In the moment Carpathian hit the ground, Mael was already moving, a blur of determination racing toward the Plinth. The decision was made in the space of a heartbeat, the argument settled by action, Mael's resolve crystallizing into a sacrifice that would mark the cavern's history.

Teleri, recognizing the turning tide of battle, called forth her most devastating Summoning. One none would dare presume to request of her, for it was once a Forbidden Summon.

But desperate times, as it is said, require measures of equal desperation.

Her voice, a haunting melody of power and dread, rose above the cacophony of combat. From the ground erupted the Climber, a horrifying mass of necrotic hands, thousands strong, reaching up from the earth's depths to ensnare the Templars. The hands gripped with unyielding strength, halting the Templars' advance, their desperation ignored by the cavern as the walls continued their remorseless closure.

Nox, caught in the grip of the Summon, could only watch in rage as Mael, solemn and determined, reached the Plinth.

"Mael, no!" Carpathian called out.

"See to Lonnaigh!" Mael shouted in reply. "Watch over my sister, Carpathian!"

Before the words even finished passing his lips, the Plinth's shadowy tendrils lashed out, binding the warrior with a voracity that spoke of centuries spent waiting for such a sacrifice.

The cavern, satisfied with its offering of flesh, acquiesced, and the Door of the Divine opened, the path to salvation making itself known. A blinding light entered the cavern, causing all those inside to seek cover for their eyes.

Mael fell to his knees as the cavern's tears continued rising around him, and in a final act, he offered a strained nod toward the now illuminated exit and issued both a command and a farewell as the tendrils ensnared him and the water baptized him with an awful consecration.

"Run, you fools," he urged, his voice barely more than a whisper.

As Xanaraxa and Zerastian aided Carpathian to his feet, the weight of the moment settled upon him with a crushing finality. His gaze, locked on Mael—now destined to be forever entwined with the Purgatory Plinth and bathed in a sea of pain—was a frenzy of grief and guilt. The decision, though made by Mael, felt like Carpathian's own failure.

Carpathian's power, the Mezmer within him, responded to his turmoil, flowing out in an uncontrollable rush. The air crackled with energy, the ancient stones of the cavern vibrating with the force of his grief, seeming to revel in it. The remaining Templars, ensnared by the Climber's deathly grasp, could only watch in horror as the chamber quaked and shuddered under the weight of Carpathian's wrath.

Xanaraxa, her eyes wide with concern, and Zerastian, her expression grim, realized the danger. Carpathian's anger, unbridled and unchecked, threatened to cause the cavern to erupt in raging white water, destroying everything in a blind quest for vengeance. They exchanged a look, a silent agreement, and acted.

They grasped Carpathian firmly, pulling him away from the sight of Mael's sacrifice. Teleri, her own face expressing a veneer of sorrow and understanding, joined them. She worked to make her voice a soothing counterpoint to the chaos, urging, "Carpathian, we must go. For Mael. For us all."

"No," he said, and the power surged further, channels of disruption shattering the foundation of the room itself. "No, this is not the path we take. I will not allow it!"

His overwhelming aura, his Resonance flaring—the peak of Steelshard, pounding dangerously against the door of Manasteel—forced all numbered here to their knees. Even Nox, defiant as they were, could not abide the unvarnished might of the Saviour.

Threatening destruction, Carpathian's Mezmer roared in his form, more deific monstrosity in this moment than he was man. He poured his fury into the Purgatory Plinth, hoping to disrupt its hold on his friend and brother, but it was not enough. It was grown now to contain power orders of magnitude above his own. It lapped at his strength, drinking it in eagerly, consuming the Mezmer he pressed into it. And then demanded more.

So be it, he thought bitterly. Let this be the true sacrifice. There will be nothing left of this but ruin. As long as there is breath in my body, I will continue to—

But, at that moment, Carpathian dropped. His body went limp, and he very nearly collapsed into the virulent Tears of Judgment, but Xanaraxa swooped to catch him before his flesh made contact with its watery anguish.

Pergamon loomed over Carpathian's wilted form in Xanaraxa's arms, his own heart torn. Pergamon, whose debt was to the World Saviour and whose principal purpose was to aid him, had severed the Saviour's filial bond to save him from his own folly.

Then, he gathered his wits about him and thundered, "We must go!" acting—as was his burden in the rare moments when Carpathian was unable to issue such commands himself—as the surrogate for Carpathian's authority.

"No!" Nox screeched, the Troll's body already mostly receded into the stone, the might of the Climber wrenching him from the Primary Plane. "No! I can't have failed!"

Decision made, sacrifice accepted, Xanaraxa placed Carpathian onto Pergamon's back, and the remaining Heart Guard—incomplete and heavy with guilt—turned and fled through the opening and into the light, the hysterical, terrified roars of the Templars and the Cavern Troll being forcibly dragged below the rising tide to the lower plane fading as the cavern's jaws snapped shut with a final, echoing boom.

CHAPTER FORTY-EIGHT

Lonnaigh, don't!" I shout, as it appears the adrenaline coursing through her has caused her to forget—or at least ignore—the pain in her wounded leg.

But my behest lands empty. It's beyond too late; she is already dashing head-long into the knee-deep water in which her brother kneels.

There is, I suppose, a faint chance she won't experience the deleterious effects of the Tears of Judgment if she's able to avoid letting it touch her exposed—

Oh. No. She's diving forward, headfirst, swimming to reach him. Okay. So much for not letting it get all over her; she's practically drinking it. Drinking in the sorrow. Drinking in the pain. Ingesting eons of agony, heartbreak, and loss directly into her lungs.

Oof. That's gonna sting.

At the very moment she begins her freestyle stroke (which—and I know this isn't the time to dwell on it, but I'd be remiss not to mention it—is excellent; she has just perfect form), Mael's eyes open wide, like headlamps. He looks like some-one who's been knocked unconscious and is just coming to, gazing around to try and understand where they are. Which, in a way, I suppose is what's happened.

"LONNN!" he bellows long and loud as he struggles to his feet.

And I'm blown away. For a couple of reasons.

First, the physical specimen that is Mael Anderbariach is a sight to behold. I like to think I'm pretty good at crafting imagery, but nothing I ever set down in writing has done justice to the person I see in front of me. I'm not sure anything could, because no amount of language can begin to capture the utter magnifi-cence of what's on display.

The size and strength and all that observable stuff is remarkable, yes, but I've actually seen that kind of thing before. I once met Dwayne Johnson (FKA "The Rock") at an event, and I was taken by both the mass and the charisma of the guy. Super impressive.

This is something else.

There is a kinetic energy radiating from Mael that is out of relation to any-thing I've ever known. It's almost supernatural. Literally. The most extreme ver-sion of what is possible in the natural world. I wish I had the time to stand properly in awe of it, because not to dignify Mael with my full respect feels like an insult to nature itself.

So, that's the first thing.

The second thing blowing my mind is that he has been here, chained by some type of Mezmeric ether and forced to remain plunged in an unceasing pool of torment, for who knows how long. At least two whole books. I'm not sure how many Lunar Cycles that translates to in Meridia Standard Time, but it's gotta be a lot. And I can't imagine that the guy has had anything to eat or drink in all that time either, apart from the black smoke writhing around his frame and tunneling itself throughout his body like some kind of macabre IV drip. Brittany noted a few Lunar Rotations ago that one thing all machines have in common is that they need fuel, but whatever fuel is pumping its way into Mael has to be akin to someone being fed a steady diet of arsenic and carpet cleaner.

And yet, even given *all* that, upon seeing his sister, he has managed to rise to his feet and call out her name.

With all that I have witnessed in my life and all that I imagine I am still yet to see, nothing has, nor can I believe anything ever will, compare to this moment for its sheer inexplicability and reinforcement of what the power of love is capable of manifesting.

(Yes, I know that "Power of Love" is another Huey Lewis and the News song, but it can't be helped. That's the best descriptor for what I'm watching, so it'll just have to stand for now.)

All those various epiphanies and wonders dart through my brain in less than a second, and in that time, Mael has managed to erupt to his full height and begun to echo the same caution I offered as I watched Lonnaigh race into the water.

"LONNAIGH! STAY BACK!"

But, of course, it's too late. Both Mael and I are attempting to close the barn door after the horse is already out, has led itself to water, and is chugging it down as it frantically freestyle-strokes its way to reach its brother.

And, suddenly (because all of what's happening couldn't *possibly* be enough), there is a loud, shrill, high-pitched squeal in the chamber, like a nineteenth century factory whistle, or train wheels careening to a stop, or a thousand tea kettles reaching a boil at the same time . . .

. . . Or, perhaps, the imprisoned spirit of a screeching Cavern Troll struggling to break free.

Tavrella, Brittany, and I cover our ears. Perg, of course, cannot, since he has no hands, so he just yells, "Make it stop! I don't like it!"

I look to see if I can identify where it's coming from and realize that it's broadcasting from, quite literally, everywhere. The whisps of black smoke ensconcing Mael are now roiling and bucking like an overfull basket of annoyed pit vipers as he tries to unshackle himself.

Beyond that, it's causing the water in which he's standing to begin thrashing as well. Convulsing. Rising and falling in waves of increasing size. It starts splashing up onto edges of the, I suppose, shore upon which we stand and, at the same time, the walls begin weeping anew as the form of what I can only assume is the overinflated, spectral residue of Nox begins taking shape, emerging from within the cavern rock.

"Jesus Christ!" I yell, barely able to hear myself over the wailing.

"What is that?!" Brittany screams. Then, realizing . . . "Oh, shit! Is that Nox?!"

"I think so!"

"What do we do?!"

"I dunno, but don't let the waves touch you!"

I say it out of reflex, not because I really need to; no one is going to be eager to allow themselves to get drenched by a splatter of melancholy if they can help it.

Well, no one but Lonnaigh, who now confronts the inevitable consequence of her rash decision.

Halfway to reaching her brother, her frantic swim turns to a slow crawl, and the bucking lake created by the Tears of Judgment (making it, I suppose, a Lake of Judgment) swoops around her completely, pulling her under. She begins convulsing, reaching for the sky and screaming Mael's name, not in the way of want or as a request for aid, but as though she is experiencing the loss of him all over again. As if he's not right in front of her.

It kind of resembles the cover art for Dio's *Holy Diver* album. Which is cool as hell when it's artwork on the cover of a classic metal record, but tragic and terrifying when you see it happening to someone you know.

That she is being pulled under, physically, is of only secondary significance. If that were all that was happening, I feel confident that Lonnaigh, even in her wounded state, could resist. It is the less obvious way in which she is being drawn down that is the actual concern. The hurt and sadness she has worked so hard to mask and keep at bay is the true agent weakening her resolve as she is drowned in an unforgiving vat of grief.

Seeing his sister being dragged under the surface and into the depths of despair, Mael screams, "NOOOOO!" jerking his body hard against the virtual restraints holding him back. She's just out of his reach, and try as he might, he's unable to get himself free to grasp her before she is pulled down to some other place, just like Nox was wrenched from the Primary Plane in this same room.

And, all the while, Nox's titanic, corporeal form keeps growing as the incessant screeching gets louder, and louder, and louder, and—

"Bruce!" Brittany screams my name, either forgetting or not caring to call me Carpathian. "You have to do something!"

"What?" I yell back over the baleful howl of the Cavern Troll.

"I don't know!"

K. Well, *that's* not helpful.

Dammit. Think, Bruce, think.

"*I am, Bruce. I'm also at a loss.*"

"*I wasn't actually asking you to weigh in, Bruce. I was just . . . Never mind!*"

SCREEEEEEEEEEEEEEEEEEEEEEEEEEECH!

God, the sound is . . . It's making it hard to concentrate. I need to try and remember . . .

When I first started banging out the Cavern of Sorrows beats, I jotted down, like, half a dozen ideas for how Carpathian and crew could get free from here. I settled on Mael offering himself up in sacrifice, but there were other notions swirling around in my head that got written on little scraps of paper or put as notes into my phone. A lot of them were dependent on the incredibly overpowered version of Carpathian that existed by the time he got to book eight, but at least a couple of them were . . . well . . . lazy.

SCREEEEEEEEEEEEEEEEEEEEEEEEECH!

One of them came to me when I was having a crack in my pool repaired. I was watching the guys drain the water with the pool pump so that they could put in a new liner, and it occurred to me, *I suppose I could always just put in a lever or something that would turn off the water and drain it from the cavern. Maybe the same lever could even open the Door of the Divine. Easy-peasy lemon squeezy, everybody gets free.*

I almost immediately dispensed with the idea because I figured 1) Brittany would hate it and accuse me of not trying hard enough, and 2) she'd be right. Riftbreakerers would likely revolt at something so obviously intended to be a bail out, like eagles conveniently scooping up Sam and Frodo as Mordor crumbles around them in *Return of the King*.

(Which, full disclosure, was another idea I toyed with: Tossing Nox into a "Well of Sorrow" and then having Teleri Summon up a Tentasaurian or Drakonar to fly everyone to safety. But even I wouldn't have attempted that. There's *homage* and then there's outright plagiarism.)

Irrespective of what defines inspiration versus what defines thievery, the point is that I did come up with a bunch of options for escaping the cavern. The question, of course, is: Because I never wrote it in the book, will it still exist? Whether I was coming up with ideas or they were being funneled through my brain by some unknown Meridian force, do they count if they never made it into the final draft?

SCREEEEEEEEEEEEEEEEEEEEEEEEEECH!

I scan the area, trying to get a lock on anything out of the ordinary, when my vision is drawn to an anomaly. There, on the far side of the expansive chamber, partially shrouded from view by gnarled and protruding rock . . . is a lever.

It's an odd sight. A simple-looking man-made object that stands in opposition to the wild, Mezmeric yet natural contours of the cavern. But it's there. A random idea that I scribbled out once upon a time is here in the chamber.

"*Ugh. A lever? Really, Bruce?*"

"*Don't start, Bruce. You try coming up with escape mechanisms for ten books.*"

The only problem with attempting to pull the lever and seeing what happens . . .

SCREEEEEEEEEEEEEEEEEEEEEEEEEEECH!

. . . is . . .

SCREEEEEEEEEEEEEEEEEEEEEEEEEEECH!

. . . how do I get to it?

SCREEEEEEEEEEEEEEEEEEEEEEEEEEECH!

"Make it stop, homes! Snail ears are notoriously fragile!"

The lever is all the way on the other side of the area. To get to it, I'm gonna have to dodge:

1. Walls alive with a giant Troll ghost.
2. A plinth that shoots out mist restraints.

3. Just generally . . . sad-boy water.

All to attempt to reach what may or may not be a successful deus ex machina. Wait. *Wait.* A deus ex machina. That's what the Heart is. A literal deus ex machina that's a machina ex deus.

> **Indeed. Hello, there. Glad you remembered! Was just about to give you a gentle nudge! All good, though. Understand that it's still quite new and might take you a bit of time to recollect what tools you possess. Especially as you gain more of them! But that's perhaps a lecture for another day, yes? In the meantime! Perhaps you should . . .** *slow things down a bit* **. . . that you might take fullest advantage of your marginally more** *efficient movements* **in such a state. (You should activate Control, is the prompt. In the event any of that was unclear.)**
> **[COURTESY MESSAGE #20}**

ZZZZZWWWWWAAAAAHHHHHMMMMM.

And, just like that, every . . . thing . . . slows.

If I had to estimate how much faster I'm able to move now, compared to everything else that Control is, um, controlling, I'd guess it's maybe ten percent. Not nearly as much faster as I'd like to be motoring, but any advantage I can get, I will take. Happily.

Seeing the faces of my friends contorted by fear, rage, and . . . rageful fear is a troubling sight. I know I wrote about Carpathian having trouble sleeping, but now, I fully understand why.

Thump-thump. Thump-thump.

I manage to step back just in time to avoid being hit in the face by a fountain of water that splashes up and out of the pool, where I realize I can now only see the tip of Lonnaigh's fingers. It didn't look that deep when Mael was kneeling in it, but with the pace of the thrashing slowed down, I can see . . .

The water around her is morphed into a fist. A mirror of the Climber's fist that grasped Nox. A copy. A replica. A karmic retribution.

With one eye on the Heart's draining icon telling me how much time I have, and one eye on the path in front of me, I make my way toward the not-so-far, yet oh-so-far-away lever tantalizing me to it from the other side of the room.

Splaaaaash. Splaaaaash.

Each one of my footfalls landing in the pool sends rivulets of water flying into the air. I'm shielding myself with my arms to avoid it landing on my face or otherwise saturating me. It's already a gamble, since this suit is mesh, and I don't know what kind of mesh, so I have no clue if it's permeable or not. I'll find out in short order, I suppose.

Glancing down to see Lonnaigh's disappearing form, I have half a mind to stop and help her, but I don't have the time to spend pulling Lonnaigh free from the water's grasp if I also hope to make it to the lever before the clock runs out.

So, despite my misgivings, I keep moving.

I make eye contact with Mael as I pass the Plinth. The black, smoky chains pitching up and down in slow motion with his labored attempt to get free make him look like some sort of unholy Cirque du Soleil performer.

He stares me in the face with a look of confusion. And then the word "Carrrpaaaaathi—?" starts to leave his lips. But I have no time to indulge the query. We'll get to all that teary reunion stuff later. (Technically, I suppose, this is already a teary reunion. But I mean more of the nice kind.)

Thump-thump. Thump-thump.

I don't have that much longer; maybe a quarter of the Heart icon remains filled. Nox's face, bleeding out of the wall, mouth contorted in an agonized wail, is right beside me. I'm trying not to look over; it's not like I'm going to forget it's there.

Fun thing about Control: It doesn't make sound disappear. It doesn't do whatever the hell Oscillating Vortex did when we went into hyperdrive, so the earsplitting screech is still screechy and earsplitting. It just now happens to also be really, really drawn out. So, that's pleasant. (It's not. I'm being sarcastic.)

Thump-thump. Thump-thump.

I have maybe five or six thumps left to thump by the time I reach the lever.

Thump.

I grab hold of it and . . .

Thump.

. . . it won't move. Like it's rusted in place or ground into the wall.

Thump.

ARE YOU FREAKIN' KIDDING ME?!

Thump.

Calm, Bruce, calm. You can do this. You're Ironspark, for crying out loud!

Thump.

Just take a breath, grab the lever with one hand, raise the Blade of the Starfallen into the air with the other, and shout, "Byyy theee pooooower ooooof Graaaaay-skuuuuull!" (Which I do, and which comes out all slow and soupy, but which only makes it sound more dramatic if you ask me.) *as you . . .*

Thump.

Push . . .

Time's up.

DOWN!

SHWOOOOOOOOOOOMMMMMPPP.

The Control Spell wears off and, unlike the first times when I used it and it felt like water was draining out of my ears, this time, water *literally* starts draining from the pool.

Holy shit, it worked! Thank you, little scrap of paper I wrote a lazy idea on!

So many things happen at the same time, I can't even catalogue them.

In no particular and a completely unknowable order:

• The water that Mael was in starts draining, like a whirlpool.

- The screech from Nox sounds like it's happening backward. More like a *CHEEEEEEEEEEEEEEEEEEEEEEEEEERCS!*
- The weeping of the walls begins drying up.
- The black smoke chains *rip* free from Mael's body as he roars at the sky.

And, I would argue most importantly:

- The Door of the Divine opens, letting in bright, Meridian morning suns light that fills the chamber with a hopeful glow.

I shield my eyes from the glare and order, "Everyone out! Grab Lonnaigh, let's go!"

Which is when the interior of the chamber starts to rumble and shake like it's a 9.0 on the Richter scale, and . . .

The Cavern of Sorrows begins collapsing in on itself.

CHAPTER FORTY-NINE

What did you do?!" Brittany calls to me from across the chamber.

"I just pulled this lever here!"

"Why?"

"I thought it might let us out!"

"You *thought?*"

"I wasn't sure!"

"Why would you pull a lever when you weren't sure what it would do?!"

"Because you told me I had to do something!"

"So this is my fault?!"

"I'm not saying— SHIT!"

I dive out of the way to avoid a falling chunk of ceiling. I should have been more specific when I jotted down "*Maybe a lever that lets them escape?*" and made it clear that it shouldn't also be a booby trap that triggers the collapse of the entire joint. This is a textbook "Don't disturb Pharaoh's tomb" kind of repercussion.

Note to self: Be more precise going forward.

"Lonnaigh!" Mael yells, now free of his bindings and dashing forward in the draining pool of water to rescue his sister.

I'm closest to the opening of the cavern. The Door of the Divine is right there. Falling stone is threatening to block the exit. If I want to be assured of making it out of here, I should run toward the light right now.

Obviously, there's no way in seven hells I'm going to do that, so there's no point in even creating a scintilla of doubt, but I'm just saying, that's what I should *do.*

Instead, I run in the same direction Mael is headed to help grab Lonnaigh up and get out of here. Brittany, Tavrella, and Perg are convening to meet in the middle as well.

The thing is . . . when we all converge on the nearly drained pool, what we find . . .

"LON!" Mael thunders.

. . . is not her.

She's not there.

She should be.

But she's not.

The bed is now dry, but Lonnaigh's body is not in it. The Tears of Judgment appear to have dragged her to . . . I have no idea. I don't know where the pool drains out. Maybe a water treatment facility? Perhaps we'll get lucky, and the municipality that governs the Cavern of Sorrows will run it through a Mezmer purifier, and instead of Tears of Judgment, Lonnaigh will wind up swimming in a pool of happy fun times in a few hours?

It's clear Mael doesn't think so because he commences pounding at the hard rock of the dried pool basin with his bare fists, shattering the floor of the cavern with each monstrous blow.

"LONNAIGH!" he rages.

BOOM! CRACK!

The sound of the cavern collapsing around us marries with Mael's vicious strikes. It seems like rather than saving his sister, all he's doing is hastening the chamber's implosion.

"Homie, we gotta—Look out!" Perg yells just as I glance to see that the Plinth has cracked at its base and is falling over like a giant redwood, but with flailing, black cables of fetid Mezmer instead of branches. To be fair: Both will end your life if they fall on you, but at least the giant redwood would look pretty while it's pancaking you to death.

I start to throw my arm up reflexively to brace myself for the impact, but Perg slides over just in time, allowing the Plinth to instead shatter across the back of his shell. He screams something in Spanish that I don't understand, and his shell—the ultimate durability of which I have wondered over a couple of times—answers my unasked question of just how much abuse it can withstand and *cracks open* while the obelisk splinters like an icicle falling from the awning of a building onto the sidewalk.

"Perg!" Brittany shrieks, wrapping her five-foot-three-inch frame around the snail's battered body, attempting to protect him from further injury. Which is nice but somewhat futile, given that her own body is much more fragile than his. But, y'know, it's not like anyone's thinking super clearly at the moment.

The coils of black Mezmer mist, now untethered to any kind of home base, boomerang around the room like bullwhips made of sulfuric lightning.

One of the bolts sails my way, and I slash at it instinctively with the Blade of the Starfallen. And, just as happened with the Shadowscorpions, it converts the dark silhouette of punishing Mezmer into something more like the tail of a dying comet, which then explodes in a harmless shower of golden sparks. Or . . . comparatively harmless, I should say, because . . .

. . . the light shower manages to somehow spark the ground on fire.

The ground.

Made of *stone*.

On *fire*.

I'm gonna need to take a Meridian physics class or something, because this shit here don't make no good sense.

So. To recap:

• Collapsing cavern.
• Massive Troll ghost shrieking in a bloodcurdling reverse scream.
• Angry giant smashing the ground with his fists.
• Broken-shelled snail familiar.
• Sorcerer sidekick who's clearly still reeling from whatever trauma memories she experienced.

- Alchemist who . . . continues just staring at me with a small smile on her face, which is starting to weird me out.
- *Fire.*
- And the person who demanded this Quest in the first place sucked into some other dimension of pain and unrelenting torment. Probably.

And I used to think meeting publishing deadlines was stressful.

BOOM!

Yet another chunk of ceiling falls near the exit. We need to make our escape, or we're going to be trapped, and all of this will have been for naught.

"We have to go! Now! Like, *now* now!"

Tavrella, Brittany, and Perg do as I urge, with Tavrella and Brittany leading the shell-shattered snail across the room and up the ramp that leads through the door to our liberation, dodging fallen debris as they hurry along.

Mael makes no moves to come, continuing to pound at the earth.

Or, I guess, the Meridia? Is it still called earth if it's not on earth*? Is this a proper use of my mental function right now? It is not.*

"Mael!" It's the first time I've addressed him directly. It's a surreal feeling to call him by name. "Mael, we need to get out! Come on!"

I reach for his shoulder, but he throws me off, damn near ripping my arm out of the socket. He continues pounding at the floor and yelling Lonnaigh's name as boulder-size rocks rain down and the fire spreads out around us.

"Mael!" I shout again, reaching for him once more. He stands and spins. The fullness of his seven feet looms over me as he looks into my eyes, panting, shoulders heaving, fists clutched tightly and dripping with blood from barraging the ground.

"Why did you bring her here?!" he shouts.

It's very, *very* intimidating, and in almost any other circumstance I could see myself cowering away, trying to deflect or placate. But here, now, I find it in me to push back. "Why did—? I didn't! She brought *me* here!"

His eyes tighten like he can't understand what I'm saying, and he cocks his head. "What do you mean?"

"She offered the Quest! I accepted!"

He looks me over, baffled, as if only just seeing me for the first time. "Why?! What has happened? What—?"

BOOM!

Another falling rock misses us by inches.

"I get it! You're out of the loop! I'll fill you in, but we have to get out of here first! Please, Mael! She's gone from this place! Whatever hope there is of finding her again, it won't happen now! Please! Come with me!"

Something about either what I say or the way I say it seems to register, because after a moment's more hesitation and a planet-shaking "GRAAAHHHHH!" wrenching itself from the pit of Mael's soul and out of his mouth, he looks to the soon-to-be inaccessible Door of the Divine and . . . runs. I take a tiny breath, grip the Blade in my hand, and tear off behind him, making it up to the cavern opening just as—

CRAAAAAAAAAAAAAAACK!

The entire rest of the ceiling ruptures and comes rocketing to the ground. There's only a sliver of daylight left visible at the base of the exit, the collection of falling rock having created a tiny alcove of space through which we might be able to crawl our way out. But there's no time to crawl. In less than a fraction of a fraction of a fraction of a fractional amount of a fraction (i.e., *very* little) of time, the whole cavern will be rubble, and Mael and I will be buried inside.

Mael, observing the same splinter of daylight I do, throws his body to the ground like a baseball player trying to steal home plate and slides his way through the egress.

Holy shit, that was fresh as fudge, I think, recognizing that if I'm to have any hope of making it out of here not looking like Flat Stanley, I'm gonna have to pull off the same move. So, despite the fact that my high school baseball coach suggested I, quote, *"consider joining the chess team instead,"* I roll the dice on the belief that new Bruce has more agility and grace than the guy who once tripped and got a concussion making his way to the batter's box, emulating what I just watched Mael pull.

And it frickin' works.

Ha! Take that, Coach Pendleton!

I go sailing through the slender opening, arms crossed in front of me, blade pressed against my chest, looking like I'm a knight of the Round Table coming down a water slide at Six Flags Hurricane Harbor, just before . . .

BOOMBOOMBOOMBOOMBOOMBOOMBOOMBOOMBOOM! BOOM!

. . .

BOOM!

The inside of the cavern gives way to the inevitability of its demise.

Sliding to a resting position just beyond the mouth of the escape route, there is a moment's silence. It allows me a chance to stare up at the morning sky, bright suns high overhead casting a pastoral glow across the plain. It's still a rocky, barren, desolate plain, just like the rest of Meridia, but all things considered, I'll take it. I breathe out, and a Notification appears.

Congratulations!
Quest: "Rescue Mael from the Cavern of Sorrows."
[COMPLETE]

Though you lost one of your number, you did complete the Quest. Well done. Golf clap, golf clap. Upgrades and Verifications available upon your next visit to a Pulse Well.
[COURTESY MESSAGE #21]

I blink the words away and roll myself to my feet. Tavrella, Brittany, and Perg are standing a few paces away. Brittany and Perg look awestruck.

"Homie, that shit was incredible."

"You okay?" Brit asks.

"Yeah, yeah, I'm . . . I'll be fine. You?"

"I guess."

"My shell is jacked, bro," Perg notes.

"I know. Does it hurt?"

"Not exactly. Feels more like . . . I don't know what to compare it to. What's the kind of massage that feels good and bad at the same time?"

"Deep tissue?" I hazard.

"Yeah, sure. Probably like that."

"I can likely repair it," Tavrella offers.

"You can?" I ask.

"If we're able to find an alchemist's shoppe that has binding meal, I should be able to merge it back together."

Before the matter may be discussed further, I hear another "GRAAAHHH!" and turn to see Mael punching hard upon the now covered cavern opening. Flecks of blood spatter the stone.

I gesture for the others to hang back and approach him carefully.

"Mael," I attempt. He stops banging but doesn't turn. "Mael?" I hazard again.

Which is when I feel a crushing blow to my chest.

I say *feel* because I don't even see it coming. The impact of the punch assails me before I'm aware it's going to happen. The force of it sends me flying through the air, and I crash onto the desert floor ten feet away, still clutching onto the Blade. I'm struggling to catch my breath, the world spinning.

Three thoughts:

1. Mael has been bound to the Purgatory Plinth, trapped nearly up to his waist in a Lake of Judgment for a long, long time.

2. My Physical Attribute is now Ironspark.

3. If either of those two things were not true, I'd be deader than Julius Caesar right now.

As it stands, it just hurts *really* bad, like falling from a ten-foot ladder and landing on your chest. Painful but survivable. I can't imagine I'll be able to take too many more of these, however, without using up a whole bunch of my brand-new Marrowmancy.

Mael comes stalking over to me, very clearly pissed and, I guess, understandably so? I mean, I didn't technically do anything wrong, but anger's gotta land somewhere, and right now, the repository for his anger over what's happened to Lonnaigh appears to be old Bruce.

It occurs to me that I can maybe run a quick diagnostic check on where things stand inside of Mael, as he was part of Carpathian's Heart Guard, so, theoretically, he should now be part of *mine* as well?

This is new territory, running a real-world check-in on someone who was one of Carpathian's closest allies, so I have no idea how it's going to shake out, but I will the Heart to do its assessment before Mael gives me another thump.

However, it seems to be having a difficult time. It's making a noise. An actual noise. A *WHHHSSSSSHHHHHHHHHH* kind of a deal. Like when the hard drive in an old PS4 gets dusty and you can hear it whirring loudly inside the housing.

Then, the display pops up, but it's odd, fractal, only displaying partial information.

Mael Anderbariach

Foundation:
Pulsariel

Mezmer Type:
Two-Type

Resonance Tier:
Ironspark [Cursed]

The content is there, but the letters are all garbled like in one of those movies from the nineties about hackers. Like *Sneakers*. Or . . . *Hackers*.

Reading through what I can make out, my heart (metaphorical, not literal) sinks. In the books, Mael's Resonance Tier was to the height of Steelshard, nearly Manasteel. But now, according to this assessment, it's at Ironspark. Cursed Ironspark at that. (Whatever that means. Can't be ideal.) He's definitely diminished, and I have to assume the cavern's impact on him is also what's affecting his demeanor. The Mael I wrote about was calm, strategic, even-keeled. That Mael would never have sucker punched Carpathian in the chest and stalked over to him like a bloodthirsty lion. I guess a few Lunar Cycles of unceasing torture changes a person.

I'm gonna have to try and charm my way outta this.

"Mael, Mael, Mael, listen," I say, scrambling to my feet, backing up, and putting my hands in the air in a position of surrender. Although one of them is still holding a legendary weapon of ass-whooping, so . . .

POP.

I make it small. And I have now used up both of my storage slots.

I continue trying to cool Mael out.

"Mael, please, let's just . . ."

He reaches out for me, attempting to grab the mesh suit, but it's so formfitting that he can't get purchase. He bats at my chest like a cat trying to grab a ball of yarn as I attempt to block the swats. He finally stops smacking at me and asks, "What the hells are you wearing?"

I drop my arms from their elbows-forward defensive posture and tell him, "Lonnaigh gave it to me. It's from the Annex."

His head cocks to the side. "The Annex?" I nod. "Why do you need spoils from the Annex? It's all far inferior to your own bounty." Then he notices. "Where is it all? Your weapons? Your artifacts? Your garments?"

"I . . . don't have them anymore. Except the Blade of the Starfallen. Which is here." I hold up the mini Blade between my thumb and forefinger before tucking it into a bracer for now.

He squints at me. "What happened to it? Why is it all no longer in your possession?"

I take a breath. "Because . . . I . . . died."

He blinks. Shakes his head. His dreadlocks wave back and forth across his monumental bare shoulders. "You what?"

"I died?"

"You . . . died."

I nod slowly. He pokes me in the chest like he's trying to see if I'm real. "Ow." He studies me more. "You've been resurrected?"

"Uh, yeah? Yeah. Resurrected, remorted, reconstituted, recarbonified, the whole nine."

His nostrils flare slightly as he breathes. "Carpathian Einzgear, the World Saviour . . . died. How?"

"Y'know, it's a long story" Like, ten books long. "But the point is . . . I'm back. And I'm here to, y'know, sort out unfinished business, like getting you free from that cavern. So . . . I mean"—I lift both thumbs—"Yay?"

"Lonnaigh," he grits out. It appears my charm offensive is falling flat.

"I know, I know. But listen, just . . . She's an Anderbariach, right? That's who she is. If anyone can survive . . . whatever it is that happened in there, it's her. I mean . . . Look!" I point to the tattoo on the back of his hand, the Tri-Venn; it's still glowing. Not with as much vigor as one might prefer, but it shines. "See! She's not gone. She's still with you. Us. And—"

Quite abruptly, Mael raises his hand to his head and staggers back. He sits hard on the ground with a mighty thud, spent. After watching for a moment, I approach and sit beside him. I look to Brittany, who silently indicates, "*Do you want us to come over?*" but I nod her off.

I don't speak for several seconds, allowing the silence to rest. Mael stares at some unknowable point in the distance, looking at something only he can see. Rage now gone, he appears to be like one of those Tibetan monks who do nothing but meditate all day for a decade and then, when they finally emerge from their meditation, they can, like, levitate and shit.

After many long moments, he says, "I wished, many times, that *I* might die."

I don't speak right away. Because, honestly, of course he did. How could he not?

Eventually I work up the courage to ask, "Why didn't you? Just . . . let go?"

He breathes heavily. In. Out. Then says, "I was not given a choice."

"What . . . do you mean?"

"The cavern would not allow it. The Plinth poured its poison into me, keeping me alive, not allowing me the release of death, ensuring that I would for eternity be forced to bathe in the waters of pain that the cavern perpetually replenished."

Jesus Christ. I knew it was a bad scene, but . . .

"How did you not . . . ?"

"Go mad?"

I mean, to my eye, the guy definitely went mad, but I'm sure as hells not gonna say it. "Yeah. Sure. How did you, uh, avoid going . . . ? Yes."

He's quiet for a second before saying, "I remembered Xanaraxa's counsel."

It takes me a tick, but then I realize. "You mean the thing she said about hope?"

He nods. "I repeated it to myself over and over. Thousands of times. 'If the wish is for pain be gone, to embrace the coming of the dawn, free from struggle and hurt and sorrow, then hold not hope, that there may be 'morrow.'"

. . . I remember when I wrote that.

I just thought they were some cool bars that a six-armed philosopher-poet might spit, and I thought it was a nice callback for Carpathian to think it again as he lay dying in the last book. But I never imagined it would be the credo someone would use to help them endure what should have been an unendurable torment.

He goes on. "I did not consider the past. I did not imagine a future. When the sorrow would well up to overtake me, I remembered that it did not exist because *I* did not exist. No harm can come to that which is not there."

Another long pause. I can feel myself getting anxious, because I have less than twenty-four Earth hours to get back to Santus Luminous and complete the Almeister Quest, which is—not to put too fine a point on it—a big frickin' deal. So . . .

"Listen, Mael, first of all, I'm sorry about . . . everything. Truly. I don't know if you'll ever know just how sorry I am. But here's the thing. Almeister—you know Almeister—Almeister is, um, well, he's been captured, see? And he's in the Tower of Zuria, and we only have—"

"Why did she call you *Bruce?*"

Beat. Beat. Beat . . . Beat.

"What's that now?"

"In the cavern. Nightwind. She said, 'Bruce, you have to do something.'"

I swallow. Hard. It feels like I just got caught cheating on a test.

"Did she?"

He turns to look at me. "You do not speak as I remember." And that ten-year-monk, look-right-through-you glare he has causes me to shudder.

"I, uh . . . y'know. Remort. And all."

His eye twitches. Almost imperceptibly, but it does. Then he stands and begins walking.

In the opposite direction from Tavrella, Brittany, and Perg.

"Where are you going?" I ask.

"To Garr Haven."

"Uh—"

"I am going to gather my clan and seek to find what has become of Lonnaigh."

"But . . ." I start, then decide that I can't possibly tell him about Garr Haven. Not yet. Not now.

So, I run after him to try and convince him to stay with us. He should be eased into his new reality (something I wasn't given the privilege of, so I know), but as much as that, we need his help. "But Mael, no, please, listen. We could use your, um . . ." I pull myself together and try to talk like Carpathian. "Mael Anderbariach! Your Saviour needs you! Your Heart Guard needs you! There are Quests yet untended! It is not a request, Mael!"

He stops, turns, looks at me. It causes me to freeze in my tracks.

"I asked one thing. One thing of Carpathian Einzgear. I asked that he watch after my sister. Protect her. Keep her safe." Blood rushes to my cheeks, and I resist the desire to stare at my feet.

"My Heart Guard?" he says, lifting the back of his hand. "Is here. And my Saviour"—he taps himself lightly on his chest—"is here."

He turns and begins walking away again.

I don't try to stop him this time.

Moping over to meet the remaining three, I fish in my bracer for my mini Blade of the Starfallen and hand it to Brittany.

"What's happening?" she asks. "Where's Mael going?"

"Garr Haven."

"But—"

"I know. Doesn't matter. Can you map us back to the car?"

She stares at me for a second before pulling the map out. "Yeah. Yeah, sure."

I take a breath and look at Tavrella. "You don't have to come along on this, you know."

She smiles gently and says, "I do."

I chew at the inside of my mouth. "I'm sorry."

"Fer what, lad?"

"For getting you into this situation."

Her smile widens, almost making her eyes disappear, and then she says the oddest thing.

She says, "Ye didn't, my boy. I was already here."

I start to ask what she means, but before I can, she glances at the map and walks past me, rubbing me on the arm as she goes. "This way is it then, yeah?"

I watch her leave. Brittany accompanies her. Perg shuffles along behind. I observe Mael as he continues disappearing in the distance. Then, I take in the rock-covered opening to the cavern. Finally, I turn my head to stare at the sky. Where a Notification appears.

It is understandable that you are engaged in quite a bit of inner confusion and turmoil right now, but it would be remiss not to

prompt that you now have but [One Lunar Rotation] remaining to complete the Quest: "Rescue Almeister from Imprisonment in the Tower of Zuria." So, despite the emotional state in which you find yourself, it's probably best that you "get to steppin'," as they say. (It's always something, isn't it?)
[COURTESY MESSAGE #22}

Yep.
It definitely is always *something*.

THE 'BURBS

TOWER OF ZURIA
[UNDISCOVERED]

OLD DOWNTOWN

THE DOME

ARCH OF RAYLION

ALCHEMIST'S SHOPPE

ACT FIVE

EXODUS (FIRST ATTEMPT)

CHAPTER FIFTY

Should we be out in the open like this?" Brittany asks.

"No. But let's give Tavrella another minute. She says this is a friendly place."

"Friendly to who, homes?" Perg asks.

It's a reasonable question.

Brit and I are scrunched down inside of Sheila—who is parked in an alley next to the alchemist's shoppe that Tavrella says she knows the owner of—waiting for her to come out and tell us if it's safe for us to go inside and fix up Perg's cracked shell.

Perg, back in his traditional snail size, sits on the dashboard, keeping a lookout. This is the most developed part of Santus Luminous, the most industrialized, so to speak, and the likeliest place for the word to have spread wide that Carpathian Einzgear has returned, along with a bounty on his head. So, we're crouched down, hoping no one comes upon us before we can get our plans together for how we intend to rescue Almeister prior to the clock running out.

The suns are already starting to dip a little lower in the sky as nightfall approaches. We lost some time coming back through the portal. Somehow, Sheila misheard Arch of Raylion as "Arch of Rail Eon," and we first got deposited in what we determined is the Meridian equivalent of Lisbon. Brittany's updated map told us we were in a place called "Ulyssippo," which she said is the original Latin name for Lisbon. Since I never wrote about it, I have no idea how Meridia knows Latin, but maybe because Brittany helped come up with a lot of the place names, it's just aware of the same things she is. Not sure, and not sure it matters.

What matters is that we skidded to a stop in an open square and almost wound up falling into the equivalent of the Atlantic Ocean, so we had to pull it together and try again. And again. And again. Because there wasn't enough runway to get Sheila up to a hundred and forty-one point six two two kilostrydes per hour, so the residents of Ulyssippo got to lean out of their windows and watch as Sheila tried over and over to activate Quick Travel. It turned into something of an impromptu sporting event, with the citizens cheering us as we'd hit the portal, and then collectively "aww" in disappointment when we failed.

After the seventh try, it finally worked.

And now we're here. With the Tower looming in the distance like a giant sundial, reminding me that my Quest timer is running low. (As if the actual Quest timer that is still counting down on the PCM of my car wasn't enough.)

The Tower. A monolith of ancient power and inscrutable purpose.

Well, its initial purpose was inscrutable. Now, its purpose is very much scrutable. It's a message to John Q. Public of Meridia that they shouldn't screw with DONG, the Council, any of them, because any organism that can properly occupy and inhabit such a villainous lighthouse of bad vibes is clearly one you don't want to try to rebel against. Fascism 101, really. Make yourself look too tough to overcome, and people will fall in line. (In an early draft, it was actually going to be called the Tower of Orwellia, but that seemed heavy-handed.)

Ultimately, the Tower of Zuria is a symbol, I suppose, for all manner of bureaucratic malfeasance and overreach. I was working for a city agency when I started writing Riftbreaker, after all. So, it's both an ominous, foreboding fantasy tower housing the mystical Nexus Core, and the Ninth Guardian's base of operations from which the executive, legislative, and judicial functions of Meridia are carried out. Laws are passed, prisoners are held, and the Ninth Guardian sits presiding over all.

Might and Mezmer meet the monotonous and mundane.

The base of the Tower is broad, carved from a stone that seems to drink in the light, a dark slate gray that verges on black in the afternoon light. The material is unlike anything else in the region, its surface smooth but for the intricate carvings that spiral up its length, symbols and Mezmeric scripts pulsing with an inner light that ebbs and flows with the wind.

As the eye travels upward, the Tower tapers gradually, though not evenly. Around its midsection, a series of balconies and buttresses jut outward, adorned with statues of mythical creatures and figures of lore, each sculpted with painstaking detail and covered in a patina that tells of their unimaginable age.

Farther up, the Tower splits into several spires, each twisting skyward like the fingers of a hand reaching out to grasp the heavens. And in one of them, Almeister sits, waiting for the mockery of justice that is set to take place in just a few hours.

Between the spires, arches and bridges connect, creating a lattice of pathways that hint at the complexity and vastness of the interior. An interior, it should be noted, that has never been seen by anyone non-Templar or Disciple.

In truth, I didn't attempt to write about what could possibly be inside simply because I didn't want to yank my own leash too short. Nothing's more of a drag than limiting yourself, only to realize later that you gave a thing eight floors when the story demands twenty, and now you have to have Retcon Johnson show up to save the day. But I wish I had, at least, some sort of working idea of what's inside. I never had Brittany make any kind of sketch or anything for the Tower. I always shooed it off, thinking of it as a Future Bruce problem.

"Did you call me, Bruce?"

"No, Bruce. Sorry. I was just thinking about Future Bruce from before."

"Oh. You mean Future 'Theoretical' Bruce, as opposed to Future 'Actual' Bruce."

"I guess? Is that what you are? Future Actual Bruce?"

"No, I think you're actually Future Actual Bruce. It's possible I might be Present Theoretical Retroactive Self-Survival Bruce."

". . . What?"

"I know. It gets complicated."

. . .

Anyway . . .

I have no clue what's going on behind the walls. And even with Brittany's advanced Map Maker Ability, the maps we have just show a giant gray area, like the cavern did. It would appear that what goes on in any area not already charted that happens to be under the Ninth Guardian's control is unknowable until and unless you're able to breach it.

What I do know is that at the very top of the Tower, the central spire pierces the sky, its tip a gleaming beacon of light that is visible for miles around, even through the thickest fog or darkest night. (I always thought that was cool, until some people on the Riftbreaker Wiki went through the books and pointed out every instance of spooky, suggestively phallic constructions in the story. Turns out, there're a lot. Which, in my defense, says more about other people's interest in seeking that stuff out than it does in me trying to make innuendos.)

"Says the guy who created a global cult called DONG."

"Oh, shut up, Bruce."

The air around the Tower pulses with energy, a tangible pressure that causes one's skin to tingle and hairs to stand on end, as if the atmosphere is charged with expectation, or perhaps warning. The ground around its base is barren, the earth scorched and devoid of life, suggesting that the Tower's defenses are not limited to its physical structure. The long-ago verdant Fields of Rendalia are now nothing but burnt soil, the name of the place a cruel reminder of what once was and is likely never to be again.

Man. I know it's scary, and it sucks and all, but I have to say: It's kind of baller in a gothic fantasy kind of way.

"Hey," I say to Brit, "you okay?"

"I mean . . . No. But I'm fine. Why?"

"I dunno. You just ask me all the time, and . . . what went down back at the cavern—"

"I'm fine."

"You sure, girlie? 'Cause I ain't gonna lie to you—you did not seem fine."

"I'm. Fine."

"Okay," I reply. "Just know that if at any point you decide you're not, and you don't wanna—"

"Bruce? Shut up."

"No, seriously. Both of you. If you don't wanna—"

"Homegirl's right, fool. *Cállate la boca.*"

"I know, but I'm just saying—"

Knock knock!

"Ah!" Brittany, Perg, and I jump as Tavrella raps on the driver's side window. "We're good. Come with me."

The back room of the alchemist's shoppe is stacked to the ceiling with potions and brews and remedies and concoctions of all kinds. Tavrella finishes applying what looks, more or less, like drywall Spackle to Perg's tiny shell.

"There ye are. Good as new; maybe e'en better. I used the fast-dry, extra-hardening meal. Probably going to leave a bit of a mark, but not too noticeable."

Perg glances at himself in a mirror on the wall. "All good. *A las chicas les gustan las cicatrices.*"

"How do you know the owner of this place?" Brit asks Tavrella.

"We had a bit of a flirtation once upon a time. Nothin' serious. *We* didn't really have alchemy, ironically, but we've remained friends."

"Alright," I sigh out, thinking. "Let's talk about how we're going to make this thing happen. As we learned the hard way"—I look to Brit—"a frontal assault, even with a full army and a bunch of Summoned Tentasaurians and Zephyrixia isn't the way to go. They just have too much Mezmer to confront with a traditional attack. And, besides, we have anything but an army; we're even lighter on muscle than we had hoped to be, so let's discuss other viable ways of getting to Almeister." Everyone nods in agreement. And nods. And nods. And nods. And says nothing. "Okay, cool. Off to a great start."

"Well," Brittany finally says, "instead of putting the focus on what we don't have, let's maybe think about what we do. And can use to our advantage. Since they're big and we're small, then we're mobile and they're slow. We're hidden and they're exposed. Let's fight only the battles we know we can win; capture their weapons and use them against them."

I stare at her for a second, then suck my teeth and whisper, "That's Gene Hackman."

"What?"

"You're quoting Gene Hackman's character from *Enemy of the State.*"

"Am I?" I nod. "Well, it's not stealing if you don't know you're doing it, right?" I throw my arms up. She goes on. "Okay, fine, fine! Sorry. But . . . it's not wrong. I mean, there's a reason one of the Quest requirements is Stealth, right? Let's not complicate the simple. You were required to have the Blade of the Starfallen and some kind of Stealth to take on this challenge. Let's focus on what specific advantages those two things gain you."

"Well, the Blade is the Blade. It counteracts ritual, dark Mezmer, turning it into light. And, it would seem, can start fires that burn stone. And CloakRender does what it does, but it doesn't last very long, so . . ."

"It *didn't.* Before. Surely, after what we've been through, you've earned some upgrades."

That's a fair point. I need to get more into the habit of remembering that I can check on that.

Yes, you do! So glad you recalled!
(Note: Prompts will continue to aid you if you choose to wait too terribly long, but not forever. Eventually, you will be expected to care for your own needs without assistance. One's Saviour tush cannot be wiped forever, as the saying goes!)
{COURTESY MESSAGE #23}

I'm bothered by the fact that these are called Courtesy Messages, as they never feel terribly courteous. But, putting that aside, I access my Heart Guard Evaluation, and this is what I see:

[Carpathian Einzgear, aka "World Saviour"]

>Mezmer Type:
All-Type

>Foundation:
Synchron

>Resonance Tier:
Etherflint

>Highest Affinities:
Elemist (Stoneheart) [Experienced]
Mutamorph [Above Average]
Aetherpulse [Above Average]

>Statistics:
Mental: *Etherflint Level 8*
Physical: *Ironspark Level 1*
Aura: *Etherflint Level 7*
Animus: *Etherflint Level 9*

>Armament(s):
Mechanical Heart
[Elder Tier] Blade of the Starfallen

> Inventory:
[Medium Tier] Stoneheart Gloves
[Elder Tier] Blade of the Starfallen

>Abilities:
Scaredy Cat
Sharpshooter

>Spell(s):
Control
CloakRender I [Aetherpulse]
Marrowmancy [Mutamorph]
Toxin Dart [Mutamorph]
[1 New Spell Available (Please visit a Pulse Well)]

>Spell(s) available for advancement:
CloakRender I
Marrowmancy
Toxin Dart

She's right. I have earned advancement opportunities for all of my Spells, *and* I have a new Spell available, not to mention being boosted up quite a bit in my statistical levels.

I'm maybe a *little* surprised that I don't have more new Spells or Abilities on offer? But, at the end of the day, I suppose I'd rather gain strength in the things I currently have some dexterity with rather than just keep on adding stuff to my list of talents, or whatever, that I'd then just have to build up. My "box of cereal/ Netflix Syndrome" condition is much benefitted by being offered fewer chances to make questionable decisions. Nothing worse than looking at a whole toolbox of gleaming objects that you don't quite know how to use, aka being a jackass of all trades.

So, on the one hand, what I can see that I have waiting for me is encouraging. On the other hand . . .

Carpathian had achieved "Perfection" in his Affinities, and his Resonance Tier was already Manasteel by the time he took on the Tower. Buuuuut, he *was* on a suicide mission, so . . .

Doesn't really matter. This is what I've got to work with. Carpathian was also a Three-Type, and I'm All-Type, so there is an argument to be made that my opportunity to draw Spells from any strain of Mezmer gives me a unique advantage in that regard.

(I'm trying to convince myself that I really believe that last part, but I left my rose-colored glasses back on the edge of that well, so it's a little harder to fool myself than it used to be.)

I check to see how yoked Brit and Perg are looking.

[Teleri Nightwind]
[Heart Guard Member]
Mezmer Type:
Three-Type

>Foundation:
Vanguard

>Resonance Tier:
Etherflint

>Affinity:
Convocationist: [High]

Function (Warmarked): [Average]
Stellari: [Average]

>Statistics:
Mental: *Etherflint Level 5*
Physical: *Etherflint Level 6*
Aura: *Etherflint Level 4*
Animus: *Etherflint Level 3*

>Armament(s):
Summoner's Cape

>Abilities:
Map Maker [Advanced]
Beast Mastery [Intermediate]

>Spell(s):
Summoner of Something [Convocationist] - [Novice]
Randolf's Radiant Ray [Stellari] - [Beginner]

[Pergamon Slow Bottom]
[Heart Guard Member]

Mezmer Type:
One-Type

Foundation:
Oracul

>Resonance Tier:
Etherflint

>Affinity:
Mutamorph

Statistics:
>Mental: *Etherflint Level 7*
>Physical: *Etherflint Level 3*
>Aura: *Etherflint Level 4*
>Animus: *Etherflint Level 7*

> Abilities:
Service Mount

>Spell(s):
Philological Consciousness

Insight
Exoskeletal Enlarge

Know what's compelling?
"*What, Bruce?*"
"*Sorry, Bruce. I was just thinking it rhetorically.*"
"*Oh. Well, tell me anyway. Now I'm curious.*"
What's compelling is how quickly we all seem to be advancing. I know I had things operate pretty slowly in the books for the most part, but Brit and Perg seem to be climbing the strengths ladder unusually fast. And I'm advancing even more robustly than they are. I know that I'm catching more heat here than Carpathian did at the beginning of his journey, but still. It took him the equivalent of *months* to get to where I am now, and he was already moving quicker than the default setting of the average Joe on Meridia, who typically took years to advance. It's like I jumped on board an OP trolley car, but what I thought was a steam engine has turned out to be a bullet train. Not complaining, but definitely curious.

And speaking of curious . . . Another Notification now appears in front of me. A strange one.

(Attention: You have [Two] outstanding requests for Heart Guard membership. Please visit a Pulse Well to [Review] and [Approve] or [Deny] these requests.)

Odd. I'm familiar with the protocol; that's how Xanaraxa, Zerastian, Teleri, Mael, Pergamon, all of 'em joined up with the Heart Guard in the books. But who . . . ?

I look over at Tavrella. She's preparing some kind of mixture, loading it into vials, and sliding them into the bandolier slots across her chest. She sees me looking at her, stops mixing, and smiles at me with her usual, kind, gentle, pacifying-yet-mildly-indecipherable smile.

"Tavrella?" I say aloud.

"Aye?" She tilts her head. Her long, silver hair washes over her shoulder.

"Have you . . . requested to be part of my Heart Guard?"

She shrugs. "If'n you'll have me."

I look to Brit, who raises her eyebrows and lifts her hands in a *Suuuuure?* gesture. I try to get a read from Perg as well, but in his smaller size, I can't really make out his features.

"Um . . ."

"I don't have Mezmer about me as ye three, certain, but there are other things I can do to help ye along." She gestures around us at all the potions and vials.

"With access to proper resources, I can make useful materiel. At the least, I can be an extra set of hands when it comes to creatin' a distraction and so forth."

"Well, Tavrella, I appreciate it, but, I mean . . . are you sure? Assuming we pull off this Tower rescue, we'll still be far from done. There's a lot more we have to . . . As, um, remorts, we're obligated to, y'know, sort out some of the things that went awry when we were here before. So, in some ways . . ." I pause, swallow. ". . . we're just getting started."

Her smile widens. She lets out a short, quiet, almost sad little laugh. And it might simply be a trick of the afternoon suns light catching the floating dust motes and glinting off the bottles in the room . . . but I feel like I can see a tear forming in her eye. "Aye. I know," she says. "That's why. I'd like to be with you this time. On yer journey."

The shiver that runs down my spine is something for which I cannot account, but it spreads out and causes my whole body to tremble.

". . . Okay then. Um. Okay. Well, then as soon as we can get to a Pulse Well, we'll . . . Yeah. We'll do it."

She bows her head in a slow, single nod, something between an affirmation and a prayer. Brittany must see me fidgeting because she whispers, "You okay?"

"Yeah, yeah. No, all good. Just . . . The Notification said I have *two* requests to join, so who's the—?"

Before I can finish the sentence, muffled sounds waft through the door from the front room; the shoppe part of the shoppe. It sounds like an argument. I can hear the voice of someone saying, with great agitation, "*Where are they?*"

Thump-thump. Thump-thump.

My Heart speeds up. My muscles tense.

"Brit?"

"Yeah?"

"Fish out the Blade and the gloves?"

"Copy." She digs in her pocket.

"Perg?"

"Homie?"

"Get ready to biggen up."

"*Sí señor,*" he responds.

But before we can get our battle faces fully affixed . . .

BOOM!

The door to the back room *slams* open, and in walks . . .

"Oh my! You're here! Here you are! Here! You're here! It's really you! You're here!"

". . . Persephone?!"

She runs over and throws her arms around my neck, virtually draping herself on me.

"You're here, you're here, you're here!" She buries her face in my shoulder and keeps saying it over and over again with a kind of almost drunken relief.

The gruff voice of Tavrella's associate, the shoppe keeper, comes from the open doorway. "Alright. So you do know this one, then," he says. "Tried to barrel right past me."

"Yes, no, yes, I . . ." I'm attempting to affirm that Persephone is a friend, but the burrowed nuzzling she's doing against my neck is making it hard to focus. As is the mere fact that she's alive and here. Also, I'm distracted by how she smells. She smells good, but not good in the way she smelled in Bell's View. Good in a way that I am familiar with but can't *imagine* that—

"Good enough," the shoppe keeper replies. "So, guess that means you know this one as well."

At that, someone walks in who—if you had given me a thousand guesses; maybe ten thousand—I never would have predicted.

He strolls casually, seemingly unbothered by anything in the world. Preternaturally unconcerned. I use the word *preternaturally*, specifically, owing to the fact it is the most apt in this situation. Because I don't just mean the lack of concern is preternatural; I mean that the individual *themself* is preternatural. Bizarre. Uncanny. Inexplicable. Quite literally paranormal.

They take a deep, long drag from the joint on which they're toking, blow a radiating puff of ganja smoke into the air—filling my nostrils with even more of the scent than the already robust amount I'm getting from Persephone's hair—and say . . .

"Carpathian EinzGEAR! WHA GWAAN, ME GEN'RAL?!"

. . .

". . . *Jameson?*"

CHAPTER FIFTY-ONE

"Once Upon a Time in Meridia."
Part 2

AGHHHHHHHHHHH!"

The scream blaring forth from the lungs of Persephone Vizardsdottir echoed throughout the abandoned streets of Bell's View like a warning siren. And, as is also often the case with warning sirens, it could not do much to ward off the violent onslaught, instead only adding to the anarchic pandemonium on display. There was no one to come to her aid. No help to be found. The village had been deserted by all but she, and in short order, Persephone would likewise be dispatched.

The jaws of the Ronine ripped into her flesh, and the claws and sharp teeth of the Rapprentices followed their leader, gnawing, biting, and lacerating the young woman's body as though they might never be sated. A handful of Templars stood by and laughed as she flailed and pitched, watching the mass of crafted venality—designed to hunt the Saviour but denied their chance to fulfill their mission this time—let loose their frustrations on Persephone instead.

Not to be outdone in feelings of aggravation, and certainly not one to allow any other than himself to unleash the final, felling blow, Moridius Wreathnestle pushed by the Templars he captained and stepped in close to Persephone, joining the orgy of pain being inflicted on her by creatures of invention, and whispered in her ear, over the noise of her own life ending:

"You're lucky, lass. This is nothing compared to what we'll do to your *Saviour*."

Then he activated his switchsaw and, as he stared hard into her terrified eyes, disemboweled the girl, allowing the rodents to feast on her entrails.

At least, that was how it appeared to the *actual* Persephone Vizardsdottir, who was a block away, peering out at the scene from around the corner of a burned-out curio shoppe.

She was able to hear the words the Templar spoke, owing to her Dreamweaver's bond with the duplicate of herself she had sacrificed to the mob; she was also, unfortunately, able to feel a hint of the pain her copy suffered, but the authentic Persephone was free of the actual, physical circumstances that befell her facsimile.

She winced with regret as the phantasmic version of herself was torn asunder, but she also concluded that the best thing she could do now would be to take flight as surreptitiously as possible and make an attempt at reuniting with the Saviour and his cadre as soon as achievable. So, despite her simmering desire to unleash an array of Spells upon the assailants—Spells that, given her historical focus on Spells of Enchantment rather than Spells of War, may or may not have been that effective anyway—she turned and scurried in the other direction, prepared to vanish quietly and disappear under the blanket of night.

But then . . . she saw something. Something that slowed her. Something glistening, black and shiny and impressive under the glow of the moons light. And she decided it was the least she was owed, given the cost she had just paid with her other self.

The magecycle Persephone Vizardsdottir *borrowed* from whichever Templar had carelessly left it running back in Bell's View as they assaulted what they thought was *her* pulled into the unruly parking area in front of Jeomandi's Pub and Pints: A Place Where Friends Meet.

The sun was now risen, and she knew she needed not to dally. Traveling on an absconded Templar magecycle was risk enough. Doing so in the broad suns light of Meridia, particularly when one was presumed to be dead, was risk too much.

She powered off the vehicle and dismounted, sweeping down her skirt and making herself appear as presentable as possible. Although, she had heard of Jeomandi's and knew that presentability was not of the highest priority at this place.

She could not articulate exactly what had compelled her to find the tavern. She only knew that something inside her, a force beyond her usual understanding, had guided her. She felt it instinctively. Somewhere inside her chest, there was a beacon leading her, and she chose not to question it.

Entering the pub, she was struck still for a moment by the sight that greeted her.

There was a stalagmite protruding up from the floor. An odd design element, she thought, but Persephone was famously nonjudgmental regarding other people's tastes.

She assumed, however, that the visceral debris, the abandoned Viking helmet, the two dead Templars, and the one diagonally carved Grubble were not aesthetic choices and far more likely the result of Carpathian having visited. She hoped that none of the viscera she could see was his.

There were a few patrons still gathered inside, nursing their drinks in the dim gloom of the poorly lit hostelry, but none of them seemed to show much interest in Persephone's arrival. They instead just kept their heads down and their focuses on losing their sordid memories in chalices of Rilkawing's Toxic Ale. One denizen did hazard a look up. A Satyr. A Satyr eating a meat pie.

The Satyr made eye contact with Persephone, and that was all the invitation the young woman needed to make an approach.

"Hello," she said, arriving tableside and smiling at the horned, hooved, furry-legged meat pie enthusiast.

The Satyr did not return the greeting, choosing instead to grunt and turn away.

"Erm . . . what happened here?" she asked. "Do you happen to know?"

Once more, the Satyr grunted, then stood to carry his meat pie to the bar where, perhaps, he could be left to devour it in peace. He kicked the lower half of the Grubble body out of the way, took a seat on a stool, grabbed up a flagon of whatever was still sitting on the bar top, took a sip, and continued attempting to, if not enjoy, at least consume his meal.

Persephone approached once more, assuming the stool beside him.

"I don't want to be a bother; I really don't. I'm just wondering if you happen to have seen a friend of mine."

"I don't see nobody," the Satyr mumbled.

"Right. Yes. Well. This friend is quite well known. And, moreover, his face is easily identifiable from the photo right there . . ." She pointed at the WANTED poster featuring the face of Carpathian Einzgear that lay near her on the bar. She was not surprised. She had assumed that DONG and the High Council would have launched a fulsome effort to capture the Saviour. So, she simply picked up the sheet of paper, held it beside her head, and smiled. "So, you know . . . My friend is not 'nobody.' And thus, perhaps you've laid eyes on him? Recently?"

The Satyr started to become agitated, shifting on his stool. "I told you . . ." he ground out.

"I know," Persephone interrupted. "But, good sir, I'm just curious if—"

Like lightning, the Satyr reached into the satchel he had strung across his chest and pulled out a blade. A long, twisted-looking thing that appeared not to have been cleaned in a very long time. He held its tip at Persephone's throat. "You know what they say about curiosity, ain'tcha? It kills."

The beautiful young woman with the impossibly red hair should have been frightened. She should have apologized and removed herself immediately. But she did not. In fact, she didn't even flinch. She just blinked once—slowly—sighed lightly, allowed her smile to tighten, and before he could understand how it had happened, the Satyr found himself lifted into the air, being choked by hands he could not see, and discovered that his own dagger was also floating in front of him, pointing directly at his wooly crotch.

"What's happening?" he choked out, struggling for air.

Persephone Vizardsdottir let out a small sound, something between an amused groan and a pitying laugh. "I think you might be mistaken. I don't believe it's curiosity that they say kills. I'm reasonably confident it's ignorance."

As the magecycle pulled to a stop near the entrance to Garr Haven in Mt. Taum-Sauk, Persephone felt the sensation in her chest, which had ceased to provide her guidance after she departed Jeomandi's, finally begin to palpitate once more.

It had been four Lunar Rotations since the Satyr (whom Persephone eventually placed back on his stool and even fetched for him a fresh meat pie from behind the untended bar) told her that someone in a cat mask had come into the pub to rescue Carpathian and his traveling companions. It racked her brain. Who would have come to Jeomandi's on the Saviour's behalf? And adorned in a cat mask, at that?

She had spent four Lunar Rotations—four long, sleepless Lunar Rotations—

attempting to piece together the fragments of information she had into something cohesive that might lead her to what—or, more exactly, who—she was looking for.

Cat mask. Cat mask, she thought.

Unsure of where to begin, she went to the first reasonable location she could conceive of: A feline rescue organization that she knew to exist near Santus Luminous, in the berg of Floraisient. She thought, perhaps, the cat-visaged hero from Jeomandi's might have come from here, owing to the fact that during the Battle of Floraisient, Carpathian had famously stopped DONG from laying fire to the organization's facade. His declaration that "There may be more than one way to skin a cat, but there are far more ways to skin a Templar! Touch one whisker on these kittens' heads, and you'll find out just how many!" had become the stuff of legend.

Just thinking about the Saviour's unyielding devotion to the weakest on Meridia made her weak herself. In her knees. And . . . wherever else she allowed her emotions to rest.

But she found no luck there. None of the kindly feline redeemers she spoke with had even heard the Saviour was returned, much less possessed the requisite Abilities with a switchsaw that Satyr reported the cat mask wearer as showcasing.

Four Lunar Rotations. For four Lunar Rotations, she wandered and wondered. Finally, with no easy revelations appearing before her, she dared to do the unthinkable. She braved approaching the Tower of Zuria itself. She knew not what she might endeavor upon when she arrived there, but she considered the possibility that perhaps Carpathian had already alighted upon the Tower and was setting about the business of rescuing her father.

But, when she arrived within a kilostryde of the looming structure—as close as she could risk approaching alone—she felt nothing. No indication in her chest that she was on the right path at all. But then, she heard klaxons, alarms sounding with a fearsome tolling. And shortly thereafter, a phalanx of Templars, escorted by the fearsome Ronine itself, set off from the Tower and roared past where she took cover in a dried-up ravine.

Once they had cleared, she once again took an accounting of the feeling in her chest that had been guiding her previously, and found . . . that the divining rod indicating the probable location of Carpathian's spirit was pointing her in the direction the Templars had just gone.

And so, careful to make sure she was neither seen nor followed, she began trailing behind the Templar battalion, tracking where they led.

And now that she had arrived, she felt stupid for not realizing sooner: Mt. Taum-Sauk. Where her father had told her Clan Catarinci maintained Garr Haven. Of course. Clan Catarinci. She admonished herself for her absence of deductive logic. She was no Hemlock Soames, the famed detective, that was sure.

She was just about to make her approach to the entrance of the famed garage when the door to Garr Haven, the one hidden behind the rock, burst open, and out charged . . . *Sheila,* the vehicle she had seen in Bell's View. The one to which Carpathian was the Titleholder. And behind the wheel, Carpathian himself. A smile bloomed on her face as full as the roses that once used to exist on this plane, or so she had heard. She had never seen such a thing as fantastical as roses herself, but in her imagination, they were beautiful beyond reckoning, bright and full of hope.

The bloom came off the rose of her cheeks quickly, however, when she saw the Templars and the Ronine in frantic pursuit of her Saviour. For the faintest of moments, she considered chasing after them herself, but then, something inside her compelled her to continue forward to Garr Haven instead. To examine what might have occurred to compel such a desperate escape.

But when she crept close to the entrance and peered into the mighty garage, laying her eyes on what rested within, she suddenly wished she had not.

She was not at all prepared for the horror that awaited her inside . . .

CHAPTER FIFTY-TWO

And then blah, blah, blah, etcetera, I got very emotional and confused, but then I reconstituted Jameson here, and he told me what happened—which explains why whatever the beacon inside me is that indicates where I might find you was severed for four Lunar Rotations; because you were, ostensibly, severed from yourself. I got even more emotional for a minute, but then he helped calm me down with some of the relaxing Mezmeric herbs he possesses, I felt much better, and I subsequently let the now *restored* beacon inside me"—she taps several times at her chest—"lead us to wherever it thought I might find you next. Which it did!" She giggles, snorts, and grabs my shoulders, shaking me like a polaroid picture. "And here you are!"

She is higher than a kite wearing a jetpack.

The shoppe keeper grunts, "Anybody else I should be expecting?"

"No, no, I don't— I don't think— Perseph— Can you just—?" I push away from her enthusiastic sorcerer-handling of me, and she retracts her arms, attempting to tamp down her vegetally induced enthusiasm. "No. No, we're not expecting anyone else. Thank you."

The shoppe keeper snorts and says, "Lotta people unhappy about what happened when you last confronted the Tower."

"I know."

"Not everybody gets to come back like you have, you know."

"I know."

"So finish the job right this time, yeah?" He bows his head and glares at me over the top of his shoppe keeper's glasses. It lands on me in a very specific way. I don't know how to describe it, but it feels . . . important to assure him.

I nod at him, firmly, definitively, with great purpose. ". . . I will."

He nods back, says, "It's about to be nightfall," and leaves, closing the door behind him.

I take a breath, look back at Persephone, who still bubbles with giddiness, and put my hands in the air in a gesture of "let's all try and settle." "Alright, just. Slow down. No blah, blah, blah, etcetera. That's not . . . Tell me how, *exactly*, you were able to, uh, recarbonify him?"

Jameson takes a pull from his spliff. "She use dem *biiiiig* magic, me breddren." Then he sees Tavrella for the first time and smiles wide. "Tav! Me sistren! Wha gwaan, star?"

"Hey, Jay." They slap palms, and he hugs her leg.

"Where me Lon-Lon? And me big bredda, May? You nah fine him? Dem not 'round now?" Tavrella looks at him, shakes her head somberly. "Bumbo . . ." Jameson says to himself quietly, taking another draw.

"We'll talk about all that later," I interject. There's much to say, and I intend to say it, but we need to move on at present if I'm going to "finish the job right." So, "What *biiiiig* magic?" I ask the extra-chill monkey, my voice fighting off incredulity in an attempt at calm reason. "And how can I understand you?" I immediately put the same question out to everyone else. "How can I understand him? He was speaking Macaque back in Garr Haven. You were speaking Macaque back in Garr Haven."

Persephone, literally abuzz (and also *pretty* flirty), says, "Well," as she boosts herself up onto the big mixing table in the middle of the room and plops down, "you saw the scene at Garr Haven." She shudders. "Awful . . ." She drifts off, getting a thousand-yard stare, seeing the nightmare tableau in her mind, I imagine. She shakes her mane of red hair, casting off whatever she's recalling, and goes on. "But then, I noticed there was a wisp of smoke rising from one of the pools of . . ." She stops again. Chokes up a little.

"You okay?" I ask, reaching out and touching her arm.

She nods quickly, goes, "Mm-hmm," and then continues. "So, I picked up the herb stick from which the smoke was emanating, realizing that it would likely still have some centralized energy on it, some directed lifeforce that hadn't been decarbonified."

"You thought there might be some spit still on it."

"Exactly right, so I used . . ." And here she hesitates dramatically, appearing almost ashamed. Or embarrassed. Or like she thinks she's going to get in trouble. She cups her hands around her mouth and whispers, "*A Ritual.*" She then bites her lip and retracts her head, waiting for someone to be mad at her, I think.

". . . *Okaaay?*" I'm trying to figure out why she's being weird about it.

She appears surprised, and maybe a little disappointed? "Did you hear me? I said I performed . . . *a ritual.*"

"Yeah, no, I heard you. What kind?" I just wanna know how she did it and if she'd be able to do it again. Because this seems like the kind of thing that could come in *very* handy.

"I . . . I broke one of Father's cardinal rules. I combined a Mezmeric Ritual with a Spell I was comfortable with. Something . . . not entirely orthodox." She cringes.

"Okay. Seph? Oh. Are you fine if I call you Seph? Just . . . Persephone is four syllables, and time is of—"

"Yes," she says, coquettishly. "I like it."

Jesus, she is distractingly cute. She has more of Mollie about her than I even knew.

"Eyes on the prize, Bruce. Time to be a fighter, not a mildly incompetent lover."

"Cool," I go on. "Seph, because time is of . . . I'm gonna need you to speed this up a little. What did you do, precisely, to bring Jameson back to . . . being Jameson after all that happened there?" I gesture vaguely at the monkey, as if I can sweep away the memories of what happened in Garr Haven.

"I understand. Alright, so." She claps her hands together once. "What I had to do was draw a Ritual Circle with salt chalk, which prepares the area for a Death Conversation Spell, which is a simple Spell on its own meant to extract information from the spirit of the recently deceased. But then, I *fused* it with Comport Familiar, which is a Ritual Spell to Summon a spectral ally. It was a bit of a gamble, mixing the two, but I needed to know what happened there. I mean, I saw you flee with the Templars chasing you—"

"Bumboclaat Templar pussyholes! Suck yuh mada me say dem now!"

"Indeed," Seph says. "So, I activated the Spell, and the power that surged forth was overwhelming, like opening a window in a great storm. My own Mezmer was being drawn out forcefully, as if being sucked away. To maintain the Spell and the Ritual, I had to continuously pour my Mezmer into it, trying desperately to hold on to the Death Conversation Spell."

"So you were essentially straddling two realms, pouring your essence into this jerry-rigged, hybrid Spell to keep it anchored?" Brittany asks, seeming a little in awe.

"Yeah . . . You were doing all that?" I throw in, attempting to sound equally in awe, but honestly a little out of my depth. Brit's granular knowledge of Mezmeric systems is admittedly stronger than mine.

"I suppose that's right, yes," Seph responds.

"Holy shit," Brit exclaims. "You could've—"

"I know." Seph shrugs. "But I've never yet been lost myself. Had the worst occurred, there's a chance I could also have become a reconstitute."

"It's not guaranteed," Brit notes.

"I'm aware, but it was in service to a greater good, so . . ." She gets quiet. I think the buzz might be wearing off a little. Or else, I'm just now contact high from Jameson's billowing cloud of Mary Jane, and we're all on an equal playing field of plant-based alteration.

"In any case, finding myself caught between worlds, the boundary began to blur, and I was within the *gray spaces*, the distinct lines that mark life from death, reality from the ethereal. My hand, submerged in the current of Mezmer, groped blindly in liminal space. Then, amidst the chaos, a thread, faint and nearly missed among the stronger currents, drifted to within my grasp. It was a lifeline in the truest sense, a connection back to the world I knew, trailing from the other side. I seized it, not with my fingers but with my will.

"The pull was immediate, fierce, as if by grabbing it, I had also tethered myself to be drawn into the void. Yet, desperately, I wrenched this thread back toward our plane, toward the circle I had so carefully drawn. The target of my improvised Spellcraft was a simian figure lying inert and so very far from the spark of life."

I take this in, thinking about the fact that I was hoping we'd be able to utilize this trick of hers at our discretion. "So, this isn't really something you can just knock out whenever you feel like, huh?"

She sighs with a measure of amusement. "Oh, Carpathian Einzgear . . ."

Huh. She just called me by my full name, and I didn't hate it. Or, she called me by Carpathian's full—Whatever! She used two names, and I'm not salty about it. Worth noting. That's all.

"Carpathian Einzgear," she says again, and again I don't mind. "Binding that thread to him was as attempting to stitch together a quilt of water using only needle and thread."

". . . Right. Okay, so that's a *no* on rolling it out willy-nilly."

Seph giggles before continuing. "Comport Familiar was designed to bridge worlds for a moment to summon an ally, not to tether a soul back to flesh. And yet, that's exactly what I aimed to do. Death Conversation, on the other hand, is intended to extract mere whispers from the beyond, but I was using it as a lifeline pulling a spirit back into the mortal coil."

"So . . ." Brittany starts. "So you're saying, basically, that Jameson . . ."

"He is the Jameson he was before, but also he is not. He is entangled with the essence of a familiar now, a melding of two spirits into something new. As far as I can discern, he doesn't see himself as just Jameson or as just the familiar but as both simultaneously."

Everyone turns slowly to look at the monkey, who seems unperturbed by the existential crisis he represents, content in his hybrid existence.

"Mi deh yah, yuh know," he shrugs.

"So that's why I can understand him now? Because he's your familiar?" I ask.

"Yeah, girlie. You put that Philological hoo-ha on him like you did me?" Perg asks.

"Oh, no. No, he could already speak, but I don't understand Macaque. I've heard it's quite challenging to master—"

"Eh. *Kutuboto nome kay randafeldo*," Brit tosses out, and then—realizing once again that she didn't know she can speak Macaque, I suppose—blinks to herself in the way someone does when they just pulled off a feat they were unaware they had it in them to accomplish.

"But I did need desperately to know what had transpired at the garage, obviously, so I cast over him a Spell of Lexicological Semasiology."

"Of course," I reply. Then decide to stop pretending. "No, sorry, a what now?"

"A Spell of Lexicological Semasiology. Which, of course, creates dialectical neutrality."

I don't even bother this time, looking instead to Brit.

"It's not . . ." She takes a breath, huffs, and says, "Semasiology is a branch of linguistics that studies the meaning of words, since, as we know, words are made up to begin with and don't have any actual meaning beyond the meanings we give them. Which is why I think it's funny when people get so bent out of shape when they hear the word 'fuck,' but that's a soapbox for another tirade. So, a Lexicological Semasiology Spell simply makes it so that everybody can understand everybody else. That's all."

"Oh. Okay. Got it."

I don't got it, and she can tell. And seeing that I'm clearly dumber than either she or I want me to be, she gestures me over to her, draws my ear to her mouth, and whispers, "Think of it as a Babel Fish, only without the fish."

Ah. Okay. *Now* I got it. Sometimes, you've just gotta relate it back to something Bruce's overfull brain can understand.

So . . . alright then.

I stroke at my chin, noticing that my beard is starting to fill out, and take in the crew assembled before me. In an odd twist of fate, we do now have an extra pair of hands, just as I was planning on bringing with to take on the Tower. They're not two relentless warriors of legend who are battle tried and indominable, but . . . Well. They're here.

I'm not certain what value Jameson adds? Explicitly? But maybe he can smoke somebody out, and they'll be too lifted to fight.

Also, I can't help but laugh to myself ever so slightly about the fact that Jameson's "dialectical neutrality" translates to me hearing him speak with a Jamaican Patois. I can only imagine what my audiobook narrator would have done if I had written this into the books and told him he had no choice. (*"It's not my fault! It's literally how he speaks!"*) I'm sure it would have turned into a whole, big thing. Ha.

But thinking about that—about something that would have seemed so important in my old life—highlights briefly how easy and good I had it not so very long ago, and how I failed to honor that in the way I probably should have. So, I send the thought away as quickly as it came and refocus myself on the task in front of us.

So. That's Jameson. TBD.

Persephone, on the other hand, is, in fact, a sorcerer, and that's not nothing. She survived an assault by Templars and monster rats by herself, stole a magecycle, roughed up a Satyr, and then managed to find me using nothing other than the instincts inside of herself telling her where to go. So I'm really glad she's here. For probably a few reasons.

To which end . . .

"Seph?"

"Yes, Carpathian?" She bats her eyes at me, I *think* unconsciously?

"Would you like to join my Heart Guard?"

I have no idea why I ask. The answer is so insanely obvious as be to tattooed on my eyeballs, but as Perg said earlier, there's a little thing called consent. Don't wanna be out here misreading signals, even if the signals I'm getting are written in flashing neon with arrows pointing at them and a declaration above them that states, "You are picking up what's being laid down, brother!"

As soon as the words leave my mouth, her breath hitches. She honestly looks like she's about to hyperventilate, in the same way some people get when they see a cute puppy and have to do everything in their power not to crush its tiny head because of how badly they just wanna squeeze the pumpkin out of it.

After several seconds of gasping for air, she finally clears her throat, tamping down her eagerness in a completely unconvincing way, and says, "Yes, I think I would like that very much, please, thank you."

"Okay, excellent. So, alright!" (I now try to turn on that Carpathian energy that I've both flirted with and felt overtake me once or twice. Let's see if I can make it something that just becomes habit.) "Here's what we've gotta do. We need to hit a Pulse Well ASAP so that we can sort out what our strategy is gonna be. *Teleri?*" Brit is staring at Jameson and doesn't respond right away. I whistle at her. "Teleri . . . T. Night . . . Hello?"

"Huh? Oh, sorry. Yeah?"

"Put on your tactician cap. Let's start letting some incursion ideas swirl around."

"Copy."

"Super. Okay. So, now we need to find the nearest Temple of the Body. Stat. Tavrella? You don't happen to know where one might be, do you? Or maybe your friend does?"

"Aye, I know where we can find one."

"You do? Excellent. Where?"

"Here."

She pulls on a tall shelf of potions and elixirs, and it swings open wide, revealing a Temple of the Body that looks like a CrossFit gym. Spartan, but has all you need.

". . . Really?" I say. "There just *happens* to be one? Right here?"

"Aye," she replies unassumingly. "Why?"

"I don't . . . It just seems . . . awfully convenient."

"Would ye rather it be awfully inconvenient?"

"Yeah, fair point."

I start walking toward it, but then stop.

I'm hesitant.

And I don't friggin' wanna be. I really don't. I don't wanna be one of those reluctant heroes who makes everybody moan at them because they won't just get out of their head and step up to do what must be done. *I get it.* That is the upside, if there is one, to being so in my head all the time. It has allowed me to become self-aware as shit. I know my strengths. And my weaknesses.

Or, at least, I think I do. It strikes me that other people don't always see the same things we do when we look in the mirror. And honestly, just because I'm me, does that mean I'm right? That I know myself better than they do?

Maybe. But maybe not.

I look at the five faces staring back at me (well, four; I still can't really make out Perg's features, but I know he's watching me) and think for a second. This is insanity. We're walking into a situation that is, most probably, going to end very, very badly. Like (insert famous movie and/or book about an overmatched posse confronting impossible odds here), the likelihood of this going our way is slim to none.

But.

This crew seems to believe in me. Perg and Brit could have peaced out any time but continue to insist on staying with me. And Tavrella and Persephone have actively asked if they can be even *more* a part of this thing than they already are.

That has to mean something.

I've made mistakes in my life. Who hasn't? But mine are uniquely mine and mine to own.

I really, really screwed the Mael thing up. I couldn't even have predicted how badly.

I can't let any more people down.

Or snails.

Or macaques, for that matter.

Or citizens of Meridia.

Or people who invested their time and energy into caring about me.

Or reading me.

Or simply believing in me.

So . . .

I narrow my eyes, nod to my group of unexpected but Heartwarmingly willing apostles, sort of reflexively bump my heels together, and say, "Alright, then. We're off to save the wizard."

CHAPTER FIFTY-THREE

A*re you receiving this?*" Brittany asks.

"*Yes, I'm—*"

"*Hello? Testing? Can you see this message?*" Persephone.

"*Yes, I can—*"

"*Check, check, one two. You getting this, homie?*"

"*Yes, I have y—*"

"*Is it working?*" Tavrella.

After some self-deliberation in the Pulse Well, I chose to select a Spell called "Mezmeric Microblather." It's a Communication Spell that allows me to connect remotely with my Heart Guard via what is, basically, text messaging. Messages pop up in front of me, just as Notifications do, and more importantly, Messages from me will actually appear before them, and only they can see it. Since we're absent any kind of high-tech earpieces or even low-tech walkie-talkies, seemed like a good idea to have a way to stay in touch on this mission.

And, as normally no one but the World Saviour gets the added privilege of being able to receive Notifications at will, everyone is quite excited to be able to lay their eyes on their own private Messages without the aid of a Pulse Well for the first time. The problem is that since it's currently a Level One Spell, while I can Message them as much as I want, the number they can send to me is restricted to five, and I don't want them to burn through their Mezmeric data plans just asking if I'm seeing the communiqués.

Especially when they're all still standing right next to me.

I turn to look at them and whisper aloud, "Yes, I see all of your Messages! Don't use them up before we get inside!"

We're roughly a football pitch's length away from the base of the Tower (non-American football, which should be evident from the use of the word *pitch*, but you never know), hiding behind an abandoned public conveyance vehicle. Since the definition of insanity is doing the same thing repeatedly and expecting a different result, and since the last time Carpathian was here he tried to attack the Tower by just marching right across the Fields of Rendalia up to the front door of the Tower with a massive fighting force in tow to start a ruckus, *we* are *sneaking* across the Fields of Rendalia up to the front door of the Tower with *an appreciably smaller and less well-equipped* fighting force in tow to start a ruckus.

It is still non compos mentis, but at least it's a new brand of psychotic.

A couple of Templars stand guard in front of the gargantuan metal door that serves as the only way into the Tower. I imagine they're kind of like the King's Guard who "protect" the entry to Buckingham Palace in that their role is largely ceremonial. There's no actual need for them, as the Tower is pretty much impenetrable and no one would be crazy enough to try taking it on anyway, but it can't hurt as part of the show. Basically, they're a yard sign for a home alarm. They lean against their magecycles and pass a flask back and forth in the moons light.

Night is fully upon us. We have precious little time to pull this rescue off. Everything is going to need to go perfectly.

The chances of which are pretty much zero.

After I stepped out of the Pulse Well, having accepted Tavrella and Seph into my Heart Guard, added the Communication Spell, bumped up my CloakRender and Marrowmancy to their current caps, and had Brit and Perg do the same for their Spells and Attributes, I was feeling pretty good. I was juiced up, boosted up, and ready to Bruce it up. But I was quickly brought back to Meridia when Brit informed me that she was having trouble coming up with anything resembling a coherent plan.

I only tasked *her* with conjuring something up because . . . Well, because historically, I'm slapdash as hell, and she's incredibly organized. But even she, with all her proclivities for problem-solving and detail handling, wasn't able to pull together the necessary calculus required to assemble a course of action. As she was quick to point out, we don't have a way to see inside, so we don't know the full layout, how much resistance we'll find, what the Tower's weaknesses are, if any, or, in fact, *how* we plan on getting inside assuming it isn't Mezmerically enchanted to know when someone is trespassing and, I dunno, incinerate us on the spot.

All of which is not . . . ideal.

And, obviously, we have no time to do recon or seek those particulars in any way. Thus, we're just flying by the seat of our mesh suits, so to speak.

So I made the decision for all of us on what I believe is our best bet. Brit was right with her stolen *Enemy of the State* quote. We use what we have; the Quest requirements are there for a reason. It's up to me to figure out how they're supposed to be utilized. Classic puzzle solving. So . . . I go Stealth. Using Toxin Darts, I take out the Templars out front, get inside (*how* is still monumentally unclear), single-handedly take down anyone and anything else I see (who knows what or how many that will be), clearing the way for the others to make it in, and once the threats are cleared and everyone is inside, we fan out and try to find Almeister.

Which is, to put it mildly, a *terrible* plan.

I had been hoping I'd be able to come up with some kind of cool, *Ocean's Eleven, Twelve,* or *8,* heist-y type of a thing with lots of fake-outs and misdirects and stuff.

Instead, what we have is more like that scene in *Pulp Fiction* when Jules and Vincent show up at Jimmie's house with a dead Marvin in the back seat of their car. Harvey Keitel's character, Winston Wolfe, who is this big-shot cleaner-slash-problem solver arrives, and it seems like he's gonna do some top-drawer, extra-fresh, next-level *Mission Impossible* shit . . . but all he really does is spray them down with a hose, throw some blankets in the back of the car, and then have them drive it to a junkyard where Julia Sweeney is waiting for them for some reason.

I mean, it *seems* kind of awesome the first time you watch it? Like, "Oh, this dude wears a tuxedo at eight in the morning and has all the answers!" But, when you think about it more . . . all he did was just not freak out and tell everyone to do some very basic, obvious shit.

But here's the thing: The reason it *is* cool is because The Wolf did, in fact, give everyone involved the thing they needed to get out of the situation they found themselves in. Which was for someone to just take charge and run the show. At the end of the day, that's a huge part of any plan's success. Having someone who remains calm when others are flipping their shit. Someone at the helm.

So . . . again . . . we're probably doomed.

But. I'm doing my best.

"Alright," I whisper, forcing myself to remain composed and rational. In charge. The kind of leader who keeps their cool and demands respect. "So, far and away, the likeliest place Almeister is being held is at the top. Up there." I point.

"Why so?" Brit asks.

"Because that's where I wrote he was—" I cut myself off. "Um. Because that's where *it was told to me* that he was, uh, being held. By the Super Vizier. When I last encountered her. Here. When we fought. And she, um, killed . . . me."

Nailed it.

"How do we get up there? It's, like . . . I dunno. But it's high. Climbing up there could take all night, and we only have until dawn, when the trial begins, to complete the Quest."

"Thank you for the recap. I don't know yet how we get there. I'm hopeful that the answer to that will be revealed once we're inside."

"And how, exactly, do we get inside? Have we figured out that part yet?"

"No. But I'm hopeful that will be revealed when we get closer to the Tower."

"But how—?"

"I don't know! But standing here asking questions that can't be answered right now isn't going to help, so let's just make moves!"

It comes out much more stridently than I anticipated. A hush takes over the space. Finally, Persephone, now finally returned from her magic carpet ride, says, "Very well. If we believe that is the place Father is being held, then that is where we shall seek him."

"No," I respond, still a little heated.

"No?" Seph asks.

"No," I repeat, more firmly. "Not we. *I* will seek Almeister, and the rest of you will attempt to find the Nexus Core."

"The Nexus Core?" Brit asks.

"Yes. *The Nexus Core.*"

"But that's not part of the Quest."

"It doesn't matter. We are here *now*, and we need to do all we can *now* to weaken DONG."

"I mean, okay, but—"

"It's not a request, Nightwind."

Brittany looks at me like I've lost my damn mind. And maybe I have. One of them, at least.

"Nope. Still here, Bruce."

"Not now, Bruce."

Finishing the job right means finishing the job *right*. Freeing Almeister, setting things straight that I sent awry? Obviously we're gonna do that. But that's the *least* we can do. I handled the Mael thing badly, but I also allowed myself to be strong-armed into it, kind of. I need to be deliberate moving forward. Less Bruce Silver and more Carpathian Einzgear.

So, I go on explaining my stance on the matter. "Until Mezmer can once again flow freely to all the citizens of Meridia, we cannot rest. None are liberated from the tyranny of DONG until all are liberated from the tyranny of DONG!"

Part of me is worried that sounds as stupid as I think it sounds? But it has caused Persephone to look at me a little gooey, so maybe it was actually inspiring in some way. And that causes me to feel . . . Well, to feel myself. (As in, "my man is *feelin'* himself, yo." Like that.)

"Alright, then. So that's the plan, yes?" Nods all around. But I want verbal responses, I decide, so I repeat, "I said . . . That's the plan, *YES?*"

General mumbles of "aye," "yes," "sure, homie," and a semi-snarky, "Whatever you say, *Dad*," from Brit.

"And whatcha gon' want me do then, me big boss?" Jameson asks, taking a slow pull from his doob, which must have some kind of Mezmer in it, given how it never seems to burn out.

"You should stay here. Keep a lookout. You're not in the Heart Guard; there's no way for you to communicate with the rest of us if something were to go wrong."

He looks at me foul, like this is completely unacceptable.

"Nah, nah me, Jah. Saviour mine . . . Jameson, him can do bad ting too. Bring more fyah upon dem Templar. Me no gon' stay quiet after what dem done to me clan now, big boss man."

"Jameson . . ." I don't know Jameson's last name. "I'm giving you an explicit order. And I need you to obey it."

Ugh. I know this is how I have to handle things. Or, at least I think it is, but something about it makes me feel weird. I need to stand by it, though, even if it makes me uncomfortable.

Jameson, small as he is, puffs his chest out and says, "Ya tink Jameson can't raise hackle? Bring dem dat big choble?"

"No. That's not it. I think you're perfectly capable of bringing . . . choble. However—"

"Ya galang bout yuh business, big boss man. Jameson gon' do what he do, me big Saviour."

And . . . he storms off. Just goes off on his own in defiance of what I told him to do, which does not make me feel all that in charge.

"Jameson! Jameson, come back here! Listen to me! You come back here right this second!"

But he's gone, mumbling to himself in Patois.

There's a beat before Perg says, "I gotta be honest? I can't understand half of what that fool is saying."

"Godsdammit," I hear myself utter as I turn to Persephone. "Is this because he's been remorted? Is he going to be impossible to control? I thought Grease Monkeys were team players!"

"I—" Seph starts before Tavrella cuts her off.

"He's scared."

"What?" I ask, turning sharply.

"I say he's scared. Just as we all are. And he wants to play a role. He wants to feel important. He's just right worked up. Remember, they killed everyone. Everyone he knew. Everyone he loved. All of 'em. Dead," Tavrella points out. "Ye have to imagine how ye'd feel."

That settles hard upon us. I know what it feels like to lose someone. So does Brittany. So does Persephone, in her way. I don't know if Perg ever lost anyone before I got him and brought him home to the aquarium—I mean, we've only been talking for like a week and haven't had a chance to get that deep into his backstory—but he seems to be nodding his tiny head along with the rest of us, so I guess he at least gets it in theory.

"Yeah, okay," I exhale. "Well, let's just . . . We'll go after him later. Let's just hope he doesn't do anything too . . . something." I have no idea what he might do. If we're lucky, he'll just find some munchies and take a nap.

I reach out my hand to Brittany. "Blade."

She leers at me, fishes around, pulls out the mini Blade of the Starfallen and the Stoneheart gloves. I take them from her, making both full size, and then hand her back the gloves.

"You hang on to these."

"Why?"

"The Quest requirements only indicate that I need the Blade, but let's bring everything we've got, just in case."

I grip the Blade of the Starfallen tightly in my hand, peer around the side of the conveyance vehicle, and take in the intimidating structure before me. Pulling my head back, I see four deeply earnest faces watching, waiting to take their cues.

I swallow hard, straighten my back, and say, "Well, it has been a privilege playing with you tonight."

". . . What?" Seph asks. "What do you mean, playing with us?"

Brittany sighs. "It's from *Titanic*."

"Titanic?"

"The movie."

"Movie?"

"Doesn't matter. He's just being dramatic. It's very much Carpathian's way when he's about to do something dangerous. To, y'know, send everyone into the situation with a sense of pride."

Persephone cocks her head. "Well then, it has been a pleasure playing with you as well, Saviour!"

In the light of the moons, I see Brittany roll her eyes. (Which, truthfully, I can't even be mad about. It's probably the appropriate response to everything that's going on.)

I take in everyone one last time, and when I get to Tavrella, she winks at me. And a feeling of calm—genuine calm—washes over my whole body.

I check in with my Heart . . .

Thump-thump. Thump-thump.

Take a deep, meditative breath . . .

Thump-thump. Thump-thump.

And then . . .

"Can you see me?"

"No, you're gone," Brit replies. Her attitude softens a little, and she adds, "Go get 'em."

Without another word, I start off toward the Tower, creepin' and peepin'.

Glancing down at my hand, I take note that the Blade has also vanished. A slightly deeper dive into the dimensions of CloakRender confirmed that any inanimate object I'm touching is likewise made invisible by the Spell, so clothes, weapons, etc., also remain unseen as long as the Spell is in effect. The same is not true for people, however. Unlike the Cerulean Tunic of the Seafarer, for example, which will blanket anyone touching it with the ability to vanish, CloakRender applies exclusively to the Spell bearer. Not even Heart Guard members can share in it, even with my Synchron Foundation.

Which is the kind of thing that, if I wrote it in a book, would, I'm sure, create a whole conversation online about *why* it doesn't work that way. I'm confident someone would suggest it violates the rules of the world or something. But, turns out, the real world doesn't play by the rules and just does whatever the hell it wants, especially when it comes to making my tasks here just, like, twenty percent harder than they need to be, causing me to once again question: What, *exactly*, does the System want? Why did it bring me here? What is its endgame in my being on Meridia? My capacity for "Trusting The System" feels like it keeps getting tested, and tests of faith are so not my jam.

But, at the moment, the *why* is inconsequential. The *what* is all that matters. And *what* I have to do is . . .

Thwoomp. Thwoomp.

The opening lyrics to the song "Sharp Darts" by The Streets (*Sharp darts, spitting masters, spitting darts faster, shut up, I'm the driver, you're the passenger*) garage-beat rhymes its way through my thoughts as two Toxin Darts, right into the necks of the Templars standing out front, send them collapsing to the ground.

I'm right up on them when I let loose with the Mutamorph Spell. Like, literally just paces away. The Toxin Darts find their exact pinpoint targets, right in the carotid arteries of the two guards. And they never had any idea I was here.

This is strong coffee, this CloakRender combined with Sharpshooter thing.

Thump-thump. Thump-thump.

Checking in with the Heart, seems like I've still got about three-quarters worth of CloakRender left. It lasted only seconds when I first used it at Jeomandi's, so proportionally, I'd say I've now got probably about a minute's worth of disappearing time. I'm not gonna be able to stay hidden and go rampaging through the Tower, leaving knocked out Templars in my wake, without having to pause periodically to let it fill back up, but it's better than nothing. At this moment, I just need to get inside, see how many bad guys there are wandering around, and take down as many as I can before I give the all clear for Team Heart Guard.

"*How's it going?*" Brittany Messages.

"*Fine. But don't use your Messages just to check-in! I'll let you know when it's clear!*"

"*Now that no one can hear what I'm saying, I need to say this: Stop being a dick, dude.*"

"*I'm not being a dick! But even if I were being a dick, also don't use your Messages just to tell me* not *to be a dick! That's an even worse use of the Spell!*"

I wait to see if she's planning on squandering another one, but no additional Message comes. Somewhere deep in my gut I can feel her cursing at me, though.

Standing this close to the base of the Tower is like being up against the foundation of the Burj Khalifa in Dubai or something. I've never been, but from the images I've seen and what I've read, you can't really grasp the enormity and scale of the thing until you're right there.

I crane my invisible neck back to look up, barely making out the top. It bleeds into the night sky and disappears in the heavens above.

How in the hell are we gonna get up there?

And then there's the gate. It is a great, wide thing that looks to be literally impossible to breach. Not just, "Oh man, this is gonna be tough," but *literally* impossible.

I'm suddenly wishing I had an Ability that allowed me to spy weaknesses in objects, like Teleri has in the books, so I might be able to spot a crack somewhere in the base that would allow me to exploit it. Or that I had taken on a Sticky Hands Spell or something when I had the chance. I didn't because those are primarily Rogue's Spells intended for thieving, but it now occurs to me that I could use it to do things like, oh, I dunno, *scale walls.* I could make it up invisibly to an opening above and crawl in that way.

Because now that I'm standing here, I'm confronting the fact that I genuinely do not have any idea how I'm going to get inside. I'm aware I've highlighted it multiple times, but it really does bear repeating: Ours is a *terrible* plan.

And then, out of nowhere, the ancient runes carved into the base begin throbbing with energy, like they have detected a presence that doesn't belong here, and they're not happy about it? Or . . . I'm not sure, but they pulse and glow and start absolutely humming. Literally.

My Heart beats heavy in time with the humming.

Thump-thump. Thump-thump. Hmm-hmm. Hmm-hmm.

And . . .

Thump-thump. Thump-thump. Hmm-hmm. Hmm-hmm.

At the exact same moment . . .

Thump-thump. Thump-thump. Hmm-hmm. Hmm-hmm.

The hilt of the Blade in my hand gets hot. Real hot. Like iPhone-in-the-sun hot.

"Ow!"

I start to drop it, but then remember that if I do, it will immediately become visible to anyone around. And while I don't actually see anybody else at the moment (which, honestly, seems weird—as written, the Tower of Zuria was always teeming with activity), I don't want to risk it. So, I just grit my teeth and force myself not to let go of the handle.

Thump-thump. Thump-thump. Hmm-hmm. Hmm-hmm.

My Heart is pounding, my arm is shaking as I try to keep from dropping the Blade, and the glyphs on the wall are shining like the wheels on a newly restored and polished 1965 Shelby Cobra.

And then the big, imposing, unbreachable door . . .

Begins slowly swinging open.

CHAPTER FIFTY-FOUR

Homie? We see the door opening. You in yet?"

The Message from Perg shows up just as the gate finishes swinging open wide and stops with a mighty *CHUNK.*

Thump-thump. Thump-thump.

A System Notification appears.

[Blade of the Starfallen] successfully employed. [Gate of the Astral Guardian] unlocked. Entrance to the Tower of Zuria granted. (Told you to Trust the System, O' ye of little faith. As they say.) {COURTESY MESSAGE #24}

"Homie? Homegirl didn't want to use up all of her Messages."

"So she asked me to check in."

Jesus Christ! He messages like a fifteen-year-old! Instead of one Message with all of the info in one place, he just used up three of *his* five Messages for no reason!

"Yes! Yes! I'm here! Don't write anything back! Just give me a minute!"

Dear god. Counting the first one he sent to see if I was getting them, he's now used four of his five!

That's it. I'm taking away his Messaging privileges and giving them to someone who knows how to use them responsibly. Maybe Tavrella.

But I'll deal with that later. For now, I step forward to see what—

"Carpathian?

"Tavrella?! What's wrong? Is everything okay?"

"Aye, we're fine."

"Then what—?"

"Pergamon just wants to know if you're mad at him."

"Are you ser—? Tavrella, please! Counting the first one you sent, you've just used . . ." I count quickly in my head, *"four of your five Messages! Don't send any more unless it's absolutely urgent! Please!"*

I cannot believe that—

"Alright. I won't."

ARRGGHH!

I send a group Notification.

"Everyone stop Messaging!! Stop!! Save your Messages! I'll send you a Party update as soon as I know what's going on! For the love of Richemerion, just hang on!"

I wait for half a second to see what happens, all my senses on high alert. Then, glancing at the icon and noting that I have just about half of the CloakRender Spell left until it will need to refill itself, I seize advantage of the fact that I'm still invisible for another few moments and race as swiftly as I can into the dark of the Tower, Toxin Darts at the ready, set to put as many lower-tier baddies to permasleep as possible, but I stop dead in my tracks when I see . . .

Nothing.

No one is here.

I mean no one. At all.

And looking around at the inside of the Tower, I *think* I understand why?

Because where I'm standing looks like, well . . . It looks like . . .

A lobby.

An office-building lobby.

A gigantic, fantasy-tinged, office-building lobby, but an office-building lobby nonetheless.

I'm not sure what I was expecting, but it was definitely more akin to some kind of medieval keep than what this is. But it kind of explains why there's no one here. In the lobby, anyway. I mean, it's night; the lobby is shut down. Obviously, there are people here somewhere—the night shift—and I'm, no doubt, going to have to deal with someone jumping out at me at some point all *Last of Us* style, but the hustle and bustle of daily activity is currently in repose.

Which I'm now guessing is why Stealth is a requirement. Taking on the Tower can't be achieved via some big, bloody battle, like Carpathian tried. It requires more finesse and nuance and . . . thoughtfulness. Carpathian had it all wrong. Or, *I* had it . . . Whatever. Less "flow state" and more "know state" is what's needed. (I get that "know state" is a stupid expression, but I also tend to rhyme when I get anxious. As is well established, I contain multitudes. I'm a multi-dude.)

Standing in the lobby, there's something about it that . . . feels familiar somehow. Like, I've definitely seen it before; I just can't remember exactly where.

Walking on my tiptoes even though I'm still invisible (because you never know), I look around, taking the place in.

There are intricate tapestries hanging all about, emblazoned with—for lack of a better word—a logo? An owl, sitting majestically (for an owl) on the top of what I am interpreting as a map of Merida as seen from space. Based on the image, the planet we're on looks like it's an oval, as opposed to a perfect sphere, and the owl holds the egg-shaped world in its owl talons as though it's carrying it along through the infinite. Sure enough, above the owl's head are the letters D.O.N.G. DONG. Disciples of the Ninth Guardian. (I don't care how many times I hear it or say it, it's never not going to make me annoyed.)

The floor, made of the same unknown stone that comprises the exterior, reflects the soft glow of chandeliers hanging from the high ceiling. (I can hear Brit asking, "How are they powered?" *I dunno, Brit. Somewhere inside this joint is the Nexus Core, the primary source of Mezmer for the whole planet, the very thing from which all life on Meridia draws its power, so the fact that they've figured out how to have indoor lighting shouldn't be all that shocking.*)

To the left and right of the lobby are corridors with plaques above them engraved with the name of what awaits beyond. Names like: "Ministry of Mezmeric Allocation," "Department of Templar Affairs," "High Council Meeting

Rooms." They appear to have entry restrictions. Walls of shimmering Mezmer prohibit admittance without some kind of key. An access panel sits to the side of each restricted corridor.

And, near one of the corridors, something that says "Portal Lift. Upper Tower Access Only," along with another access panel.

That's it. That's how we get to the top. We're going to have to figure out how to bypass the Mezmeric locks . . .

I continue my scan of the space and see, directly in front of me, in the center of the Goliathan room, a grand reception desk standing unoccupied, with a smaller pedestal affixed to the front. Something about the pedestal in particular is intriguing.

I move in to get a closer look, and that's when I hear . . .

Eiiiiinnnzzzgggeeeeeaaaaarrr.

The Ronine's call is soft, whisperlike, as though it's coming from far away. But it answers the question of whether or not anyone knows I'm around.

Thump-thump. Thump-thump.

CloakRender's time is almost up. I arrive in front of the pedestal and look down to discover . . . it's a touch screen.

Seriously.

A touch screen.

Kind of diamond shaped.

Looking more or less exactly like you'd find in any one of a thousand office buildings on Earth.

Or, more specifically, exactly like the one in . . .

Thump-thump. Thump-thump.

Oh, for the love of . . . It hits me like a spellsword to the back of the head.

Thump-thump. Thump-thump.

I know what this all reminds me of.

Thump-thump. Thump-thump.

The Nakatomi Building.

It's the Nakatomi Building, aka Nakatomi Plaza, aka Nakatomi *Tower.*

From the greatest action-slash-Christmas movie ever made—*Die Hard.*

Are you kiddi—?

Schwink!

CloakRender: [Time Expired]

I glance down at myself, and here I am. All of me. Mesh suited with the Blade of the Starfallen gripped in my sweaty palm for the world to see.

I look around. Still no one. The sound of my own breath and my Heart beating feel like they're echoing all throughout the lobby. If there is someone here, they're definitely going to hear me.

I swallow hard and press the touch screen, which lights up. Words appear in an array of languages that I don't know, but about halfway down, I see, in English:

Welcome to the Tower of Zuria.
Please select the keypad of your preferred language to enter the name
of the person you are here to see.

This is so f'ing bizarre.

I scroll through until a QWERTY keypad using the Latin alphabet appears, and I begin typing: A-L—

It autocompletes all names that it has in its database.

Albaziel Mertronix
Aldornicon Russenflevel
Alfatrosian Mesticialrandillyusmortooshbam III
Alma Smith

K. That last one seems out of place, but, regardless, no Almeister.

"Maybe he's listed under his maiden name, Bruce."

". . . What?"

"In Die Hard, *John McClane types in Holly McClane at first, but then realizes she's using her maiden name, Holly Gennaro."*

"I don't think that's it."

"Maybe because he's not an employee and just an independent contractor?"

"He's not a . . . He's a prisoner, Bruce! Not a 1099 worker!"

"Right, right. Maybe you have to start with 'prisoner,' then. Like, 'Prisoner so-and-so'?"

What the hell? Worth a shot. I tap in P-R-I-S—

A bevy of names roll out alphabetically.

Prisoner Aaaaaaaaaaaron Razedefine
Prisoner Aaaaaaaaaaron Quipterronase
Prisoner Aaaaaaaaaaron Brixexporch
Prisoner Aaaaaaaaaron . . .

There are an unusually high number of Aarons, each one with one less *A* in the first part of their name than the one before. I scroll until I get past them all and find the Als.

Prisoner Alastair Stairala
Prisoner Albumin Creatine
Prisoner Almeister The Wizard

There he is, his name right in front of me. The very first character besides Carpathian about whom I wrote. The person who selected Carpathian Einzgear and conditioned him to become the World Saviour.

I press on his name, and it shows exactly where he's being held.

Prisoner Almeister The Wizard
Guardian Block
Upper Tower

And then a map appears, confirming what I already knew. He's at the very, very top, in the apex portion of the Tower. Which, from where I'm standing looking up, seems like it might as well be back in the universe from which I came for how impossible it seems to reach.

I turn my head to the Portal Lift that grants admission to that part of the structure, cordoned off by a Mezmer field that requires some kind of key to pass through.

How do we get our hands on a key?

"*I dunno, Bruce. Look around. Maybe there's one hidden behind a plant somewhere like in* The Outlast Trials?"

"*You really think it would be that easy, Bruce? Just break open a box or something?*"

"*I dunno, Bruce. Maybe. Or maybe that security guard has one.*"

"*What security—? Oh shit!*"

I turn my head just in time to see a big, lumbering Templar—round gut hanging over the front of his pants—buttoning up his trousers and refastening his Templar belt. A bear claw dangles out of his mouth. (Not the pastry; an actual bear claw. It does look glazed, though.)

Before he sees me, I close my eyes and try to force CloakRender back into being. Since there's no sound or indicator or anything, I have to look down to see if I'm not here. But, when I glance at my hand, I see the Blade plain as day. I force the icon to appear; it's still filling back up.

Shit. Shit. What do I do?

He finishes buckling his belt, looks up, and sees me. He blinks like he's not sure what's in front of him. I go to raise my hands, but one of them happens to be holding a legendary blade of slaying and opening gates and stuff, and upon seeing that . . .

"Oi! Don't move!"

He fumbles at his waist for his switchsaw, trying to get it unholstered, but it appears to be stuck. It's both cartoonishly silly and sad. But more than that, it's my opportunity.

Thwoomp.

The Sharpshot Toxin Dart hits him in the neck, and he drops like a . . . Like a big ol' Templar who just got hit in the neck with a Sharpshot Toxin Dart.

I stay stock-still for a moment, watching my CloakRender icon continue to fill back up while waiting to see if anyone heard all that and is on their way. After almost a full minute, when I'm sure no one is coming and see CloakRender finally top itself back off for another use, I make my way carefully over to the fallen Templar.

I'm now seeing what the Toxin Darts do to a person. Like, what they actually do.

It's pretty awful.

His face has almost immediately transformed, taking on an eerie and haunting appearance. Veins stand out starkly against his skin, tracing a dark and twisted network beneath the surface like ominous rivers on a map. They possess a sickly shade of purple coupled with a deep, spectral blue. And they're not static—they writhe beneath the skin, as if struggling against an unseen force to escape.

I'm trying to focus on the fact that he was about to pull out a switchsaw and attempt to unalive me, so, quid pro murder attempt, but still . . . I wish I could unsee what I've done.

I have to move my eyes away from his thrombotic mug so that I don't get too hung up on it, and that's when I notice . . .

Cards. Like, key cards. Like a bunch of key cards hanging from a lanyard on his belt.

Well, would you look at that.

Despite my desire to not touch the guy I just killed, I reach down anyway, unbuckle the belt he just rebuckled, and slide the stack of cards free. They don't have words on them telling me what they might unlock, but they are color coded, which is the next best thing.

So, alright. I now have a way to get around in here, it looks like. Let me Message the Heart Guard and tell them that—

"Hey."

The voice comes from behind. I spin like a dervish, wrist snapped back, ready to fire a Toxin Dart, looking for all the world, I imagine, like a low-rent Spider-Man, but . . .

"It's me, it's me, it's me!" Brittany exclaims, arms raised in surrender. The rest of the Heart Guard is with her.

"What the hells are you all doing here?" I whisper-shout. "I told you I'd Message you."

"Well, you didn't, and it was taking a long time. And you were so snippy about us not using up our Messages that we figured we'd come see what was happening in here." She looks at the felled Templar. "Ugh. What the hell *is* happening? Where is everyone?"

EIIIIINNNNZZZGGGEEEAAARRR . . .

The Ronine's warning is louder now. I look up and around at the Tower. "They're here."

"What is that?" Persephone asks, pointing at the key cards in my hand.

"What's going to give us access to where we need to go. Come on."

I lead the Heart Guard over to the touch screen.

"What's this?" Brit asks.

"The info console for the building."

"It looks just like the one in *Die*—"

"Yes, I know. Look."

I point at Almeister's name and location. There's a breath of silence as the gravity of the moment lands on everyone. I toss the key cards down on the reception desk and sift through until I see the honey-golden looking one that matches the color of the Mezmer blockade guarding the Portal Lift.

"Okay," I say. "I'm going after Almeister. The rest of you look for the Nexus Core; bonus points if you unlock it and let Mezmer flow wide. Extra bonus points if you also find the lair of the Ninth Guardian. Extra-extra bonus points if you manage to take down the Tower in the process. But I'll settle for everyone getting out alive before dawn breaks. Let's not get too obsessed with punching above our weight."

"Carpathian," Seph speaks up.

"Yes?"

"I know that you wish to go alone to rescue Father, but . . ."

"Yes?"

"Just . . . you've already been lost to us once. If you are lost again . . ."

She trails off, a pitiable sadness in her eyes.

"I'll be fine."

"You're absolutely certain I can't come with you? I can help. I—"

"You can also help Teleri and Pergamon find the Nexus Core. In fact, you're likely of more value in that regard with your individual Abilities and Spells. In some ways, you know Meridia better than we do at present." Brit and I share an "Ain't that the truth" glance. "Besides, we need to communicate, and you only have nine Messages left between the four of you."

She starts to protest again, but then halts and nods with a tiny pout on her lips.

Ugh. Pretty and sad kills me. Gets me every time, dammit.

I huff a challenged sigh. "Okay, look, how about if Tavrella comes with me? Tavrella, you up for that?"

"Aye. 'Ever I'm needed fer."

I look to Seph. "She's already used all of her Messages anyway. And she's strapped." I indicate the vials of alchemical potions on her chest. "She has my back."

Seph appears to hold her breath and she nods once more, accepting this as sufficient.

"Excellent. So we'll head up, and you three find the Nexus Core. See if anything on the map looks like 'Engine Room' or 'Mezmer-Generating Facility' or whatever. Bring the rest of the key cards with you."

I check in with the Quest Timer.

Time Remaining for Completion of Quest:
"Rescue Almeister from Imprisonment in the Tower of Zuria."
[Half a Lunar Rotation]

Damn, I wish we had Zerastian with us; her Technomancy would be useful. It has aided us substantially on more than one occasion.

Whoa. Okay. That was absolutely a Carpathian thought that just ran through my brain, unsolicited. Not sure what that means, exactly, but it's not an objectively wrong thought, so . . . Maybe Zerastian will be the next one to try and seek out. But for what's left of this Quest . . .

"Everybody good?"

Nods all around. I take the key card for the Portal Lift, and Tavrella and I scoot over, my head still on a swivel as we move. Because, on balance, this has been way, way too easy thus far. I know one shouldn't look a gift Tower incursion in the buttresses, but there's no way things should have been able to go this smoothly.

A mishmash of thoughts.

Trust the System.

The System merely is.

You didn't choose Riftbreaker.

Riftbreaker chose you.

I place the key card against the access panel and, just as I had hoped, the wall of Mezmer slides away, allowing us to step on board the lift. I press the key card against a similar panel inside and select Upper Tower. As the lift begins moving us upward, I stare at the uncountably long list of levels printed above the door, while the sound of . . .

EIIIIINNNZZZGGGEEEAAARRRRRRRRRRRRRRRR.

. . . ringing in my ears grows louder.

CHAPTER FIFTY-FIVE

Steady, lad?" Tavrella asks as the lift carries us toward the sky.

"Yeah, why?"

"'Cause yer hand is shakin'."

I look down to see the Blade is jittering against my thigh. Shit. I have enough stacked against me without accidently slicing off my own damn leg like some kind of Kickelmustron, so I force myself to chill.

Chill. Ha. That's all I wanted to do when I killed off Carpathian. Just put this world aside, turn my brain off, and find my footing again. But instead of solid ground, I'm about a kilostryde above Meridia in a portal lift being ferried to what I just know in my Heart of Hearts is going to be some kind of mayhem factory.

I look at Tavrella. "I'll fix the thing with Lonnaigh. And Mael. I'm not sure how, but I'll make that all right."

She takes me by my free hand. "I know ye will." She squeezes me once and lets go. Then she says, "Ye and that Persephone. What's going on there?"

"Sorry?"

"I know blind folk who'd be able to see there's something between ye. She yer lady friend?"

"Oh, uh . . ."

"Sorry, don't mean to presume. Lads yer preference? None of the above? Forgive me. I'm an old woman; I sometimes forget how the world works now."

"Oh, no, that's— That's not— No, I like women. In that way. In a huggy, kissy way, I mean."

She nods. "So she *is* yer lady friend, then?

"I don't, uh . . ." Something about this line of questioning is making me weirdly self-conscious. Partially because I don't exactly know how to answer, but there's also something else that I can't quite . . . "Um. Maybe?" I manage.

We're getting close to the top. It feels like we're not moving at all, but the numbers are flying by. And since she's asking me a question, it's now that awkward thing where I feel obligated to make small talk in return.

"Sooooo . . . how 'bout you?"

"How 'bout me what, lad?"

"You . . . with anyone? Or . . . ?" It's a dumb question, but I'm historically bad with this kind of thing.

"Not anymore."

"Oh. I see. Did they, uh . . . ?"

"He. No, he's still alive. Far as I know."

"Oh. Didn't work out?"

"Not exactly."

I pause, then ask, "You mean it didn't *exactly* work out? Or 'not exactly' it *didn't* work out."

She smiles. "Little column A, little column B, I suppose. It weren't nobody's fault. Things just happen; not always a reason. Not one can be pointed to, anyway. Feel like always trying to find meanin' in every little thing that happens to us keeps us from livin' the life we're s'posed to be. Like I say to folk, if'n ye have the time to be worried 'bout something, means everything is fine right now."

"What? That's so funny. That's what *I*—"

"*Now arriving: Upper Tower. Guardian Block.*"

The mellow lift voice precedes the lift juddering to a halt and another wall of Mezmer sliding away. It opens into a long, wide corridor with an ominous-looking door at the far end.

We step off the lift and Tavrella asks, "Ye think he's down there, then?"

"Yeah. I do."

"Yer sure?"

"Pretty sure."

"Why?"

I blow out my lips and reply, "Because I understand how things here work . . ."

We begin making our way down the hall. I'm moving without a great deal of hesitation owing to the fact that, assuming we're still following video-gamer-ish logic, once we enter the room with Almeister, it's likely to trigger some other kind of flow of baddies from the walls or something. Though, given how disruptively Meridia behaves, we might also get sucker punched before we get there, so I remain on tenterhooks out of an abundance of caution.

We reach the grand door at the end, unmolested, to find there's another access panel. I hold the key card up against it, and there's a *click*. I look to Tavrella who, yet again, winks at me, and then push open the door to find . . .

Thump-thump. Thump-thump.

The room is empty.

It's also not in any way like I imagined it. Beyond the fact that there's no Almeister here, I mean. In my mind, Almeister's cell was kind of like the place in the Tower of London where Richard II was imprisoned. Cold, austere, y'know, a cell. This is more like . . . I dunno. It's half junior suite at the Four Seasons and half sanctuary.

It's comfortable looking. There are plush sofas and a pretty nice-looking bed, but there's also all kinds of Ninth Guardian–themed iconography everywhere. Notably, an altar that has the same owl imagery I saw downstairs. Candles burn all around the room, as if some kind of ceremony has been taking place. The smell of lilac is particularly strong in here.

"Where is he?" Tavrella asks.

"I . . . don't know." Looking at the burning candles and the state of the room, someone was here not that very long ago. But they're certainly not here now. I glance out through a large window and see that we are, quite literally, close enough to the weird, geometric stars that we could reach out and touch them.

I make my way up to the altar where most of the candles are placed to see if there's anything that might tell me anything. And what I find is . . . one very specific thing that tells me everything.

A flyer. A piece of parchment that reads:

"Preparations for the trial of Almeister The Wizard will be taking place this evening in the Grand Courtroom on Middle Level B, Quadrant A, Section D, so that the proceedings begin promptly at dawn. Attendance for all those present in the Tower is mandatory."

A chill races through me. "Shit!"

"What is it?" Tavrella asks, coming to join me.

I show her the parchment. "The Quest is to rescue him from *imprisonment.* I assumed—I figured he'd be—I mean, I thought I'd have until . . ."

I shoot a look at the window again and, from this high up, can see the suns of Meridia starting to rise in the distance, along the far edge of the horizon.

"Dammit!" I immediately go to send a group Message to the Heart Guard.

. . . But I can't pull it up.

Tavrella notices the look on my face. "What's wrong?"

"I'm not sure. I can't seem to . . ." Once again, I attempt to Message, and once again, I can't access it. "The Microblather Spell isn't working."

"Really?"

"Really."

I don't like this. At all. My Carpathy-sense is tingling. Something is very wrong.

"C'mon," I say, "we need to get out of here."

"What's—?"

"I'm not sure, but we have to go."

We start to head off, but I stop before I get even a step in the direction of the door. Because . . . sitting on the altar . . . is a book.

At a quick glance, there is nothing special about it. It is not fancy and leather bound. It doesn't have gilded pages. It doesn't appear to be enchanted or Mezmeric in any way. But there is still something about it that makes my breath catch in my throat.

The title.

The title is what stops me from darting out to complete the Quest.

The title of the book.

The title that reads . . .

The Gospel According to Brucillian

CHAPTER FIFTY-SIX

This is it?" I ask Tavrella, picking the book up and showing her the cover. "This is the book that's saying whatever kinds of things it's saying about . . . me?"

She tries to grab it out of my hand, but I pull it back. "Lad," she starts, "put it down. Don't bother with it. I told ye; it's a lot of faff."

"What's a copy of it doing in the Tower?"

She shakes her head. "Dunno. Propaganda? My guess is the whole thing is fabricated by the Ninth Guardian to turn favor against ye. But ye can't fret about that. Ye do what ye've come back here to do, and folks'll come round. Let's just get to—"

I don't let her finish her sentence before I crack open the cover and look at the first page, which starts off almost like a child's fairy tale. It reads, "'Once Upon a Time in Meridia. Part 1.'"

But before my eyes can scan the page to read more . . .

BOOM!

Annnnnd, trigger the baddies.

"Don't make a move, Saviour! Stand back! Put down your weapon!"

I know the voice. It's a voice I last heard screaming Draven's name in Garr Haven when I used the Stoneheart Gloves to end his life.

"Yolanda," I spit, half startled and half not even remotely surprised. She's leading a squadron of Templars who come bursting into the room behind her. They didn't even have the decency to wait until I went back into the hall and jump out at me from any one of those closed doors, like proper villains.

I decide that despite her request that I not move, stand back, and put down my weapon, I'm going to choose to do the opposite of every one of those things. So, I do move, leap forward, and lunge at her with the Blade of the Starfallen. She and the others immediately draw their weapons, which, to my wonder, aren't switchsaws. In fact, they aren't Mezmer-powered weapons at all. They're holding swords. And not spellswords or fireblades or anything of the like. Just regular old, run-of-the-mill, everyday swords.

Odd.

Well, whatever. Not gonna look an archaic weapon fight in the hilt.

But before I can make a move to come at them, one of the Templars grabs Tavrella just as she's going for a vial from her bandolier.

"No, ya don't!" he shouts as he wrestles her hand away from her chest and pins it behind her back, holding his unenchanted Templar blade against her throat. The blade may not be packed with Mezmer, but it still looks like it could open an artery.

Keeping the Blade of the Starfallen pointed at Yolanda, I throw my free hand up to sharpshoot the one holding my alchemist friend who's always smiling at me right in the throat with a Toxin Dart. Honestly, it doesn't even have to be that sharp a shot. I'm happy to hit him in the head, eye, wherever I can that will take him out and expedite us getting away from this situation as quickly as possible.

I force a Dart to fly free and . . . it doesn't. Nothing happens. Nothing zips forth from within me, Dart or otherwise. *What the hells? Am I out? Is there a limit I didn't know about?*

The Templar holding Tavrella laughs. "Ha! Problem, Saviour? Having a little trouble with the old Spellcasting?"

Being mocked isn't usually the sort of thing that bothers me too much. I have a strong tendency toward super self-deprecation, so I'm usually already talking shit to myself about myself in ways that put to candy-eyed shame whatever someone else can think to say to me. Also, I work with words for a living, and as Brittany says, they only have meaning if you give them meaning. So, I can choose which ones to take seriously and which not to.

However . . .

I'm tired, I'm stressed, I'm under threat, and I'm sick of people and things trying to kill me, so this is one of those rare occasions where someone trolling me is harshing my mellow pretty bad. (Not as bad as the actual, literal Troll in the Cavern of Sorrows who tried to bring an entire dungeon down on my head, but that guy's a professional. This Templar's a part-time, amateur troll at best.)

Nonetheless, I decide that I'm going to go ahead and tap into another of my Spells, my likely favorite, my old standby, what has now become a classic—Control.

I'll just slow this situation down long enough to . . . Enough to . . . Long en— Enou—

What the hell is going on?! I should've heard a *ZZZZZWWWAAAAAH-HHMMMMMM* by now, and everything should be slow rolling so that I can put in some dirty work on these chumps.

But it's not.

What is this?! Why don't my Spells work?!

I try to check in with my Heart to see if it knows what's going on, but . . . nothing. No response from the Heart at all. I try to send a Message to Brit once again, but once again, I can't even pull it up. Everything—all my resources—have gone completely dead.

What have they done to me?

"Don't bother, Saviour," says Yolanda. "I mean, part of me wants to just let ya fritter away trying to get your Mezmer to work, but it won't. Not here. This entire part of the Tower is Mezmer resistant. Ya didn't know that?"

Mezmer resistant?! I absolutely did not know that.

"'Course ya didn't. No way the mistress could've gotten you all the way up here if you had. She said you'd come. Said Carpathian the Saviour had too much hubris not to try another *daring rescue*, even after he led so many to their deaths the last time. Just can't help yourself. And now, you've gone and done it again." She smirks.

Done it again? Brit, Perg, Seph . . . Doe she mean . . . ?

"What are you talking about?"

She ignores the question and goes on. "But this time 'round, she said just go ahead and let ya make it in, yeah? Get ya up here, amidst the stars. Away from Meridia's pull and the effects of what Mezmer ya might have in ya."

Is Yolanda saying that . . . that Mezmer is like a cell phone signal?! That when I'm this far away from the planet's network of Mezmer towers or whatever, I can't get service?

Rhetorical; that seems to be exactly what she's saying. Being this far away from the planet is like Kryptonite, I guess. On Earth, Superman has all kinds of powers, but on Krypton, he's just another dude. So, up here, I'm . . . just . . . me?

That's why *they're* not carrying Mezmeric weapons. Because it doesn't work for them up here either. Oh, shit . . . *That's* why they had Almeister imprisoned in this room. Because otherwise, he would've been able to use his wizarding wizardry to escape. Duh.

Man. I can't believe how much there is I have failed to understand about this place. There were so many plot holes that I never even considered closing the loop on. Jesus Christ.

"And," Yolanda goes on, "of course, when we dispatch you here in a moment, there'll be no possibility of your remorting again. Probably wouldn't, anyway, since you used up your one already, but better safe than sorry. I would ask if ya have any final words, but honestly, I don't really care, so—"

"Wait!" I say as she steps toward me. I need a minute to figure out what I'm going to do.

"Why should I wait, Saviour? Did you wait before you ran Draven through?!"

It's a legit complaint. I get that. But I also note that she is, in fact, waiting, so I seize on the pause to stall in whatever way I can.

"Why . . . Then why are you going through with the trial?! For Almeister? If the goal was just to get me here, and now I'm here, why bother with the whole dog and pony show?"

"What's a dog?" she asks.

"What's a pony?" another of the Templars adds.

"I . . . A . . . A . . ." I try to remember the names of the animal comps that exist here for dogs and ponies. *Oh! Right.* "A snufflepuss and whinny clomper show?"

Yolanda's chest heaves, and she gets a malevolent smile. "'Cause. He's going to stand up there, in front of all of Meridia, and disavow ya."

". . . What?"

"He's going to tell everyone about the false prophet that is Carpathian Einzgear. And that the one they call Brucillian, the one yet to arrive, the one who was always here, the one they call the Creator, the Created, and the Eternal, is the *true* Saviour. The *true* Saviour who is aligned with the Ninth Guardian. The one who will tell the people of Meridia not to resist. To comply. To spread the word that there is no ruler but the Ninth Guardian, and Brucillian is their messenger."

I feel confused. And dizzy. And obviously, those things are related.

What the . . . ?

The abundance of bafflement that I'm feeling has put me into a worse state of mind than if I'd just started swinging my Blade and said damn the consequences. Stalling for time has innervated me to a degree that I feel stuck in mud. It's like when Control is active, but it's only happening to me, and it's everyone else who is moving at full speed.

Yolanda makes to shove her longsword right through my meshy gullet, but before I can react in any way, two things happen.

1. Tavrella elbows the Templar holding her in the stomach, wheels away, and smashes the dude in the head with a vial from her bandolier. Whatever was inside the vial is obviously devoid of any Mezmeric properties, but a nasty chemical burn in the face will sting, no matter who you are. The Templar staggers back, caterwauling and rubbing at his eyes.

And,

2. Backup arrives.

"Ya tink ya gaan run 'round do dem fuckery on me Tavrella nah? Ya bald-head bumboclaat Templar yah! Me gwaan licky boom boom down!"

Jameson, coming from out of nowhere, rampages into the room with all the spirited retribution that one could possibly expect from an enraged macaque.

He wields a lead pipe. That's it. No Spells, no tricks, no Mezmer, just a long-ass metal rod that he starts swinging away with, knocking Templars stupid with loud *CLANGS* every time he cracks one in the dome. He is undistilled fury, and Templars all reap the whirlwind. It's like watching a scene from *Planet of the Apes* combined with an old Tasmanian Devil cartoon.

And before you can say, "Guess who's coming to dinner? Natty Dreadlocks," he's knocked the entire platoon the hell out. He stands in the middle of the fallen bodies, teeth bared and chest heaving, eyes wild with bloodlust, looking like he's not even close to done.

"Ya dun mess wit' da bad bwai," he says, dropping the pipe and letting it clank to the floor.

"Jameson! How did you get up here?" I ask in my astonishment.

"Me a monkey, man. You no tink me know how climb?"

"You scaled the whole thing?!"

"Only halfway. To a landin'. Then me climb inside an open window and take de 'mergency stairs."

. . . Okay. So be it.

"We have to find the others and let them know DONG knows we're here," I say in a hurry.

"What 'bout dem?" Jameson points to the bundle of downed Templars, looking like an unconscious pit of rats clumped up on the ground.

"What about them?"

"Me just bang on de brain. We gon' need finish dem job."

I shudder a tiny bit. I get what he's saying. I know that if we don't . . . finish dem job . . . that there's a nonzero chance we'll see them again. But I just don't know if I can.

"It'll be fine. Come on," I say, starting for the door. Tavrella follows, but Jameson doesn't move to join us.

"After what dem do, you just gwaan let dem go on 'bout dey business? You don't tink—?"

His pleading is interrupted by the sound of . . .

SHIIIIINK.

The look on Jameson's face as Yolanda's blade pierces his body is an equal measure of pain and disbelief, just like the look on Draven's face when he was impaled by the rock I sent through him. She withdraws it just as quickly as she lanced him through, staggers to her feet, and takes advantage of our shock to grab Tavrella (who has now been snatched hostage a second time in less than five minutes) and use her as a shield. Blood trickles down the side of Yolanda's face, and any vague remnant in my imagination of Yolanda being a funny sidekick character has been fully washed away by a rushing river of violence and contempt.

Jameson's body falls limp to the floor, the noise of his labored breathing the only sound in the room for a brief moment before Yolanda says, "Key card."

"What?"

"Key card! Now!" She presses the blade's edge against Tavrella's throat, and a trickle of red spills out.

"Okay, okay," I say, grabbing the keycard from where I placed it near the altar and handing it over to her outstretched hand. "Where are you going? Where are you taking her?"

"Just stay back, Einzgear! You took someone I cared about. You done *all* the things you done! YOU DID THIS! And you have to pay! YOU have to pay! And you will. You will pay dearly. Dearly!"

I feel like an old computer with a nearly full hard drive that has been asked to perform more than it can process. Like there are too many apps and programs open, and it hasn't got the necessary memory available to execute all that's being asked of it, so the little pinwheel thing just spins and spins and gives no indication of when it might start functioning again. Or if.

The good news, if there is any, is that I think I am finally 'round the bend on being shocked or surprised anymore. As long as I am still on Meridia—however long that might be—I don't think I'll be capable of being caught unprepared again. My brain has been placed in a fiery furnace, just like Shadrach, Meshach, and Abednego. But, unlike them, it hasn't made it out unscathed because of some sort of divine intervention. It's been fully melted and rendered down into its most malleable form, the upside of which is that it can now be reshaped into whatever I want it to be.

As Yolanda pulls Tavrella with her down the corridor toward the Portal Lift, I note that Tavrella is still smiling at me, that ever-present twinkle still in her eye.

And it's just then that something . . .

Something catches my own eye.

Something in my periphery.

Something outside the window of the room, high up in the rapidly dwindling night sky.

I try to keep one eye on the action in front of me while turning the other to the window. *Which is, I'm pretty sure, impossible. For me at least. I did once know a guy who could* kind of *make one of his eyeballs—*

"*Stop, Bruce! Focus!*"

I have to look. I have to turn my head to see if what I think I'm seeing is actually . . .

So I do. I turn my head.

And I see . . .

It is.

What I thought I glimpsed out of the corner of my vision does actually appear to be there. It's not possible for it to be. There's no way it could. But . . . it is.

A butterfly.

A beautiful, multicolored butterfly flapping its wings. And, what's more, it's framed by a rainbow.

A rainbow that couldn't possibly exist for dozens of reasons, but it does. It is. It's here. Just like the rainbow that appeared in the Cavern of Sorrows. Just like . . .

Just like the rainbow that appeared at the cemetery the day of my mom's funeral.

It had been raining all that morning, but right as the graveside service began, the rain stopped, and a rainbow showed up.

A huge, arcing rainbow.

A huge arc.

An arc. Like . . .

Like a portal.

I am overcome by a set of emotions that I haven't felt in years and years and years. It washes over me and through me and threatens to drown me. It's even more powerful than Mezmer. If I had to give it a name, I suppose I'd call it . . . revelation.

I know why she feels so familiar. Why I feel so safe in her company. Why being near her is so pacifying. I understand who she is. How did I not recognize . . . ?

And, as if to emphasize the point, leaving no uncertainty, the very moment it dawns upon me, Tavrella calls out, "Everything's going to be alright, lad! I promise! Just keep doing what you're doing! *It's trouble worth getting into!*"

And winks at me.

. . .

And then there is what I imagine to be the longest dolly zoom in the history of long dolly zooms as I am once again proven wrong . . . and the remaining liquified matter that used to be my brain oozes out of my ears.

CHAPTER FIFTY-SEVEN

Goddammit! I told him he wasn't allowed to go into that house!"

I'm in my room and can hear Dad's shouting from all the way down the hall in the kitchen. That's normal. He has a big voice. It carries. And he's always shouting about something.

"Tom, stop. Just calm down," Mom says. Her voice is quieter, so I get up from my bed, where I'm huddled under the covers, and go over to the door, opening it a crack so I can try and hear what they're saying.

"Ella, I swear, you coddle the boy too much. He needs to toughen up."

"He just fell into a pit full of rats adventuring to find another world. How tough do you want him to be?"

"Ella—"

"He's a boy, Tom. And right now, he's scared to death. You yelling at him isn't gonna help anything."

"Might make him understand that what I say goes."

"I think all it'll do is make him more afraid, which will then just make him more determined to do what he wants in spite of what you say to prove to himself that he's not afraid."

"When did you become a child psychologist?"

"Stop. I'm around kids all day; I know how they react to things. But, more specifically, I know our son and how he reacts to things . . . because I know you. And how you do."

"Hell does that mean?"

"Two days ago, you told me that you backed the bus up to pick up that old woman who's always running late, even though your supervisor told you not to do it again and that you'd get reprimanded if you did."

"I don't see what that has to do with—"

"You defied a direct order because you wanted to do the right thing. You're a good man."

"You're comparing helping an old woman with trying to find an imaginary portal to another dimension, or whatever the hell? I don't—"

"That's not what I'm saying. I'm saying that—"

But before Mom can finish her sentence, she has a coughing fit. It's a bad one this time. I feel like it's starting to get worse.

"Shit. C'mon, sit down . . . Here. Here's some water. There ya go. Small sips. Don't . . . That's right. You okay? You gonna be alright?"

Mom coughs once or twice more, then says, "I'm fine."

There's a long pause in their talking before Dad asks, "Do you think we should try to find a new doctor? Seems like this one's not—"

"It's not the doctor's fault, Tom."

"Ell—"

"*We're doing what we can. Things will be what they'll be; no sense in worrying about what's going to happen. If you have the time to worry, it means we're okay now. Today. So, let's just be here. Okay? Let's just be here now.*"

There's another long time with neither one of them saying anything. I wish I could see what was happening, but I don't wanna make Dad madder by going into the kitchen, so I stay here with my head peeking out into the hallway.

After probably a minute, Mom says, "Let me go check on him."

Then Dad says something that I can't make out. He's talking softer now than I'm used to hearing him talk. Mom says something back, then I hear her start to come to my room, so I close the door, jump back into bed, and pull the covers up. She comes in just as I get underneath.

"Bruce?" Mom calls, walking over to me. She smells nice. She'd been out in the garden earlier, and she smells like those flowers she likes, the ones she's always worrying over. The ones that the butterflies seem to like so much. Lilacs, I think she calls them. She's holding a blue Freezer Pop. They're my favorite. "Hey, buddy. How you doing?"

"I'm okay."

She sits on the edge, hands me the Freezer Pop, and strokes my hair as I suck on the blue ice.

"That was pretty scary what happened, huh?" she asks.

"Nah," I lie, not wanting to show anything like weakness. "I was just worried that one was gonna bite me. Then I'd have to get a rabies shot. Rats have rabies, did you know that?"

She smiles. "I did know that, yeah."

I feel my eyebrows scrunch up when I say, "I'm sorry."

She keeps stroking my hair. "I know, honey. It's okay." A quiet moment passes before she finally asks, "Was it worth it?"

I bite my lip and think. "I dunno. There wasn't a door to anywhere else or anything good. Just a buncha jerk rabies-carrying rats."

She laughs, which makes me calm down even more. She's always laughing or smiling or winking at me, and it always makes me feel calm. It's nice. And I don't want to mess up the nice moment, but there's something on my mind that I need to ask, so I finally decide to just do it.

"Mom?"

"Hm?"

"Why doesn't Dad like me?"

Her eyes narrow; they look kinda sad. She doesn't look sad often, and I hate it when it seems like she might be. I hope I didn't do that. Make her sad.

"Honey, Dad likes you. He loves you. He just doesn't always know how to show it."

"Why not?"

She thinks for a minute then says, "Do you understand what I do? For work?"

"You're a teacher."

"Do you know what kind?"

"High school?"

"Yes. But I mean what I teach. I teach chemistry. Do you know what that is?"

"*It's like . . . science. Right?*"

"*That is exactly what it is. So, there's a thing in science that has to do with the way objects come together, and the way they don't. It's called a 'bond.' And it gets complicated, but basically it says that things that are opposite from each other attract, and things that are the same kind of . . . well, they push against one another.*"

"*Okay.*" I try to follow along as I drink down the melted blue at the bottom of the plastic Freezer Pop sleeve.

"*Now, people are much more complicated than that, and it takes something a lot bigger than science to explain why we do the things we do, but my point is just . . . that you and your dad are a lot alike, sweetie.*"

It's not the first time I've heard her say it, but I don't get it. I don't think Dad and I are anything alike. And I can feel myself getting worked up at the idea. "*No, we're not!*"

"*Shh, shh, it's okay. It's not a bad thing. You're both very strong-willed and determined; you just have different ways of showing it. And what I'm trying to say is that's why sometimes it might seem like Dad is being hard on you. Because he sees a lot of himself in you.*"

I want to understand, but I can't make it make sense. "*I don't get it. If he sees me as being like him, then why wouldn't he be nicer? Doesn't it mean that he's just being hard on himself?*"

She smiles, pushes my hair back, and says, "*You are incredibly smart. You know that?*"

"*I am?*"

"*You are. And you've got a good heart.*" *She puts her hand on my chest, then takes the Freezer Pop wrapper, puts it down on the nightstand, and picks up the copy of* The Lion, the Witch, and the Wardrobe *that she's been reading to me.*

"*C'mon, scooch over; we're almost at the end.*"

I move to the side, and she crawls into bed next to me, pulling the blankets around both of us.

"*You good?*" *she asks. I nod, and she leans over and kisses me on the head.* "*Everything's going to be alright, Bruce. I promise. 'Kay?*"

"*Okay, Mom.*"

She takes a deep breath . . . and starts reading.

"'*Chapter Seventeen. The Hunting of the White Stag. The battle was all over a few minutes after their arrival. Most of the enemy had been killed in the first charge of Aslan and his companions . . .*'"

I'm vibrating. I can barely stand. I press the Blade into the floor and brace myself on the hilt.

I mean, she *looks* nothing like her, and she *sounds* nothing like her, but . . .

She is.

She *has* to be.

Mom.

Ella Silvert née Tavares.

How did I not see it? Her name, for Christ's sake! How the hell could I miss it?! If it was a snake, it would have bit me and then strangled me and then swallowed me whole.

"Don't be so hard on yourself, Bruce. How could you have known to even look for it?"

"The other voice. The one we both heard in Jeomandi's and then in Garr Haven saying that everything's going to be alright. Do you think . . . ?"

"Dunno, Bruce. Maybe?"

But how? How *is she here?*

A thought occurs to me. *Am I dead? Did I somehow die and not realize it, and this is some kind of afterlife? Like, a do-over or . . . ?*

Shit. Shit, shit, shit. I dunno, but—!

I break into a sprint, racing down the hallway to grab her back before Yolanda can make off with her as a captive. Yolanda taps the key card against the panel, and the doors start to open.

"Let her go!" I call down the long corridor. "You let her go! Now!"

Yolanda, eyes fixed on me, narrows her gaze. "Like I said, Einzgear! You'll pay! Dearly!"

And then she drags the blade across Tavrella's throat, sending a fountain of blood spraying forth from her neck, before dropping her body to the ground, stepping aboard the lift, and smirking at me with a venomous satisfaction in her eyes as the doors close shut.

"TAVRELLA!" I scream with a kind of fear that I haven't felt in years.

Arriving by her side, I hear her gagging, watch her grasping at her wound in a futile attempt to staunch the bleeding. I fall to my knees and grab her head up. I don't know why; I don't think there's a thing I can do to help her. But . . . I just need to hold her, I suppose.

Because I wasn't allowed to touch her the first time. I was hurried away so that I wouldn't see her in her final moment. So, here, now, I'm doing the only thing I can do, which is to be as close to her as I can.

And then I realize . . .

Marrowmancy! I have Marrowmancy, and with my Synchron Foundation, I might be able to extend it to a member of my Heart Guard! Of which Tavrella is now one! I can . . .

No. I can't. I can't access my Mezmer here. I'm . . .

I'm as helpless as a six-year-old boy being rushed out of a hospital room.

"Jesus," I hear myself saying. "Jesus, Tavrella, I . . . Please, please, please, I'm sorry."

The urgent begging gives way quickly to sobbing, which gives way to me pounding my fist into the floor. Just as Mael did.

"Don't . . ." I think I hear. She's struggling to speak, choking on her own blood.

"What?" I ask, leaning my head down to hear her. "Wha-wha-what? Are you saying?"

"Don't . . ." she forces out, which hurts my heart, but I want to know what she has to say, so I make no attempt to stop her trying. "Don't . . . be sorry. It's been worth it."

EIIIIINNNZZZGGGEEEAAARRR!

The Ronine. It's close now. So very close. It disrupts my shock. My sorrow. My mourning.

And it causes another realization to manifest in my brain. A confirmation, really.

They know.

The Ninth Guardian. They *know* who I am. I don't know if the Super Vizier does, or if any of the other Disciples do, but *they* know. The Ninth Guardian knows.

The flow state, the plot holes, all the chaotic bedlam that spilled out onto the page. Brit and Elizabeth Gilbert were right.

I didn't choose this world.

It chose me.

But why? *Why* me? If the Ninth Guardian knows I'm just a guy called Bruce Silvert from St. Louis, Missouri, then how did I get picked to be the one who—?

"Me gen'ral?"

The sound comes from down the hall. I barely hear it over the noise inside my brain, but it cuts through just enough, and I look up to see Jameson staggering into the corridor, clutching himself around the belly. Somehow, he's still alive.

I'm torn about what to do. I don't want to leave Tavrella's side, but . . . But looking down into her eyes, which appear to have changed color and now look more like the warm, chestnut brown that I remember Mom's eyes being, I see that the life has been fully drained from them. They're still kind. Still hopeful. Still generous and encouraging. But they're also empty.

I force myself to choke down a final sob and then place her head on the floor of the Tower as softly as I can, looking one final time into her face before standing and running down to greet the not quite mortally wounded macaque.

"Jameson," I breathe. "How are you—?"

"Me herb," he says, cutting me off.

"What?"

"Me herb. It in me pocket. Gimme me herb now, big boss?" I fish in the pocket of his coveralls and find his everlasting doob smoker. "Fyah?"

I search in his other pocket and find a lighter that has a picture of a sexy-looking chimpanzee painted on the side, and light him smoke. Um . . . light the joint, I mean. (It's easy to fall into his pattern of speech.)

I wish Jameson and I had met under different circumstances. I can see us sitting on a beach somewhere together, passing a fatty back and forth. But. That's not how it went.

He looks around me, seeing Tavrella's body lying at the end of the hallway.

"Me big sistah?" he asks.

I don't answer, just tighten my jaw and shake my head. He nods, a tear falling from his eye. I start to lift him up to bring him with me.

"Ow, ow," he groans, resisting. "Whatcha doin', me Saviour?"

"I'm not leaving you here."

"No, me boss. Ya got big ting still do. Leave ol' Jameson here. De blade miss de main important part. Me irie."

"No. No way. You're not irie, and I'm not leaving you behind." I let go of him for a second. "Wait here."

"Where ya goin, me big bredda?"

"We need to slow your bleeding."

I step back into the room with the downed Templars and tear a piece of cloth from one of them to take and wrap around Jameson's wound. I'm just finishing ripping a piece of fabric free when I hear something behind me.

Movement. One of the other Templars is coming to.

I think about everything that's happened that's led me to this moment, and I don't just mean since I got transported here—I mean in my whole life. From as far back as I can remember to this very second. From my mom dying, and my retreat into a world of fantasy and of fiction—of diversion and deflection—to this moment now. This moment here. This moment in which . . . In which . . . In which I can see the culmination of all the things that have shaped me into the person I am today. Everything that makes me me.

And I wonder if it's all a lie.

Did I not make the choices I thought I've made? My whole existence, have I, in fact, been guided and manipulated by some greater power for some unknown reason? Have I been encouraged to "Trust the System" just to keep me docile? Compliant?

. . . Distracted?

I step over to the groggy Templar, moaning and struggling to become alert, and look her in her woozy face. My jaw tightens, and I get sad. Because I can feel a kind of empathy for this person despite myself. This Templar whose name I don't know and who probably has a vast and complicated life's story of their own that I'd be surprised to learn.

I wonder if they're like me—just a puppet being controlled by some unseen hand, unaware that the choices they think are theirs really belong to someone else. Would they make the same decisions if they knew? At their core, is *this* who they are, or are they just clay that was molded into the thing they've become? Are they truly in service to something drawn of evil, or are they just confused, deceived, and ignorant?

I wonder what *their* father was like when *they* were growing up.

And in the field of thoughts through which I find myself wandering, I stumble over something. Words I wrote. Words the Super Vizier once uttered to Carpathian.

"It gnaws at you, killing. Eats you from the inside. It is a drink from a cup that poisons the soul. Unless . . . you simply embrace it; let it become a part of you. It is the only path to freedom in a fractured world."

I consider the words as I look at this unfortunate spirit, this perceived foe who was likely manipulated into doing the things they have done, just as I have been.

And I feel pity. Deep, pained pity. They were eaten from the inside through no fault of their own.

My spirit aches for her—for this poor, deceived Templar—as I lift high the Blade of the Starfallen and drive it right through her unsuspecting heart.

She doesn't even yelp. Life just exhales out of her body on one long, final gasp. And she dies. Just like that. No Mezmer, no Spells, no special Abilities. Simply a sharp blade through the beating muscle that, until this very moment, pumped life throughout her fragile body.

And as I proceed to drive the Blade of the Starfallen through the chests of the other unconscious Templars scattered on the floor, I begin to weep. Not sob or gnash my teeth or anything, just weep quietly as I dispatch them to wherever their spirits will be sent next. I can't tell if the tears are because I feel sorrow about what I'm doing or if they're because I feel sorrow that I feel not even the slightest bit of regret about it at all.

After I have pierced the sternum of the final Templar and am back in the hall, scooping up Jameson, I hear the loudest, most unbridled, most frantic "*EIIIIINNNNZZZGGGEEEAAARRR!*" to date.

"Ye hear dat, me gen'ral?"

"Yeah. I hear it."

"'Tis it, den?"

"It's . . ."

I'm not sure how to answer. How to describe it. How to explain that it's this thing that was made to hunt Carpathian, but it's also the thing that chases *me*. That has chased me since long before I even knew it existed. Maybe since long before it actually did.

"It's a monster."

"Monsta? What kind monsta?"

I look back down the hall at Tavrella's body. I shut my eyes. I think of the story. Of *The Lion, the Witch, and the Wardrobe*. And I think I finally realize what it actually is. The Ronine. What it really, *truly* is.

"A monster that came from behind a door I need to close now."

Hello. It appears your Mezmeric functions have been offline. You will be pleased to know that you once again have full functionality. It is good to see that you managed to survive without the use of your Spells and Abilities for the period of time you were rendered Mezmerically impotent. Bully. For. You.
{COURTESY MESSAGE #25}

Jameson and I are on the emergency stairs, racing down to try and get to Middle Level B, Quadrant A, Section D. (Which, as I'm thinking it, just realized is an acronym for BAD, and now I wanna beat the hell out of everyone involved in the manufacture of this place just for being so cheesy.)

"Ah!"

Jameson jolts in pain as I jump down several stairs at once and bang onto a landing.

"Sorry!"

Honestly, I'm blown away that the dude is still alive; he took a shank through the torso. He might be as tough as I am when I'm at full capacity, or else the much-maligned plant of mystical healing that he continues puffing is offering proof of why it's inexplicable that it's still not decriminalized everywhere on Earth. (The pro-pot lobby should use Jameson on their posters. "*This macaque was speared through the chest and remained alive due to the restorative powers of Nurse Mary Jane Weederstrong.*")

I immediately send a group Message.

"*Hello? Check one two. Check one two. Is anyone receiving this?*"

I wait for a reply. And wait. And wait. And wait. Nothing. *Dammit.* What's happened to them? Why aren't they respond—

"*Bruce? Bruce, are you there?*"

Oh shit! Brittany! She's alive!

"*Hey! Is everyone alright?*" I ping back.

"*Yeah,*" she Messages, "*are you? We tried to send you a Message earlier, but it wouldn't go through. We think we found where the Core is housed, in an area called 'Recycling.' And part of the reason we think that is because when we got to this section of the Tower it was, like, insanely fucking guarded, and we almost took serious casualties, but between the three of us we beat the guards back and we're all okay, but holy shit the security here was tight, and right now Perg is biggened up and using his shell like a battering ram to try and break down a door that's definitely guarded by some kind of Mezmer that we can't penetrate, and I know this is a lot of info to send in a message, but this is the last Message I get, so I'm dumping out everything I can think of, and I think you would have been super impressed if you could have actually seen it all go down, but you weren't here, so, oh well, maybe we'll describe it in detail when we have more time. Also, is it weird that there's a Message limit but no limit on character count? I think it is, but—Oh shit, it looks like Perg might have made it through, hold on, if there's more info I'll have Seph Message you!*"

I send a Message back that reads simply, "*Copy. Almeister moved. Trial already started. Middle Level B, Quadrant A, Section D. Headed there now.*"

There's much more to communicate, obviously, but reading through Brit's Message causes me to realize that must be what I sound like a lot of the time, and it makes me understand why I used to get tired so easily. That shit looks exhausting.

"*Carpathian?*"

"*. . . Persephone?*"

"*You say Father's trial has begun?*"

"Yes. I'm on my way."

There's a pause before she replies. . . .

"I'm coming."

"What? No. No, Seph, stay with Perg and Brit. It's too dangerous, and they may need you. I've got it. I promise. Seph? Persephone? Are you there?"

I've lost count of who's used what number of Messages, so I don't know if she's out or if she still has one left and is just ignoring me. If it's the prior, there's nothing I can do. And if it's the latter, I can't really be mad about being ghosted. I ghosted her for nine-and-a-half books, after all.

I can feel my strength returning and tell Jameson, "Hold on, this may hurt a little," as I begin leaping full levels at a time, just skying my way down like I'm a parkour megabeast.

"Blood fyah, dat sting!" JTM (Jameson the Macaque, obviously) shouts.

"I know, I know! But just hold on! We're almost—"

CRASH!

I land, hard, smashing through the floor upon which I have made impact and falling I don't know how many levels before coming to rest abruptly, flat on my back, Jameson clutched to my chest like I've got him in a Baby Björn while managing not to lacerate either of us with the Blade of the Starfallen.

"You okay?" I ask, coughing, trying to get a sense of where I am.

"Me been better. Me been . . . No. Me never been worse. But Jameson tink him live."

I try to shake the cobwebs off and catch my breath. And it's in the stillness that I feel something. Where I've landed . . . it doesn't feel completely solid. It feels like there's something moving beneath me. Writhing, almost. And that's when I hear, *EIIIINNZZGGEEAARR!* booming, echoing all around me, and realize that what I feel moving underneath and now crawling on top of me are . . .

Rapprentices. Dozens upon dozens of Rapprentices.

They seem to be racing from somewhere below to cover my whole body. To consume me. And, behind them, on the stairs coming up, I now hear . . .

THUD. THUD. THUD.

. . . as the Ronine makes its ascent to join its unholy spawn.

CHAPTER FIFTY-EIGHT

B*ruce? Bruce?"*

"*Who's that? Who's there?"*

"*Everything's going to be alright, Bruce. I promise."*

"Big Saviour! Dem rat-cat comin', me boss! Wake now, me gen'ral!"

Jameson's voice snaps me back. Back to an absolutely horrible set of circumstances that has me wishing I had never complained about having to drive a late-night route from time to time. I'd take hauling around drunk teenagers throwing up on my bus at one in the morning over what's happening now any time.

"*EIIIIIIIIIIIIIIIIIIINNNNNNNNNNNZZZZZGGGGGEEEEEAAAAAR!*"

The Ronine lets loose with one last, bone-shaking cry as it lands on the platform where I'm currently flat on my back, being overrun by its chittering, nattering, vomit-borne progeny.

"Dey tryin' get into me mouth, big boss!" Jameson shouts.

I hear him. He's lucky. They're trying to get into my soul.

I run through my mental inventory of Spells and Abilities that could help in this situation: disappear, slow down time, shoot these monstrosities with Toxin Darts . . . run. But all of those feel like trying to put out a house fire with a water pistol, and not a Super Soaker or something but one of those crappy little plastic ones you used to be able to find in the lame-o toy aisle when you'd go to the drugstore to fill a prescription. (They might still sell them. I haven't looked in a while. Not the point.)

The point is that I know, full well, that even if I beat it back, anything I do to battle this thing is just gonna be a temporary fix. As Persephone said, it was designed for the sole purpose of defeating Carpathian Einzgear, the World Saviour, and until it has fulfilled that purpose, it will not rest, it will not stop, it will not quit.

And that's me. *I'm* Carpathian Einzgear.

I mean, I'm not, insofar as I never did all the things Carpathian did in the books. I didn't live those experiences, but we did share them. And in that way, I'm as much Carpathian as anyone who read the books or believed in him or embraced what he stands for.

So, I guess, I am Carpathian in the same way that I am Spartacus; aka, I am he, as you are he, as you are me, and we are all together. (Goo goo g'joob.)

But . . .

I'm also Bruce Silvert. And the forces that brought me here know that. And the forces that brought me here, for whatever reason, are testing that.

So . . .

I make no attempt to rid myself of the Rapprentices pouring over my body. The only reason I stand up is so that I can remove Jameson from having to endure their torment. They're not here for him; they're here for me. So, as I manage myself to my feet, I place Jameson off to the side, near a door above which a sign reads, Middle Level B.

Well, would you look at that. I'm here.

I'm exactly where I'm supposed to be.

I place the Blade of the Starfallen on the ground next to the macaque.

"Whatcha doin', me Saviour? Ya gon' need de Blade!"

"No, I don't," I say quietly. Partially because I feel no need to yell, and partially because I now also have Rapprentices crawling into my mouth.

They're literally all over me. You can't even see the mesh suit anymore because of how covered I am in tiny rodents. (That aren't actually all that tiny. They're of a pretty decent size, honestly, but compared to the Ronine, they're petite-ish.)

"Then how ya gon' fight dem big monsta?!" Jameson asks anxiously.

I pull one of the Rapprentices off my lips so I can speak clearly, and tell him, ". . . I'm not."

The Ronine steps toward me, its face once again in mine. Rapprentices scurry across my eyes, obscuring my vision. The Ronine nudges one of them out of the way so it can get a clear look at me, and—I'm pretty sure I'm not making this up—smiles at me. A distorted, broken, cruel smile, like it will finally fulfill its promise, and then, perhaps, it will be able to rest.

I understand how it feels.

So.

I take a step back, Rapprentices clinging to my body, and hold my arms out wide to the side.

Now, I'm not blind to the obvious Judeo-Christian imagery this evokes. You'd be hard-pressed not to note the parallels. Guy called the *Saviour*, standing crucifix style while his tormentors revel in his presumed suffering? I mean, I wouldn't *write* something like that, given how on-the-nose it seems, but I'm not writing it; it's happening to me, so what're you gonna do?

I continue holding my arms out, an open invitation to the beast to do its worst. To have at me. To do what it will.

It growls deep in its throat the now familiar, "*EIIINNNZZZGGG-EEEAAARRR.*"

And in response, I say, "Yep. That's me. Einzgear. I'm here. Let's get it over with."

It growls again, quieter, this time presenting the name as a question, as it did in Garr Haven. "*EIIINNNZZZGGGEEEAAARRR?*"

And it is at this point that a curious thing happens . . .

It backs up. Just a step. But definitely away from me.

So. I step forward.

"Where are you going? It's me. Carpathian Einzgear. The one for whom you were built. The one you are commanded to seek. Here I am. Come along, now."

It takes another step back. I take another step forward. And when I do, some of the Rapprentices fall away. They let go of me and scurry back toward their master.

"Stop. Why aren't you finishing the job? I'm right here. Let's be done with this."

A handful more of the Rapprentices flee, scurrying down my legs and running off to gather around the Ronine's feet. Bunching up. As if they're protecting it.

The Ronine is now at the edge of the landing, and one of its rear paws slips. It stumbles, falling back down a couple of steps before catching itself. I keep marching forward.

"Don't run. Don't leave. You have something you want of me? Something you need? Claim it. Claim what it is you desire of me. But you must grasp it. *You* must. I'm not just going to give it to you. Not anymore. You have to take it. So take it."

The Rapprentices hiss and squeal as I take one step down the stairs then another, following as the Ronine looks around, trying to figure out where to go. Lost. Stripped of power.

And then . . .

It begins to whimper. To whine and to shake. To cower. Afraid I'm going to hurt *it*.

I stop walking and stand over the creature. The invention. The product of someone's overactive imagination. Watching as its eyes widen and it opens its mouth as if trying to speak. After a long, long moment of struggle, it finally manages a sound. Not one I've heard before; a long, mournful, *Oooooooooooooooooooooooooo*.

So, I mean, okay . . .

There's a part of me that wants to believe what it's saying is *Bruuuuuuu-uuuuuuuuuuuuuuce* and just can't form the consonants. Because that would be both poetic and allegorical in some kind of really profound way that, if I were to write it in a book, might even compel someone to debate its meaning in a literature class someday. (A high school lit class, to be sure. No chance anyone would ever write their graduate thesis on a Bruce Silver tome.)

But another part of me believes that it's just a wail—a lost, sorrow-filled cry—because it has been stripped of its purpose and now finds itself adrift. A strange animal in a strange land with no understanding of itself.

Its giant frame quivers as I approach, like a homeless dog who's been kicked one time too many and can't tell the difference between someone coming toward it with cruel intentions and someone approaching it as a friend. And, if I'm being totally, completely, unabashedly, one hundred percent honest . . . I'm not sure which I am, either, until . . .

I reach out and begin to stroke its filthy rat mane. At first, it hisses at me, but then, when it realizes that I pose no threat, it begins to relax ever so slightly. The tension in its bones lets loose a bit, and it eyes me warily.

"That's right," I whisper. "S'okay. You don't have to be scared. Not anymore." It's unclear who I'm talking to.

"Damn, me breddren. Ya dun gon' tame da beast, now."

I look over my shoulder to find Jameson standing at the edge of the landing, holding his wound and smoking away.

"Stay here with it," I say, moving to exit through the door to Middle Level B.

"Here? What me gon' do here?"

406   JOHNATHAN MCCLAIN AND SETH MCDUFFEE

"You two . . . protect each other."

"Each other? Dis one here on de side o' right, now?"

"Is anyone?"

"Him got a name, den?" Jameson asks just as I open the stairwell door.

I think for a second. The first rat reference that pops into my head is the movie *Willard*, and the first lion name that shows up is the first one I ever remember hearing as a child.

So, I decide to combine the two.

"Waslan. His name is *Was*lan," I say, moving forward and letting the door close behind me.

CHAPTER FIFTY-NINE

I'm back in a section of the Tower that looks more like Tolkien than it does *Blade Runner.*

They must have had about fifty different architects working on this place. Containing multitudes is one thing, but the design aesthetic of this joint is absolutely schizophrenic.

I've gotten turned around twice looking for Quadrant A, Section D. I opened one door where I think I saw a sleeping Hydra. Could've just been three Tentasaurians napping on each other, but I feel like I know a Hydra when I see a Hydra.

Whatever it was, it was a good reminder that the Tower is still crawling with things that can wax me, so I need to stay on my guard. Thus, I'm using CloakRender to move around until it wears off, then pausing in the shadows before activating it again. The staying in the shadows part is getting marginally more difficult, however, due to the fact that the suns rising in the north are beginning to show themselves more and more. I am very, very much running out of time.

I'm still not completely sure what will happen if I don't successfully pull off this rescue. At the very least, I won't get any of the answers I seek, and Persephone will be incredibly bummed. At worst . . . Who knows? Any superlative badness I could think to assign will surely be dwarfed by whatever the actual worst thing turns out to be.

As if by thinking about her I have summoned her, I get a Message:

"Carpathian. It's Persephone. You know. Seph. This is my last available Message, so Teleri, Pergamon, and I wanted to let you know that we've run into a problem. It seems—"

It seems? It seems what?! The message cut off at the most important part! Whatever happens after "it seems" is the thing a person usually most needs to know!

Schwink!

CloakRender: [Time Expired]

Shit.

I duck into an alcove to hide while I wait for CloakRender to fill back up again, and also to send Persephone a Message.

"Seph, your Message cut off. What happened? Are you all okay?"

Of course she can't answer, but not asking feels weird. I go on.

"If you see this and are still thinking about coming to the courtroom, don't. I'm near there now, but haven't had a chance to look inside yet. Until I can get eyes on what's happening, it's too dangerous. Give me just—"

"Carpathian?"

Ah!

I jump and spin, Blade of the Starfallen at the ready, to see Seph standing right behind me, along with Brit and Perg in his, I guess we'll call it, Café Grande size (aka medium, aka baby pony size). All three of them, just standing there, looking at me.

I drag them out of the corridor and into an alcove.

"What are you doing here?"

"We needed to find you," Seph explains. "I accidentally sent my last Message before I had completed its composition. Clumsy Messaging on my part. New Spell for me."

"I saw. What happened? What problem did you run into?"

"We found where the Nexus Core is stored," Brit says.

"You did?!"

"Yeah."

"Okay, so—"

"It's not there."

". . . Excuse me?"

"I said, it's not there."

"Yeah, no, I heard you. What do you mean, 'it's not there'? Where is it?"

"Homie, if we knew that, we wouldn't be here now, fool. We'd be going after it. Also, I cracked my shell *again* breaking down the magic door. Where's old girl Tav?"

My poker face doesn't choose to make an appearance because Brit says immediately, "Oh, no. Did—?"

"Not now." I point to a window we can see from here. The black of night is now fully a light blue. "I want to hear about the Core, I wanna tell you everything that's happened, but we don't have time. I need to get into the courtroom."

"Do you have a plan for such?" Persephone asks.

"Yeah. As soon as my CloakRender fills back up, I'm going to go dark, creep in, see what the seven hells is happening, and figure out what next from there."

"That's a terrible plan," Brit says.

"No shit! We have nothing *but* terrible plans! But you don't take the field with the team you want; you attack a thing with the tools you have!"

"That's a mixed metaphor, homie. That's not like you. I don't think you're in any mental state to—"

"Shut up! Just shut up! Not in the godsdamn mood!"

It doesn't really come out all that angry, more overwhelmed. But it does get everyone to dummy up for a second, which is why I'm able to hear light chatter coming from down the hallway.

"If we get a reprimand because you couldn't find your robe, mate . . ."

"It's not my fault! It was still in the wash! Facilities needs to have a look at the launderation mechanisms in the Housekeeping division."

Two Templars. Twins. Motoring toward the courtroom. One is buttoned up in a formal Templar robe—the kind Templars wear, historically, in fantasy worlds—and the other is working to get theirs on over their black, semitranslucent magecycle gear. They hustle right past us.

I hand the Blade to Brittany. "Hold this." I focus, look down at myself, see that I am now no longer visible, step into the open corridor, and . . .

Thwoomp. Thwoomp.

I drag them back into the alcove and am disrobing one of them just as CloakRender wears off.

"You seem to be getting much more comfortable whacking fools, homie." Brit gives Perg an admonishing smack. "What? I mean it as a compliment," he says.

Persephone begins stripping the robe from the other downed Templar.

"What are you doing?" I ask.

"Obviously, I am coming with you."

"Seph . . ."

"Carpathian . . . He is *my father.*"

Looking into her eyes, seeing her resoluteness, I realize there's no way I'm going to keep her from coming in with me. I get it. Replace *Father* with . . . And I get it.

"Okay, fine, let's go."

"What should we do?" Brit asks.

"Find the emergency stairwell door. Jameson is there; he's hurt. Help him."

"Jameson? How—"

"Also . . . the Ronine is there."

"What?!"

"Again, lots to go over, not a lot of time. Just . . . Perg?"

"Yeah, big homie?"

"You are, ironically, the only one left with a Message, correct?" His moustache raises as he smiles. "What?"

"I think that is, in fact, an exemplary use of 'ironic.'"

"Amazing. You *do* have one left, do you not?"

"*Sí, señor.*"

"Don't use it until I reach out for your twenty. If we get out of that room alive, we'll need to coordinate exfil." I see Brittany smirk. It looks kind of . . . proud.

I grab the Blade back, breathe in, breathe out, throw the hood of the robe over my head so that it covers my face, and with a crisp nod, head to the courtroom door.

There is no way of predicting, even a little bit, what awaits us on the other side. This whole thing could be another elaborate ambush; there's just no Meridian way to know. But as we stand before the door, my hand on the elaborately engraved handle, we're about to find out.

"You ready?"

Persephone nods. Though it's uncertain, a nod is a nod. I pull open the great door and we find . . .

. . . that we are very likely screwed like a jackrabbit in heat.

It's a packed house, absolutely filled to the rafters. And that's saying something, because the place is the size of Radio City Music Hall. Maybe bigger. The owl logo I've now seen all around is everywhere. It continues to itch at my brain because I know I've seen it somewhere before, but I never described anything like it in the books.

Why does it seem so much like a thing I should know?

There are at least three, four, maybe even five thousand seats in the gallery, all of them filled with bodies. Human, Dwarf, Elf, Centaur, Ogre, an entire section filled with some beings that look like they have pumpkins for heads . . .

And that's just sitting down. It's SRO, filled to the brim with Disciples of the Ninth Guardian. Unsurprisingly, the Guardian does not appear to be in attendance, but every other form of Guardian lover is here.

We have to angle our way past some husky, pretty ripe-smelling Viking types as we make our way in. They turn on us, looking like they want to get all kinds of froggy at being disturbed thus, but when they see we're wearing Templar robes, they step aside and let us through.

As we approach the front of the Titanic-size theater (because that's what it is—a place for a performance, not an exercise in justice), I see the Templar section. Several of them have their hoods up as we do, but some let them flop casually behind their heads, draping on their necks. Notably, standing right at the front of the pack chatting, two Templars I know well. Or, as well as I hope to. Moridius Wreathnestle and Yolanda HoneyBunny.

I start to head in their direction. Persephone's hand on my arm stops me.

"What are you doing?" she asks.

"I'm going to carve Yolanda's eyes out of her skull. Maybe Moridius's too."

I start away again, but she tightens her grip. "Carpathian . . ."

I turn to see her face; it is lined with worry and urgency. She lifts her chin toward the front of the room, so I turn my attention that way and see . . .

A dais, standing before the crowd. And on the dais . . .

A cage. A cage with bars made of glowing light.

And inside . . . Almeister.

Almeister the Wizard, looking so very much like I ever imagined him, i.e., Ian McShane.

I could spend a lot of time working through in my brain the exact language needed to articulate how he appears, but for the sake of simplicity, the guy looks like Ian McShane but a little skinnier and with longer hair. It's really that simple.

Except he's stripped of anything that makes him seem regal or wizard-y and is instead wearing an old white dressing gown, paper-thin, paper-white skeletal legs protruding out of the bottom like some ancient hospital patient robbed of his dignity.

He wears no shoes, and I see him wiggling his naked toes as though he's trying to maintain balance. His shoulders slump. His legs quiver. His bound hands shake in a palsied manner.

The things tying his wrists aren't chains but ethereal bands of Mezmer that hum softly.

More than the binding of his limbs, however, it appears his spirit is bound, all energy and will beaten out of him, either literally or otherwise.

I glance at Persephone. She turns her face against her hood so that I can't see the tears she's fighting to keep from falling.

The murmur of thousands of different souls embodying dozens of different species speaking in multiple languages has a tremendously disorienting effect, and I have to take a moment. I adjust the Blade of the Starfallen beneath my robe, clutching it tightly like a child clutching on to a teddy bear for comfort.

"Oi!" a Templar I don't know shouts toward us. "Traycon! Raycon!" We look their way and see they're waving us over to join the Templar throng who have their own section near the front. I hesitate.

"What shall we do?" Persephone asks.

"Just . . . walk slowly while I think," I tell her.

We start edging in the direction of the several hundred or more robed Templars, passing, as we shuffle along, a special box with a sign letting all know that there sits . . . the High Council.

The High Council itself.

The High Council which, of course, is made up of—by my quick head count—a dozen wizards. A dozen. Wizards.

Great.

That's just great.

Not only are we going to have to confront Templars, Vikings, and whatever the hell the Pumpkin Heads are, but now the wizards of the High Council too. That's just super.

As we arrive at the teeming cluster of Templars, a voice bellows, loud, piercing through the din in the room. At the front of the hall, adjacent to the dais upon which Almeister's cage sits, a guy who looks like the Thing from the Fantastic Four announces:

"All rise! The High Court of Meridia will now be in order! Their Eminence Jellicollum Umlaut Kippledendlefreem presiding!"

A figure robed in deep blue and purple enters. The person wearing the garb looks like the anthropomorphized version of the word "Harrumph," and appears to be the . . . chief justice? Head magistrate? Law king? Judgey Judgerson? Whatever. They are clearly the one in charge.

They come up behind the bench and take what I feel is an inordinately long time getting settled. And with every shift and adjustment of their magnificent rump, another second passes that brings us closer to dawn. I decide to risk checking in with the Heart and trust that no one but me will be able to see what it says.

Time Remaining for Completion of Quest:
"Rescue Almeister from Imprisonment in the Tower of Zuria."
[NOT LONG NOW]

That's helpful.

Finally, the presiding judge person speaks.

"You may be seated." The clamor of thousands of bodies sitting as one sweeps the room. "First, I'd like to thank the High Council and the barristers for agreeing to move up the trial a bit. I have a game of Weasel Catch calendared for later this morning and didn't want to have to change it."

God. The legal system really does work the same everywhere.

"So! Let us begin then, yes? Yes. No need to answer; it was rhetorical. Would the barrister bringing the case on behalf of the Meridian people like to make an opening statement?"

"I would, Your Eminence."

The Super Vizier. I didn't see her buried amid the shroud of bodies, but she's the one presenting the case against Almeister. I see her take a sip of water, which, I'm assuming, means she's actually physically here this time and not just another apparition.

"Thank you, Your Eminence. Esteemed Councilors, Templars, and guardians of the realm," she begins, her voice carrying the weight of her office. "We convene under the mandate of the law to address a matter most grave. As established, before us stands Almeister The Wizard, accused of treachery against the Ninth Guardian, the High Council, and all DONGs everywhere!"

There's a general murmur of agreement, and I can't help but feel, despite the circumstances, how ridiculous it is that no one, not *one* person *ever* snorts at the casual use of *DONG*.

And "DONGs" doesn't even make sense! That technically means "Disciple of the Ninth GuardianS," plural, when what she *actually* intends is "DiscipleS of the Ninth Guardian." There is but one Ninth Guardian who has multiple disciples, not multiple—

Oh, forget it.

"And," she goes on speechifying, "of conspiracy with forces that threaten the very fabric of our society."

Again, I look to Seph. Again, she attempts to hide her face.

"The charges laid before you, Almeister The Wizard, have been deliberated with utmost solemnity," the Super Vizier continues with an insincere gravity, as if the outcome of this so-called trial was not already predetermined. "Yet, in the spirit of our laws and customs, you are granted a final opportunity to disavow your allegiance to Carpathian, the so-called *World Saviour*, and declare before this gathering your renunciation of his cause."

The chamber falls silent. All eyes turn to Almeister, who shuffles his arthritic feet.

But, before he can offer a word, the voice of Jabba the Judge calls out, "Hold, please. Before such declarations can be made, we must await confirmation from the Transistor. Madame Engineer, what is the status of the broadcast preparations?"

Off to the side, where a court reporter might normally sit, a woman with a complex array of tools and devices works feverishly over a contraption that radiates energy.

Oh shit. I know what this is.

In book six, the same book that saw the character of Rufrict introduced, Draven buying a gift for his niece, and Almeister remorted, the concept of a Mezmeric Telosphere Transistor was introduced. There needed to be a way to communicate the news of Almeister's rearrival on Meridia. An APB, basically. So I created (or, as I'm coming to accept, whoever's been funneling the stories of this dump into my head let me become aware of) a Meridian version of TV or a streaming platform or whatever you wanna call it. It's a marvel of Mezmeric engineering, capable of projecting thoughts and declarations across vast distances.

So, it's live streaming . . . but magic.

"We are . . . um, *moments* away, Your Eminence," she replies without looking up, her hands moving with practiced precision. "The etheric alignments are nearly harmonized."

The assembly watches, a collective breath held in suspense, as the engineer finalizes her adjustments. Suddenly, the air vibrates with the impending moment of truth as the machine roars to life.

"Excellent! We may now proceed with the formalities of the renunciation," declares the overseer. "Unless defense counsel has anything they might wish to proffer that would otherwise provoke a stay of some kind?"

The "defense counsel" appears to be preoccupied flirting with the Elven Templar sitting just behind her.

"Counselor . . ." the head judge person prompts. "Have you . . . anything?"

The pathetic attempt at propriety is almost more insulting than the trial itself.

"Uh . . ." She looks through some papers, drops some on the floor, tosses a few in the air. "No, Your Eminence. Think we're good." She gives a thumbs-up.

"Almeister The Wizard," the mass of flesh behind the bench says, "you have a statement you wish to make?"

Almeister, shaggy hair draping over his face, nods his head slightly.

"And you make it of your own free will? With no, uh, yadda yadda or blah blah?"

A long pause before Almeister once again nods, this time with even less commitment.

"Very well. You may begin."

Almeister shuffles from side to side. There must be some amplification system inside his mobile prison cell because I hear him clear his throat.

Shit. I have to do something. Now. If he starts speaking and says a bunch of scandalous shit about me, what has already been a difficult task—surviving this world—is going to become impossible. *Think. Think.*

My best instinct is to just throw Control up right now, see how many Toxin Darts I can land in suckers' necks, and attempt to break Almeister free before I'm mowed down by a wall of hot fire, probably both figuratively and literally. The High Council wizards in here would have me smoked before I made it to the cage. Who knows what Mezmer they're packing.

Think, Bruce, think!

Bruce?

Bruce? Are you there?

The other Bruce in my brain has disappeared like a damn deserter, leaving me alone to figure this thing out. *Man, when you can't trust your broken psyche to have your back . . .*

But then . . . I am saved. Sort of. I think? Maybe? Probably not. But at least there's a stay. Because the Super Vizier calls out . . .

"Your Eminence? Before we proceed. If I may?"

All heads turn as one to focus on her.

"Yes, Mistress Vizier? You have something to add?"

"I don't, Your Eminence. But there *is* someone here who might wish to speak."

Thump-thump. Thump-thump.

Sweat forms on my brow as my grip tightens around the Blade. She looks right at me and points.

"Carpathian Einzgear. He should be allowed to say something on his own behalf, wouldn't you agree? Since he has gone through all the trouble to be here."

There is a collective gasp that sounds like a hurricane sweeping through the room.

The Super Vizier and I make eye contact. She smiles. I grind my teeth.

She revels in the shock and awe for a moment before she smiles and asks me directly, "So? Anything you would care to add? Saviour?"

CHAPTER SIXTY

Silvert! Has anyone seen Silvert?"

I hear my supervisor's voice from outside the break room, where I'm working on something I just started playing around with called Riftbreaker. I'm not sure what it's about yet; not exactly. But it's flowing out of me, leading me where the story seems to want me to take it. It's a pretty cool feeling.

I feed Crystal a bit of the banana I brought with me for lunch as boss lady enters, already deep into a fight with me that I didn't even know we were having.

"There you are. God . . . Dammit. Why is that goddamn monkey here again? I told— Fuck it. Silvert? I just reviewed the onboard footage from your route yesterday."

". . . Okay."

"You backed your bus up?"

"Sorry?"

"Your bus. The thing you drive. For your goddamn job."

I sigh, try to laugh it off. "Yes, ma'am, I know what a bus is."

I hate that I'm laughing like I'm making some kind of apology. Like I'm already accepting blame for whatever she's about to lay at my feet. Like she's not the one being an asshole.

"So then you know how the bus works, right? How your job works. Your job is to drive forward, not back it up in the middle of the street."

"Ma'am, I—"

"Bruce, I. SAW. IT," she yells. Crystal ducks around the side of my arm to hide.

"Ma'am, I'm sorry, I—"

"Some old lady. You backed up to let some old lady on?"

"Oh. Oh, that. I mean, I saw her running to catch up after I had pulled away, so I stopped and . . . maybe I moved back like a foot? So she wouldn't be in traffic? But—"

"Jesus Christ. Always needing to play the hero, just like your father." Every muscle in my body stiffens at that. "Always making excuses. I've been doing this job for thirty-five years, and in all the time I've been here, there are two things I know I can count on no matter what. That Tom and Bruce Silvert will be a pain in my ass."

About a hundred thoughts run through my head to say in reply, but what comes out is . . . "That's one thing."

"What?"

"You said two things that you can count on. Me and my dad being a pain in your ass. Technically, it's only one thing, just broken up between two people."

She starts to shake. I think her head is going to explode. Like in Scanners.

"That's it; you're getting written up. And know that any bonus you were expecting this year will reflect your blatant disregard for protocol."

"Ma'am, I'm sorry. It wasn't my intention—"

"I don't give a shit about your intentions! Intentions are irrelevant!" She points at my notepad. "Unlike in your little fantasy fiction universe or whatever the hell it is you're doing there, in the real world, actions have consequences, Silvert."

She storms out. Crystal pulls her head out from hiding and sticks her tongue out at the always angry woman as she stomps away.

I watch the open doorway through which she exited, wishing that when she stepped through it, it would take her someplace else. Someplace far away where I wouldn't have to see her again, instead of just back to her office, where I imagine she'll sit around thinking up new ways to be all over my back.

There has to be a way to . . . I can't . . . There just has to be something better out there.

I break off another small piece of banana and hand it to Crystal. Adjusting her beret on her furry little head, I say aloud, "Someday. Someday, I'll figure out how to get outta here."

But, for now, I crumple up the empty paper bag that held my lunch, toss it into the trash can, Kobe style, and trudge back out to the depot to face "real life" once again.

🪶🪶🪶

"Einzg—? Carpa—Here?!" The overfilled bag of air behind the bench blusters.

There is a general rumble of disbelief as the Super Vizier, still looking at me with an insipid smile on her face, tilts her head to the side as if to say, "Good luck," and then makes her way quickly out of a side door to let whatever chaos she hath unleashed do its work. It feels very much like a Super Vizier thing to have done. Set the wrecking ball in motion and then move aside as it executes its demolition.

I look to Almeister, who is squinting at me, as if he's not sure he can believe what he's seeing. And then . . .

"Don't let him near the wizard! Don't let him escape!" Moridius's voice echoes above the din of the thousands of assembled DsONG (Nope. I get it now. It may be a grammatically correct acronym, but it just sounds weird.), and the courtroom erupts into pandemonium.

I'm momentarily frozen by the overwhelming odds facing me. Until you've had several thousand angry cultists rise as one against you in a closed environment like this, you can't know how you're going to react. My reaction is, at the moment, a gulp and a fumbling to draw the Blade out from underneath my pilfered robe.

Fortunately, Persephone wastes no time. She shoves me behind her, throws off her Templar robe, and immediately starts weaving her hands through the air, fingers tracing sigils that glow with the intensity of a star being born. It's kind of like the move I've seen from Brittany, but with an insouciance born of practice. A casual kind of perfection.

She whispers something—the name of the Spell, perhaps—and the air ripples around us as first dozens, then *multiple* dozens of her flood the space.

Copies. Just like the ones she produced at the battle in Bell's View. But this time, she is fabricating a proper battalion of spectral Persephone duplicates. They flicker in and out of solidity, a mesmerizing (not to be confused with Mezmerating, although they're that too) army of partially tangible illusions that dart forward to meet the onslaught on our behalf.

They're not capable of engaging fully, as they are only ideas, reflections, symbols of the sorcerer herself, but they are able to provide enough of a disruption and distraction that it affords the real Persephone space to shout at me, "Father! Get Father!"

I start to make my way to the dais to see how I can rupture the Mezmeric cage holding the wizard captive, but as I do, the entire High Council rises as one, an assembly of entities whose very auras press down with an oppressive force, a manifestation of power that seems to thicken the air around me. Their robes, elaborate declarations of Mezmeric significance, flutter dramatically, stirred not by any mundane breeze but by the surge of energy that courses through them. As they stand, a collective embodiment of might and majesty, they begin to unleash their displeasure.

And by that, I mean they start blasting holes in the joint.

"Court is adjourned!" the roly-poly jurist from behind the bench shouts, ducking to the floor and scrambling out of the auditorium.

The High Council wizards, with deliberate motions, summon forth Mezmeric Spells of a caliber I've not yet witnessed with my own eyes. Beams of light, upturned rock, and a . . . like . . . fog made out of rose petals(?) have turned the monumental courtroom into the big alien takeover scene from *Independence Day*. Everything they're tossing out is a corruption of the natural order. These aren't just blasts of energy but calculated strikes, each one weaving through the air with sinister precision, seeking out Persephone's spectral Mary Kates and Ashleys, ripping through them one by one to mute their attention-pulling impact.

The duplicates, in a mirroring of the integrity and discipline of the original herself, meet their ends with grace, especially given the violence of their destruction. As the array of Spells find their marks, the illusions don't simply fade but are instantly obliterated, disintegrating into clouds of smoke that dissipate into the charged air. The destruction of each clone is marked by a sound—a whisper of perfectly cut screams—haunting and brief, as if the essence of the Spell mourns its own demise.

Attempting to ignore it and focus on retrieving Almeister is like trying not to break an egg in the middle of a tornado, but I'm doing my best. Screams fill the air, a disharmonic convergence that drowns out individual cries. All of the thousands present have become a mass of confusion and fear, a stampede of bodies scrambling for safety in a place where no corner is untouched by the melee.

Somehow, in the midst of all this, I manage to reach the dais.

"Almeister! Stand back!"

The old man looks at me, his eyes narrowed and his mouth agape. "Car . . . *pathian?*" he says, sounding befuddled.

Rather than answer, I go to strike at the Mezmeric lock on the cage with the Blade of the Starfallen, hoping that its inherent power is sufficient to break the bonds that bind.

But, unfortunately, I don't get to find out, as a blast of energy from . . . I don't know where, sends me reeling backward, tumbling ass over teakettle across the great room. I hit the wall, hard, and feel my arm—my Blade-wielding arm, no less—rip out of the socket.

"Son of a biscuit!"

I see Persephone, looking less like the elixir-making, shy and retiring, sweet-faced Spellcaster I think of her as and more like . . . I dunno . . . Menhit, the Nubian goddess of war, whose name translates, literally, as she who sacrifices or she who massacres, because, at the moment, Seph is doing both. Even as her illusions take the brunt of the attacks, she's hurling Pyreheart fury back at the High Council. Spheres of fire, bright and consuming, arc through the air, each one bursting with the heat of a fiery furnace. They explode against shields of Mezmer, creating shock waves that ripple out, knocking back the less prepared attendees.

The calamity is absolute.

Meanwhile . . .

Thump-thump. Thump-thump.

There's me. Slumped against a wall. Nursing my arm ouchie. And that simply won't do.

Marrowmancy, the Mutamorph Spell I selected anticipating that I wasn't going to be able to duck and dodge boo-boos forever. I have it available.

Yes, you do! Good job, squire! You're becoming better and better at thinking for yourself. Oh, they grow up so fast . . .
{COURTESY MESSAGE #26}

I focus in on my Spell Center (which—side note, not the time to talk about it, but—is getting much easier to conceptualize) and focus the Marrowmancy into the raging ache in my busted shoulder.

POP, I feel it snap back into place.

Oh, snap! Literally! This is gonna rule!

And good thing I found my way into it as successfully as I have, because now a mace, swinging with the kind of enthusiasm usually reserved for birthday piñatas, whistles through the air where my head was moments before. The dodge is pure instinct, a side roll that results in me winding up face-to-face with a terrified-looking . . . Bridge Troll? Beardless Dwarf? Kind-of-agitated Munchkin? (The ones from the movie, not the pastry balls.) Whatever they are, the surprise on their face mirrors mine, as if we've both stumbled into the wrong party and are too polite to mention it.

Our eyes lock in a moment of silent "*My, oh my, what have we gotten ourselves into?*" before the unspoken truce is shattered by the crackling of a Scorchheart Spell slicing the air toward us.

It's a split-second decision—one born of the primal urge to survive rather than any strategic genius—but with a nudge less gentle than I'd like to admit, I redirect my newfound ally into the path of the Spell. Their expression of betrayal would be almost comical if the stakes weren't so damn high.

I race back toward the dais, calling a "Sorry, mate!" over my shoulder at the immolated unfortunate. The ethics of my actions weigh heavily for a fleeting second, but urgent self-preservation has a way of browbeating moral quandaries into the back seat. Also, pretty much everyone here stands in support of an evil empire, so I choose to feel like I'm on the right side of history. Freed from immediate danger, I weave, hack, and slash my way back to Almeister as Persephone maintains her noble defense.

BOOF is the sound of me deflecting a blast of energy with the Blade. *CLANG* is the sound of me smashing it into the shield of a too-tall Viking. *WHOOSH* is the sound of me striking a foe who is turned into a streaming rain of energy.

Just as I start to think I might actually make it to my goal, a stray Spell ricochets off a Viking shield. But its trajectory is altered in a stroke of freak luck. (Or freak misfortune, depending on whether or not you're the one it lands on.) I'm the lucky one in this instance. The pumpkin-headed person it hits right in the . . . Well, right in the pumpkin probably feels less fortunate as their pumpkin explodes, just like when you throw one off a balcony onto the concrete below. (Which, in one instance of youthful Halloween exuberance, I may have done ten or fifteen times before the cops showed up.)

Just as I am once again near enough to Almeister to attempt freeing him, I note that Persephone's duplicates are dwindling, the High Council's power too immense for even her clever tricks to withstand indefinitely. I know Almeister is the prize, but I can't let Seph go down. I can't abandon her again, even if it is in service to rescuing her father. I have to do both. Be there for Persephone *and* rescue Almeister. I *can* do both.

I'm just not sure how.

"What are you doing?" Seph shouts as I race to her side, batting away a Sneakrillian Templar she didn't see coming up behind her. Why would she? Their primary skill set is built right into their name. Only reason I saw it is because I know what to look for, which is the fact that, by design, they sneak up on someone exactly the way Sylvester the Cat would sneak up on Tweety Bird. Which is funny right up to the point when they disembowel you.

"There are too many! Too powerful! We need more backup! Or . . . something!" I shout back, swiping the Blade at the Sneakrillian and watching it explode into a shower of light.

Persephone and I are back-to-back, fighting off assailants like we're Neo and Trinity.

"I am going to attempt something," Persephone calls over her shoulder. "Stand guard over me!"

"What does it look like I'm trying to do?! What are you going to attempt?!"

Her response sends a shiver down my spine. "My lone Steelshard Spell!"

Oh. OH *SHIT. Steelshard?!*

The revelation hits me like a bolt of microwaved divinity.

Up until this moment, the nature of her power has been a bit of a mystery. I glimpsed her capacity for putting in work in Bell's View, and she previously mentioned that she had a single Spell at one Tier higher than her current orientation, but *Steelshard*?

That's not just powerful—it's monumental. Epic. Biblical in its scope.

That means her actual Resonance Tier is full-blown Ironspark, and based on the rules of logic governing such things, she has to have at least a *high* Ironspark rating in her Aura stat to even attempt to gain a mastery over a Steelshard Spell.

I guess spending an inordinate amount of time alone in a town, pining for some dude to come back, gives one lots of time to work on their Mezmer game. In the hierarchy of magical prowess, this places her not just above me but in a league that rivals Mael. Before the . . . unpleasantness, anyway. Man, she has really been holding back on what she's capable of.

Your playing small doesn't serve the world, Seph!

With no time to process the enormity of this revelation, I spring into action, positioning myself as a bulwark between her and what is, right now, the world. I lift the Blade of the Starfallen, readying it in my hands. My Heart hammers against my ribcage, not just from the adrenaline of battle but from the weight of the responsibility now resting on my shoulders. Protect Persephone. Protect her at all costs.

She gives me a sharp nod and warns, "I'll have only perhaps a minute before the Spell ends!"

Seems to be the default here. Everything lasts about a damn minute. Speaks very poorly for the concept of intelligent design.

She begins.

Her arms rise and my ears pop as Mezmer, pure and raw, swirls around her, coalescing into a barrier of shimmering light that envelops her form, not unlike Storm from X-Men commanding the elements with a mere gesture. The air around us crackles with energy, the atmosphere charged with her power. Hell, it even smells like ozone up in this piece now. I can feel the force radiating from her, a tangible thing that sends ripples through the virtual fabric of the room.

The barrier around her is a beacon, drawing eyes and, inevitably, aggression. I steel myself, tightening my grip on the Blade. If the barrier is our fortress, then I am its gatekeeper. And I'll be *damned* if I'm letting anything through. And I mean *anything*.

"No, you don't!" I shout at a small chipmunk-looking thing that I stab into a pool of energy with the Blade. "Don't test me, chipmunk!"

As the energetic strength of her influence on the air around us starts to coalesce, I notice something that . . . well . . . that's super flippin' strange.

The emerging figures taking shape and emanating out of the swirl of cosmic glitter aren't the backup, reserve replicas of Persephone I'm expecting. As they gain definition, I note there's something strikingly familiar about them. The curve of the shoulder, the set of the stance, an unmistakable silhouette.

The extra aid she's beckoning, the cavalry she's calling up, the regiment of equipped fighters she's trusting to prevent us being sponged from the planet is . . .

Me.

CHAPTER SIXTY-ONE

What are you doing?" I bellow as I see Moridius now advancing our way, switch-saw in one hand and fireblade in the other.

He's actually doing us *kind* of a favor? In that he's chopping down anyone who stands in between him and us, so, the enemy of my enemy is my friend? I guess?

Persephone doesn't answer. I shout a second question. "Seph?! What's happening?"

Because the figures solidifying in the air above us are, in fact, me. Bruce. Of House Silvert. But, also, they're . . . not. They're me as I've never been; me as I could only dream of being, clad in the legendary armor I have described countless times as Carpathian's own. The armor's intricate details, its mythic contours, wrap around these versions of me in a display of power and promise that's breathtakingly personal.

This isn't just a summoning—it's a revelation. A mirror held up not to show me as I am but as I could be.

And more importantly . . . how she sees me.

The realization dishes me up a plate of awe with a side order of acute vulnerability.

I am the superweapon. *I* am the champion arrayed for battle. Not in the shadows of what was but in the full might of what I can become. It is a weighty declaration of faith, of potential recognized and called forth in the most dramatic of fashions. Here, under the watchful gaze of myriad foes, I'm a legion of Bruces, each donned in the armor that symbolizes ultimate valor and strength. Each a testament to a belief in me that I've scarcely dared hold myself.

A belief in the notion that *I* can be an ideal. *I* can become a symbol of hope clad in the armor of legends. Me. I can.

And I gotta tell you . . . the feeling is pretty awe-inspiring. (Also, *massively* intimidating, but for the most part, kinda awesome.)

As the Brucepathians solidify, the entire venue gasps collectively. The other-worldly warriors hover in the air, an ethereal army ready at Persephone's command. The silence stretches, a taut string ready to snap.

And then . . . it does.

"False prophet!" Moridius screams, letting free a blast from his fireblade. It arcs toward one of the newly formed Brucepathians, rocketing through the eerie stillness almost gleefully.

The Brucepathian raises an armored gauntlet and *BLOCKS* it. The blast, cast with motif d'obliterate, is deflected with a proficiency that causes Moridius to stop his charge and stare with the rest of the madding crowd. Persephone's Spell-work has not only summoned fully corporeal beings into existence but imbued them with a resilience that scoffs at the notion of a single hit taking them down. They're not illusions—they are menace.

Persephone Vizardsdottir, child of Almeister, has achieved something extraordinary: She's outgrown her own lineage. She isn't the Pyreheart or Dreamweave Mezmer seen before on this plane. She is something else, something more.

If I were to place a bet (which I don't really anymore since I developed a little bit of a DraftKings addiction, but if I *did*), my money would be on this being a manifestation of Nexabind Mezmer. Which means that Persephone, in casting these Brucepathians, has revealed herself to be at least a Three-Type Sorcerer.

The Brucepathians spring into action, a blur of movement, poetry, and violence intertwined. They slice, they stab, they punch, they kick. They are a whirlwind of martial prowess that needs no extra Mezmer to underscore its effectiveness. Their flight, the only hint of their mystical origin, allows them to maneuver with a grace that's appalling, each movement an ode to Persephone's skill and intent.

"KILL THE SPELLCASTER!" Moridius commands, and suddenly, Seph and I find ourselves yet again the focal point of a renewed onslaught.

But the Brucepathians, my spectral counterparts, don't falter. If anything, the command serves as a clarion call, galvanizing them into even fiercer action. They move with a synchrony that's uncanny, each one an extension of Persephone's will. Their blocks become more determined, their strikes more precise, a blossoming corsage of combat that unfolds with each passing second.

Three of the Brucepathians race to the dais. For a moment, I think *they're* going to rescue Almeister, but they don't. Perhaps they can't, since they're not me, just representations of me. It's not *their* Quest. It's mine. But they do position themselves as guardians of the cage, preventing any DONG with a notion to get saucy from pressing up on the wizard.

The advancing hoard that sees Persephone as the prime target comes upon us with intentions as clear as the unyielding malice in their eyes. They charge, a mass of anger come to life, attempting to encircle us entirely, pin us in.

I'm torn between fear, something akin to duty, and an overwhelming sense of solidarity with this woman who, with unbelievable confidence, conjured an army of *me* to stand as her ultimate defense. Sure, there's a sea of enemies, each probably more versed in the art of war than I am. Sure, they likely outclass me, given I'm only Etherflint Tier. But then I remember: I'm not just any Bruce, Mordechai, or Harry waiting to be yanked from the clutches of a dragon. My physical stats are at Ironspark, and in my hand I wield the Blade of the goddamn Starfallen.

So let's pull up your knickers, butterbean, and get to wilding the hell out.

In a scene that calls back to battling the Shadowscorpions, enemies who attempt to breach our makeshift perimeter meet the righteous, steadfast edge of the Blade. And as the enemies press in, a need fuels my movements to prove not only to this room full of assholes but to myself that I am *not the one* to be jerking around. The Blade of the Starfallen sings with each contact, abolishing darkness and turning it into light, its edge a harbinger of doom for those foolish enough to think me an easy target.

Awkwardness gives way to a fluidity of motion that surprises me. It's as if the very essence of combat has seeped into my bones, guiding my movements with an intuition. Strikes I would have hesitated over are starting to flow naturally, the

Blade a concentrated ball of pure, unthinking will. I dodge Mezmeric blasts with fluid grace, the occasional hit absorbed, but not enough to deter my momentum.

I'm saying I'm coming correct with the chop-chop.

Still, some dumb goons manage to close in on Persephone, their Spells targeting the orb of light that cocoons her.

CRACK!

CRACK!

CRACK!

Each attack against it sends ripples of further panic through me, as the orb's shell of protection is threatening to crack like a dinosaur egg. (Which I say because it's big, not because I presume to know how, exactly, dinosaur eggs are cracked.)

Since, unlike the Brucepathians and complementary extra Persephones, the Blade of the Starfallen is but one of one, I also start unleashing Toxin Darts with Sharpshooter accuracy, their targets collapsing even as I engage the next threat. The Blade continues dancing in my other hand, a striking viper made of steel that finds its mark again and again.

The pandemonium is all-encompassing. With each passing moment, I lean further afield, the Blade of the Starfallen carving a path through those who would see us undone.

That's when a peculiar sensation begins to overtake me. It's as if I'm not alone in my own body, as if there's another presence. This otherness, this spectral co-pilot, doesn't give me a sense of being *extra* but of having an incompleteness to it, like I'm only half the man I used to be and there's a shadow hanging over me. I'm both participant and spectator, caught in the throes of violence yet somehow detached, observing through a lens that isn't entirely my own.

One of the owls catches my eye. One of the icons of power that embellish the space. And I have this immense feeling, quite unexpectedly, that . . . everything is, indeed, going to be alright. It's like a glance through a keyhole into the future that shows me a green field, a flowing waterfall, and a world at peace.

"*I told you everything was going to be alright, Bruce.*"

"*Who is that? Who are you who keeps invading my thoughts? Tell me who you are!*"

Rather than an answer, I am instead responded to by an attack that slices through the din. An icy blade, billowing with frozen vapor, aimed with lethal precision at Persephone's flickering Mezmer shell.

Yolanda. Mouth twisted in rage and pain, her Frostheart-conjured weapon a glacial-silver flash of intent aimed directly at Persephone.

Instincts now fueled by my dual consciousness propel me forward, my Blade clashing with hers. I expect the power and force of the Blade of the Starfallen to simply diffuse her weapon into a burst of confetti, but instead, our swords meet with a juddering *CLANG* that sings of old grudges. And new.

Yolanda presses the attack and, well, she is *strong*. Like, appreciably stronger than she should be. Like Moridius, she is clearly the beneficiary of being one of the Super Vizier's favorites, with the attendant Mezmer boost that affords.

As her formidable strength presses against mine, the clash of our blades a jazzy, upbeat love song to her power, the unthinkable happens. The Blade of the Starfallen, though unbreakable, is forced back by the sheer might of her continued assault, and in a heart-stopping moment, it grazes Persephone's protective Mezmer shield. The contact, slight as it may be, is enough. The shield bursts like a soap bubble under a child's finger, leaving Persephone exposed, the Mezmer that cocooned her dissipating into the air with a sigh of light.

"NOW!" Moridius screams, indicating to all the Templars (and, I suppose, anyone else who wants to get in on the action) that Persephone is exposed.

The sudden breach throws me off-balance, my stance crumbling, and I stagger backward. Yolanda, the predator, sensing her moment, leaps at me, vapor-trailing blade arcing through the air, aiming to end this in one decisive blow.

Then, in the blink of an eye, everything shifts.

Time stretches, elongating, and I find myself ensnared in a slow-motion scape, the world around me looking like a living fresco of the Rubens painting *The Fall of the Damned*.

ZZZZZZZZZZWWWWWAAAAAHHHHHMMMMM.

I've activated Control.

I didn't think about it; instinct took over. And in this dilated slice of reality, something extraordinary unfolds. With the slow-motion disintegration of her shield, a cascade of Pyreheart energy begins unraveling around Persephone, painting the air with strokes of fire waiting to be reclaimed. Persephone's Pyreheart Mezmer, woven from the same fabric as my own Affinity for Elemist Mezmer, becomes visible to me in a way it hasn't before.

My Synchron Foundation, until now a potential only barely tapped, surges to the forefront.

Driven by a reaction that bypasses thought, I reach for that dissipating energy, the Pyreheart Mezmer calling to the very core of my being. My hands, my Heart (actual and metaphorical), my very soul extends, grasping at the flames that dance on the edge of perception, pulling them toward me with a desperation born of necessity.

Control has already saved me more times than I can count. Now, it merges with this newfound connection to the Pyreheart Mezmer. My Blade of the Starfallen (and right now, it is *very* much mine) becomes a conduit, a focal point for this torrent of elemental fury I'm barely beginning to understand.

I move swifter than the world around me, navigating past the protracted stillness like a thief in the night scampering free as the world sleeps, and I'm in front of Yolanda, my Blade coming down to parry the Templar's lethal strike, when . . .

The Blade of the Starfallen erupts in flames.

SHWOOOOOOOOOOOOOOOOOMMMMMPPP.

The sparking of the Blade appears to cause Control to cease as the sword becomes a brilliant, roaring inferno that transforms it into a swirling pillar of "Oh girl, you done messed up now." Fire encases the steel, and Yolanda, caught off guard by this sudden blaze staring her right in her face, falters, eyes widening.

I lunge. She throws up a parry, and our blades clash with a spark. She's quick, ducking under my swing, her counter slicing through the air just inches from my face. I can feel the whoosh as it narrowly avoids giving me an unrequested rhinoplasty. I retaliate with a rapid succession of jabs, but she weaves through each attempted strike.

There is no way she's *just* a Templar. My previous impression of her as a charming, slow-of-wit Snug the Joiner–like figure has been disabused like a mother scratcher. She's something else. Or, at the least, she has been grown into something else by the forces at play.

And, as if bolstered by my realization, with another comingled strike, twist, and shove, the unthinkable happens: She sends the Blade of the Starfallen flying from my grip and knocks me to the ground.

The sword spins, end over end, away from me, a fiery missile landing on top of the bench where the fat magistrate sat moments ago—the bench adjacent to where Almeister remains trapped in his cage—and, as we learned in the Cavern of Sorrows, since shit here defies the laws of geology as I have previously understood them . . . it *lights the massive theatre of the absurd aflame.*

WHOOOOOOSHHH!

The entire back wall of the place turns into a scene out of Dante's Inferno like it was nothing more than accelerant-doused tissue paper. (Meridia is an extremely flammable world.)

"Jesus!" I roll out of the way as Yolanda's sword crashes down, and when I circle around, this is what I see:

1. Yolanda, rearing back to land a killing strike.

2. Moridius, aiming his switchsaw at Persephone.

3. A collection of Pumpkin Heads and Dwarves, Ishilden, Squee Ballers, RyderDies, Elves, Templars, Who-the-hell-ever else, crowding around Almeister's cage, fighting to get past the trio of Brucepathians trying to protect it.

4. Brucepathians and Secondary Persephones being torn asunder by the Mezmer of the wizards of the High Council.

And all of this playing out against a backdrop of conflagrating brimstone that appears to be spreading in slow motion.

To be clear: Control is not active. It appears to have been malfunctioned by the inflaming of the Blade. But still, all seems slow to me. Which, y'know, is a thing that I hear happens to a person right before they're about to die, so . . . that tracks.

For a moment, lying here on the ground, I swear all I can hear are echoes of rats scrabbling over my tiny body in the dark. In bitter contrast to the feeling of invulnerability I had just moments ago, I now feel completely without power—but not in a helpless way; in an accepting way. In an understanding way. In the way that Carpathian likely felt at the end of the final book. In a way that says, "*You can stop fighting now. It's okay. Rest.*"

It's the look I saw in Mom's eyes before I was hurried out of the hospital room. I only glimpsed it for a second, but I saw it. Acquiescence at the end of a long-suffered fight. It made me sad, but in some way, it also made me feel relieved. For her. Because she was fighting a battle she was never going to win and had become okay with it.

The only thing that's bumming me out is that I wish I had answers to the many questions that want explanations. *How did I get here? Why am I here? Where is here? Who is the Ninth Guardian? Did they do this to me? Why have they done this to me? Tavrella . . .*

So, with few cards left to play and only one chip left in my pile, I decide to just throw it in. Toss out the only question I think I actually have a chance of getting an answer to.

I send a Message to the last member of my Heart Guard who can respond.

"Perg? Things aren't great here. You should run if you can. Where are you?"

And just before Yolanda's blade meets my skull, Moridius's switchsaw sends a blast through the real Persephone this time, and the blood-lusting horde does away with what remains of what was once known as the Rebellion, Meridia's last hope, I get a response.

"We're right here, big homie."

KA-BOOOOOOOOOOOM!

"EIIIIINNNNNZZZGGGEEEEEAAARRRRR!"

CHAPTER SIXTY-TWO

"E*IIIIINNNNNZZZGGGEEEEEAAARRRRR!*" the beckoning call of Waslan shouts a second time as the beast tears into the room. But it doesn't sound the way it did before, like it did when it was beckoning Einzgear. It's more like it's using the word as a clarion call, a shout of rebellion, of liberation.

It barrels into the space behind Perg, who is currently in his largest, Garr Haven size. Maybe even bigger. The crack in his shell he suffered breaking down the door to the missing Nexus Core looks like a crag in the side of a boulder, but it hasn't stopped him from demolishing the entrance to the courtroom and creating a thirty-foot-wide opening leading to the corridor beyond. A hazy light shines into the space from a window in the hallway.

Dawn, it would appear, has arrived.

"How ya like me now, motherfuckers?!" Brittany shouts from her place atop the Ronine's back. The lion section. She rides upon it, cape flowing behind her, looking like a deathcore Joan of Arc or some damn thing.

"Zimmi, bredda an sistah! Ya gun try send Jameson 'way like de lamb? But me come back ridin' de lion, now as a god, ya know!" Jameson stands atop Waslan's head, fresh metal rod in hand, looking like he's feeling much better.

And behind this confederacy of chaos . . . Rapprentices.

And I mean, *Rapprentices*. Thousands upon thousands of them. *Thousands*. They stampede into the room and immediately begin attacking . . . well, everyone. Every living thing they see, they are on top of and all over and up into.

It wasn't an echo from my past that I heard. It was a pandemonium of unanticipated allies torpedoing their way to my aid. Well, that's a hell of a thing, isn't it?

General mayhem ensues, with all the screaming and horror one might expect, but my eyes remain focused on Yolanda and Moridius, both of whom . . . turn tail and run, Moridius actually carving through anyone in his way with both blade and switchsaw. And I mean *anyone*, Templars included. He and Yolanda make their way to the door through which the Super Vizier exited earlier.

I leap to my feet, braving the various pockets of flame engorging the courtroom to reach the Blade of the Starfallen.

"Carpathian!" Persephone cries out. "Father!"

I see that the inferno is reaching his cell. The three Brucepathians are using whatever they have possession of to keep the fire from consuming the cage, but their function is at least partially controlled by Seph's own dominion over them, and now that her bond is severed, so too is their aptitude for aid. The best they seem to be able to do is drape their bodies over the enclosure in an attempt to allow the fire to burn *them* alive before it reaches Almeister.

Shadrach, Meshach, Abednego. Shadrach, Meshach, Abednego.

In the biblical story, the three young men were saved by a fourth man seen walking around in the fiery furnace. A man no one expected. A savior.

I grab the Blade, leap above a gout of fire to reach the dais, *SLAM* down on the Mezmerated chains with the torch Blade, and they burst open, freeing Almeister and sparing the versions of me from having to self-sacrifice.

Today, at least.

I experience a brief quiet that violates logic as each of the three Brucepathians regard me with looks of approval, gentle nods, and then . . .

They disappear. Just evaporate and go back to wherever Persephone summoned them from.

Meanwhile, Rapprentices tear flesh and create havoc; Waslan spins its tail, bares its teeth, and does all it can to keep Brittany and Jameson safe; for her part, Brit lashes out with Randolf's Radiant Ray *and* the Stoneheart gloves *at the same time*, sending radiant rock flying like fireballs. Which, of course, further accelerates the now quickly spreading conflagration, tornadoing up anyone on the receiving end of that *biiiiig* magic like their names are Dorothy and Toto. Those who manage to dodge Triple-R Stonefire wind up catching a good, old-fashioned buck-a-buck to the dome from Jameson's boom stick. And Perg just stomps around, Godzilla-ing fools as the fire spreads, breaking through the ceiling and the floor and spreading to other levels of the Tower.

I scoop Almeister in my arms and race him over to Seph. "Take him! Get him out of here! Now!" I place him in her embrace, watch for a second as the love for her father and her relief at seeing him returned to her company washes over her, and then start off in the direction the Super Vizier fled.

"Where are you going?"

"I'll find you!"

"But—"

"Just go! All of you, go!" I poke hard at my chest, indicating my Heart. "I'll find you!"

I turn my back on my Party and run straight through a curtain of purple fire and out the door, which leads to stairs. Stairs that appear to only go up. Which is irritating, but whatcha gonna do?

The stairwell is filled with smoke and—as it would appear that one of the things on Meridia that operates as it does on Earth is that smoke rises—it looks like I'm going to be breathing in that good old monoxide all along my climb.

I bound up the first set of stairs, initially taking the levels an entire flight at a time, but the higher I go, the harder it gets. Perhaps because I'm giving myself magical black lung, but I suspect it also has to do with the fact that the farther up I get, the less I have access to my full complement of Mezmer. By the time I get to a plateau that has a door marked "Management," I can barely breathe.

This has to be it. The sign above the door looks exactly like the sign above my old supervisor's office in St. Louis.

I grab the handle and struggle to pull it open. Once through, I become dizzy. And not just because I'm massively oxygen depleted, but because I have stepped back in time. Back to when I worked for St. Louis Transit. The layout, the furniture, the drab paint job . . . it's all as I remember.

I stagger forward, hoping that they're still here. That the Super Vizier and Moridius haven't run off yet. That they came back here for some reason.

I stumble past empty desks, papers scattered everywhere, and toward the office marked "Super Vizier."

Jackpot. She's in there; I see her through the glass. She appears to be . . . shredding something. Getting rid of . . . I can't even imagine. But I don't know that I give a shit.

The fire from the Blade has gone out, also Mezmer depleted, but it's still a big damn frickin' sword, so I draw in as much breath as my constricted lungs can handle, and I kick the door in.

Sort of.

It's glass, so my foot just kind of shatters it. Fortunately, I'm wearing the old-school Templar garb, which does a decent job of protecting my skin, Mezmer or no.

"Look at me!" I command of her, stepping into her office.

The Super Vizier doesn't really react. She just finishes the last of her paper shredding, turns slowly, sees me, shakes her head slightly, and says, "Why, oh why, won't you just die?"

"You'd be surprised how much I hear that."

She laughs slightly, steps to her desk, sits down, and gestures for me to take a seat as well. I don't. I remain still, watching her as black smoke rises from below, encircling her.

"So. What can I do for you?"

"What did you do with it?" I ask.

She presses her lips together, looking perplexed. "Do with what?"

"Don't, okay? Just . . . don't act all . . . the way you're acting. The Nexus Core. What did you do with the Nexus Core?"

". . . I don't know what you mean."

I step forward, slamming the Blade down on her desk, hard, causing papers to fly everywhere. "Don't lie to me!" She remains unmoved, listening. "Teleri. Teleri Nightwind. You know, 'the brains of the operation'? She says she found where you keep it but that it's gone. Where is it?"

She stares at me, squints her eyes, and says, "How would she have found where we keep it?"

". . . What?"

She chuckles lightly to herself like I'm a silly little kid who amuses her. "You think we would keep the greatest source of power on the planet in a place where everyone would think to look for it? The Tower? The most obvious physical structure on Meridia? Do you think we're that oblivious?"

No. No, I think you'd keep it here because that's where I wrote that it was.

"Um . . ."

"*I* don't even know where the Nexus Core is. There's only one person who knows."

She lets it hang in the air, almost tempting me to say, "The Ninth Guardian," as though I'm in some poorly written, overly script-polished action flick that condescends to its audience by feeling the need to spoon-feed them every little thing.

But . . . because I'm *not* saying it, now I wonder if that is, in fact, who she means.

So . . . I . . .

Goddammit.

"You mean the Ninth Guardian, right? That's who you're talking about? The Ninth Guardian? The Ninth Guardian is the one who knows where it is? The Ninth Guardian?"

She shakes her head a little, like she's tired.

"May I ask you a question, Einzgear?"

The billowing smoke is completely enveloping the floor now.

"Sure, why not? We have time."

"Why?"

"Why what?"

"Why do you fight so hard? Why do you care so much?"

I consider the question. If I'm being brutally honest with myself, it's a good one.

I set my jaw and offer the best answer I can come up with. (That I also happen to believe.) "Because. Because . . . life is hard. You and the Ninth Guardian and all of you have *made* life hard. And people . . . they need hope. They need to be able to believe in something. Something that takes away the feelings of despair they have when they look out their windows at the world you've created. They need to hold on to the promise that a better world exists. One that they can aspire to. Be a part of. And they've put their trust in me to deliver on that promise, so I owe it to them to not give up."

She looks like she just got sleepy.

"Aw. That's sweet. But it's incredibly naive."

She stands, crosses around her desk to position herself before me, and moves the Blade aside with her hand as if she hasn't a worry in the universe.

"They don't care about *you.* They don't *know* you. If you were no longer here, they'd . . . They'd find someone else to give them *hope.* Look how quickly so many of them have already turned away from you and given over to this wild Brucillian fantasy. They don't care about 'Carpathian Einzgear.' They just harbor some childlike belief that there's actually a mystical 'saviour' out there who will come and rescue them from their dismal realities. There isn't."

She smiles. *Taking something good and turning it into an object of despair.*

"There is no Saviour. Not really. You know that as well as I do. It's a costume you've agreed to wear, but at the end of the day, it's a fiction. All of this"—she sweeps her arm around the room—"is a fiction. So, again I ask, why do you fight so hard?"

I stare at her because . . . because I don't know if she knows the full scope of what she's implying or if it's just coincidence. Either way, it's got me a little off-balance.

She shakes her head sadly, slowly. "You could've been done with it. You made a good decision. Before. When you gave in. Quit. You could've just let it go and drifted away into the quiet solitude of evermore. But you *had* to come back. And now, look what you've done."

I am resisting the urge to fall into the chair because she has definitely knee-capped me.

It's getting brutally hot, fire creeping into the corners of the room, lapping at the walls.

We face one another, her smirking, me attempting not to blink first. (Which I mean in a completely metaphorical way, since I'm blinking five times a second to try and keep the smoldering air from burning my eyes.)

"I have a proposition for you," she whispers so that I have to strain above the crackle of the literal Towering inferno. "Join us."

I stop myself from saying, "What?" choosing instead to just think it real hard.

"It would be so much easier," she says. "Don't you remember? When you were a simple conveyance conductor? How worry-free life was? It could be that way again. The weight you carry now, the burdens you shoulder—all gone. And, not to reduce it to basic arithmetic, but we do have a new benefits pack-age that I think—"

"ENOUGH!" I bellow, slamming the Blade down close to her a second time. As before, she doesn't react. "Who. Is. The. Ninth. Guardian?"

Her chest rises and falls on a heavy sigh. Breathing in the acrid smoke doesn't seem to bother her in the least; it appears as though she enjoys it. "You're asking the wrong question."

I concentrate my focus. "Then what's the right question?"

"The right question to ask is not *who* the Guardian is, but *why* they are."

Before I can press the matter further, the Super Vizier dashes to the side, away from me. At first, I think it's to attempt an escape, but then I realize it's so she can avoid the sharp steel that is protruding from my stomach. Or, possibly, the *other* sharp steel protruding from my chest.

SHINK. SHINK.

Both swords retract, and I turn to find Moridius Wreathnestle and Yolanda Honeybunny looking at me, their blades drenched red with my blood.

"That's for Draven," Yolanda says dispassionately.

"And for Charlemond," Moridius offers, adding, "Technically a second time, I suppose."

I fall back onto the Super Vizier's desk, still clutching the Blade. She moves to join the two, and all three of them stare at me.

"*Last* time," the Super Vizier suggests to Moridius. "The *last* time you shall have to do it. There is no Mezmer here that can revive him, no allies who can whisper mystic, ancient incantations," she says in a cynical, mocking tone. "This will be his final resting place, as it should have been all along, I suspect."

There's a moment of thick solemnity before her tenor changes and she says, "Anyhoo! Yolanda, excellent work. Your bonus this year shall reflect your commitment to seeing your tasks through to completion."

"Thank you, Mistress."

"Moridius, grab the Blade of the Starfallen and let's be on our way. For all his failures, he has managed to wreck the Tower. Let's be generous and allow him his final moment to at least bask in the achievement of that."

My grip tightens around the hilt as Moridius steps to fetch it from me, but before he can . . .

CRASH! BOOM! BOOM!

For a moment, I think it's maybe Brittany using the Stoneheart Gloves to throw up a barrier between us, but then I recognize it as more flames exploding from the floor.

"Alright, fine," the Super Vizier says, exasperated. "Let's just go, then."

She takes a breath as if she's going to add one last pointed, too-clever-by-half thing to me, but then she just groans. And with that, Yolanda, Moridius, and the Super Vizier dash off, leaving me to my end.

Well . . .

I guess this is it. I'm out of moves. No sense in fighting it. I hope the rest of the team was able to get Almeister to safety. I'm glad Persephone got her dad back. That's nice. I hope Brit and Perg are able to find the rest of the Heart Guard— Zerastian, Xanaraxa—and, obviously, help Mael bring Lonnaigh back. Eh. That'll be able to happen. I feel sure of it.

"*Bruce?*" I call for the voice in my head. "*Bruce? You there? Hello?*"

No answer. That's a bummer. Nobody wants to die alone, but, y'know, we don't always get what we want, so . . .

"Bruce?"

Huh?

The voice doesn't sound like the one inside my head. It doesn't sound like it's coming from inside my head at all. It sounds like it's coming from . . . the doorway.

"Bruce? Are you okay?"

Who is that? I know this voice, but it can't be. Unless it is . . .

And then I smell it.

Lilac.

The soft, delicate fragrance somehow penetrating the odor of burning Tower and, more distractingly, the burning flesh of those still trapped inside.

I try to lift my head to see, but it hurts too much, so I remain flat on my back on the desk, staring at the ceiling, until finally a face appears above, looking down at me, smiling.

Mom.

She looks like she's coming in from the garden. The garden she took such good care of that, sadly, dried up and went fallow after she died and there was no one left to care for it.

She's wearing her sun hat and her gardening gloves. She pulls the gloves off, puts them in her pocket, and then sits casually on the desk next to me.

"Mom?"

She strokes my sweat-soaked hair.

"Shh. I'm here, honey. Oof. Looks like you got a little cut there, sweetie."

"Yeah. Yeah. Little bit."

"Oh, babe. I wish I had a Freezer Pop for you, but I'm fresh out."

"That's okay," I tell her. "It's just nice to see you."

"It's nice to see you too, baby."

CRASH! CRASH! BOOM!

"Mom, you shouldn't be here. It's dangerous."

"Oh, come on; it's not gonna bother me. But you should get out of here while you still can."

"I . . . I don't know if I can. I'm not sure my legs work."

"Of course they do. Bruce, you're the most resilient person I've ever known."

"I am?"

"Absolutely. Look at all you've managed to accomplish even when you had things stacked against you that would cause most people to just give up. You're not a quitter."

I start to cry. "I dunno, Mom. I think maybe I might be."

"Bruce Thomas Silvert, you are not, and I will not let someone talk about my son that way."

I laugh a little through my tears. It hurts. In all the ways.

There's a moment of silence as the Tower continues falling around us and Mom continues stroking my head. Finally, she says, "Let me ask you this, and then I won't bother you about it anymore."

". . . Okay."

"Has it been worth it? If it hasn't . . . well, then I guess, do whatever you want. But if it *has* . . . then you really need to keep going."

I think about it for a second; not in a specific way. Just let the idea swirl as the world melts around me. Then . . .

"Can you help me up?" I ask her.

"Sorry, sweetie. I wish I could. But you're gonna have to get up on your own. You can. You've done it hundreds of times."

I swallow. Take in her words. ". . . Yeah. Okay, Mom."

". . . Okay."

She moves her hand away from my head and I grunt, hard, as I force myself into a sitting position. I have no idea how I'm alive. I really don't. No Spells, no Abilities, and two sword wounds in my torso. This shit seems impossible, yet . . . here I am. Sitting up.

I slide off the desk, working hard to stay on my feet.

"How do I get out?" I ask.

"It's a great question. I think—and I'm sorry to be the bearer of bad news—but I think *that's* likely your best bet."

She points at a window that's been blown out by the fire, suns shining through.

"The window? But, Mom . . . If this doesn't kill me"—I point at the gashes in my body—"the fall definitely will."

She shrugs. "Maybe. Maybe not. Who can say? I think you just have to . . . trust the System. I know; it sucks."

I nod. "Will I see you again?"

"I mean, I don't make the rules, but I'd be willing to bet on it. *You* shouldn't—not with your DraftKings problem. But I would."

I want to give her a hug, a kiss on the cheek, something. But, somehow, I know that's not possible, so I just make my way to the window and pull myself up to stand on the sill.

I look back to say goodbye, and when I do, I see that . . .

She isn't alone.

Tavrella is with her.

They stand side by side, holding hands.

I lift my hand to them in a goodbye, and they raise their free hands in return.

They wink in unison, smile. I smile back.

Then, I turn away, stare long and hard into the face of a new morning rising on Meridia . . .

And jump.

CHAPTER SIXTY-THREE

Seasons of Rebellion, Riftbreaker Book One, Chapter One

As the suns rose high above the plains of the world known as Meridia, Carpathian Einzgear, a young public conveyance conductor for the city of Santus Luminous, sat behind the wheel of his assigned vehicle, allowing on his usual cadre of morning passengers. He said hello to each guest boarding the vehicle, and they said hello back. Everyone always felt happy in the company of the young man. He was a hard fellow to dislike.

And it had been a good start to the day for the smiling, cheerful, generally unbothered Einzgear. He had woken early, feeling hopeful about the day to come. He could not point to a specific reason why he felt thus. He just knew that something about this day felt . . . right.

Perhaps it was that the owner of the corner shoppe where Carpathian purchased his daily body fuel had given him a free puff pastry this morning. Or perhaps it was that he had heard big announcements were coming from within the Office of Public Conveyance; he was hoping for a grand bonus this year. Or perhaps it was simply that he did not typically allow himself to dwell on that which some might otherwise find irksome.

In truth, it was ever the latter, a condition in him borne of necessity and fostered over many years. However, unbeknownst to him, that was all set to change.

As the final passenger settled in their seat, Carpathian pulled away from the stop, only to glance in the rearview mirror and see someone running to catch up. A man. An old man, by the looks of him. An old wizard, to be precise.

Carpathian had not seen the wizard before. He was not one of the usual attendants on this route so far as Carpathian could remember.

The conveyance conductor knew the policy. Stopping for passengers once the conveyance had resumed motion was forbidden. He had been reprimanded on more than one occasion for the infraction.

But . . .

He could not help himself. The poor fellow seemed to be struggling and, despite a small voice in his head telling him not to . . . Carpathian stopped. Not only did he stop—he backed up slightly to provide room for the old gentleman to board.

Opening the doors, the elderly wizard stepped up, using his staff to assist himself, and said, "Thank you. Thank you. It was most important that I catch the right bus."

"The right bus?" Carpathian asked.

"Yes, yes," the old man replied. "Yes. The right bus."

"I see. And this is it? You're sure this is the right one?"

The wizard looked at the conveyance conductor with a gleam in his eye and said, "It is. It is, indeed . . ."

CHAPTER SIXTY-FOUR

SHIT! OW!"

So . . . here's something funny. The Drakonar statue mounted on the side of the Tower as would be a gargoyle on Earth isn't actually the thing that has stopped me falling. It definitely *slowed* me down, but it's actually one of the bridges that connects the part of the Tower I leapt from to another section of Tower that's just about completely draped in flames that has *stopped* me.

Feels like a real fifty-fifty call on whether or not this is a good thing. Plus side? I fell a hell of a lot less than if I'd made it all the way to the ground. Negative side? I'm still stuck on a burning tower, sporting two major stab wounds and— I'm relatively certain—however many broken bones a person can have. There are normally two hundred and six bones in the human body (thanks, Discovery Science), so I'm guessing that the fractures I've just suffered have doubled or tripled that number? Assuming you can count bone *fragments* as bones.

My mesh suit is ripped to shreds. I'm absolutely busted to bits. I feel like I probably look like Tobey Maguire after the Green Goblin fight.

Oh, god, oh, it hurts. Oh, man, I do so wish I could use Mezmer. What's the old saying? I'd rather have Marrowmancy and not need it than need a full-body transfusion?

Thump-thump. Thump-thump.

Oh, dammit, and now my Heart is pumping again, which means that the blood flowing out of me is probably just gonna flow faster and—

Wait. My Heart is pumping again? My Heart is pumping again!

Am I close enough to Meridia's surface that things are functional once more?

Yes! You are! You are back online, you survivor, you! Of course, as you already know, you are in an absolute wreck of a state. But! There is some very exciting news to share. Please stand by (or lie there in agony) while that information processes.
{COURTESY MESSAGE #27}

Exciting news? What exciting—

Congratulations!
Quest: "Rescue Almeister from Imprisonment in the Tower of Zuria."
[COMPLETE]

You have successfully completed a very difficult Quest indeed! And! You destroyed a tower in the process! A whole tower. And you

managed all this while losing only [One] of your number! Huzzah! Upgrades and Verifications available upon your next visit to a Pulse Well. And one has to imagine they're going to be baller. As you might say. (Side Note: To make it to a Pulse Well, you should use Marrowmancy. And quick.) [COURTESY MESSAGE #28}

Losing one of my number. Losing *one* . . . of my number. Feels like I lost a whole lot more than that. But, if I don't want to lose a whole lot more still, I need to try and heal my body at least. That I can try and do now.

As for everything else, well, as Tavrella said: Some wounds just take time.

I groan in discomfort and concentrate as much as my mind will allow to invoke the Marrowmancy Spell. A sudden acute pain sears through me, far more intense than I anticipated. And then, something really nifty happens: Unlike my healing in the Pulse Well, which felt magical and euphoric, the pain morphs into something even more bizarre and terrifying.

My bones don't just ache—they feel like they're shifting, realigning . . . draining? It's like the very essence of my skeletal structure is being siphoned off.

Then, it happens.

From the gashes and punctures, tendrils of dark, dark red and yellow ooze out, the color of bone marrow mingling with the early-morning light. Kind of beautiful, in a grotesquely fascinating way. The ribbons snake around my wounds with a life of their own, like that scene in *Akira* when Tesuo tries to control his powers and instead starts morphing. Except this isn't an award-winning 1980s anime; it's alarmingly real and happening in my own flesh.

(Where are the butterflies?! Where are the goddamn butterflies?)

The tendrils writhe and twist, growing out of my body, weaving over and under each other in a dance of healing and horror. My skin is knitting back together, and for every moment I'm able to keep my focus, the Spell continues its grim work.

Sharp spikes of pain punctuate the process, each followed by a wave of relief so profound it's almost cruel. Bones snap back into alignment, cobbling themselves together with a sound both sickening and satisfying. My dermis, torn and ragged moments before, renews under the ministrations of these helpful yet macabre little tendrils.

When the ordeal is finally over, the tendrils consolidate and retreat, slipping through the pores. It's like watching a knot of snakes withdraw into the sand.

I push myself to my feet, take a step, and—

CRAAAAAAAAAAACK! BOOOOOOOOM!

Okay, so that part of the bridge is gone. Not great.

Not a lot of real estate left to hold me up here. I wonder if . . .

It's still a long way down. I wonder if I jumped again, maybe I could just Marrowmancy myself back together when I hit the ground?

"I dunno. I wouldn't do that, Bruce."

"Bruce?! Is that you?! I thought you were gone."

"No. No, I'm still here. I just needed a break. Things got pretty intense."

"Yeah. So next time, maybe gimme a heads up before you bail, 'kay?"

"Will do, Bruce. I will. My bad."

"So, you don't think I should jump?"

"I mean, you could. It'd probably be fine? But wouldn't it be easier to just hitch a ride on that Tentasaurian?"

"What Tentasaurian?"

"The Tentasaurian flying right at you."

I look to the side and— Holy shit, there's a Tentasaurian flying right at me.

It comes directly next to my tiny remaining section of bridge and stops in front of my face. And then . . . it speaks. Sort of. I actually hear it in my mind. Its voice is . . . Well, it sounds a lot like you'd expect a Tentasaurian to sound, I guess.

"Bruce?"

"Uh . . . yeah?"

"It's me. It's Brittany."

"Brit? How—?"

"Seems like this is a thing I can do now. Summon 'em and communicate through 'em or something. Whatever. Point is, you can hear me?"

"Yeah, I can hear you. Where are you?"

"We're in Sheila. She was being a real asshole about letting us drive without you, but Persephone sweet-talked her into it. We're bringing Almeister back to Bell's View."

"How's he doing?"

"Pretty fucked up. How about you? Did you find the Super Vizier? Figure out what happened to the Core?"

"Yes and no. It's a . . . It's a story; I'll tell you when we meet up. Lemme figure out how to get out of here and—"

"Jump on."

". . . What?"

"Jump on. That's why I sent Carol for you."

"Carol? This is Carol?"

The Tentasaurian flaps a wing at me in salutation.

"Yeah. Get on board."

"Seriously?"

"Yes. Seriously. Why?"

"I dunno. Just feels kinda . . ."

"Kinda what?"

"Derivative."

"Of what?"

"I mean, LOTR. *Thrones.* Um . . . *How to Train Your Dragon* . . ."

"Bro, fuck derivative. Get on Carol and get back to Bell's View so we can figure out what the hell we do now."

". . . Yeah. Okay."

Carol the Tentasaurian turns her body so I can climb onto her back, which I do *just* as the bridge upon which I'm standing gives way and crumbles like part of a glacier breaking off and collapsing into the sea.

Before we head back to Bell's View, Carol aids the Tower's final downfall along by spewing a streaming torrent of fire from within her belly onto the remaining structure, further expediting the demise of the once oppressive monument to avarice and control.

As the last remnants of the fortification give way and it dissolves from the sky with one final screaming attempt at maintaining its integrity, I look to the ground below and see throngs of citizens staring up at the sky, pointing at me as Carol and I fly away into the morning suns.

Carol deposits me close to Persephone's workshop and then is off into the sky again. It was an unexpectedly smooth trip over. I have to remember to give her five stars.

I look around to make sure the coast is clear. I don't see any possible threats, but I don't suppose I will. Something that occurs to me is that, with the Tower destroyed, the Super Vizier, the Ninth Guardian, DONG, et al. will need to establish a new base of operations. Santus Luminous may no longer be the primary seat of power in Meridia. The great, wide world that is this planet is a thing that I am going to have to explore in its fullness if I am to continue my goal of bringing down the Guardian.

Is that my goal? Bringing down the Guardian? I thought my goal was just to figure out how to get home.

"*These things are not mutually exclusive, Bruce.*"

"*Yeah, I know, Bruce. But . . .*"

Screw it. Not today. That's a tortured conversation with myself I can have another Lunar Rotation.

I trot to the workshop and find Waslan sitting outside the door, keeping watch.

I look at the Ronine. It looks back. I lift my chin. "Hey." The beast nods. "I'm gonna just . . ." I point at the door, and it steps aside, granting me access. I nod in appreciation and move past, politely but cautiously. Because here's the thing: I'm glad we're cool now . . . but it's still half a rat. And let's be honest—that's kinda creepy.

Anyway, I open the door, knocking as I do, because you never know. Someone might be getting out of the shower.

Inside, I find Perg in his miniature pony format and Jameson mid-conversation. Jameson is offering his spliff to Perg, who appears to be declining.

"It not bad ting. It open ya mind, ya hear me now."

"A week ago, I sat in an aquarium eating *estúpidos* eggshells and sleeping. Now I can get big, get small, talk and shit. How much more open does my mind need to be, fool?"

"Hey," I greet.

"Yo, big homie. What up, fool? How you doing? What's the update?"

"Um . . . a lot. We should have a group chat. Like, an actual one. Talk things out. Hit a Pulse Well. See what's what. Y'know."

"Word."

"Your shell?"

"It's okay. When we grabbed Sheila, we hit up the alchemist's shoppe and scooped a bunch of stuff, including shell-repair paste or whatever. I suppose it's *technically* stealing, since the shoppe keeper wasn't there, but the door was open, so—"

"Great," I cut him off.

There's a beat before he adds, "So . . . Tavrella . . . She . . . ?"

"Where are the others?"

". . . They're in the back."

I nod. Look to Jameson. "And you're good?"

"Yes, me Saviour. Teleri, she done use dem ray on me, ya hear."

"Ray? Randolf's Radiant Ray?"

"Dem de one. She done cauterize me body, me spirit, proper up, nah."

"She . . . *healed you* . . . using Randolf's Radiant Ray?"

"Ya nah hear me just say dat very ting?"

". . . Okay."

I have questions, but I can't continue indulging a deep dive into every new revelation I have. It's what I want to do. It's what I know to do. It's what I have done in my life. Allow my thoughts to amble and naval-gaze and wander down paths of wonder for no other reason than it kept me from having to confront certain realities. But it's a luxury I can no longer indulge.

Because Meridia is dangerous. Meridia is impatient. And Meridia is my reality.

I step into the back where I find Seph and Brit sitting next to a bed upon which rests the sleeping body of one Almeister T. Wizard.

"Hey."

Seph and Brit's heads snap my way.

"Carpathian! How are—?" Seph starts to ask, but I put up a hand to stop her.

"I'm fine. How's he? Doing any better?"

"Physically, he is weak. But I believe he will be able to return to form soon enough," Brit answers. Surprisingly. Because that's not how Brit tends to talk. I make a face. "What?" she asks, sounding more like herself, as in the *what* is sharp and annoyed.

"Nothing, just . . . Nothing. How about . . . ?" I point at my head, indicating *How's his brain?*

Persephone has a fretted look about her. "That is . . . less clear. He has been . . ."

"He's been rambling a little," Brit finishes for her.

"About what?"

"Carp— You. The System. Something about a prophecy. I'm not totally sure."

"But he has called for you," Persephone reiterates. "Multiple times."

I nod to myself. Step over to the bed. Pull up a chair. Sit.

Thump-THUMP. Thump-THUMP.

Being this close to him is causing my Heart to try and punch its way out of my chest. This moment has been haunting the edges of my mind since this whole crazy business began.

He must be able to hear it. Or maybe he can just feel my presence. Either way, he stirs.

"Carpathian? Carpathian, is that you?" His voice is ragged and raw—gravelly. Which is how I had imagined him sounding (in part because of the voice the audiobook guy gave him), but he sounds older than I anticipated. More gnarled even. Tired.

He reaches out his hand. I glance at Seph and Brit. Seph nods and smiles. Brit shrugs like, *I dunno, dude, take the old guy's hand.*

I do. I lace his knotted, weathered fingers through mine and squeeze gently.

I start to speak, but my voice hitches. Because . . . Because even after everything . . . something about saying what I'm about to say feels different. Like once I say it now, here, to this old man, it really, *really* becomes the truth. I will be owning it. There will be no walking back. It will become indelible. Absolute.

I will be committed. For good.

I rock back and forth in the chair slightly, gearing myself up to generate the words, like a skydiver readying themselves to leap into a great, wide, unceasing sky. Finally, I just let it out.

"Yes, Almeister. It's me. It's Carpathian. I'm here."

I will every bit of truth and earnestness I can muster into the words, and a wave of calm washes over me, offering a fleeting shelter from the anxiety that had been building. My parachute opens, and I am floating through the atmosphere, filled more with wonder than fear. Because, for the first time—*truly* for the first time—I think I might . . . believe what I said.

He turns his head to see me. His eyes glisten. I smile, squeeze his hand ever so slightly tighter still, and breathe into the moment. He stares and stares and stares. It looks like he can't believe I'm real. (I know how he feels.)

His eyes widen, as if seeing me for the very first time. He crooks his neck, ruffling his mane of white hair against the pillow upon which his head rests, takes a long beat to really drink in the image of me smiling at him . . . then he pulls his hand free from mine and says:

". . . You're not Carpathian."

EPILOGUE

"Once Upon a Time in Meridia."
Part 3

The Super Vizier led the way through the dark, damp tunnel, her strides long and purposeful. Moridius, ever devoted, trailed behind. He struggled to keep pace, both physically and mentally, though his love for her remained undimmed by the harsh new realities they faced.

Their march was tense, the Super Vizier's fury palpable. The aftermath of the chaos at the Tower had left a bitter taste in her mouth indeed, and her mind raced with thoughts of the destruction, the time it would take to sort through the rubble and repair what had been lost. If repair was even possible. Likelier, she thought, that an entirely new structure would need to be built.

And not simply a physical one.

But more than that, what was irking her at this moment was the news she had received that, somehow, despite all evidence to the contrary . . . the Saviour had survived.

Defying odds, logic, and the promise she had made to see it done right this time, the one known to the world as Carpathian Einzgear lived.

Moridius, sensing her turmoil, attempted to offer some semblance of comfort, his voice a cautious whisper in the echoing tunnel.

"Can it be so bad? Surely, we will recov—"

She stopped so abruptly that Moridius almost collided with her. Turning to face him, her expression projected nothing so much as cold wrath wrapped in disbelief.

"Recover?" she declared, her tone scornful. "*Recover?* The Tower was *burned*. To. The Ground. De-stroyed. There is no knowing how long it will take to restore what has been ruined. We lost half of the High Council, for the love of Kentavion."

Moridius nodded. He was well aware of what their inexplicably failed attempt to end the life of the Saviour had cost.

He was also well aware of the opportunity it presented.

"So . . . there are empty seats, then. On the High Council. That need be filled."

The Super Vizier once more maintained her forward gaze.

"Yes. There are. And they'll need to be filled quickly. This time not merely with *wizards*," she said the word with contempt, "who know not battle. Can't believe we wasted good Mezmer on some of those fools. Most of them merely pontificate and cogitate, working on their precious Spells for academic purposes, rendering themselves useless when it comes time for an actual confrontation. For, make no mistake, there will be another confrontation; it is inevitable. And the remorted Saviour will only continue growing stronger. *Again.*"

Misinterpreting the Super Vizier's words as a veiled invitation, Moridius ventured a suggestion cloaked in a veneer of subtlety that was anything but.

"Perhaps, then," he began, "bein' there's a fair number of seats to fill, perhaps there's room for some . . . new style of leadership? Someone with *actual* experience on the ground, say?"

His hint was as delicate as a sledgehammer, eyes searching for a sign of approval.

The Super Vizier stopped dead in her tracks again, turning to face him with a countenance that was equal parts disbelief and amusement. She snorted, a sound that cut him near his feelings in a way with which he was uncomfortable.

"Are you . . . Are you suggesting . . . yourself?" The idea seemed to amuse her, but not in the way Moridius had hoped.

"I'm just sayin'. I know him. Einzgear. And I feel like—"

She stroked his cheek. "My dear, sweet Moridius. No. Your place is here, by my side. That's where your truest value lies. I *need* you, dearest."

It was consolation draped in the illusion of importance; her version of a pep talk.

Moridius Wreathnestle knew good and well what she was doing, but one of his love languages was allowing her to think him stupider than he was. It seemed to give her joy, so he made no attempt to dissuade her perception.

"Of course, Mistress," he agreed amiably. "Have you begun thinking then, at all, about where you might seek candidates to replace the seats lost?"

"A bit," she replied without elaboration. "You'd be surprised by some of those who have already made enthusiastic overtures to become part of our number."

"Not sure I'd be that surprised. It's a great honor."

She didn't respond with words, simply gave him a placating smile and stroked his arm before returning to their perambulation.

They approached a heavy door that marked the end of their underground exit. With a casual flick of her wrist, she summoned her Mezmer, the door wrenching from its hinges with a screech of twisted metal. She flung it aside as if it were no more than parchment, revealing the sunlit expanse of a secluded beach beyond.

The sight of the water glinting with morning rays and the ship waiting a short distance away seemed to lift the Super Vizier's spirits. Moridius, on the other hand, thought of all the things that he wished could have gone differently. He was not keen to be on the seas. The open road was his home, and he found himself concerned that he might not see the firm soil of Meridia again for some time.

There was a flash from the ship, indicating it was safe to board. Without another word, the Super Vizier strode toward the waiting vessel. Moridius felt his feet hesitating to move, but after a moment, he forced himself to follow suit, shadowing his paramour and superior.

Once settled on the deck of the watercraft, the Templar allowed himself a moment to reflect. The Saviour, while being an absolute fondle goblin in Moridius's eyes (a locution that he knew was no longer approved of in polite society, but that he still used privately with his mates and in his own mind), was an estimable foe. More than estimable. And Moridius found himself very nearly in admiration of the man despite how much it tortured him to admit it.

"Do we have a strategy?" he asked.

"For what?"

"For how, exactly, we plan to battle the Saviour."

"You mean beyond the already successful plan to continue exposing his fraudulence to the whole of Meridia?"

"Yeah. Beyond that."

The Super Vizier studied her beau. He may have been her consort, but he was also her subordinate, and, in this moment, she did not care for his tone.

"That is why we are here. On this vessel." Moridius studied her, questioningly. "We know that he will be seeking the treasures he lost when he reconstituted. Whatever else he may strive to achieve, it is become clear that reestablishing his primary allies and tools of rebellion are chief amongst his goals."

"So . . ."

"So, we must find and assume possession of the Cerulean Tunic of the Seafarer before he has the opportunity." Moridius looked somehow dissatisfied with this response. "You're making a face. Stop that. Why are you making a face?"

"I understand the logic, I reckon, but it's one item. How much value is there in preventing him fetching one item?"

"Enough," she replied.

"How do we even know that he'll seek the Tunic next? What about his other items? The Gauntlet of Sorenthali? The Obsidian Shield of—"

"He will be incentivized."

"Incentivized how?"

"The Tunic is not the only thing he will be coming for."

"What are you talking about, not the only thing he'll be coming for?"

Before she could answer, the ship lurched. Then it lurched again, attempting to embark but, for some reason, failing to set to sea.

"What's all that?" Moridius wondered aloud.

But then, confusion gave way to something more like disbelief as he turned his head to find the source of the obstruction to the ship's departure making itself known.

The Super Vizier pressed against the Templar and purred, "It's not *what* I'm talking about that he'll be coming for, my dear . . . It's *who*."

Stepping onto the deck, still holding the rigging that kept the boat moored to the dock—the rigging that the hands gripping it had used to physically restrain the mighty ship using nothing more than the strength inside the body to which the hands belonged—was a figure. A figure as imposing as a storm cloud. A giant of a man with dark skin, dreadlocks, and dripping with seawater as if he'd just emerged from the deepest depths of the ocean himself, like a mythic beast.

"You weren't planning on leaving without me, were you?"

Moridius stared, awestruck. Dumbfounded. In complete and utter disbelief.

"As I said . . ." the Super Vizier, smiling wide, whispered into the Templar's ear as the legendary warrior with the glowing Tri-Venn tattoo on the back of his hand tossed the thick coils of rigging onto the deck, "you'd be surprised by some of those who wish to join us."

ABOUT THE AUTHORS

Johnathan McClain is an award-winning actor, screenwriter, novelist, and audio-book narrator who did not set out to have such a diverse set of careers but has embraced life's unpredictabilities.

As an actor, his extensive resumé includes a notable turn as Megan Draper's agent, Alan Silver, on the final season of AMC's critically acclaimed drama *Mad Men* as well as appearing as the lead of the TV Land comedy series, *Retired at 35*—starring alongside late Hollywood icons George Segal and Jessica Walter—among dozens of other TV series, films, and plays.

As a writer and producer, Johnathan's feature film debut, *The Outfit*, cowritten with Oscar winner Graham Moore and starring Mark Rylance, Zoey Deutch, Dylan O'Brien, and Johnny Flynn, was produced by FilmNation and distributed internationally by Focus Features in the spring of 2022. He has also created, written, and produced two television series which, unlike his film, have yet to be captured on camera.

As an audiobook narrator, Johnathan has recorded approximately 200 titles ranging from sci-fi, to romance, to non-fiction, to fantasy, to LitRPG, and everything in between. He is the recipient of multiple Audiofile Earphone Awards, SOVAS nominations, and an Audie for his narration of Amie Kaufman and Jay Kristoff's #1 *New York Times*–bestselling sci-fi novel, *Illuminae*, which won the Audie Award for audiobook of the year for multivoiced narration in 2016.

He lives in Los Angeles with his wife, Laura.

Seth McDuffee is the literary equivalent of a mullet: business in the front, party in the back. When he's not penning bestsellers like *Good Boy* and the Big Sneaky Barbarian series, he fancies himself a musician, a marketer, and moonlights as the host and dungeon master of the wildly popular podcast, *The d20 Syndicate*.

A towering giant with hair long enough to give Rapunzel a complex, Seth began his writing career shortly after his crushing defeat in the first round of a third-grade spelling bee. (The word was "bologna," and he's been trying to prove it's a made-up word ever since.)

When not busy disappointing elementary school spelling judges or annoying his neighbors with his ten-hour renditions of "Wagon Wheel" on the theremin, Seth can be found in his kitchen, where he uses his classical culinary training to perfect the art of microwaving Hot Pockets.

Critics have called his work "mostly readable" and "probably not plagiarized." His mother thinks he's very handsome. He lives in the Midwest with his tiny, irritating dog, and bombshell fiancée, Michaela.

Podium

DISCOVER MORE

STORIES
UNBOUND

PodiumEntertainment.com

Printed in the USA
CPSIA information can be obtained
at www.ICGtesting.com
JSHW022140270824
68853JS00006B/7

9 781039 455405